ACCLAIM FOR

The Stories of

VLADIMIR NABOKOV

"[This collection] brings the reader closer to his magic. . . . Those who know Nabokov the novelist and have forgotten that Nabokov the story writer exists now have a precious gift in their hands." —*Los Angeles Times Book Review*

"His English is an extraordinary instrument, at once infinitely delicate and muscularly robust: no other writer of our time, not even Joyce, can catch the shifting play of the world's light and shade as he does." —*Boston Globe*

"These stories are wonders of the English language." —*San Francisco Chronicle*

"It startles, then it provokes, and finally it satisfies in a way that a more domesticated fiction cannot. . . . An enduring tribute to Nabokov's ability to charm . . . and inspire." —*Atlanta Journal-Constitution*

"They offer a startling, cloudless view of a writer's development. . . . The effect of such felicities en masse is not only addictive; they point to the finesse of Nabokov's ear [and] to the extreme and unembarrassable weirdness of his invention, the plain flights of his fancy." —*The New Yorker*

The Stories of

VLADIMIR NABOKOV

Vladimir Nabokov was born in St. Petersburg on April 23, 1899. His family fled to Germany in 1919, during the Bolshevik Revolution. Nabokov studied French and Russian literature at Trinity College, Cambridge, from 1919 to 1923, then lived in Berlin (1923–1937) and Paris (1937–1940), where he began writing, mainly in Russian, under the pseudonym Sirin. In 1940 he moved to the United States, where he pursued a brilliant literary career (as a poet, novelist, critic, and translator) while teaching literature at Wellesley, Stanford, Cornell, and Harvard. The monumental success of his novel *Lolita* (1955) enabled him to give up teaching and devote himself fully to his writing. In 1961 he moved to Montreux, Switzerland, where he died in 1977. Recognized as one of this century's master prose stylists in both Russian and English, he translated a number of his original English works—including *Lolita*—into Russian, and collaborated on English translations of his original Russian works.

INTERNATIONAL

The Stories of

VLADIMIR NABOKOV

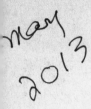

May 2013

NYC

The Stories of

VLADIMIR NABOKOV

TO IGOR

with warmest wishes for Joy
in your life

your Jacques

J'ambroise

VINTAGE INTERNATIONAL

Vintage Books

A Division of Random House, Inc.

New York

The Library of Congress has cataloged
the Knopf edition as follows:
Nabokov, Vladimir Vladimirovich, 1899–1977.
[Short stories]
The stories of Vladimir Nabokov.—1st American ed.
p. cm.
ISBN: 0-394-58615-8
I. Manners and customs—Fiction. I. Title.
PS3527.A15A6 1995
813'.54—dc20 95-23466

Vintage ISBN: 0-679-72997-6

www.vintagebooks.com

Printed in the United States of America
20 19 18 17 16 15 14

To Véra

Contents

← a favorite

Preface

HAVING APPEARED individually in periodicals and in various assortments in previous volumes, fifty-two of Vladimir Nabokov's stories were eventually published, during his lifetime, in four definitive English collections: *Nabokov's Dozen* and three other thirteen-story "dozens"—*A Russian Beauty and Other Stories*, *Tyrants Destroyed and Other Stories*, and *Details of a Sunset and Other Stories*.

Nabokov had long expressed the intention of issuing a final batch, but was not sure whether there were enough stories that met his standard to make up a fifth Nabokovian—or numerical—dozen. His creative life was too full, and was truncated too suddenly, for him to make a final selection. He had penciled a brief list of stories he considered worthy of publication and labeled it "bottom of the barrel." He was referring, he explained to me, not to their quality, but to the fact that, among the materials available for consultation at the moment, they were the final ones worthy of publication. Nonetheless, after our archive had been organized and thoroughly checked, Véra Nabokov and I came up with a happy total of thirteen, all of which, in our circumspect estimation, Nabokov might have deemed suitable. Hence Nabokov's "bottom of the barrel" list, reproduced following this preface, should be considered partial and preliminary; it contains only eight of the thirteen newly collected stories, and also includes *The Enchanter*, which does not appear in the present collection but has been published in English as a separate short novel (New York, Putnam's, 1986; New York, Vintage International, 1991). Nor do the author's working titles correspond in every case to those decided upon for this volume.

From the list entitled "Stories written in English," also reproduced following the preface, Nabokov omitted "First Love" (first published in *The New Yorker* as "Colette"), either through an oversight or because of its transformation into a chapter of *Speak, Memory* (original title: *Conclusive Evidence*). Some alignment instructions—albeit in Russian—in the upper left-hand corner suggest that this list was a fair copy prepared for typing. The two facsimile lists contain a few inaccuracies. "The Vane Sisters," for example, was written in 1951.

The four "definitive" volumes mentioned above had been painstakingly assorted and orchestrated by Nabokov using various criteria—theme, period, atmosphere, uniformity, variety. It is appropriate that each of them conserve its "book" identity for future publication as well. The thirteen stories published in France and Italy as, respectively, *La Vénitienne* and *La veneziana* have also perhaps earned the right to appear as a separate English-language volume. These thirteen have made other individual and collective debuts in Europe, and the four previous dozens have appeared worldwide, sometimes in different constellations such as the recent *Russkaya Dyuzhena (Russian Dozen)* in Israel. I shall not touch on publication in post-Perestroyka Russia, which, with few exceptions, has been mega-copy piracy in every sense until now, although improvements shimmer on the horizon.

The present comprehensive collection, while not intended to eclipse the previous groupings, is deliberately arranged in chronological sequence, or the best possible approximation thereof. To this end, the order used in previous volumes has occasionally been altered, and the newly collected pieces have been integrated where appropriate. Date of composition was the criterion of choice. When this was not available or not dependable, date of first publication or other mentions became the guide. Eleven of the newly incorporated thirteen have never before been translated into English. Five of them remained unpublished until the recent appearance of the "new" thirteen in several European languages. Further bibliographical essentials and certain other interesting details appear at the back of this volume.

One obvious bonus of the new arrangement is a convenient overview of Nabokov's development as a writer of fiction. It is interesting, too, that the vectors are not always linear, and a strikingly mature short story may suddenly crop up amid the younger, simpler tales. While illuminating the evolution of the creative process, and affording exciting insights into the themes and methods to be used later—particularly in the novels—Vladimir Nabokov's stories are nevertheless among his most immediately accessible work. Even when linked in some way to the larger fictions, they are self-contained. Even when they can be read on more than one level, they require few literary prerequisites. They offer the reader immediate gratification whether or not he has ventured into Nabokov's larger and more complex writings or delved into his personal history.

My translations of the "new" thirteen are my responsibility alone. The translation of most of the previously published Russian stories was the fruit of a cloudless collaboration between father and son, but the father had authorial license to alter his own texts in their translated form as, on occasion, he deemed appropriate. It is conceivable he might have done so, here and there, with the newly translated stories as well. It goes without saying that, as lone translator, the only liberty I have taken was the correction of the obvious slip or typo, and of editorial blunders from the past. The worst of those was the omission of the entire, wonderful, final page of "The Assistant Producer" in all English-language editions, it seems, subsequent to the first. Incidentally, in the song that twice meanders through the story, the Don Cossack who heaves his bride into the Volga is Stenka Razin.

I confess that, during the long gestation of this collection, I have taken advantage of queries and comments from hawk-eyed translators and editors of recent and concurrent translations into other tongues, and of fine-toothed inspections by those who are publishing a few of the stories individually in English. No matter how intense and pedantic the checking, a flounder or several will slip through the net. Nevertheless, future editors and translators should be aware that the present volume reflects what, at the time of its publication, are the most accurate versions of the English texts and, especially with regard to the thirteen newly collected pieces, of the underlying Russian originals (which were at times very hard to decipher, contained possible or probable author's or copyist's slips necessitating sometimes difficult decisions, and on occasion had one or more variants).

To be fair, I would like to acknowledge, with gratitude, spontaneously submitted draft translations of two stories. One came from Charles Nicol, the other from Gene Barabtarlo. Both are appreciated, and both yielded *trouvailles*. However, in order to maintain an appropriately homogeneous style, I have stuck, by and large, to my own English locutions. I am indebted to Brian Boyd, Dieter Zimmer, and Michael Juliar for their invaluable bibliographical research. Above all, I am grateful to Véra Nabokov for her infinite wisdom, her superlative judgment, and the willpower that compelled her, with failing eyesight and enfeebled hands, to jot a preliminary translation of several passages of "Gods" in her very last days.

It would take much more than a brief preface to trace themes, methods, and images as they weave and develop in these stories, or the echoes of Nabokov's youth in Russia, his university years in England, the émigré period in Germany and France, and the America he was inventing, as he put it, after having invented Europe. To choose at random from the thirteen newly collected stories, "La Veneziana," with its astonishing twist, echoes Nabokov's love for painting (to which he intended, as a boy, to dedicate his life) against a backdrop that includes tennis, which he played and described with a special flair. The other twelve range from fable ("The Dragon") and political intrigue ("Russian Spoken Here") to a poetical, personal impressionism ("Sounds" and "Gods").

Nabokov gives in his notes (which appear at the end of this volume) certain insights regarding the previously collected stories. Among the many things one might add is the eerie doubling of space-time (in "Terra Incognita" and "The Visit to the Museum") that foreshadows the atmosphere of *Ada, Pale Fire,* and, to a degree, *Transparent Things* and *Look at the Harlequins!* Nabokov's predilection for butterflies is a central theme of "The Aurelian" and flickers through many other stories. But what is stranger, music, for which he never professed a special love, often figures prominently in his writing ("Sounds," "Bachmann," "Music," "The Assistant Producer").

Particularly touching to me personally is the sublimation, in "Lance" (as my father told me), of what my parents experienced in my mountain-climbing days. But perhaps the deepest, most important theme, be it subject or undercurrent, is Nabokov's contempt for cruelty—the cruelty of humans, the cruelty of fate—and here the instances are too numerous to name.

DMITRI NABOKOV
St. Petersburg, Russia, and Montreux, Switzerland
June 1995

A note from Georg Heepe, editorial director of Rowohlt Verlag, Hamburg, traces the discovery of "Easter Rain," now appended to this edition. It reads in part:

When we were preparing the first German edition of the complete stories in 1987–88, Nabokov scholar Dieter Zimmer searched all the accessible libraries, likely and unlikely, for the April 1925 issue of the Russian émigré magazine *Russkoe Ekho* that he knew included "Easter Rain." He went even into what was then East Berlin on a day's permit, and thought of the Deutsche Buecherei in Leipzig as well. But the chance seemed too slight, the bureaucratic procedures too forbidding. And there was one more consideration. There would have been no copy machines.

We had published the stories without "Easter Rain" when he heard rumors that a scholar residing in Sweden had found the story in Leipzig. The Iron Curtain had been raised by then, and he went to check. There it was: a complete set of *Russkoe Ekho*. And now they had Xerox machines.

Thus "Easter Rain"—first discovered by Svetlana Polsky, though we only learned her name some years later; translated into English in collaboration with Peter Constantine for the Spring 2002 issue of *Conjunctions*—now joins this volume.

DMITRI NABOKOV
Vevy, Switzerland
May 2002

[Bottom of the Barrel]

The Wingstroke	(Udar kryla, 1924)
Vengeance	(Mest', 1924)
	(Blagost', 1924)
The Seaport	(Port, 1924)
Gods	(Bogi, 1924)
The Fight	(Draka, 1924)
The Razor	(Britva, 1926)
Christmas Tale	(Rozhdestvenskiy rasskaz, 1928)
The Enchanter	(Volshebnik, 1939)

[unpublished]

Stories written in English

1   The Assistant Producer, 1943
                                      in N's Dozen
                              [missing last page]
                                      See A. Appel

2   That in Aleppo Once, 1943

3   A Forgotten Poet, 1944

4   Time and Ebb, 1945

5   Conversation Piece   1945

6   Signs and Symbols   1948

7   Lance   1952

8   Scenes from the Life of a Double Monster 1958

9   The Vane Sisters 1959

The Stories of

VLADIMIR NABOKOV

THE WOOD-SPRITE

I WAS pensively penning the outline of the inkstand's circular, quivering shadow. In a distant room a clock struck the hour, while I, dreamer that I am, imagined someone was knocking at the door, softly at first, then louder and louder. He knocked twelve times and paused expectantly.

"Yes, I'm here, come in. . . ."

The doorknob creaked timidly, the flame of the runny candle tilted, and he hopped sidewise out of a rectangle of shadow, hunched, gray, powdered with the pollen of the frosty, starry night.

I knew his face—oh, how long I had known it!

His right eye was still in the shadows, the left peered at me timorously, elongated, smoky-green. The pupil glowed like a point of rust. . . . That mossy-gray tuft on his temple, the pale-silver, scarcely noticeable eyebrow, the comical wrinkle near his whiskerless mouth—how all this teased and vaguely vexed my memory!

I got up. He stepped forward.

His shabby little coat seemed to be buttoned wrong—on the female side. In his hand he held a cap—no, a dark-colored, poorly tied bundle, and there was no sign of any cap. . . .

Yes, of course I knew him—perhaps had even been fond of him, only I simply could not place the where and the when of our meetings. And we must have met often, otherwise I would not have had such a firm recollection of those cranberry lips, those pointy ears, that amusing Adam's apple. . . .

With a welcoming murmur I shook his light, cold hand, and touched the back of a shabby armchair. He perched like a crow on a tree stump, and began speaking hurriedly.

"It's so scary in the streets. So I dropped in. Dropped in to visit you. Do you recognize me? You and I, we used to romp together and

3

halloo at each other for days at a time. Back in the old country. Don't tell me you've forgotten?"

His voice literally blinded me. I felt dazzled and dizzy—I remembered the happiness, the echoing, endless, irreplaceable happiness. . . .

No, it can't be: I'm alone. . . . It's only some capricious delirium. Yet there really was somebody sitting next to me, bony and implausible, with long-eared German bootees, and his voice tintinnabulated, rustled—golden, luscious-green, familiar—while the words were so simple, so human. . . .

"There—you remember. Yes, I am a former Forest Elf, a mischievous sprite. And here I am, forced to flee like everyone else."

He heaved a deep sigh, and once again I had visions of billowing nimbus, lofty leafy undulations, bright flashes of birch bark like splashes of sea foam, against a dulcet, perpetual, hum. . . . He bent toward me and glanced gently into my eyes. "Remember our forest, fir so black, birch all white? They've cut it all down. The grief was unbearable—I saw my dear birches crackling and falling, and how could I help? Into the marshes they drove me, I wept and I howled, I boomed like a bittern, then left lickety-split for a neighboring pinewood.

"There I pined, and could not stop sobbing. I had barely grown used to it, and lo, there was no more pinewood, just blue-tinted cinders. Had to do some more tramping. Found myself a wood—a wonderful wood it was, thick, dark, and cool. Yet somehow it was just not the same thing. In the old days I'd frolic from dawn until dusk, whistle furiously, clap my hands, frighten passersby. You remember yourself—you lost your way once in a dark nook of my woods, you and some little white dress, and I kept tying the paths up in knots, spinning the tree trunks, twinkling through the foliage. Spent the whole night playing tricks. But I was only fooling around, it was all in jest, vilify me as they might. But now I sobered up, for my new abode was not a merry one. Day and night strange things crackled around me. At first I thought a fellow elf was lurking there; I called, then listened. Something crackled, something rumbled. . . . But no, those were not the kinds of sounds we make. Once, toward evening, I skipped out into a glade, and what do I see? People lying around, some on their backs, some on their bellies. Well, I think, I'll wake them up, I'll get them moving! And I went to work shaking boughs, bombarding with cones, rustling, hooting. . . . I toiled away for a whole hour, all to no avail. Then I took a closer look, and I was horror-struck. Here's a man with his head hanging by one flimsy crimson thread, there's one with a heap of thick worms for a stomach. . . . I could not endure it. I let out a howl, jumped in the air, and off I ran. . . .

"Long I wandered through different forests, but I could find no peace. Either it was stillness, desolation, mortal boredom, or such horror it's better not to think about it. At last I made up my mind and changed into a bumpkin, a tramp with a knapsack, and left for good: Rus', adieu! Here a kindred spirit, a Water-Sprite, gave me a hand. Poor fellow was on the run too. He kept marveling, kept saying—what times are upon us, a real calamity! And even if, in olden times, he had had his fun, used to lure people down (a hospitable one, he was!), in recompense how he petted and pampered them on the gold river bottom, with what songs he bewitched them! These days, he says, only dead men come floating by, floating in batches, enormous numbers of them, and the river's moisture is like blood, thick, warm, sticky, and there's nothing for him to breathe. . . . And so he took me with him.

"He went off to knock about some distant sea, and put me ashore on a foggy coast—go, brother, find yourself some friendly foliage. But I found nothing, and ended up here in this foreign, terrifying city of stone. Thus I turned into a human, complete with proper starched collars and bootees, and I've even learned human talk. . . ."

He fell silent. His eyes glistened like wet leaves, his arms were crossed, and, by the wavering light of the drowning candle, some pale strands combed to the left shimmered so strangely.

"I know you too are pining," his voice shimmered again, "but your pining, compared to mine, my tempestuous, turbulent pining, is but the even breathing of one who is asleep. And think about it: not one of our Tribe is there left in Rus'. Some of us swirled away like wisps of fog, others scattered over the world. Our native rivers are melancholy, there is no frisky hand to splash up the moon-gleams. Silent are the orphaned bluebells that remain, by chance, unmown, the pale-blue *gusli* that once served my rival, the ethereal Field-Sprite, for his songs. The shaggy, friendly, household spirit, in tears, has forsaken your besmirched, humiliated home, and the groves have withered, the pathetically luminous, magically somber groves. . . .

"It was we, Rus', who were your inspiration, your unfathomable beauty, your agelong enchantment! And we are all gone, gone, driven into exile by a crazed surveyor.

"My friend, soon I shall die, say something to me, tell me that you love me, a homeless phantom, come sit closer, give me your hand. . . ."

The candle sputtered and went out. Cold fingers touched my palm. The familiar melancholy laugh pealed and fell still.

When I turned on the light there was no one in the armchair. . . . No one! . . . Nothing was left but a wondrously subtle scent in the room, of birch, of humid moss. . . .

RUSSIAN SPOKEN HERE

M ARTIN MARTINICH'S tobacco shop is located in a corner building. No wonder tobacco shops have a predilection for corners, for Martin's business is booming. The window is of modest size, but well arranged. Small mirrors make the display come alive. At the bottom, amid the hollows of hilly azure velvet, nestles a motley of cigarette boxes with names couched in the glossy international dialect that serves for hotel names as well; higher up, rows of cigars grin in their lightweight boxes.

In his day Martin was a well-off landowner. He is famed in my childhood recollections for a remarkable tractor, while his son Petya and I succumbed simultaneously to Meyn Ried and scarlet fever, so that now, after fifteen years chock-full of all kinds of things, I enjoyed stopping by the tobacco shop on that lively corner where Martin sold his wares.

Since last year, moreover, we have more than reminiscences in common. Martin has a secret, and I have been made party to that secret. "So, everything as usual?" I ask in a whisper, and he, glancing over his shoulder, replies just as softly, "Yes, thank heaven, all is quiet." The secret is a quite extraordinary one. I recall how I was leaving for Paris and stayed at Martin's till evening the day before. A man's soul can be compared to a department store and his eyes to twin display windows. Judging by Martin's eyes, warm, brown tints were in fashion. Judging by those eyes, the merchandise inside his soul was of superb quality. And what a luxuriant beard, fairly glistening with robust Russian gray. And his shoulders, his stature, his mien. . . . At one time they used to say he could slit a handkerchief with a sword—one of the exploits of Richard Coeur de Lion. Now a fellow émigré would say with envy, "The man did not give in!"

His wife was a puffy, gentle old woman with a mole by her left nostril. Ever since the time of revolutionary ordeals her face had had a touching tic: she would give quick sidewise glances skyward. Petya had the same imposing physique as his father. I was fond of his mild-mannered glumness and unexpected humor. He had a large, flaccid face (about which his father used to say, "What a mug—three days would not suffice to circumnavigate it") and reddish-brown, permanently tousled hair. Petya owned a tiny cinema in a sparsely populated part of town, which brought a very modest income. And there we have the whole family.

I spent that day before my departure sitting by the counter and watching Martin receive his customers—first he would lean lightly, with two fingers, on the countertop, then step to the shelves, produce a box with a flourish, and ask, as he opened it with his thumbnail, *"Einen Rauchen?"*—I remember that day for a special reason: Petya suddenly came in from the street, disheveled and livid with rage. Martin's niece had decided to return to her mother in Moscow, and Petya had just been to see the diplomatic representatives. While one of the representatives was giving him some information, another, who was obviously involved with the government political directorate, whispered barely audibly, "All kinds of White Guard scum keep hanging around."

"I could have made mincemeat of him," said Petya, slamming his fist into his palm, "but unfortunately I could not forget about my aunt in Moscow."

"You already have a peccadillo or two on your conscience," good-naturedly rumbled Martin. He was alluding to a most amusing incident. Not long ago, on his nameday, Petya had visited the Soviet bookstore, whose presence blemishes one of Berlin's most charming streets. They sell not only books there, but also various handmade bric-a-brac. Petya selected a hammer adorned with poppies and emblazoned with an inscription typical for a Bolshevik hammer. The clerk inquired if he would like something else. Petya said, "Yes, I would," nodding at a small plaster bust of Mister Ulyanov.* He paid fifteen marks for bust and hammer, whereupon, without a word, right there on the counter, he popped that bust with that hammer, and with such force that Mister Ulyanov disintegrated.

I was fond of that story, just as I was fond, for instance, of the dear silly sayings from unforgettable childhood that warm the cockles of one's heart. Martin's words made me glance with a laugh at Petya. But Petya jerked his shoulder sullenly and scowled. Martin rummaged in

*Lenin's real name. —D.N.

the drawer and proffered him the most expensive cigarette in the shop. But even this did not dispel Petya's gloom.

I returned to Berlin a half-year later. One Sunday morning I felt an urge to see Martin. On weekdays you could get through via the shop, since his apartment—three rooms and kitchen—was directly behind it. But of course on a Sunday morning the shop was closed, and the window had shut its grated visor. I glanced rapidly through the grating at the red and gold boxes, at the swarthy cigars, at the modest inscription in a corner: "Russian spoken here," remarked that the display had in some way grown even gayer, and walked through the courtyard to Martin's place. Strange thing—Martin himself appeared to me even jollier, jauntier, more radiant than before. And Petya was downright unrecognizable: his oily, shaggy locks were combed back, a broad, vaguely bashful smile did not leave his lips, he kept a kind of sated silence, and a curious, joyous preoccupation, as if he carried a precious cargo within him, softened his every movement. Only the mother was pale as ever, and the same touching tic flashed across her face like faint summer lightning. We sat in their neat parlor, and I knew that the other two rooms—Petya's bedroom and that of his parents—were just as cozy and clean, and I found that an agreeable thought. I sipped tea with lemon, listened to Martin's mellifluous speech, and I could not rid myself of the impression that something new had appeared in their apartment, some kind of joyous, mysterious palpitation, as happens, for instance, in a home where there is a young mother-to-be. Once or twice Martin glanced with a preoccupied air at his son, whereupon the other would promptly rise, leave the room, and, on his return, nod discreetly toward his father, as if to say everything was going splendidly.

There was also something new and, to me, enigmatic in the old man's conversation. We were talking about Paris and the French, and suddenly he inquired, "Tell me, my friend, what's the largest prison in Paris?" I replied I didn't know and started telling him about a French revue that featured blue-painted women.

"You think that's something!" interrupted Martin. "They say, for example, that women scratch the plaster off the walls in prison and use it to powder their faces, necks, or whatever." In confirmation of his words he fetched from his bedroom a thick tome by a German criminologist and located in it a chapter about the routine of prison life. I tried changing the subject, but, no matter what theme I selected, Martin steered it with artful convolutions so that suddenly we would find ourselves discussing the humaneness of life imprisonment as opposed to execution, or the ingenious methods invented by criminals to break out into the free world.

I was puzzled. Petya, who loved anything mechanical, was picking with a penknife at the springs of his watch and chuckling to himself. His mother worked at her needlepoint, now and then nudging the toast or the jam toward me. Martin, clutching his disheveled beard with all five fingers, gave me a sidelong flash of his tawny eye, and suddenly something within him let go. He banged the palm of his hand on the table and turned to his son. "I can't stand it any longer, Petya—I'm going to tell him everything before I burst." Petya nodded silently. Martin's wife was getting up to go to the kitchen. "What a chatterbox you are," she said, shaking her head indulgently. Martin placed his hand on my shoulder, gave me such a shake that, had I been an apple tree in the garden, the apples would literally have come tumbling off me, and glanced into my face. "I'm warning you," he said. "I'm about to tell you such a secret, such a secret . . . that I just don't know. Mind you—mum's the word! Understand?"

And, leaning close to me, bathing me in the odor of tobacco and his own pungent old-man smell, Martin told me a truly remarkable tale.*

"It happened," began Martin, "shortly after your departure. In walked a customer. He had obviously not noticed the sign in the window, for he addressed me in German. Let me emphasize this: if he had noticed the sign he would not have entered a modest émigré shop. I recognized him right off as a Russian by his pronunciation. Had a Russian mug too. I, of course, launched into Russian, asked him what price range, what kind. He gave me a look of disagreeable surprise: 'What made you think I was Russian?' I gave him a perfectly friendly answer, as I recall, and began counting out his cigarettes. At that moment Petya entered. When he saw my customer he said with utter calm, 'Now here's a pleasant encounter.' Then my Petya walks up close to him and bangs him on the cheek with his fist. The other froze. As Petya explained to me later, what had happened was not just a knock-out with the victim crumpling to the floor, but a special kind of knock-out: it turns out Petya had delivered a delayed-action punch, and the man went out on his feet. And looked as if he were sleeping standing up. Then he started slowly tilting back like a tower. Here Petya walked around behind him and caught him under the armpits. It was all highly unexpected. Petya said, 'Give me a hand, Dad.' I asked what he thought he was doing. Petya only repeated, 'Give me a hand.' I know

---

*In this narrative, all traits and distinguishing marks that might hint at the identity of the real Martin are of course deliberately distorted. I mention this so that curiosity seekers will not search in vain for the "tobacco shop in the corner building." —V.N.

my Petya well—no point in smirking, Petya—and know he has his feet on the ground, ponders his actions, and does not knock people unconscious for nothing. We dragged the unconscious one from the shop into the corridor and on to Petya's room. Right then I heard a ring—someone had stepped into the shop. Good thing, of course, that it hadn't happened earlier. Back into the shop I went, made my sale, then, luckily, my wife arrived with the shopping, and I immediately put her to work at the counter while I, without a word, went lickety-split into Petya's room. The man was lying with eyes closed on the floor, while Petya was sitting at his table, examining in a pensive kind of way certain objects like that large leather cigar case, half a dozen obscene postcards, a wallet, a passport, an old but apparently efficient revolver. He explained right away: as I'm sure you have imagined, these items came from the man's pockets, and the man himself was none other than the representative—you remember Petya's story—who made the crack about the White scum, yes, yes, the very same one! And, judging by certain papers, he was a GPU man if I ever saw one. 'Well and good,' I say to Petya, 'so you've punched a guy in the mug. Whether he deserved it or not is a different matter, but please explain to me, what do you intend to do now? Evidently you forgot all about your aunt in Moscow.' 'Yes, I did,' said Petya. 'We must think of something.'

"And we did. First we got hold of some stout rope, and plugged his mouth with a towel. While we were working on him he came to and opened one eye. Upon closer examination, let me tell you, the mug turned out to be not only repulsive but stupid as well—some kind of mange on his forehead, mustache, bulbous nose. Leaving him lying on the floor, Petya and I settled down comfortably nearby and started a judicial inquiry. We debated for a good while. We were concerned not so much with the affront itself—that was a trifle, of course—as much as with his entire profession, so to speak, and with the deeds he had committed in Russia. The defendant was allowed to have the last word. When we relieved his mouth of the towel, he gave a kind of moan, gagged, but said nothing except 'You wait, you just wait. . . .' The towel was retied, and the session resumed. The votes were split at first. Petya demanded the death sentence. I found that he deserved to die, but proposed substituting life imprisonment for execution. Petya thought it over and concurred. I added that although he had certainly committed crimes, we were unable to ascertain this; that his employment in itself alone constituted a crime; that our duty was limited to rendering him harmless, nothing more. Now listen to the rest.

"We have a bathroom at the end of the corridor. Dark, very dark little room, with an enameled iron bathtub. The water goes on strike pretty often. There is an occasional cockroach. The room is so dark because the window is extremely narrow and is situated right under the ceiling, and besides, right opposite the window, three feet away or less, there's a good, solid brick wall. And it was here in this nook that we decided to keep the prisoner. It was Petya's idea—yes, yes, Petya, give Caesar his due. First of all, of course, the cell had to be prepared. We began by dragging the prisoner into the corridor so he would be close by while we worked. And here my wife, who had just locked up the shop for the night and was on her way to the kitchen, saw us. She was amazed, even indignant, but then understood our reasoning. Docile girl. Petya began by dismembering a stout table we had in the kitchen—knocked off its legs and used the resulting board to hammer shut the bathroom window. Then he unscrewed the taps, removed the cylindrical water heater, and laid a mattress on the bathroom floor. Of course next day we added various improvements: we changed the lock, installed a deadbolt, reinforced the window board with metal—and all of it, of course, without making too much noise. As you know, we have no neighbors, but nonetheless it behooved us to act cautiously. The result was a real prison cell, and there we put the GPU chap. We undid the rope, untied the towel, warned him that if he started yelling we would reswaddle him, and for a long time; then, satisfied that he had understood for whom the mattress had been placed in the bathtub, we locked the door and, taking turns, stood guard all night.

"That moment marked the beginning of a new life for us. I was no longer simply Martin Martinich, but Martin Martinich the head warden. At first the inmate was so stunned by what had happened that his behavior was subdued. Soon, however, he reverted to a normal state and, when we brought his dinner, launched into a hurricane of foul language. I cannot repeat the man's obscenities; I shall limit myself to saying that he placed my dear late mother in the most curious situations. It was decided to inculcate in him thoroughly the nature of his legal status. I explained that he would remain imprisoned until the end of his days; that if I died first I would transmit him to Petya like a bequest; that my son in his turn would transmit him to my future grandson and so forth, causing him to become a kind of family tradition. A family jewel. I mentioned in passing that, in the unlikely eventuality of our having to move to a different Berlin flat, he would be tied up, placed in a special trunk, and would make the move with us easy as pie. I went on to explain to him that in one case only would he be granted amnesty. Namely, he would be released the day the Bolshevik bubble burst. Finally I promised that he would be well fed—far better than when, in my time, I had been locked up by the Cheka—and that, by way of special privilege, he would receive books. And in fact, to this day I don't believe he has once complained about the food. True, at first Petya proposed that he be fed dried roach, but search as he might, that Soviet fish was unavailable in Berlin. We are obliged to give him bourgeois food. Exactly at eight every morning Petya and I go in and place by his tub a bowl of hot soup with meat and a loaf of gray bread. At the same time we take out the chamber pot, a clever apparatus we acquired just for him. At three he gets a glass of tea, at seven some more soup. This nutritional system is modeled on the one in use in the best European jails.

"The books were more of a problem. We held a family council for starters, and stopped at three titles: *Prince Serebryaniy*, Krylov's *Fables*, and *Around the World in Eighty Days*. He announced that he would not read those 'White Guard pamphlets,' but we left him the books, and we have every reason to believe that he read them with pleasure.

"His mood was changeable. He grew quiet. Evidently he was cooking up something. Maybe he hoped the police would start looking for him. We checked the papers, but there was not a word about the vanished Cheka agent. Most likely the other representatives had decided the man had simply defected, and had preferred to bury the affair. To this pensive period belongs his attempt to slip away, or at least to get word to the outside world. He trudged about his cell, probably reached for the window, tried to pry the planks loose, tried pounding, but we made some threat or other and the pounding ceased. And once, when Petya went in there alone, the man lunged at him. Petya grabbed him in a gentle bear hug and sat him back in the tub. After this occurrence he underwent another change, became very good-natured, even joked on occasion, and finally attempted to bribe us. He offered us an enormous sum, promising to obtain it through somebody. When this did not help either, he started whimpering, then went back to swearing worse than before. At the moment he is at a stage of grim submissiveness, which, I'm afraid, bodes no good.

"We take him for a daily walk in the corridor, and twice a week we air him out by an open window; naturally we take all necessary precautions to prevent him from yelling. On Saturdays he takes a bath. We ourselves have to wash in the kitchen. On Sundays I give him short lectures and let him smoke three cigarettes—in my presence, of course. What are these lectures about? All sorts of things. Pushkin, for instance, or Ancient Greece. Only one subject is omitted—politics. He is totally deprived of politics. Just as if such a thing did not exist on the face of the earth. And you know what? Ever since I have kept one Soviet agent locked up, ever since I have served the Fatherland, I am simply a different man. Jaunty and happy. And business has looked up, so there is no great problem supporting him either. He costs me twenty marks or so a month, counting the electric bill: it's completely dark in there, so from eight a.m. to eight p.m. one weak lightbulb is left on.

"You ask, what milieu is he from? Well, how shall I put it. . . . He is twenty-four years old, he is a peasant, it is unlikely that he finished even a village school, he was what is called 'an honest Communist,' studied only political literacy, which in our book signifies trying to make blockheads out of knuckleheads—that's all I know. Oh, if you want I'll show him to you, only remember, mum's the word!"

Martin went into the corridor. Petya and I followed. The old man in his cozy house jacket really did look like a prison warden. He produced the key as he walked, and there was something almost professional in the way he inserted it in the lock. The lock crunched twice, and Martin threw open the door. Far from being some ill-lit hole, it was a splendid, spacious bathroom, of the kind one finds in comfortable German dwellings. Electric light, bright yet pleasing to the eye, burned behind a merry, ornate shade. A mirror glistened on the left-hand wall. On the night table by the bathtub there were books, a peeled orange on a lustrous plate, and an untouched bottle of beer. In the white bathtub, on a mattress covered with a clean sheet, with a large pillow under the back of his head, lay a well-fed, bright-eyed fellow with a long growth of beard, in a bathrobe (a hand-me-down from the master) and warm, soft slippers.

"Well, what do you say?" Martin asked me.

I found the scene comical and did not know what to answer. "That's where the window used to be," Martin indicated with his finger. Sure enough, the window was boarded up to perfection.

The prisoner yawned and turned toward the wall. We went out. Martin fondled the bolt with a smile. "Fat chance he'll ever escape," he said, and then added pensively, "I would be curious to know, though, just how many years he'll spend in there. . . ."

SOUNDS

I T WAS necessary to shut the window: rain was striking the sill and splashing the parquet and armchairs. With a fresh, slippery sound, enormous silver specters sped through the garden, through the foliage, along the orange sand. The drainpipe rattled and choked. You were playing Bach. The piano had raised its lacquered wing, under the wing lay a lyre, and little hammers were rippling across the strings. The brocade rug, crumpling into coarse folds, had slid partway off the piano's tail, dropping an opened opus onto the floor. Every now and then, through the frenzy of the fugue, your ring would clink on the keys as, incessantly, magnificently, the June shower slashed the windowpanes. And you, without interrupting your playing, and slightly tilting your head, were exclaiming, in time to the beat, "The rain, the rain . . . I am go-ing to drown it out. . . ."

But you could not.

Abandoning the albums that lay on the table like velvet coffins, I watched you and listened to the fugue, the rain. A feeling of freshness welled in me like the fragrance of wet carnations that trickled down everywhere, from the shelves, from the piano's wing, from the oblong diamonds of the chandelier.

I had a feeling of enraptured equilibrium as I sensed the musical relationship between the silvery specters of rain and your inclined shoulders, which would give a shudder when you pressed your fingers into the rippling luster. And when I withdrew deep into myself the whole world seemed like that—homogeneous, congruent, bound by the laws of harmony. I myself, you, the carnations, at that instant all became vertical chords on musical staves. I realized that everything in the world was an interplay of identical particles comprising different kinds of consonance: the trees, the water, you . . . All was unified,

14

equivalent, divine. You got up. Rain was still mowing down the sunlight. The puddles looked like holes in the dark sand, apertures onto some other heavens that were gliding past underground. On a bench, glistening like Danish china, lay your forgotten racquet; the strings had turned brown from the rain, and the frame had twisted into a figure eight.

When we entered the lane, I felt a bit giddy from the motley of shadows and the aroma of mushroom rot.

I recall you within a chance patch of sunlight. You had sharp elbows and pale, dusty-looking eyes. When you spoke, you would carve the air with the riblike edge of your little hand and the glint of a bracelet on your thin wrist. Your hair would melt as it merged with the sunlit air that quivered around it. You smoked copiously and nervously. You exhaled through both nostrils, obliquely flicking off the ash. Your dove-gray manor was five versts from ours. Its interior was reverberant, sumptuous, and cool. A photograph of it had appeared in a glossy metropolitan magazine. Almost every morning, I would leap onto the leather wedge of my bicycle and rustle along the path, through the woods, then along the highway and through the village, then along another path toward you. You counted on your husband's not coming in September. And we feared nothing, you and I—not your servants' gossip, not my family's suspicions. Each of us, in a different way, trusted fate.

Your love was a bit muted, as was your voice. One might say you loved askance, and you never spoke about love. You were one of those habitually untalkative women, to whose silence one immediately grows accustomed. But now and then something in you burst forth. Then your giant Bechstein would thunder, or else, gazing mistily straight ahead, you would tell me hilarious anecdotes you had heard from your husband or from his regimental comrades. I remember your hands—elongated, pale hands with bluish veins.

On that happy day when the rain was lashing and you played so unexpectedly well came the resolution of the nebulous something that had imperceptibly arisen between us after our first weeks of love. I realized that you had no power over me, that it was not you alone who were my lover but the entire earth. It was as if my soul had extended countless sensitive feelers, and I lived within everything, perceiving simultaneously Niagara Falls thundering far beyond the ocean and the long golden drops rustling and pattering in the lane. I glanced at a birch tree's shiny bark and suddenly felt that, in place of arms, I possessed inclined branches covered with little wet leaves and, instead of legs, a thousand slender roots, twining into the earth, imbibing it. I wanted to transfuse myself thus into all of nature, to experience what it was like to be an old boletus mushroom with its spongy yellow underside, or a dragonfly, or the solar sphere. I felt so happy that I suddenly burst out laughing, and kissed you on the clavicle and nape. I would even have recited a poem to you, but you detested poetry.

You smiled a thin smile and said, "It's nice after the rain." Then you thought for a minute and added, "You know, I just remembered— I've been invited to tea today at . . . what's his name . . . Pal Palych's. He's a real bore. But, you know, I must go."

Pal Palych was an old acquaintance of mine. We would be fishing together and, all of a sudden, in a creaky little tenor, he would break into "The Evening Bells." I was very fond of him. A fiery drop fell from a leaf right onto my lips. I offered to accompany you.

You gave a shivery shrug. "We'll be bored to death there. This is awful." You glanced at your wrist and sighed. "Time to go. I must change my shoes."

In your misty bedroom, the sunlight, having penetrated the low-ered Venetian blinds, formed two golden ladders on the floor. You said something in your muted voice. Outside the window, the trees breathed and dripped with a contented rustle. And I, smiling at that rustle, lightly and unavidly embraced you.

It happened like this. On one bank of the river was your park, your meadows, and on the other stood the village. The highway was deeply rutted in places. The mud was a lush violet, and the grooves contained bubbly, café-au-lait water. The oblique shadows of black log isbas ex-tended with particular clarity.

We walked in the shade along a well-trodden path, past a grocery, past an inn with an emerald sign, past sun-filled courtyards emanating the aromas of manure and of fresh hay.

The schoolhouse was new, constructed of stone, with maples planted around it. On its threshold a peasant woman's white calves gleamed as she wrung out a rag into a bucket.

You inquired, "Is Pal Palych in?" The woman, with her freckles and braids, squinted against the sun. "He is, he is." The pail tinkled as she pushed it with her heel. "Come in, ma'am. They'll be in the workshop."

We creaked along a dark hallway, then through a spacious classroom.

I glanced in passing at an azure map, and thought, That's how all of Russia is—sunlight and hollows. . . . In a corner sparkled a crushed piece of chalk.

Farther on, in the small workshop, there was a pleasant smell of carpenter's glue and pine sawdust. Coatless, puffy, and sweaty, his left leg extended, Pal Palych was planing away appetizingly at a groaning white board. His moist, bald pate rocked to and fro in a dusty ray of sunlight. On the floor under the workbench, the shavings curled like flimsy locks.

I said loudly, "Pal Palych, you have guests!"

He gave a start, immediately got flustered, bestowed a polite smack on the hand you raised with such a listless, familiar gesture, and for an instant poured his damp fingers into my hand and gave it a shake. His face looked as if it had been fashioned of buttery modeling clay, with its limp mustache and unexpected furrows.

"Sorry—I'm not dressed, you see," he said with a guilty smile. He grabbed a pair of shirt cuffs that had been standing like cylinders side by side on the windowsill, and pulled them on hastily.

"What are you working on?" you asked with a glint of your bracelet. Pal Palych was struggling into his jacket with sweeping motions. "Nothing, just puttering," he sputtered, stumbling slightly on the labial consonants. "It's a kind of little shelf. Haven't finished yet. I still have to sand and lacquer it. But take a look at this—I call it the Fly. . . ." With a spinning rub of his joined palms, he launched a miniature wooden helicopter, which soared with a buzzing sound, bumped on the ceiling, and dropped.

The shadow of a polite smile flitted across your face. "Oh, silly me," Pal Palych started again. "You were expected upstairs, my friends. . . . This door squeaks. Sorry. Allow me to go first. I'm afraid my place is a mess. . . ."

"I think he forgot he invited me," you said in English as we began climbing the creaky staircase.

I was watching your back, the silk checks of your blouse. From somewhere downstairs, probably the courtyard, came a resonant peasant-woman voice, "Gerosim! Hey, Gerosim!" And suddenly it was supremely clear to me that, for centuries, the world had been blooming, withering, spinning, changing solely in order that now, at this instant, it might combine and fuse into a vertical chord the voice that had resounded downstairs, the motion of your silken shoulder blades, and the scent of pine boards.

Pal Palych's room was sunny and somewhat cramped. A crimson rug with a yellow lion embroidered in its center was nailed to the wall above the bed. On another wall hung a framed chapter from *Anna Karenin*, set in such a way that the interplay of dark and light type together with the clever placement of the lines formed Tolstoy's face.

Rubbing his hands together, our host seated you. As he did so, he knocked an album off the table with the flap of his jacket. He retrieved it. Tea, yogurt, and some insipid biscuits appeared. From a dresser drawer, Pal Palych produced a flowery tin of Landrin hard candy. When he stooped, a fold of pimply skin bulged behind his collar. The down of a spiderweb on the windowsill contained a yellow, dead bumblebee. "Where is Sarajevo?" you asked suddenly, rustling a newspaper page that you had listlessly picked up from a chair. Pal Palych, busy pouring tea, replied, "In Serbia."

And, with a trembling hand, he carefully gave you the steaming glass in its silver stand.

"There you are. May I offer you some biscuits? . . . And what are they throwing bombs for?" he addressed me with a jerk of his shoulders.

I was examining, for the hundredth time, a massive glass paperweight. The glass contained pinkish azure and St. Isaac's Cathedral specked with golden sandy grains. You laughed and read aloud, "Yesterday, a merchant of the Second Guild named Yeroshin was arrested at the Quisisana Restaurant. It turned out that Yeroshin, under the pretext of . . ." You laughed again. "No, the rest is indecent."

Pal Palych grew flustered, flushed a brownish shade of red, and dropped his spoon. Maple leaves glistened immediately beneath the windows. A wagon rattled past. From somewhere came the plaintive, tender cry "Ice—cream! . . ."

He began talking about school, about drunkenness, about the trout that had appeared in the river. I started scrutinizing him, and had the feeling I was really seeing him for the first time, even though we were old acquaintances. An image of him from our first encounter must have remained impressed on my brain and never changed, like something accepted and grown habitual. When thinking in passing about Pal Palych, I had the impression for some reason that he had not only a dark-blond mustache but even a matching little beard. An imaginary beard is a characteristic of many Russian faces. Now, having given him a special look, so to speak, with an internal eye, I saw that in reality his chin was rounded, hairless,* and had a slight cleft. He had a fleshy nose, and I noticed, on his left eyelid, a pimplelike mole I would have dearly loved to cut off—but cutting would have meant killing. That little grain contained him, totally and exclusively. When I realized all this, and examined all of him, I made the slightest of motions, as if nudging my soul to start it sliding downhill, and glided inside Pal Palych, made myself comfortable inside him, and felt from within, as it were, that growth on his wrinkly eyelid, the starched winglets of his collar, and the fly crawling across his bald spot. I examined all of him with limpid, mobile eyes. The yellow lion over the bed now seemed an old acquaintance, as if it had been on my wall since childhood. The colored postcard, enclosed in its convex glass, became extraordinary, graceful, joyous. It was not you sitting in front of me, in the low wicker armchair to which my back had grown accustomed, but the benefactress of the school, a taciturn lady I hardly knew. And right away, with the same lightness of movement, I glided into you too, perceived the ribbon of a garter above your knee and, a little higher, the tickle of batiste, and thought, in your stead, that it was boring, it was hot, one wanted to smoke. At that instant you produced a gold case from your purse and inserted a cigarette into your holder. And I was within everything—you, the cigarette, the holder, Pal Palych scrabbling awkwardly with his match, the glass paperweight, the dead bumblebee on the windowsill.

Many years have sailed by, and I do not know where he is now, timid, puffy Pal Palych. Sometimes, though, when he is the last thing I am thinking about, I see him in a dream, transposed into the setting of my current existence. He enters a room with his fussy, smiling gait, faded panama in hand; he bows as he walks; he mops his bald spot and ruddy neck with an enormous handkerchief. And when I dream of him you invariably traverse my dream, looking lazy and wearing a low-belted silk top.

· · ·

*The sharp-eyed bilingual reader familiar with the original Russian may note the substitution of "hairless" for "irresolute." The two words resemble each other in Russian, and "irresolute" was almost certainly the result of a copyist's slip. —D.N.

I was not loquacious on that wonderfully happy day. I gulped the slippery flakes of curds and strained to hear every sound. When Pal Palych fell silent, I could hear his stomach muttering—a delicate squeak, followed by a tiny gurgle. Whereupon he would demonstratively clear his throat and hurriedly start talking about something. Stumbling, at a loss for the right word, he would frown and drum his fingertips on the table. You reclined in the low armchair, impassive and silent. Turning your head sidewise and lifting your angular elbow, you would glance at me from under your lashes as you adjusted the hairpins in back. You thought I felt awkward in front of Pal Palych because you and I had arrived together, and he might have an inkling about our relationship. And I was amused that you were thinking this, and amused by the dim, melancholy way Pal Palych blushed when you deliberately mentioned your husband and his work.

In front of the school, the sun's hot ochre had splashed beneath the maples. From the threshold, Pal Palych bowed, thanking us for dropping by, then he bowed again from the doorway, and a thermometer sparkled, glassy-white, on the outside wall.

When we had left the village, crossed the bridge, and were climbing the path toward your house, I took you under the elbow, and you flashed that special sidelong smile that told me you were happy. Suddenly I had the desire to tell you about Pal Palych's little wrinkles, about the spangled St. Isaac's, but, as soon as I began, I had a feeling the wrong words were coming out, bizarre words, and when you tenderly said, "Decadent," I changed the subject. I knew what you needed: simple feelings, simple words. Your silence was effortless and windless, like the silence of clouds or plants. All silence is the recognition of a mystery. There was much about you that seemed mysterious.

A workman in a puffed blouse was resonantly and firmly sharpening his scythe. Butterflies floated above the unmowed scabious flowers. Toward us along the path came a young girl with a pale-green kerchief on her shoulders and daisies in her dark hair. I had already seen her three times or so, and her thin, tanned neck had stuck in my memory. As she passed, she gave you an attentive touch of her barely slanted eyes. Then, hopping carefully across the ditch, she disappeared behind the alders. A silvery tremor traversed the matte-textured bushes. You said, "I bet she was having herself a nice walk in my park. How I detest these vacationers. . . ." A fox terrier, a plump old bitch, was trotting along the path after her owner. You adored dogs. The little animal crawled up to us on its belly, wriggling, its ears laid back. It rolled over under your proffered hand, showing its pink underbelly, covered with gray maplike spots. "Why, you sweetheart," you said with your special, petting-ruffling voice.

The fox terrier, having rolled around for a while, gave a dainty little squeal and trotted on, scuttling across the ditch.

When we were already approaching the low park gate, you decided you wanted to smoke, but, after rummaging in your handbag, you softly clucked, "How silly of me. I left the holder at his place." You touched my shoulder. "Dearest, run and fetch it. Otherwise I cannot smoke." I laughed as I kissed your fluttery eyelashes and your narrow smile.

You cried out after me, "Just hurry!" I set off at a run, not because there was any great rush, but because everything around me was running—the iridescence of the bushes, the shadows of the clouds on the damp grass, the purplish flowers scurrying for their lives into a gully before the mower's lightning.

Some ten minutes later, panting hotly, I was climbing the steps to the schoolhouse. I banged on the brown door with my fist. A mattress spring squeaked inside. I turned the handle, but the door was locked. "Who's there?" came Pal Palych's flustered voice.

I shouted, "Come on, let me in!" The mattress clinked again, and there was a slapping of unshod feet. "What do you lock yourself in for, Pal Palych?" I noticed right away that his eyes were red.

"Come in, come in. . . . Glad to see you. You see, I was asleep. Come on in."

"We forgot a cigarette holder here," I said, trying not to look at him.

We finally found the green-enameled tube under the armchair. I stuck it in my pocket. Pal Palych was trumpeting into his handkerchief.

"She's a wonderful person," he said inopportunely, sitting down heavily on the bed. He sighed and looked askance. "There's something about a Russian woman, a certain—" He got all wrinkled up and rubbed his brow. "A certain"—he emitted a gentle grunt—"spirit of self-sacrifice. There is nothing more sublime in the world. That extraordinarily subtle, extraordinarily sublime spirit of self-sacrifice." He joined his hands behind his head and broke into a lyrical smile.

"Extraordinarily . . ." He fell silent, then asked, already with a different tone, one that he often used to make me laugh, "And what else do you have to tell me, my friend?" I felt like giving him a hug, saying something full of warmth, something he needed. "You ought to go for a walk, Pal Palych. Why mope in a stuffy room?"

He gave a dismissive wave. "I've seen all there is to see. You do nothing b-but get all hot out there. . . ." He wiped his puffy eyes and his mustache with a downward motion of his hand. "Maybe tonight I'll go do some fishing." The pimplelike mole on his wrinkled eyelid twitched.

One ought to have asked him, "Dear Pal Palych, why were you lying down just now with your face buried in the pillow? Is it just hay fever, or some major grief? Have you ever loved a woman? And why cry on a day like this, with this nice sunshine and the puddles outside? . . ."

"Well, I have to run, Pal Palych," I said, glancing at the abandoned glasses, the typographically re-created Tolstoy, and the boots with earlike loops under the table.

Two flies settled on the red floor. One climbed on top of the other. They buzzed and flew apart.

"No hard feelings," Pal Palych said with a slow exhalation. He shook his head. "I'll grin and bear it—go, don't let me keep you."

I was running again along the path, next to the alder bushes. I felt that I had bathed in another's grief, that I was radiant with his tears. The feeling was a happy one, which I have since experienced only rarely: at the sight of a bowed tree, a pierced glove, a horse's eye. It was happy because it had a harmonious flow. It was happy as any movement or radiance is happy. I had once been splintered into a million beings and objects. Today I am one; tomorrow I shall splinter again. And thus everything in the world decants and modulates. That day I was on the crest of a wave. I knew that all my surroundings were notes of one and the same harmony, knew—secretly—the source and the inevitable resolution of the sounds assembled for an instant, and the new chord that would be engendered by each of the dispersing notes. My soul's musical ear knew and comprehended everything.

You met me on the paved section of the garden, by the veranda steps, and your first words were, "My husband called from town while I was gone. He's coming on the ten o'clock. Something must have happened. Maybe he's being transferred."

A wagtail, like a blue-gray wind, quickstepped across the sand. A pause, two or three steps, another pause, more steps. The wagtail, the cigarette holder in my hand, your words, the spots of sunlight on your dress . . . It could not have been otherwise.

"I know what you're thinking," you said, knitting your eyebrows. "You're thinking someone will tell him and so forth. But it makes no difference. . . . You know what I've . . ."

I looked you straight in the face. I looked with all my soul, directly. I collided with you. Your eyes were limpid, as if a pellicle of silken paper had fluttered off them—the kind that sheathes illustrations in precious books. And, for the first time, your voice was limpid too. "You know what I've decided? Listen. I cannot live without you. That's exactly what I'll tell him. He'll give me a divorce right away. And then, say in the fall, we could . . ."

I interrupted you with my silence. A spot of sunlight slid from your skirt onto the sand as you moved slightly away.

What could I say to you? Could I invoke freedom, captivity, say I did not love you enough? No, that was all wrong.

An instant passed. During that instant, much happened in the world: somewhere a giant steamship went to the bottom, a war was declared, a genius was born. The instant was gone.

"Here's your cigarette holder," I said. "It was under the armchair. And you know, when I went in, Pal Palych must have been . . ."

You said, "Good. Now you may leave." You turned and ran quickly up the steps. You took hold of the glass door's handle, and could not open it right away. It must have been torture for you.

I stood in the garden for a while amid the sweetish damp. Then, hands thrust deep into my pockets, I walked along the dappled sand around the house. At the front porch, I found my bicycle. Leaning on the low horns of the handlebar, I rolled off along the park lane. Toads lay here and there. I inadvertently ran over one. *Pop* under the tire. At the end of the lane there was a bench. I leaned the bicycle against a tree trunk and sat down on the invitingly white plank. I thought about how, in the next couple of days, I would get a letter from you, how you would beckon and I would not return. Your house glided into a marvelous, melancholy distance with its winged piano, the dusty volumes of *The Art Review*, the silhouettes in their circular frames. It was delicious losing you. You went off, jerking angularly at the glass door. But a different you departed otherwise, opening your pale eyes under my joyous kisses.

I sat thus until evening. Midges, as if jerked by invisible threads, darted up and down. Suddenly, somewhere nearby, I became aware of a bright dapple—it was your dress, and you were—

Had not the final vibrations died away? Therefore, I felt uneasy that you were here again, somewhere off to the side, beyond my field of vision, that you were walking, approaching. With an effort, I turned my face. It was not you but that girl with the greenish scarf—remember, the one we ran into? And that fox terrier of hers with its comical belly? . . .

She walked past, through gaps in the foliage, and crossed the little bridge leading to a small kiosk with stained-glass windows. The girl is bored, she is strolling through your park; I shall probably make her acquaintance by and by.

I rose slowly, slowly rode out of the motionless park onto the main road, straight into an enormous sunset, and, on the far side of a curve, overtook a carriage. It was your coachman, Semyon, driving at a walk toward the station. When he saw me, he slowly removed his cap, smoothed the glossy strands on the back of his head, then replaced it. A checkered lap rug lay folded on the seat. An intriguing reflection flashed in the eye of the black gelding. And when, with motionless pedals, I flew downhill toward the river, I saw from the bridge the panama and rounded shoulders of Pal Palych, who was sitting below on a projection of the bathing booth, with a fishing rod in his fist.

I braked, and stopped with my hand on the railing.

"Hey, hey, Pal Palych! How're they biting?" He looked upward, and gave me a nice, homey kind of wave.

A bat darted above the rose-colored mirror surface. The reflection of the foliage looked like black lace. Pal Palych, from afar, was shouting something, beckoning with his hand. A second Pal Palych quivered in the black ripples. Laughing aloud, I pushed away from the handrail.

I passed the isbas in one soundless sweep along the firmly packed path. Mooing sounds floated past through the lusterless air; some skittles flew up with a clatter. Then, farther along, on the highway, in the vastness of the sunset, amid the faintly vaporous fields, there was silence.

WINGSTROKE

1

WHEN the curved tip of one ski crosses the other, you tumble forward. The scalding snow goes up your sleeves, and it is very hard to get back on your feet. Kern, who had not skied for a long time, rapidly worked up a sweat. Feeling slightly dizzy, he yanked off the woolen cap that had been tickling his ears, and brushed the moist sparks from his eyelashes.

All was merriment and azure in front of the six-story hotel. The trees stood disembodied in the radiance. Countless ski tracks flowed like shadowy hair down the shoulders of the snowy hills. And all around, a gigantic whiteness rushed heavenward and sparkled, unfettered, in the sky.

Kern's skis creaked as he made his way up the slope. Noticing his broad shoulders, his equine profile, and the robust gloss on his cheekbones, the English girl he had met yesterday, the third day since his arrival, had taken him for a compatriot. Isabel, Airborne Isabel, as she was dubbed by a crowd of sleek and swarthy young men of the Argentine type, who scurried everywhere in her wake: to the hotel ballroom, up the padded stairs, along the snowy slopes in a play of sparkling dust. Her mien was airy and impetuous, her mouth so red it seemed the Creator had scooped up some torrid carmine and slapped a handful on the nether part of her face. Laughter flitted in her down-flecked eyes. A Spanish comb stood erect like a wing in the steep wave of her black, satin-sheeny hair. This was how Kern had seen her yesterday, when the slightly hollow din of the gong summoned her to dinner from Room 35. And the fact that they were neighbors, and that the number of her room was that of his years, and that she was seated across from him at the long table d'hôte, tall, vivacious, in a low-cut black dress, with a band of black silk on her bare neck—all this seemed

25

so significant to Kern that it made a rift in the dull melancholy that had already oppressed him for half a year.

It was Isabel who spoke first, and that did not surprise him. In this huge hotel that blazed, isolated, in a cleft between the mountains, life pulsed tipsy and lighthearted after the dead War years. Besides, to her, to Isabel, nothing was forbidden—not the sidelong flutter of eyelashes, not the melody of laughter in her voice as she said, handing Kern the ashtray, "I think you and I are the only English here," and added, inclining tableward a translucent shoulder restrained by a black ribbon-like strap, "Not counting, of course, a half-dozen little old ladies, and that character over there with the turned-around collar."

Kern replied, "You're mistaken. I have no homeland. It's true I spent many years in London. Besides—"

The next morning, after a half-year of indifference, he suddenly felt the pleasure of entering the deafening cone of an ice-cold shower. At nine, after a substantial and sensible breakfast, he crunched off on his skis across the reddish sand scattered on the naked glare of the path before the hotel veranda. When he had mounted the snowy slope, herringbone-style as befits a skier, there, amid checkered knickers and flushed faces, was Isabel.

She greeted him English fashion—with but the flourish of a smile. Her skis were iridescent with olive-gold. Snow clung to the intricate straps that held her feet. There was an unfeminine strength about her feet and legs, shapely in their sturdy boots and tightly wound puttees. A purple shadow glided behind her along the crusty surface as, hands nonchalantly thrust into the pockets of her leather jacket and her left ski slightly advanced, she sped off down the slope, ever faster, scarf flying, amid sprays of powdered snow. Then, at full speed, she made a sharp turn with one knee deeply flexed, straightened again, and sped on, past the firs, past the turquoise skating rink. A pair of youths in colorful sweaters and a famous Swedish sportsman with a terra-cotta face and colorless, combed-back hair rushed past behind her.

A little later Kern ran into her again near a bluish track along which people flashed with a faint clatter, belly-down on their flat sleds like woolly frogs. With a glint of her skis Isabel disappeared behind the bend of a snowbank, and when Kern, ashamed of his awkward movements, overtook her in a soft hollow amid silver-frosted boughs, she wiggled her fingers in the air, stamped her skis, and was off again. Kern stood for a time among the violet shadows, and suddenly felt a whiff of the familiar terror of silence. The lacework of the branches in the enamel-like air had the chill of a terrifying fairy tale. The trees, the intricate shadows, his own skis all looked strangely toylike. He realized

that he was tired, that he had a blistered heel, and, snagging some protruding branches, he turned back. Skaters glided mechanically across
the smooth turquoise. On the snow slope beyond, the terra-cotta
Swede was helping up a snow-covered, lanky chap with horn-rimmed
glasses, who was floundering in the sparkling powder like some awkward bird. Like a detached wing, a ski that had come off his foot was
sliding down the hill.

Back in his room, Kern changed and, at the sound of the gong's
hollow clanging, rang and ordered cold roast beef, some grapes, and a
flask of Chianti.

He had a nagging ache in his shoulders and thighs.

Had no business chasing after her, he thought. A man sticks a pair
of boards on his feet and proceeds to savor the law of gravity.
Ridiculous.

Around four he went down to the spacious reading room, where
the mouth of the fireplace exhaled orange heat and invisible people sat
in deep leather armchairs with their legs extending from under open
newspapers. On a long oaken table lay a disorderly pile of magazines
full of advertisements for toilet supplies, dancing girls, and parliamentary top hats. Kern picked out a ragged copy of the *Tattler* from the
previous June and, for a long time, examined the smile of the woman
who had, for seven years, been his wife. He recalled her dead face,
which had become so cold and hard, and some letters he had found in
a small box.

He pushed aside the magazine, his fingernail squeaking on the
glossy page.

Then, moving his shoulders laboriously and wheezing on his short
pipe, he went out onto the enormous enclosed veranda, where a
chilled band was playing and people in bright scarves were drinking
strong tea, ready to rush out again into the cold, onto the slopes that
shone with a humming shimmer through the wide windowpanes. With
searching eyes, he scanned the veranda. Somebody's curious gaze
pricked him like a needle touching the nerve of a tooth. He turned
back abruptly.

In the billiard room, which he had entered sidewise as the oak door
yielded to his push, Monfiori, a pale, red-haired little fellow who recognized only the Bible and the carom, was bent over the emerald
cloth, sliding his cue back and forth as he aimed at a ball. Kern had
made his acquaintance recently, and the man had promptly showered
him with citations from the Holy Scriptures. He said he was writing a
major book in which he demonstrated that, if one construed the Book
of Job in a certain way, then . . . But Kern had stopped listening, for

his attention had suddenly been caught by his interlocutor's ears—pointed ears, packed with canary-colored dust, with reddish fluff on their tips.

The balls clicked and scattered. Raising his eyebrows, Monfiori proposed a game. He had melancholy, slightly bulbous, caprine eyes.

Kern had already accepted, and had even rubbed some chalk on the tip of his cue, but, suddenly sensing a wave of dreadful ennui that made the pit of his stomach ache and his ears ring, said he had a pain in his elbow, glanced out as he passed a window at the mountains' sugary sheen, and returned to the reading room.

There, with his legs intertwined and one patent-leather shoe twitching, he again examined the pearl-gray photograph, the childlike eyes and shaded lips of the London beauty who had been his wife. The first night after her self-inflicted death he followed a woman who smiled at him on a foggy street corner, taking revenge on God, love, and fate.

And now came this Isabel with that red smear for a mouth. If one could only . . .

He clenched his teeth and the muscles of his strong jaws rippled. His entire past life seemed a shaky row of varicolored screens with which he shielded himself from cosmic drafts. Isabel was but the latest bright scrap. How many there had already been of these silk rags, and how he had tried to hang them across the gaping black gap! Voyages, books in delicate bindings, and seven years of ecstatic love. They billowed, these scraps, with the wind outside, tore, fell one by one. The gap cannot be hidden, the abyss breathes and sucks everything in. This he understood when the detective in suede gloves . . .

Kern sensed that he was rocking back and forth, and that some pale girl with pink eyebrows was looking at him from behind a magazine. He took a *Times* from the table and opened the giant sheets. Paper bedspread across the chasm. People invent crimes, museums, games, only to escape from the unknown, from the vertiginous sky. And now this Isabel . . .

He tossed the paper aside, rubbed his forehead with an enormous fist, and again felt someone's wondering gaze on him. Then he slowly walked out of the room, past the reading feet, past the fireplace's orange jaw. He lost his way in the resounding corridors, found himself in some hallway, where the white legs of a bowed chair were reflected by the parquet and a broad painting hung on the wall of William Tell piercing the apple on his son's head; then he examined at length his clean-shaven, heavy face, the blood streaks on the whites of his eyes, his checked bow tie in the glistening mirror of a bright bathroom where water gurgled musically and a golden cigarette butt discarded by someone floated in the porcelain depths.

Beyond the windows the snows were dimming and turning blue. Delicate hues illumined the sky. The flaps of the revolving door at the entrance to the din-filled vestibule slowly glinted as they admitted clouds of vapor and snorting, florid-faced people tired after their snowy games. The stairs breathed with footfalls, exclamations, laughter. Then the hotel grew still: everyone was dressing for dinner.

Kern, who had fallen into a vague torpor in his armchair in his twilit room, was awakened by the gong's vibrations. Reveling in his newfound energy, he turned on the lights, inserted cuff links into a fresh, starched shirt, extracted a flattened pair of black pants from under the squeaking press. Five minutes later, aware of a cool lightness, the firmness of the hair on the top of his head, and every detail of his well-creased clothes, he went down to the dining room.

Isabel was not there. Soup was served, then fish, but she did not appear.

Kern examined with revulsion the dull-bronzed youths, the brick-hued face of an old woman with a beauty spot dissimulating a pimple, a man with goatish eyes, and fixed his gloomy gaze on a curly little pyramid of hyacinths in a green pot.

She appeared only when, in the hall where William Tell hung, the instruments of a Negro band had started pounding and moaning.

She smelled of chill air and perfume. Her hair looked moist. Something about her face stunned Kern.

She smiled a brilliant smile, and adjusted the black ribbon on her translucent shoulder.

"You know, I just got back. Barely had time to change and wolf down a sandwich."

Kern asked: "Don't tell me you've been skiing all this time? Why, it's completely dark out."

She gave him an intense look, and Kern realized what had astonished him: her eyes, which sparkled as if they were dusted with frost.

Isabel began gliding softly along the dovelike vowels of English speech: "Of course. It was extraordinary. I hurtled down the slopes in the dark, I flew off the bumps. Right up into the stars."

"You might have killed yourself," said Kern.

She repeated, narrowing her downy eyes, "Right up into the stars," and added, with a glint of her bare clavicle, "and now I want to dance."

The Negro band rattled and wailed in the hall. Japanese lanterns floated colorfully. Moving on tiptoe, alternating quick steps with suspended ones, his palm pressed to hers, Kern advanced, at close quarters, on Isabel. One step, and her slender leg would press into him; another, and she would resiliently yield. The fragrant freshness of her hair tickled his temple, and he could feel, under the edge of his right hand, the supple undulations of her bared back. With bated breath he would enter breaks in the music, then glide on from measure to measure. . . . Around him floated past the intense faces of angular couples with perversely absent eyes. And the opaque song of the strings was punctuated by the patter of primitive little hammers.

The music accelerated, swelled, and ended with a clatter. Everything stopped. Then came applause, demanding more of the same. But the musicians had decided to have a rest.

Pulling a handkerchief out of his cuff and mopping his brow, Kern set off after Isabel, who, with a flutter of her black fan, was heading for the door. They sat down side by side on some wide stairs.

Not looking at him, she said, "Sorry—I had the feeling I was still amid the snow and stars. I didn't even notice whether you danced well or not."

Kern glanced at her as if not hearing, and she was indeed immersed in her own radiant thoughts, thoughts unknown to him.

One step lower sat a youth in a very narrow jacket and a skinny girl with a birthmark on her shoulder blade. When the music started again, the youth invited Isabel to dance a Boston. Kern had to dance with the skinny girl. She smelled of slightly sour lavender. Colored paper streamers swirled out through the hall, tangling themselves about the dancers. One of the musicians stuck on a white mustache, and for some reason Kern felt ashamed for him. When the dance was over he abandoned his partner and rushed off in search of Isabel. She was nowhere to be seen—not at the buffet nor on the staircase.

That's it—bedtime, was Kern's terse thought.

Back in his room he held the drape aside before lying down, and, without thinking, looked into the night. Reflections of windows lay on the dark snow in front of the hotel. In the distance, the metallic summits floated in a funereal radiance.

He had the sensation he had glanced into death. He pulled the folds together tightly so that not a ray of night could leak into the room. But when he switched off the light and lay down, he noticed a glint coming from the edge of a glass shelf. He got up and fiddled a long time around the window, cursing the splashes of moonlight. The floor was cold as marble.

When Kern loosened the cord of his pajamas and closed his eyes, slippery slopes started to rush beneath him. A hollow pounding began in his heart, as if it had kept silent all day and was now taking advantage of the quiet. He began feeling frightened as he listened to this pounding. He recalled how once, on a very windy day, he was passing a butcher's shop with his wife, and a carcass rocked on its hook with a dull thudding against the wall. That was how his heart felt now. His wife, meanwhile, had her eyes narrowed against the wind and was holding her hat as she said that the wind and the sea were driving her crazy, that they must leave, they must leave. . . .

Kern rolled over onto his other side—gingerly, so his chest would not burst from the convex blows.

"Can't go on like this," he mumbled into the pillow, forlornly folding up his legs. He lay for a while on his back peering at the ceiling, at the wan gleams that had penetrated, as piercing as his ribs.

When his eyes closed again, silent sparks started to glide in front of him, then infinitely unwinding transparent spirals. Isabel's snowy eyes and fiery mouth flashed past, then came sparks and spirals again. For an instant his heart retracted into a lacerating knot. Then it swelled and gave a thump.

Can't go on like this, I'll go crazy. No future, just a black wall. There's nothing left.

He had the impression that the paper streamers were slithering down his face, rustling and ripping into narrow shreds. And the Japanese lanterns flowed with colored undulations in the parquet. He was dancing, advancing.

If I could just unclench her, flip her open. . . . And then . . .

And death seemed to him like a gliding dream, a fluffy fall. No thoughts, no palpitations, no aches.

The lunar ribs on the ceiling had imperceptibly moved. Footfalls passed quietly along the corridor, a lock clicked somewhere, a soft ringing flew past; then footfalls again, the mutter and murmur of footfalls.

That means the ball is over, thought Kern. He turned his stuffy pillow over.

Now, all around, there was an immense, gradually cooling silence. Only his heart oscillated, taut and heavy. Kern groped on the bedside table, located the pitcher, took a swallow from the spout. An icy streamlet scalded his neck and collarbone.

He started thinking of methods to induce sleep. He imagined waves rhythmically running up onto a shoreline. Then plump gray sheep slowly tumbling over a fence. One sheep, two, three . . .

Isabel is asleep next door, thought Kern. Isabel is asleep, wearing yellow pajamas, probably. Yellow becomes her. Spanish color. If I scratched on the wall with my fingernail she'd hear me. Damned palpitations . . .

He fell asleep at the very moment he had begun trying to decide whether there was any point in turning on the light and reading something for a while. There's a French novel lying on the armchair. The ivory knife glides, cutting the pages. One, two . . .

He came to in the middle of the room, awakened by a sense of unbearable horror. The horror had knocked him off the bed. He had dreamt that the wall next to which stood his bed had begun slowly collapsing onto him—so he had recoiled with a spasmodic exhalation.

Kern found the headboard by touch, and would have gone back to sleep immediately if it had not been for a noise he heard through the wall. He did not understand right away where this noise was coming from, and the act of straining his hearing made his consciousness, which was ready to glide down the slope of sleep, abruptly grow lucid. The noise occurred again: a twang, followed by the rich sonority of guitar strings.

Kern remembered—it was Isabel who was in the next room. Right away, as if in response to his thought, came a peal of her laughter. Twice, thrice, the guitar throbbed and dissolved. Then an odd, intermittent bark sounded and ceased.

Seated on his bed, Kern listened in wonder. He pictured a bizarre scene: Isabel with a guitar and a huge Great Dane looking up at her with blissful eyes. He put his ear to the chilly wall. The bark rang out again, the guitar twanged as from a fillip, and a strange rustle began undulating as if an ample wind were whirling there in the next room. The rustle stretched out into a low whistle, and once again the night filled with silence. Then a frame banged—Isabel had shut the window.

Indefatigable girl, he thought—the dog, the guitar, the icy drafts.

Now all was quiet. Having expelled all those noises from her room, Isabel had probably gone to bed and was now asleep.

"Damn it! I don't understand anything. I don't have anything. Damn it, damn it," moaned Kern, burying himself in the pillow. A leaden fatigue was compressing his temples. His legs ached and tingled unbearably. He groaned in the darkness for a long time, turning heavily from side to side. The rays on the ceiling were long since extinguished.

2
_____

The next day Isabel did not appear until lunchtime.

Since morning the sky had been blindingly white and the sun had been moonlike. Then snow began falling, slowly and vertically. The dense flakes, like ornamental spots on a white veil, curtained the view of the mountains, the heavily laden firs, the dulled turquoise of the rink. The plump, soft particles of snow rustled against the window-panes, falling, falling without end. If one watched them for long, one had the impression the entire hotel was slowly drifting upward.

"I was so tired last night," Isabel was saying to her neighbor, a young man with a high olive forehead and piercing eyes, "so tired I decided to loll in bed."

"You look stunning today," drawled the young man with exotic courtesy.

She inflated her nostrils derisively.

Looking at her through the hyacinths, Kern said coldly, "I didn't know, Miss Isabel, that you had a dog in your room, as well as a guitar."

Her downy eyes seemed to narrow even more, against a breeze of embarrassment. Then she beamed with a smile, all carmine and ivory.

"You overdid it on the dance floor last night, Mr. Kern," she replied. The olive youth and the little fellow who recognized only Bible and billiards laughed, the first with a hearty ha-ha, the second very softly, with raised eyebrows.

Kern said with a frown, "I'd like to ask you not to play at night. I don't have an easy time falling asleep."

Isabel slashed his face with a rapid, radiant glance.

"You had better ask your dreams, not me, about that."

And she began talking to her neighbor about the next day's ski competition.

For some minutes already Kern had felt his lips stretching into a spasmodic, uncontrollable sneer. It twitched agonizingly in the corners of his mouth, and he suddenly felt like yanking the tablecloth off the table, hurling the pot with the hyacinths against the wall.

He rose, trying to conceal his unbearable tremor, and, seeing no one, went out of the room.

"What's happening to me," he questioned his anguish. "What's going on here?"

He kicked his suitcase open and started packing. He immediately felt dizzy. He stopped and again began pacing the room. Angrily he stuffed his short pipe. He sat down in the armchair by the window, beyond which the snow was falling with nauseating regularity.

He had come to this hotel, to this wintry, stylish nook called Zermatt, in order to fuse the sensation of white silence with the pleasure of lighthearted, motley encounters, for total solitude was what he feared most. But now he understood that human faces were also intolerable to him, that the snow made his head ring, and that he lacked the inspired vitality and tender perseverance without which passion is powerless. While for Isabel, probably, life consisted of a splendid ski run, of impetuous laughter, of perfume and frosty air.

Who is she? A heliotype diva, broken free? Or the runaway daughter of a swaggering, bilious lord? Or just one of those women from Paris . . . And where does her money come from? Slightly vulgar thought . . .

She does have the dog, though, and it's pointless for her to deny it. Some sleek-haired Great Dane. With a cold nose and warm ears. Still snowing, too, Kern thought haphazardly. And, in my suitcase—a spring seemed to pop open, with a clink, in his brain—I have a Parabellum.

Until evening he again ambled about the hotel, or made dry rustling noises with the newspapers in the reading room. From the vestibule window he saw Isabel, the Swede, and several young men with jackets pulled on over fringed sweaters getting into a swanlike curved sleigh. The roan horses made their merry harnesses ring. The snow was falling silent and dense. Isabel, all spangled with small white stars, was shouting and laughing amid her companions. And when the sled started with a jerk and sped off, she rocked backward, clapping her fur-mittened hands in the air.

Kern turned away from the window.

Go ahead, enjoy your ride. . . . It makes no difference. . . .

Then, during dinner, he tried not to look at her. She was filled with a merry, festive gaiety, and paid no attention to him. At nine the Negro music began moaning and clattering again. Kern, in a state of feverish languor, was standing by the doorjamb, gazing at the clinched couples and at Isabel's curly fan.

A soft voice said next to his ear, "Would you care to go to the bar?"

He turned and saw the melancholy caprine eyes, the ears with their reddish fuzz.

Amid the crimson penumbra of the bar the glass tables reflected the flounces of the lampshades.

On high stools at the metal counter sat three men, all three wearing white gaiters, their legs retracted, sucking through straws on bright-colored drinks. On the other side of the bar, where varicolored bottles sparkled on the shelves like a collection of convex beetles, a fleshy, black-mustachioed man in a cherry-colored dinner jacket was mixing cocktails with extraordinary dexterity. Kern and Monfiori selected a table in the bar's velvet depths. A waiter opened a long list of beverages, gingerly and reverently, like an antiquary exhibiting a precious book.

"We're going to have a glass of each in succession," said Monfiori in his melancholy, slightly hollow voice, "and when we get to the end we'll start over, choosing only the ones we found to our liking. Perhaps we'll stop at one and keep savoring it for a long time. Then we'll go back to the beginning again."

He gave the waiter a pensive look. "Is that clear?"

The part in the waiter's hair tipped forward.

"This is known as the roaming of Bacchus," Monfiori told Kern with a doleful chuckle. "Some people approach their daily life in the same way."

Kern stifled a tremulous yawn. "You know this ends by making you throw up."

Monfiori sighed, swigged, smacked his lips, and marked the first item on the list with an X, using an automatic pencil. Two deep furrows ran from the wings of his nose to the corners of his thin mouth.

After his third glass Kern lit a cigarette in silence. After his sixth drink—an oversweet concoction of chocolate and champagne—he had the urge to talk.

He exhaled a megaphone of smoke. Narrowing his eyes, he tapped the ashes from his cigarette with a yellowed nail.

"Tell me, Monfiori, what do you think of this—what's her name—Isabel?"

"You'll get nowhere with her," replied Monfiori. "She belongs to the slippery species. All she seeks is fleeting contact."

"But she plays the guitar at night, and fusses with her dog. That's not good, is it?" said Kern, goggling his eyes at his glass.

With another sigh, Monfiori said, "Why don't you drop her. After all . . ."

"Sounds to me like envy—" began Kern.

The other quietly interrupted him: "She's a woman. And I, you see, have other tastes." Clearing his throat modestly, he made another X.

The ruby drinks were replaced by golden ones. Kern had the feeling his blood was turning sweet. His head was growing foggy. The white spats left the bar. The drumming and crooning of the distant music ceased.

"You say one must be selective . . . ," he spoke thickly and limply, "while I have reached a point . . . Listen to this, for instance—I once had a wife. She fell in love with someone else. He turned out to be a thief. He stole cars, necklaces, furs. . . . And she poisoned herself. With strychnine."

"And do you believe in God?" asked Monfiori with the air of a man getting on his hobby horse. "There is God, after all."

Kern gave an artificial laugh.

"Biblical God. . . . Gaseous vertebrate. . . . I am not a believer."

"That's from Huxley," insinuatingly observed Monfiori. "There was a biblical God, though. . . . The point is that He is not alone; there are numerous biblical Gods. . . . A host. My favorite one is . . . 'He sneezes and there is light. He has eyes like the eyelashes of dawn.' Do you understand what this means? Do you? And there is more: '. . . the fleshy parts of his body are solidly interconnected, and they won't budge.' Well? Well? Do you understand?"

"Wait a minute," shouted Kern.

"No, no—you must think about it. 'He transforms the sea into a seething ointment; he leaves behind a trail of radiance; the abyss is akin to a patch of gray hair!' "

"Wait, will you," interrupted Kern. "I want to tell you that I have decided to kill myself. . . ."

Monfiori gave him an opaque, attentive look, covering his glass with his palm. He was silent for a time.

"Just as I thought," he began with unexpected gentleness. "To-night, as you were watching the people dancing, and before that, when you got up from the table . . . There was something about your face . . . The crease between the brows . . . That special one . . . I understood right away . . ." He fell silent, caressing the table's edge.

"Listen to what I'm going to tell you," he continued, lowering his heavy, purplish eyelids with their wartlike lashes. "I search everywhere for the likes of you—in expensive hotels, on trains, in seaside resorts, at night on the quays of big cities." A dreamy little sneer fleeted across his lips.

"I recall, in Florence once . . ." He raised his doelike eyes. "Listen, Kern—I'd like to be present when you do it. . . . May I?"

Kern, in a numb slouch, sensed a chill in his chest under his starched shirt. *We're both drunk*, the words rushed through his brain, *and he's spooky.*

"May I?" repeated Monfiori with a pout, "Pretty please?" (touch of clammy, hairy little hand).

With a jerk and a groggy sway Kern rose from his chair.

"Go to hell! Let me out. . . . I was joking. . . ."

The attentive gaze of Monfiori's leechy eyes did not waver.

"I've had enough of you! I've had enough of everything." Kern dashed off with a splashlike gesture of his hands. Monfiori's gaze came unstuck with what seemed like a smack.

"Murk! Puppet! . . . Wordplay! . . . Basta! . . ."

He banged his hip painfully on the edge of the table. The raspberry fatty behind his vacillating bar puffed out his white shirtfront and began to float, as though in a curved mirror, amid his bottles. Kern traversed the gliding ripples of the carpet and, with his shoulder, shoved a falling glass door.

The hotel was fast asleep. Mounting the cushiony stairs with difficulty, he located his room. A key protruded from the adjoining door. Someone had forgotten to lock himself in. Flowers meandered in the dim light of the corridor. Once he was in his room he spent a long time groping along the wall in search of the light switch. Then he collapsed into an armchair by the window.

It struck him that he must write certain letters, farewell letters. But the syrupy drinks had weakened him. His ears filled with a dense, hollow din, and gelid waves breathed on his brow. He had to write a letter, and there was something else troubling him. As if he had left home and forgotten his wallet. The mirrory blackness of the window reflected his stripelike collar and his pale forehead. He had splashed some intoxicating drops on his shirtfront. He must write that letter . . . no, that wasn't it. Suddenly something flashed in his mind's eye. The key! The key protruding from the neighboring door. . . .

Kern rose ponderously and went out into the dimly lit corridor. From the enormous key dangled a shiny wafer with the number 35. He stopped in front of this white door. There was an avid tremor in his legs.

A frosty wind lashed his brow. The window of the spacious, illuminated bedroom was wide open. On the wide bed, in open-collared yellow pajamas, Isabel lay supine. A pale hand drooped, with a smouldering cigarette between its fingers. Sleep must have overcome her without warning.

Kern approached the bed. He banged his knee against a chair, on which a guitar uttered a faint twang. Isabel's blue hair lay in tight circles on the pillow. He took a look at her dark eyelids, at the delicate shadow between her breasts. He touched the blanket. Her eyes opened immediately. Then, in a hunchbacked kind of stance, Kern said: "I need your love. Tomorrow I shall shoot myself."

He had never dreamt that a woman, even if taken by surprise, could be so startled. First Isabel remained motionless, then she lunged, looking back at the open window, slipping instantly from the bed, and rushed past Kern with bowed head, as if expecting a blow from above.

The door slammed. Some sheets of letter paper fluttered from the table.

Kern remained standing in the middle of the spacious bright room. Some grapes glowed purple and gold on the night table.

"Madwoman," he said aloud.

He laboriously shifted his shoulders. Like a steed he trembled with a prolonged shiver from the cold. Then, suddenly, he froze motionless.

Outside the window, swelling, flying, a joyous barking sound approached by agitated jolts. In a wink the square of black night in the window opening filled and came aboil with solid, boisterous fur. In one broad and noisy sweep this roughish fur obscured the night sky from one window frame to the other. Another instant and it swelled tensely, obliquely burst in, and unfolded. Amid the whistling spread of agitated fur flashed a white face. Kern grabbed the guitar by its fingerboard and, with all his strength, struck the white face flying at him. Like some fluffy tempest, the giant wing's rib knocked him off his feet. He was overwhelmed by an animal smell. Kern rose with a lurch.

In the center of the room lay an enormous angel.

He occupied the entire room, the entire hotel, the entire world. His right wing had bent, leaning its angle against the mirrored dresser. The left one swung ponderously, catching on the legs of an overturned chair. The chair banged back and forth on the floor. The brown fur of the wings steamed, iridescent with frost. Deafened by the blow, the angel propped itself on its palms like a sphinx. Blue veins swelled on its white hands, and hollows of shadow showed on its shoulders next to the clavicles. Its elongated, myopic-looking eyes, pale-green like predawn air, gazed at Kern without blinking from beneath straight, joined brows.

Suffocating from the pungent odor of wet fur, Kern stood motionless in the apathy of ultimate fear, examining the giant, steamy wings and the white face.

A hollow din began beyond the door in the corridor, and Kern was overcome by a different emotion: heart-rending shame. He was ashamed to the point of pain, of horror, that in a moment someone might come in and find him and this incredible creature.

The angel heaved a noisy breath, moved. But his arms had grown weak, and he collapsed on his chest. A wing jerked. Grinding his teeth, trying not to look, Kern stooped over him, took hold of the mound of damp, odorous fur and the cold, sticky shoulders. He noticed with sickening horror that the angel's feet were pale and boneless, and that he would be unable to stand on them. The angel did not resist. Kern hurriedly pulled him toward the wardrobe, flung open the mirrored door, began pushing and squeezing the wings into the creaking depths. He seized them by their ribs, trying to bend them and pack them in. Unfurling flaps of fur kept slapping him in the chest. At last he closed the door with a solid shove. At that instant there came a lacerating, unbearable shriek, the shriek of an animal crushed by a wheel. He had slammed the door on one of the wings, that was it. A small corner of the wing protruded from the crack. Opening the door slightly, Kern shoved the curly wedge in with his hand. He turned the key.

It grew very quiet. Kern felt hot tears running down his face. He took a breath and rushed for the corridor. Isabel lay next to the wall, a cowering heap of black silk. He gathered her in his arms, carried her into his room, and lowered her onto the bed. Then he snatched from his suitcase the heavy Parabellum, slammed the clip home, ran out holding his breath, and burst into Room 35.

The two halves of a broken plate lay, all white, on the carpet. The grapes were scattered.

Kern saw himself in the mirrored door of the wardrobe: a lock of hair fallen over an eyebrow, a starched dress shirtfront spattered with red, the lengthwise glint of the pistol's barrel.

"Must finish it off," he exclaimed tonelessly, and opened the wardrobe.

There was nothing but a gust of odorous fluff. Oily brown tufts eddying about the room. The wardrobe was empty. On its floor lay a white squashed hatbox.

Kern approached the window and looked out. Furry little clouds were gliding across the moon and breathing dim rainbows around it. He shut the casements, put the chair back in its place, and kicked some brown tufts under the bed. Then he cautiously went out into the corridor. It was quiet as before. People sleep soundly in mountain hotels.

And when he returned to his room what he saw was Isabel with her bare feet hanging from the bed, trembling, with her head between her hands. He felt ashamed, as he had, not long ago, when the angel was looking at him with its odd greenish eyes.

"Tell me, where is he?" asked Isabel breathlessly.

Kern turned away, went to the desk, sat down, opened the blotter, and replied, "I don't know."

Isabel retracted her bare feet onto the bed.

"May I stay here with you for now? I'm so frightened. . . ."

Kern gave a silent nod. Dominating the tremor of his hand, he started writing. Isabel began speaking again, in an agitated, toneless voice, but for some reason it appeared to Kern that her fright was of the female, earthly variety.

"I met him yesterday as I was flying on my skis in the dark. Last night he came to me."

Trying not to listen, Kern wrote in a bold hand:

"My dear friend, this is my last letter. I could never forget how you helped me when disaster crashed down on me. He probably lives on a peak where he hunts alpine eagles and feeds on their meat. . . ."

Catching himself, he slashed that out and took another sheet. Isabel was sobbing with her face buried in the pillow.

"What shall I do now? He'll come after me for revenge. . . . Oh, my God. . . ."

"My dear friend," Kern wrote quickly, *"she sought unforgettable caresses and now she will give birth to a winged little beast. . . ."* Oh, damn! He crumpled the sheet.

"Try to get some sleep," he addressed Isabel over his shoulder, "and leave tomorrow. For a monastery."

Her shoulders shook rapidly. Then she grew still.

Kern wrote. Before him smiled the eyes of the one person in the world with whom he could freely speak or remain silent. He wrote to that person that life was finished, that he had begun feeling of late that, in place of the future, a black wall was looming ever closer, and that now something had happened after which a man cannot and must not continue living. *"At noon tomorrow I shall die,"* wrote Kern, *"tomorrow, because I want to die in full command of my faculties, in the sober light of day. And right now I am in too deep a state of shock."*

When he had finished he sat down in the armchair by the window. Isabel was sleeping, her breathing barely audible. An oppressive fatigue girdled his shoulders. Sleep descended like a soft fog.

3
_____

He was awakened by a knock on the door. Frosty azure was pouring through the window.

"Come in," he said, stretching.

The waiter noiselessly set a tray with a cup of tea on the table and exited with a bow.

Laughing to himself, Kern thought, "And here I am in a rumpled dinner jacket."

Then, instantly, he remembered what had happened during the night. He shuddered and glanced at the bed. Isabel was gone. Must have returned to her room with the approach of morning. And by now she has undoubtedly left. . . . He had a momentary vision of brown, crumbly wings. Getting up quickly, he opened the door to the corridor.

"Listen," he called to the waiter's departing back. "Take a letter with you."

He went to the desk and rummaged about. The fellow was waiting at the door. Kern slapped all his pockets and took a look under the armchair.

"You may go. I'll give it to the porter later."

The parted hair bent forward, and the door closed softly.

Kern was distressed at having lost the letter. That letter in particular. He had said in it so well, so smoothly and simply, all that needed to be said. Now he could not recall the words. Only senseless sentences surfaced. Yes, the letter had been a masterpiece.

He began writing anew, but it came out cold and rhetorical. He sealed the letter and neatly wrote the address.

He felt a strange lightness in his heart. He would shoot himself at noon, and after all, a man who has resolved to kill himself is a god.

The sugary snow glistened outside the window. He felt drawn out there, for the last time.

The shadows of frosted trees lay on the snow like blue plumes. Sleigh bells jingled somewhere, densely and merrily. There were lots of people out, girls in fur caps moving timorously and awkwardly on their skis, young men exhaling clouds of laughter as they called loudly to each other, elderly people ruddy from the effort, and some sinewy blue-eyed oldster dragging a velvet-covered sled. Kern thought in passing, why not give the old chap a whack in the face, a backhanded one, just for the fun of it, for now everything was permissible. He broke out laughing. He had not felt so good in a long time.

Everyone was drifting to the area where the ski-jumping competition had begun. The site consisted of a steep descent merging halfway down into a snowy platform, which ended abruptly, forming a right-angled projection. A skier glided down the steep section and flew off the projecting ramp into the azure air. He flew with outstretched arms, landed upright on the continuation of the slope, and glided on. The Swede had just broken his own recent record and, far below, in a whirlwind of silvery dust, turned sharply with one bent leg extended.

Two others, in black sweaters, sped past, jumped, and resiliently hit the snow.

"Isabel is jumping next," said a soft voice at Kern's shoulder. Kern thought rapidly, Don't tell me she is still here. . . . How can she . . . and looked at the speaker. It was Monfiori. In a top hat, pushed over his protruding ears, and a little black coat with strips of faded velvet on the collar, he stood out drolly amid the woolly crowd. Should I tell him? thought Kern.

He rejected with revulsion the smelly brown wings—must not think about that.

Isabel mounted the hill. She turned to say something to her companion, gaily, gaily as always. This gaiety gave Kern a scary feeling. He caught what seemed a fleeting glimpse of something above the snows, above the glassy hotel, above the toylike people—a shudder, a shimmer . . .

"And how are you today?" asked Monfiori, rubbing his lifeless hands.

Simultaneously voices rang out around them: "Isabel! Airborne Isabel!"

Kern threw back his head. She was hurtling down the steep slope. For an instant he saw her bright face, her glistening lashes. With a soft whistling sound she skimmed off the trampoline, flew up, hung motionless, crucified in midair. And then . . .

No one, of course, could have expected it. In full flight Isabel crumpled spasmodically, fell like a stone, and started rolling amid the snowbursts of her cartwheeling skis.

Right away she was hidden from view by the backs of people rushing toward her. Kern slowly approached with hunched shoulders. He saw it vividly in his mind's eye, as if it were written in a large hand: revenge, wingstroke. The Swede and the lanky type in horn-rimmed glasses bent over Isabel. With professional gestures the bespectacled man was palpating her motionless body. He muttered, "I can't understand it—her rib cage is crushed. . . ."

He raised up her head. There was a glimpse of her dead, seemingly denuded face.

Kern turned with a crunch of his heel and strode off resolutely toward the hotel. Beside him trotted Monfiori, running ahead, peeking into his eyes.

"I am going upstairs to my room now," said Kern, trying to swallow his sobbing laughter, to restrain it. "Upstairs . . . If you wish to accompany me . . ."

The laughter neared his throat and bubbled over. Kern was climbing the stairs like a blind man. Monfiori was supporting him, meekly and hastily.

GODS

H ERE is what I see in your eyes right now: rainy night, narrow street, streetlamps gliding away into the distance. The water runs down the drainpipes from steeply sloping roofs. Under the snake's-mouth of each pipe stands a green-hooped bucket. Rows of buckets line the black walls on either side of the street. I watch as they fill with cold mercury. The pluvial mercury swells and overflows. The bareheaded lamps float in the distance, their rays standing on end in the rainy murk. The water in the buckets is overflowing.

Thus I gain entry to your overcast eyes, to a narrow alley of black glimmer where the nocturnal rain gurgles and rustles. Give me a smile. Why do you look at me so balefully and darkly? It's morning. All night the stars shrieked with infant voices and, on the roof, someone lacerated and caressed a violin with a sharp bow. Look, the sun slowly crossed the wall like a blazing sail. You emanate an enveloping smoky haze. Dust starts swirling in your eyes, millions of golden worlds. You smiled!

We go out on the balcony. It's spring. Below, in the middle of the street, a yellow-curled boy works lickety-split, sketching a god. The god stretches from one sidewalk to the other. The boy is clutching a piece of chalk in his hand, a little piece of white charcoal and he's squatting, circling, drawing with broad strokes. This white god has large white buttons and turned-out feet. Crucified on the asphalt, he looks skyward with round eyes. He has a white arc for a mouth. A log-sized cigar has appeared in his mouth. With helical jabs the boy makes spirals representing smoke. Arms akimbo, he contemplates his work. He adds another button. . . . A window frame clanked across the way; a female voice, enormous and happy, rang out summoning him. The boy gave the chalk a punt and dashed inside. On the purplish asphalt remained the white geometric god, gazing skyward.

44

Your eyes again grew murky. I realized, of course, what you were remembering. In a corner of our bedroom, under the icon, there is a colored rubber ball. Sometimes it hops softly and sadly from the table and rolls gently on the floor.

Put it back in its place under the icon, and then why don't we go take a walk?

Spring air. A little downy. See those lindens lining the street? Black boughs covered with wet green spangles. All the trees in the world are journeying somewhere. Perpetual pilgrimage. Remember, when we were on our way here, to this city, the trees traveling past the windows of our railroad car? Remember the twelve poplars conferring about how to cross the river? Earlier, still, in the Crimea, I once saw a cypress bending over an almond tree in bloom. Once upon a time the cypress had been a big, tall chimney sweep with a brush on a wire and a ladder under his arm. Head over heels in love, poor fellow, with a little laundry maid, pink as almond petals. Now they have met at last, and are on their way somewhere together. Her pink apron balloons in the breeze; he bends toward her timidly, as if still worried he might get some soot on her. First-rate fable.

All trees are pilgrims. They have their Messiah, whom they seek. Their Messiah is a regal Lebanese cedar, or perhaps he is quite small, some totally inconspicuous little shrub in the tundra. . . .

Today some lindens are passing through town. There was an attempt to restrain them. Circular fencing was erected around their trunks. But they move all the same. . . .

The roofs blaze like oblique, sun-blinded mirrors. A winged woman stands on a windowsill washing the panes. She bends over, pouts, brushes a strand of flaming hair from her face. The air is faintly redolent of gasoline and lindens. Who can tell, today, just what emanations gently greeted a guest entering a Pompeian atrium? A half-century from now no one will know the smells that prevailed in our streets and rooms. They will excavate some military hero of stone, of which there are hundreds in every city, and heave a sigh for Phidias of yore. Everything in the world is beautiful, but Man only recognizes beauty if he sees it either seldom or from afar. . . . Listen . . . today, we are gods! Our blue shadows are enormous. We move in a gigantic, joyous world. A tall pillar on the corner is tightly swathed in wet canvases, across which a paintbrush has scattered colored whirlwinds. The old woman who sells papers has curling gray hairs on her chin, and mad light-blue eyes. Unruly newspapers stick chaotically out of her pouch. Their large type makes me think of flying zebras.

A bus stops at its signpost. Upstairs the conductor ba-bangs with his palm on the iron gunwale. The helmsman gives his huge wheel a mighty turn. A mounting, labored moan, a brief grinding sound. The wide tires have left silver imprints on the asphalt. Today, on this sunny day, anything is possible. Look—a man has jumped from a roof onto a wire and is walking on it, splitting with laughter, his arms widespread, high over the rocking street. Look—two buildings have just had a harmonious game of leapfrog; number three ended up between one and two; it did not fully settle right away—I saw a gap below it, a narrow band of sunlight. And a woman stopped in the middle of a square, threw back her head, and started singing; a crowd gathered around her, then surged back: an empty dress lies on the asphalt, and up in the sky there's a transparent cloudlet.

You're laughing. When you laugh, I want to transform the entire world so it will mirror you. But your eyes are instantly extinguished. You say, passionately, fearfully, "Would you like to go . . . there? Would you? It's lovely there today, everything's in bloom. . . ."

Certainly it's all in bloom, certainly we'll go. For aren't you and I gods? . . . I sense in my blood the rotation of unexplorable universes. . . .

Listen—I want to run all my life, screaming at the top of my lungs. Let all of life be an unfettered howl. Like the crowd greeting the gladiator.

Don't stop to think, don't interrupt the scream, exhale, release life's rapture. Everything is blooming. Everything is flying. Everything is screaming, choking on its screams. Laughter. Running. Let-down hair. That is all there is to life.

They are leading camels along the street, on the way from the circus to the zoo. Their plump humps list and sway. Their long, gentle faces are turned up a little, dreamily. How can death exist when they lead camels along a springtime street? At the corner, an unexpected whiff of Russian foliage; a beggar, a divine monstrosity, turned all inside out, feet growing out of armpits, proffers, with a wet, shaggy paw, a bunch of greenish lilies-of-the-val . . . I bump a passerby with my shoulder. . . . Momentary collision of two giants. Merrily, magnificently, he swings at me with his lacquered cane. The tip, on the backswing, breaks a shopwindow behind him. Zigzags shoot across the shiny glass. No—it's only the splash of mirrored sunlight in my eyes. Butterfly, butterfly! Black with scarlet bands. . . . A scrap of velvet. . . . It swoops above the asphalt, soars over a speeding car and a tall building, into the humid azure of the April sky. Another, identical butterfly once settled on the white border of an arena; Lesbia, senator's daughter, gracile, dark-eyed, with a gold ribbon on her forehead, entranced by the palpitating wings, missed the split second, the whirlwind of blinding dust, in which the bull-like neck of one combatant crunched under the other's naked knee.

Today my soul is filled with gladiators, sunlight, the world's din. . . .

We descend a wide staircase into a long, dim underground chamber. Flagstones resound vibrantly under our steps. Representations of burning sinners adorn the gray walls. Black thunder, in the distance, swells in velvet folds. It bursts forth all around us. We rush headlong, as if awaiting a god. We are packed inside a glassy glitter. We gather momentum. We hurtle into a black chasm and speed with a hollow din far underground, hanging on to leather straps. With a pop the amber lamps are extinguished for an instant, during which flimsy globules burn with a hot light in the dark—the bulging eyes of demons, or perhaps our fellow passengers' cigars.

The lights come back on. Look, over there—the tall man in a black overcoat standing by the car's glass door. I faintly recognize that narrow, yellowish face, the bony hump of his nose. Thin lips compressed, attentive furrow between heavy brows, he listens to something being explained by another man, pale as a plaster mask, with a small, circular, sculpted beard. I am certain they are speaking in terza rima. And your neighbor, that lady in the pale-yellow coat sitting with lowered lashes—could that be Dante's Beatrice? Out of the dank nether world we emerge anew into the sunlight. The cemetery is on the distant outskirts. Edifices have grown sparser. Greenish voids. I recall how this same capital looked on an old print.

We walk against the wind along imposing fences. On the same kind of sunny, tremulous day as this we'll head back north, to Russia. There will be very few flowers, only the yellow stars of dandelions along the ditches. The dove-gray telegraph poles will hum at our approach. When, beyond the curve, my heart is jabbed by the firs, the red sand, the corner of the house, I shall totter and fall prone.

Look! Above the vacant green expanses, high in the sky, an airplane progresses with a bassy ring like an aeolian harp. Its glass wings are glinting. Beautiful, no? Oh, listen—here is something that happened in Paris, about 150 years ago. Early one morning—it was autumn, and the trees floated in soft orange masses along the boulevards into the tender sky—early one morning, the merchants had assembled in the marketplace; the stands filled with moist, glistening apples; there were whiffs of honey and damp hay. An old fellow with white down in his auricles was unhurriedly setting up cages containing various birds that fidgeted in the chilly air; then he sleepily reclined on a mat, for the auroral fog still obscured the gilt hands on the town hall's black dial. He had scarcely gone to sleep when someone started tugging at his shoulder. Up jumped the oldster, and saw before him an out-of-breath young man. He was lanky, skinny, with a small head and a pointed little nose. His waistcoat—silvery with black stripes—was buttoned askew, the ribbon on his pigtail had come undone, one of his white stockings was sagging in bunched wrinkles. "I need a bird, any bird—a chicken will do," said the young man, having given the cages a cursory, agitated glance. The old man gingerly extracted a small white hen, which put up a fluffy struggle in his swarthy hands. "What's wrong—is it sick?" asked the young man, as if discussing a cow. "Sick? My little fish's belly!" mildly swore the oldster.

The young man flung him a shiny coin and ran off amid the stands, the hen pressed to his bosom. Then he stopped, turned abruptly with a whip of his pigtail, and ran back to the old vendor.

"I need the cage too," he said.

When he went off at last, holding the chicken with the cage in his outstretched hand and swinging the other arm, as if he were carrying a bucket, the old man gave a snort and lay back down on his mat. How business went that day and what happened to him afterwards is of no concern to us at all.

As for the young man, he was none other than the son of the renowned physicist Charles. Charles glanced over his spectacles at the little hen, gave the cage a flick of his yellow fingernail, and said, "Fine—now we have a passenger as well." Then, with a severe glint of his eyeglasses, he added, "As for you and me, my boy, we'll take our time. God only knows what the air is like up there in the clouds."

The same day, at the appointed hour on the Champs de Mars, before an astonished crowd, an enormous, lightweight dome, embroidered with Chinese arabesques, with a gilded gondola attached by silken cords, slowly swelled as it filled with hydrogen. Charles and his son busied themselves amid streams of smoke blown sideways by the wind. The hen peered through the wire netting of her cage with one beady eye, her head tilted to one side. All around moved colorful, spangled caftans, airy women's dresses, straw hats; and, when the sphere lurched upward, the old physicist followed it with his gaze, then broke into tears on his son's shoulder, and a hundred hands on every side began waving handkerchiefs and ribbons. Fragile clouds floated through the tender, sunny sky. The earth receded, quivery, light-green, covered with scudding shadows and the fiery splashes of trees. Far below some toy horsemen hurtled past—but soon the sphere rose out of sight. The hen kept peering downward with one little eye.

The flight lasted all day. The day concluded with an ample, vivid sunset. When night fell, the sphere began slowly descending. Once upon a time, in a village on the shore of the Loire, there lived a gentle, wily-eyed peasant. Out he goes into the field at dawn. In the middle of the field he sees a marvel: an immense heap of motley silk. Nearby, overturned, lay a little cage. A chicken, all white, as if modeled out of snow, was thrusting its head through mesh and intermittently moving its beak, as it searched for small insects in the grass. At first the peasant had a fright, but then he realized that it was simply a present from the Virgin Mary, whose hair floated through the air like autumn spider-webs. The silk his wife sold off piecemeal in the nearby town, the little gilded gondola became a crib for their tightly swaddled firstborn, and the chicken was dispatched to the backyard.

Listen on.

Some time elapsed, and then one fine day, as he passed a hillock of chaff at the barn gate, the peasant heard a happy clucking. He stooped. The hen popped out of the green dust and hawked at the sun as she waddled rapidly and not without some pride. While, amid the chaff, hot and sleek, glowed four golden eggs. And no wonder. At the wind's mercy, the hen had traversed the entire flush of the sunset, and the sun, a fiery cock with a crimson crest, had done some fluttering over her.

I don't know if the peasant understood. For a long time he stood motionless, blinking and squinting from the brilliance and holding in his palms the still warm, whole, golden eggs. Then, his sabots rattling, he rushed across the yard with such a howl that his hired hand thought he must have lopped off a finger with his axe. . . .

Of course all this happened a long, long time ago, long before the aviator Latham, having crashed in mid-Channel, sat, if you will, on the dragonfly tail of his submerging *Antoinette*, smoking a yellowed ciga-rette in the wind, and watching as, high in the sky, in his little stubby-winged machine, his rival Blériot flew for the first time from Calais to England's sugary shores.

But I cannot overcome your anguish. Why have your eyes again filled with darkness? No, don't say anything. I know everything. You mustn't cry. He can hear my fable, there's no doubt at all he can hear it. It is to him that it's addressed. Words have no borders. Try to un-derstand! You look at me so balefully and darkly. I recollect the night after the funeral. You were unable to stay home. You and I went out into the glossy slush. Lost our way. Ended up in some strange, narrow street. I did not make out its name, but could see it was inverted, mir-rorlike, in the glass of a streetlamp. The lamps were floating off into the distance. Water dripped from the roofs. The buckets lining both sides of the street, along black walls, were filling with cold mercury. Filling and overflowing. And suddenly, helplessly spreading your hands, you spoke:

"But he was so little, and so warm. . . ."

Forgive me if I am incapable of weeping, of simple human weeping, but instead keep singing and running somewhere, clutching at whatever wings fly past, tall, disheveled, with a wave of suntan on my forehead. Forgive me. That's how it must be.

We walk slowly along the fences. The cemetery is already near. There it is, an islet of vernal white and green amid some dusty vacant land. Now you go on alone. I'll wait for you here. Your eyes gave a quick, embarrassed smile. You know me well. . . . The wicket-gate squeaked, then banged shut. I sit alone on the sparse grass. A short way off there is a vegetable garden with some purple cabbage. Beyond the vacant lot, factory buildings, buoyant brick behemoths, float in the azure mist. At my feet, a squashed tin glints rustily inside a funnel of sand. Around me, silence and a kind of spring emptiness. There is no death. The wind comes tumbling upon me from behind like a limp doll and tickles my neck with its downy paw. There can be no death.

My heart, too, has soared through the dawn. You and I shall have a new, golden son, a creation of your tears and my fables. Today I understood the beauty of intersecting wires in the sky, and the hazy mosaic of factory chimneys, and this rusty tin with its inside-out, semi-detached, serrated lid. The wan grass hurries, hurries somewhere along the dusty billows of the vacant lot. I raise my arms. The sunlight glides across my skin. My skin is covered with multicolored sparkles.

And I want to rise up, throw my arms open for a vast embrace, address an ample, luminous discourse to the invisible crowds. I would start like this:

"O rainbow-colored gods . . ."

A MATTER OF CHANCE

H E HAD a job as a waiter in the international dining car of a German fast train. His name was Aleksey Lvovich Luzhin.

He had left Russia five years before, in 1919, and since then, as he made his way from city to city, had tried a good number of trades and occupations: he had worked as a farm laborer in Turkey, a messenger in Vienna, a housepainter, a sales clerk, and so forth. Now, on either side of the diner, the meadows, the hills overgrown with heather, the pine groves flowed on and on, and the bouillon steamed and splashed in the thick cups on the tray that he nimbly carried along the narrow aisle between the window tables. He waited with masterful dispatch, forking up from the dish he carried slices of beef or ham, depositing them on the plates, and in the process rapidly dipping his close-cropped head, with its tensed forehead and black, bushy eyebrows.

The car would arrive in Berlin at five p.m., and at seven it would depart in the opposite direction, toward the French border. Luzhin lived on a kind of steel seesaw: he had time to think and reminisce only at night, in a narrow nook that smelled of fish and dirty socks. His most frequent recollections were of a house in St. Petersburg, of his study there, with those leather buttons on the curves of overstuffed furniture, and of his wife Lena, of whom he had had no news for five years. At present, he felt his life wasting away. Too-frequent sniffs of cocaine had ravaged his mind; the little sores on the inside of his nostrils were eating into the septum.

When he smiled, his large teeth would flash with an especially clean luster, and this Russian ivory smile somehow endeared him to the other two waiters—Hugo, a thickset, fair-haired Berliner who made out the checks, and quick, red-haired, sharp-nosed Max, who resembled a fox, and whose job it was to take coffee and beer to the compartments. Lately, however, Luzhin smiled less often.

During the leisure hours when the crystal-bright waves of the drug beat at him, penetrating his thoughts with their radiance and transforming the least trifle into an ethereal miracle, he painstakingly noted on a sheet of paper all the various steps he intended to take in order to trace his wife. As he scribbled, with all those sensations still blissfully taut, his jottings seemed exceedingly important and correct to him. In the morning, however, when his head ached and his shirt felt clammy and sticky, he looked with bored disgust at the jerky, blurry lines. Recently, though, another idea had begun to occupy his thoughts. He began, with the same diligence, to elaborate a plan for his own death; he would draw a kind of graph indicating the rise and fall of his sense of fear; and, finally, so as to simplify matters, he set himself a definite date—the night between the first and second of August. His interest was aroused not so much by death itself as by all the details preceding it, and he would get so involved with these details that death itself would be forgotten. But as soon as he sobered up, the picturesque setting of this or that fanciful method of self-destruction would pale, and only one thing remained clear: his life had wasted away to nothing and there was no use continuing it.

The first day of August ran its course. At six-thirty in the evening, in the vast, dimly lit buffet of the Berlin station, old Princess Maria Ukhtomski sat at a bare table, obese, all in black, with a sallow face like a eunuch's. There were few people around. The brass counterweights of the suspended lamps glimmered under the high, misty ceiling. Now and then a chair was moved back with a hollow reverberation.

Princess Ukhtomski cast a stern glance at the gilt hand of the wall clock. The hand lurched forward. A minute later it shuddered again. The old lady rose, picked up her glossy black *sac de voyage* and, leaning on her big-knobbed man's cane, shuffled toward the exit.

A porter was waiting for her at the gate. The train was backing into the station. One after another, the lugubrious, iron-colored German carriages moved past. The varnished brown teak of one sleeping car bore under the center window a sign with the inscription BERLIN–PARIS; that international car, as well as the teak-lined diner, in a window of which she glimpsed the protruding elbows and head of a carroty-haired waiter, were alone reminiscent of the severely elegant prewar Nord-Express.

The train stopped with a clang of bumpers, and a long, sibilant sigh of brakes.

The porter installed Princess Ukhtomski in a second-class compartment of a Schnellzug car—a smoking compartment as she requested. In one corner, by the window, a man in a beige suit with an insolent face and an olive complexion was already trimming a cigar.

The old Princess settled across from him. She checked, with a slow, deliberate look, whether all her things had been placed in the overhead net. Two suitcases and a basket. All there. And the glossy *sac de voyage* in her lap. Her lips made a stern chewing movement.

A German couple lumbered into the compartment, breathing heavily.

Then, a minute before the train's departure, in came a young woman with a big painted mouth and a tight black toque that covered her forehead. She arranged her belongings and stepped out into the corridor. The man in the beige suit glanced after her. She raised the window with inexperienced jerks and leaned out to say good-bye to someone. The Princess caught the patter of Russian speech.

The train started. The young woman returned to the compartment. That smile that lingered on her face died out, and was replaced by a weary look. The brick rear walls of houses went gliding past; one of them displayed the painted advertisement of a colossal cigarette, stuffed with what looked like golden straw. The roofs, wet from a rainstorm, glistened under the rays of the low sun.

Old Princess Ukhtomski could control herself no longer. She inquired gently in Russian: "Do you mind if I put my bag here?"

The woman gave a start and replied, "Not at all, please do."

The olive-and-beige man in the corner peered at her over his paper.

"Well, I'm on my way to Paris," volunteered the Princess with a slight sigh. "I have a son there. I am afraid to stay in Germany, you know."

She produced an ample handkerchief from her *sac de voyage* and firmly wiped her nose, left to right and back again.

"Yes, afraid. People say there's going to be a Communist revolution in Berlin. Have you heard anything?"

The young woman shook her head. She glanced suspiciously at the man with the paper and at the German couple.

"I don't know anything. I arrived from Russia, from Petersburg, the day before yesterday."

Princess Ukhtomski's plump, sallow face expressed intense curiosity. Her diminutive eyebrows crept upward.

"You don't say!"

With her eyes fixed on the tip of her gray shoe, the woman said rapidly, in a soft voice: "Yes, a kindhearted person helped me to get out. I'm going to Paris too now. I have relatives there."

She started taking off her gloves. A gold wedding ring slipped off her finger. Quickly she caught it.

"I keep losing my ring. Must have grown thinner or something."

She fell silent, blinking her lashes. Through the corridor window beyond the glass compartment door the even row of telegraph wires could be seen swooping upward.

Princess Ukhtomski moved closer to her neighbor.

"Tell me," she inquired in a loud whisper. "The sovietchiks aren't doing so well now, are they?"

A telegraph pole, black against the sunset, flew past, interrupting the smooth ascent of the wires. They dropped as a flag drops when the wind stops blowing. Then furtively they began rising again. The express was traveling swiftly between the airy walls of a spacious fire-bright evening. From somewhere in the ceilings of the compartments a slight crackling kept coming, as if rain were falling on the steel roofs. The German cars swayed violently. The international one, its interior upholstered in blue cloth, rode more smoothly and silently than the others. Three waiters were laying the tables in the diner. One of them, with close-cropped hair and beetling brows, was thinking about the little vial in his breast pocket. He kept licking his lips and sniffling. The vial contained a crystalline powder and bore the brand name Kramm. He was distributing knives and forks and inserting sealed bottles into rings on the tables, when suddenly he could stand it no longer. He flashed a fluttered smile toward Max Fuchs, who was lowering the thick blinds, and darted across the unsteady connecting platform into the next car. He locked himself in the toilet. Carefully calculating the jolts of the train, he poured a small mound of the powder on his thumbnail; greedily applied it to one nostril, then to the other; in-haled; with a flip of his tongue licked the sparkling dust off his nail; blinked hard a couple of times from the rubbery bitterness, and left the toilet, boozy and buoyant, his head filling with icy delicious air. As he crossed the diaphragm on his way back into the diner, he thought: how simple it would be to die right now! He smiled. He had best wait till nightfall. It would be a pity to cut short the effect of the enchant-ing poison.

"Give me the reservation slips, Hugo. I'll go hand them out."

"No, let Max go. Max works faster. Here, Max."

The red-haired waiter clutched the book of coupons in his freckled fist. He slipped like a fox between the tables and into the blue corridor of the sleeper. Five distinct harp strings swooped desperately upward alongside the windows. The sky was darkening. In the second-class compartment of a German car an old woman in black, resembling a eunuch, heard out with subdued *ochs* the account of a distant, dreary life.

"And your husband—did he stay behind?"

The young woman's eyes opened wide and she shook her head: "No. He has been abroad for quite a time. Just happened that way. In the very beginning of the Revolution he traveled south to Odessa. They were after him. I was supposed to join him there, but didn't get out in time."

"Terrible, terrible. And you have had no news of him?"

"None. I remember I decided he was dead. Started to wear my ring on the chain of my cross—I was afraid they'd take that away too. Then, in Berlin, friends told me that he was alive. Somebody had seen him. Only yesterday I put a notice in the émigré paper."

She hastily produced a folded page of the *Rul'* from her tattered silk vanity bag.

"Here, take a look."

Princess Ukhtomski put on her glasses and read: "Elena Nikolayevna Luzhin seeks her husband Aleksey Lvovich Luzhin."

"Luzhin?" she queried, taking off her glasses. "Could it be Lev Sergeich's son? He had two boys. I don't recall their names—"

Elena smiled radiantly. "Oh, how nice. That's a surprise. Don't tell me you knew his father."

"Of course, of course," began the Princess in a complacent and kindly tone. "Lyovushka Luzhin, formerly of the Uhlans. Our estates were adjacent. He used to visit us."

"He died," interposed Elena.

"Yes, yes, I heard. May his soul rest in peace. He would always arrive with his borzoi hound. I don't remember his boys well, though. I've been abroad since 1917. The younger one had light hair, I believe. And he had a stutter."

Elena smiled again.

"No, no, that was his elder brother."

"Oh, well, I got them mixed up, my dear," the Princess said comfortably. "My memory is not so good. I wouldn't even have remembered Lyovushka if you had not mentioned him yourself. But now it all comes back to me. He used to ride over for evening tea and— Oh, let me tell you—" The Princess moved a little closer and went on, in a clear, slightly lilting voice, without sadness, for she knew that happy things can only be spoken of in a happy way, without grieving because they have vanished:

"Let me tell you," she went on, "we had a set of amusing plates— with a gold rim running around and, in the very center, a mosquito so lifelike that anyone who didn't know tried to brush it off."

The compartment door opened. A red-haired waiter was handing out reservation slips for dinner. Elena took one. So did the man sitting in the corner, who for some time had been trying to catch her eye.

"I brought my own food," said the Princess. "Ham and a bun."

Max went through all the cars and trotted back to the diner. In passing, he nudged his Russian fellow worker, who was standing in the car's vestibule with a napkin under his arm. Luzhin looked after Max with glistening, anxious eyes. He felt a cool, ticklish vacuum replacing his bones and organs, as if his whole body were about to sneeze the next instant, expelling his soul. He imagined for the hundredth time how he would arrange his death. He calculated every little detail, as if he were composing a chess problem. He planned to get off at night at a certain station, walk around the motionless car and place his head against the buffer's shieldlike end when another car, that was to be coupled on, approached the waiting one. The buffers would clash. Between their meeting ends would be his bowed head. It would burst like a soap bubble and turn into iridescent air. He should get a good foothold on the crosstie and press his temple firmly against the cold metal of the bumper.

"Can't you hear me? Time to go make the dinner call."

It was now Hugo speaking. Luzhin responded with a frightened smile and did what he was told, opening for an instant the compartment doors as he went, announcing loudly and hurriedly, "First call for dinner!"

In one compartment his eye fell fleetingly on the plump, yellowish face of an old woman who was unwrapping a sandwich. He was struck by something very familiar about that face. As he hurried back through the cars, he kept thinking who she might be. It was as if he had already seen her in a dream. The sensation that his body would sneeze up his soul any instant now became more concrete—any moment now I'll remember whom that old woman resembled. But the more he strained his mind, the more irritatingly the recollection would slip away. He was morose when he returned to the diner, with his nostrils dilating and a spasm in his throat that would not let him swallow.

"Oh, the hell with her—what nonsense."

The passengers, walking unsteadily and holding on to the walls, began to move through the corridors in the direction of the diner. Reflections were already glimmering in the darkened windows, even though a yellow streak of sunset was still visible there. Elena Luzhin noticed with alarm that the man in the beige suit had waited to get up when she had. He had nasty, glassy, protuberant eyes that seemed filled with dark iodine. He walked along the passage in such a way as almost to step on her, and when a jolt threw her off balance (the cars were rocking violently) he would pointedly clear his throat. For some reason she suddenly thought he must be a spy, an informer, and she knew it was silly to think so—she was no longer in Russia, after all—yet she could not get rid of the idea.

He said something as they passed through the corridor of the sleeper. She quickened her step. She crossed the joggy connecting plates to the diner, which came after the sleeper. And here, suddenly, in the vestibule of the diner, with a kind of rough tenderness the man clutched her by the upper arm. She stifled a scream and yanked away her arm so violently that she nearly lost her footing.

The man said in German, with a foreign accent, "My precious!"

Elena made a sudden about-face. Back she went, across the connecting platform, through the sleeping car, across another platform. She felt unbearably hurt. She would rather not have dinner at all than sit facing that boorish monster. "God knows what he took me for," she reflected, "and all just because I use lipstick."

"What's the matter, my dear? Aren't you having dinner?"

Princess Ukhtomski had a ham sandwich in her hand.

"No, I don't feel like it any more. Excuse me, I'm going to take a nap."

The old woman raised her thin brows in surprise, then resumed munching.

As for Elena, she leaned her head back and pretended to sleep. Soon she did doze off. Her pale, tired face twitched occasionally. The wings of her nose shone where the powder had worn off. Princess Ukhtomski lit a cigarette that had a long cardboard mouthpiece.

A half-hour later the man returned, sat down imperturbably in his corner, and worked on his back teeth with a toothpick for a while. Then he shut his eyes, fidgeted a little, and curtained his head with a flap of his overcoat, which was hanging on a hook by the window. Another half-hour went by and the train slowed. Platform lights passed like specters alongside the fogged-up windows. The car stopped with a prolonged sigh of relief. Sounds could be heard: somebody coughing

in the next compartment, footsteps running past on the station platform. The train stood for a long time, while distant nocturnal whistles
called out to each other. Then it jolted and began to move.

Elena awoke. The Princess was dozing, her open mouth a black
cave. The German couple was gone. The man, his face covered by his
coat, slept too, his legs grotesquely spread.

Elena licked her dry lips and wearily rubbed her forehead. Suddenly
she gave a start: the ring was missing from her fourth finger.

For an instant she gazed, motionless, at her naked hand. Then,
with a pounding heart, she began searching hastily on the seat, on the
floor. She glanced at the man's sharp knee.

"Oh, my Lord, of course—I must have dropped it on the way to
the dining car when I jerked free—"

She hurried out of the compartment; arms spread, swaying this way
and that, holding back her tears, she traversed one car, another. She
reached the end of the sleeping car and, through the rear door, saw
nothing but air, emptiness, the night sky, the dark wedge of the road-
bed disappearing into the distance.

She thought she had got mixed up and gone the wrong way. With
a sob, she headed back.

Next to her, by the toilet door, stood a little old woman wearing a
gray apron and an armband, who resembled a night nurse. She was
holding a little bucket with a brush sticking out of it.

"They uncoupled the diner," said the little old woman, and for
some reason sighed. "After Cologne there will be another."

In the diner that had remained behind under the vault of a station and
would continue only next morning to France, the waiters were cleaning up, folding the tablecloths. Luzhin finished, and stood in the open
doorway of the car's vestibule. The station was dark and deserted.
Some distance away a lamp shone like a humid star through a gray
cloud of smoke. The torrent of rails glistened slightly. He could not
understand why the face of the old lady with the sandwich had disturbed him so deeply. Everything else was clear, only this one blind
spot remained.

Red-haired, sharp-nosed Max also came out into the vestibule. He
was sweeping the floor. He noticed a glint of gold in a corner. He bent
down. It was a ring. He hid it in his waistcoat pocket and gave a quick
look around to see if anyone had noticed. Luzhin's back was motionless in the doorway. Max cautiously took out the ring; by the dim light
he distinguished a word in script and some figures engraved on the in-

side. Must be Chinese, he thought. Actually, the inscription read "1-VIII-1915. ALEKSEY." He returned the ring to his pocket.

Luzhin's back moved. Quietly he got off the car. He walked diagonally to the next track, with a calm, relaxed gait, as if taking a stroll.

A through train now thundered into the station. Luzhin went to the edge of the platform and hopped down. The cinders crunched under his heel.

At that instant, the locomotive came at him in one hungry bound. Max, totally unaware of what happened, watched from a distance as the lighted windows flew past in one continuous stripe.

THE SEAPORT

THE low-ceilinged barbershop smelled of stale roses. Horseflies hummed hotly, heavily. The sunlight blazed on the floor in puddles of molten honey, gave the lotion bottles tweaks of sparkle, transluced through the long curtain hanging in the entrance, a curtain of clay beads and little sections of bamboo strung alternately on close-hung cord, which would disintegrate in an iridescent clitter-clatter every time someone entered and shouldered it aside. Before him, in the murkish glass, Nikitin saw his own tanned face, the long sculptured strands of his shiny hair, the glitter of the scissors that chirred above his ear, and his eyes were attentive and severe, as always happens when you contemplate yourself in mirrors. He had arrived in this ancient port in the south of France the day before, from Constantinople, where life had grown unbearable for him. That morning he had been to the Russian Consulate and the employment office, had roamed about the town, which, down narrow alleyways, crept seaward, and now, exhausted, prostrated by the heat, he had dropped in to have a haircut and to refresh his head. The floor around his chair was already strewn with small bright mice—the cuttings of his hair. The barber filled his palm with lather. A delicious chill ran through the crown of his head as the barber's fingers firmly rubbed in the thick foam. Then an icy gush made his heart jump, and a fluffy towel went to work on his face and his wet hair.

Parting the undulating rain of curtain with his shoulder, Nikitin went out into a steep alley. Its right side was in the shade; on the left a narrow stream quivered along the curb in the torrid radiance; a black-haired, toothless girl with swarthy freckles was collecting the shimmering rivulet with her resonant pail; and the stream, the sun, the violet shade—everything was flowing and slithering downward to

60

the sea: another step and, in the distance, between some walls, loomed its compact sapphire brilliance. Infrequent pedestrians walked on the shady side. Nikitin happened upon a climbing Negro in a Colonial uniform, with a face like a wet galosh. On the sidewalk stood a straw chair from whose seat a cat departed with a cushioned bound. A brassy Provençal voice started jabbering in some window. A green shutter banged. On a vendor's stand, amid purple mollusks that gave off a whiff of seaweed, lay lemons shot with granulated gold.

Reaching the sea, Nikitin paused to look excitedly at the dense blue that, in the distance, modulated into blinding silver, and at the play of light delicately dappling the white topside of a yacht. Then, unsteady from the heat, he went in search of the small Russian restaurant whose address he had noted on a wall of the consulate.

The restaurant, like the barbershop, was hot and none too clean. In back, on a wide counter, appetizers and fruit showed through billows of protective grayish muslin. Nikitin sat down and squared his shoulders; his shirt stuck to his back. At a nearby table sat two Russians, evidently sailors of a French vessel, and, a little farther off, a solitary old fellow in gold-rimmed glasses was making smacking and sucking noises as he lapped borscht from his spoon. The proprietress, wiping her puffy hands with a towel, gave the newcomer a maternal look. Two shaggy pups were rolling on the floor in a flurry of little paws. Nikitin whistled, and a shabby old bitch with green mucus at the corners of her gentle eyes came and put her muzzle in his lap.

One of the seamen addressed him in a composed and unhurried tone: "Send her away. She'll get fleas all over you."

Nikitin cosseted the dog's head a little and raised his radiant eyes.

"Oh, I'm not afraid of that. . . . Constantinople . . . The barracks . . . You can imagine . . ."

"Just get here?" asked the seaman. Even voice. Mesh T-shirt. All cool and competent. Dark hair neatly trimmed in back. Clear forehead. Overall appearance decent and placid.

"Last night," Nikitin replied.

The borscht and the fiery dark wine made him sweat even more. He was happy to relax and have a peaceful chat. Bright sunlight poured through the aperture of the door together with the tremulous sparkle of the alley rivulet; from his corner under the gas meter, the elderly Russian's spectacles scintillated.

"Looking for work?" asked the other sailor, who was middle-aged, blue-eyed, had a pale walrus mustache, and was also clean-cut, well groomed, levigated by sun and salty wind.

Nikitin said with a smile, "I certainly am. . . . Today I went to the employment office. . . . They have jobs planting telegraph poles, weaving hawsers—I'm just not sure. . . ."

"Come work with us," said the black-haired one. "As a stoker or something. No nonsense there, you can take my word. . . . Ah, there you are, Lyalya—our profound respects!"

A young girl entered, wearing a white hat, with a sweet, plain face. She made her way among the tables and smiled, first at the puppies, then at the seamen. Nikitin had asked them something but forgot his question as he watched the girl and the motion of her low hips, by which you can always recognize a Russian damsel. The owner gave her daughter a tender look, as if to say, "You poor tired thing," for she had probably spent all morning in an office, or else worked in a store. There was something touchingly homespun about her that made you think of violet soap and a summer flag stop in a birch forest. There was no France outside the door, of course. Those mincing movements . . . Sunny nonsense.

"No, it's not complicated at all," the seaman was saying, "here's how it works—you have an iron bucket and a coal pit. You start scraping. Lightly at first, so long as the coal goes sliding down into the bucket by itself, then you scrape harder. When you've filled the bucket you set it on a cart. You roll it over to the chief stoker. A bang of his shovel and—one!—the firebox door's open, a heave of the same shovel and—two!—in goes the coal—you know, fanned out so it will come down evenly. Precision work. Keep your eye on the dial, and if that pressure drops . . ."

In a window that gave on the street appeared the head and shoulders of a man wearing a panama and a white suit.

"How are you, Lyalya dearest?"

He leaned his elbows on the windowsill.

"Of course it *is* hot in there, a real furnace—you wear nothing to work but pants and a mesh T-shirt. The T-shirt is black when you're finished. As I was saying, about the pressure—'fur' forms in the firebox, an incrustation hard as stone, which you break up with a poker this long. Tough work. But afterwards, when you pop out on deck, the sunshine feels cool even if you're in the tropics. You shower, then down you go to your quarters, straight into your hammock—that's heaven, let me tell you. . . ."

Meanwhile, at the window: "And he insists he saw me in a car, you see?" (Lyalya in a high-pitched, excited voice).

Her interlocutor, the gentleman in white, stood leaning on the sill from the outside, and the square window framed his rounded shoulders, his soft, shaven face half-lit by the sun—a Russian who had been lucky.

"He goes on to tell me I was wearing a lilac dress, when I don't even own a lilac dress," yelped Lyalya, "and he persists: '*zhay voo zasyur.*'"

The seaman who had been talking to Nikitin turned and asked, "Couldn't you speak Russian?"

The man in the window said, "I managed to get this music, Lyalya. Remember?"

That was the momentary aura, and it felt almost deliberate, as if someone were having fun inventing this girl, this conversation, this small Russian restaurant in a foreign port—an aura of dear workaday provincial Russia, and right away, by some miraculous, secret association of thoughts, the world appeared grander to Nikitin, he yearned to sail the oceans, to put into legendary bays, to eavesdrop everywhere on other people's souls.

"You asked what run we're on? Indochina," spontaneously said the seaman.

Nikitin pensively tapped a cigarette out of its case; a gold eagle was etched on the wooden lid.

"Must be wonderful."

"What do you think? Sure it is."

"Well, tell me about it. Something about Shanghai, or Colombo."

"Shanghai? I've seen it. Warm drizzle, red sand. Humid as a greenhouse. As for Ceylon, for instance, I didn't get ashore to visit it—it was my watch, you know."

Shoulders hunched, the white-jacketed man was saying something to Lyalya through the window, softly and significantly. She listened, her head cocked, fondling the dog's curled-over ear with one hand. Extending its fire-pink tongue, panting joyously and rapidly, the dog looked through the sunny chink of the door, most likely debating whether or not it was worthwhile to go lie some more on the hot threshold. And the dog seemed to be thinking in Russian.

Nikitin asked, "Where should I apply?"

The seaman winked at his mate, as if to say, "See, I brought him round." Then he said, "It's very simple. Tomorrow morning bright and early you go to the Old Port, and at Pier Two you'll find our *Jean-Bart*. Have a chat with the first mate. I think he'll hire you."

Nikitin took a keen and candid look at the man's clear, intelligent forehead. "What were you before, in Russia?" he asked.

The man shrugged and gave a wry smile.

"What was he? A fool," Droopy Mustache answered for him in a bass voice.

Later they both got up. The younger man pulled out the wallet he carried inserted in the front of his pants behind his belt buckle, in the manner of French sailors. Something elicited a high-pitched laugh from Lyalya as she came up and gave them her hand (palm probably a little damp). The pups were tumbling about the floor. The man standing at the window turned away, whistling absently and tenderly. Nikitin paid and went out leisurely into the sunlight.

It was about five in the afternoon. The sea's blueness, glimpsed at the far ends of alleys, hurt his eyes. The circular screens of the outdoor toilets were ablaze.

He returned to his squalid hotel and, slowly stretching his intertwined hands behind his head, collapsed onto the bed in a state of blissful solar inebriation. He dreamt he was an officer again, walking along a Crimean slope overgrown with milkweed and oak shrubs, mowing off the downy heads of thistles as he went. He awoke because he had started laughing in his sleep; he awoke, and the window had already turned a twilight blue.

He leaned out into the cool chasm, meditating: Wandering women. Some of them Russian. What a big star.

He smoothed his hair, rubbed the dust off the knobby tips of his shoes with a corner of the blanket, checked his wallet—only five francs left—and went out to roam some more and revel in his solitary idleness.

Now it was more crowded than it had been in the afternoon. Along the alleys that descended toward the sea, people were sitting, cooling off. Girl in a kerchief with spangles. . . . Flutter of eyelashes. . . . Paunchy shopkeeper, sitting astride a straw chair, elbows propped on its reversed back, smoking, with a flap of shirt protruding on his belly from beneath his unbuttoned waistcoat. Children hopping in a squatting posture as they sailed little paper boats, by the light of a streetlamp, in the black streamlet running next to the narrow sidewalk. There were smells of fish and wine. From the sailors' taverns, which shone with a yellow gleam, came the labored sound of hurdy-gurdies, the pounding of palms on tables, metallic exclamations. And, in the upper part of town, along the main avenue, the evening crowds shuffled and laughed, and women's slender ankles and the white shoes of naval officers flashed beneath clouds of acacias. Here and there, like the colored flames of some petrified fireworks display, cafés blazed in the purple twilight. Round tables right out on the sidewalk, shadows of black plane trees on the striped awning, illuminated from within. Nikitin stopped, picturing a mug of beer, ice-cold and heavy. Inside, beyond the tables, a violin wrung its sounds as if they were human hands, accompanied by the full-bodied resonance of a rippling harp. The more banal the music, the closer it is to the heart.

At an outer table sat a weary streetwalker all in green, swinging the pointed tip of her shoe.

I'll have the beer, decided Nikitin. No I won't . . . Then again . . .

The woman had doll-like eyes. There was something very familiar about those eyes, about those elongated, shapely legs. Gathering up her purse, she got up as if in a hurry to get somewhere. She wore a long jacketlike top of knitted emerald silk that adhered low on her hips. Past she went, squinting from the music.

It would be strange indeed, mused Nikitin. Something akin to a falling star hurtled through his memory, and, forgetting about his beer, he followed her as she turned into a dark, glistening alley. A streetlamp stretched her shadow. The shadow flashed along a wall and skewed. She walked slowly and Nikitin checked his pace, afraid, for some reason, to overtake her.

Yes, there's no question. . . . God, this is wonderful. . . .

The woman stopped on the curb. A crimson bulb burned over a black door. Nikitin walked past, came back, circled the woman, stopped. With a cooing laugh she uttered a French word of endearment.

In the wan light, Nikitin saw her pretty, fatigued face, and the moist luster of her minute teeth.

"Listen," he said in Russian, simply and softly. "We've known each other a long time, so why not speak our native language?"

She raised her eyebrows. "Inglish? Yew spik Inglish?"

Nikitin gave her an intent look, then repeated somewhat helplessly, "Come, you know and I know."

"*T'es Polonais, alors?*" inquired the woman, dragging out the final rolled syllable as they do in the South.

Nikitin gave up with a sardonic smile, thrust a five-franc note into her hand, turned quickly, and started across the sloping square. An instant later he heard rapid footfalls behind him, and breathing, and the rustle of a dress. He looked back. There was no one. The square was deserted and dark. The night wind propelled a newspaper sheet across the flagstones.

He heaved a sigh, smiled once more, thrust his fists deep into his pockets, and, looking at the stars, which flashed and waned as if fanned by a gigantic bellows, began descending seaward. He sat down on the ancient wharf with his feet dangling over the edge, above the rhythmic, moonlit swaying of the waves, and sat thus for a long time, head thrown back, leaning on the palms of his stretched-back hands.

A falling star shot by with the suddenness of a missed heartbeat. A strong, clean gust blew through his hair, pale in the nocturnal radiance.

REVENGE

1

O STEND, the stone wharf, the gray strand, the distant row of hotels, were all slowly rotating as they receded into the turquoise haze of an autumn day.

The professor wrapped his legs in a tartan lap robe, and the chaise longue creaked as he reclined into its canvas comfort. The clean, ochre-red deck was crowded but quiet. The boilers heaved discreetly.

An English girl in worsted stockings, indicating the professor with a motion of her eyebrow, addressed her brother who was standing nearby: "Looks like Sheldon, doesn't he?"

Sheldon was a comic actor, a bald giant with a round, flabby face. "He's really enjoying the sea," the girl added sotto voce. Whereupon, I regret to say, she drops out of my story.

Her brother, an ungainly, red-haired student on his way back to his university after the summer holidays, took the pipe out of his mouth and said, "He's our biology professor. Capital old chap. Must say hello to him." He approached the professor, who, lifting his heavy eyelids, recognized one of the worst and most diligent of his pupils.

"Ought to be a splendid crossing," said the student, giving a light squeeze to the large, cold hand that was proffered him.

"I hope so," replied the professor, stroking his gray cheek with his fingers. "Yes, I hope so," he repeated weightily, "I hope so."

The student gave the two suitcases standing next to the deck chair a cursory glance. One of them was a dignified veteran, covered with the white traces of old travel labels, like bird droppings on a monument. The other one—brand-new, orange-colored, with gleaming locks—for some reason caught his attention.

"Let me move that suitcase before it falls over," he offered, to keep up the conversation.

The professor chuckled. He did look like that silver-browed comic, or else like an aging boxer. . . .

"The suitcase, you say? Know what I have in it?" he inquired, with a hint of irritation in his voice. "Can't guess? A marvelous object! A special kind of coat hanger . . ."

"A German invention, sir?" the student prompted, remembering that the biologist had just been to Berlin for a scientific congress.

The professor gave a hearty, creaking laugh, and a golden tooth flashed like a flame. "A divine invention, my friend—divine. Something everybody needs. Why, you travel with the same kind of thing yourself. Eh? Or perhaps you're a polyp?" The student grinned. He knew that the professor was given to obscure jokes. The old man was the object of much gossip at the university. They said he tortured his spouse, a very young woman. The student had seen her once. A skinny thing, with incredible eyes. "And how is your wife, sir?" asked the red-haired student.

The professor replied, "I shall be frank with you, dear friend. I've been struggling with myself for quite some some time, but now I feel compelled to tell you. . . . My dear friend, I like to travel in silence. I trust you'll forgive me."

But here the student, whistling in embarrassment and sharing his sister's lot, departs forever from these pages.

The biology professor, meanwhile, pulled his black felt hat down over his bristly brows to shield his eyes against the sea's dazzling shimmer, and sank into a semblance of sleep. The sunlight falling on his gray, clean-shaven face, with its large nose and heavy chin, made it seem freshly modeled out of moist clay. Whenever a flimsy autumn cloud happened to screen the sun, the face would suddenly darken, dry out, and petrify. It was all, of course, alternating light and shade rather than a reflection of his thoughts. If his thoughts had indeed been reflected on his face, the professor would have hardly been a pretty sight. The trouble was that he had received a report the other day from the private detective he had hired in London that his wife was unfaithful to him. An intercepted letter, written in her minuscule, familiar hand, began, *"My dear darling Jack, I am still all full of your last kiss."* The professor's name was certainly not Jack—that was the whole point. The perception made him feel neither surprise nor pain, not even masculine vexation, but only hatred, sharp and cold as a lancet. He realized with utter clarity that he would murder his wife. There could be no qualms. One had only to devise the most excruciating, the most ingenious method. As he reclined in the deck chair, he reviewed for the hundredth time all the methods of torture described by travelers and medieval scholars. Not one of them, so far, seemed adequately painful. In the distance, at the verge of the green shimmer, the sugary-white cliffs of Dover were materializing, and he had still not made a decision. The steamer fell silent and, gently rocking, docked. The professor followed his porter down the gangplank. The customs officer, after rattling off the items ineligible for import, asked him to open a suitcase—the new, orange one. The professor turned the lightweight key in its lock and swung open the leather flap. Some Russian lady behind him loudly exclaimed, "Good Lord!" and gave a nervous laugh. Two Belgians standing on either side of the professor cocked their heads and gave a kind of upward glance. One shrugged his shoulders and the other gave a soft whistle, while the English turned away with indifference. The official, dumbfounded, goggled his eyes at the suitcase's contents. Everybody felt very creepy and uncomfortable. The biologist phlegmatically gave his name, mentioning the university museum. Expressions cleared up. Only a few ladies were chagrined to learn that no crime had been committed.

"But why do you transport it in a suitcase?" inquired the official with respectful reproach, gingerly lowering the flap and chalking a scrawl on the bright leather. "I was in a hurry," said the professor with a fatigued squint. "No time to hammer together a crate. In any case it's a valuable object and not something I'd send in the baggage hold." And, with a stooped but springy gait, the professor crossed to the railway platform past a policeman who resembled a gargantuan toy. But suddenly he paused as if remembering something and mumbled with a radiant, kindly smile, "There—I have it. A most clever method." Whereupon he heaved a sigh of relief and purchased two bananas, a pack of cigarettes, newspapers reminiscent of crackling bedsheets, and, a few minutes later, was speeding in a comfortable compartment of the Continental Express along the scintillating sea, the white cliffs, the emerald pastures of Kent.

2

They were wonderful eyes indeed, with pupils like glossy inkdrops on dove-gray satin. Her hair was cut short and golden-pale in hue, a luxuriant topping of fluff. She was small, upright, flat-chested. She had been expecting her husband since yesterday, and knew for certain he would arrive today. Wearing a gray, open-necked dress and velvet slippers, she was sitting on a peacock ottoman in the parlor, thinking what a pity it was her husband did not believe in ghosts and openly despised the young medium, a Scot with pale, delicate eyelashes, who occasionally visited her. After all, odd things did happen to her. Recently, in her sleep, she had had a vision of a dead youth with whom, before she was married, she had strolled in the twilight, when the blackberry blooms seem so ghostly white. Next morning, still aquiver, she had penciled a letter to him—a letter to her dream. In this letter she had lied to poor Jack. She had, in fact, nearly forgotten about him; she loved her excruciating husband with a fearful but faithful love; yet she wanted to send a little warmth to this dear spectral visitor, to reassure him with some words from earth. The letter vanished mysteriously from her writing pad, and the same night she dreamt of a long table, from under which Jack suddenly emerged, nodding to her gratefully. Now, for some reason, she felt uneasy when recalling that dream, almost as if she had cheated on her husband with a ghost.

The drawing room was warm and festive. On the wide, low windowsill lay a silk cushion, bright yellow with violet stripes.

The professor arrived just when she had decided his ship must have gone to the bottom. Glancing out the window, she saw the black top of a taxi, the driver's proffered palm, and the massive shoulders of her husband who had bent down his head as he paid. She flew through the rooms and trotted downstairs swinging her thin, bared arms.

He was climbing toward her, stooped, in an ample coat. Behind him a servant carried his suitcases.

She pressed against his woolen scarf, playfully bending back the heel of one slender, gray-stockinged leg. He kissed her warm temple. With a good-natured smile he lifted away her arms. "I'm covered with dust. . . . Wait. . . . ," he mumbled, holding her by the wrists. Frowning, she tossed her head and the pale conflagration of her hair. The professor stooped and kissed her on the lips with another little grin.

At supper, thrusting out the white breastplate of his starched shirt and energetically moving his glossy cheekbones, he recounted his brief journey. He was reservedly jolly. The curved silk lapels of his dinner jacket, his bulldog jaw, his massive bald head with ironlike veins on its temples—all this aroused in his wife an exquisite pity: the pity she always felt because, as he studied the minutiae of life, he refused to enter her world, where the poetry of de la Mare flowed and infinitely tender astral spirits hurtled.

"Well, did your ghosts come knocking while I was away?" he asked, reading her thoughts. She wanted to tell him about the dream, the letter, but felt somehow guilty.

"You know something," he went on, sprinkling sugar on some pink rhubarb, "you and your friends are playing with fire. There can be really terrifying occurrences. One Viennese doctor told me about some incredible metamorphoses the other day. Some woman—some kind of fortune-telling hysteric—died, of a heart attack I think, and, when the doctor undressed her (it all happened in a Hungarian hut, by candlelight), he was stunned at the sight of her body; it was entirely covered with a reddish sheen, was soft and slimy to the touch, and, upon closer examination, he realized that this plump, taut cadaver consisted entirely of narrow, circular bands of skin, as if it were all bound evenly and tightly by invisible strings, something like that advertisement for French tires, the man whose body is all tires. Except that in her case these tires were very thin and pale red. And, as the doctor watched, the corpse gradually began to unwind like a huge ball of yarn. . . . Her body was a thin, endless worm, which was disentangling itself and crawling, slithering out through the crack under the door while, on the bed, there remained a naked, white, still humid skeleton. Yet this woman had a husband, who had once kissed her—kissed that worm."

The professor poured himself a glass of port the color of mahogany and began gulping the rich liquid, without taking his narrowed eyes off his wife's face. Her thin, pale shoulders gave a shiver. "You yourself don't realize what a terrifying thing you've told me," she said in agitation. "So the woman's ghost disappeared into a worm. It's all terrifying. . . ."

"I sometimes think," said the professor, ponderously shooting a cuff and examining his blunt fingers, "that, in the final analysis, my science is an idle illusion, that it is we who have invented the laws of physics, that anything—absolutely anything—can happen. Those who abandon themselves to such thoughts go mad. . . ."

He stifled a yawn, tapping his clenched fist against his lips.

"What's come over you, my dear?" his wife exclaimed softly. "You never spoke this way before. . . . I thought you knew everything, had everything mapped out. . . ."

For an instant the professor's nostrils flared spasmodically, and a gold fang flashed. But his face quickly regained its flabby state. He stretched and got up from the table. "I'm babbling nonsense," he said calmly and tenderly. "I'm tired. I'll go to bed. Don't turn on the light when you come in. Get right into bed with me—with me," he repeated meaningfully and tenderly, as he had not spoken for a long time.

These words resounded gently within her when she remained alone in the drawing room.

She had been married to him for five years and, despite her husband's capricious disposition, his frequent outbursts of unjustified jealousy, his silences, sullenness, and incomprehension, she felt happy, for she loved and pitied him. She, all slender and white, and he, massive, bald, with tufts of gray wool in the middle of his chest, made an impossible, monstrous couple—and yet she enjoyed his infrequent, forceful caresses.

A chrysanthemum, in its vase on the mantel, dropped several curled petals with a dry rustle. She gave a start and her heart jolted disagreeably as she remembered that the air was always filled with phantoms, that even her scientist husband had noted their fearsome apparitions.

She recalled how Jackie had popped out from under the table and started nodding his head with an eerie tenderness. It seemed to her that all the objects in the room were watching her expectantly. She was chilled by a wind of fear. She quickly left the drawing room, restraining an absurd cry. She caught her breath and thought, What a silly thing I am, really. . . . In the bathroom she spent a long time examining the sparkling pupils of her eyes. Her small face, capped by fluffy gold, seemed unfamiliar to her.

Feeling light as a young girl, with nothing on but a lace nightgown, trying not to brush against the furniture, she went to the darkened bedroom. She extended her arms to locate the headboard of the bed, and lay down on its edge. She knew she was not alone, that her husband was lying beside her. For a few instants she motionlessly gazed upward, feeling the fierce, muffled pounding of her heart.

When her eyes had become accustomed to the dark, intersected by the stripes of moonlight pouring through the muslin blind, she turned her head toward her husband. He was lying with his back to her, wrapped in the blanket. All she could see was the bald crown of his head, which seemed extraordinarily sleek and white in the puddle of moonlight.

He's not asleep, she thought affectionately. If he were, he would be snoring a little.

She smiled and, with her whole body, slid over toward her husband, spreading her arms under the covers for the familiar embrace. Her fingers felt some smooth ribs. Her knee struck a smooth bone. A skull, its black eye sockets rotating, rolled from its pillow onto her shoulder.

• • •

Electric light flooded the room. The professor, in his crude dinner jacket, his starched bosom, eyes, and enormous forehead glistening, emerged from behind a screen and approached the bed.

The blanket and sheets, jumbled together, slithered to the rug. His wife lay dead, embracing the white, hastily cobbled skeleton of a hunchback that the professor had acquired abroad for the university museum.

BENEFICENCE

I HAD inherited the studio from a photographer. A lilac-hued canvas still stood by the wall, depicting part of a balustrade and a whitish urn against the background of an indistinct garden. And it was in a wicker armchair, as if on the very threshold of those gouache depths, that I sat, thinking of you, until morning. It got very cold at daybreak. Roughcast clay heads gradually floated out of the murk into the dusty haze. One of them (your likeness) was wrapped in a wet rag. I traversed this hazy chamber—something crumbled and crackled underfoot—and, with the end of a long pole, hooked and pulled open in succession the black curtains that hung like shreds of tattered banners across the slanting glass. Having ushered in the morning—a squinty, wretched morning—I started laughing, and had no idea why; perhaps it was simply because I had spent the entire night sitting in a wicker armchair, surrounded by rubbish and shards of plaster of Paris, amid the dust of congealed plasticine, thinking of you.

Here is the kind of feeling I would experience whenever your name was mentioned in my presence: a bolt of black, a scented, forceful motion—that's how you threw back your arms when adjusting your veil. Long had I loved you; why, I know not. With your deceitful, savage ways, dwelling as you did in idle melancholy.

Recently I had come across an empty matchbox on your bedside table. On it there was a small funereal mound of ashes and a golden cigarette butt—a coarse, masculine one. I implored you to explain. You laughed unpleasantly. Then you burst into tears and I, forgiving everything, embraced your knees and pressed my wet eyelashes to the warm black silk. After that I did not see you for two weeks.

The autumn morning shimmered in the breeze. I carefully stood the pole in a corner. The tiled roofs of Berlin were visible through the window's broad span, their outlines varying with the iridescent inner irregularities of the glass; in their midst, a distant cupola rose like a bronze watermelon. The clouds were scudding, rupturing, fleetingly revealing an astonished, gossamer autumnal blue.

The day before I had spoken to you on the phone. It was I who had given in and called. We agreed to meet today at the Brandenburg Gate. Your voice, through the beelike hum, was remote and anxious. It kept sliding into the distance and vanishing. I spoke to you with tightly shut eyes, and felt like crying. My love for you was the throbbing, welling warmth of tears. That is exactly how I imagined paradise: silence and tears, and the warm silk of your knees. This you could not comprehend.

After dinner, when I went outside to meet you, my head began to whirl from the crisp air and the torrents of yellow sunlight. Every ray echoed in my temples. Large, rustling, russet leaves waddled as they raced along the sidewalk.

I reflected while I walked that you would probably not come to the rendezvous. And that, if you did, we would quarrel again anyway. I knew only how to sculpt and how to love. This was not enough for you.

The massive gates. Wide-hipped buses squeezing through the portals and rolling on down the boulevard, which receded into the restless blue glitter of the windy day. I waited for you under an oppressive vault, between chilly columns, near the grate of the guardhouse window. People everywhere: Berlin clerks were leaving their offices, ill-shaven, each with a briefcase under his arm and, in his eyes, the turbid nausea that comes when you smoke a bad cigar on an empty stomach—their weary, predatory faces, their high starched collars, flashed by endlessly; a woman passed with a red straw hat and a gray karakul coat; then a youth in velvet pants buttoned under the knees; and others still.

I waited, leaning on my cane, in the cold shadow of the corner columns. I did not believe you would come.

By one of the columns, near the guardhouse window, was a stand with postcards, maps, fan-spreads of colored photos, and by it on a stool sat a brown little old woman, short-legged, plump, with a round, speckled face, and she too was waiting.

I wondered which of us would wait longer, and who would come first—a customer, or you. The old woman's mien conveyed something like this: "I just happen to be here. . . . I sat down for a minute. . . . Yes, there's some kind of stand nearby, with excellent, curious knickknacks. . . . But I have nothing to do with it. . . ."

People passed ceaselessly between the columns, skirting the corner of the guardhouse; some glanced at the postcards. The old woman would tense every nerve and fix her bright tiny eyes on the passerby, as if transmitting a thought: Buy it, buy it. . . . But the other, after a quick survey of the colored cards and the gray ones, walked on, and she, with seeming indifference, lowered her eyes and went back to the red book she was holding in her lap.

I did not believe you would come. But I waited for you as I had never waited before, smoking restlessly, peeking beyond the gate toward the uncluttered plaza at the start of the boulevard; then I would retreat anew into my nook, trying not to give the appearance of waiting, trying to imagine that you were walking, approaching while I was not looking, that if I took another peek around that corner I would see your seal-fur coat and the black lace hanging from your hat brim down over your eyes—and I deliberately did not look, cherishing the self-deception.

There was a rush of cold wind. The woman got up and started pushing her postcards more firmly into their slots. She wore a kind of yellow velours jacket with gathers at the waist. The hem of her brown skirt was hiked up higher in front than in back, which made her look as if she were thrusting out her belly when she walked. I could make out meek, kindhearted creases on her round little hat and her worn duck bootees. She was busily arranging her tray of wares. Her book, a guide to Berlin, lay on the stool, and the autumn wind absently turned the pages and ruffled the map that had fallen out from them like a flight of stairs.

I was getting cold. My cigarette smouldered lopsidedly and bitterly. I felt the waves of a hostile chill on my chest. No customer had appeared.

Meanwhile the knickknack woman got back on her perch and, since the stool was too tall for her, she had to do some squirming, with the soles of her blunt bootees leaving the sidewalk by turns. I tossed away the cigarette and flicked it with the end of my cane, provoking a fiery spray.

An hour had passed already, maybe more. How could I think you would come? The sky had imperceptibly turned into one continuous storm cloud, the passersby walked even faster, hunched over, holding on to their hats, and a lady who was crossing the square opened her umbrella as she went. It would be a real miracle if you were to arrive now.

The old woman had meticulously placed a marker in her book and paused as if lost in thought. My guess is she was conjuring up a rich foreigner from the Adlon Hotel who would buy all her wares, and overpay, and order more, many more picture postcards and guide-books of all kinds. And she probably was not very warm either in that velours jacket. You *had* promised you would come. I remembered the phone call, and the fleeting shadow of your voice. God, how I wanted to see you. The ill wind started gusting again. I turned up my collar.

Suddenly the window of the guardhouse opened, and a green soldier hailed the old woman. She quickly scrambled down from her stool and, with her thrust-out belly, scuttled up to the window. With a relaxed motion, the soldier handed her a streaming mug and closed the sash. His green shoulder turned and withdrew into the murky depths.

Gingerly carrying the mug, the woman returned to her seat. It was coffee with milk, judging by the brown fringe of skin sticking to the rim.

Then she began drinking. I have never seen a person drink with such utter, profound, concentrated relish. She forgot her stand, the postcards, the chill wind, her American client, she just sipped, sucked, disappeared totally into her coffee—exactly as I forgot about my vigil and saw only the velours jacket, the bliss-dimmed eyes, the stubby hands clutching the mug in their woolen mittens. She drank for a long time, drank in slow swallows, reverently licking off the fringe of skin, heating her palms on the warm tin. And a dark, sweet warmth poured into my soul. My soul, too, was drinking and heating itself, and the brown little woman tasted of coffee with milk.

She finished. For a moment she paused, motionless. Then she rose and headed for the window to return the mug.

But she stopped halfway, and her lips gathered into a little smile. She scuttled rapidly back to her stand, snatched up two colored postcards, and, hurrying back to the iron grille of the window, softly tapped on the glass with her small woolly fist. The grille opened, a green sleeve glided out, with a gleaming button on the cuff, and she thrust mug and cards into the dark window with a series of hasty nods. The soldier, examining the photographs, turned away into the interior, slowly shutting the sash behind him.

Here I became aware of the world's tenderness, the profound beneficence of all that surrounded me, the blissful bond between me and all of creation, and I realized that the joy I had sought in you was not only secreted within you, but breathed around me everywhere, in the speeding street sounds, in the hem of a comically lifted skirt, in the metallic yet tender drone of the wind, in the autumn clouds bloated with rain. I realized that the world does not represent a struggle at all, or a predaceous sequence of chance events, but shimmering bliss, beneficent trepidation, a gift bestowed on us and unappreciated.

And at that instant you arrived at last—or, rather, not you but a German couple, he in a raincoat, legs in long stockings like green bottles; she slender and tall, in a panther coat. They approached the stand, the man began selecting, and my little old coffeewoman, flushed, puffed up, looked now into his eyes, now at the cards, fussing, moving her eyebrows tensely like an old cabbie urging on his nag with his whole body. But the German had barely had time to pick something out when, with a shrug of her shoulder, his wife tugged him away by the sleeve. It was then I noticed that she resembled you. The similarity was not in the features, not in the clothes, but in that squeamish, unkind grimace, in that cursory, indifferent glance. The two of them walked on without buying anything, and the old woman only smiled, replaced her postcards in their slots, and again became absorbed in her red book. There was no point in waiting any longer. I departed along darkening streets, peering into the faces of passersby, capturing smiles and amazing little motions—the bobbing of a girl's pigtail as she tossed a ball against a wall, the heavenly melancholy reflected in a horse's purplish, oval eye. I captured and collected all of it. The oblique, plump raindrops grew more frequent, and I recalled the cool coziness of my studio, the muscles, foreheads, and strands of hair that I had modeled, and felt in my fingers the subtle tingle of my thought starting to sculpt.

It grew dark. The rain was gusting. The wind greeted me turbulently at every corner. Then a streetcar clanged past, its windows agleam with amber, its interior filled with black silhouettes. I hopped aboard as it passed and began drying my rain-soaked hands.

The people in the car looked sullen and swayed sleepily. The black windowpanes were specked with a multitude of minute raindrops, like a night sky overcast with a beadwork of stars. We were clattering along a street lined with noisy chestnut trees, and I kept imagining that the humid boughs were lashing the windows. And when the tram halted one could hear, overhead, the chestnuts plucked by the wind knocking against the roof. Knock—then again, resiliently, gently: knock, knock. The tram would chime and start, the gleam of the streetlamps shattered in the wet glass, and, with a sensation of poignant happiness, I awaited the repetition of those meek, lofty sounds. The brakes slammed on for a stop. Again a round, solitary chestnut dropped, and, after a moment, another thumped and rolled along the roof: knock, knock. . . .

DETAILS OF A SUNSET

T HE last streetcar was disappearing in the mirrorlike murk of the street and, along the wire above it, a spark of Bengal light, crackling and quivering, sped into the distance like a blue star.

"Well, might as well just plod along, even though you are pretty drunk, Mark, pretty drunk. . . ."

The spark went out. The roofs glistened in the moonlight, silvery angles broken by oblique black cracks.

Through this mirrory darkness he staggered home: Mark Standfuss, a salesclerk, a demigod, fair-haired Mark, a lucky fellow with a high starched collar. At the back of his neck, above the white line of that collar, his hair ended in a funny, boyish little tag that had escaped the barber's scissors. That little tag was what made Klara fall in love with him, and she swore that it was true love, that she had quite forgotten the handsome ruined foreigner who last year had rented a room from her mother, Frau Heise.

"And yet, Mark, you're drunk. . . ."

That evening there had been beer and songs with friends in honor of Mark and russet-haired, pale Klara, and in a week they would be married; then there would be a lifetime of bliss and peace, and of nights with her, the red blaze of her hair spreading all over the pillow, and, in the morning, again her quiet laughter, the green dress, the coolness of her bare arms.

In the middle of a square stood a black wigwam: the tram tracks were being repaired. He remembered how today he had got under her short sleeve, and kissed the touching scar from her smallpox vaccination. And now he was walking home, unsteady on his feet from too much happiness and too much drink, swinging his slender cane, and among the dark houses on the opposite side of the empty street a night echo clop-clopped in time with his footfalls; but grew silent when he turned at the corner where the same man as always, in apron and peaked cap, stood by his grill, selling frankfurters, crying out in a tender and sad birdlike whistle: *"Würstchen, würstchen . . ."*

Mark felt a sort of delicious pity for the frankfurters, the moon, the blue spark that had receded along the wire, and, as he tensed his body against a friendly fence, he was overcome with laughter, and, bending, exhaled into a little round hole in the boards the words "Klara, Klara, oh my darling!"

On the other side of the fence, in a gap between the buildings, was a rectangular vacant lot. Several moving vans stood there like enormous coffins. They were bloated from their loads. Heaven knows what was piled inside them. Oakwood trunks, probably, and chandeliers like iron spiders, and the heavy skeleton of a double bed. The moon cast a hard glare on the vans. To the left of the lot, huge black hearts were flattened against a bare rear wall—the shadows, many times magnified, of the leaves of a linden tree that stood next to a streetlamp on the edge of the sidewalk.

Mark was still chuckling as he climbed the dark stairs to his floor. He reached the final step, but mistakenly raised his foot again, and it came down awkwardly with a bang. While he was groping in the dark in search of the keyhole, his bamboo cane slipped out from under his arm and, with a subdued little clatter, slid down the staircase. Mark held his breath. He thought the cane would turn with the stairs and knock its way down to the bottom. But the high-pitched wooden click abruptly ceased. Must have stopped. He grinned with relief and, holding on to the banister (the beer singing in his hollow head), started to descend again. He nearly fell, and sat down heavily on a step, as he groped around with his hands.

Upstairs the door onto the landing opened. Frau Standfuss, with a kerosene lamp in her hand, half-dressed, eyes blinking, the haze of her hair showing from beneath her nightcap, came out and called, "Is that you, Mark?"

A yellow wedge of light encompassed the banisters, the stairs, and his cane, and Mark, panting and pleased, climbed up again to the landing, and his black, hunchbacked shadow followed him up along the wall.

Then, in the dimly lit room, divided by a red screen, the following conversation took place:

"You've had too much to drink, Mark."

"No, no, Mother . . . I'm so happy . . ."

"You've got yourself all dirty, Mark. Your hand is black. . . . ."

". . . so very happy. . . . Ah, that feels good . . . water's nice and cold. Pour some on the top of my head . . . more. . . . Everybody congratulated me, and with good reason. . . . Pour some more on."

"But they say she was in love with somebody else such a short time ago—a foreign adventurer of some kind. Left without paying five marks he owed Frau Heise. . . ."

"Oh, stop—you don't understand anything. . . . We did such a lot of singing today. . . . Look, I've lost a button. . . . I think they'll double my salary when I get married. . . ."

"Come on, go to bed. . . . You're all dirty, and your new pants too."

That night Mark had an unpleasant dream. He saw his late father. His father came up to him, with an odd smile on his pale, sweaty face, seized Mark under the arms, and began to tickle him silently, violently, and relentlessly.

He only remembered that dream after he had arrived at the store where he worked, and he remembered it because a friend of his, jolly Adolf, poked him in the ribs. For one instant something flew open in his soul, momentarily froze still in surprise, and slammed shut. Then again everything became easy and limpid, and the neckties he offered his customers smiled brightly, in sympathy with his happiness. He knew he would see Klara that evening—he would only run home for dinner, then go straight to her house. . . . The other day, when he was telling her how cozily and tenderly they would live, she had suddenly burst into tears. Of course Mark had understood that these were tears of joy (as she herself explained); she began whirling about the room, her skirt like a green sail, and then she started rapidly smoothing her glossy hair, the color of apricot jam, in front of the mirror. And her face was pale and bewildered, also from happiness, of course. It was all so natural, after all. . . .

"A striped one? Why certainly."

He knotted the tie on his hand, and turned it this way and that, enticing the customer. Nimbly he opened the flat cardboard boxes. . . .

Meanwhile his mother had a visitor: Frau Heise. She had come without warning, and her face was tear-stained. Gingerly, almost as if she were afraid of breaking into pieces, she lowered herself onto a stool in the tiny, spotless kitchen where Frau Standfuss was washing the dishes. A two-dimensional wooden pig hung on the wall, and a half-open matchbox with one burnt match lay on the stove.

"I have come to you with bad news, Frau Standfuss."

The other woman froze, clutching a plate to her chest.

"It's about Klara. Yes. She has lost her senses. That lodger of mine came back today—you know, the one I told you about. And Klara has gone mad. Yes, it all happened this morning. . . . She never wants to see your son again. . . . You gave her the material for a new dress; it will be returned to you. And here is a letter for Mark. Klara's gone mad. I don't know what to think. . . ."

Meanwhile Mark had finished work and was already on his way home. Crew-cut Adolf walked him all the way to his house. They both stopped, shook hands, and Mark gave a shove with his shoulder to the door which opened into cool emptiness.

"Why go home? The heck with it. Let's have a bite somewhere, you and I." Adolf stood, propping himself on his cane as if it were a tail. "The heck with it, Mark. . . ."

Mark gave his cheek an irresolute rub, then laughed. "All right. Only it's my treat."

When, half an hour later, he came out of the pub and said good-bye to his friend, the flush of a fiery sunset filled the vista of the canal, and a rain-streaked bridge in the distance was margined by a narrow rim of gold along which passed tiny black figures.

He glanced at his watch and decided to go straight to his fiancée's without stopping at his mother's. His happiness and the limpidity of the evening air made his head spin a little. An arrow of bright copper struck the lacquered shoe of a fop jumping out of a car. The puddles, which still had not dried, surrounded by the bruise of dark damp (the live eyes of the asphalt), reflected the soft incandescence of the evening. The houses were as gray as ever; yet the roofs, the moldings above the upper floors, the gilt-edged lightning rods, the stone cupolas, the colonnettes—which nobody notices during the day, for day people seldom look up—were now bathed in rich ochre, the sunset's airy warmth, and thus they seemed unexpected and magical, those upper protrusions, balconies, cornices, pillars, contrasting sharply, because of their tawny brilliance, with the drab façades beneath.

Oh, how happy I am, Mark kept musing, how everything around celebrates my happiness.

As he sat in the tram he tenderly, lovingly examined his fellow passengers. He had such a young face, had Mark, with pink pimples on the chin, glad luminous eyes, an untrimmed tag at the hollow of his nape. . . . One would think fate might have spared him.

In a few moments I'll see Klara, he thought. She'll meet me at the door. She'll say she barely survived until evening.

He gave a start. He had missed the stop where he should have got off. On the way to the exit he tripped over the feet of a fat gentleman who was reading a medical journal; Mark wanted to tip his hat but nearly fell: the streetcar was turning with a screech. He grabbed an overhead strap and managed to keep his balance. The man slowly retracted his short legs with a phlegmy and cross growl. He had a gray mustache which twisted up pugnaciously. Mark gave him a guilty smile and reached the front end of the car. He grasped the iron handrails with both hands, leaned forward, calculated his jump. Down below, the asphalt streamed past, smooth and glistening. Mark jumped. There was a burn of friction against his soles, and his legs started running by themselves, his feet stamping with involuntary resonance. Several odd things occurred simultaneously: from the front of the car, as it swayed away from Mark, the conductor emitted a furious shout; the shiny asphalt swept upward like the seat of a swing; a roaring mass hit Mark from behind. He felt as if a thick thunderbolt had gone through him from head to toe, and then nothing. He was standing alone on the glossy asphalt. He looked around. He saw, at a distance, his own figure, the slender back of Mark Standfuss, who was walking diagonally across the street as if nothing had happened. Marveling, he caught up with himself in one easy sweep, and now it was he nearing the sidewalk, his entire frame filled with a gradually diminishing vibration.

That was stupid. Almost got run over by a bus. . . .

The street was wide and gay. The colors of the sunset had invaded half of the sky. Upper stories and roofs were bathed in glorious light. Up there, Mark could discern translucent porticoes, friezes and frescoes, trellises covered with orange roses, winged statues that lifted skyward golden, unbearably blazing lyres. In bright undulations, ethereally, festively, these architectonic enchantments were receding into the heavenly distance, and Mark could not understand how he had never noticed before those galleries, those temples suspended on high.

He banged his knee painfully. That black fence again. He could not help laughing as he recognized the vans beyond. There they stood, like gigantic coffins. Whatever might they conceal within? Treasures? The skeletons of giants? Or dusty mountains of sumptuous furniture?

Oh, I must have a look. Or else Klara will ask, and I shan't know.

He gave a quick nudge to the door of one of the vans and went inside. Empty. Empty, except for one little straw chair in the center, comically poised askew on three legs.

Mark shrugged and went out on the opposite side. Once again the hot evening glow gushed into sight. And now in front of him was the familiar wrought-iron wicket, and further on Klara's window, crossed by a green branch. Klara herself opened the gate, and stood waiting, lifting her bared elbows, adjusting her hair. The russet tufts of her armpits showed through the sunlit openings of her short sleeves.

Mark, laughing noiselessly, ran up to embrace her. He pressed his cheek against the warm, green silk of her dress.

Her hands came to rest on his head.

"I was so lonely all day, Mark. But now you are here."

She opened the door, and Mark immediately found himself in the dining room, which struck him as being inordinately spacious and bright.

"When people are as happy as we are now," she said, "they can do without a hallway," Klara spoke in a passionate whisper, and he felt that her words had some special, wonderful meaning.

And in the dining room, around the snow-white oval of the table-cloth, sat a number of people, none of whom Mark had seen before at his fiancée's house. Among them was Adolf, swarthy, with his square-shaped head; there was also that short-legged, big-bellied old man who had been reading a medical journal in the tram and was still grumbling.

Mark greeted the company with a shy nod and sat down beside Klara, and in that same instant felt, as he had a short time ago, a bolt of atrocious pain pass through his whole frame. He writhed, and Klara's green dress floated away, diminished, and turned into the green shade of a lamp. The lamp was swaying on its cord. Mark was lying beneath it, with that inconceivable pain crushing his body, and nothing could be distinguished save that oscillating lamp, and his ribs were pressing against his heart, making it impossible to breathe, and some-one was bending his leg, straining to break it, in a moment it would crack. He freed himself somehow, the lamp glowed green again, and Mark saw himself sitting a little way off, beside Klara, and no sooner had he seen it than he found himself brushing his knee against her warm silk skirt. And Klara was laughing, her head thrown back.

He felt an urge to tell about what had just happened, and, address-ing all those present—jolly Adolf, the irritable fat man—uttered with an effort: "The foreigner is offering the aforementioned prayers on the river. . . ."

It seemed to him that he had made everything clear, and apparently they had all understood. . . . Klara, with a little pout, pinched his cheek: "My poor darling. It'll be all right. . . ."

He began to feel tired and sleepy. He put his arm around Klara's neck, drew her to him, and lay back. And then the pain pounced upon him again, and everything became clear.

Mark was lying supine, mutilated and bandaged, and the lamp was not swinging any longer. The familiar fat man with the mustache, now a doctor in a white gown, made worried growling small noises as he peered into the pupils of Mark's eyes. And what pain! . . . God, in a moment his heart would be impaled on a rib and burst . . . God, any instant now. . . . This is silly. Why isn't Klara here? . . .

The doctor frowned and clucked his tongue.

Mark no longer breathed, Mark had departed—whither, into what other dreams, none can tell.

THE THUNDERSTORM

A T T H E corner of an otherwise ordinary West Berlin street, under the canopy of a linden in full bloom, I was enveloped by a fierce fragrance. Masses of mist were ascending in the night sky and, when the last star-filled hollow had been absorbed, the wind, a blind phantom, covering his face with his sleeves, swept low through the deserted street. In lusterless darkness, over the iron shutter of a barbershop, its suspended shield—a gilt shaving basin—began swinging like a pendulum.

I came home and found the wind waiting for me in the room: it banged the casement window—and staged a prompt reflux when I shut the door behind me. Under my window there was a deep courtyard where, in the daytime, shirts, crucified on sun-bright clotheslines, shone through the lilac bushes. Out of that yard voices would rise now and then: the melancholy barking of ragmen or empty-bottle buyers; sometimes, the wail of a crippled violin; and, once, an obese blond woman stationed herself in the center of the yard and broke into such lovely song that maids leaned out of all the windows, bending their bare necks. Then, when she had finished, there was a moment of extraordinary stillness; only my landlady, a slatternly widow, was heard sobbing and blowing her nose in the corridor.

In that yard now a stifling gloom swelled, but then the blind wind, which had helplessly slithered into its depths, once again began reaching upward, and suddenly it regained its sight, swept up and, in the amber apertures of the black wall opposite, the silhouettes of arms and disheveled heads began to dart, as escaping windows were being caught and their frames resonantly and firmly locked. The lights went out. The next moment an avalanche of dull sound, the sound of distant thunder, came into motion, and started tumbling through the dark-violet sky. And again all grew still as it had when the beggar woman finished her song, her hands clasped to her ample bosom.

In this silence I fell asleep, exhausted by the happiness of my day, a happiness I cannot describe in writing, and my dream was full of you.

I woke up because the night had begun crashing to pieces. A wild, pale glitter was flying across the sky like a rapid reflection of colossal spokes. One crash after another rent the sky. The rain came down in a spacious and sonorous flow.

I was intoxicated by those bluish tremors, by the keen, volatile chill. I went up to the wet window ledge and inhaled the unearthly air, which made my heart ring like glass.

Ever nearer, ever more grandly, the prophet's chariot rumbled across the clouds. The light of madness, of piercing visions, illumined the nocturnal world, the metal slopes of roofs, the fleeing lilac bushes. The Thunder-god, a white-haired giant with a furious beard blown back over his shoulder by the wind, dressed in the flying folds of a dazzling raiment, stood, leaning backward, in his fiery chariot, restraining with tensed arms his tremendous, jet-black steeds, their manes a violet blaze. They had broken away from the driver's control, they scattered sparkles of crackling foam, the chariot careened, and the flustered prophet tugged at the reins in vain. His face was distorted by the blast and the strain; the whirlwind, blowing back the folds of his garment, bared a mighty knee; the steeds tossed their blazing manes and rushed on ever more violently, down, down along the clouds. Then, with thunderous hooves, they hurtled across a shiny rooftop, the chariot lurched, Elijah staggered, and the steeds, maddened by the touch of mortal metal, sprang skyward again. The prophet was pitched out. One wheel came off. From my window I saw its enormous fiery hoop roll down the roof, teeter at the edge, and jump off into darkness, while the steeds, dragging the overturned chariot, were already speeding along the highest clouds; the rumble died down, and the stormy blaze vanished in livid chasms.

The Thunder-god, who had fallen onto the roof, rose heavily. His sandals started slipping; he broke a dormer window with his foot, grunted, and, with a sweep of his arm grasped a chimney to steady himself. He slowly turned his frowning face as his eyes searched for something—probably the wheel that had flown off its golden axle. Then he glanced upward, his fingers clutching at his ruffled beard, shook his head crossly—this was probably not the first time that it happened—and, limping slightly, began a cautious descent.

In great excitement I tore myself away from the window, hurried to put on my dressing gown, and ran down the steep staircase straight to the courtyard. The storm had blown over but a waft of rain still lingered in the air. To the east an exquisite pallor was invading the sky.

The courtyard, which from above had seemed to brim with dense darkness, contained, in fact, nothing more than a delicate, melting mist. On its central patch of turf darkened by the damp, a lean, stoop-shouldered old man in a drenched robe stood muttering something and looking around him. Upon seeing me, he blinked angrily and said, "That you, Elisha?"

I bowed. The prophet clucked his tongue, scratching the while his bald brown spot.

"Lost a wheel. Find it for me, will you?"

The rain had now ceased. Enormous flame-colored clouds collected above the roofs. The shrubs, the fence, the glistening kennel, were floating in the bluish, drowsy air around us. We groped for a long time in various corners. The old man kept grunting, hitching up the heavy hem of his robe, splashing through the puddles with his round-toed sandals, and a bright drop hung from the tip of his large, bony nose. As I brushed aside a low branch of lilac, I noticed, on a pile of rubbish, amid broken glass, a narrow-rimmed iron wheel that must have belonged to a baby carriage. The old man exhaled warm relief above my ear. Hastily, even a little brusquely, he pushed me aside, and snatched up the rusty hoop. With a joyful wink he said, "So that's where it rolled."

Then he stared at me, his white eyebrows came together in a frown, and, as if remembering something, he said in an impressive voice, "Turn away, Elisha."

I obeyed, even shutting my eyes. I stood like that for a minute or so, and then could not control my curiosity any longer.

The courtyard was empty, except for the old, shaggy dog with its graying muzzle that had thrust its head out of the kennel and was looking up, like a person, with frightened hazel eyes. I looked up too. Elijah had scrambled onto the roof, the iron hoop glimmering behind his back. Above the black chimneys a curly auroral cloud loomed like an orange-hued mountain and, beyond it, a second and a third. The hushed dog and I watched together as the prophet, who had reached the crest of the roof, calmly and unhurriedly stepped upon the cloud and continued to climb, treading heavily on masses of mellow fire. . . .

Sunlight shot through his wheel whereupon it became at once huge and golden, and Elijah himself now seemed robed in flame, blending with the paradisal cloud along which he walked higher and higher until he disappeared in a glorious gorge of the sky.

Only then did the decrepit dog break into a hoarse morning bark. Ripples ran across the bright surface of a rain puddle. The light breeze stirred the geraniums on the balconies. Two or three windows awakened. In my soaked bedslippers and worn dressing gown I ran out into the street to overtake the first, sleepy tramcar, and pulling the skirts of my gown around me, and laughing to myself as I ran, I imagined how, in a few moments, I would be in your house and start telling you about that night's midair accident, and the cross old prophet who fell into my yard.

LA VENEZIANA

1

IN FRONT of the red-hued castle, amid luxuriant elms, there was a vividly green grass court. Early that morning the gardener had smoothed it with a stone roller, extirpated a couple of daisies, redrawn the lines on the lawn with liquid chalk, and tightly strung a resilient new net between the posts. From a nearby village the butler had brought a carton within which reposed a dozen balls, white as snow, fuzzy to the touch, still light, still virgin, each wrapped like a precious fruit in its own sheet of transparent paper.

It was about five in the afternoon. The ripe sunshine dozed here and there on the grass and the tree trunks, filtered through the leaves, and placidly bathed the court, which had now come alive. There were four players: the Colonel himself (the castle's proprietor), Mrs. McGore, the host's son Frank, and Simpson, a college friend of his.

A person's motions while playing, like his handwriting in quieter moments, tell a good deal about him. Judging by the Colonel's blunt, stiff strokes, by the tense expression on his fleshy face that looked as if it had just spat out the massive gray mustache towering above his lip; by the fact that, in spite of the heat, he did not unbutton his shirt collar; and by the way he served, legs firmly planted apart like two white poles, one might conclude, firstly, that he had never been a good player, and, secondly, that he was a staid, old-fashioned, stubborn man, subject to occasional outbursts of seething anger. In fact, having hit the ball into the rhododendrons, he would exhale a terse oath through his teeth, or goggle his fishlike eyes at his racquet as if he could not forgive it for such a humiliating miss. Simpson, his partner by chance, a skinny blond youth with meek but mad eyes that fluttered and glinted behind his pince-nez like limp light-blue butterflies, was trying to play as best he could, although the Colonel, of course, never expressed his vexation when the loss of a point was the other's fault. But no matter how hard Simpson tried, no matter how he leaped about, none of his shots were successful. He felt as if he were coming apart at the seams, as if it were his timidity that kept him from hitting accurately, and that, instead of an instrument of play, meticulously and ingeniously assembled out of resonant, amber catgut strung on a superbly calculated frame, he was holding a clumsy dry log from which the ball would rebound with a painful crack, ending up in the net or in the bushes, and even managing to knock the straw hat off the circular pate of Mr. McGore, who was standing beside the court and watching with no great interest as his young wife Maureen and the lightfooted, nimble Frank defeated their perspiring opponents.

If McGore, an old connoisseur of art, and restorer, reframer, and recanvaser of even older paintings, who regarded the world as a rather poor study daubed with unstable paints on a flimsy canvas, had been the kind of curious and impartial spectator it is sometimes so expedient to attract, he might have concluded that tall, dark-haired, cheerful Maureen lived with the same carefree manner with which she played, and that Frank carried over into life as well his ability to return the most difficult shot with graceful ease. But, just as handwriting can often fool a fortune-teller by its superficial simplicity, the game of this white-clad couple in truth revealed nothing more than that Maureen played weak, soft, listless, female tennis, while Frank tried not to whack the ball too hard, recalling that he was not in a university tournament but in his father's park. He moved effortlessly toward the ball, and the long stroke gave a sense of physical fulfillment: every motion tends to describe a full circle, and even though, at its midpoint, it is transformed into the ball's linear flight, its invisible continuation is nevertheless instantaneously perceived by the hand and runs up the muscles all the way to the shoulder, and it is precisely this prolonged internal scintilla that makes the stroke fulfilling. With a phlegmatic smile on his clean-shaven, suntanned face, his bared flawless teeth flashing, Frank would rise on his toes and, without visible effort, swing his naked forearm. That ample arc contained an electric kind of force and the ball would rebound with a particularly taut and accurate ring from his racquet's strings.

He had arrived that morning with his friend to vacation at his father's, and had found Mr. and Mrs. McGore whom he already knew and who had been visiting at the castle for more than a month; the Colonel, inflamed by a noble passion for paintings, willingly forgave McGore his foreign origin, his unsociable nature, and his lack of humor in exchange for the assistance this famous art expert gave him and for the magnificent, priceless canvases he procured. Especially magnificent was the Colonel's most recent acquisition, the portrait of a woman by Luciani, sold to him by McGore for a most sumptuous sum.

Today, McGore, at the insistence of his wife who was familiar with the Colonel's punctiliousness, had put on a pale summer suit instead of the frock coat he usually wore, but he still did not pass his host's muster: his shirt was starched and had pearl buttons, which was, of course, inappropriate. Also not very appropriate were his reddish-yellow half-boots and the absence of the trouser cuffs the late king had instantaneously made fashionable when he once had to traverse some puddles to cross the road; nor did the old straw hat with a gnawed-looking rim from behind which poked McGore's gray curls appear especially elegant. He had a somewhat simian face, with a protuberant mouth, a long gap between nose and lip, and a whole complex system of wrinkles, so that one could probably read his face as if it were a palm. As he watched the ball flying back and forth across the net, his little greenish eyes darted right, left, right, and paused to blink lazily when the ball's flight was interrupted. The vivid white of three pairs of flannels and one short, cheerful skirt contrasted beautifully in the brilliant sunlight with the apple-hued verdure, but, as we have already remarked, Mr. McGore considered life's Creator only a second-rate imitator of the masters whom he had been studying for forty years.

Meanwhile Frank and Maureen, having won five straight games, were about to win the sixth. Frank, who was serving, tossed the ball high with his left hand, leaned far back as if he were about to fall over, then immediately lunged forward with a broad arching motion, his glossy racquet giving a glancing blow to the ball, which shot across the net and bounced like white lightning past Simpson, who gave it a helpless sidewise look.

"That's it," said the Colonel.

Simpson felt greatly relieved. He was too ashamed of his inept strokes to be capable of enthusiasm for the game, and this shame was intensified by the extraordinary attraction he felt for Maureen. All the players bowed to each other as was the custom, and Maureen gave a sidelong smile as she adjusted the strap on her bared shoulder. Her husband was applauding with an air of indifference.

"We must have a game of singles," remarked the Colonel, slapping his son on the back with gusto as the latter, baring his teeth, pulled on his white, crimson-striped club blazer with a violet emblem on one side.

"Tea!" said Maureen. "I'm dying for some tea."

Everyone moved into the shadow of a giant elm, where the butler and the black-and-white maid had set up a portable table. There was tea dark as Munich beer, sandwiches consisting of cucumber slices on rectangles of crustless bread, a swarthy cake pocked with black raisins, and large strawberries with cream. There were also several earthenware bottles of ginger ale.

"In my days," began the Colonel, lowering himself with ponderous relish into a folding canvas chair, "we preferred real, full-blooded English sports: rugby, cricket, hunting. There is something foreign about today's games, something skinny-legged. I am a staunch advocate of manly holds, juicy meat, an evening bottle of port—which does not prevent me," concluded the Colonel, as he smoothed his large mustache with a little brush, "from enjoying robust old paintings that have the luster of that same hearty wine."

"By the way, Colonel, the *Veneziana* has been hung," said McGore in his dreary voice, laying his hat on the lawn by his chair and rubbing the crown of his head, naked as a knee, around which still curled thick, dirty gray locks. "I picked the best-lighted spot in the gallery. They have rigged a lamp over it. I'd like you to have a look."

The Colonel fixed his glistening eyes in turn on his son, on the embarrassed Simpson, and on Maureen, who was laughing and grimacing from the hot tea.

"My dear Simpson," he exclaimed emphatically, pouncing on his chosen prey, "you haven't seen it yet! Pardon me for tearing you away from your sandwich, my friend, but I feel obligated to show you my new painting. The connoisseurs are going crazy over it. Come on. Of course I don't dare ask Frank."

Frank made a jovial bow. "You're right, Father. Paintings perturb me."

"We'll be right back, Mrs. McGore," said the Colonel as he got up. "Careful, you're going to step on the bottle," he addressed Simpson, who had also risen. "Prepare to be showered with beauty."

The three of them headed for the house across the softly sunlit lawn. Narrowing his eyes, Frank looked after them, looked down at McGore's hat abandoned on the grass by the chair (it exhibited to God, to the blue heavens, to the sun, its whitish underside with a dark greasy spot in the center, on the imprint of a Viennese hat shop), and then, turning toward Maureen, said a few words that will doubtless surprise the unperceptive reader. Maureen was sitting in a low armchair, covered with trembling ringlets of sunlight, pressing the gilt meshwork of the racquet to her forehead, and her face immediately became older and more severe when Frank said, "Now then, Maureen. It's time for us to make a decision. . . ."

2

McGore and the Colonel, like two guards, led Simpson into a cool, spacious hall, where paintings glistened on the walls and there was no furniture other than an oval table of glossy black wood standing in the center, all four of its legs reflected in the mirrorlike walnut-yellow of the parquet. Having conducted their prisoner to a large canvas in an opaque gilded frame, the Colonel and McGore stopped, the former with his hands in his pockets, the latter pensively picking some dry gray pollenlike matter out of his nostril and scattering it with a light rolling rub of his fingers.

The painting was very fine indeed. Luciani had portrayed the Venetian beauty in half-profile, standing against a warm, black background. Rose-tinted cloth revealed her prominent, dark-hued neck, with extraordinarily tender folds beneath the ear, and the gray lynx fur with which her cherry-red mantlet was trimmed was slipping off her left shoulder. With the elongated fingers of her right hand spread in pairs, she seemed to have been on the point of adjusting the falling fur but to have frozen motionless, her hazel, uniformly dark eyes gazing fixedly, languidly from the canvas. Her left hand, with white ripples of cambric encircling the wrist, was holding a basket of yellow fruit; the narrow crown of her headdress glowed atop her dark-chestnut hair. On the left the black was interrupted by a large right-angled opening straight into the twilight air and the bluish-green chasm of the cloudy evening.

Yet it was not those details of stupendous umbral interplay, nor the dark-hued warmth of the entire painting, that struck Simpson. It was something else. Tilting his head slightly to one side and blushing instantly, he said, "God, how she resembles—"

"My wife," finished McGore in a bored voice, scattering his dry pollen.

"It's incredibly good," whispered Simpson, tilting his head the other way, "incredibly . . ."

"Sebastiano Luciani," said the Colonel, complacently narrowing his eyes, "was born at the end of the fifteenth century in Venice and died in the mid-sixteenth in Rome. His teachers were Bellini and Giorgione and his rivals Michelangelo and Raffaello. As you can see, he synthesized in his work the power of the former and the tenderness of the latter. It's true he was not overly fond of Santi, and here it was not just a matter of professional vanity—legend has it that our artist was taken with a Roman lady called Margherita, known subsequently as 'la Fornarina.' Fifteen years before his death he took monastic vows upon receiving from Clement VII a simple and profitable appointment. Ever since then he has been known as Fra Sebastiano del Piombo. *Piombo* means 'lead,' for his duties consisted of applying enormous lead seals to the fiery papal bulls. A dissolute monk, he was fond of carousing and composed indifferent sonnets. But what a master. . . ."

The Colonel gave Simpson a quick glance, noting with satisfaction the impression the painting had made on his speechless guest.

It should again be emphasized, however, that Simpson, unaccustomed as he was to the contemplation of artwork, of course could not fully appreciate the mastery of Sebastiano del Piombo, and the one thing that fascinated him—apart, of course, from the purely physiological effect of the splendid colors on his optic nerves—was the resemblance he had immediately noticed, even though he was seeing Maureen for the first time. And the remarkable thing was that the Veneziana's face—the sleek forehead, bathed, as it were, in the recondite gloss of some olivaster moon, the totally dark eyes, the placidly expectant expression of her gently joined lips—clarified for him the real beauty of that other Maureen who kept laughing, narrowing her eyes, shifting her pupils in a constant struggle with the sunlight whose bright maculae glided across her white frock as she separated the rustling leaves with her racquet in search of a ball that had rolled into hiding.

Taking advantage of the liberty that an English host allows his guests, Simpson did not return to the tea table, but set off across the garden, rounding the star-shaped flower beds, and soon losing his way amid the checkerboard shadows of an avenue in the park, with its smell of fern and decaying leaves. The enormous trees were so old that their branches had had to be propped up by rusted braces, and they hunched over massively like dilapidated giants on iron crutches.

"God, what a stunning painting," Simpson whispered again. He walked unhurriedly, waving his racquet, stooped, his rubber soles lightly slapping. One must picture him clearly: gaunt, reddish-haired, clad in rumpled white trousers and a baggy gray jacket with half-belt; and also take careful note of the lightweight, rimless pince-nez on his pockmarked buttonlike nose, his weak, slightly mad eyes, and the freckles on his convex forehead, his cheekbones, and his neck, red from the summer sun.

He was in his second year at university, lived modestly, and diligently attended lectures on theology. He and Frank became friends not only because fate had assigned them the same apartment (consisting of two bedrooms and a common parlor), but, above all, like most weak-willed, bashful, secretly rapturous people, he involuntarily clung to someone in whom everything was vivid and firm—teeth, muscles, the physical strength of the soul, which is willpower. For his part, Frank, the pride of his college, who rowed in a racing scull and flew across the field with a leather watermelon under his arm, who knew how to land a punch on the very tip of the chin where there is the same kind of funny bone as in the elbow, a punch that would put an adversary to sleep—this extraordinary, universally liked Frank found something very flattering to his vanity in his friendship with the weak, awkward Simpson. Simpson, incidentally, was privy to something odd that Frank concealed from his other chums, who knew him only as a fine athlete and an exuberant chap, paying no attention whatever to occasional rumors that Frank was exceptionally good at drawing but showed his drawings to no one. He never spoke about art, was ever ready to sing and swig and carouse, yet suddenly a strange gloom would come over him and he would not leave his room or let anyone in, and only his roommate, lowly Simpson, would see what he was up to. What Frank created during these two or three days of ill-humored isolation he either hid or destroyed, and then, as if having paid an agonizing tribute to his vice, he would again become his merry, uncomplicated self. Only once did he bring this up with Simpson.

"You see," he said, wrinkling his limpid forehead and forcefully knocking the ashes from his pipe, "I feel that there is something about art, and painting in particular, that is effeminate, morbid, unworthy of a strong man. I try to struggle with this demon because I know how it can ruin people. If I yield to it completely, then, instead of a peaceful, ordered existence with finite distress and finite delights, with those precise rules without which any game loses its appeal, I shall be doomed to constant chaos, tumult, God knows what. I'll be tormented to my dying day, I shall become like one of those wretches I've run into in Chelsea, those vain, long-haired fools in velvet jackets—harried, weak, enamored only of their sticky palettes. . . ."

But the demon must have been very potent. At the end of the winter semester, without a word to his father (thereby hurting him deeply), Frank went off in third class to Italy, to return a month later directly to the university, suntanned and joyous, as if he had rid himself once and for all of the murky fever of creation.

Then, with the advent of summer vacation, he invited Simpson for a stay at his father's and Simpson accepted in a burst of gratitude, for he was thinking with horror of the usual return home to his peaceful northern town where some shocking crime occurred every month, and to his parson father, a gentle, harmless, but totally insane man who devoted more attention to his harp and his chamber metaphysics than to his flock.

The contemplation of beauty, whether it be a uniquely tinted sunset, a radiant face, or a work of art, makes us glance back unwittingly at our personal past and juxtapose ourselves and our inner being with the utterly unattainable beauty revealed to us. That is why Simpson, in front of whom the long-dead Venetian girl had just risen in her cambric and velvet, now reminisced, as he ambled along the violet dirt of the lane, soundless at this evening hour; he reminisced about his friendship with Frank, about his father's harp, about his own cramped, cheerless youth. The resonant forest stillness was complemented now and then by the crackle of a branch touched one knew not by whom. A red squirrel scurried down a tree trunk, ran across to a neighboring trunk with its bushy tail erect, and darted up again. In the soft flow of sunlight between two tongues of foliage midges circled like golden dust, and a bumblebee, entangled in the heavy lacework of a fern, already buzzed with a more reserved, evening tone.

Simpson sat down on a bench spattered with the white traces of dried bird droppings, and hunched over, propping his sharp elbows on his knees. He sensed the onset of an auditory hallucination that had afflicted him since childhood. When in a meadow, or, as now, in a quiet, already duskening wood, he would involuntarily begin to wonder if, through this silence, he might perhaps hear the entire, enormous world traversing space with a melodious whistle, the bustle of distant cities, the pounding of sea waves, the singing of telegraph wires above the deserts. Gradually his hearing, guided by his thoughts, began to detect those sounds in earnest. He could hear the chugging of a train, even though the tracks might have been dozens of miles away; then the clanging and screeching of wheels and—as his recondite hearing grew ever more acute—the passengers' voices, their coughs and laughter, the rustling of their newspapers, and, finally, plunging totally into his acoustic mirage, he clearly distinguished their heartbeat, and the rolling crescendo of that beat, that drone, that clangor, deafened Simpson. He opened his eyes with a shudder and realized that the pounding was that of his own heart.

"Lugano, Como, Venice . . . ," he murmured as he sat on the bench under a soundless hazelnut tree, and right away he heard the subdued plashing of sunny towns, and then, closer, the tinkling of bells, the whistle of pigeon wings, a high-pitched laugh akin to the laugh of Maureen, and the ceaseless shuffling of unseen passersby. He wanted to halt his hearing there, but his hearing, like a torrent, rushed ever deeper. Another instant and, unable now to halt his extraordinary plunge, he was hearing not only their footfalls but their hearts. Millions of hearts were swelling and thundering, and Simpson, coming fully to his senses, realized that *all* those sounds, *all* those hearts were concentrated in the frenzied beat of his own.

He raised his head. A light wind, like the motion of a silk cape, passed along the avenue. The sun's rays were a gentle yellow.

He rose with a feeble smile and, forgetting his racquet on the bench, went toward the house. It was time to dress for dinner.

3
———————

"It's hot with this fur on, though! No, Colonel, it's only cat. It's true my Venetian rival wore something more expensive. But the color is the same, isn't it? A perfect likeness, in short."

"If I dared I'd coat you with varnish, and send Luciani's canvas up to the attic," courteously countered the Colonel, who, in spite of his strict principles, was not averse to challenging a lady as attractive as Maureen to a flirtatious verbal duel.

"I would split with laughter," she parried.

"I fear, Mrs. McGore, that we make a terribly poor background for you," said Frank, with a broad, boyish grin. "We are crude, complacent anachronisms. Now if your husband were to don a coat of armor—"

"Fiddlesticks," said McGore. "The impression of antiquity can be evoked as easily as the impression of color by pressing one's upper eyelid. On occasion I allow myself the luxury of imagining today's world, our machines, our fashions, as they will appear to our descendants four or five hundred years hence. I assure you that I feel as ancient as a Renaissance monk."

"Have some more wine, my dear Simpson," offered the Colonel.

Bashful, quiet Simpson, who was seated between McGore and his wife, had put his large fork to work prematurely, during the second course when he should have used the small one, so that he had only the small fork and a large knife for the meat course, and now, as he manipulated them, one of his hands had a kind of limp. When the main course was brought around the second time, he helped himself out of nervousness, then noticed he was the only one eating and everyone was waiting impatiently for him to finish. He got so flustered that he pushed away his still-full plate, nearly knocked over his glass, and began slowly reddening. He had already come ablaze several times during dinner, not because he actually had something to be ashamed about, but because he thought how he might blush for no reason, and then the pink blood colored his cheeks, his forehead, even his neck, and it was no more possible to halt that blind, agonizing, hot flush than to confine the emerging sun behind its cloud. At the first such onset he deliberately dropped his napkin, but, when he raised his head, he was a fearful sight: at any moment his starched collar would catch fire too. Another time he tried to suppress the onslaught of the hot, silent wave by addressing a question to Maureen—whether or not she liked playing lawn tennis—but Maureen, alas, did not hear him, asked him what he had said, whereupon, as he repeated his foolish phrase, Simpson instantly blushed to the point of tears and Maureen, out of charity, turned away and started on some other topic.

The fact that he was sitting next to her, sensing the warmth of her cheek and of her shoulder, from which, as in the painting, the gray fur was slipping, and that she seemed about to pull it up, but stopped at Simpson's question, extending and twining her slender, elongated fingers, filled him with such languor that there was a moist sparkle in his eyes from the crystal blaze of the wineglasses, and he kept imagining that the circular table was an illuminated island, slowly revolving, floating somewhere, gently carrying off those seated around it. Through the open French windows one could see, in the distance, the skittle shapes of the terrace balustrade, and the breath of the blue night air was stifling. Maureen's nostrils inhaled this air; her soft, totally dark eyes remained unsmiling as they glided from face to face, even when a smile would faintly raise a corner of her tender, unpainted lips. Her face remained within a somewhat swarthy shadow, and only her forehead was bathed by the levigate light. She said fatuous, funny things. Everyone laughed, and the wine gave the Colonel a nice flush. McGore, who was peeling an apple, encircled it with his palm like a monkey, his small face with its halo of gray hair wrinkled from the effort, and the silver knife tightly clutched in his dark, hairy fist detached endless spirals of red and yellow peel. Frank's face was not visible to Simpson, since between them stood a bouquet of flaming, fleshy dahlias in a sparkling vase.

After supper, which ended with port and coffee, the Colonel, Maureen, and Frank sat down to play bridge, with a dummy since the other two did not play.

The old restorer went out, bandy-legged, onto the darkened balcony and Simpson followed, feeling Maureen's warmth recede behind him.

McGore eased himself with a grunt into a wicker chair near the balustrade and offered Simpson a cigar. Simpson perched sideways on the railing and lit up awkwardly, narrowing his eyes and inflating his cheeks.

"I guess you liked that old rake del Piombo's Venetian lass," said McGore, releasing a rosy puff of smoke into the dark.

"Very much," replied Simpson, and added, "Of course, I don't know anything about pictures—"

"All the same, you liked it," nodded McGore. "Splendid. That's the first step toward understanding. I, for one, have dedicated my whole life to this."

"She looks absolutely real," Simpson said pensively. "It's enough to make one believe mysterious tales about portraits coming to life. I read somewhere that some king descended from a canvas, and, as soon as—"

McGore dissolved in a subdued, brittle laugh. "That's nonsense, of course. But another phenomenon does occur—the inverse, so to speak."

Simpson glanced at him. In the dark of the night his starched shirtfront bulged like a whitish hump, and the flame of his cigar, like a ruby pinecone, illumined his small, wrinkled face from below. He had had a lot of wine and was, apparently, in the mood to talk.

"Here is what happens," McGore continued unhurriedly. "Instead of inviting a painted figure to step out of its frame, imagine someone managing to step into the picture himself. Makes you laugh, doesn't it? And yet I've done it many a time. I have had the good fortune of visiting all the art museums of Europe, from The Hague to Petersburg and from London to Madrid. When I found a painting I particularly liked, I would stand directly in front of it and concentrate all my willpower on one thought: to enter it. It was an eerie sensation, of course. I felt like the apostle about to step off his bark onto the water's surface. But what bliss ensued! Let us say I was facing a Flemish canvas, with the Holy Family in the foreground, against a smooth, limpid, landscape. You know, with a road zigzagging like a white snake, and green hills. Then, finally, I would take the plunge. I broke free from real life and entered the painting. A miraculous sensation! The coolness, the placid air permeated with wax and incense. I became a living part of the painting and everything around me came alive. The pilgrims' silhouettes on the road began to move. The Virgin Mary was saying something in a rapid Flemish patter. The wind rippled through the conventional flowers. The clouds were gliding. . . . But the delight did not last long. I would get the feeling that I was softly congealing, cohering with the canvas, merging into a film of oil color. Then I would shut my eyes tight, yank with all my strength, and leap out. There was a gentle plop, as when you pull your foot out of the mud. I would open my eyes, and find myself lying on the floor beneath a splendid but lifeless painting."

Simpson listened with attention and embarrassment. When McGore paused, he gave a barely perceptible start and looked around. Everything was as before. Below, the garden breathed the darkness, one could see the dimly lit dining room through the glass door, and, in the distance, through another open doorway, a bright corner of the parlor with three figures playing cards. What strange things McGore was saying! . . .

"You understand, don't you," he continued, shaking off some scaly ash, "that in another instant the painting would have sucked me in forever. I would have vanished into its depths and lived on in its landscape, or else, grown weak with terror, and lacking the strength either to return to the real world or to penetrate the new dimension, I would have jelled into a figure painted on the canvas, like the anachronism Frank was talking about. Yet, despite the danger, I have yielded to temptation time after time. . . . Oh, my friend, I've fallen in love with Madonnas! I remember my first infatuation—a Madonna with an azure corona, by the delicate Raffaello. . . . Beyond her, at a distance, two men stood by a column, calmly chatting. I eavesdropped on their conversation—they were discussing the worth of some dagger. . . . But the most enchanting Madonna of all comes from the brush of Bernardo Luini. All his creations contain the quiet and the delicacy of the lake on whose shore he was born, Lago Maggiore. The most delicate of masters. His name even yielded a new adjective, *luinesco*. His best Madonna has long, caressingly lowered eyes, and her apparel has light-blue, rose-red, misty-orange tints. A gaseous, rippling haze encircles her brow, and that of her reddish-haired infant. He raises a pale apple toward her, she looks at it lowering her gentle, elongated eyes . . . Luinesque eyes . . . God, how I kissed them. . . ."

McGore fell silent and a dreamy smile tinged his thin lips, lighted by the cigar's flame. Simpson held his breath and, as before, felt he was slowly gliding off into the night.

"Complications did occur," McGore went on after clearing his throat. "I got an ache in my kidneys after a goblet of strong cider that a plump Rubens bacchante once served me, and I caught such a chill on the foggy, yellow skating rink of one of the Dutchmen that I went on coughing and bringing up phlegm for a whole month. That's the kind of thing that can happen, Mr. Simpson."

McGore's chair creaked as he rose and straightened his waistcoat. "Got carried away," he remarked dryly. "Time for bed. God knows how long they'll go on slapping their cards about. I'm off—good night."

He crossed the dining room and the parlor, nodding to the players as he went, and disappeared in the shadows beyond. Simpson was left alone on his balustrade. His ears rang with McGore's high-pitched voice. The magnificent starry night reached to the very balcony, and the enormous velvety shapes of the black trees were motionless. Through the French window, beyond a band of darkness, he could see the pink-hued parlor lamp, the table, the players' faces rouged by the light. He saw the Colonel rise. Frank followed suit. From afar, as if over the telephone, came the Colonel's voice. "I'm an old man, I turn in early. Good night, Mrs. McGore."

And Maureen's laughing voice: "I'll go in a minute too. Or else my husband will be cross with me. . . ."

Simpson heard the door close in the distance behind the Colonel. Then an extraordinary thing happened. From his vantage point in the darkness he saw Maureen and Frank, now alone far off in that lacuna of mellow light, slip into each other's arms, he saw Maureen fling back her head and bend it back farther and farther beneath Frank's violent and prolonged kiss. Then, catching up her fallen fur and giving Frank's hair a ruffle, she disappeared into the distance with a muffled slam of the door. Frank smoothed his hair with a smile, thrust his hands in his pockets, and, whistling softly, crossed the dining room on his way to the balcony. Simpson was so flabbergasted that he froze still, his fingers clutching the railing, and gazed with horror as the starched shirtfront and the dark shoulder approached through the glistening glass. When he came out onto the balcony and saw his friend's silhouette in the dark, Frank gave a slight shudder and bit his lip.

Simpson awkwardly crawled off the railing. His legs were trembling. He made a heroic effort: "Marvelous night. McGore and I have been chatting out here."

Frank said calmly, "He lies a lot, that McGore. On the other hand, when he gets going he's worth a listen."

"Yes, it's very curious. . . ." lamely concurred Simpson.

"The Big Dipper," said Frank and yawned with his mouth closed. Then, in an even voice, he added, "Of course I know that you are a perfect gentleman, Simpson."

4

Next morning a warm drizzle came pattering, shimmering, stretching in thin threads across the dark background of the forest's depths. Only three people came down for breakfast—first the Colonel and listless, wan Simpson; then Frank, fresh, bathed, shaved to a high gloss, with an innocent smile on his overly thin lips.

The Colonel was markedly out of spirits. The night before, during the bridge game, he had noticed something. Bending down hastily to retrieve a dropped card, he had seen Frank's knee pressed against Maureen's. This must be stopped immediately. For some time already the Colonel had had an inkling that something was not right. No wonder Frank had rushed off to Rome, where the McGores always went in the spring. His son was free to do as he liked, but to stand for something like this here, at home, in the ancestral castle—no, the most stringent measures must be taken immediately.

The Colonel's displeasure had a disastrous effect on Simpson. He had the impression that his presence was a burden to his host, and was at a loss for a subject of conversation. Only Frank was placidly jovial as always, and, his teeth asparkle, munched with gusto on hot toast spread with orange marmalade.

When they had finished their coffee, the Colonel lit his pipe and rose.

"Didn't you want to take a look at the new car, Frank? Let's walk over to the garage. Nothing to do in this rain anyway."

Then, sensing that poor Simpson had remained mentally suspended in midair, the Colonel added, "I've got a few good books here, my dear Simpson. Help yourself if you wish."

Simpson came to with a start and pulled some bulky red volume down from the shelf. It turned out to be the *Veterinary Herald* for 1895.

"I need to have a little talk with you," began the Colonel when he and Frank had tugged on their crackling raincoats and walked out into a mist of rain.

Frank gave his father a rapid glance.

"How shall I put it," he pondered, puffing on his pipe. "Listen, Frank," he said, taking the plunge—and the wet gravel crunched more succulently under his soles—"it has come to my attention, it doesn't matter how, or, to put it more simply, I have noticed . . . Dammit,

Frank, what I mean is, what kind of relations do you have with McGore's wife?"

Frank replied quietly and coolly, "I'd rather not discuss that with you, Father," meanwhile thinking angrily to himself: what a scoundrel—he did rat on me!

"Obviously I cannot demand—" began the Colonel, and stopped short. At tennis, after the first bad shot, he still managed to control himself.

"Might be a good idea to fix this footbridge," remarked Frank, hitting a rotten timber with his heel.

"To hell with the bridge!" said the Colonel. This was his second miss, and the veins swelled on his forehead in an irate vee.

The chauffeur, who had been banging around with some buckets by the garage gates, yanked off his checkered cap upon seeing his master. He was a short, stocky man with a cropped yellow mustache.

"Morning, sir," he said amiably and pushed open one of the gates with his shoulder. In the petrol-and-leather-scented penumbra glimmered an enormous, black, brand-new Rolls-Royce.

"And now let us take a walk in the park," said the Colonel in a toneless voice when Frank had had his fill of examining cylinders and levers.

The first thing that happened in the park was that a large, cold drop of water fell from a branch, inside the Colonel's collar. And actually it was this drop that made the cup overflow. After a masticating movement of his lips, as though rehearsing the words, he abruptly thundered: "I warn you, Frank, in my house I shall not stand for any adventures of the French-novel genre. Furthermore, McGore is my friend—can you understand that or not?"

Frank picked up the racquet Simpson had forgotten on the bench the previous day. The damp had turned it into a figure eight. Rotten racquet, Frank thought with revulsion. His father's words were pounding ponderously past: "I shall not stand for it," he was saying. "If you cannot behave properly, then leave. I am displeased with you, Frank, I am terribly displeased with you. There is something about you that I don't understand. At university you do poorly at your studies. In Italy God knows what you were up to. They tell me you paint. I suppose I'm not worthy of being shown your daubings. Yes, daubings. I can imagine. . . . A genius indeed! For you doubtless consider yourself a genius, or, even better, a futurist. And now we have these love affairs to boot. . . . In short, unless—"

Here the Colonel noticed that Frank was whistling softly and nonchalantly through his teeth. The Colonel stopped and goggled his eyes.

Frank flung the twisted racquet into the bushes like a boomerang, smiled, and said, "This is all poppycock, Father. I read in a book on the Afghanistan war about what you did there and what you were decorated for. It was absolutely foolish, featherbrained, suicidal, but it was an exploit. That is what counts. While your disquisitions are poppycock. Good day."

And the Colonel remained standing alone in the middle of the lane, frozen in wonderment and wrath.

5
———

The distinctive feature of everything extant is its monotony. We partake of food at predetermined hours because the planets, like trains that are never late, depart and arrive at predetermined times. The average person cannot imagine life without such a strictly established timetable. But a playful and sacrilegious mind will find much to amuse it imagining how people would exist if the day lasted ten hours today, eighty-five tomorrow, and after tomorrow a few minutes. One can say a priori that, in England, such uncertainty with regard to the exact duration of the coming day would lead first of all to an extraordinary proliferation of betting and sundry other gambling arrangements. One could lose his entire fortune because a day lasted a few more hours than he had supposed on the eve. The planets would become like racehorses, and what excitement would be aroused by some sorrel Mars as it tackled the final celestial hurdle! Astronomers would assume bookmakers' functions, the god Apollo would be depicted in a flaming jockey cap, and the world would merrily go mad.

Unfortunately, however, that is not the way things are. Exactitude is always grim, and our calendars, where the world's existence is calculated in advance, are like the schedule of some inexorable examination. Of course there is something soothing and insouciant about this regimen devised by a cosmic Frederick Taylor. Yet how splendidly, how radiantly the world's monotony is interrupted now and then by the book of a genius, a comet, a crime, or even simply by a single sleepless night. Our laws, though—our pulse, our digestion are firmly linked to the harmonious motion of the stars, and any attempt to disturb this regularity is punished, at worst by beheading, at best by a headache. Then again, the world was unquestionably created with good intentions and it is no one's fault if it sometimes grows boring, if the music of the spheres reminds some of us of the endless repetitions of a hurdy-gurdy.

Simpson was particularly conscious of this monotony. He found it somehow terrifying that today, too, breakfast would be followed by lunch, tea by supper, with inviolable regularity. He wanted to scream at the thought that things would continue like that all his life, he wanted to struggle like someone who has awakened in his coffin. The drizzle was still shimmering outside the window, and having to stay indoors made his ears ring as they do when you have a fever. McGore spent the whole day in the workshop that had been set up for him in one of the castle's towers. He was busy restoring the varnish of a small, dark picture painted on wood. The workshop smelled of glue, turpentine, and garlic, which is used for removing greasy spots from paintings. On a small carpenter's bench near the press sparkled retorts containing hydrochloric acid and alcohol; scattered about lay scraps of flannel, nostriled sponges, assorted scrapers. McGore was wearing an old dressing gown, glasses, a shirt with no starched collar, and a stud nearly the size of a doorbell button protruding right under his Adam's apple; his neck was thin, gray, and covered with senile excrescences, and a black skullcap covered his bald spot. With a delicate rotary rubbing of his fingers already familiar to the reader, he was sprinkling a pinch of ground tar, carefully rubbing it into the painting so that the old, yellowed varnish, abraded by the powdery particles, itself turned into dry dust.

The castle's other denizens sat in the parlor. The Colonel had angrily unfolded a giant newspaper and, as he gradually cooled down, was reading aloud an emphatically conservative article. Then Maureen and Frank got involved in a game of Ping-Pong. The little celluloid ball, with its crackly, melancholy ring, flew back and forth across the green net intersecting the long table, and of course Frank played masterfully, moving only his wrist as he nimbly flicked the thin wooden paddle left and right.

Simpson traversed all the rooms, biting his lips and adjusting his pince-nez. Eventually he reached the gallery. Pale as death, carefully closing behind him the heavy, silent door, he tiptoed up to Fra Bastiano del Piombo's *Veneziana*. She greeted him with her familiar opaque gaze, and her long fingers paused on their way to her fur wrap, to the slipping crimson folds. Caressed by a whiff of honeyed darkness, he glanced into the depths of the window that interrupted the black background. Sand-tinted clouds stretched across the greenish blue; toward them rose dark, fractured cliffs amid which wound a pale-hued trail, while lower down there were indistinct wooden huts, and, in one of them, Simpson thought he saw a point of light flicker for an instant. As he peered through this ethereal window, he sensed that the Venetian lady was smiling, but his swift glance failed to catch that smile; only the shaded right corner of her gently joined lips was slightly raised. At that moment something within him deliciously gave way, and he yielded totally to the picture's warm enchantment. One must bear in mind that he was a man of morbidly rapturous temperament, that he had no idea of life's realities, and that, for him, impressionability took the place of intellect. A cold tremor, like a quick dry hand, brushed his back, and he realized immediately what he must do. However, when he looked around and saw the sheen of parquet, the table, and the blind white gloss of the paintings where the drizzly light pouring through the window fell on them, he had a feeling of shame and fear. And, in spite of another momentary surge of the previous enchantment, he already knew that he could hardly carry out what, a minute ago, he could have done unthinkingly.

Fixing his eyes on the Veneziana's face, he backed away from her and suddenly flung his arms apart. His coccyx banged painfully on something. He looked around and saw the black table behind him. Trying to think about nothing, he climbed onto it, stood up fully erect facing the Venetian lady, and once again, with an upward sweep of his arms, prepared to fly to her.

"Astonishing way to admire a painting. Invented it yourself, did you?"

It was Frank. He was standing, legs apart, in the doorway and gazing at Simpson with icy derision.

With a wild glint of pince-nez lenses in his direction, Simpson staggered awkwardly, like an alarmed lunatic. Then he hunched over, flushed hotly, and clambered clumsily to the floor.

Frank's face wrinkled with acute revulsion as he silently left the room. Simpson lunged after him.

"Please, I beg you, don't tell anyone. . . ." Without turning or stopping, Frank gave a squeamish shrug.

6
————

Toward evening the rain unexpectedly ceased. Someone, remembering, had turned off the taps. A humid orange sunset came aquiver amid the boughs, broadened, was reflected in all the puddles simultaneously. Dour little McGore was dislodged from his tower by force.

He smelled of turpentine, and had burned his hand with a hot iron. He reluctantly pulled on his black coat, turned up the collar, and went out with the others for a stroll. Only Simpson stayed home, on the pretext that he absolutely must answer a letter brought by the evening post. Actually no answer was required, since it was from the university milkman and demanded immediate payment of a bill for two shillings and ninepence.

For a long time Simpson sat in the advancing twilight, leaning back aimlessly in the leather armchair. Then, with a shudder, he realized he was falling asleep, and started thinking how he could get away from the castle as quickly as possible. The simplest way would be to say his father was ill: like many bashful people, Simpson was capable of lying without batting an eyelash. Yet it was difficult for him to leave. Something dark and delicious held him back. How attractive the dark rocks looked in the fenestral chasm. . . . What a joy it would be to embrace her shoulder, take from her left hand the basket with its yellow fruit, to walk off peacefully with her along that pale path into the penumbra of the Venetian evening. . . .

Once again he caught himself falling asleep. He got up and washed his hands. From downstairs sounded the spherical, dignified dinner gong.

Thus from constellation to constellation, from meal to meal, proceeds the world, and so does this tale. But its monotony will now be broken by an incredible miracle, an unheard-of adventure. Of course neither McGore, who had again painstakingly freed of glossy red ribbons the faceted nudity of an apple, nor the Colonel, once more agreeably flushed after four glasses of port (not to mention two of white Burgundy) had any way of knowing what woes the morrow would bring. Dinner was followed by the invariable game of bridge, during which the Colonel noticed with pleasure that Frank and Maureen did not even glance at each other. McGore went off to work; Simpson seated himself in a corner and opened a portfolio of prints, glancing only a couple of times from his corner at the players, having marveled in passing that Frank was so cold toward him, while Maureen seemed to have faded somehow, to have yielded her place to another. . . . How insignificant these thoughts were compared to the sublime anticipation, the enormous excitement that he now tried to outwit by examining indistinct lithographs.

When they were parting company, and Maureen nodded to him with a good-night smile, he absently, unabashedly, smiled back.

7

_____

That night, sometime after one o'clock, the old watchman, who had once worked as groom for the Colonel's father, was, as usual, taking a short walk along the park lanes. He knew perfectly well that his duty was purely perfunctory, since the location was exceptionally peaceful. He invariably turned in at eight, the alarm would go off with a clatter at one, and the watchman (a giant of an old fellow with venerable gray side-whiskers, which, incidentally, the gardener's children liked to tug) would awaken, light up his pipe, and clamber out into the night. Having once made the rounds of the dark, tranquil park, he would return to his small room, immediately undress, and, clad only in an imperishable undershirt that went very well with his whiskers, go back to bed and sleep through till morning.

That night, however, the old watchman noticed something that was not to his liking. He noticed from the park that one window of the castle was feebly illuminated. He knew with absolute precision that it was a window of the hall where the precious paintings were hung. Since he was an exceptionally cowardly old chap, he decided to pretend to himself that he had not noticed that strange light. But his conscientiousness got the upper hand, and he calmly determined that, while it was his duty to ascertain that there were no thieves in the park, he had no obligation to chase thieves within the house. And having thus determined, the old man went back to his quarters with a clear conscience—he lived in a little brick house by the garage—and straightaway fell into a dead man's sleep, which would have been impervious even to the roar of the new black car, had someone started it up in jest, deliberately opening the muffler cutout.

Thus the pleasant, innocuous old fellow, like some guardian angel, momentarily traverses this narrative and rapidly vanishes into the misty domains whence he was evoked by a whim of the pen.

8

_____

But something really did happen in the castle.

Simpson awoke exactly at midnight. He had just fallen asleep and, as sometimes happens, the very act of falling asleep was what woke him. Propping himself on one arm, he looked into the darkness. His heart was thumping rapidly because he sensed that Maureen had entered his room. Just now, in his momentary dream, he had been talking to her, helping her climb the waxen path between black cliffs with their occasional glossy, oil-paint fissures. Now and then a dulcet breeze made the narrow white headdress quiver gently, like a sheet of thin paper, on her dark hair.

With a stifled exclamation Simpson felt for the switch. The light came in a spurt. There was no one in the room. He felt an acute sting of disappointment and lapsed into thought, shaking his head like a drunk. Then, moving drowsily, he rose from the bed and started to dress, listlessly smacking his lips. He was guided by a vague sensation that he must dress severely and smartly. So it was with a kind of somnolent meticulousness that he buttoned his low waistcoat on his belly, tied the black bow of his tie, and for a long time pinched with two fingers at a nonexistent little worm on the satin lapel of his jacket. Vaguely recollecting that the simplest way into the gallery was from outdoors, he slipped out like a silent breeze through the French window into the dark, humid garden. Looking as if they had been doused with mercury, black bushes glistened in the starlight. Somewhere an owl was hooting. With a light, quick step Simpson walked across the lawn, amid gray bushes, rounding the massive house. For a moment he was sobered by the night's freshness and the intensely shining stars. He stopped, bent over, and then collapsed like an empty suit of clothes onto the grass in the narrow interstice between flower bed and castle wall. A wave of drowsiness came over him, and he tried to shake it off with a jerk of his shoulder. He had to hurry. She was waiting. He thought he heard her insistent whisper. . . .

He was unaware of how he had got up, gone indoors, and switched on the lights, bathing Luciani's canvas in a warm sheen. The Venetian girl stood half-facing him, alive and three-dimensional. Her dark eyes gazed into his without the sparkle, the rosy fabric of her blouse set off with an unhabitual warmth the dark-hued beauty of her neck and the delicate creases under her ear. A gently mocking smile was frozen at the right corner of her expectantly joined lips. Her long fingers, spread in twos, stretched toward her shoulder, from which the fur and velvet were about to fall.

And Simpson, with a profound sigh, moved toward her and effortlessly entered the painting. A marvelous freshness immediately made his head spin. There was a scent of myrtle and of wax, with a very faint whiff of lemon. He was standing in a bare black room of some kind, by a window that opened on evening, and at his very side stood a real, Venetian, Maureen—tall, gorgeous, all aglow from within. He realized that the miracle had happened, and slowly moved toward her. With a sidewise smile la Veneziana gently adjusted her fur and, lowering her hand into her basket, handed him a small lemon. Without taking his eyes off her now playfully mobile eyes, he accepted the yellow fruit from her hand, and, as soon as he felt its firm, roughish coolness and the dry warmth of her long fingers, an incredible bliss came to a boil within him and began deliciously burbling. Then, with a start, he looked behind him toward the window. There, along a pale path amid some rocks, walked blue silhouettes with hoods and small lanterns. Simpson looked about the room in which he was standing, but without any awareness of a floor beneath his feet. In the distance, instead of a fourth wall, a far, familiar hall glimmered like water, with the black island of a table at its center. It was then that a sudden terror made him compress the cold little lemon. The enchantment had dissolved. He tried looking to his left at the girl but was unable to turn his neck. He was mired like a fly in honey—he gave a jerk and got stuck, feeling his blood and flesh and clothing turning into paint, growing into the varnish, drying on the canvas. He had become part of the painting, depicted in a ridiculous pose next to the Veneziana, and, directly in front of him, even more distinct than before, stretched the hall, filled with live, terrestrial air that, henceforth, he would not breathe.

9

Next morning McGore woke up earlier than usual. With his bare, hairy feet, with toenails like black pearls, he groped for his slippers, and softly padded along the corridor to the door of his wife's room. They had had no conjugal relations for more than a year, but he nevertheless visited her every morning and watched with powerless excitement while she did her hair, jerking her head energetically as the comb chirruped through the chestnut wing of the taut tresses. Today, entering her room at this early hour, he found the bed made and a sheet of paper pinned to the headboard. McGore produced from the pocket of his dressing gown an enormous eyeglass case and, without putting on the glasses but simply holding them up to his eyes, leaned over the pillow and read the minute, familiar writing on the pinned note. When he had finished he meticulously replaced his glasses in their case, unpinned and folded the sheet, stood lost in thought for an instant, and then shuffled resolutely out of the room. In the corridor he collided with the manservant, who glanced at him with alarm.

"What, is the Colonel up already?" asked McGore.

The manservant answered hurriedly, "Yes, sir. The Colonel is in the picture gallery. I'm afraid, sir, that he's very cross. I was sent to wake up the young gentleman."

Without waiting to hear him out, wrapping his mouse-colored robe around him as he went, McGore set off quickly for the gallery. Also in his dressing gown, from beneath which protruded the folds of his striped pajama bottoms, the Colonel was pacing to and fro along the wall. His mustache bristled and his crimson-flushed countenance was terrifying to behold. Seeing McGore, he stopped, and, after some preliminary lip-chewing, roared, "Here, have a good look!"

McGore, to whom the Colonel's ire mattered little, nevertheless inadvertently looked where his hand was pointing and saw something truly incredible. On the Luciani canvas, next to the Venetian girl, an additional figure had appeared. It was an excellent, if hastily executed, portrait of Simpson. Gaunt, his black jacket strongly highlighted by the lighter background, his feet turned oddly outward, he extended his hands as if in supplication, and his pallid face was distorted by a pitiful, frantic expression.

"Like it?" the Colonel inquired furiously. "No worse than Bastiano himself, is it? The vile brat! That's his revenge for my kindhearted advice. Just wait . . ."

The waiter came in, distraught.

"Mr. Frank is not in his room, sir. And his things are gone. Mr. Simpson has disappeared too, sir. He must have gone out for a stroll, sir, seeing as how it's such a fine morning."

"To hell with the morning!" thundered the Colonel. "This very instant, I want—"

"May I be so bold as to inform you," meekly added the waiter, "that the chauffeur was just here and said the new motor car had disappeared from the garage."

"Colonel," McGore said softly, "I think I can explain what's happened."

He glanced at the waiter, who tiptoed out.

"Now then," went on McGore in a bored tone, "your supposition that it was indeed your son who painted in that figure is doubtless right. But, in addition, I gather from a note that was left for me that he departed at daybreak with my wife."

The Colonel was a gentleman and an Englishman. He immediately felt that to vent one's anger in front of a man whose wife had just run off was improper. Therefore, he went over to a window, swallowed half his anger and blew the other half outdoors, smoothed his mustache, and, regaining his calm, addressed McGore.

"Allow me, my dear friend," he said courteously, "to assure you of my sincerest, deepest sympathy, rather than dwell on the wrath I feel toward the perpetrator of your calamity. Nevertheless, while I understand the state you are in, I must—I am obliged, my friend—to ask an immediate favor of you. Your art will rescue my honor. Today I am expecting young Lord Northwick from London, the owner, as you know, of another painting by the same del Piombo."

McGore nodded. "I'll bring the necessary implements, Colonel."

He was back in a couple of minutes, still in his dressing gown, carrying a wooden case. He opened it immediately, produced a bottle of ammonia, a roll of cotton wool, rags, scrapers, and went to work. As he scraped and rubbed Simpson's dark figure and white face from the varnish he did not give a thought to what he was doing, and what he *was* thinking about should not arouse the curiosity of a reader respectful of another's grief. In half an hour Simpson's portrait was completely gone, and the slightly damp paints of which he had consisted remained on McGore's rags.

"Remarkable," said the Colonel. "Remarkable. Poor Simpson has disappeared without a trace."

On occasion some chance remark sets off very important thoughts. This is what happened now to McGore who, as he was gathering his instruments, suddenly stopped short with a shocked tremor.

How strange, he thought, how very strange. Is it possible that— He looked at the rags with the paint sticking to them, and abruptly, with an odd frown, wadded them together and tossed them out the window by which he had been working. Then he ran his palm across his forehead with a frightened glance at the Colonel—who, interpreting his agitation differently, was trying not to look at him—and, with uncharacteristic haste, went out of the hall straight into the garden.

There, beneath the window, between the wall and the rhododendrons, the gardener stood scratching the top of his head over a man in black lying facedown on the lawn. McGore quickly approached.

Moving his arm, the man turned over. Then, with a flustered smirk, he got up.

"Simpson, for heaven's sake, what's happened?" asked McGore, peering into his pale countenance.

Simpson gave another laugh.

"I'm awfully sorry. . . . It's so silly. . . . I went out for a stroll last night and fell right asleep, here on the grass. Ow, I'm all aches and pains. . . . I had a monstrous dream. . . . What time is it?"

Left alone, the gardener gave a disapproving shake of his head as he looked at the matted lawn. Then he bent down and picked up a small dark lemon bearing the imprint of five fingers. He stuck the lemon in his pocket and went to fetch the stone roller he had left on the tennis court.

10

Thus the dry, wrinkled fruit the gardener happened to find remains the only riddle of this whole tale. The chauffeur, dispatched to the station, returned with the black car and a note Frank had inserted into the leather pouch above the seat.

The Colonel read it aloud to McGore:

"Dear Father," wrote Frank, *"I have fulfilled two of your wishes. You did not want any romances going on in your house, so I am leaving, and taking with me the woman without whom I cannot live. You also wanted to see a sample of my art. That is why I made you a portrait of my former friend, whom you can tell for me, by the way, that informers only make me laugh. I painted him at night, from memory, so if the resemblance is imperfect it is from lack of time, poor light, and my understandable haste. Your new car runs fine. I am leaving it for you at the station garage."*

"Splendid," hissed the Colonel. "Except I'd be very curious to know what money you're going to live on."

McGore, paling like a fetus in alcohol, cleared his throat and said, "There is no reason to conceal the truth from you, Colonel. Luciani never painted your *Veneziana*. It is nothing more than a magnificent imitation."

The Colonel slowly rose.

"It was done by your son," went on McGore, and suddenly the corners of his mouth began to tremble and drop. "In Rome. I procured the canvas and paints for him. He seduced me with his talent. Half the sum you paid went to him. Oh, dear God . . ."

The Colonel's jaw muscles contracted as he looked at the dirty handkerchief with which McGore was wiping his eyes and realized the poor fellow was not joking.

Then he turned and looked at *la Veneziana*. Her forehead glowed against the dark background, her long fingers glowed more gently, the lynx fur was slipping bewitchingly from her shoulder, and there was a secretly mocking smile at the corner of her lips.

"I'm proud of my son," calmly said the Colonel.

BACHMANN

T HERE was a fleeting mention in the newspapers not long ago
that the once famous pianist and composer Bachmann had
died, forgotten by the world, in the Swiss hamlet of Marival,
at the St. Angelica Home. This brought to my mind the story about a
woman who loved him. It was told me by the impresario Sack. Here
it is.

Mme. Perov met Bachmann some ten years before his death. In
those days the golden throb of the deep and demented music he
played was already being preserved on wax, as well as being heard live
in the world's most famous concert halls. Well, one evening—one of
those limpid-blue autumn evenings when one feels more afraid of old
age than of death—Mme. Perov received a note from a friend. It read,
*"I want to show you Bachmann. He will be at my house after the concert
tonight. Do come."*

I imagine with particular clarity how she put on a black, décolleté
dress, flicked perfume onto her neck and shoulders, took her fan and
her turquoise knobbed cane, cast a parting glance at herself in the tri-
fold depths of a tall mirror, and sunk into a reverie that lasted all the
way to her friend's house. She knew that she was plain and too thin,
and that her skin was pale to the point of sickliness; yet this faded
woman, with the face of a madonna that had not quite come out, was
attractive thanks to the very things she was ashamed of: the pallor of
her complexion, and a barely perceptible limp, which obliged her to
carry a cane. Her husband, an energetic and astute businessman, was
away on a trip. Sack did not know him personally.

When Mme. Perov entered the smallish, violet-lighted drawing
room where her friend, a stout, noisy lady with an amethyst diadem,
was fluttering heavily from guest to guest, her attention was immediately attracted by a tall man with a clean-shaven, lightly powdered face

who stood leaning his elbow on the case of the piano, and entertaining with some story three ladies grouped around him. The tails of his dress coat had a substantial-looking, particularly thick silk lining, and, as he talked, he kept tossing back his dark, glossy hair, at the same time inflating the wings of his nose, which was very white and had a rather elegant hump. There was something about his entire figure benevolent, brilliant, and disagreeable.

"The acoustics were terrible!" he was saying, with a twitch of his shoulder, "and everybody in the audience had a cold. You know how it is: let one person clear his throat, and right away several others join in, and off we go." He smiled, throwing back his hair. "Like dogs at night exchanging barks in a village!"

Mme. Perov approached, leaning slightly on her cane, and said the first thing that came into her head:

"You must be tired after your concert, Mr. Bachmann?"

He bowed, very flattered.

"That's a little mistake, madame. The name is Sack. I am only the impresario of our Maestro."

All three ladies laughed. Mme. Perov lost countenance, but laughed too. She knew about Bachmann's amazing playing only from hearsay, and had never seen a picture of him. At that moment the hostess surged toward her, embraced her, and with a mere motion of the eyes as if imparting a secret, indicated the far end of the room, whispering, "There he is—look."

Only then did she see Bachmann. He was standing a little away from the other guests. His short legs in baggy black trousers were set wide apart. He stood reading a newspaper. He held the rumpled page close up to his eyes, and moved his lips as semiliterate people do when reading. He was short, balding, with a modest lick of hair athwart the top of his head. He wore a starched turndown collar that seemed too large for him. Without taking his eyes off the paper he absentmindedly checked the fly of his trousers with one finger, and his lips began to move with even greater concentration. He had a very funny small rounded blue chin that resembled a sea urchin.

"Don't be surprised," said Sack, "he is a barbarian in the literal sense of the word—as soon as he arrives at a party he immediately picks up something and starts reading."

Bachmann suddenly sensed that everybody was looking at him. He slowly turned his face and, raising his bushy eyebrows, smiled a wonderful, timid smile that made his entire face break out in soft little wrinkles.

The hostess hurried toward him.

"Maestro," she said, "allow me to present another of your admirers, Mme. Perov."

He thrust out a boneless, dampish hand. "Very glad, very glad indeed."

And once again he immersed himself in his newspaper.

Mme. Perov stepped away. Pinkish spots appeared on her cheekbones. The joyous to-and-fro flicker of her black fan, gleaming with jet, made the fair curls on her temples flutter. Sack told me later that on that first evening she had impressed him as an extraordinarily "temperamental," as he put it, extraordinarily high-strung woman, despite her unpainted lips and severe hairdo.

"Those two were worth each other," he confided to me with a sigh. "As for Bachmann, he was a hopeless case, a man completely devoid of brains. And then, he drank, you know. The evening they met I had to whisk him away as on wings. He had demanded cognac all of a sudden, and he wasn't supposed to, he wasn't supposed to at all. In fact, we had begged him: 'For five days don't drink, for just five days'—he had to play those five concerts, you see. 'It's a contract, Bachmann, don't forget.' Imagine, some poet fellow in a humor magazine actually made a play on 'unsure feet' and 'forfeit'! We were literally on our last legs. And moreover, you know, he was cranky, capricious, grubby. An absolutely abnormal individual. But how he played . . ."

And, giving his thinning mane a shake, Sack rolled his eyes in silence.

As Sack and I looked through the newspaper clippings pasted in an album as heavy as a coffin, I became convinced that it was precisely then, in the days of Bachmann's first encounters with Mme. Perov, that began the real, worldwide—but, oh, how transitory!—fame of that astonishing person. When and where they became lovers, nobody knows. But after the soirée at her friend's house she began to attend all of Bachmann's concerts, no matter in what city they took place. She always sat in the first row, very straight, smooth-haired, in a black, open-necked dress. Somebody nicknamed her the Lame Madonna.

Bachmann would walk onstage rapidly, as if escaping from an enemy or simply from irksome hands. Ignoring the audience, he would hurry up to the piano and, bending over the round stool, would begin tenderly turning the wooden disc of the seat, seeking a certain mathematically precise level. All the while he would coo, softly and earnestly, appealing to the stool in three languages. He would go on fussing thus for quite a while. English audiences were touched, French, diverted, German, annoyed. When he found the right level, Bachmann would give the stool a loving little pat and seat himself, feeling for the pedals with the soles of his ancient pumps. Then he would take out an ample, unclean handkerchief and, while meticulously wiping his hands with it, would examine the first row of seats with a mischievous yet timid twinkle. At last he would bring his hands down softly onto the keys. Suddenly, though, a tortured little muscle would twitch under one eye; clucking his tongue, he would climb off the stool and again begin rotating its tenderly creaking disc.

Sack thinks that when she came home after hearing Bachmann for the first time, Mme. Perov sat down by the window and remained there till dawn, sighing and smiling. He insists that never before had Bachmann played with such beauty, such frenzy, and that subsequently, with every performance, his playing became still more beautiful, still more frenzied. With incomparable artistry, Bachmann would summon and resolve the voices of counterpoint, cause dissonant chords to evoke an impression of marvelous harmonies, and, in his Triple Fugue, pursue the theme, gracefully, passionately toying with it, as a cat with a mouse: he would pretend he had let it escape, then, suddenly, in a flash of sly glee, bending over the keys, he would overtake it with a triumphant swoop. Then, when his engagement in that city was over, he would disappear for several days and go on a binge.

The habitués of the dubious little taverns burning venomously amid the fog of a gloomy suburb would see a small stocky man with untidy hair around a bald spot and moist eyes pink like sores, who would always choose an out-of-the-way corner, but would gladly buy a drink for anybody who happened to importune him. An old little piano tuner, long since fallen into decay, who drank with him on several occasions, decided that he followed the same trade, since Bachmann, when drunk, would drum on the table with his fingers and, in a thin, high voice, sing a very exact A. Sometimes a hardworking prostitute with high cheekbones would lead him off to her place. Sometimes he tore the violin out of the tavern fiddler's hands, stamped on it, and was thrashed in punishment. He mixed with gamblers, sailors, athletes incapacitated by hernias, as well as with a guild of quiet, courteous thieves.

For nights on end Sack and Mme. Perov would look for him. It is true that Sack searched only when it was necessary to get him in shape for a concert. Sometimes they found him, and sometimes, bleary-eyed, dirty, collarless, he would appear at Mme. Perov's of his own accord;

the sweet, silent lady would put him to bed, and only after two or three days would she telephone Sack to tell him that Bachmann had been found.

He combined a kind of unearthly shyness with the prankishness of a spoiled brat. He hardly talked to Mme. Perov at all. When she remonstrated with him and tried to take him by the hands, he would break away and hit her on the fingers with shrill cries, as if the merest touch caused him impatient pain, and presently he would crawl under the blanket and sob for a long time. Sack would come and say it was time to leave for London or Rome, and take Bachmann away.

Their strange liaison lasted three years. When a more or less reanimated Bachmann was served up to the audience, Mme. Perov would invariably be sitting in the first row. On long trips they would take adjoining rooms. Mme. Perov saw her husband several times during this period. He, of course, like everybody else, knew about her rapturous and faithful passion, but he did not interfere and lived his own life.

"Bachmann made her existence a torment," Sack kept repeating. "It is incomprehensible how she could have loved him. The mystery of the female heart! Once, when they were at somebody's house together, I saw the Maestro with my own eyes suddenly begin snapping his teeth at her, like a monkey, and you know why? Because she wanted to straighten his tie. But in those days there was genius in his playing. To that period belongs his Symphony in D Minor and several complex fugues. No one saw him writing them. The most interesting is the so-called Golden Fugue. Have you heard it? Its thematic development is totally original. But I was telling you about his whims and his growing lunacy. Well, here's how it was. Three years passed, and then, one night in Munich, where he was performing . . ."

And as Sack neared the end of his story, he narrowed his eyes more sadly and more impressively.

It seems that the night of his arrival in Munich Bachmann escaped from the hotel where he had stopped as usual with Mme. Perov. Three days remained before the concert, and therefore Sack was in a state of hysterical alarm. Bachmann could not be found. It was late autumn, with a lot of rain. Mme. Perov caught cold and took to her bed. Sack, with two detectives, continued to check the bars.

On the day of the concert the police telephoned to say that Bachmann had been located. They had picked him up in the street during the night and he had had an excellent bit of sleep at the station. Without a word Sack drove him from the police station to the theater, consigned him like an object to his assistants, and went to the hotel to get Bachmann's tailcoat. He told Mme. Perov through the door what had happened. Then he returned to the theater.

Bachmann, his black felt hat pushed down onto his brows, was sitting in his dressing room, sadly tapping the table with one finger. People fussed and whispered around him. An hour later the audience began taking their places in the huge hall. The white, brightly lit stage, adorned by sculptured organ pipes on either side, the gleaming black piano, with upraised wing, and the humble mushroom of its stool—all awaited in solemn idleness a man with moist, soft hands who would soon fill with a hurricane of sound the piano, the stage, and the enormous hall, where, like pale worms, women's shoulders and men's bald pates moved and glistened.

And now Bachmann has trotted onstage. Paying no attention to the thunder of welcome that rose like a compact cone and fell apart in scattered, dying claps, he began rotating the disc of the stool, cooing avidly, and, having patted it, sat down at the piano. Wiping his hands, he glanced toward the first row with his timid smile. Abruptly his smile vanished and Bachmann grimaced. The handkerchief fell to the floor. His attentive gaze slid once again across the faces—and stumbled, as it were, upon reaching the empty seat in the center. Bachmann slammed down the lid, got up, walked out to the very edge of the stage, and, rolling his eyes and raising his bent arms like a ballerina, executed two or three ridiculous *pas*. The audience froze. From the back seats came a burst of laughter. Bachmann stopped, said something that nobody could hear, and then, with a sweeping, archlike motion, showed the whole house a fico.

"It happened so suddenly," went Sack's account, "that I could not get there in time to help. I bumped into him when, after the fig—instead of the fugue—he was leaving the stage. I asked him, 'Bachmann, where are you going?' He uttered an obscenity and disappeared into the greenroom."

Then Sack himself walked out on the stage, to a storm of wrath and mirth. He raised his hand, managed to obtain silence, and gave his firm promise that the concert would take place. Upon entering the greenroom he found Bachmann sitting there as though nothing had happened, his lips moving as he read the printed program.

Sack glanced at those present and, raising a brow meaningfully, rushed to the telephone and called Mme. Perov. For a long time he could get no answer; at last something clicked and he heard her feeble voice.

"Come here this instant," jabbered Sack, striking the telephone book with the side of his hand. "Bachmann won't play without you. It's a terrible scandal! The audience is beginning to— What?— What's that?— Yes, yes, I keep telling you he refuses. Hello? Oh, damn!—I've been cut off. . . ."

Mme. Perov was worse. The doctor, who had visited her twice that day, had looked with dismay at the mercury that had climbed so high along the red ladder in its glass tube. As she hung up—the telephone was by the bed—she probably smiled happily. Tremulous and unsteady on her feet, she started to dress. An unbearable pain kept stabbing her in the chest, but happiness called to her through the haze and hum of the fever. I imagine for some reason that when she started pulling on her stockings, the silk kept catching on the toenails of her icy feet. She arranged her hair as best she could, wrapped herself in a brown fur coat, and went out, cane in hand. She told the doorman to call a taxi. The black pavement glistened. The handle of the car door was wet and ice-cold. All the way during the ride that vague, happy smile must have remained on her lips, and the sound of the motor and the hiss of the tires blended with the hot humming in her temples. When she reached the theater, she saw crowds of people opening angry umbrellas as they tumbled out into the street. She was almost knocked off her feet, but managed to squeeze through. In the greenroom Sack was pacing back and forth, clutching now at his left cheek, now at his right.

"I was in an utter rage!" he told me. "While I was struggling with the telephone, the Maestro escaped. He said he was going to the toilet, and slipped away. When Mme. Perov arrived I pounced on her— why hadn't she been sitting in the theater? You understand, I absolutely did not take into account the fact that she was ill. She asked me, 'So he's back at the hotel now? So we passed each other on the way?' And I was in a furious state, shouting, 'The hell with hotels— he's in some bar! Some bar! Some bar!' Then I gave up and rushed off. Had to rescue the ticket seller."

And Mme. Perov, trembling and smiling, went to search for Bachmann. She knew approximately where to look for him, and it was thither, to that dark, dreadful quarter that an astonished driver took her. When she reached the street where, according to Sack, Bachmann had been found the day before, she let the taxi go and, leaning on her cane, began walking along the uneven sidewalk, under the slanting streams of black rain. She entered all the bars one by one. Bursts of raucous music deafened her and men looked her over insolently. She would glance around the smoky, spinning, motley tavern and go back out into the lashing night. Soon it began to seem to her that she was continuously entering one and the same bar, and an agonizing weakness descended upon her shoulders. She walked, limping and emitting barely audible moans, holding tightly the turquoise knob of her cane in her cold hand. A policeman who had been watching her for some time approached with a slow, professional step and asked for her address, then firmly and gently led her over to a horse cab on night duty. In the creaking, evil-smelling murk of the cab she lost consciousness and, when she came to, the door was open and the driver, in a shiny oilskin cape, was giving her little pokes in the shoulder with the butt of his whip. Upon finding herself in the warm corridor of the hotel, she was overcome by a feeling of complete indifference to everything. She pushed open the door of her room and went in. Bachmann was sitting on her bed, barefoot and in a nightshirt, with a plaid blanket humped over his shoulders. He was drumming with two fingers on the marble top of the night table, while using his other hand to make dots on a sheet of music paper with an indelible pencil. So absorbed was he that he did not notice the door open. She uttered a soft, moanlike "ach." Bachmann gave a start. The blanket started to slide off his shoulders.

I think this was the only happy night in Mme. Perov's life. I think that these two, the deranged musician and the dying woman, that night found words the greatest poets never dreamt of. When the indignant Sack arrived at the hotel the next morning, Bachmann sat there with an ecstatic, silent smile, contemplating Mme. Perov, who was lying across the wide bed, unconscious under the plaid blanket. Nobody could know what Bachmann was thinking as he looked at the burning face of his mistress and listened to her spasmodic breathing; probably he interpreted in his own fashion the agitation of her body, the flutter and fire of a fatal illness, not the least idea of which entered his head. Sack called the doctor. At first Bachmann looked at them distrustfully, with a timid smile; then he clutched at the doctor's shoulder, ran back, struck himself on the forehead, and began tossing to and fro and gnashing his teeth. She died the same day, without regaining consciousness. The expression of happiness never left her face. On the night table Sack found a crumpled sheet of music paper, but no one was able to decipher the violet dots of music scattered over it.

"I took him away immediately," Sack went on. "I was afraid of what would happen when the husband arrived, you can understand. Poor Bachmann was as limp as a rag doll and kept plugging his ears with his fingers. He would cry out as though someone were tickling him, 'Stop those sounds! Enough, enough music!' I don't really know what gave him such a shock: between you and me, he never loved that unfortunate woman. In any case, she was his undoing. After the funeral Bachmann disappeared without leaving a trace. You can still find his name in the advertisements of player-piano firms, but, generally speaking, he has been forgotten. It was only six years later that fate brought us together again. For an instant only. I was waiting for a train at a small station in Switzerland. It was a glorious evening, I recall. I was not alone. Yes, a woman—but that's a different libretto. And then, what do you know, I see a small crowd gathered around a short man in a shabby black coat and black hat. He was thrusting a coin into a music box, and sobbing uncontrollably. He would put in a coin, listen to the tinny melody, and sob. Then the roll or something broke down. The coin jammed. He began shaking the box, wept louder, gave up, and went away. I recognized him immediately, but, you understand, I was not alone, I was with a lady, and there were people around, sort of gaping. It would have been awkward to go up to him and say *Wie geht's dir*, Bachmann?"

THE DRAGON

H E L I V E D in reclusion in a deep, murky cave, in the very heart of a rocky mountain, feeding only on bats, rats, and mold. Occasionally, it is true, stalactite hunters or snoopy travelers would come peeking into the cave, and that was a tasty treat. Other pleasant memories included a brigand attempting to flee from justice, and two dogs that were once let loose to ascertain if the passage did not go clear through the mountain. The surrounding country was wild, porous snow lay here and there on the rock, and waterfalls rumbled with an icy roar. He had hatched some thousand years ago, and, perhaps because it had happened rather unexpectedly—the enormous egg was cracked open by a lightning bolt one stormy night—the dragon had turned out cowardly and not overly bright. Besides, he was strongly affected by his mother's death. . . . She had long terrorized the neighboring villages, had spat flames, and the king would get cross, and around her lair incessantly prowled knights, whom she would crunch to pieces like walnuts. But once, when she had swallowed a plump royal chef and dozed off on a sun-warmed rock, the great Ganon himself galloped up in iron armor, on a black steed under silver netting. The poor sleepy thing went rearing up, her green and red humps flashing like bonfires, and the charging knight thrust his swift lance into her smooth white breast. She crashed to the ground, and promptly, out of the pink wound, sidled the corpulent chef with her enormous, steaming heart under his arm.

The young dragon saw all this from a hiding place behind the rock and, forever after, could not think about knights without a shudder. He withdrew into the depths of a cave, whence he never emerged. Thus passed ten centuries, equivalent to twenty dragon years.

Then, suddenly, he fell prey to unbearable melancholy. . . . In fact, the spoiled food from the cave was provoking ferocious gastric alarms, revolting rumblings, and pain. He spent nine years making up his mind, and on the tenth, he did. Slowly and cautiously, gathering in and extending the rings of his tail, he clambered out of his cave.

Immediately he sensed that it was spring. The black rocks, washed by a recent downpour, were ashimmer; the sunlight boiled in the overflowing mountain torrent; the air was redolent of wild game. And the dragon, broadly inflating his flaming nostrils, started his descent into the valley. His satiny belly, white as a water lily, nearly touched the ground, crimson blotches stood out on his bloated green flanks, and the sturdy scales merged, on his back, into a jagged conflagration, a ridge of double ruddy humps, diminishing in size toward the potently, flexibly twitching tail. His head was smooth and greenish, bubbles of fiery mucus hung from his soft, warty underlip, and his giant, scaly paws left deep tracks, star-shaped concavities.

The first thing he saw upon descending into the valley was a railroad train traveling along rocky slopes. The dragon's first reaction was delight, since he mistook the train for a relative he could play with. Moreover, he thought that beneath that shiny, hard-looking shell there must surely be some tender meat. So he set off in pursuit, his feet slapping with a hollow, damp noise, but, just as he was about to gobble up the last car, the train sped into a tunnel. The dragon stopped, thrust his head into the black lair into which his quarry had vanished, but there was no way he could get in there. He dispatched a couple of torrid sneezes into the depths, then retracted his head, sat on his haunches, and began waiting—who knows, it might come running out again. After waiting some time he shook his head and moved on. At that instant a train did come scurrying out of the dark lair, gave a sly flash of window glass, and disappeared behind a curve. The dragon gave a hurt look over his shoulder and, raising his tail like a plume, resumed his journey.

Dusk was falling. Fog floated above the meadows. The gigantic beast, big as a live mountain, was seen by some homeward-bound peasants, who remained petrified with awe. A little auto speeding along the highway had all four of its tires blow out from fright, bounced, and ended up in the ditch. But the dragon walked on, noticing nothing; from afar came the hot scent of concentrated crowds of humans, and that is where he was headed. And, against the blue expanse of the night sky, there loomed before him black factory smokestacks, guardians of a large industrial town.

The main personages of this town were two: the owner of the Miracle Tobacco Company and that of the Big Helmet Tobacco Company. Between them raged age-old, subtle hostilities, about which one could write an entire epic poem. They were rivals in everything—the motley colors of their advertisements, their distribution techniques, pricing, and labor relations—but no one could say which had the upper hand. That memorable night, the owner of the Miracle Company stayed very late at his office. Nearby on his desk lay a stack of new, freshly printed advertisements that workmen from the cooperative were to plaster around the city at daybreak.

Suddenly a bell pierced the silence of the night and, a few moments later, entered a pale, haggard man with a burdocklike wart on his right cheek. The factory owner knew him: he was the proprietor of a model tavern the Miracle Company had set up on the outskirts.

"It's going on two in the morning, my friend. The only justification I can find for your visit is an event of unheard-of importance."

"That's exactly the case," said the tavern keeper in a calm voice, although his wart was twitching. This is what he reported:

He was bundling off five thoroughly soused old laborers. They must have seen something highly curious outdoors, for they all broke out laughing—"Oh-ho-ho," rumbled one of the voices, "I must have had one glass too many, if I see, big as life, the hydra of counterrevo—"

He did not have time to finish, for there was a surge of terrifying, ponderous noise, and someone screamed. The tavern keeper stepped outside to have a look. A monster, glimmering in the murk like a moist mountain, was swallowing something large with its head thrown back, which made its whitish neck swell with alternating hillocks; it swallowed and licked its chops, its whole body rocked, and it gently lay down in the middle of the street.

"I think it must have dozed off," finished the tavern keeper, restraining the twitching wart with his finger.

The factory owner got up. The robust fillings of his teeth flashed with the golden fire of inspiration. The arrival of a live dragon aroused in him no other feelings than the passionate desire that guided him in every instance—the desire to inflict a defeat on the rival firm.

"Eureka," he exclaimed. "Listen, my good man, are there any other witnesses?"

"I don't think so," the other replied. "Everybody was in bed, and I decided not to wake anyone and came straight to you. So as to avoid panic."

The factory owner donned his hat.

"Splendid. Take this—no, not the whole pile, thirty or forty sheets will do—and bring along this can, and the brush too. There, now show me the way."

They went out into the dark night and were soon at the quiet street at the end of which, according to the tavern keeper, reposed a monster. First, by the light of a lone, yellow streetlamp, they saw a policeman standing on his head in the middle of the pavement. It turned out later that, while making his nightly rounds, he had come upon the dragon and had such a fright that he turned upside down and remained petrified in that attitude. The factory owner, a man with the size and strength of a gorilla, turned him right side up and leaned him against the lightpost; then he approached the dragon. The dragon was asleep, and no wonder. The individuals he had devoured, it so happened, were totally impregnated with wine, and had popped succulently between his jaws. The alcohol on an empty stomach had gone straight to his head and he had lowered the pellicles of his eyelids with a blissful smile. He lay on his belly with his front paws folded under, and the glow of the streetlamp highlighted the glistening arcs of the double vertebral protuberances.

"Set up the ladder," said the factory owner. "I'll do the pasting myself."

And, choosing flat spots on the slimy green flanks of the monster, he began unhurriedly brushing paste on the scaly skin and affixing ample advertising posters. When he had used all the sheets, he gave the brave tavern keeper a meaningful handshake and, chomping on his cigar, returned home.

Morning came, a magnificent spring morning softened by a lilac haze. And suddenly the street came alive with a merry, excited din, doors and windows slammed, people poured into the street, mingling with those who were hurrying somewhere, laughing as they went. What they saw was a perfectly lifelike dragon, all covered with colorful advertisements, slapping listlessly along the asphalt. One poster was even stuck to the bald crown of his head. "SMOKE ONLY MIRACLE BRAND," rollicked the blue and crimson letters of the ads. "ONLY FOOLS DON'T SMOKE MY CIGARETTES," "MIRACLE TOBACCO TURNS AIR INTO HONEY," "MIRACLE, MIRACLE, MIRACLE!"

It really is a miracle, laughed the crowd, and how is it done—is it a machine or are there people inside?

The dragon was feeling rotten after his involuntary binge. The cheap wine now made him sick to his stomach, his whole body felt weak, and the thought of breakfast was out of the question. Besides, he was now overcome by an acute sense of shame, the excruciating shyness of a creature that finds itself amid a crowd for the first time. Frankly speaking, he very much wished to return as soon as possible to his cave, but that would have been even more shameful—therefore, he continued his grim progress through the town. Several men with placards on their backs protected him from the curious and from urchins who wanted to slip under his white belly, clamber onto his lofty backbone, or touch his snout. Music played, people gaped from every window, behind the dragon automobiles drove single file, and in one of them slouched the factory owner, the hero of the day.

The dragon walked without looking at anybody, dismayed by the incomprehensible merriment that he aroused.

Meanwhile, in a sunlit office, along a carpet soft as moss, paced to and fro with clenched fists the rival manufacturer, owner of the Big Helmet Company. At an open window, observing the procession, stood his girlfriend, a diminutive tightrope dancer.

"This is an outrage," croaked over and again the manufacturer, a middle-aged, bald man with blue-gray bags of flabby skin under his eyes. "The police ought to put a stop to this scandal. . . . When did he manage to cobble together this stuffed dummy?"

"Ralph," the dancer suddenly cried, clapping her hands. "I know what you should do. We have a number at the circus called The Joust, and—"

In a torrid whisper, goggling her doll-like, mascara-lined eyes, she told him her plan. The manufacturer beamed. An instant later he was already on the phone with the circus manager.

"So," said the manufacturer, hanging up. "The dummy is made of inflated rubber. We'll see what's left of it if we give it a good prick."

Meanwhile the dragon had crossed the bridge, passed the marketplace and the Gothic cathedral, which aroused some pretty repugnant memories, continued along the main boulevard, and was traversing a broad square when, parting the crowd, a knight unexpectedly came charging at him. The knight wore iron armor, visor lowered, a funereal plume on his helmet, and rode a ponderous black horse in silvery netting. Arms bearers—women dressed as pages—walked alongside, carrying picturesque, hastily devised banners heralding "BIG HELMET," "SMOKE ONLY BIG HELMET," "BIG HELMET BEATS THEM ALL." The circus rider impersonating the knight spurred his steed and clenched his lance. But the steed for some reason started backing, spurting foam, then suddenly reared up and sat heavily on its haunches. The knight tumbled to the asphalt, with such a clatter one might think someone had thrown all the dishes out the window. But the dragon did not see this. At the knight's first move he had stopped abruptly, then rapidly turned, knocking down a pair of curious old women standing on a balcony with his tail as he did so, and, squashing the scattering spectators, had taken flight. He was out of the town in a single bound, flew across the fields, scrambled up the rocky slopes, and dove into his bottomless cavern. There he collapsed onto his back, paws folded and showing his satiny, white, shuddering belly to the dark vaults, heaved a deep breath, closed his astonished eyes, and died.

CHRISTMAS

1

AFTER walking back from the village to his manor across the dimming snows, Sleptsov sat down in a corner, on a plush-covered chair which he never remembered using before. It was the kind of thing that happens after some great calamity. Not your brother but a chance acquaintance, a vague country neighbor to whom you never paid much attention, with whom in normal times you exchange scarcely a word, is the one who comforts you wisely and gently, and hands you your dropped hat after the funeral service is over, and you are reeling from grief, your teeth chattering, your eyes blinded by tears. The same can be said of inanimate objects. Any room, even the coziest and the most absurdly small, in the little-used wing of a great country house has an unlived-in corner. And it was such a corner in which Sleptsov sat.

The wing was connected by a wooden gallery, now encumbered with our huge north Russian snowdrifts, to the master house, used only in summer. There was no need to awaken it, to heat it: the master had come from Petersburg for only a couple of days and had settled in the annex, where it was a simple matter to get the stoves of white Dutch tile going.

The master sat in his corner, on that plush chair, as in a doctor's waiting room. The room floated in darkness; the dense blue of early evening filtered through the crystal feathers of frost on the window-pane. Ivan, the quiet, portly valet, who had recently shaved off his mustache and now looked like his late father, the family butler, brought in a kerosene lamp, all trimmed and brimming with light. He set it on a small table, and noiselessly caged it within its pink silk shade. For an instant a tilted mirror reflected his lit ear and cropped gray hair. Then he withdrew and the door gave a subdued creak.

Sleptsov raised his hand from his knee and slowly examined it. A

drop of candle wax had stuck and hardened in the thin fold of skin between two fingers. He spread his fingers and the little white scale
cracked.

2

The following morning, after a night spent in nonsensical, fragmentary
dreams totally unrelated to his grief, as Sleptsov stepped out into the
cold veranda, a floorboard emitted a merry pistol crack underfoot, and
the reflections of the many-colored panes formed paradisal lozenges on
the whitewashed cushionless window seats. The outer door resisted at
first, then opened with a luscious crunch, and the dazzling frost hit his
face. The reddish sand providently sprinkled on the ice coating the
porch steps resembled cinnamon, and thick icicles shot with greenish
blue hung from the eaves. The snowdrifts reached all the way to the
windows of the annex, tightly gripping the snug little wooden structure in their frosty clutches. The creamy white mounds of what were
flower beds in summer swelled slightly above the level snow in front of
the porch, and farther off loomed the radiance of the park, where
every black branchlet was rimmed with silver, and the firs seemed to
draw in their green paws under their bright plump load.

Wearing high felt boots and a short fur-lined coat with a karakul
collar, Sleptsov strode off slowly along a straight path, the only one
cleared of snow, into that blinding distant landscape. He was amazed
to be still alive, and able to perceive the brilliance of the snow and feel
his front teeth ache from the cold. He even noticed that a snow-
covered bush resembled a fountain and that a dog had left a series of
saffron marks on the slope of a snowdrift, which had burned through
its crust. A little farther, the supports of a footbridge stuck out of the
snow, and there Sleptsov stopped. Bitterly, angrily, he pushed the
thick, fluffy covering off the parapet. He vividly recalled how this
bridge looked in summer. There was his son walking along the slippery
planks, flecked with aments, and deftly plucking off with his net a butterfly that had settled on the railing. Now the boy sees his father.
Forever-lost laughter plays on his face, under the turned-down brim of
a straw hat burned dark by the sun; his hand toys with the chainlet of
the leather purse attached to his belt, his dear, smooth, suntanned legs
in their serge shorts and soaked sandals assume their usual cheerful
widespread stance. Just recently, in Petersburg, after having babbled in

his delirium about school, about his bicycle, about some great Oriental moth, he died, and yesterday Sleptsov had taken the coffin—weighed down, it seemed, with an entire lifetime—to the country, into the family vault near the village church.

It was quiet as it can only be on a bright, frosty day. Sleptsov raised his leg high, stepped off the path and, leaving blue pits behind him in the snow, made his way among the trunks of amazingly white trees to the spot where the park dropped off toward the river. Far below, ice blocks sparkled near a hole cut in the smooth expanse of white and, on the opposite bank, very straight columns of pink smoke stood above the snowy roofs of log cabins. Sleptsov took off his karakul cap and leaned against a tree trunk. Somewhere far away peasants were chopping wood—every blow bounced resonantly skyward—and beyond the light silver mist of trees, high above the squat isbas, the sun caught the equanimous radiance of the cross on the church.

3
———

That was where he headed after lunch, in an old sleigh with a high straight back. The cod of the black stallion clacked strongly in the frosty air, the white plumes of low branches glided overhead, and the ruts in front gave off a silvery blue sheen. When he arrived he sat for an hour or so by the grave, resting a heavy, woolen-gloved hand on the iron of the railing that burned his hand through the wool. He came home with a slight sense of disappointment, as if there, in the burial vault, he had been even further removed from his son than here, where the countless summer tracks of his rapid sandals were preserved beneath the snow.

In the evening, overcome by a fit of intense sadness, he had the main house unlocked. When the door swung open with a weighty wail, and a whiff of special, unwintery coolness came from the sonorous iron-barred vestibule, Sleptsov took the lamp with its tin reflector from the watchman's hand and entered the house alone. The parquet floors crackled eerily under his step. Room after room filled with yellow light, and the shrouded furniture seemed unfamiliar; instead of a tinkling chandelier, a soundless bag hung from the ceiling; and Sleptsov's enormous shadow, slowly extending one arm, floated across the wall and over the gray squares of curtained paintings.

He went into the room which had been his son's study in summer, set the lamp on the window ledge, and, breaking his fingernails as he did so, opened the folding shutters, even though all was darkness outside. In the blue glass the yellow flame of the slightly smoky lamp appeared, and his large, bearded face showed momentarily.

He sat down at the bare desk and sternly, from under bent brows, examined the pale wallpaper with its garlands of bluish roses; a narrow officelike cabinet, with sliding drawers from top to bottom; the couch and armchairs under slipcovers; and suddenly, dropping his head onto the desk, he started to shake, passionately, noisily, pressing first his lips, then his wet cheek, to the cold, dusty wood and clutching at its far corners.

In the desk he found a notebook, spreading boards, supplies of black pins, and an English biscuit tin that contained a large exotic cocoon which had cost three rubles. It was papery to the touch and seemed made of a brown folded leaf. His son had remembered it during his sickness, regretting that he had left it behind, but consoling himself with the thought that the chrysalid inside was probably dead. He also found a torn net: a tarlatan bag on a collapsible hoop (and the muslin still smelled of summer and sun-hot grass).

Then, bending lower and lower and sobbing with his whole body, he began pulling out one by one the glass-topped drawers of the cabinet. In the dim lamplight the even files of specimens shone silklike under the glass. Here, in this room, on that very desk, his son had spread the wings of his captures. He would first pin the carefully killed insect in the cork-bottomed groove of the setting board, between the adjustable strips of wood, and fasten down flat with pinned strips of paper the still fresh, soft wings. They had now dried long ago and been transferred to the cabinet—those spectacular Swallowtails, those dazzling Coppers and Blues, and the various Fritillaries, some mounted in a supine position to display the mother-of-pearl undersides. His son used to pronounce their Latin names with a moan of triumph or in an arch aside of disdain. And the moths, the moths, the first Aspen Hawk of five summers ago!

4

The night was smoke-blue and moonlit; thin clouds were scattered about the sky but did not touch the delicate, icy moon. The trees, masses of gray frost, cast dark shadows on the drifts, which scintillated here and there with metallic sparks. In the plush-upholstered, well-heated room of the annex Ivan had placed a two-foot fir tree in a clay pot on the table, and was just attaching a candle to its cruciform tip when Sleptsov returned from the main house, chilled, red-eyed, with gray dust smears on his cheek, carrying a wooden case under his arm. Seeing the Christmas tree on the table, he asked absently: "What's that?"

Relieving him of the case, Ivan answered in a low, mellow voice: "There's a holiday coming up tomorrow."

"No, take it away," said Sleptsov with a frown, while thinking, Can this be Christmas Eve? How could I have forgotten?

Ivan gently insisted: "It's nice and green. Let it stand for a while."

"Please take it away," repeated Sleptsov, and bent over the case he had brought. In it he had gathered his son's belongings—the folding butterfly net, the biscuit tin with the pear-shaped cocoon, the spreading board, the pins in their lacquered box, the blue notebook. Half of the first page had been torn out, and its remaining fragment contained part of a French dictation. There followed daily entries, names of captured butterflies, and other notes:

"Walked across the bog as far as Borovichi, . . ."

"Raining today. Played checkers with Father, then read Goncharov's Frigate, *a deadly bore."*

"Marvelous hot day. Rode my bike in the evening. A midge got in my eye. Deliberately rode by her dacha twice, but didn't see her . . ."

Sleptsov raised his head, swallowed something hot and huge. Of whom was his son writing?

"Rode my bike as usual," he read on, *"Our eyes nearly met. My darling, my love . . ."*

"This is unthinkable," whispered Sleptsov. "I'll never know. . . ."

He bent over again, avidly deciphering the childish handwriting that slanted up then curved down in the margin.

"Saw a fresh specimen of the Camberwell Beauty today. That means autumn is here. Rain in the evening. She has probably left, and we didn't even get acquainted. Farewell, my darling. I feel terribly sad. . . ."

"He never said anything to me. . . ." Sleptsov tried to remember, rubbing his forehead with his palm.

On the last page there was an ink drawing: the hind view of an elephant—two thick pillars, the corners of two ears, and a tiny tail.

Sleptsov got up. He shook his head, restraining yet another onrush of hideous sobs.

"I–can't–bear–it–any–longer," he drawled between groans, repeating even more slowly, "I—can't—bear—it—any—longer. . . ."

"It's Christmas tomorrow," came the abrupt reminder, "and I'm going to die. Of course. It's so simple. This very night . . ."

He pulled out a handkerchief and dried his eyes, his beard, his cheeks. Dark streaks remained on the handkerchief.

". . . death," Sleptsov said softly, as if concluding a long sentence.

The clock ticked. Frost patterns overlapped on the blue glass of the window. The open notebook shone radiantly on the table; next to it the light went through the muslin of the butterfly net, and glistened on a corner of the open tin. Sleptsov pressed his eyes shut, and had a fleeting sensation that earthly life lay before him, totally bared and comprehensible—and ghastly in its sadness, humiliatingly pointless, sterile, devoid of miracles. . . .

At that instant there was a sudden snap—a thin sound like that of an overstretched rubber band breaking. Sleptsov opened his eyes. The cocoon in the biscuit tin had burst at its tip, and a black, wrinkled creature the size of a mouse was crawling up the wall above the table. It stopped, holding on to the surface with six black furry feet, and started palpitating strangely. It had emerged from the chrysalid because a man overcome with grief had transferred a tin box to his warm room, and the warmth had penetrated its taut leaf-and-silk envelope; it had awaited this moment so long, had collected its strength so tensely, and now, having broken out, it was slowly and miraculously expanding. Gradually the wrinkled tissues, the velvety fringes, unfurled; the fan-pleated veins grew firmer as they filled with air. It became a winged thing imperceptibly, as a maturing face imperceptibly becomes beautiful. And its wings—still feeble, still moist—kept growing and unfolding, and now they were developed to the limit set for them by God, and there, on the wall, instead of a little lump of life, instead of a dark mouse, was a great *Attacus* moth like those that fly, birdlike, around lamps in the Indian dusk.

And then those thick black wings, with a glazy eyespot on each and a purplish bloom dusting their hooked foretips, took a full breath under the impulse of tender, ravishing, almost human happiness.

A LETTER THAT NEVER
REACHED RUSSIA

M Y CHARMING, dear, distant one, I presume you cannot
have forgotten anything in the more than eight years of our
separation, if you manage to remember even the gray-
haired, azure-liveried watchman who did not bother us in the least
when we would meet, skipping school, on a frosty Petersburg morning, in the Suvorov Museum, so dusty, so small, so similar to a glori-
fied snuffbox. How ardently we kissed behind a waxen grenadier's
back! And later, when we came out of that antique dust, how dazzled
we were by the silvery blaze of the Tavricheski Park, and how odd it
was to hear the cheery, avid, deep-fetched grunts of soldiers, lunging
on command, slithering across the icy ground, plunging a bayonet into
the straw-bellied German-helmeted dummy in the middle of a Petersburg street.

Yes, I know that I had sworn, in my previous letter to you, not to
mention the past, especially the trifles in our shared past; for we authors in exile are supposed to possess a lofty pudicity of expression, and
yet, here I am, from the very first lines, disdaining that right to sublime imperfection, and defeating with epithets the recollection on
which you touched with such lightness and grace. Not of the past, my
love, do I wish to speak to you.

It is night. At night one perceives with a special intensity the immobility of objects—the lamp, the furniture, the framed photographs on
one's desk. Now and then the water gulps and gurgles in its hidden
pipes as if sobs were rising to the throat of the house. At night I go
out for a stroll. Reflections of streetlamps trickle across the damp Berlin asphalt whose surface resembles a film of black grease with puddles
nestling in its wrinkles. Here and there a garnet-red light glows over a
fire-alarm box. A glass column, full of liquid yellow light, stands at the
streetcar stop, and, for some reason, I get such a blissful, melancholy

sensation when, late at night, its wheels screeching around the bend, a tram hurtles past, empty. Through its windows one can clearly see the rows of brightly lit brown seats between which a lone ticket collector with a black satchel at his side makes his way, reeling a bit and thus looking a little tight—as he moves against the direction of the car's travel.

As I wander along some silent, dark street, I like to hear a man coming home. The man himself is not visible in the darkness, and you never know beforehand which front door will come alive to accept a key with grinding condescension, swing open, pause, retained by the counterweight, slam shut; the key will grind again from the inside, and, in the depths beyond the glass pane of the door, a soft radiance will linger for one marvelous minute.

A car rolls by on pillars of wet light. It is black, with a yellow stripe beneath the windows. It trumpets gruffly into the ear of the night, and its shadow passes under my feet. By now the street is totally deserted—except for an aged Great Dane whose claws rap on the sidewalk as it reluctantly takes for a walk a listless, pretty, hatless girl with an opened umbrella. When she passes under the garnet bulb (on her left, above the fire alarm), a single taut, black segment of her umbrella reddens damply.

And beyond the bend, above the sidewalk—how unexpectedly!—the front of a cinema ripples in diamonds. Inside, on its rectangular, moon-pale screen you can watch more-or-less skillfully trained mimes: the huge face of a girl with gray, shimmering eyes and black lips traversed vertically by glistening cracks, approaches from the screen, keeps growing as it gazes into the dark hall, and a wonderful, long, shining tear runs down one cheek. And occasionally (a heavenly moment!) there appears real life, unaware that it is being filmed: a chance crowd, bright waters, a noiselessly but visibly rustling tree.

Farther on, at the corner of a square, a stout prostitute in black furs slowly walks to and fro, stopping occasionally in front of a harshly lighted shop window where a rouged woman of wax shows off to night wanderers her streamy, emerald gown and the shiny silk of her peach-colored stockings. I like to observe this placid middle-aged whore, as she is approached by an elderly man with a mustache, who came on business that morning from Papenburg (first he passes her and takes two backward glances). She will conduct him unhurriedly to a room in a nearby building, which, in the daytime, is quite undistinguishable from other, equally ordinary buildings. A polite and impassive old porter keeps an all-night vigil in the unlighted front hall. At the top of a steep staircase an equally impassive old woman will unlock with sage unconcern an unoccupied room and receive payment for it.

And do you know with what a marvelous clatter the brightly lit train, all its windows laughing, sweeps across the bridge above the street! Probably it goes no farther than the suburbs, but in that instant the darkness beneath the black span of the bridge is filled with such mighty metallic music that I cannot help imagining the sunny lands toward which I shall depart as soon as I have procured those extra hundred marks for which I long so blandly, so lightheartedly.

I am so lighthearted that sometimes I even enjoy watching people dancing in the local café. Many fellow exiles of mine denounce indignantly (and in this indignation there is a pinch of pleasure) fashionable abominations, including current dances. But fashion is a creature of man's mediocrity, a certain level of life, the vulgarity of equality, and to denounce it means admitting that mediocrity can create something (whether it be a form of government or a new kind of hairdo) worth making a fuss about. And of course these so-called modern dances of ours are actually anything but modern: the craze goes back to the days of the Directoire, for then as now women's dresses were worn next to the skin, and the musicians were Negroes. Fashion breathes through the centuries: the dome-shaped crinoline of the middle 1800s was the full inhalation of fashion's breath, followed by exhalation: narrowing skirts, close dances. Our dances, after all, are very natural and pretty innocent, and sometimes—in London ballrooms—perfectly graceful in their monotony. We all remember what Pushkin wrote about the waltz: "monotonous and mad." It's all the same thing. As for the deterioration of morals . . . Here's what I found in D'Agricourt's memoirs: "I know nothing more depraved than the minuet, which they see fit to dance in our cities."

And so I enjoy watching, in the *cafés dansants* here, how "pair after pair flick by," to quote Pushkin again. Amusingly made-up eyes sparkle with simple human merriment. Black-trousered and light-stockinged legs touch. Feet turn this way and that. And meanwhile, outside the door, waits my faithful, my lonely night with its moist reflections, hooting cars, and gusts of high-blowing wind.

On that kind of night, at the Russian Orthodox cemetery far outside the city, an old lady of seventy committed suicide on the grave of her recently deceased husband. I happened to go there the next morning, and the watchman, a badly crippled veteran of the Denikin campaign, moving on crutches that creaked with every swing of his body, showed me the white cross on which she hanged herself, and the yellow strands still adhering where the rope ("brand-new one," he said gently) had chafed. Most mysterious and enchanting of all, though, were the crescent-shaped prints left by her heels, tiny as a child's, on the damp soil by the plinth. "She trampled the ground a bit, poor thing, but apart from that there's no mess at all," observed the watchman calmly, and, glancing at those yellow strands and at those little depressions, I suddenly realized that one can distinguish a naive smile even in death. Possibly, dear, my main reason for writing this letter is to tell you of that easy, gentle end. Thus the Berlin night resolved itself.

Listen: I am ideally happy. My happiness is a kind of challenge. As I wander along the streets and the squares and the paths by the canal, absently sensing the lips of dampness through my worn soles, I carry proudly my ineffable happiness. The centuries will roll by, and schoolboys will yawn over the history of our upheavals; everything will pass, but my happiness, dear, my happiness will remain, in the moist reflection of a streetlamp, in the cautious bend of stone steps that descend into the canal's black waters, in the smiles of a dancing couple, in everything with which God so generously surrounds human loneliness.

THE FIGHT

IN THE morning, if the sun was inviting, I would leave Berlin to go swimming. At the end of the trolley line, on a green bench, sat the motormen, stocky fellows in enormous blunt-toed boots, resting, savoring their smokes, from time to time rubbing their massive, metal-redolent hands, and watching a man in a wet leather apron water the flowering sweetbriar along the tracks nearby; the water gushed in a flexible silvery fan from the glistening hose, now flying in the sunlight, now smoothly swooping over the palpitating shrubs. Clutching my rolled-up towel under my arm, I passed by them, striding swiftly toward the edge of the forest. There, the thickly growing slender pine trunks, rough and brown below, flesh-colored higher up, were speckled with fragments of shadow, and the sickly grass underneath was strewn with scraps of newspaper and scraps of sunlight that seemed to supplement each other. Suddenly the sky gaily parted the trees, and I descended along the silvery waves of sand toward the lake, where the voices of bathers would burst forth and subside and dark heads could be glimpsed bobbing on the smooth, luminous surface. All over the sloping bank lay supine or prone bodies with every possible shade of suntan; some still had a pinkish rash on their shoulder blades, others glowed like copper or were the color of strong coffee with cream. I would discard my shirt, and right away the sun overwhelmed me with its blind tenderness.

And every morning, punctually at nine o'clock, the same man would appear next to me. He was a bowlegged, elderly German in trousers and jacket of semimilitary cut, with a large bald head that the sun had smoothed to a red sheen. He brought along an umbrella the color of an aged raven and a neatly tied bundle, which immediately separated into a gray blanket, a beach towel, and a batch of newspapers. He carefully spread the blanket on the sand and, stripping to the

141

bathing trunks he had providently worn under his trousers, arranged himself most comfortably on the blanket, adjusted the umbrella over his head so that his face alone would be in the shade, and went to work on his newspapers. I observed him out of the corner of my eye, noting the dark, woolly, combed-looking growth on his strong crooked legs, and his plump belly with the deep navel gazing heavenward like an eye, and I amused myself trying to guess who this pious sun-worshipper might be.

We spent hours lolling on the sand. Summer clouds glided by in a fluctuating caravan—camel-shaped clouds, tent-shaped clouds. The sun tried to slip in between them, but they would sweep over it with their blinding edge; the air grew dim, then the sun ripened again, but it was the opposite bank that would be illumined first—we remained in the even, colorless shade, while over there the warm light had already spread itself. The shadows of the pines revived on the sand; small naked figures flared up, modeled out of sunlight; and, all of a sudden, like an enormous happy oculus, the radiance opened to engulf our side as well. Then I jumped to my feet, and the gray sand softly scalded my soles as I ran toward the water, which I parted noisily with my body. How nice it was to dry off afterwards in the blazing sun and feel its stealthy lips greedily drink the cool pearls remaining on one's body!

My German slaps shut his umbrella and, his crooked calves cautiously quivering, descends in his turn toward the water, where he first wets his head, as elderly bathers do, and then starts swimming with sweeping gestures. A vendor of hard candy passes along the lakeshore, hawking his wares. Two others, in bathing suits, hurry past with a pail of cucumbers, and my neighbors in the sun, somewhat coarse, beautifully built fellows, pick up the terse calls of the vendors in artful imitation. A naked infant, all black because of the wet sand sticking to him, waddles past me, and his soft little beak bounces drolly between his plump, clumsy little legs. Close by sits his mother, an attractive young woman, half undressed; she is combing out her long dark hair, holding the hairpins between her teeth. Farther, at the very edge of the forest, sun-browned youths play a hard game of catch, flinging their soccer ball one-handed in a motion that revives the immortal gesture of the Discobolus; and now a breeze sets the pines aboil with an Attic rustle, and I dream that our entire world, like that large, firm ball, has flown back in a wondrous arc into the grip of a naked pagan god. Meanwhile an airplane, with an aeolian exclamation, soars above the pines, and one of the swarthy athletes interrupts his game to gaze at the sky where two blue wings speed toward the sun with a rapturous Daedalian hum.

I wish to tell all this to my neighbor when, breathing heavily, and baring his uneven teeth, he comes out of the water and lies down again on the sand, and it is only my lack of German words that keeps him from understanding me. He does not understand me but still answers with a smile that involves his entire being, the brilliant bald spot on his head, the black thicket of his mustache, his jolly meaty belly with a woolly path running down its center.

His profession was revealed to me, in time, by sheer accident. Once, at twilight, when the roar of motorcars became muffled and the hillocks of oranges on hawkers' carts acquired a southern brightness in the blue air, I happened to stroll through a distant district and drop into a tavern to quench the evening thirst so familiar to urban vagabonds. My merry German stood behind the glistening bar, letting a thick yellow stream spurt from the spigot, trimming off the foam with a small wooden spatula, and letting it spill lavishly over the rim. A massive, ponderous wagon driver with a monstrous gray mustache leaned on the bar, watching the spigot and listening to the beer, which hissed like horse urine. The host raised his eyes, grinned a friendly grin, poured a beer for me too, and flung my coin into the drawer with a clink. Next to him, a young girl in a checkered dress, fair-haired, with pointed pink elbows, was washing glasses and nimbly drying them with a squeaky cloth. That same night, I learned that she was his daughter, that her name was Emma, and that his last name was Krause. I sat down in a corner and started unhurriedly sipping the light, white-maned beer, with its faintly metallic aftertaste. The tavern was of the usual type—a couple of posters advertising drinks, some deer antlers, and a low, dark ceiling festooned with paper flaglets, remnants of some festival or other. Beyond the bar, bottles glistened on the shelves, and higher up an old-fashioned, hut-shaped cuckoo clock tocked resonantly. A cast-iron stove dragged its annulate pipe along the wall, then folded it into the overhead motley of the flags. The dirty white of the cardboard beer-mug coasters stood out against the bare sturdy tables. At one of the tables, a sleepy man with appetizing folds of fat on his nape, and a glum, white-toothed fellow—a typesetter or an electrician, judging by his appearance—were shooting craps. All was quiet and peaceful. Unhurriedly, the clock kept breaking off dry little sections of time. Emma clinked her glasses and kept glancing at the corner where, in a narrow mirror bisected by the gold lettering of an advertisement, was reflected the sharp profile of the electrician and his hand holding up the conical black cup with the dice.

The next morning, I walked again past the stocky motormen, past the fan of spraying water in which momentarily hovered a glorious rainbow, and found myself again on the sunlit shore, where Krause was already reclining. He thrust his sweaty face out from under his umbrella and began talking—about the water, about the heat. I lay down, squinting to keep out the sun, and when I reopened my eyes everything around me was a light blue. All of a sudden, among the pines of the sun-dappled lakeside road, a small van drove up, followed by a policeman on a bicycle. Inside the van, yelping desperately, a small captured dog thrashed about. Krause raised himself up and yelled at the top of his voice, "Watch out! Dogcatcher!" At once someone took up that shout, and it passed from throat to throat, curving around the circular lake, outdistancing the catcher, and the forewarned owners ran for their dogs, hurriedly muzzled them, and clicked on leashes. Krause listened with pleasure as the resounding repetitions receded, and said with a good-natured wink, "There. That's the last one he'll get."

I began to visit his tavern fairly often. I very much liked Emma—her naked elbows, the small birdlike face, the vapid, tender eyes. But what I liked most was the way she looked at her lover, the electrician, as he lazily leaned on the bar. I had a side view of him—the baleful, malevolent wrinkle beside his mouth, his glowing, wolflike eye, the blue bristles on his sunken, long-unshaven cheek. She looked at him with such apprehension and such love when he spoke to her while transfixing her with his unflinching gaze, and she nodded so trustingly, with her pale lips half open, that I, in my corner, had a blissful sensation of joy and well-being, as if God had confirmed to me the immortality of the soul or a genius had praised my books. I also committed to memory the electrician's hand, wet with beer foam; the thumb of that hand gripping the mug; the huge black nail with a crack in the middle.

The last time I was there, the evening, as I remember it, was muggy and pregnant with the promise of an electrical storm. Then the wind began gusting violently and people in the square ran for the subway stairs; in the ashen dark outside, the wind tore at their clothes as in the painting *The Destruction of Pompeii*. The host felt hot in the dim little tavern; he had unbuttoned his collar and was gloomily eating his supper in the company of two shopkeepers. It was getting late and the rain was rustling against the windowpanes when the electrician arrived. He was soaking wet and chilled, and muttered something in annoyance when he saw that Emma was not at the bar. Krause kept silent, munching on a boulder-gray sausage.

I sensed that something extraordinary was about to happen. I had had a lot to drink, and my soul—my avid, sharp-eyed inner self—craved a spectacle. It all began very simply. The electrician walked to the bar, casually poured himself a glass of brandy from a flat bottle, swallowed, wiped his mouth with his wrist, gave his cap a slap, and headed for the door. Krause lowered his knife and fork crosswise onto his plate and loudly said, "Wait! That'll be twenty pfennigs!"

The electrician, with his hand already on the doorknob, looked back. "I thought I was at home here."

"You don't intend to pay?" asked Krause.

Emma suddenly appeared from beneath the clock at the back of the bar, looked at her father, then at her lover, and froze. Above her, the cuckoo hopped out of its hut and hid again.

"Leave me alone," the electrician said slowly, and went out.

Whereupon, with astounding agility, Krause rushed after him, yanking open the door.

I drank the rest of my beer and ran out too, feeling a gust of moist wind rush pleasantly over my face.

They were standing face-to-face on the black, rain-lustrous sidewalk, and both were yelling. I could not catch all the words in the crescendo of this roaring ruckus, but there was one word that was distinctly and continually repeated: *twenty, twenty, twenty.* Several people had already stopped to have a look at the quarrel—I myself was enthralled by it, by the reflections of the streetlamp on the distorted faces, the strained sinew in Krause's naked neck; for some reason it brought back a splendid scuffle I had once had in a seaport dive with a beetle-black Italian, during which my hand had somehow got into his mouth and I had fiercely tried to squeeze, to tear, the wet skin inside his cheek.

The electrician and Krause yelled louder and louder. Past me slipped Emma and stopped, not daring to approach, only shouting in desperation, "Otto! Father! Otto! Father!" And at each of her shouts the swell of a contained, expectant cackle ran through the small crowd.

The two men switched to hand-to-hand combat eagerly, with a muffled thumping of fists. The electrician hit in silence, while Krause emitted a short grunt with every blow. Skinny Otto's back bent; some dark blood began to trickle from one nostril. Suddenly he tried to seize the heavy hand that was pummeling his face, but, failing in this, swayed and crashed facedown onto the sidewalk. People ran toward him, screening him from my sight.

I remembered having left my hat on the table and went back into the tavern. Inside, it seemed oddly light and quiet. Emma sat at a corner table with her head lying on an outstretched arm. I went over to her and stroked her hair. She raised her tear-stained face, then dropped her head again. I cautiously kissed the delicate part in her kitchen-scented hair, found my hat, and walked out.

In the street, a crowd was still gathered. Krause, breathing heavily, the way he did when he came out of the lake, was explaining something to a policeman.

I neither know nor wish to know who was wrong and who was right in this affair. The story could have been given a different twist, and made to depict compassionately how a girl's happiness had been mortified for the sake of a copper coin, how Emma spent the whole night crying, and how, after falling asleep toward morning, she saw again, in her dreams, the frenzied face of her father as he pummeled her lover. Or perhaps what matters is not the human pain or joy at all but, rather, the play of shadow and light on a live body, the harmony of trifles assembled on this particular day, at this particular moment, in a unique and inimitable way.

THE RETURN OF CHORB

T HE KELLERS left the opera house at a late hour. In that pacific German city, where the very air seemed a little lusterless and where a transverse row of ripples had kept shading gently the reflected cathedral for well over seven centuries, Wagner was a leisurely affair presented with relish so as to overgorge one with music. After the opera Keller took his wife to a smart nightclub renowned for its white wine. It was past one in the morning when their car, flippantly lit on the inside, sped through lifeless streets to deposit them at the iron wicket of their small but dignified private house. Keller, a thickset old German, closely resembling Oom Paul Kruger, was the first to step down on the sidewalk, across which the loopy shadows of leaves stirred in the streetlamp's gray glimmer. For an instant his starched shirtfront and the droplets of bugles trimming his wife's dress caught the light as she disengaged a stout leg and climbed out of the car in her turn. The maid met them in the vestibule and, still carried by the momentum of the news, told them in a frightened whisper about Chorb's having called. Frau Keller's chubby face, whose everlasting freshness somehow agreed with her Russian merchant-class parentage, quivered and reddened with agitation.

"He said she was ill?"

The maid whispered still faster. Keller stroked his gray brush of hair with his fat palm, and an old man's frown overcast his large, somewhat simian face, with its long upper lip and deep furrows.

"I simply refuse to wait till tomorrow," muttered Frau Keller, shaking her head as she gyrated heavily on one spot, trying to catch the end of the veil that covered her auburn wig. "We'll go there at once. Oh dear, oh dear! No wonder there's been no letters for quite a month."

Keller punched his gibus open and said in his precise, slightly guttural Russian: "The man is insane. How dare he, if she's ill, take her a second time to that vile hotel?"

But they were wrong, of course, in thinking that their daughter was ill. Chorb said so to the maid only because it was easier to utter. In point of fact he had returned alone from abroad and only now realized that, like it or not, he would have to explain how his wife had perished, and why he had written nothing about it to his in-laws. It was all very difficult. How was he to explain that he wished to possess his grief all by himself, without tainting it by any foreign substance and without sharing it with any other soul? Her death appeared to him as a most rare, almost unheard-of occurrence; nothing, it seemed to him, could be purer than such a death, caused by the impact of an electric stream, the same stream which, when poured into glass receptacles, yields the purest and brightest light.

Ever since that spring day when, on the white highway a dozen kilometers from Nice, she had touched, laughing, the live wire of a storm-felled pole, Chorb's entire world ceased to sound like a world: it retreated at once, and even the dead body that he carried in his arms to the nearest village struck him as something alien and needless.

In Nice, where she had to be buried, the disagreeable consumptive clergyman kept in vain pressing him for details: Chorb responded only with a languid smile. He sat daylong on the shingly beach, cupping colored pebbles and letting them flow from hand to hand; and then, suddenly, without waiting for the funeral, he traveled back to Germany.

He passed in reverse through all the spots they had visited together during their honeymoon journey. In Switzerland where they had wintered and where the apple trees were now in their last bloom, he recognized nothing except the hotels. As to the Black Forest, through which they had hiked in the preceding autumn, the chill of the spring did not impede memory. And just as he had tried, on the southern beach, to find again that unique rounded black pebble with the regular little white belt, which she had happened to show him on the eve of their last ramble, so now he did his best to look up all the roadside items that retained her exclamation mark: the special profile of a cliff, a hut roofed with a layer of silvery-gray scales, a black fir tree and a footbridge over a white torrent, and something which one might be inclined to regard as a kind of fatidic prefiguration: the radial span of a spider's web between two telegraph wires that were beaded with droplets of mist. She accompanied him: her little boots stepped rapidly, and her hands never stopped moving, moving—to pluck a leaf from a bush or stroke a rock wall in passing—light, laughing hands that knew no repose. He saw her small face with its dense dark freckles, and her wide eyes, whose pale greenish hue was that of the shards of glass licked smooth by the sea waves. He thought that if he managed to gather all the little things they had noticed together—if he re-created thus the near past—her image would grow immortal and replace her forever. Nighttime, though, was unendurable. Night imbued with sudden terror her irrational presence. He hardly slept at all during the three weeks of his trek—and now he got off, quite drugged with fatigue, at the railway station, which had been last autumn their point of departure from the quiet town where he had met and married her.

It was around eight o'clock of the evening. Beyond the houses the cathedral tower was sharply set off in black against a golden-red stripe of sunset. In the station square stood in file the selfsame decrepit fiacres. The identical newspaper seller uttered his hollow crepuscular cry. The same black poodle with apathetic eyes was in the act of raising a thin hindleg near a Morris pillar, straight at the scarlet lettering of a playbill announcing *Parsifal*.

Chorb's luggage consisted of a suitcase and a big tawny trunk. A fiacre took him through the town. The cabby kept indolently flapping his reins, while steadying the trunk with one hand. Chorb remembered that she whom he never named liked to take rides in cabs.

In a lane at the corner of the municipal opera house there was an old three-storied hotel of a disreputable type with rooms that were let by the week, or by the hour. Its black paint had peeled off in geographical patterns; ragged lace curtained its bleary windows; its inconspicuous front door was never locked. A pale but jaunty lackey led Chorb down a crooked corridor reeking of dampness and boiled cabbage into a room which Chorb recognized—by the picture of a pink *baigneuse* in a gilt frame over the bed—as the very one in which he and his wife had spent their first night together. Everything amused her then—the fat man in his shirtsleeves who was vomiting right in the passage, and the fact of their having chosen by chance such a beastly hotel, and the presence of a lovely blond hair in the washbasin; but what tickled her most was the way they had escaped from her house. Immediately upon coming home from church she ran up to her room to change, while downstairs the guests were gathering for supper. Her father, in a dress coat of sturdy cloth, with a flabby grin on his apish face, clapped this or that man on the shoulder and served ponies of brandy himself. Her mother, in the meantime, led her closest friends, two by two, to inspect the bedroom meant for the young couple: with tender emotion, whispering under her breath, she pointed out the colossal eiderdown, the orange blossoms, the two pairs of brand-new bedroom slippers—large checkered ones, and tiny red ones with pompons—that she had aligned on the bedside rug, across which a Gothic inscription ran: "WE ARE TOGETHER UNTO THE TOMB." Presently, everybody moved toward the hors d'oeuvres—and Chorb and his wife, after the briefest of consultations, fled through the back door, and only on the following morning, half an hour before the express train was to leave, reappeared to collect their luggage. Frau Keller had sobbed all night; her husband, who had always regarded Chorb (destitute Russian émigré and littérateur) with suspicion, now cursed his daughter's choice, the cost of the liquor, the local police that could do nothing. And several times, after the Chorbs had gone, the old man went to look at the hotel in the lane behind the opera house, and henceforward that black, purblind house became an object of disgust and attraction to him like the recollection of a crime.

While the trunk was being brought in, Chorb kept staring at the rosy chromo. When the door closed, he bent over the trunk and unlocked it. In a corner of the room, behind a loose strip of wallpaper, a mouse made a scuffing noise and then raced like a toy on rollers. Chorb turned on his heel with a start. The lightbulb hanging from the ceiling on a cord swayed ever so gently, and the shadow of the cord glided across the green couch and broke at its edge. It was on that couch that he had slept on his nuptial night. She, on the regular bed, could be heard breathing with the even rhythm of a child. That night he had kissed her once—on the hollow of the throat—that had been all in the way of lovemaking.

The mouse was busy again. There exist small sounds that are more frightening than gunfire. Chorb left the trunk alone and paced the room a couple of times. A moth struck the lamp with a ping. Chorb wrenched the door open and went out.

On the way downstairs he realized how weary he was, and when he found himself in the alley the blurry blue of the May night made him dizzy. Upon turning into the boulevard he walked faster. A square. A stone *Herzog*. The black masses of the City Park. Chestnut trees now were in flower. *Then*, it had been autumn. He had gone for a long stroll with her on the eve of the wedding. How good was the earthy, damp, somewhat violety smell of the dead leaves strewing the sidewalk! On those enchanting overcast days the sky would be of a dull white, and the small twig-reflecting puddle in the middle of the black pavement resembled an insufficiently developed photograph. The graystone villas were separated by the mellow and motionless foliage of yellowing trees, and in front of the Kellers' house the leaves of a withering poplar had acquired the tone of transparent grapes. One glimpsed, too, a few birches behind the bars of the gate; ivy solidly muffed some of their boles, and Chorb made a point of telling her that ivy never grew on birches in Russia, and she remarked that the foxy tints of their minute leaves reminded her of spots of tender rust upon ironed linen. Oaks and chestnuts lined the sidewalk; their black bark was velveted with green rot; every now and then a leaf broke away to fly athwart the street like a scrap of wrapping paper. She attempted to catch it on the wing by means of a child's spade found near a heap of pink bricks at a spot where the street was under repair. A little way off the funnel of a workers' van emitted gray-blue smoke which drifted aslant and dissolved between the branches—and a resting workman, one hand on his hip, contemplated the young lady, as light as a dead leaf, dancing about with that little spade in her raised hand. She skipped, she laughed. Chorb, hunching his back a bit, walked behind her—and it seemed to him that happiness itself had that smell, the smell of dead leaves.

At present he hardly recognized the street, encumbered as it was with the nocturnal opulence of chestnut trees. A streetlamp glinted in front; over the glass a branch drooped, and several leaves at its end, saturated with light, were quite translucent. He came nearer. The shadow of the wicket, its checkerwork all distorted, swept up toward him from the sidewalk to entangle his feet. Beyond the gate, and beyond a dim gravel walk, loomed the front of the familiar house, dark except for the light in one open window. Within that amber chasm the housemaid was in the act of spreading with an ample sweep of her arms a snow-bright sheet on a bed. Loudly and curtly Chorb called out to her. With one hand he still gripped the wicket and the dewy touch of iron against his palm was the keenest of all memories.

The maid was already hurrying toward him. As she was to tell Frau Keller later, what struck her first was the fact that Chorb remained standing silently on the sidewalk although she had unlocked the little gate at once. "He had no hat," she related, "and the light of the streetlamp fell on his forehead, and his forehead was all sweaty, and the hair was glued to it by the sweat. I told him master and mistress were at the theater. I asked him why he was alone. His eyes were blazing, their look terrified me, and he seemed not to have shaved for quite a time. He said softly: 'Tell them that she is ill.' I asked: 'Where are you staying?' He said: 'Same old place,' and then added: 'That does not matter. I'll call again in the morning.' I suggested he wait—but he didn't reply and went away."

Thus Chorb traveled back to the very source of his recollections, an agonizing and yet blissful test now drawing to a close. All there remained was but a single night to be spent in that first chamber of their marriage, and by tomorrow the test would be passed and her image made perfect.

But as he trudged back to the hotel, up the boulevard, where on all the benches in the blue darkness sat hazy figures, Chorb suddenly understood that, despite exhaustion, he would not be able to sleep alone in that room with its naked bulb and whispery crannies. He reached the square and plodded along the city's main avenue—and now he knew what must be done. His quest, however, lasted a long while: This was a quiet and chaste town, and the secret by-street where one could buy love was unknown to Chorb. Only after an hour of helpless wandering, which caused his ears to sing and his feet to burn, did he enter that little lane—whereupon he accosted at once the first girl who hailed him.

"The night," said Chorb, scarcely unclenching his teeth.

The girl cocked her head, swung her handbag, and replied: "Twenty-five."

He nodded. Only much later, having glanced at her casually, Chorb noted with indifference that she was pretty enough, though considerably jaded, and that her bobbed hair was blond.

She had been in that hotel several times before, with other customers, and the wan, sharp-nosed lackey, who was tripping down as they were going upstairs, gave her an amiable wink. While Chorb and she walked along the corridor, they could hear, from behind one of the doors, a bed creaking, rhythmically and weightily, as if a log were being sawed in two. A few doors farther the same monotonous creak came from another room, and as they passed by the girl looked back at Chorb with an expression of cold playfulness.

In silence he ushered her into his room—and immediately, with a profound anticipation of sleep, started to tear off his collar from its stud. The girl came up very close to him: "And what about a small present?" she suggested, smiling.

Dreamily, absentmindedly, Chorb considered her, as he slowly grasped what she meant.

Upon receiving the banknotes, she carefully arranged them in her bag, uttered a light little sigh, and again rubbed herself against him.

"Shall I undress?" she asked with a shake of her bob.

"Yes, go to bed," muttered Chorb. "I'll give you some more in the morning."

The girl began to undo hastily the buttons of her blouse, and kept glancing at him askance, being slightly taken aback by his abstraction and gloom. He shed his clothes quickly and carelessly, got into the bed, and turned to the wall.

"This fellow likes kinky stuff," vaguely conjectured the girl. With slow hands she folded her chemise, placed it upon a chair. Chorb was already fast asleep.

The girl wandered around the room. She noticed that the lid of the trunk standing by the window was slightly ajar; by squatting on her heels, she managed to peep under the lid's edge. Blinking and cautiously stretching out her bare arm, she palpated a woman's dress, a stocking, scraps of silk—all this stuffed in anyhow and smelling so nice that it made her feel sad.

Presently she straightened up, yawned, scratched her thigh, and, just as she was, naked, but in her stockings, drew aside the window curtain. Behind the curtain the casement was open and one could make out, in the velvety depths, a corner of the opera house, the black shoulder of a stone Orpheus outlined against the blue of the night, and a row of light along the dim façade which slanted off into darkness. Down there, far away, diminutive dark silhouettes swarmed as they emerged from bright doorways onto the semicircular layers of illumined porch steps, to which glided up cars with shimmering headlights and smooth glistening tops. Only when the breakup was over and the brightness gone, the girl closed the curtain again. She switched off the light and stretched on the bed beside Chorb. Just before falling asleep she caught herself thinking that once or twice she had already been in that room: she remembered the pink picture on its wall.

Her sleep lasted not more than an hour: a ghastly deep-drawn howl roused her. It was Chorb screaming. He had woken up sometime after midnight, had turned on his side, and had seen his wife lying beside him. He screamed horribly, with visceral force. The white specter of a woman sprang off the bed. When, trembling, she turned on the light, Chorb was sitting among the tumbled bedclothes, his back to the wall, and through his spread fingers one eye could be seen burning with a mad flame. Then he slowly uncovered his face, slowly recognized the girl. With a frightened mutter she was hastily putting on her chemise.

And Chorb heaved a sigh of relief, for he realized that the ordeal was over. He moved onto the green couch, and sat there, clasping his hairy shins and with a meaningless smile contemplating the harlot.

That smile increased her terror; she turned away, did up one last hook, laced her boots, busied herself with the putting on of her hat.

At this moment the sound of voices and footsteps came from the corridor.

One could hear the voice of the lackey repeating mournfully: "But look here, there's a lady with him." And an irate guttural voice kept insisting: "But I'm telling you she's my daughter."

The footsteps stopped at the door. A knock followed.

The girl snatched her bag from the table and resolutely flung the door open. In front of her stood an amazed old gentleman in a lusterless top hat, a pearl stud gleaming in his starched shirt. From over his shoulder peered the tear-stained face of a stout lady with a veil on her hair. Behind them the puny pale lackey strained up on tiptoe, making big eyes and gesturing invitingly. The girl understood his signs and shot out into the corridor, past the old man, who turned his head in her wake with the same puzzled look and then crossed the threshold with his companion. The door closed. The girl and the lackey remained in the corridor. They exchanged a frightened glance and bent their heads to listen. But in the room all was silence. It seemed incredible that inside there should be three people. Not a single sound came from there.

"They don't speak," whispered the lackey, and put his finger to his lips.

A GUIDE TO BERLIN

I N T H E morning I visited the zoo and now I am entering a pub with my friend and usual pot companion. Its sky-blue sign bears a white inscription, "LÖWENBRÄU," accompanied by the portrait of a lion with a winking eye and mug of beer. We sit down and I start telling my friend about utility pipes, streetcars, and other important matters.

1 THE PIPES

In front of the house where I live a gigantic black pipe lies along the outer edge of the sidewalk. A couple of feet away, in the same file, lies another, then a third and a fourth—the street's iron entrails, still idle, not yet lowered into the ground, deep under the asphalt. For the first few days after they were unloaded, with a hollow clanging, from trucks, little boys would run on them up and down and crawl on all fours through those round tunnels, but a week later nobody was playing any more and thick snow was falling instead; and now, when, cautiously probing the treacherous glaze of the sidewalk with my thick rubberheeled stick, I go out in the flat gray light of early morning, an even stripe of fresh snow stretches along the upper side of each black pipe while up the interior slope at the very mouth of the pipe which is nearest to the turn of the tracks, the reflection of a still illumined tram sweeps up like bright-orange heat lightning. Today someone wrote "Otto" with his finger on the strip of virgin snow and I thought how beautifully that name, with its two soft *o*'s flanking the pair of gentle consonants, suited the silent layer of snow upon that pipe with its two orifices and its tacit tunnel.

2 THE STREETCAR

The streetcar will vanish in twenty years or so, just as the horse-drawn tram has vanished. Already I feel it has an air of antiquity, a kind of old-fashioned charm. Everything about it is a little clumsy and rickety, and if a curve is taken a little too fast, and the trolley pole jumps the wire, and the conductor, or even one of the passengers, leans out over the car's stern, looks up, and jiggles the cord until the pole is back in place, I always think that the coach driver of old must sometimes have dropped his whip, reined in his four-horse team, sent after it the lad in long-skirted livery who sat beside him on the box and gave piercing blasts on his horn while, clattering over the cobblestones, the coach swung through a village.

The conductor who gives out tickets has very unusual hands. They work as nimbly as those of a pianist, but instead of being limp, sweaty, and soft-nailed, the ticketman's hands are so coarse that when you are pouring change into his palm and happen to touch that palm, which seems to have developed a harsh chitinous crust, you feel a kind of moral discomfort. They are extraordinarily agile and efficient hands, despite their roughness and the thickness of the fingers. I watch him with curiosity as he clamps the ticket with his broad black fingernail and punches it in two places, rummages in his leather purse, scoops up coins to make change, immediately slaps the purse shut, and yanks the bell cord, or, with a shove of his thumb, throws open the special little window in the forward door to hand tickets to people on the front platform. And all the time the car sways, passengers standing in the aisle grab at the overhead straps, and surge back and forth—but he will not drop a single coin or a single ticket torn from his roll. In these winter days the bottom half of the forward door is curtained with green cloth, the windows are clouded with frost, Christmas trees for sale throng the edge of the sidewalk at each stop, the passengers' feet are numb with cold, and sometimes a gray worsted mitten clothes the conductor's hand. At the end of the line the front car uncouples, enters a siding, runs around the remaining one, and approaches it from behind. There is something reminiscent of a submissive female in the way the second car waits as the first, male, trolley, sending up a small crackling flame, rolls up and couples on. And (minus the biological metaphor) I am reminded of how, some eighteen years ago in Petersburg, the horses used to be unhitched and led around the pot-bellied blue tram.

The horse-drawn tram has vanished, and so will the trolley, and some eccentric Berlin writer in the twenties of the twenty-first century, wishing to portray our time, will go to a museum of technological history and locate a hundred-year-old streetcar, yellow, uncouth, with old-fashioned curved seats, and in a museum of old costumes dig up a black, shiny-buttoned conductor's uniform. Then he will go home and compile a description of Berlin streets in bygone days. Everything, every trifle, will be valuable and meaningful: the conductor's purse, the advertisement over the window, that peculiar jolting motion which our great-grandchildren will perhaps imagine—everything will be ennobled and justified by its age.

I think that here lies the sense of literary creation: to portray ordinary objects as they will be reflected in the kindly mirrors of future times; to find in the objects around us the fragrant tenderness that only posterity will discern and appreciate in the far-off times when every trifle of our plain everyday life will become exquisite and festive in its own right: the times when a man who might put on the most ordinary jacket of today will be dressed up for an elegant masquerade.

3 WORK

Here are examples of various kinds of work that I observe from the crammed tram, in which a compassionate woman can always be relied upon to cede me her window seat—while trying not to look too closely at me.

At an intersection the pavement has been torn up next to the track; by turns, four workmen are pounding an iron stake with mallets; the first one strikes, and the second is already lowering his mallet with a sweeping, accurate swing; the second mallet crashes down and is rising skyward as the third and then the fourth bang down in rhythmical succession. I listen to their unhurried clanging, like four repeated notes of an iron carillon.

A young white-capped baker flashes by on his tricycle; there is something angelic about a lad dusted with flour. A van jingles past with cases on its roof containing rows of emerald-glittering empty bottles, collected from taverns. A long, black larch tree mysteriously travels by in a cart. The tree lies flat; its tip quivers gently, while the earth-covered roots, enveloped in sturdy burlap, form an enormous beige bomblike sphere at its base. A postman, who has placed the mouth of a sack under a cobalt-colored mailbox, fastens it on from below, and secretly, invisibly, with a hurried rustling, the box empties and the postman claps shut the square jaws of the bag, now grown full and heavy. But perhaps fairest of all are the carcasses, chrome yellow, with pink blotches, and arabesques, piled on a truck, and the man in apron and leather hood with a long neck flap who heaves each carcass onto his back and, hunched over, carries it across the sidewalk into the butcher's red shop.

4 EDEN

Every large city has its own, man-made Eden on earth.

If churches speak to us of the Gospel, zoos remind us of the solemn, and tender, beginning of the Old Testament. The only sad part is that this artificial Eden is all behind bars, although it is also true that if there were no enclosures the very first dingo would savage me. It is Eden nonetheless, insofar as man is able to reproduce it, and it is with good reason that the large hotel across from the Berlin Zoo is named after that garden.

In the wintertime, when the tropical animals have been hidden away, I recommend visiting the amphibian, insect, and fish houses. Rows of illuminated displays behind glass in the dimly lit hall resemble the portholes through which Captain Nemo gazed out of his submarine at the sea creatures undulating among the ruins of Atlantis. Behind the glass, in bright recesses, transparent fishes glide with flashing fins, marine flowers breathe, and, on a patch of sand, lies a live, crimson five-pointed star. This, then, is where the notorious emblem originated—at the very bottom of the ocean, in the murk of sunken Atlantica, which long ago lived through various upheavals while pottering about topical utopias and other inanities that cripple us today.

Oh, do not omit to watch the giant tortoises being fed. These ponderous, ancient corneous cupolas were brought from the Galápagos Islands. With a decrepit kind of circumspection, a wrinkly flat head and two totally useless paws emerge in slow motion from under the two-hundred-pound dome. And with its thick, spongy tongue, suggesting somehow that of a cacological idiot slackly vomiting his monstrous speech, the turtle sticks its head into a heap of wet vegetables and messily munches their leaves.

But that dome above it—ah, that dome, that ageless, well-rubbed, dull bronze, that splendid burden of time . . .

5 THE PUB

"That's a very poor guide," my usual pot companion says glumly. "Who cares about how you took a streetcar and went to the Berlin Aquarium?"

The pub in which he and I are sitting is divided into two parts, one large, the other somewhat smaller. A billiard table occupies the center of the former; there are a few tables in the corners; a bar faces the entrance, and bottles stand on shelves behind the bar. On the wall, between the windows, newspapers and magazines mounted on shot staffs hang like paper banners. At the far end there is a wide passageway, through which one sees a cramped little room with a green couch under a mirror, out of which an oval table with a checked oilcloth topples and takes up its solid position in front of the couch. That room is part of the publican's humble little apartment. There his wife, with faded looks and big breasts, is feeding soup to a blond child.

"It's of no interest," my friend affirms with a mournful yawn. "What do trams and tortoises matter? And anyway the whole thing is simply a bore. A boring, foreign city, and expensive to live in, too . . ."

From our place near the bar one can make out very distinctly the couch, the mirror, and the table in the background beyond the passage. The woman is clearing the table. Propped on his elbows, the child attentively examines an illustrated magazine on its useless handle.

"What do you see down there?" asks my companion and turns slowly, with a sigh, and the chair creaks heavily under him.

There, under the mirror, the child still sits alone. But he is now looking our way. From there he can see the inside of the tavern—the green island of the billiard table, the ivory ball he is forbidden to touch, the metallic gloss of the bar, a pair of fat truckers at one table and the two of us at another. He has long since grown used to this scene and is not dismayed by its proximity. Yet there is one thing I know. Whatever happens to him in life, he will always remember the picture he saw every day of his childhood from the little room where he was fed his soup. He will remember the billiard table and the coatless evening visitor who used to draw back his sharp white elbow and hit the ball with his cue, and the blue-gray cigar smoke, and the din of voices, and my empty right sleeve and scarred face, and his father behind the bar, filling a mug for me from the tap.

"I can't understand what you see down there," says my friend, turning back toward me.

What indeed! How can I demonstrate to him that I have glimpsed somebody's future recollection?

A NURSERY TALE

1

F ANTASY, the flutter, the rapture of fantasy! Erwin knew these things well. In a tram, he would always sit on the right-hand side, so as to be nearer the sidewalk. Twice daily, from the tram he took to the office and back, Erwin looked out of the window and collected his harem. Happy, happy Erwin, to dwell in such a convenient, such a fairy-tale German town!

He covered one sidewalk in the morning, on his way to work, and the other in the late afternoon, on his way home. First one, then the other was bathed in voluptuous sunlight, for the sun also went and returned. We should bear in mind that Erwin was so morbidly shy that only once in his life, taunted by rascally comrades, he had accosted a woman, and she had said quietly: "You ought to be ashamed of yourself. Leave me alone." Thereafter, he had avoided conversation with strange young ladies. In compensation, separated from the street by a windowpane, clutching to his ribs a black briefcase, wearing scuffed trousers with a pinstripe, and stretching one leg under the opposite seat (if unoccupied), Erwin looked boldly and freely at passing girls, and then would suddenly bite his nether lip: this signified the capture of a new concubine; whereupon he would set her aside, as it were, and his swift gaze, jumping like a compass needle, was already seeking out the next one. Those beauties were far from him, and therefore the sweetness of free choice could not be affected by sullen timidity. If, however, a girl happened to sit down across from him, and a certain twinge told him that she was pretty, he would retract his leg from under her seat with all the signs of a gruffness quite uncharacteristic of his young age—and could not bring himself to take stock of her: the bones of his forehead—right here, over the eyebrows—ached from shyness, as if an iron helmet were restricting his temples and preventing him from raising his eyes; and what a relief it was when she got

161

up and went toward the exit. Then, feigning casual abstraction, he looked—shameless Erwin did look—following her receding back, swallowing whole her adorable nape and silk-hosed calves, and thus, after all, would he add her to his fabulous harem! The leg would again be stretched, again the bright sidewalk would flow past the window, and again, his thin pale nose with a noticeable depression at the tip directed streetward, Erwin would accumulate his slave girls. And this is fantasy, the flutter, the rapture of fantasy!

2

One Saturday, on a frivolous evening in May, Erwin was sitting at a sidewalk table. He watched the tripping throng of the avenue, now and then biting his lip with a quick incisor. The entire sky was tinged with pink and the streetlamps and shop-sign bulbs glowed with a kind of unearthly light in the gathering dusk. The first lilacs were being hawked by an anemic but pretty young girl. Rather fittingly the café phonograph was singing the Flower Aria from *Faust*.

A tall middle-aged lady in a charcoal tailor-made suit, heavily, yet not ungracefully, swinging her hips, made her way among the sidewalk tables. There was no vacant one. Finally, she put one hand in a glossy black glove upon the back of the empty chair opposite Erwin.

"May I?" queried her unsmiling eyes from under the short veil of her velvet hat.

"Yes, certainly," answered Erwin, slightly rising and ducking. He was not awed by such solid-built women with thickly powdered, somewhat masculine jowls.

Down onto the table with a resolute thud went her oversize handbag. She ordered a cup of coffee and a wedge of apple tart. Her deep voice was somewhat hoarse but pleasant.

The vast sky, suffused with dull rose, grew darker. A tram screeched by, inundating the asphalt with the radiant tears of its lights. And short-skirted beauties walked by. Erwin's glance followed them.

I want this one, he thought, noticing his nether lip. And that one, too.

"I think it could be arranged," said his vis-à-vis in the same calm husky tones in which she had addressed the waiter.

Erwin almost fell off his chair. The lady looked intently at him, as she pulled off one glove to tackle her coffee. Her made-up eyes shone cold and hard, like showy false jewels. Dark pouches swelled under them, and—what seldom occurs in the case of women, even elderly women—hairs grew out of her feline-shaped nostrils. The shed glove revealed a big wrinkled hand with long, convex, beautiful fingernails.

"Don't be surprised," she said with a wry smile. She muffled a yawn and added: "In point of fact, I am the Devil."

Shy, naive Erwin took this to be a figure of speech, but the lady, lowering her voice, continued as follows:

"Those who imagine me with horns and a thick tail are greatly mistaken. Only once did I appear in that shape, to some Byzantine imbecile, and I really don't know why it was such a damned success. I am born three or four times every two centuries. In the 1870s, some fifty years ago, I was buried, with picturesque honors and a great shedding of blood, on a hill above a cluster of African villages of which I had been ruler. My term there was a rest after more stringent incarnations. Now I am a German-born woman whose last husband—I had, I think, three in all—was of French extraction, a Professor Monde. In recent years I have driven several young men to suicide, caused a well-known artist to copy and multiply the picture of the Westminster Abbey on the pound note, incited a virtuous family man— But there is really nothing to brag about. This has been a pretty banal avatar, and I am fed up with it."

She gobbled up her slice of tart and Erwin, mumbling something, reached for his hat, which had fallen under the table.

"No, don't go yet," said Frau Monde, simultaneously beckoning the waiter. "I am offering you something. I am offering you a harem. And if you are still skeptical of my power— See that old gentleman in tortoiseshell glasses crossing the street? Let's have him hit by a tram."

Erwin, blinking, turned streetward. As the old man reached the tracks he took out his handkerchief and was about to sneeze into it. At the same instant, a tram flashed, screeched, and rolled past. From both sides of the avenue people rushed toward the tracks. The old gentleman, his glasses and handkerchief gone, was sitting on the asphalt. Someone helped him up. He stood, sheepishly shaking his head, brushing his coat sleeves with the palms of his hands, and wiggling one leg to test its condition.

"I said 'hit by a tram,' not 'run over,' which I might also have said," remarked Frau Monde coolly, as she worked a thick cigarette into an enameled holder. "In any case, this is an example."

She blew two streams of gray smoke through her nostrils and again fixed Erwin with her hard bright eyes.

"I liked you immediately. That shyness, that bold imagination. You reminded me of an innocent, though hugely endowed, young monk whom I knew in Tuscany. This is my penultimate night. Being a woman has its points, but being an aging woman is hell, if you will pardon me the expression. Moreover, I made such mischief the other day—you will soon read about it in all the papers—that I had better get out of this life. Next Monday I plan to be born elsewhere. The Siberian slut I have chosen shall be the mother of a marvelous, monstrous man."

"I see," said Erwin.

"Well, my dear boy," continued Frau Monde, demolishing her second piece of pastry, "I intend, before going, to have a bit of innocent fun. Here is what I suggest. Tomorrow, from noon to midnight you can select by your usual method" (with heavy humor Frau Monde sucked in her lower lip with a succulent hiss) "all the girls you fancy. Before my departure, I shall have them gathered and placed at your complete disposal. You will keep them until you have enjoyed them all. How does that strike you, *amico*?"

Erwin dropped his eyes and said softly: "If it is all true, it would be a great happiness."

"All right then," she said, and licked the remains of whipped cream off her spoon: "All right. One condition, nevertheless, must be set. No, it is not what you are thinking. As I told you, I have arranged my next incarnation. *Your* soul I do not require. Now this is the condition: the total of your choices between noon and midnight must be an odd number. This is essential and final. Otherwise I can do nothing for you."

Erwin cleared his throat and asked, almost in a whisper: "But— how shall I know? Let's say I've chosen one—what then?"

"Nothing," said Frau Monde. "Your feeling, your desire, are a command in themselves. However, in order that you may be sure that the deal stands, I shall have a sign given you every time—a smile, not necessarily addressed to you, a chance word in the crowd, a sudden patch of color—that sort of thing. Don't worry, you'll know."

"And—and—" mumbled Erwin, shuffling his feet under the table: "—and where is it all going to—uh—happen? I have only a very small room."

"Don't worry about that either," said Frau Monde, and her corset creaked as she rose. "Now it's time you went home. No harm in getting a good night's rest. I'll give you a lift."

In the open taxi, with the dark wind streaming between starry sky and glistening asphalt, poor Erwin felt tremendously elated. Frau

Monde sat erect, her crossed legs forming a sharp angle, and the city lights flashed in her gemlike eyes.

"Here's your house," she said, touching Erwin's shoulder. *"Au revoir."*

3

Many are the dreams that can be brought on by a mug of dark beer laced with brandy. Thus reflected Erwin when he awoke the next morning—he must have been drunk, and the talk with that funny female was all fancy. This rhetorical turn often occurs in fairy tales and, as in fairy tales, our young man soon realized he was wrong.

He went out just as the church clock had begun the laborious task of striking noon. Sunday bells joined in excitedly, and a bright breeze ruffled the Persian lilacs around the public lavatory in the small park near his house. Pigeons settled on an old stone *Herzog* or waddled along the sandbox where little children, their flannel behinds sticking up, were digging with toy scoops and playing with wooden trains. The lustrous leaves of the lindens moved in the wind; their ace-of-spades shadows quivered on the graveled path and climbed in an airy flock the trouser legs and skirts of the strollers, racing up and scattering over shoulders and faces, and once again the whole flock slipped back onto the ground, where, barely stirring, they lay in wait for the next foot passenger. In this variegated setting, Erwin noticed a girl in a white dress who had squatted down to tousle with two fingers a fat shaggy pup with warts on its belly. The inclination of her head bared the back of her neck, revealing the ripple of her vertebrae, the fair bloom, the tender hollow between her shoulder blades, and the sun through the leaves found fiery strands in her chestnut hair. Still playing with the puppy, she half-rose from her haunches and clapped her hands above it. The fat little animal rolled over on the gravel, ran off a few feet, and toppled on its side. Erwin sat down on a bench and cast a timid and avid glance at her face.

He saw her so clearly, with such piercing and perfect force of perception, that, it seemed, nothing new about her features might have been disclosed by years of previous intimacy. Her palish lips twitched as if repeating every small soft movement of the puppy; her eyelashes beat so brightly as to look like the raylets of her beaming eyes; but most enchanting, perhaps, was the curve of her cheek, now slightly in profile; that dipping line no words, of course, could describe. She started running, showing nice legs, and the puppy tumbled in her wake like a woolly ball. In sudden awareness of his miraculous might, Erwin caught his breath and awaited the promised signal. At that moment the girl turned her head as she ran and flashed a smile at the plump little creature that could barely keep up with her.

"Number one," Erwin said to himself with unwonted complacency, and got up from his bench.

He followed the graveled path with scraping footsteps, in gaudy, reddish-yellow shoes worn only on Sundays. He left the oasis of the diminutive park and crossed over to Amadeus Boulevard. Did his eyes rove? Oh, they did. But, maybe, because the girl in white had somehow left a sunnier mark than any remembered impression, some dancing blind spot prevented him from finding another sweetheart. Soon, however, the blot dissolved, and near a glazed pillar with the tramway timetable our friend observed two young ladies—sisters, or even twins, to judge by their striking resemblance—who were discussing a streetcar route in vibrant, echoing voices. Both were small and slim, dressed in black silk, with saucy eyes and painted lips.

"That's exactly the tram you want," one of them kept saying.

"Both, please," Erwin requested quickly.

"Yes, of course," said the other in response to her sister's words.

Erwin continued along the boulevard. He knew all the smart streets where the best possibilities existed.

"Three," he said to himself. "Odd number. So far so good. And if it were midnight right now—"

Swinging her handbag she was coming down the steps of the Leilla, one of the best local hotels. Her big blue-chinned companion slowed down behind her to light his cigar. The lady was lovely, hatless, bobhaired, with a fringe on her forehead that made her look like a boy actor in the part of a damsel. As she went by, now closely escorted by our ridiculous rival, Erwin remarked simultaneously the crimson artificial rose in the lapel of her jacket and the advertisement on a billboard: a blond-mustachioed Turk and, in large letters, the word "YES!," under which it said in smaller characters: "I SMOKE ONLY THE ROSE OF THE ORIENT."

That made four, divisible by two, and Erwin felt eager to restore the odd-number rigmarole without delay. In a lane off the boulevard there was a cheap restaurant which he sometimes frequented on Sundays when sick of his landlady's fare. Among the girls he had happened to note at one time or another there had been a wench who worked in that place. He entered and ordered his favorite dish: blood sausage and sauerkraut. His table was next to the telephone. A man in a bowler called a number and started to jabber as ardently as a hound that has picked up the scent of a hare. Erwin's glance wandered toward the bar—and there was the girl he had seen three or four times before. She was beautiful in a drab, freckled way, if beauty can be drably russet. As she raised her bare arms to place her washed beer steins he saw the red tufts of her armpits.

"All right, all right!" barked the man into the mouthpiece.

With a sigh of relief enriched by a belch, Erwin left the restaurant. He felt heavy and in need of a nap. To tell the truth, the new shoes pinched like crabs. The weather had changed. The air was sultry. Great domed clouds grew and crowded one another in the hot sky. The streets were becoming deserted. One could feel the houses fill to the brim with Sunday-afternoon snores. Erwin boarded a streetcar.

The tram started to roll. Erwin turned his pale face, shining with sweat, to the window, but no girls walked. While paying his fare he noticed, on the other side of the aisle, a woman sitting with her back to him. She wore a black velvet hat, and a light frock patterned with intertwined chrysanthemums against a semitransparent mauve background through which showed the shoulder straps of her slip. The lady's statuesque bulk made Erwin curious to glimpse her face. When her hat moved and, like a black ship, started to turn, he first looked away as usual, glanced in feigned abstraction at a youth sitting opposite him, at his own fingernails, at a red-cheeked little old man dozing in the rear of the car, and, having thus established a point of departure justifying further castings-around, Erwin shifted his casual gaze to the lady now looking his way. It was Frau Monde. Her full, no-longer-young face was blotchily flushed from the heat, her mannish eyebrows bristled above her piercing prismatic eyes, a slightly sardonic smile curled up the corners of her compressed lips.

"Good afternoon," she said in her soft husky voice: "Come sit over here. Now we can have a chat. How are things going?"

"Only five," replied Erwin with embarrassment.

"Excellent. An odd number. I would advise you to stop there. And at midnight—ah, yes, I don't think I told you—at midnight you are to come to Hoffmann Street. Know where that is? Look between Number Twelve and Fourteen. The vacant lot there will be replaced by a villa with a walled garden. The girls of your choice will be waiting for you on cushions and rugs. I shall meet you at the garden gate—but it is understood," she added with a subtle smile, "I shan't intrude. You'll remember the address? There will be a brand-new streetlight in front of the gate."

"Oh, one thing," said Erwin, collecting his courage. "Let them be dressed at first—I mean let them look just as they were when I chose them—and let them be very merry and loving."

"Why, naturally," she replied, "everything will be just as you wish whether you tell me or not. Otherwise there was no point in starting the whole business, *n'est-ce pas?* Confess, though, my dear boy—you were on the brink of enrolling me in your harem. No, no, have no fear, I am kidding you. Well, that's your stop. Very wise to call it a day. Five is fine. See you a few secs after midnight, ha-ha."

4
————

Upon reaching his room, Erwin took off his shoes and stretched out on the bed. He woke up toward evening. A mellifluous tenor at full blast streamed from a neighbor's phonograph: *"I vant to be happee—"*

Erwin started thinking back: Number one, the Maiden in White, she's the most artless of the lot. I may have been a little hasty. Oh, well, no harm done. Then the Twins near the pillar of glass. Gay, painted young things. With them I'm sure to have fun. Then number four, Leilla the Rose, resembling a boy. That's, perhaps, the best one. And finally, the Fox in the ale-house. Not bad either. But only five. That's not very many!

He lay prone for a while with his hands behind his head, listening to the tenor, who kept wanting to be happy: Five. No, that's absurd. Pity it's not Monday morning: those three shopgirls the other day—oh, there are so many more beauties waiting to be found! And I can always throw in a streetwalker at the last moment.

Erwin put on his regular pair of shoes, brushed his hair, and hurried out.

By nine o'clock he had collected two more. One of them he noticed in a café where he had a sandwich and two drams of Dutch gin. She was talking with great animation to her companion, a beard-fingering foreigner, in an impenetrable language—Polish or Russian—and her gray eyes had a slight slant, her thin aquiline nose wrinkled when she laughed, and her elegant legs were exposed to the knee. While Erwin watched her quick gestures, the reckless way in which she tap-tapped cigarette ash all over the table, a German word, like a window, flashed open in her Slavic speech, and this chance word (*"offenbar"*) was the "evident" sign. The other girl, number seven on the list, turned up at the Chinese-style entrance of a small amusement park. She wore a scarlet blouse with a bright-green skirt, and her bare neck swelled as she shrieked in glee, fighting off a couple of slap-happy young boors who were grabbing her by the hips and trying to make her accompany them.

"I'm willing, I'm willing!" she cried out at last, and was rushed away.

Varicolored paper lanterns enlivened the place. A sledgelike affair with wailing passengers hurtled down a serpentine channel, disappeared in the angled arcades of medieval scenery, and dived into a new abyss with new howls. Inside a shed, on four bicycle seats (there were no wheels, just the frames, pedals, and handlebars), sat four girls in jerseys and shorts—a red one, a blue one, a green one, a yellow one— their bare legs working at full tilt. Above them hung a dial on which moved four pointers, red, blue, green, and yellow. At first the blue one was first, then the green overtook it. A man with a whistle stood by and collected the coins of the few simpletons who wanted to place their bets. Erwin stared at those magnificent legs, naked nearly up to the groin and pedaling with passionate power.

They must be terrific dancers, he thought; I could use all four.

The pointers obediently gathered into one bunch and came to a stop.

"Dead heat!" shouted the man with the whistle. "A sensational finish!"

Erwin drank a glass of lemonade, consulted his watch, and made for the exit.

Eleven o'clock and eleven women. That will do, I suppose.

He narrowed his eyes as he imagined the pleasures awaiting him. He was glad he had remembered to put on clean underwear.

How slyly Frau Monde put it, reflected Erwin with a smile. Of course she will spy on me and why not? It will add some spice.

He walked, looking down, shaking his head delightedly, and only rarely glancing up to check the street names. Hoffmann Street, he knew, was quite far, but he still had an hour, so there was no need to hurry. Again, as on the previous night, the sky swarmed with stars and the asphalt glistened like smooth water, absorbing and lengthening the magic lights of the town. He passed a large cinema whose radiance flooded the sidewalk, and at the next corner a short peal of childish laughter caused him to raise his eyes.

He saw before him a tall elderly man in evening clothes with a little girl walking beside—a child of fourteen or so in a low-cut black party dress. The whole city knew the elderly man from his portraits. He was a famous poet, a senile swan, living all alone in a distant suburb. He strode with a kind of ponderous grace; his hair, the hue of soiled cotton wool, reached over his ears from beneath his fedora. A stud in the triangle of his starched shirt caught the gleam of a lamp, and his long bony nose cast a wedge of shadow on one side of his thin-lipped mouth. In the same tremulous instant Erwin's glance lit on the face of the child mincing at the old poet's side; there was something odd about that face, odd was the flitting glance of her much too shiny eyes, and if she were not just a little girl—the old man's granddaughter, no doubt—one might suspect that her lips were touched up with rouge. She walked swinging her hips very, very slightly, her legs moved closer together, she was asking her companion something in a ringing voice—and although Erwin gave no command mentally, he knew that his swift secret wish had been fulfilled.

"Oh, of course, of course," replied the old man coaxingly, bending toward the child.

They passed, Erwin caught a whiff of perfume. He looked back, then went on.

"Hey, careful," he suddenly muttered as it dawned upon him that this made twelve—an even number: I must find one more—within half an hour.

It vexed him a little to go on searching, but at the same time he was pleased to be given yet another chance.

I'll pick up one on the way, he said to himself, allaying a trace of panic. I'm sure to find one!

"Maybe, it will be the nicest of all," he remarked aloud as he peered into the glossy night.

And a few minutes later he experienced the familiar delicious contraction—that chill in the solar plexus. A woman in front of him was walking along with rapid and light steps. He saw her only from the back and could not have explained why he yearned so poignantly to overtake precisely *her* and have a look at her face. One might, naturally, find random words to describe her bearing, the movement of her shoulders, the silhouette of her hat—but what is the use? Something beyond visible outlines, some kind of special atmosphere, an ethereal excitement, lured Erwin on and on. He marched fast and still could not catch up with her; the humid reflections of lights flickered before him; she tripped along steadily, and her black shadow would sweep up, as it entered a streetlamp's aura, glide across a wall, twist around its edge, and vanish.

"Goodness, I've got to see her face," Erwin muttered. "And time is flying."

Presently he forgot about time. That strange silent chase in the night intoxicated him. He managed at last to overtake her and went on, far ahead, but had not the courage to look back at her and merely slowed down, whereupon she passed him in her turn and so fast that he did not have time to raise his eyes. Again he was walking ten paces behind her and by then he knew, without seeing her face, that she was his main prize. Streets burst into colored light, petered out, glowed again; a square had to be crossed, a space of sleek blackness, and once more with a brief click of her high-heeled shoe the woman stepped onto a sidewalk, with Erwin behind, bewildered, disembodied, dizzy from the misty lights, the damp night, the chase.

What enticed him? Not her gait, not her shape, but something else, bewitching and overwhelming, as if a tense shimmer surrounded her: mere fantasy, maybe, the flutter, the rapture of fantasy, or maybe it was that which changes a man's entire life with one divine stroke—Erwin knew nothing, he just sped after her over asphalt and stone, which seemed also dematerialized in the iridescent night.

Then trees, vernal lindens, joined the hunt: they advanced whispering on either side, overhead, all around him; the little black hearts of their shadows intermingled at the foot of each streetlamp, and their delicate sticky aroma encouraged him.

Once again Erwin came near. One more step, and he would be abreast of her. She stopped abruptly at an iron wicket and fished out her keys from her handbag. Erwin's momentum almost made him bump into her. She turned her face toward him, and by the light a streetlamp cast through emerald leaves, he recognized the girl who had been playing that morning with a woolly black pup on a graveled path, and immediately remembered, immediately understood all her charm, tender warmth, priceless radiance.

He stood staring at her with a wretched smile.

"You ought to be ashamed of yourself," she said quietly. "Leave me alone."

The little gate opened, and slammed. Erwin remained standing under the hushed lindens. He looked around, not knowing which way to go. A few paces away, he saw two blazing bubbles: a car standing by the sidewalk. He went up to it and touched the motionless, dummylike chauffeur on the shoulder.

"Tell me what street is this? I'm lost."

"Hoffmann Street," said the dummy dryly.

And then a familiar, husky, soft voice spoke out of the depths of the car.

"Hello. It's me."

Erwin leaned a hand on the car door and limply responded.

"I am bored to death," said the voice, "I'm waiting here for my boyfriend. He is bringing the poison. He and I are dying at dawn. How are you?"

"Even number," said Erwin, running his finger along the dusty door.

"Yes, I know," calmly rejoined Frau Monde. "Number thirteen turned out to be number one. You bungled the job rather badly."

"A pity," said Erwin.

"A pity," she echoed, and yawned.

Erwin bowed, kissed her large black glove, stuffed with five out-spread fingers, and with a little cough turned into the darkness. He walked with a heavy step, his legs ached, he was oppressed by the thought that tomorrow was Monday and it would be hard to get up.

TERROR

HERE is what sometimes happened to me: after spending the first part of the night at my desk—that part when night trudges heavily uphill—I would emerge from the trance of my task at the exact moment when night had reached the summit and was teetering on that crest, ready to roll down into the haze of dawn; I would get up from my chair, feeling chilly and utterly spent, turn on the light in my bedroom, and suddenly see myself in the looking glass. Then it would go like this: during the time I had been deep at work, I had grown disacquainted with myself, a sensation akin to what one may experience when meeting a close friend after years of separation: for a few empty, lucid, but numb moments you see him in an entirely different light even though you realize that the frost of this mysterious anesthesia will presently wear off, and the person you are looking at will revive, glow with warmth, resume his old place, becoming again so familiar that no effort of the will could possibly make you recapture that fleeting sensation of estrangedness. Precisely thus I now stood considering my own reflection in the glass and failing to recognize it as mine. And the more keenly I examined my face—those unblinking alien eyes, that sheen of tiny hairs along the jaw, that shade along the nose—and the more insistently I told myself "This is I, this is So-and-so," the less clear it became *why* this should be "I," the harder I found it to make the face in the mirror merge with that "I" whose identity I failed to grasp. When I spoke of my odd sensations, people justly observed that the path I had taken led to the madhouse. In point of fact, once or twice, late at night, I peered so lengthily at my reflection that a creepy feeling came over me and I put out the light in a hurry. Yet next morning, while shaving, it would never occur to me to question the reality of my image.

Another thing: at night, in bed, I would abruptly remember that I

173

was mortal. What then took place within my mind was much the same as happens in a huge theater if the lights suddenly go out, and someone shrilly screams in the swift-winged darkness, and other voices join in, resulting in a blind tempest, with the black thunder of panic growing—until suddenly the lights come on again, and the performance of the play is blandly resumed. Thus would my soul choke for a moment while, lying supine, eyes wide open, I tried with all my might to conquer fear, rationalize death, come to terms with it on a day-by-day basis, without appealing to any creed or philosophy. In the end, one tells oneself that death is still far away, that there will be plenty of time to reason everything out, and yet one knows that one never will do it, and again, in the dark, from the cheapest seats, in one's private theater where warm live thoughts about dear earthly trifles have panicked, there comes a shriek—and presently subsides when one turns over in bed and starts to think of some different matter.

I assume that those sensations—the perplexity before the mirror at night or the sudden pang of death's foretaste—are familiar to many, and if I dwell on them it is only because they contain just a small particle of that supreme terror that I was destined once to experience. Supreme terror, special terror—I am groping for the exact term but my store of ready-made words, which in vain I keep trying on, does not contain even one that will fit.

I led a happy life. I had a girl. I remember well the torture of our first separation. I had gone on a business trip abroad, and upon my return she met me at the station. I saw her standing on the platform, caged as it were in tawny sunlight, a dusty cone of which had just penetrated through the station's glazed vault. Her face kept rhythmically turning to and fro as the train windows slowly glided by to a stop. With her I always felt easy and at rest. Once only—and here again I feel what a clumsy instrument human speech is. Still, I would like to explain. It is really such nonsense, so ephemeral: we are alone in her room, I write while she darns a silk stocking stretched taut over the back of a wooden spoon, her head bent low; one ear, translucently pink, is half concealed by a strand of fair hair, and the small pearls around her neck gleam touchingly, and her tender cheek appears sunken because of the assiduous pout of her lips. All at once, for no reason at all, I become terrified of her presence. This is far more terrifying than the fact that somehow, for a split second, my mind did not register her identity in the dusty sun of the station. I am terrified by there being another person in the room with me; I am terrified by the very notion of *another person*. No wonder lunatics don't recognize relatives. But she raises her head, all her features participate in the quick smile she gives me—and no trace is left now of the odd terror I felt a moment ago. Let me repeat: this happened only one single time, and I took it to be a silly trick of my nerves, forgetting that on lonely nights before a lonely mirror I had experienced something quite similar.

She was my mistress for nearly three years. I know that many people could not understand our relationship. They were at a loss to explain what there was in that naive little maiden to attract and hold a poet's affection, but good God! how I loved her unassuming prettiness, gaiety, friendliness, the birdlike flutterings of her soul. It was exactly that gentle simplicity of hers that protected me: to her, everything in the world had a kind of everyday clarity, and it would even seem to me that she knew what awaited us after death, so that there was no reason for us to discuss that topic. At the end of our third year together I again was obliged to go away, for a rather long time. On the eve of my departure we went to the opera. She sat down for a moment on the crimson little sofa in the darkish, rather mysterious vestibule of our loge to take off her huge gray snowboots, from which I helped her to extricate her slender silk-clad legs—and I thought of those delicate moths that hatch from bulky shaggy cocoons. We moved to the front of our box. We were gay as we bent over the rosy abyss of the house while waiting for the raising of the curtain, a solid old screen with pale-gold decorations depicting scenes from various operas—Ruslan in his pointed helmet, Lenski in his carrick. With her bare elbow she almost knocked down from the plush parapet her little nacreous opera glass.

Then, when all in the audience had taken their seats, and the orchestra drew in its breath and prepared to blast forth, something happened: every light went out in the huge rosy theater, and such a dense darkness swooped upon us that I thought I had gone blind. In this darkness everything at once began to move, a shiver of panic began to rise and resolved itself in feminine cries, and because men's voices very loudly called for calm, the cries became more and more riotous. I laughed and began talking to her, but then felt that she had clutched my wrist and was silently worrying my cuff. When light again filled the house I saw that she was pale and that her teeth were clenched. I helped her to get out of the loge. She shook her head, chiding herself with a deprecatory smile for her childish fright—but then burst into tears and asked to be taken home. It was only in the close carriage that she regained her composure and, pressing her crumpled handkerchief to her swimming bright eyes, began to explain how sad she felt about my going away tomorrow, and how wrong it would have been to spend our last evening at the opera, among strangers.

Twelve hours later I was in a train compartment, looking out of the window at the misty winter sky, the inflamed little eye of the sun, which kept up with the train, the white snow-covered fields which kept endlessly opening up like a giant fan of swan's down. It was in the foreign city I reached next day that I was to have my encounter with supreme terror.

To begin with, I slept badly for three nights in a row and did not sleep at all during the fourth. In recent years I had lost the habit of solitude, and now those solitary nights caused me acute unrelieved anguish. The first night I saw my girl in dream: sunlight flooded her room, and she sat on the bed wearing only a lacy nightgown, and laughed, and laughed, could not stop laughing. I recalled my dream quite by accident, a couple of hours later, as I was passing a lingerie store, and upon remembering it realized that all that had been so gay in my dream—her lace, her thrown-back head, her laughter—was now, in my waking state, frightening. Yet, I could not explain to myself why that lacy laughing dream was now so unpleasant, so hideous. I had a lot of things to take care of, and I smoked a lot, and all the time I was aware of the feeling that I absolutely must maintain rigid control over myself. When getting ready for bed in my hotel room, I would deliberately whistle or hum but would start like a fearful child at the slightest noise behind me, such as the flop of my jacket slipping from the chairback to the floor.

On the fifth day, after a bad night, I took time out for a stroll. I wish the part of my story to which I am coming now could be set in italics; no, not even italics would do: I need some new, unique kind of type. Insomnia had left me with an exceptionally receptive void within my mind. My head seemed made of glass, and the slight cramp in my calves had also a vitreous character. As soon as I came out of the hotel— Yes, now I think I have found the right words. I hasten to write them down before they fade. When I came out on the street, I suddenly saw the world such as it really *is*. You see, we find comfort in telling ourselves that the world could not exist without us, that it exists only inasmuch as we ourselves exist, inasmuch as we can represent it to ourselves. Death, infinite space, galaxies, all this is frightening, exactly because it transcends the limits of our perception. Well—on that terrible day when, devastated by a sleepless night, I stepped out into the center of an incidental city, and saw houses, trees, automobiles, people, my mind abruptly refused to accept them as "houses," "trees," and so forth—as something connected with ordinary human life. My line of communication with the world snapped, I was on my own and the world was on *its* own, and *that* world was devoid of sense. I saw the actual essence of all things. I looked at houses and they had lost their usual meaning—that is, all that we think when looking at a house: a certain architectural style, the sort of rooms inside, ugly house, comfortable house—all this had evaporated, leaving nothing but an absurd shell, the same way an absurd sound is left after one has repeated sufficiently long the commonest word without heeding its meaning: house, howss, whowss. It was the same with trees, the same with people. I understood the horror of a human face. Anatomy, sexual distinctions, the notion of "legs," "arms," "clothes"—all that was abolished, and there remained in front of me a mere *something*—not even a creature, for that too is a human concept, but merely *something* moving past. In vain did I try to master my terror by recalling how once in my childhood, on waking up, I raised my still sleepy eyes while pressing the back of my neck to my low pillow and saw, leaning toward me over the bed head, an incomprehensible face, noseless, with a hussar's black mustache just below its octopus eyes, and with teeth set in its forehead. I sat up with a shriek and immediately the mustache became eyebrows and the entire face was transformed into that of my mother, which I had glimpsed at first in an unwonted upside-down aspect.

And now, too, I tried to "sit up" mentally, so that the visible world might resume its everyday position—but I did not succeed. On the contrary: the closer I peered at people the more absurd their appearance looked to me. Overwhelmed with terror, I sought support in some basic idea, some better brick than the Cartesian one, with the help of which to begin the reconstruction of the simple, natural, habitual world as we know it. By that time I was resting, I believe, on the bench of a public park. I have no precise recollection of my actions. Just as a man who is having a heart attack on a sidewalk does not give a hoot for the passersby, the sun, the beauty of an ancient cathedral, and has only one concern: to breathe, so I too had but one desire: not to go mad. I am convinced that nobody ever saw the world the way I saw it during those moments, in all its terrifying nakedness and terrifying absurdity. Near me a dog was sniffing the snow. I was tortured by my efforts to recognize what "dog" might mean, and because I had been staring at it hard, it crept up to me trustingly, and I felt so nauseated that I got up from the bench and walked away. It was then that my terror reached its highest point. I gave up struggling. I was no longer a man, but a naked eye, an aimless glance moving in an absurd world. The very sight of a human face made me want to scream.

Presently I found myself again at the entrance of my hotel. Some-one came up to me, pronounced my name, and thrust a folded slip of paper into my limp hand. Automatically I unfolded it, and at once my terror vanished. Everything around me became again ordinary and un-obtrusive: the hotel, the changing reflections in the glass of the revolv-ing door, the familiar face of the bellboy who had handed me the telegram. I now stood in the middle of the spacious vestibule. A man with a pipe and a checked cap brushed against me in passing and gravely apologized. I felt astonishment and an intense, unbearable but quite human pain. The telegram said she was dying.

While I traveled back, while I sat at her bedside, it never occurred to me to analyze the meaning of being and nonbeing, and no longer was I terrified by those thoughts. The woman I loved more than any-thing on earth was dying. This was all I saw or felt.

She did not recognize me when my knee thudded against the side of her bed. She lay, propped up on huge pillows, under huge blankets, herself so small, with hair brushed back from the forehead revealing the narrow scar on her temple ordinarily concealed by a strand brushed low over it. She did not recognize my living presence, but by the slight smile that raised once or twice the corners of her lips, I knew that she saw me in her quiet delirium, in her dying fancy—so that there were two of me standing before her: I myself, whom she did not see, and my double, who was invisible to me. And then I remained alone: my double died with her.

Her death saved me from insanity. Plain human grief filled my life so completely that there was no room left for any other emotion. But time flows, and her image within me becomes ever more perfect, ever more lifeless. The details of the past, the live little memories, fade im-perceptibly, go out one by one, or in twos and threes, the way lights go out, now here now there, in the windows of a house where people are falling asleep. And I know that my brain is doomed, that the terror I experienced once, the helpless fear of existing, will sometime over-take me again, and that then there will be no salvation.

RAZOR

His regimental comrades had good reason to dub him "Razor." The man's face lacked a façade. When his acquaintances thought of him they could imagine him only in profile, and that profile was remarkable: nose sharp as a draftsman's triangle; chin sturdy as an elbow; long, soft eyelashes characteristic of certain very obstinate, very cruel people. His name was Ivanov.

That nickname of former days contained a strange clairvoyance. It is not rare for a man called Stone or Stein to become a perfectly good mineralogist. Captain Ivanov, after an epic escape and sundry insipid ordeals, had ended up in Berlin, and chosen the very trade at which his nickname had hinted—that of a barber.

He worked in a small but clean barbershop that also employed two young professionals, who treated "the Russian captain" with jovial respect. Then there was the owner, a dour lump of a man who would spin the handle of the cash register with a silvery sound, and also a manicurist, anemic and translucent as if she had been drained dry by the contact of innumerable fingers placed, in batches of five, on the small velvet cushion in front of her.

Ivanov was very good at his work, although he was somewhat handicapped by his poor knowledge of German. However, he soon figured out how to deal with the problem: tack a *"nicht"* onto the first sentence, an interrogative *"was?"* onto the next, then *"nicht"* again, continuing to alternate in the same way. And even though it was only in Berlin that he had learned haircutting, it was remarkable how closely his manner resembled that of the tonsors back in Russia, with their well-known penchant for a lot of superfluous scissor-clicking—they'll click away, take aim, and snip a lock or two, then keep their blades going lickety-split in the air as if impelled by inertia. This deft, gratuitous whirring was the very thing that earned him the respect of his colleagues.

Without doubt scissors and razors are weapons, and there was something about this metallic chirr that gratified Ivanov's warlike soul. He was a rancorous, keen-witted man. His vast, noble, splendid homeland had been ruined by some dull buffoon for the sake of a well-turned scarlet phrase, and this he could not forgive. Like a tightly coiled spring, vengeance lurked, biding its time, within his soul.

One very hot, bluish summer morning, taking advantage of the nearly total absence of customers during those workaday hours, both of Ivanov's colleagues took an hour off. Their employer, dying from the heat and from long-ripening desire, had silently escorted the pale, unresisting little manicurist to a back room. Left alone in the sun-drenched shop, Ivanov glanced through one newspaper, then lit a cigarette and, all in white, stepped outside the doorway and started watching the passersby.

People flashed past, accompanied by their blue shadows, which broke over the edge of the sidewalk and glided fearlessly underneath the glittering wheels of cars that left ribbonlike imprints on the heat-softened asphalt, resembling the ornate lacework of snakes. Suddenly a short, thickset gentleman in black suit and bowler, with a black briefcase under his arm, turned off the sidewalk and headed straight for white Ivanov. Blinking from the sun, Ivanov stepped aside to let him into the barbershop.

The newcomer's reflection appeared in all the mirrors at once: in profile, three-quarter-face, and showing the waxen bald spot in back from which the black bowler had ascended to snag a hat hook. And when the man turned squarely toward the mirrors, which sparkled above marble surfaces aglitter with green and gold scent bottles, Ivanov instantly recognized that mobile, puffy face with the piercing little eyes and a plump mole by the right lobe of his nose.

The gentleman silently sat down in front of the mirror, then, mumbling indistinctly, tapped his untidy cheek with a stubby finger: Meaning, I want a shave. In a kind of astonished haze, Ivanov spread a sheet over him, whipped up some tepid lather in a porcelain bowl, started brushing it on to the man's cheeks, rounded chin, and upper lip, gingerly circumnavigated the mole, began rubbing in the foam with his index finger. But he did all this mechanically, so shaken was he by having encountered this person again.

Now a flimsy white mask of soap covered the man's face up to his eyes, minuscule eyes that glittered like the tiny wheels of a watch movement. Ivanov had opened his razor and begun to sharpen it on a strap when he recovered from his amazement and realized that this man was in his power.

Then, bending over the waxy bald spot, he brought the blue blade close to the soapy mask and said very softly, "My respects to you, comrade. How long has it been since you left our part of the world? No, don't move, please, or I might cut you prematurely."

The glittering little wheels started moving faster, glanced at Ivanov's sharp profile, and stopped. Ivanov removed some excess flakes of lather with the blunt side of the razor and continued, "I remember you very well, comrade. Sorry if I find it distasteful to pronounce your name. I remember how you interrogated me some six years ago, in Kharkov. I remember your signature, dear friend. . . . But, as you see, I am still alive."

Then the following happened. The little eyes darted about, then suddenly shut tight, eyelids compressed like those of the savage who thought closing his eyes made him invisible.

Ivanov tenderly moved his blade along the cold, rustling cheek.

"We're absolutely alone, comrade. Understand? One little slip of the razor, and right away there will be a good deal of blood. Here is where the carotid throbs. So there will a good deal, even a great deal of blood. But first I want your face decently shaved, and, besides, I have something to recount to you."

Cautiously, with two fingers, Ivanov lifted the fleshy tip of the man's nose and, with the same tenderness, began shaving above the upper lip.

"The point, comrade, is that I remember everything. I remember perfectly, and I want you to remember too. . . ." And, in a soft voice, Ivanov began his account, as he unhurriedly shaved the recumbent, motionless face. The tale he told must have been terrifying indeed, because from time to time his hand would stop, and he would stoop very close to the gentleman sitting like a corpse under the shroudlike sheet, his convex eyelids lowered.

"That is all," Ivanov said with a sigh, "that's the whole story. Tell me, what do you think would be a suitable atonement for all that? What is considered an equivalent of a sharp sword? And again, keep in mind that we are utterly, totally alone."

"Corpses are always shaved," went on Ivanov, running the blade upward along the stretched skin of the man's neck. "Those sentenced to death are shaved too. And now I am shaving you. Do you realize what is going to happen next?"

The man sat without stirring or opening his eyes. Now the lathery mask was gone from his face. Traces of foam remained only on his cheekbones and near his ears. This tensed, eyeless, fat face was so pallid that Ivanov wondered if he had not suffered a fit of paralysis. But when he pressed the flat surface of the razor to the man's neck, his entire body gave a twitch. He did not, however, open his eyes.

Ivanov gave the man's face a quick wipe and spat some talcum on him from a pneumatic dispenser. "That will do for you," he said. "I'm satisfied. You may leave." With squeamish haste he yanked the sheet off the man's shoulders. The other remained seated.

"Get up, you ninny," shouted Ivanov, pulling him up by the sleeve. The man froze, with firmly shut eyes, in the middle of the shop. Ivanov clapped the bowler on his head, thrust the briefcase under his arm, and swiveled him toward the door. Only then did the man jerk into motion. His shut-eyed face flashed in all the mirrors. He stepped like an automaton through the door that Ivanov was holding open, and, with the same mechanical gait, clutching his briefcase with an outstretched petrified hand, gazing into the sunny blur of the street with the glazed eyes of a Greek statue, he was gone.

THE PASSENGER

"YES, Life is more talented than we," sighed the writer, tapping the cardboard mouthpiece of his Russian cigarette against the lid of his case. "The plots Life thinks up now and then! How can we compete with that goddess? Her works are untranslatable, indescribable."

"Copyright by the author," suggested the critic, smiling; he was a modest, myopic man with slim, restless fingers.

"Our last recourse, then, is to cheat," continued the writer, absentmindedly throwing a match into the critic's empty wineglass. "All that's left to us is to treat her creations as a film producer does a famous novel. The producer needs to prevent servant maids from being bored on Saturday nights; therefore he alters the novel beyond recognition; minces it, turns it inside out, throws out hundreds of episodes, introduces new characters and incidents he has invented himself—and all this for the sole purpose of having an entertaining film unfold without a hitch, punishing virtue in the beginning and vice at the end, a film perfectly natural in terms of its own conventions and, above all, furnished with an unexpected but all-resolving outcome. Exactly thus do we, writers, alter the themes of Life to suit us in our drive toward some kind of conventional harmony, some kind of artistic conciseness. We spice our savorless plagiarisms with our own devices. We think that Life's performance is too sweeping, too uneven, that her genius is too untidy. To indulge our readers we cut out of Life's untrammeled novels our neat little tales for the use of schoolchildren. Allow me, in this connection, to impart to you the following experience.

"I happened to be traveling in the sleeping car of an express. I love the process of settling into viatic quarters—the cool linen of the berth, the slow passage of the station's departing lights as they start moving behind the black windowpane. I remember how pleased I was that there was nobody in the bunk above me. I undressed, I lay down supine with my hands clasped under my head, and the lightness of the scant regulation blanket was a treat in comparison to the puffiness of hotel featherbeds. After some private musings—at the time I was anxious to write a story about the life of railway-car cleaning women—I put out the light and was soon asleep. And here let me use a device cropping up with dreary frequency in the sort of story to which mine promises to belong. Here it is—that old device which you must know so well: 'In the middle of the night I woke up suddenly.' What follows, however, is something less stale. I woke up and saw a foot."

"Excuse me, a what?" interrupted the modest critic, leaning forward and lifting his finger.

"I saw a foot," repeated the writer. "The compartment was now lighted. The train stood at a station. It was a man's foot, a foot of considerable size, in a coarse sock, through which the bluish toenail had worked a hole. It was planted solidly on a step of the bed ladder close to my face, and its owner, concealed from my sight by the upper bunk roofing me, was just on the point of making a last effort to hoist himself onto his ledge. I had ample time to inspect that foot in its gray, black-checkered sock and also part of the leg: the violet vee of the garter on the side of the stout calf and its little hairs nastily sticking out through the mesh of the long underwear. It was altogether a most repellent limb. While I looked, it tensed, the tenacious big toe moved once or twice; then, finally, the whole extremity vigorously pushed off and soared out of sight. From above came grunting and snuffling sounds leading one to conclude that the man was preparing to sleep. The light went out, and a few moments later the train jerked into motion.

"I don't know how to explain it to you, but that limb anguished me most oppressively. A resilient varicolored reptile. I found it disturbing that all I knew of the man was that evil-looking leg. His figure, his face, I never saw. His berth, which formed a low, dark ceiling over me, now seemed to have come lower; I almost felt its weight. No matter how hard I tried to imagine the aspect of my nocturnal fellow traveler all I could visualize was that conspicuous toenail which showed its bluish mother-of-pearl sheen through a hole in the wool of the sock. It may seem strange, in a general way, that such trifles should bother me, but, per contra, is not every writer precisely a person who bothers about trifles? Anyhow, sleep did not come. I kept listening—had my unknown companion started to snore? Apparently he was not snoring but moaning. Of course, the knocking of train wheels at night is known to encourage aural hallucinations; yet I could not get over the impression that from up there, above me, came sounds of an unusual nature. I raised myself on one elbow. The sounds grew more distinct. The man on the upper berth was sobbing."

"What's that?" interrupted the critic. "Sobbing? I see. Sorry—didn't quite catch what you said." And, again dropping his hands in his lap and inclining his head to one side, the critic went on listening to the narrator.

"Yes, he was sobbing, and his sobs were atrocious. They choked him; he would noisily let his breath out as if having drunk at one gulp a quart of water, whereupon there followed rapid spasms of weeping with the mouth shut—the frightful parody of a cackle—and again he would draw in air and again let it out in short expirations of sobbing, with his mouth now open—to judge by the ha-ha-ing note. And all this against the shaky background of hammering wheels, which by this token became something like a moving stairway along which his sobs went up and came down. I lay motionless and listened—and felt, incidentally, that my face in the dark looked awfully silly, for it is always embarrassing to hear a stranger sobbing. And mind you, I was helplessly shackled to him by the fact of our sharing the same two-berth compartment, in the same unconcernedly rushing train. And he did not stop weeping; those dreadful arduous sobs kept up with me: we both—I below, the listener, and he overhead, the weeping one—sped sideways into night's remoteness at eighty kilometers an hour, and only a railway crash could have cleft our involuntary link.

"After a while he seemed to stop crying, but no sooner was I about to drop off than his sobs started to swell again and I even seemed to hear unintelligible words which he uttered in a kind of sepulchral, belly-deep voice between convulsive sighs. He was silent again, only snuffling a bit, and I lay with my eyes closed and saw in fancy his disgusting foot in its checkered sock. Somehow or other I managed to fall asleep; and at half past five the conductor wrenched the door open to call me. Sitting on my bed—and knocking my head every minute against the edge of the upper berth—I hurried to dress. Before going out with my bags into the corridor, I turned to look up at the upper berth, but the man was lying with his back to me, and had covered his head with his blanket. It was morning in the corridor, the sun had just risen, the fresh, blue shadow of the train ran over the grass, over the shrubs, swept sinuously up the slopes, rippled across the trunks of flickering birches—and an oblong pondlet shone dazzlingly in the middle of a field, then narrowed, dwindled to a silvery slit, and with a rapid clatter a cottage scuttled by, the tail of a road whisked under a crossing gate—and once more the numberless birches dizzied one with their flickering, sun-flecked palisade.

"The only other people in the corridor were two women with sleepy, sloppily made-up faces, and a little old man wearing suede gloves and a traveling cap. I detest rising early: for me the most ravishing dawn in the world cannot replace the hours of delicious morning sleep; and therefore I limited myself to a grumpy nod when the old gentleman asked me if I, too, was getting off at . . . he mentioned a big town where we were due in ten or fifteen minutes.

"The birches suddenly dispersed, half a dozen small houses poured down a hill, some of them, in their haste, barely missing being run over by the train; then a huge purple-red factory strode by flashing its windowpanes; somebody's chocolate hailed us from a ten-yard poster; another factory followed with its bright glass and chimneys; in short, there happened what usually happens when one is nearing a city. But all at once, to our surprise, the train braked convulsively and pulled up at a desolate whistle-stop, where an express had seemingly no business to dawdle. I also found it surprising that several policemen stood out there on the platform. I lowered a window and leaned out. 'Shut it, please,' said one of the men politely. The passengers in the corridor displayed some agitation. A conductor passed and I asked what was the matter. 'There's a criminal on the train,' he replied, and briefly explained that in the town at which we had stopped in the middle of the night, a murder had occurred on the eve: a betrayed husband had shot his wife and her lover. The ladies exclaimed *'akh!,'* the old gentleman shook his head. Two policemen and a rosy-cheeked, plump, bowler-hatted detective who looked like a bookmaker entered the corridor. I was asked to go back to my berth. The policemen remained in the corridor, while the detective visited one compartment after another. I showed him my passport. His reddish-brown eyes glided over my face; he returned my passport. We stood, he and I, in that narrow coupé on the upper bunk of which slept a dark-cocooned figure. 'You may leave,' said the detective, and stretched his arm toward that upper darkness: 'Papers, please.' The blanketed man kept on snoring. As I lingered in the doorway, I still heard that snoring and seemed to make out through it the sibilant echoes of his nocturnal sobs. 'Please, wake up,' said the detective, raising his voice; and with a kind of professional jerk he pulled at the edge of the blanket at the sleeper's nape. The latter stirred but continued to snore. The detective shook him by the shoulder. This was rather sickening. I turned away and stared at the window across the corridor, but did not really see it, while listening with my whole being to what was happening in the compartment.

"And imagine, I heard absolutely nothing out of the ordinary. The man on the upper berth sleepily mumbled something, the detective distinctly demanded his passport, distinctly thanked him, then went out and entered another compartment. That is all. But think only how nice it would have seemed—from the writer's viewpoint, naturally—if the evil-footed, weeping passenger had turned out to be a murderer, how nicely his tears in the night could have been explained, and, what is more, how nicely all that would have fitted into the frame of my night journey, the frame of a short story. Yet, it would appear that the plan of the Author, the plan of Life, was in this case, as in all others, a hundred times nicer."

The writer sighed and fell silent, as he sucked his cigarette, which had gone out long ago and was now all chewed up and damp with saliva. The critic was gazing at him with kindly eyes.

"Confess," spoke the writer again, "that beginning with the moment when I mentioned the police and the unscheduled stop, you were sure my sobbing passenger was a criminal?"

"I know your manner," said the critic, touching his interlocutor's shoulder with the tips of his fingers and, in a gesture peculiar to him, instantly snatching back his hand. "If you were writing a detective story, your villain would have turned out to be not the person whom none of the characters suspect but the person whom everybody in the story suspects from the very beginning, thus fooling the experienced reader who is used to solutions proving to be *not* the obvious ones. I am well aware that you like to produce an impression of inexpectancy by means of the most natural denouement; but don't get carried away by your own method. There is much in life that is casual, and there is also much that is unusual. The Word is given the sublime right to enhance chance and to make of the transcendental something that is not accidental. Out of the present case, out of the dance of chance, you could have created a well-rounded story if you had transformed your fellow traveler into a murderer."

The writer sighed again.

"Yes, yes, that did occur to me. I might have added several details. I would have alluded to the passionate love he had for his wife. All kinds of inventions are possible. The trouble is that we are in the dark—maybe Life had in mind something totally different, something much more subtle and deep. The trouble is that I did not learn, and shall never learn, why the passenger cried."

"I intercede for the Word," gently said the critic. "You, as a writer of fiction, would have at least thought up some brilliant solution: your character was crying, perhaps, because he had lost his wallet at the station. I once knew someone, a grown-up man of martial appearance, who would weep or rather bawl when he had a toothache. No, thanks, no—don't pour me any more. That's sufficient, that's quite sufficient."

THE DOORBELL

S EVEN years had passed since he and she had parted in Petersburg. God, what a crush there had been at the Nikolaevsky Station! Don't stand so close—the train is about to start. Well,
here we go, good-bye, dearest. . . . She walked alongside, tall,
thin, wearing a raincoat, with a black-and-white scarf around her
neck, and a slow current carried her off backward. A Red Army recruit,
he took part, reluctantly and confusedly, in the civil war. Then, one
beautiful night, to the ecstatic stridulation of prairie crickets, he went
over to the Whites. A year later, in 1920, not long before leaving Russia, on the steep, stony Chainaya Street in Yalta, he ran into his uncle,
a Moscow lawyer. Why, yes, there was news—two letters. She was leaving for Germany and already had obtained a passport. You look fine,
young man. And at last Russia let go of him—a permanent leave, according to some. Russia had held him for a long time; he had slowly
slithered down from north to south, and Russia kept trying to keep
him in her grasp, with the taking of Tver, Kharkov, Belgorod, and various interesting little villages, but it was no use. She had in store for
him one last temptation, one last gift—the Crimea—but even that did
not help. He left. And on board the ship he made the acquaintance of
a young Englishman, a jolly chap and an athlete, who was on his way
to Africa.

Nikolay visited Africa, and Italy, and for some reason the Canary Islands, and then Africa again, where he served for a while in the Foreign Legion. At first he recalled her often, then rarely, then again more
and more often. Her second husband, the German industrialist Kind,
died during the war. He had owned a goodish bit of real estate in Berlin, and Nikolay assumed there was no danger of her going hungry
there. But how quickly time passed! Amazing! . . . Had seven whole
years really gone by?

During those years he had grown hardier, rougher, had lost an index finger, and had learned two languages—Italian and English. The color of his eyes had become lighter and their expression more candid owing to the smooth rustic tan that covered his face. He smoked a pipe. His walk, which had always had the solidity characteristic of short-legged people, now acquired a remarkable rhythm. One thing about him had not changed at all: his laugh, accompanied by a quip and a twinkle.

He had quite a time, chuckling softly and shaking his head, before he finally decided to drop everything and by easy stages make his way to Berlin. On one occasion—at a newsstand, somewhere in Italy, he noticed an émigré Russian paper, published in Berlin. He wrote to the paper to place an advertisement under Personal: So-and-so seeks So-and-so. He got no reply. On a side trip to Corsica, he met a fellow Russian, the old journalist Grushevski, who was leaving for Berlin. Make inquiries on my behalf. Perhaps you'll find her. Tell her I am alive and well. . . . But this source did not bring any news either. Now it was high time to take Berlin by storm. There, on the spot, the search would be simpler. He had a lot of trouble obtaining a German visa, and he was running out of funds. Oh, well, he would get there one way or another. . . .

And so he did. Wearing a trenchcoat and a checked cap, short and broad-shouldered, with a pipe between his teeth and a battered valise in his good hand, he exited onto the square in front of the station. There he stopped to admire a great jewel-bright advertisement that inched its way through the darkness, then vanished and started again from another point. He spent a bad night in a stuffy room in a cheap hotel, trying to think of ways to begin the search. The address bureau, the office of the Russian-language newspaper . . . Seven years. She must really have aged. It was rotten of him to have waited so long; he could have come sooner. But, ah, those years, that stupendous roaming about the world, the obscure ill-paid jobs, chances taken and chucked, the excitement of freedom, the freedom he had dreamed of in childhood! . . . It was pure Jack London. . . . And here he was again: a new city, a suspiciously itchy featherbed, and the screech of a late tram. He groped for his matches, and with a habitual movement of his index stump began pressing the soft tobacco into the pipebowl.

When traveling the way he did you forget the names of time; they are crowded out by those of places. In the morning, when Nikolay went out intending to go to the police station, the gratings were down on all the shop fronts. It was a damned Sunday. So much for the address office and the newspaper. It was also late autumn: windy weather, asters in the public gardens, a sky of solid white, yellow trees, yellow trams, the nasal honking of rheumy taxis. A chill of excitement came over him at the idea that he was in the same town as she. A fifty-pfennig coin bought him a glass of port in a cab drivers' bar, and the wine on an empty stomach had a pleasant effect. Here and there in the streets there came a sprinkling of Russian speech: ". . . *Skol'ko raz ya tebe govorila*" (". . . How many times have I told you"). And again, after the passage of several natives: ". . . He's willing to sell them to me, but frankly, I . . ." The excitement made him chuckle and finish each pipeful much more quickly than usual. ". . . Seemed to be gone, but now Grisha's down with it too. . . ." He considered going up to the next pair of Russians and asking, very politely: "Do you know by any chance Olga Kind, born Countess Karski?" They must all know each other in this bit of provincial Russia gone astray.

It was already evening, and, in the twilight, a beautiful tangerine light had filled the glassed tiers of a huge department store when Nikolay noticed, on one of the sides of a front door, a small white sign that said: "I. S. WEINER, DENTIST. FROM PETROGRAD." An unexpected recollection virtually scalded him. This fine friend of ours is pretty well decayed and must go. In the window, right in front of the torture seat, inset glass photographs displayed Swiss landscapes. . . . The window gave on Moika Street. Rinse, please. And Dr. Weiner, a fat, placid, white-gowned old man in perspicacious glasses, sorted his tinkling instruments. She used to go to him for treatment, and so did his cousins, and they even used to say to each other, when they quarreled for some reason or other, "How would you like a Weiner?" (i.e., a punch in the mouth?). Nikolay dallied in front of the door, on the point of ringing the bell, remembering it was Sunday; he thought some more and rang anyway. There was a buzzing in the lock and the door gave. He went up one flight. A maid opened the door. "No, the doctor is not receiving today." "My teeth are fine," objected Nikolay in very poor German. "Dr. Weiner is an old friend of mine. My name is Galatov—I'm sure he remembers me. . . ." "I'll tell him," said the maid.

A moment later a middle-aged man in a frogged velveteen jacket came out into the hallway. He had a carroty complexion and seemed extremely friendly. After a cheerful greeting he added in Russian, "I don't remember you, though—there must be a mistake." Nikolay looked at him and apologized: "Afraid so. I don't remember you either. I was expecting to find the Dr. Weiner who lived on Moika Street in Petersburg before the Revolution, but got the wrong one. Sorry."

"Oh, that must be a namesake of mine. A common namesake. I lived on Zagorodny Avenue."

"We all used to go to him," explained Nikolay, "and well, I thought . . . You see, I'm trying to locate a certain lady, a Madame Kind, that's the name of her second husband—"

Weiner bit his lip, looked away with an intent expression, then addressed him again. "Wait a minute. . . . I seem to recall . . . I seem to recall a Madame Kind who came to see me here not long ago and was also under the impression— We'll know for sure in a minute. Be kind enough to step into my office."

The office remained a blur in Nikolay's vision. He did not take his eyes off Weiner's impeccable calvities as the latter bent over his appointment book.

"We'll know for sure in a minute," he repeated, sunning his fingers across the pages. "We'll know for sure in just a minute. We'll know in just . . . Here we are. Frau Kind. Gold filling and some other work—which I can't make out, there's a blot here."

"And what's the first name and patronymic?" asked Nikolay, approaching the table and almost knocking off an ashtray with his cuff.

"That's in the book too. Olga Kirillovna."

"Right," said Nikolay with a sigh of relief.

"The address is Plannerstrasse fifty-nine, care of Babb," said Weiner with a smack of his lips, and rapidly copied the address on a separate slip. "Second street from here. Here you are. Very happy to be of service. Is she a relative of yours?"

"My mother," replied Nikolay.

Coming out of the dentist's, he proceeded with a somewhat quickened step. Finding her so easily astonished him, like a card trick. He had never paused to think, while traveling to Berlin, that she might long since have died or moved to a different city, and yet the trick had worked. Weiner had turned out to be a different Weiner—and yet fate found a way. Beautiful city, beautiful rain! (The pearly autumn drizzle seemed to fall in a whisper and the streets were dark.) How would she greet him—tenderly? Sadly? Or with complete calm. She had not spoiled him as a child. You are forbidden to run through the drawing room while I am playing the piano. As he grew up, he would feel more and more frequently that she did not have much use for him. Now he tried to picture her face, but his thoughts obstinately refused to take on color, and he simply could not gather in a living optical image what he knew in his mind: her tall, thin figure with that loosely assembled look about her; her dark hair with streaks of gray at the temples; her large, pale mouth; the old raincoat she had on the last time he saw her; and the tired, bitter expression of an aging woman, that seemed to have always been on her face—even before the death of his father,

Admiral Galatov, who had shot himself shortly before the Revolution. Number 51. Eight houses more.

He suddenly realized that he was unendurably, indecently perturbed, much more so than he had been, for example, that first time when he lay pressing his sweat-drenched body against the side of a cliff and aiming at an approaching whirlwind, a white scarecrow on a splendid Arabian horse. He stopped just short of Number 59, took out his pipe and a rubber tobacco pouch; stuffed the bowl slowly and carefully, without spilling a single shred; lit up, coddled the flame, drew, watched the fiery mound swell, gulped a mouthful of sweetish, tongue-prickling smoke, carefully expelled it, and with a firm, unhurried step walked up to the house.

The stairs were so dark that he stumbled a couple of times. When, in the dense blackness, he reached the second-floor landing, he struck a match and made out a gilt nameplate. Wrong name. It was only much higher that he found the odd name "Babb." The flamelet burned his fingers and went out. God, my heart is pounding. . . . He groped for the bell in the dark and rang. Then he removed the pipe from between his teeth and began waiting, feeling an agonizing smile rend his mouth.

Then he heard a lock, a bolt made a double resonant sound, and the door, as if swung by a violent wind, burst open. It was just as dark in the anteroom as on the stairs, and out of that darkness floated a vibrant, joyful voice. "The lights are out in the whole building—*eto oozhas*, it's appalling"—and Nikolay recognized at once that long emphatic "oo" and on its basis instantly reconstructed down to the most minute feature the person who now stood, still concealed by darkness, in the doorway.

"Sure, can't see a thing," said he with a laugh, and advanced toward her.

Her cry was as startled as if a strong hand had struck her. In the dark he found her arms, and shoulders, and bumped against something (probably the umbrella stand). "No, no, it's not possible . . ." she kept repeating rapidly as she backed away.

"Hold still, Mother, hold still for a minute," he said, hitting something again (this time it was the half-open front door, which shut with a great slam).

"It can't be . . . Nicky, Nick—"

He was kissing her at random, on the cheeks, on the hair, everywhere, unable to see anything in the dark but with some interior vision recognizing all of her from head to toe, and only one thing about her had changed (and even this novelty unexpectedly made him recall his earliest childhood, when she used to play the piano): the strong, elegant smell of perfume—as if those intervening years had not existed, the years of his adolescence and her widowhood, when she no longer wore perfume and faded so sorrowfully—it seemed as if nothing of that had happened, and he had passed straight from distant exile into childhood. . . . "It's you. You've come. You're really here," she prattled, pressing her soft lips against him. "It's good. . . . This is how it should be. . . ."

"Isn't there any light anywhere?" Nikolay inquired cheerfully.

She opened an inner door and said excitedly, "Yes, come on. I've lit some candles there."

"Well, let me look at you," he said, entering the flickering aura of candlelight and gazing avidly at his mother. Her dark hair had been bleached a very light strawlike shade.

"Well, don't you recognize me?" she asked, with a nervous intake of breath, then added hurriedly, "Don't stare at me like that. Come on, tell me all the news! What a tan you have . . . my goodness! Yes, tell me everything!"

That blond bob . . . And her face was made up with excruciating care. The moist streak of a tear, though, had eaten through the rosy paint, and her mascara-laden lashes were wet, and the powder on the wings of her nose had turned violet. She was wearing a glossy blue dress closed at the throat. And everything about her was unfamiliar, restless and frightening.

"You're probably expecting company, Mother," observed Nikolay, and not quite knowing what to say next, energetically threw off his overcoat.

She moved away from him toward the table, which was set for a meal and sparkled with crystal in the semidarkness; then she came back toward him, and mechanically glanced at herself in the shadow-blurred mirror.

"So many years have passed. . . . Goodness! I can hardly believe my eyes. Oh, yes, I have friends coming tonight. I'll call them off. I'll phone them. I'll do something. I must call them off. . . . Oh, Lord. . . ."

She pressed against him, palpating him to find out how real he was.

"Calm down, Mother, what's the matter with you—this is overdoing it. Let's sit down somewhere. *Comment vas-tu?* How does life treat you?" . . . And, for some reason fearing the answers to his questions, he started telling her about himself, in the snappy neat way he had, puffing on his pipe, trying to drown his astonishment in words and smoke. It turned out that, after all, she had seen his ad and had been in touch with the old journalist and been on the point of writing to Nikolay—always on the point. . . . Now that he had seen her face distorted by its make-up and her artificially fair hair he felt that her voice, too, was no longer the same. And as he described his adventures, without a moment's pause, he glanced around the half-lit, quivering room, at its awful middle-class trappings—the toy cat on the mantelpiece, the coy screen from behind which protruded the foot of the bed, the picture of Friedrich the Great playing the flute, the bookless shelf with the little vases in which the reflected lights darted up and down like mercury. . . . As his eyes roamed around he also inspected something he had previously only noticed in passing: that table—a table set for two, with liqueurs, a bottle of Asti, two tall wine glasses, and an enormous pink cake adorned with a ring of still unlit little candles. ". . . Of course, I immediately jumped out of my tent, and what do you think it turned out to be? Come on, guess!"

She seemed to emerge from a trance, and gave him a wild look (she was reclining next to him on the divan, her temples compressed between her hands, and her peach-colored stockings gave off an unfamiliar sheen).

"Aren't you listening, Mother?"

"Why, yes—I am. . . ."

And now he noticed something else: she was oddly absent, as if she were listening not to his words but to a doomful thing coming from afar, menacing and inevitable. He went on with his jolly narrative, but then stopped again and asked, "That cake—in whose honor is it? Looks awfully good."

His mother responded with a flustered smile. "Oh, it's a little stunt. I told you I was expecting company."

"It reminded me awfully of Petersburg," said Nikolay. "Remember how you once made a mistake and forgot one candle? I had turned ten, but there were only nine candles. *Tu escamotas* my birthday. I bawled my head off. And how many do we have here?"

"Oh, what does it matter?" she shouted, and rose, almost as if she wanted to block his view of the table. "Why don't you tell me instead what time it is? I must ring up and cancel the party. . . . I must do something."

"Quarter past seven," said Nikolay.

"Trop tard, trop tard!" she raised her voice again. "All right! At this point it no longer matters. . . ."

Both fell silent. She resumed her seat. Nikolay was trying to force himself to hug her, to cuddle up to her, to ask, "Listen, Mother—what has happened to you? Come on: out with it." He took another look at the brilliant table and counted the candles ringing the cake. There were twenty-five of them. Twenty-five! And he was already twenty-eight. . . .

"Please don't examine my room like that!" said his mother. "You look like a regular detective! It's a horrid hole. I would gladly move elsewhere, but I sold the villa that Kind left me." Abruptly she gave a small gasp: "Wait a minute—what was that? Did you make that noise?"

"Yes," answered Nikolay. "I'm knocking the ashes out of my pipe. But tell me: you do still have enough money? You're not having any trouble making ends meet?"

She busied herself with readjusting a ribbon on her sleeve and spoke without looking at him: "Yes. . . . Of course. He left me a few foreign stocks, a hospital and an ancient prison. A prison! . . . But I must warn you that I have barely enough to live on. For heaven's sake stop knocking with that pipe. I must warn you that I . . . That I cannot . . . Oh, you understand, Nick—it would be hard for me to support you."

"What on earth are you talking about, Mother?" exclaimed Nikolay (and at that moment, like a stupid sun issuing from behind a stupid cloud, the electric light burst forth from the ceiling). "There, we can snuff out those tapers now; it was like squatting in the Mostaga Mausoleum. You see, I do have a small supply of cash, and anyway, I like to be as free as a damned fowl of some sort. . . . Come, sit down—stop running around the room."

Tall, thin, bright blue, she stopped in front of him and now, in the full light, he saw how much she had aged, how insistently the wrinkles on her cheeks and forehead showed through the make-up. And that awful bleached hair! . . .

"You came tumbling in so suddenly," she said and, biting her lips, she consulted a small clock standing on the shelf. "Like snow out of a cloudless sky . . . It's fast. No, it's stopped. I'm having company tonight, and here you arrive. It's a crazy situation. . . ."

"Nonsense, Mother. They'll come, they'll see your son has arrived, and very soon they'll evaporate. And before the evening's over you and I will go to some music hall, and have supper somewhere. . . . I remember seeing an African show—that was really something! Imagine—about fifty Negroes, and a rather large, the size of, say—"

The doorbell buzzed loudly in the front hall. Olga Kirillovna, who had perched on the arm of a chair, gave a start and straightened up.

"Wait, I'll get it," said Nikolay, rising.

She caught him by the sleeve. Her face was twitching. The bell stopped. The caller waited.

"It must be your guests," said Nikolay. "Your twenty-five guests. We have to let them in."

His mother gave a brusque shake of her head and resumed listening intently.

"It isn't right—" began Nikolay.

She pulled at his sleeve, whispering, "Don't you dare! I don't want to . . . Don't you dare. . . ."

The bell started buzzing again, insistently and irritably this time. And it buzzed on for a long time.

"Let me go," said Nikolay. "This is silly. If somebody rings you have to answer the door. What are you frightened of?"

"Don't you dare—do you hear," she repeated, spasmodically clutching at his hand. "I implore you. . . . Nicky, Nicky, Nicky! . . . Don't!"

The bell stopped. It was replaced by a series of vigorous knocks, produced, it seemed, by the stout knob of a cane.

Nikolay headed resolutely for the front hall. But before he reached it his mother had grabbed him by the shoulders, and tried with all her might to drag him back, whispering all the while, "Don't you dare. . . . Don't you dare. . . . For God's sake! . . ."

The bell sounded again, briefly and angrily.

"It's your business," said Nikolay with a laugh and, thrusting his hands into his pockets, walked the length of the room. This is a real nightmare, he thought, and chuckled again.

The ringing had stopped. All was still. Apparently the ringer had got fed up and left. Nikolay went up to the table, contemplated the splendid cake with its bright frosting and twenty-five festive candles, and the two wineglasses. Nearby, as if hiding in the bottle's shadow, lay a small white cardboard box. He picked it up and took off the lid. It contained a brand-new, rather tasteless silver cigarette case.

"And that's that," said Nikolay.

His mother, who was half-reclining on the couch with her face buried in a cushion, was convulsed with sobs. In previous years he had often seen her cry, but then she had cried quite differently: while sitting at table, for instance, she would cry without turning her face away, and blow her nose loudly, and talk, talk, talk; yet now she was weeping so girlishly, was lying there with such abandon . . . and there was something so graceful about the curve of her spine and about the way one foot, in its velvet slipper, was touching the floor. . . . One might almost think that it was a young, blond woman crying. . . . And her crumpled handkerchief was lying on the carpet just the way it was supposed to, in that pretty scene.

Nikolay uttered a Russian grunt (*kryak*) and sat down on the edge of her couch. He *kryak*'ed again. His mother, still hiding her face, said into the cushion, "Oh, why couldn't you have come earlier? Even one year earlier . . . Just one year! . . ."

"I wouldn't know," said Nikolay.

"It's all over now," she sobbed, and tossed her light hair. "All over. I'll be fifty in May. Grown-up son comes to see aged mother. And why did you have to come right at this moment . . . tonight!"

Nikolay put on his overcoat (which, contrary to European custom, he had simply thrown into a corner), took his cap out of a pocket, and sat down by her again.

"Tomorrow morning I'll move on," he said, stroking the shiny blue silk of his mother's shoulder. "I feel an urge to head north now, to Norway, perhaps—or else out to sea for some whale fishing. I'll write you. In a year or so we'll meet again, then perhaps I'll stay longer. Don't be cross with me because of my wanderlust!"

Quickly she embraced him and pressed a wet cheek to his neck. Then she squeezed his hand and suddenly cried out in astonishment.

"Blown off by a bullet," laughed Nikolay. "Good-bye, my dearest."

She felt the smooth stub of his finger and gave it a cautious kiss. Then she put her arm around her son and walked with him to the door.

"Please write often. . . . Why are you laughing? All the powder must have come off my face?"

And no sooner had the door shut after him than she flew, her blue dress rustling, to the telephone.

AN AFFAIR OF HONOR

1

T H E accursed day when Anton Petrovich made the acquaintance of Berg existed only in theory, for his memory had not affixed to it a date label at the time, and now it was impossible to identify that day. Broadly speaking, it happened last winter around Christmas, 1926. Berg arose out of nonbeing, bowed in greeting, and settled down again—into an armchair instead of his previous nonbeing. It was at the Kurdyumovs', who lived on St. Mark Strasse, way off in the sticks, in the Moabit section of Berlin, I believe. The Kurdyumovs remained the paupers they had become after the Revolution, while Anton Petrovich and Berg, although also expatriates, had since grown somewhat richer. Now, when a dozen similar ties of a smoky, luminous shade—say that of a sunset cloud—appeared in a haberdasher's window, together with a dozen handkerchiefs in exactly the same tints, Anton Petrovich would buy both the fashionable tie and fashionable handkerchief, and every morning, on his way to the bank, would have the pleasure of encountering the same tie and the same handkerchief, worn by two or three gentlemen who were also hurrying to their offices. At one time he had business relations with Berg; Berg was indispensable, would call up five times a day, began frequenting their house, and would crack endless jokes—God, how he loved to crack jokes. The first time he came, Tanya, Anton Petrovich's wife, found that he resembled an Englishman and was very amusing. "Hello, Anton!" Berg would roar, swooping down on Anton's hand with outspread fingers (the way Russians do), and then shaking it vigorously. Berg was broadshouldered, well-built, clean-shaven, and liked to compare himself to an athletic angel. He once showed Anton Petrovich a little old black notebook. The pages were all covered with crosses, exactly five hundred twenty-three in number. "Civil war in the Crimea—a souvenir," said Berg with a slight smile, and coolly added, "Of course, I counted only those Reds I killed outright." The fact that Berg was an ex–cavalry man and had fought under General Denikin aroused Anton Petrovich's envy, and he hated when Berg would tell, in front of Tanya, of reconnaissance forays and midnight attacks. Anton Petrovich himself was short-legged, rather plump, and wore a monocle, which, in its free time, when not screwed into his eye socket, dangled on a narrow black ribbon and, when Anton Petrovich sprawled in an easy chair, would gleam like a foolish eye on his belly. A boil excised two years before had left a scar on his left cheek. This scar, as well as his coarse, cropped mustache and fat Russian nose, would twitch tensely when Anton Petrovich screwed the monocle home. "Stop making faces," Berg would say, "you won't find an uglier one."

In their glasses a light vapor floated over the tea; a half-squashed chocolate eclair on a plate released its creamy inside; Tanya, her bare elbows resting on the table and her chin leaning on her interlaced fingers, gazed upward at the drifting smoke of her cigarette, and Berg was trying to convince her that she must wear her hair short, that all women, from time immemorial, had done so, that the Venus de Milo had short hair, while Anton Petrovich heatedly and circumstantially objected, and Tanya only shrugged her shoulder, knocking the ash off her cigarette with a tap of her nail.

And then it all came to an end. One Wednesday at the end of July Anton Petrovich left for Kassel on business, and from there sent his wife a telegram that he would return on Friday. On Friday he found that he had to remain at least another week, and sent another telegram. On the following day, however, the deal fell through, and without bothering to wire a third time Anton Petrovich headed back to Berlin. He arrived about ten, tired and dissatisfied with his trip. From the street he saw that the bedroom windows of his flat were aglow, conveying the soothing news that his wife was at home. He went up to the fifth floor, with three twirls of the key unlocked the thrice-locked door, and entered. As he passed through the front hall, he heard the steady noise of running water from the bathroom. Pink and moist, Anton Petrovich thought with fond anticipation, and carried his bag on into the bedroom. In the bedroom, Berg was standing before the wardrobe mirror, putting on his tie.

Anton Petrovich mechanically lowered his little suitcase to the floor, without taking his eyes off Berg, who tilted up his impassive face, flipped back a bright length of tie, and passed it through the knot. "Above all, don't get excited," said Berg, carefully tightening the knot. "Please don't get excited. Stay perfectly calm."

Must do something, Anton Petrovich thought, but what? He felt a tremor in his legs, an absence of legs—only that cold, aching tremor. Do something quick. . . . He started pulling a glove off one hand. The glove was new and fit snugly. Anton Petrovich kept jerking his head and muttering mechanically, "Go away immediately. This is dreadful. Go away. . . ."

"I'm going, I'm going, Anton," said Berg, squaring his broad shoulders as he leisurely got into his jacket.

If I hit him, he'll hit me too, Anton Petrovich thought in a flash. He pulled off the glove with a final yank and threw it awkwardly at Berg. The glove slapped against the wall and dropped into the wash-stand pitcher.

"Good shot," said Berg.

He took his hat and cane, and headed past Anton Petrovich toward the door. "All the same, you'll have to let me out," he said. "The downstairs door is locked."

Scarcely aware of what he was doing, Anton Petrovich followed him out. As they started to go down the stairs, Berg, who was in front, suddenly began to laugh. "Sorry," he said without turning his head, "but this is awfully funny—being kicked out with such complications." At the next landing he chuckled again and accelerated his step. Anton Petrovich also quickened his pace. That dreadful rush was unseemly. . . . Berg was deliberately making him go down in leaps and bounds. What torture . . . Third floor . . . second . . . When will these stairs end? Berg flew down the remaining steps and stood waiting for Anton Petrovich, lightly tapping the floor with his cane. Anton Petrovich was breathing heavily, and had trouble getting the dancing key into the trembling lock. At last it opened.

"Try not to hate me," said Berg from the sidewalk. "Put yourself in my place. . . ."

Anton Petrovich slammed the door. From the very beginning he had had a ripening urge to slam some door or other. The noise made his ears ring. Only now, as he climbed the stairs, did he realize that his face was wet with tears. As he passed through the front hall, he heard again the noise of running water. Hopefully waiting for the tepid to grow hot. But now above that noise he could also hear Tanya's voice. She was singing loudly in the bathroom.

With an odd sense of relief, Anton Petrovich returned to the bed-room. He now saw what he had not noticed before—that both beds were tumbled and that a pink nightgown lay on his wife's. Her new evening dress and a pair of silk stockings were laid out on the sofa: ev-idently, she was getting ready to go dancing with Berg. Anton Petro-vich took his expensive fountain pen out of his breast pocket. "*I cannot bear to see you. I cannot trust myself if I see you."* He wrote standing up, bending awkwardly over the dressing table. His monocle was blurred by a large tear . . . the letters swam. . . . *"Please go away. I am leaving you some cash. I'll talk it over with Natasha tomorrow. Sleep at her house or at a hotel tonight—only please do not stay here."* He finished writing and placed the paper against the mirror, in a spot where she would be sure to see it. Beside it he put a hundred-mark note. And, passing through the front hall, he again heard his wife singing in the bathroom. She had a Gypsy kind of voice, a bewitching voice . . . happiness, a summer night, a guitar . . . she sang that night seated on a cushion in the middle of the floor, and slitted her smiling eyes as she sang. . . . He had just proposed to her . . . yes, happiness, a summer night, a moth bumping against the ceiling, "My soul I surrender to you, I love you with infinite passion. . . ." "How dreadful! How dreadful!" he kept repeating as he walked down the street. The night was very mild, with a swarm of stars. It did not matter which way he went. By now she had probably come out of the bathroom and found the note. Anton Petrovich winced as he remembered the glove. A brand-new glove afloat in a brimming pitcher. The vision of this brown wretched thing caused him to utter a cry that made a passerby start. He saw the dark shapes of huge poplars around a square and thought, Mityushin lives here someplace. Anton Petrovich called him up from a bar, which arose before him as in a dream and then receded into the distance like the taillight of a train. Mityushin let him in but he was drunk, and at first paid no attention to Anton Petrovich's livid face. A person unknown to Anton Petrovich sat in the small dim room, and a black-haired lady in a red dress lay on the couch with her back to the table, apparently asleep. Bottles gleamed on the table. Anton Petrovich had arrived in the middle of a birthday celebration, but he never understood whether it was being held for Mityushin, the fair sleeper, or the unknown man (who turned out to be a Russified German with the strange name of Gnushke). Mityushin, his rosy face beaming, introduced him to Gnushke and, indicating with a nod the generous back of the sleeping lady, remarked casually, "Adelaida Albertovna, I want you to meet a great friend of mine." The lady did not stir; Mityushin, however, did not show the least surprise, as if he had never expected her to wake up. All of this was a little bizarre and nightmarish—that empty vodka bottle with a rose stuck into its neck, that chessboard on which a higgledy-piggledy game was in progress, the sleeping lady, the drunken but quite peaceful Gnushke. . . .

"Have a drink," said Mityushin, and then suddenly raised his eyebrows. "What's the matter with you, Anton Petrovich? You look very ill."

"Yes, by all means, have a drink," with idiotic earnestness said Gnushke, a very long-faced man in a very tall collar, who resembled a dachshund.

Anton Petrovich gulped down half a cup of vodka and sat down.

"Now tell us what's happened," said Mityushin. "Don't be embarrassed in front of Henry—he is the most honest man on earth. My move, Henry, and I warn you, if after this you grab my bishop, I'll mate you in three moves. Well, out with it, Anton Petrovich."

"We'll see about that in a minute," said Gnushke, revealing a big starched cuff as he stretched out his arm. "You forgot about the pawn at h-five."

"H-five yourself," said Mityushin. "Anton Petrovich is going to tell us his story."

Anton Petrovich had some more vodka and the room went into a spin. The gliding chessboard seemed on the point of colliding with the bottles; the bottles, together with the table, set off toward the couch; the couch with mysterious Adelaida Albertovna headed for the window; and the window also started to move. This accursed motion was somehow connected with Berg, and had to be stopped—stopped at once, trampled upon, torn, destroyed. . . .

"I want you to be my second," began Anton Petrovich, and was dimly aware that the phrase sounded oddly truncated but could not correct that flaw.

"Second what?" said Mityushin absently, glancing askance at the chessboard, over which Gnushke's hand hung, its fingers wriggling.

"No, you listen to me," Anton Petrovich exclaimed with anguish in his voice. "You just listen! Let us not drink any more. This is serious, very serious."

Mityushin fixed him with his shiny blue eyes. "The game is canceled, Henry," he said, without looking at Gnushke. "This sounds serious."

"I intend to fight a duel," whispered Anton Petrovich, trying by mere optical force to hold back the table that kept floating away. "I wish to kill a certain person. His name is Berg—you may have met him at my place. I prefer not to explain my reasons. . . ."

"You can explain everything to your second," said Mityushin smugly.

"Excuse me for interfering," said Gnushke suddenly, and raised his index finger. "Remember, it has been said: 'Thou shalt not kill!' "

"The man's name is Berg," said Anton Petrovich. "I think you know him. And I need two seconds." The ambiguity could not be ignored.

"A duel," said Gnushke.

Mityushin nudged him with his elbow. "Don't interrupt, Henry."

"And that is all," Anton Petrovich concluded in a whisper and, lowering his eyes, feebly fingered the ribbon of his totally useless monocle.

Silence. The lady on the couch snored comfortably. A car passed in the street, its horn blaring.

"I'm drunk, and Henry's drunk," muttered Mityushin, "but apparently something very serious has happened." He chewed on his knuckles and looked at Gnushke. "What do you think, Henry?" Gnushke sighed.

"Tomorrow you two will call on him," said Anton Petrovich. "Select the spot, and so on. He did not leave me his card. According to the rules he should have given me his card. I threw my glove at him."

"You are acting like a noble and courageous man," said Gnushke with growing animation. "By a strange coincidence, I am not unfamiliar with these matters. A cousin of mine was also killed in a duel."

Why "also"? Anton Petrovich wondered in anguish. Can this be a portent?

Mityushin took a swallow from his cup and said jauntily: "As a friend, I cannot refuse. We'll go see Mr. Berg in the morning."

"As far as the German laws are concerned," said Gnushke, "if you kill him, they'll put you in jail for several years; if, on the other hand, you are killed, they won't bother you."

"I have taken all that into consideration," Anton Petrovich said solemnly.

Then there appeared again that beautiful expensive implement, that shiny black pen with its delicate gold nib, which in normal times would glide like a wand of velvet across the paper; now, however, Anton Petrovich's hand shook, and the table heaved like the deck of a storm-tossed ship. . . . On a sheet of foolscap that Mityushin produced, Anton Petrovich wrote a cartel of defiance to Berg, three times calling him a scoundrel and concluding with the lame sentence: *"One of us must perish."*

Having done, he burst into tears, and Gnushke, clucking his tongue, wiped the poor fellow's face with a large red-checked handkerchief, while Mityushin kept pointing at the chessboard, repeating ponderously, "You finish him off like that king there—mate in three moves and no questions asked." Anton Petrovich sobbed, and tried to brush away Gnushke's friendly hands, repeating with childish intonations, "I loved her so much, so much!"

And a new sad day was dawning.

"So at nine you will be at his house," said Anton Petrovich, lurching out of his chair.

"At nine we'll be at his house," Gnushke replied like an echo.

"We'll get in five hours of sleep," said Mityushin.

Anton Petrovich smoothed his hat into shape (he had been sitting on it all the while), caught Mityushin's hand, held it for a moment, lifted it, and pressed it to his cheek.

"Come, come, you shouldn't," mumbled Mityushin and, as before, addressed the sleeping lady, "Our friend is leaving, Adelaida Albertovna."

This time she stirred, awakened with a start, and turned over heavily. Her face was full and creased by sleep, with slanting, excessively made-up eyes. "You fellows better stop drinking," she said calmly, and turned back toward the wall.

At the corner of the street Anton Petrovich found a sleepy taxi, which whisked him with ghostly speed through the wastes of the blue-gray city and fell asleep again in front of his house. In the front hall he met Elspeth the maid, who opened her mouth and looked at him with unkind eyes, as if about to say something; but she thought better of it, and shuffled off down the corridor in her carpet slippers.

"Wait," said Anton Petrovich. "Is my wife gone?"

"It's shameful," the maid said with great emphasis. "This is a madhouse. Lug trunks in the middle of the night, turn everything upside down. . . ."

"I asked if my wife was gone," Anton Petrovich shouted in a high-pitched voice.

"She is," glumly answered Elspeth.

Anton Petrovich went on into the parlor. He decided to sleep there. The bedroom, of course, was out of the question. He turned on the light, lay down on the sofa, and covered himself with his overcoat. For some reason his left wrist felt uncomfortable. Oh, of course—my watch. He took it off and wound it, thinking at the same time, Extraordinary, how this man retains his composure—does not even forget to wind his watch. And, since he was still drunk, enormous, rhythmic waves immediately began rocking him, up and down, up and down, and he began to feel very sick. He sat up . . . the big copper ashtray . . . quick. . . . His insides gave such a heave that a pain shot through his groin . . . and it all missed the ashtray. He fell asleep right away. One foot in its black shoe and gray spat dangled from the couch, and the light (which he had quite forgotten to turn off) lent a pale gloss to his sweaty forehead.

2
————

Mityushin was a brawler and a drunkard. He could go and do all kinds of things at the least provocation. A real daredevil. One also recalls having heard about a certain friend of his who, to spite the post office, used to throw lighted matches into mailboxes. He was nicknamed the Gnut. Quite possibly it was Gnushke. Actually, all Anton Petrovich had intended to do was to spend the night at Mityushin's place. Then, suddenly, for no reason at all that talk about duels had started. . . . Oh, of course Berg must be killed; only the matter ought to have been carefully thought out first, and, if it had come to choosing seconds, they should in any case have been gentlemen. As it was, the whole thing had taken on an absurd, improper turn. Everything had been absurd and improper—beginning with the glove and ending with the ashtray. But now, of course, there was nothing to be done about it—he would have to drain this cup. . . .

He felt under the couch, where his watch had landed. Eleven. Mityushin and Gnushke have already been at Berg's. Suddenly a pleasant thought darted among the others, pushed them apart, and disappeared. What was it? Oh, of course! They had been drunk yesterday, and he had been drunk too. They must have overslept, then come to their senses and thought that he had been babbling nonsense; but the pleasant thought flashed past and vanished. It made no difference— the thing had been started and he would have to repeat to them what he had said yesterday. Still, it was odd that they had not shown up yet. A duel. What an impressive word, "duel"! I am having a duel. Hostile meeting. Single combat. Duel. "Duel" sounds best. He got up, and noticed that his trousers were terribly wrinkled. The ashtray had been removed. Elspeth must have come in while he was sleeping. How embarrassing. Must go see how things look in the bedroom. Forget his wife. She did not exist any more. Never had existed. All of that was gone. Anton Petrovich took a deep breath and opened the bedroom door. He found the maid there stuffing a crumpled newspaper into the wastebasket.

"Bring me some coffee, please," he said, and went to the dressing table. There was an envelope on it. His name; Tanya's hand. Beside it, in disorder, lay his hairbrush, his comb, his shaving brush, and an ugly, stiff glove. Anton Petrovich opened the envelope. The hundred marks and nothing else. He turned it this way and that, not knowing what to do with it.

"Elspeth. . . ."

The maid approached, glancing at him suspiciously.

"Here, take it. You were put to so much inconvenience last night, and then those other unpleasant things. . . . Go on, take it."

"One hundred marks?" the maid asked in a whisper, and then suddenly blushed crimson. Heaven only knows what rushed through her head, but she banged the wastebasket down on the floor and shouted, "No! You can't bribe me, I'm an honest woman. Just you wait, I'll tell everybody you wanted to bribe me. No! This is a madhouse. . . ." And she went out, slamming the door.

"What's wrong with her? Good Lord, what's wrong with her?" muttered Anton Petrovich in confusion, and, stepping rapidly to the door, shrieked after the maid, "Get out this minute, get out of this house!"

"That's the third person I've thrown out," he thought, his whole body trembling. "And now there is no one to bring me my coffee."

He spent a long time washing and changing, and then sat in the café across the street, glancing every so often to see if Mityushin and Gnushke were not coming. He had lots of business to attend to in town, but he could not be bothered with business. Duel. A glamorous word.

In the afternoon Natasha, Tanya's sister, appeared. She was so upset that she could barely speak. Anton Petrovich paced back and forth, giving little pats to the furniture. Tanya had arrived at her sister's flat in the middle of the night, in a terrible state, a state you simply could not imagine. Anton Petrovich suddenly found it strange to be saying *"ty"* (thou) to Natasha. After all, he was no longer married to her sister.

"I shall give her a certain sum every month under certain conditions," he said, trying to keep a rising hysterical note out of his voice.

"Money isn't the point," answered Natasha, sitting in front of him and swinging her glossily stockinged leg. "The point is that this is an absolutely awful mess."

"Thanks for coming," said Anton Petrovich, "we'll have another chat sometime, only right now I'm very busy." As he saw her to the door, he remarked casually (or at least he hoped it sounded casual), "I'm fighting a duel with him." Natasha's lips quivered; she quickly kissed him on the cheek and went out. How strange that she did not start imploring him not to fight. By all rights she ought to have implored him not to fight. In our time nobody fights duels. She is wearing the same perfume as . . . As who? No, no, he had never been married.

A little later still, at about seven, Mityushin and Gnushke arrived. They looked grim. Gnushke bowed with reserve and handed Anton Petrovich a sealed business envelope. He opened it. It began: *"I have received your extremely stupid and extremely rude message. . . ."* Anton Petrovich's monocle fell out, he reinserted it. *"I feel very sorry for you, but since you have adopted this attitude, I have no choice but to accept your challenge. Your seconds are pretty awful. Berg."*

Anton Petrovich's throat went unpleasantly dry, and there was again that ridiculous quaking in his legs.

"Sit down, sit down," he said, and himself sat down first. Gnushke sank back into an armchair, caught himself, and sat up on its edge.

"He's a highly insolent character," Mityushin said with feeling. "Imagine—he kept laughing all the while, so that I nearly punched him in the teeth."

Gnushke cleared his throat and said, "There is only one thing I can advise you to do: take careful aim, because he is also going to take careful aim."

Before Anton Petrovich's eyes flashed a notebook page covered with Xs: diagram of a cemetery.

"He is a dangerous fellow," said Gnushke, leaning back in his armchair, sinking again, and again wriggling out.

"Who's going to make the report, Henry, you or I?" asked Mityushin, chewing on a cigarette as he jerked at his lighter with his thumb.

"You'd better do it," said Gnushke.

"We've had a very busy day," began Mityushin, goggling his baby-blue eyes at Anton Petrovich. "At exactly eight-thirty Henry, who was still as tight as a drum, and I . . ."

"I protest," said Gnushke.

". . . went to call on Mr. Berg. He was sipping his coffee. Right off we handed him your little note. Which he read. And what did he do, Henry? Yes, he burst out laughing. We waited for him to finish laughing, and Henry asked what his plans were."

"No, not his plans, but how he intended to react," Gnushke corrected.

". . . to react. To this, Mr. Berg replied that he agreed to fight and that he chose pistols. We have settled all the conditions: the combatants will be placed facing each other at twenty paces. Firing will be regulated by a word of command. If nobody is dead after the first exchange, the duel may go on. And on. What else was there, Henry?"

"If it is impossible to procure real dueling pistols, then Browning automatics will be used," said Gnushke.

"Browning automatics. Having established this much, we asked Mr. Berg how to get in touch with his seconds. He went out to telephone. Then he wrote the letter you have before you. Incidentally, he kept joking all the time. The next thing we did was to go to a café to meet his two chums. I bought Gnushke a carnation for his buttonhole. It was by this carnation that they recognized us. They introduced themselves, and, well, to put it in a nutshell, everything is in order. Their names are Marx and Engels."

"That's not quite exact," interjected Gnushke. "They are Markov and Colonel Arkhangelski."

"No matter," said Mityushin and went on. "Here begins the epic part. We went out of town with these chaps to look for a suitable spot. You know Weissdorf, just beyond Wannsee. That's it. We took a walk through the woods there and found a glade, where, it turned out, these chaps had had a little picnic with their girls the other day. The glade is small, and all around there is nothing but woods. In short, the ideal spot—although, of course, you don't get the grand mountain decor as in Lermontov's fatal affair. See the state of my boots—all white with dust."

"Mine too," said Gnushke. "I must say that trip was quite a strenuous one."

There followed a pause.

"It's hot today," said Mityushin. "Even hotter than yesterday."

"Considerably hotter," said Gnushke.

With exaggerated thoroughness Mityushin began crushing his cigarette in the ashtray. Silence. Anton Petrovich's heart was beating in his throat. He tried to swallow it, but it started pounding even harder. When would the duel take place? Tomorrow? Why didn't they tell him? Maybe the day after tomorrow? It would be better the day after tomorrow. . . .

Mityushin and Gnushke exchanged glances and got up.

"We shall call for you tomorrow at six-thirty a.m.," said Mityushin. "There is no point in leaving sooner. There isn't a damn soul out there anyway."

Anton Petrovich got up too. What should he do? Thank them?

"Well, thank you, gentlemen. . . . Thank you, gentlemen. . . . Everything is settled, then. All right, then."

The others bowed.

"We must still find a doctor and the pistols," said Gnushke.

In the front hall Anton Petrovich took Mityushin by the elbow and mumbled, "You know, it's awfully silly, but you see, I don't know how to shoot, so to speak, I mean, I know how, but I've had no practice at all. . . ."

"Hm," said Mityushin, "that's too bad. Today is Sunday, otherwise you could have taken a lesson or two. That's really bad luck."

"Colonel Arkhangelski gives private shooting lessons," put in Gnushke.

"Yes," said Mityushin. "You're the smart one, aren't you? Still, what are we to do, Anton Petrovich? You know what—beginners are lucky. Put your trust in God and just press the trigger."

They left. Dusk was falling. Nobody had lowered the blinds. There must be some cheese and graham bread in the sideboard. The rooms were deserted and motionless, as if all the furniture had once breathed and moved about but had now died. A ferocious cardboard dentist bending over a panic-stricken patient of cardboard—this he had seen such a short time ago, on a blue, green, violet, ruby night, shot with fireworks, at the Luna Amusement Park. Berg took a long time aiming, the air rifle popped, the pellet hit the target, releasing a spring, and the cardboard dentist yanked out a huge tooth with a quadruple root. Tanya clapped her hands, Anton Petrovich smiled, Berg fired again, and the cardboard discs rattled as they spun, the clay pipes were shattered one after another, and the Ping-Pong ball dancing on a slender jet of water disappeared. How awful. . . . And, most awful of all, Tanya had then said jokingly, "It wouldn't be much fun fighting a duel with you." Twenty paces. Anton Petrovich went from door to window, counting the paces. Eleven. He inserted his monocle, and tried to estimate the distance. Two such rooms. Oh, if only he could manage to disable Berg at the first fire. But he did not know how to aim the thing. He was bound to miss. Here, this letter opener, for example. No, better take this paperweight. You are supposed to hold it like this and take aim. Or like this, perhaps, right up near your chin—it seems easier to do it this way. And at this instant, as he held before him the paperweight in the form of a parrot, pointing it this way and that, Anton Petrovich realized that he would be killed.

At about ten he decided to go to bed. The bedroom, though, was taboo. With great effort he found some clean bedclothes in the dresser, recased the pillow, and spread a sheet over the leather couch in the parlor. As he undressed, he thought, I am going to bed for the last time in my life. Nonsense, faintly squeaked some little particle of Anton Petrovich's soul, the same particle that had made him throw the glove, slam the door, and call Berg a scoundrel. "Nonsense!" Anton Petrovich said in a thin voice, and at once told himself it was not right to say such things. *If I think that nothing will happen to me, then the worst will happen. Everything in life always happens the other way around. It would be nice to read something—for the last time—before going to sleep.*

There I go again, he moaned inwardly. *Why "for the last time"? I am in a terrible state. I must take hold of myself. Oh, if only I were given some sign. Cards?*

He found a deck of cards on a nearby console and took the top card, a three of diamonds. *What does the three of diamonds mean chiromantically? No idea.* Then he drew, in that order, the queen of diamonds, the eight of clubs, the ace of spades. *Ah! That's bad. The ace of spades—I think that means death. But then that's a lot of nonsense, superstitious nonsense. . . . Midnight. Five past. Tomorrow has become today. I have a duel today.*

He sought peace in vain. Strange things kept happening: the book he was holding, a novel by some German writer or other, was called *The Magic Mountain*, and "mountain," in German is *Berg*; he decided that if he counted to three and a streetcar went by at "three" he would be killed, and a streetcar obliged. And then Anton Petrovich did the very worst thing a man in his situation could have done: he decided to reason out what death really meant. When he had thought along these lines for a minute or so, everything lost sense. He found it difficult to breathe. He got up, walked about the room, and took a look out the window at the pure and terrible night sky. *Must write my testament,* thought Anton Petrovich. But to make a will was, so to speak, playing with fire; it meant inspecting the contents of one's own urn in the columbarium. "Best thing is to get some sleep," he said aloud. But as soon as he closed his eyelids, Berg's grinning face would appear before him, purposively slitting one eye. He would turn on the light again, attempt to read, smoke, though he was not a regular smoker. Trivial memories floated by—a toy pistol, a path in the park, that sort of thing—and he would immediately cut short his recollections with the thought that those who are about to die always remember trifles from their past. Then the opposite thing frightened him: he realized that he was not thinking of Tanya, that he was numbed by a strange drug that made him insensitive to her absence. *She was my life and she has gone,* he thought. *I have already, unconsciously, bid life farewell, and everything is now indifferent to me, since I shall be killed. . . .* The night, meanwhile, was beginning to wane.

At about four he shuffled into the dining room and drank a glass of soda water. A mirror near which he passed reflected his striped pajamas and thinning, wispy hair. I'm going to look like my own ghost, he thought. But how can I get some sleep? How?

He wrapped himself in a lap robe, for he noticed that his teeth were chattering, and sat down in an armchair in the middle of the dim room that was slowly ascertaining itself. How will it all be? I must dress soberly, but elegantly. Tuxedo? No, that would be idiotic. A black suit, then . . . and, yes, a black tie. The new black suit. But if there's a wound, a shoulder wound, say . . . The suit will be ruined. . . . The blood, the hole, and, besides, they may start cutting off the sleeve. Nonsense, nothing of the sort is going to happen. I must wear my new black suit. And when the duel starts, I shall turn up my jacket collar—that's the custom, I think, in order to conceal the whiteness of one's shirt, probably, or simply because of the morning damp. That's how they did it in that film I saw. Then I must keep absolutely cool, and address everyone politely and calmly. Thank you, I have already fired. It is your turn now. If you do not remove that cigarette from your mouth I shall not fire. I am ready to continue. "Thank you, I have already laughed"—that's what you say to a stale joke. . . . Oh, if one could only imagine all the details! They would arrive—he, Mityushin, and Gnushke—in a car, leave the car on the road, walk into the woods. Berg and his seconds would probably be waiting there already, they always do in books. Now, there was a question: does one salute one's opponent? What does Onegin do in the opera? Perhaps a discreet tip of the hat from a distance would be just right. Then they would probably start marking off the yards and loading the pistols. What would he do meanwhile? Yes, of course—he would place one foot on a stump somewhere a little way off, and wait in a casual attitude. But what if Berg also put one foot on a stump? Berg was capable of it. . . . Mimicking me to embarrass me. That would be awful. Other possibilities would be to lean against a tree trunk, or simply sit down on the grass. Somebody (in a Pushkin story?) ate cherries from a paper bag. Yes, but you have to bring that bag to the dueling ground—looks silly. Oh, well, he would decide when the time came. Dignified and nonchalant. Then we would take our positions. Twenty yards between us. It would be then that he should turn up his collar. He would grasp the pistol like this. Colonel Angel would wave a handkerchief or count till three. And then, suddenly, something utterly terrible, something absurd would happen—an unimaginable thing, even if one thought about it for nights on end, even if one lived to be a hundred in Turkey. . . . Nice to travel, sit in cafés. . . . What does one feel when a bullet hits one between the ribs or in the forehead? Pain? Nausea? Or is there simply a bang followed by total darkness? The tenor Sobinov once crashed down so realistically that his pistol flew into the orchestra. And what if, instead, he received a ghastly wound of some kind—in one eye, or in the groin? No, Berg would kill him outright. Of course, here I've counted only the ones I killed outright. One more cross in that little black book. Unimaginable. . . .

The dining-room clock struck five: ding-dawn. With a tremendous effort, shivering and clutching at the lap robe, Anton Petrovich got up, then paused again, lost in thought, and suddenly stamped his foot, as Louis XVI stamped his when told it was time, Your Majesty, to go to the scaffold. Nothing to be done about it. Stamped his soft clumsy foot. The execution was inevitable. Time to shave, wash, and dress. Scrupulously clean underwear and the new black suit. As he inserted the opal links into his shirt cuffs, Anton Petrovich mused that opals were the stones of fate and that it was only two or three hours before the shirt would be all bloody. Where would the hole be? He stroked the shiny hairs that went down his fat warm chest, and felt so frightened that he covered his eyes with his hand. There was something pathetically independent about the way everything within him was moving now—the heart pulsating, the lungs swelling, the blood circulating, the intestines contracting—and he was leading to slaughter this tender, defenseless, inner creature, that lived so blindly, so trustingly. . . . Slaughter! He grabbed his favorite shirt, undid one button, and grunted as he plunged headfirst into the cold, white darkness of the linen enveloping him. Socks, tie. He awkwardly shined his shoes with a chamois rag. As he searched for a clean handkerchief he stumbled on a stick of rouge. He glanced into the mirror at his hideously pale face, and then tentatively touched his cheek with the crimson stuff. At first it made him look even worse than before. He licked his finger and rubbed his cheek, regretting that he had never taken a close look at how women apply make-up. A light, brick hue was finally imparted to his cheeks, and he decided it looked all right. "There, I'm ready now," he said, addressing the mirror; then came an agonizing yawn, and the mirror dissolved into tears. He rapidly scented his handkerchief, distributed papers, handkerchief, keys, and fountain pen in various pockets, and slipped into the black noose of his monocle. Pity I don't have a good pair of gloves. The pair I had was nice and new, but the left glove is widowed. The drawback inherent in duels. He sat down at his writing desk, placed his elbows on it, and began waiting, glancing now out of the window, now at the traveling clock in its folding leather case.

It was a beautiful morning. The sparrows twittered like mad in the tall linden tree under the window. A pale-blue, velvet shadow covered the street, and here and there a roof would flash silver. Anton Petrovich was cold and had an unbearable headache. A nip of brandy would be paradise. None in the house. House already deserted; master going away forever. Oh, nonsense. We insist on calmness. The front-door bell will ring in a moment. I must keep perfectly calm. The bell is going to ring right now. They are already three minutes late. Maybe they won't come? Such a marvelous summer morning. . . . Who was the last person killed in a duel in Russia? A Baron Manteuffel, twenty years ago. No, they won't come. Good. He would wait another half-hour, and then go to bed—the bedroom was losing its horror and becoming definitely attractive. Anton Petrovich opened his mouth wide, preparing to squeeze out a huge lump of yawn—he felt the crunch in his ears, the swelling under his palate—and it was then that the door-bell brutally rang. Spasmodically swallowing the unfinished yawn, Anton Petrovich went into the front hall, unlocked the door, and Mityushin and Gnushke ushered each other across the threshold.

"Time to go," said Mityushin, gazing intently at Anton Petrovich. He was wearing his usual pistachio-colored tie, but Gnushke had put on an old frock coat.

"Yes, I am ready," said Anton Petrovich, "I'll be right with you. . . ."

He left them standing in the front hall, rushed into the bedroom, and, in order to gain time, started washing his hands, while he kept repeating to himself, "What is happening? My God, what is happening?" Just five minutes ago there had still been hope, there might have been an earthquake, Berg might have died of a heart attack, fate might have intervened, suspended events, saved him.

"Anton Petrovich, hurry up," called Mityushin from the front hall. Quickly he dried his hands and joined the others.

"Yes, yes, I'm ready, let's go."

"We'll have to take the train," said Mityushin when they were outside. "Because if we arrive by taxi in the middle of the forest, and at this hour, it might seem suspicious, and the driver might tell the police. Anton Petrovich, please don't start losing your nerve."

"I'm not—don't be silly," replied Anton Petrovich with a helpless smile.

Gnushke, who had remained silent until this point, loudly blew his nose and said matter-of-factly: "Our adversary is bringing the doctor. We were unable to find dueling pistols. However, our colleagues did procure two identical Brownings."

In the taxi that was to take them to the station, they seated themselves thus: Anton Petrovich and Mityushin in back, and Gnushke facing them on the jump seat, with his legs pulled in. Anton Petrovich was again overcome by a nervous fit of yawning. That revengeful yawn he had suppressed. Again and again came that humpy spasm, so that his eyes watered. Mityushin and Gnushke looked very solemn, but at the same time seemed exceedingly pleased with themselves.

Anton Petrovich clenched his teeth and yawned with his nostrils only. Then, abruptly, he said, "I had an excellent night's sleep." He tried to think of something else to say. . . .

"Quite a few people in the streets," he said, and added, "In spite of the early hour." Mityushin and Gnushke were silent. Another fit of yawning. Oh, God. . . .

They soon arrived at the station. It seemed to Anton Petrovich that he had never traveled so fast. Gnushke bought the tickets and, holding them fanwise, went ahead. Suddenly he looked around at Mityushin and cleared his throat significantly. By the refreshment booth stood Berg. He was getting some change out of his trouser pocket, thrusting his left hand deep inside it, and holding the pocket in place with his right, the way Anglo-Saxons do in cartoons. He procured a coin in the palm of his hand and, as he handed it to the woman vendor, said something that made her laugh. Berg laughed too. He stood with legs slightly spread. He was wearing a gray flannel suit.

"Let's go around that booth," said Mityushin. "It would be awkward passing right next to him."

A strange numbness came over Anton Petrovich. Totally unconscious of what he was doing, he boarded the coach, took a window seat, removed his hat, donned it again. Only when the train jerked and began to move did his brain start working again, and in this instant he was possessed by the feeling that comes in dreams when, speeding along in a train from nowhere to nowhere, you suddenly realize that you are traveling clad only in your underpants.

"They are in the next coach," said Mityushin, taking out a cigarette case. "Why on earth do you keep yawning all the time, Anton Petrovich? It gives one the creeps."

"I always do in the morning," mechanically answered Anton Petrovich.

Pine trees, pine trees, pine trees. A sandy slope. More pine trees. Such a marvelous morning. . . .

"That frock coat, Henry, is not a success," said Mityushin. "No question about it—to put it bluntly—it just isn't."

"That is my business," said Gnushke.

Lovely, those pines. And now a gleam of water. Woods again. How touching, the world, how fragile. . . . If I could only keep from yawning again . . . jaws aching. If you restrain the yawn, your eyes begin watering. He was sitting with his face turned toward the window, listening to the wheels beating out the rhythm *Abattoir . . . abattoir . . . abattoir . . .*

"Here's what I advise you to do," said Gnushke. "Blaze at once. I advise you to aim at the center of his body—you have more of a chance that way."

"It's all a question of luck," said Mityushin. "If you hit him, fine, and if not, don't worry—he might miss too. A duel becomes real only after the first exchange. It is then that the interesting part begins, so to speak."

A station. Did not stop long. Why did they torture him so? To die today would be unthinkable. What if I faint? You have to be a good actor. . . . What can I try? What shall I do? Such a marvelous morning. . . .

"Anton Petrovich, excuse me for asking," said Mityushin, "but it's important. You don't have anything to entrust to us? I mean, papers, documents. A letter, maybe, or a will? It's the usual procedure."

Anton Petrovich shook his head.

"Pity," said Mityushin. "Never know what might happen. Take Henry and me—we're all set for a sojourn in jail. Are your affairs in order?"

Anton Petrovich nodded. He was no longer able to speak. The only way to keep from screaming was to watch the pines that kept flashing past.

"We get off in a minute," said Gnushke, and rose. Mityushin rose also. Clenching his teeth, Anton Petrovich wanted to rise too, but a jolt of the train made him fall back into his seat.

"Here we are," said Mityushin

Only then did Anton Petrovich manage to separate himself from the seat. Pressing his monocle into his eye socket, he cautiously descended to the platform. The sun welcomed him warmly.

"They are behind," said Gnushke. Anton Petrovich felt his back growing a hump. No, this is unthinkable, I must wake up.

They left the station and set out along the highway, past tiny brick houses with petunias in the windows. There was a tavern at the intersection of the highway and of a soft, white road leading off into the forest. Suddenly Anton Petrovich stopped.

"I'm awfully thirsty," he muttered. "I could do with a drop of something."

"Yes, wouldn't hurt," said Mityushin. Gnushke looked back and said, "They have left the road and turned into the woods."

"It will only take a minute," said Mityushin.

The three of them entered the tavern. A fat woman was wiping the counter with a rag. She scowled at them and poured three mugs of beer.

Anton Petrovich swallowed, choked slightly, and said, "Excuse me for a second."

"Hurry," said Mityushin, putting his mug back on the bar.

Anton Petrovich turned into the passage, followed the arrow to men, mankind, human beings, marched past the toilet, past the kitchen, gave a start when a cat darted under his feet, quickened his step, reached the end of the passage, pushed open a door, and a shower of sunlight splashed his face. He found himself in a little green yard, where hens walked about and a boy in a faded bathing suit sat on a log. Anton Petrovich rushed past him, past some elder bushes, down a couple of wooden steps and into more bushes, then suddenly slipped, for the ground sloped. Branches whipped against his face, and he pushed them aside awkwardly, diving and slipping; the slope, overgrown with elder, kept growing steeper. At last his headlong descent became uncontrollable. He slid down on tense, outspread legs, warding off the springy twigs. Then he embraced an unexpected tree at full speed, and began moving obliquely. The bushes thinned out. Ahead was a tall fence. He saw a loophole in it, rustled through the nettles, and found himself in a pine grove, where shadow-dappled laundry hung between the tree trunks near a shack. With the same purposefulness he traversed the grove and presently realized that he was again sliding downhill. Ahead of him water shimmered among the trees. He stumbled, then saw a path to his right. It led him to the lake.

An old fisherman, suntanned, the color of smoked flounder and wearing a straw hat, indicated the way to the Wannsee station. The road at first skirted the lake, then turned into the forest, and he wandered through the woods for about two hours before emerging at the railroad tracks. He trudged to the nearest station, and as he reached it a train approached. He boarded a car and squeezed in between two passengers, who glanced with curiosity at this fat, pale, moist man in black, with painted cheeks and dirty shoes, a monocle in his begrimed eye socket. Only upon reaching Berlin did he pause for a moment, or at least he had the sensation that, up to that moment, he had been fleeing continuously and only now had stopped to catch his breath and look around him. He was in a familiar square. Beside him an old flower woman with an enormous woolen bosom was selling carnations. A man in an armorlike coating of newspapers was touting the title of a local scandal sheet. A shoeshine man gave Anton Petrovich a fawning look. Anton Petrovich sighed with relief and placed his foot firmly on the stand; whereupon the man's elbows began working lickety-split.

It is all horrible, of course, he thought, as he watched the tip of his shoe begin to gleam. But I am alive, and for the moment that is the main thing. Mityushin and Gnushke had probably traveled back to town and were standing guard before his house, so he would have to wait a while for things to blow over. In no circumstances must he meet them. Much later he would go to fetch his things. And he must leave Berlin that very night. . . .

"*Dobryy den'* [Good day], Anton Petrovich," came a gentle voice right above his ear.

He gave such a start that his foot slipped off the stand. No, it was all right—false alarm. The voice belonged to a certain Leontiev, a man he had met three or four times, a journalist or something of the sort. A talkative but harmless fellow. They said his wife deceived him right and left.

"Out for a stroll?" asked Leontiev, giving him a melancholy handshake.

"Yes. No, I have various things to do," replied Anton Petrovich, thinking at the same time, "I hope he proceeds on his way, otherwise it will be quite dreadful."

Leontiev looked around, and said, as if he had made a happy discovery, "Splendid weather!"

Actually he was a pessimist and, like all pessimists, a ridiculously unobservant man. His face was ill-shaven, yellowish and long, and all of him looked clumsy, emaciated, and lugubrious, as if nature had suffered from toothache when creating him.

The shoeshine man jauntily clapped his brushes together. Anton Petrovich looked at his revived shoes.

"Which way are you headed?" asked Leontiev.

"And you?" asked Anton Petrovich.

"Makes no difference to me. I'm free right now. I can keep you company for a while." He cleared his throat and added insinuatingly, "If you allow me, of course."

"Of course, please do," mumbled Anton Petrovich. Now he's attached himself, he thought. Must find some less familiar street, or else more acquaintances will turn up. If I can only avoid meeting those two. . . .

"Well, how is life treating you?" asked Leontiev. He belonged to the breed of people who ask how life is treating you only to give a detailed account of how it is treating them.

"Oh, well, I am all right," Anton Petrovich replied. Of course he'll find out all about it afterwards. Good Lord, what a mess. "I am going this way," he said aloud, and turned sharply. Smiling sadly at his own thoughts, Leontiev almost ran into him and swayed slightly on lanky legs. "This way? All right, it's all the same to me."

What shall I do? thought Anton Petrovich. After all, I can't just keep strolling with him like this. I have to think things over and decide so much. . . . And I'm awfully tired, and my corns hurt.

As for Leontiev, he had already launched into a long story. He spoke in a level, unhurried voice. He spoke of how much he paid for his room, how hard it was to pay, how hard life was for him and his wife, how rarely one got a good landlady, how insolent theirs was with his wife.

"Adelaida Albertovna, of course, has a quick temper herself," he added with a sigh. He was one of those middle-class Russians who use the patronymic when speaking of their spouses.

They were walking along an anonymous street where the pavement was being repaired. One of the workmen had a dragon tattooed on his bare chest. Anton Petrovich wiped his forehead with his handkerchief and said: "I have some business near here. They are waiting for me. A business appointment."

"Oh, I'll walk you there," said Leontiev sadly.

Anton Petrovich surveyed the street. A sign said "HOTEL." A squalid and squat little hotel between a scaffolded building and a warehouse.

"I have to go in here," said Anton Petrovich. "Yes, this hotel. A business appointment."

Leontiev took off his torn glove and gave him a soft handshake. "Know what? I think I'll wait a while for you. Won't be long, will you?"

"Quite long, I'm afraid," said Anton Petrovich.

"Pity. You see, I wanted to talk something over with you, and ask your advice. Well, no matter. I'll wait around for a while, just in case. Maybe you'll get through early."

Anton Petrovich went into the hotel. He had no choice. It was empty and darkish inside. A disheveled person materialized from behind a desk and asked what he wanted.

"A room," Anton Petrovich answered softly.

The man pondered this, scratched his head, and demanded a deposit. Anton Petrovich handed over ten marks. A red-haired maid, rapidly wiggling her behind, led him down a long corridor and unlocked a door. He entered, heaved a deep sigh, and sat down in a low armchair of ribbed velvet. He was alone. The furniture, the bed, the washstand seemed to awake, to give him a frowning look, and go back to sleep. In this drowsy, totally unremarkable hotel room, Anton Petrovich was at last alone.

Hunching over, covering his eyes with his hand, he lapsed into thought, and before him bright, speckled images passed by, patches of sunny greenery, a boy on a log, a fisherman, Leontiev, Berg, Tanya. And, at the thought of Tanya, he moaned and hunched over even more tensely. Her voice, her dear voice. So light, so girlish, quick of eye and limb, she would perch on the sofa, tuck her legs under her, and her skirt would float up around her like a silk dome and then drop back. Or else, she would sit at the table, quite motionless, only blinking now and then, and blowing out cigarette smoke with her face upturned. It's senseless. . . . Why did you cheat? For you did cheat. What shall I do without you? Tanya! . . . Don't you see—you cheated. My darling—why? Why?

Emitting little moans and cracking his finger joints, he began pacing up and down the room, bumping against the furniture without noticing it. He happened to stop by the window and glance out into the street. At first he could not see the street because of the mist in his eyes, but presently the street appeared, with a truck at the curb, a bicyclist, an old lady gingerly stepping off the sidewalk. And along the sidewalk slowly strolled Leontiev, reading a newspaper as he went; he passed and turned the corner. And, for some reason, at the sight of Leontiev, Anton Petrovich realized just how hopeless his situation was—yes, hopeless, for there was no other word for it. Only yesterday he had been a perfectly honorable man, respected by friends, acquaintances, and fellow workers at the bank. His job! There was not even any question of it. Everything was different now: he had run down a slippery slope, and now he was at the bottom.

"But how can it be? I must decide to do something," Anton Petrovich said in a thin voice. Perhaps there was a way out? They had tormented him for a while, but enough was enough. Yes, he had to decide. He remembered the suspicious gaze of the man at the desk. What should one say to that person? Oh, obviously: "I'm going to fetch my luggage—I left it at the station." So. Good-bye forever, little hotel! The street, thank God, was now clear: Leontiev had finally given up and left. How do I get to the nearest streetcar stop? Oh, just go straight, my dear sir, and you will reach the nearest streetcar stop. No, better take a taxi. Off we go. The streets grow familiar again. Calmly, quite calmly. Tip the taxi driver. Home! Five floors. Calmly, quite calmly he went into the front hall. Then quickly opened the parlor door. My, what a surprise!

In the parlor, around the circular table, sat Mityushin, Gnushke, and Tanya. On the table stood bottles, glasses, and cups. Mityushin beamed—pink-faced, shiny-eyed, drunk as an owl. Gnushke was drunk too, and also beamed, rubbing his hands together. Tanya was sitting with her bare elbows on the table, gazing at him motionlessly. . . .

"At last!" exclaimed Mityushin, and took him by the arm. "At last you've shown up!" He added in a whisper, with a mischievous wink, "You sly-boots, you!"

Anton Petrovich now sits down and has some vodka. Mityushin and Gnushke keep giving him the same mischievous but good-natured looks. Tanya says: "You must be hungry. I'll get you a sandwich."

Yes, a big ham sandwich, with the edge of fat overlapping. She goes to make it and then Mityushin and Gnushke rush to him and begin to talk, interrupting each other.

"You lucky fellow! Just imagine—Mr. Berg also lost his nerve. Well, not 'also,' but lost his nerve anyhow. While we were waiting for you at the tavern, his seconds came in and announced that Berg had changed his mind. Those broad-shouldered bullies always turn out to be cowards. 'Gentlemen, we ask you to excuse us for having agreed to act as seconds for this scoundrel.' That's how lucky you are, Anton Petrovich! So everything is now just dandy. And you came out of it honorably, while he is disgraced forever. And, most important, your wife, when she heard about it, immediately left Berg and returned to you. And you must forgive her."

Anton Petrovich smiled broadly, got up, and started fiddling with the ribbon of his monocle. His smile slowly faded away. Such things don't happen in real life.

He looked at the moth-eaten plush, the plump bed, the washstand, and this wretched room in this wretched hotel seemed to him to be the room in which he would have to live from that day on. He sat down on the bed, took off his shoes, wiggled his toes with relief, and noticed that there was a blister on his heel, and a corresponding hole in his sock. Then he rang the bell and ordered a ham sandwich. When the maid placed the plate on the table, he deliberately looked away, but as soon as the door had shut, he grabbed the sandwich with both hands, immediately soiled his fingers and chin with the hanging margin of fat, and, grunting greedily, began to munch.

THE CHRISTMAS STORY

S ILENCE fell. Pitilessly illuminated by the lamplight, young and plump-faced, wearing a side-buttoned Russian blouse under his black jacket, his eyes tensely downcast, Anton Golïy began gathering the manuscript pages that he had discarded helter-skelter during his reading. His mentor, the critic from *Red Reality*, stared at the floor as he patted his pockets in search of some matches. The writer Novodvortsev was silent too, but his was a different, venerable, silence. Wearing a substantial pince-nez, exceptionally large of forehead, two strands of his sparse dark hair pulled across his bald pate, gray streaks on his close-cropped temples, he sat with closed eyes is if he were still listening, his heavy legs crossed and one hand compressed between a kneecap and a hamstring. This was not the first time he had been subjected to such glum, earnest rustic fictionists. And not the first time he had detected, in their immature narratives, echoes—not yet noted by the critics—of his own twenty-five years of writing; for Golïy's story was a clumsy rehash of one of his subjects, that of "The Verge," a novella he had excitedly and hopefully composed, whose publication the previous year had done nothing to enhance his secure but pallid reputation.

The critic lit a cigarette. Golïy, without raising his eyes, was stuffing his manuscript into his briefcase. But their host kept his silence, not because he did not know how to evaluate the story, but because he was waiting, meekly and drearily, in the hope that the critic might perhaps say the words that he, Novodvortsev, was embarrassed to pronounce: that the subject was Novodvortsev's, that it was Novodvortsev who had inspired the image of that taciturn fellow, selflessly devoted to his laborer grandfather, who, not by dint of education, but rather through some serene, internal power wins a psychological victory over the spiteful intellectual. But the critic, hunched on the edge of the leather couch like a large, melancholy bird, remained hopelessly silent.

Realizing yet again that he would not hear the hoped-for words, and trying to concentrate his thoughts on the fact that, after all, it was to him and not Neverov that the aspiring author had been brought for an opinion, Novodvortsev repositioned his legs, inserted his other hand between them, said with a businesslike tone, "Now, then," and, with a glance at the vein that had swelled on Goliy's forehead, began speaking in a quiet, even voice. He said the story was solidly constructed, that one felt the power of the Collective in the place where the peasants start building a school with their own means, that, in the description of Pyotr's love for Anyuta there might be imperfections of style, but one heard the call of spring and of a wholesome lust—and, all the while as he talked, he kept remembering for some reason how he had written recently to this same critic, to remind him that his twenty-fifth anniversary as an author would fall in January, but that he emphatically requested that no festivities be organized, given that his years of dedicated work for the Union were not yet over. . . .

"As for your intellectual, you didn't get him right," he was saying. "There is no real sense of his being doomed. . . ."

The critic still said nothing. He was a red-haired man, skinny and decrepit, rumored to be ill with consumption, but in reality probably healthy as a bull. He had replied, also by letter, that he approved of Novodvortsev's decision, and that had been the end of it. He must have brought Goliy by way of secret compensation. . . . Novodvortsev suddenly felt so sad—not hurt, just sad—that he stopped short and started wiping his lenses with his handkerchief, revealing quite kindly eyes.

The critic rose. "Where are you off to? It's still early," said Novodvortsev, but he got up too. Anton Goliy cleared his throat and pressed his briefcase to his side.

"He will become a writer, there's no doubt about it," said the critic with indifference, roaming about the room and stabbing the air with his spent cigarette. Humming, with a raspy sound, through his teeth, he drooped over the desk, then stood for a time by an étagère where a respectable edition of *Das Kapital* dwelt between a tattered volume of Leonid Andreyev and a nameless tome with no binding; finally, with the same stooping gait, he approached the window and drew the blue blind aside.

"Drop in sometime," Novodvortsev was meanwhile saying to Anton Goliy, who bowed jerkily and then squared his shoulders with a swagger. "When you've written something more, bring it on over."

"Heavy snowfall," said the critic, releasing the blind. "By the way, today is Christmas Eve."

He began rummaging listlessly for his coat and hat.

"In the old days, on this date, you and your confreres would be churning out Christmas copy. . . ."

"Not I," said Novodvortsev.

The critic chuckled. "Pity. You ought to do a Christmas story. New-style."

Anton Golïy coughed into his fist. "Back home we once had—" he began in a hoarse bass, then cleared his throat again.

"I'm being serious," continued the critic, climbing into his coat. "One can devise something very clever. . . . Thanks, but it's already—"

"Back home," Anton Golïy said, "We once had. A teacher. Who. Took it into his head. To do a Christmas tree for the kids. On top he stuck. A red star."

"No, that won't quite do," said the critic. "It's a little heavy-handed for a small story. You can put a keener edge on it. Struggle between two different worlds. All against a snowy background."

"One should be careful with symbols generally," glumly said Novodvortsev. "Now I have a neighbor—upstanding man, party member, active militant, yet he uses expressions like 'Golgotha of the Proletariat.' . . ."

When his guests had left he sat down at his desk and propped an ear on his thick, white hand. By the inkstand stood something akin to a square drinking glass with three pens stuck into a caviar of blue glass pellets. The object was some ten or fifteen years old—it had withstood every tumult, whole worlds had shaken apart around it—but not a single glass pellet had been lost. He selected a pen, moved a sheet of paper into place, tucked a few more sheets under it so as to write on a plumper surface. . . .

"But what about?" Novodvortsev said out loud, then pushed his chair aside with his thigh and began pacing the room. There was an unbearable ringing in his left ear.

The scoundrel said it deliberately, he thought, and, as if following in the critic's recent footsteps, went to the window.

Presumes to advise me. . . . And that derisive tone of his. . . . Probably thinks I have no originality left in me. . . . I'll go and do a real Christmas story. . . . And he himself will recollect, in print: "I drop in on him one evening and, between one thing and another, happen to suggest, 'Dmitri Dmitrievich, you ought to depict the struggle between the old order and the new against a background of so-called Christmas snow. You could carry through to its conclusion the theme you traced so remarkably in "The Verge"—remember Tumanov's dream? That's the theme I mean. . . .' And on that night was born the work which . . ."

The window gave onto a courtyard. The moon was not visible. . . . No, on second thought, there *is* a sheen coming from behind a dark chimney over there. Firewood was stacked in the courtyard, covered with a sparkling carpet of snow. In a window glowed the green dome of a lamp—someone was working at his desk, and the abacus shimmered as if its beads were made of colored glass. Suddenly, in utter silence, some lumps of snow fell from the roof's edge. Then, again, a total torpor.

He felt the tickling vacuum that always accompanied the urge to write. In this vacuum something was taking shape, growing. A new, special kind of Christmas. . . . Same old snow, brand-new conflict. . . .

He heard cautious footfalls through the wall. It was his neighbor coming home, a discreet, polite fellow, a Communist to the marrow of his bones. With an abstract rapture, a delicious expectation, Novodvortsev returned to his seat at the desk. The mood, the coloring of the developing work, was already there. He had only to create the skeleton, the subject. A Christmas tree—that's where he should start. In some homes, he imagined people who had formerly been somebody, people who were terrified, ill-tempered, doomed (he imagined them so clearly . . .), who must surely be putting paper ornaments on a fir stealthily cut down in the woods. There was no place to buy that tinsel now, and they didn't heap fir trees in the shadow of Saint Isaac's any more. . . .

Cushioned, as if bundled up in cloth, there came a knock. The door opened a couple of inches. Delicately, without poking in his head, the neighbor said, "May I bother you for a pen? A blunt one would be nice, if you have it."

Novodvortsev did.

"Thank you kindly," said the neighbor, soundlessly closing the door.

This insignificant interruption somehow weakened the image that had already been ripening. He recalled that, in "The Verge," Tumanov felt nostalgia for the pomp of former holidays. Mere repetition wouldn't do. Another recollection flashed inopportunely past. At a recent party some young woman had said to her husband, "In many ways you bear a strong resemblance to Tumanov." For a few days he felt very happy. But then he made the lady's acquaintance, and the Tumanov turned out to be her sister's fiancé. Nor had that been the first disillusionment. One critic had told him he was going to write an article on "Tumanovism." There was something infinitely flattering about that "ism," and about the small *t* with which the word began in Russian. The critic, however, had left for the Caucasus to study the Georgian poets. Yet there had been pleasant occurrences as well. For instance, a list like "Gorky, Novodvortsev, Chirikov . . ."

In an autobiography accompanying his complete works (six volumes with portrait of the author), he had described how he, the son of humble parents, had made his way in the world. His youth had, in reality, been happy. A healthy vigor, faith, successes. Twenty-five years had passed since a plump journal had carried his first story. Korolenko had liked him. He had been arrested now and then. One newspaper had been closed down on his account. Now his civic aspirations had been fulfilled. Among beginning, younger writers he felt free and at ease. His new life suited him to a T. Six volumes. His name well known. But his fame was pallid, pallid. . . .

He skipped back to the Christmas-tree image, and suddenly, for no apparent reason, remembered the parlor of a merchant family's house, a large volume of articles and poems with gilt-edged pages (a benefit edition for the poor) somehow connected with that house, the Christmas tree in the parlor, the woman he loved in those days, and all of the tree's lights reflected as a crystal quiver in her wide-open eyes when she plucked a tangerine from a high branch. It had been twenty years ago or more—how certain details stuck in one's memory. . . .

He abandoned this recollection with chagrin and imagined once again the same old shabby fir trees that, at this very moment, were surely being decorated. . . . No story there, although of course one *could* give it a keener edge. . . . Émigrés weeping around a Christmas tree, decked out in their uniforms redolent of mothballs, looking at the tree and weeping. Somewhere in Paris. Old general recalls how he used to smack his men in the teeth as he cuts an angel out of gilded cardboard. . . . He thought about a general whom he actually knew, who actually was abroad now, and there was no way he could picture him weeping as he knelt before a Christmas tree. . . .

"I'm on the right track, though," Novodvortsev said aloud, impatiently pursuing some thought that had slipped away. Then something new and unexpected began to take shape in his fancy—a European city, a well-fed, fur-clad populace. A brightly lit store window. Behind it an enormous Christmas tree, with hams stacked at its base and expensive fruit affixed to its branches. Symbol of well-being. And in front of the window, on the frozen sidewalk—

With triumphal agitation, sensing that he had found the necessary, one-and-only key, that he would write something exquisite, depict as no one had before the collision of two classes, of two worlds, he commenced writing. He wrote about the opulent tree in the shamelessly illuminated window and about the hungry worker, victim of a lockout, peering at that tree with a severe and somber gaze.

"*The insolent Christmas tree,*" wrote Novodvortsev, "*was afire with every hue of the rainbow.*"

THE POTATO ELF

ACTUALLY his name was Frederic Dobson. To his friend the conjuror, he talked about himself thus:

"There was no one in Bristol who didn't know Dobson the tailor for children's clothes. I am his son—and am proud of it out of sheer stubbornness. You should know that he drank like an old whale. Some time around 1900, a few months before I was born, my gin-soaked dad rigged up one of those waxwork cherubs, you know—sailor suit, with a lad's first long trousers—and put it in my mother's bed. It's a wonder the poor thing did not have a miscarriage. As you can well understand, I know all this only by hearsay—yet, if my kind informers were not liars, this is, apparently, the secret reason I am—"

And Fred Dobson, in a sad and good-natured gesture, would spread out his little hands. The conjuror, with his usual dreamy smile, would bend down, pick up Fred like a baby, and, sighing, place him on the top of a wardrobe, where the Potato Elf would meekly roll up and start to sneeze softly and whimper.

He was twenty, and weighed less than fifty pounds, being only a couple of inches taller than the famous Swiss dwarf, Zimmermann (dubbed "Prince Balthazar"). Like friend Zimmermann, Fred was extremely well built, and had there not been those wrinkles on his round forehead and at the corners of his narrowed eyes, as well as a rather eerie air of tension (as if he were resisting growth), our dwarf would have easily passed for a gentle eight-year-old boy. His hair, the hue of damp straw, was sleeked down and evenly parted by a line which ran up the exact middle of his head to conclude a cunning agreement with its crown. Fred walked lightly, had an easy demeanor, and danced rather well, but his very first manager deemed it wise to weight the notion of "elf" with a comic epithet upon noticing the fat nose inherited by the dwarf from his plethoric and naughty father.

The Potato Elf, by his sole aspect, aroused a storm of applause and laughter throughout England, and then in the main cities of the Continent. He differed from most dwarfs in being of a mild and friendly nature. He became greatly attached to the miniature pony Snowdrop, on which he trotted diligently around the arena of a Dutch circus; and, in Vienna, he conquered the heart of a stupid and glum giant hailing from Omsk by stretching up to him the first time he saw him and pleading like an infant to be taken up in Nurse's arms.

He usually performed not alone. In Vienna, for example, he appeared with the Russian giant and minced around him, neatly attired in striped trousers and a smart jacket, with a voluminous roll of music under his arm. He brought the giant's guitar. The giant stood like a tremendous statue and took the instrument with the motions of an automaton. A long frock coat that looked carved out of ebony, elevated heels, and a top hat with a sheen of columnar reflections increased the height of the stately three-hundred-and-fifty-pound Siberian. Thrusting out his powerful jaw, he beat the strings with one finger. Backstage, in womanish tones, he complained of giddiness. Fred grew very fond of him and even shed a few tears at the moment of separation, for he rapidly became accustomed to people. His life, like a circus horse's, went round and round with smooth monotony. One day in the dark of the wings, he tripped over a bucket of house paint and mellowly plopped into it—an occurrence he kept recalling for quite a long while as something out of the ordinary.

In this way the dwarf traveled around most of Europe, and saved money, and sang with a *castrato*-like silvery voice, and in German variety theaters the audience ate thick sandwiches and candied nuts on sticks, and in Spanish ones, sugared violets and also nuts on sticks. The world was invisible to him. There remained in his memory the same faceless abyss laughing at him, and afterwards, when the performance was over, the soft, dreamy echo of a cool night that seems of such a deep blue when you leave the theater.

Upon returning to London he found a new partner in the person of Shock, the conjuror. Shock had a tuneful delivery, slender, pale, virtually ethereal hands, and a lick of chestnut-brown hair that came down on one eyebrow. He resembled a poet more than a stage magician, and demonstrated his skill with a sort of tender and graceful melancholy, without the fussy patter characteristic of his profession. The Potato Elf assisted him amusingly and, at the end of the act, would turn up in the gallery with a cooing exclamation of joy, although a minute before everyone had seen Shock lock him up in a black box right in the middle of the stage.

All this happened in one of those London theaters where there are acrobats soaring in the tinkle-and-shiver of the trapezes, and a foreign tenor (a failure in his own country) singing barcaroles, and a ventriloquist in naval uniform, and bicyclists, and the inevitable clown-eccentric shuffling about in a minuscule hat and a waistcoat coming down to his knees.

2

Latterly Fred had been growing gloomy, and sneezing a lot, soundlessly and sadly, like a little Japanese spaniel. While not experiencing for months any hankering after a woman, the virginal dwarf would be beset now and then by sharp pangs of lone amorous anguish which went as suddenly as they came, and again, for a while, he would ignore the bare shoulders showing white beyond the velvet boundary of loges, as well as the little girl acrobats, or the Spanish dancer whose sleek thighs were revealed for a moment when the orange-red curly fluff of her nether flounces would whip up in the course of a rapid swirl.

"What you need is a female dwarf," said Shock pensively, producing with a familiar flick of finger and thumb a silver coin from the ear of the dwarf, whose little arm went up in a brushing-away curve as if chasing a fly.

That same night, as Fred, after his number, snuffling and grumbling, in bowler and tiny topcoat, was toddling along a dim backstage passage, a door came ajar with a sudden splash of gay light and two voices called him in. It was Zita and Arabella, sister acrobats, both half-undressed, suntanned, black-haired, with elongated blue eyes. A shimmer of theatrical disorder and the fragrance of lotions filled the room. The dressing table was littered with powder puffs, combs, cut-glass atomizers, hairpins in an ex–chocolate box, and rouge sticks.

The two girls instantly deafened Fred with their chatter. They tickled and squeezed the dwarf, who, glowering and empurpled with lust, rolled like a ball in the embrace of the bare-armed teases. Finally, when frolicsome Arabella drew him to her and fell backward upon the couch, Fred lost his head and began to wriggle against her, snorting and clasping her neck. In attempting to push him away, she raised her arm and, slipping under it, he lunged and glued his lips to the hot pricklish hollow of her shaven axilla. The other girl, weak with laughter, tried in vain to drag him off by his legs. At that moment the door banged open, and the French partner of the two aerialists came into the room wearing marble-white tights. Silently, without any resentment, he grabbed the dwarf by the scruff of the neck (all you heard was the snap of Fred's wing collar as one side broke loose from the stud), lifted him in the air, and threw him out like a monkey. The door slammed. Shock, who happened to be wandering past, managed to catch a glimpse of the marble-bright arm and of a black little figure with feet retracted in flight.

Fred hurt himself in falling and now lay motionless in the corridor. He was not really stunned, but had gone all limp, with eyes fixed on one point, and fast-chattering teeth.

"Bad luck, old boy," sighed the conjuror, picking him up from the floor. He palpated with translucent fingers the dwarf's round forehead and added, "I told you not to butt in. Now you got it. A dwarf woman is what you need."

Fred, his eyes bulging, said nothing.

"You'll sleep at my place tonight," decided Shock, and carried the Potato Elf toward the exit.

3

There existed also a Mrs. Shock.

She was a lady of uncertain age, with dark eyes which had a yellowish tinge around the iris. Her skinny frame, parchment complexion, lifeless black hair, a habit of strongly exhaling tobacco smoke through her nostrils, the studied untidiness of her attire and hairdo—all this could hardly attract many men, but, no doubt, was to Mr. Shock's liking, though actually he never seemed to notice his wife, as he was always engaged in imagining secret devices for his show, always appeared unreal and shifty, thinking of something else when talking about trivialities, but keenly observing everything around him when immersed in astral fancies. Nora had to be constantly on the lookout, since he never missed the occasion to contrive some small, inutile, yet subtly artful deception. There had been, for instance, that time when he amazed her by his unusual gluttony: he smacked his lips juicily, sucked chicken bones clean, again and again heaped up food on his plate; then he departed after giving his wife a sorrowful glance; and a little later the maid, giggling into her apron, informed Nora that Mr. Shock had not touched one scrap of his dinner, and had left all of it in three brand-new pans under the table.

She was the daughter of a respectable artist who painted only horses, spotty hounds, and huntsmen in pink coats. She had lived in Chelsea before her marriage, had admired the hazy Thames sunsets, taken drawing lessons, gone to ridiculous meetings attended by the local Bohemian crowd—and it was there that the ghost-gray eyes of a quiet slim man had singled her out. He talked little about himself, and was still unknown. Some people believed him to be a composer of lyrical poems. She fell headlong in love with him. The poet absentmindedly became engaged to her, and on the very first day of matrimony explained, with a sad smile, that he did not know how to write poetry, and there and then, in the middle of the conversation, he transformed an old alarm clock into a nickel-plated chronometer, and the chronometer into a miniature gold watch, which Nora had worn ever since on her wrist. She understood that nevertheless conjuror Shock was, in his own way, a poet: only she could not get used to his demonstrating his art every minute, in all circumstances. It is hard to be happy when one's husband is a mirage, a peripatetic legerdemain of a man, a deception of all five senses.

4

―――――

She was idly tapping a fingernail against the glass of a bowl in which several goldfish that looked cut out of orange peel breathed and fin-flashed when the door opened noiselessly, and Shock appeared (silk hat askew, strand of brown hair on his brow) with a little creature all screwed up in his arms.

"Brought him," said the conjuror with a sigh.

Nora thought fleetingly: Child. Lost. Found. Her dark eyes grew moist.

"Must be adopted," softly added Shock, lingering in the doorway.

The small thing suddenly came alive, mumbled something, and started to scrabble shyly against the conjuror's starched shirtfront. Nora glanced at the tiny boots in chamois spats, at the little bowler.

"I'm not so easy to fool," she sneered.

The conjuror looked at her reproachfully. Then he laid Fred on a plush couch and covered him with a lap robe.

"Blondinet roughed him up," explained Shock, and could not help adding, "Bashed him with a dumbbell. Right in the tummy."

And Nora, kindhearted as childless women frequently are, felt such an especial pity that she almost broke into tears. She proceeded to mother the dwarf, she fed him, gave him a glass of port, rubbed his forehead with eau de cologne, moistened with it his temples and the infantine hollows behind his ears.

Next morning Fred woke up early, inspected the unfamiliar room, talked to the goldfish, and after a quiet sneeze or two, settled on the ledge of the bay window like a little boy.

A melting, enchanting mist washed London's gray roofs. Somewhere in the distance an attic window was thrown open, and its pane caught a glint of sunshine. The horn of an automobile sang out in the freshness and tenderness of dawn.

Fred's thoughts dwelt on the previous day. The laughing accents of the girl tumblers got oddly mixed up with the touch of Mrs. Shock's cold fragrant hands. At first he had been ill-treated, then he had been caressed; and, mind you, he was a very affectionate, very ardent dwarf. He dwelt in fancy on the possibility of his rescuing Nora someday from a strong, brutal man resembling that Frenchman in white tights. Incongruously, there floated up the memory of a fifteen-year-old female dwarf with whom he appeared together at one time. She was a bad-tempered, sick, sharp-nosed little thing. The two were presented to the spectators as an engaged couple, and, shivering with disgust, he had to dance an intimate tango with her.

Again a lone klaxon sang out and swept by. Sunlight was beginning to infuse the mist over London's soft wilderness.

Around half-past seven the flat came to life. With an abstract smile Mr. Shock left for an unknown destination. From the dining room came the delicious smell of bacon and eggs. With her hair done anyhow, wearing a kimono embroidered with sunflowers, appeared Mrs. Shock.

After breakfast she offered Fred a perfumed cigarette with a red-petaled tip and, half-closing her eyes, had him tell her about his existence. At such narrative moments Fred's little voice deepened slightly: he spoke slowly, choosing his words, and, strange to say, that unforeseen dignity of diction became him. Bent-headed, solemn, and elastically tense, he sat sideways at Nora's feet. She reclined on the plush divan, her arms thrown back, revealing her sharp bare elbows. The dwarf, having finished his tale, lapsed into silence but still kept turning this way and that the palm of his tiny hand, as if softly continuing to speak. His black jacket, inclined face, fleshy little nose, tawny hair, and that middle parting reaching the back of his head vaguely moved Nora's heart. As she looked at him through her lashes she tried to imagine that it was not an adult dwarf sitting there, but her nonexistent little son in the act of telling her how his schoolmates bullied him. Nora stretched her hand and stroked his head lightly—and, at that moment, by an enigmatic association of thought, she called forth something else, a curious, vindictive vision.

Upon feeling those light fingers in his hair, Fred at first sat motionless, then began to lick his lips in feverish silence. His eyes, turned askance, could not detach their gaze from the green pompon on Mrs. Shock's slipper. And all at once, in some absurd and intoxicating way, everything came into motion.

5

_____

On that smoke-blue day, in the August sun, London was particularly lovely. The tender and festive sky was reflected in the smooth spread of the asphalt, the glossy pillar boxes glowed crimson at the street corners, through the Gobelin green of the park cars flashed and rolled with a low hum—the entire city shimmered and breathed in the mellow warmth, and only underground, on the platforms of the Tube, could one find a region of coolness.

Every separate day in the year is a gift presented to only one man—the happiest one; all other people use his day, to enjoy the sunshine or berate the rain, never knowing, however, to whom that day really belongs; and its fortunate owner is pleased and amused by their ignorance. A person cannot foreknow which day exactly will fall to his lot, what trifle he will remember forever: the ripple of reflected sunlight on a wall bordering water or the revolving fall of a maple leaf; and it often happens that he recognizes *his* day only in retrospection, long after he has plucked, and crumpled, and chucked under his desk the calendar leaf with the forgotten figure.

Providence granted Fred Dobson, a dwarf in mouse-gray spats, the merry August day in 1920 which began with the melodious hoot of a motor horn and the flash of a casement swung open in the distance. Children coming back from a walk told their parents, with gasps of wonder, that they had met a dwarf in a bowler hat and striped trousers, with a cane in one hand and a pair of tan gloves in the other.

After ardently kissing Nora good-bye (she was expecting visitors), the Potato Elf came out on the broad smooth street, flooded with sunlight, and instantly knew that the whole city had been created for him and only for him. A cheerful taxi driver turned down with a resounding blow the iron flag of his meter; the street started to flow past, and Fred kept slipping off the leathern seat, while chuckling and cooing under his breath.

He got out at the Hyde Park entrance, and without noticing the looks of curiosity, minced along, by the green folding chairs, by the pond, by the great rhododendron bushes, darkling under the shelter of elms and lindens, above a turf as bright and bland as billiard cloth. Riders sped past, lightly going up and down on their saddles, the yellow leather of their leggings creaking, the slender faces of their steeds springing up, their bits clinking; and expensive black motorcars, with a dazzling glitter of wheel spokes, progressed sedately over the ample lacework of violet shade.

The dwarf walked, inhaling the warm whiffs of benzine, the smell of foliage that seemed to rot with the overabundance of green sap, and twirled his cane, and pursed his lips as if about to whistle, so great was the sense of liberation and lightness overwhelming him. His mistress had seen him off with such hurried tenderness, had laughed so nervously, that he realized how much she feared that her old father, who always came to lunch, would begin to suspect something if he found a strange gentleman in the house.

That day he was seen everywhere: in the park, where a rosy nurse in a starched bonnet offered him for some reason a ride in the pram she was pushing; and in the halls of a great museum; and on the escalator that slowly crept out of rumbling depths where electric winds blew among brilliant posters; and in an elegant shop where only men's handkerchiefs were sold; and on the crest of a bus, where he was hoisted by someone's kind hands.

And after a while he became tired—all that motion and glitter dazed him, the laughing eyes staring at him got on his nerves, and he felt he must ponder carefully the ample sensation of freedom, pride, and happiness which kept accompanying him.

When finally a hungry Fred entered the familiar restaurant where all kinds of performers gathered and where his presence could not surprise anyone, and when he looked around at those people, at the old dull clown who was already drunk, at the Frenchman, a former enemy, who now gave him a friendly nod, Mr. Dobson realized with perfect clarity that never again would he appear on the stage.

The place was darkish, with not enough lamps lit inside and not enough outside day filtering in. The dull clown resembling a ruined banker, and the acrobat who looked oddly uncouth in mufti, were playing a silent game of dominoes. The Spanish dancing girl, wearing a cartwheel hat that cast a blue shadow on her eyes, sat with crossed legs all alone at a corner table. There were half a dozen people whom Fred did not know; he examined their features which years of make-up had bleached; meanwhile the waiter brought a cushion to prop him up, changed the tablecloth, nimbly laid the cover.

All at once, in the dim depths of the restaurant, Fred distinguished the delicate profile of the conjuror, who was talking in undertone to an obese old man of an American type. Fred had not expected to run here into Shock—who never frequented taverns—and in point of fact had totally forgotten about his existence. He now felt so sorry for the poor magician that, at first, he decided to conceal everything; but then it occurred to him that Nora could not cheat anyway and would probably tell her husband that very evening ("I've fallen in love with Mr. Dobson. . . . I'm leaving you")—and that she should be spared a difficult, disagreeable confession, for was he not her knight, did he not feel proud of her love, should he not, therefore, be justified in causing her husband pain, no matter the pity?

The waiter brought him a piece of kidney pie and a bottle of ginger beer. He also switched on more light. Here and there, above the dusty plush, crystal flowers glowed forth, and the dwarf saw from afar a golden gleam bring out the conjuror's chestnut forelock, and the light and shade shuttle over his tender transparent fingers. His interlocutor rose, clawing at the belt of his pants and obsequiously grinning, and Shock accompanied him to the cloakroom. The fat American donned a wide-brimmed hat, shook Shock's ethereal hand, and, still hitching up his pants, made for the exit. Momentarily one discerned a chink of lingering daylight, while the restaurant lamps glowed yellower. The door closed with a thud.

"Shock!" called the Potato Elf, wiggling his short feet under the table.

Shock came over. On his way, he pensively took a lighted cigar out of his breast pocket, inhaled, let out a puff of smoke, and put the cigar back. Nobody knew how he did it.

"Shock," said the dwarf, whose nose had reddened from the ginger beer, "I must speak to you. It is most important."

The conjuror sat down at Fred's table and leaned his elbow upon it.

"How's your head—doesn't hurt?" he inquired indifferently.

Fred wiped his lips with the napkin; he did not know how to start, still fearing to cause his friend too much anguish.

"By the way," said Shock, "tonight I appear together with you for the last time. That chap is taking me to America. Things look pretty good."

"I say, Shock—" and the dwarf, crumbling bread, groped for adequate words. "The fact is . . . Be brave, Shock. I love your wife. This morning, after you left, she and I, we two, I mean, she—"

"Only I'm a bad sailor," mused the conjuror, "and it's a week to Boston. I once sailed to India. Afterwards I felt as a leg does when it goes to sleep."

Fred, flushing purple, rubbed the tablecloth with his tiny fist. The conjuror chuckled softly at his own thoughts, and then asked, "You were about to tell me something, my little friend?"

The dwarf looked into his ghostly eyes and shook his head in confusion.

"No, no, nothing. . . . One can't talk to you."

Shock's hand stretched out—no doubt he intended to snip out a coin from Fred's ear—but for the first time in years of masterly magic, the coin, not grasped by the palm muscles firmly enough, fell out the wrong way. He caught it up and rose.

"I'm not going to eat here," said he, examining curiously the crown of the dwarf's head. "I don't care for this place."

Sulky and silent, Fred was eating a baked apple.

The conjuror quietly left. The restaurant emptied. The languorous Spanish dancer in the large hat was led off by a shy, exquisitely dressed young man with blue eyes.

Well, if he doesn't want to listen, that settles it, reflected the dwarf; he sighed with relief and decided that after all Nora would explain things better. Then he asked for notepaper and proceeded to write her a letter. It closed as follows:

Now you understand why I cannot continue to live as before. What feelings would you experience knowing that every evening the common herd rocks with laughter at the sight of your chosen one? I am breaking my contract, and tomorrow I shall be leaving. You will receive another letter from me as soon as I find a peaceful nook where after your divorce we shall be able to love one another, my Nora.

Thus ended the swift day given to a dwarf in mouse-colored spats.

6
———————

London was cautiously darkening. Street sounds blended in a soft hollow note, as if someone had stopped playing but still kept his foot on the piano pedal. The black leaves of the limes in the park were patterned against the transparent sky like aces of spades. At this or that turning, or between the funereal silhouettes of twin towers, a burning sunset was revealed like a vision.

It was Shock's custom to go home for dinner and change into professional tails so as to drive afterwards straight to the theater. That evening Nora awaited him most impatiently, quivering with evil glee. How glad she was to have now her own private secret! The image of the dwarf himself she dismissed. The dwarf was a nasty little worm.

She heard the lock of the entrance door emit its delicate click. As so often happens when one has betrayed a person, Shock's face struck her as new, as almost that of a stranger. He gave her a nod, and shamefully, sadly lowered his long-lashed eyes. He took his place opposite her at the table without a word. Nora considered his light-gray suit that made him seem still more slender, still more elusive. Her eyes lit up with warm triumph; one corner of her mouth twitched malevolently.

"How's your dwarf?" she inquired, relishing the casualness of her question. "I thought you'd bring him along."

"Haven't seen him today," answered Shock, beginning to eat. All at once he thought better of it—took out a vial, uncorked it with a careful squeak, and tipped it over a glassful of wine.

Nora expected with irritation that the wine would turn a bright blue, or become as translucent as water, but the claret did not change its hue. Shock caught his wife's glance and smiled dimly.

"For the digestion—just drops," he murmured. A shadow rippled across his face.

"Lying as usual," said Nora. "You've got an excellent stomach."

The conjuror laughed softly. Then he cleared his throat in a businesslike way, and drained his glass in one gulp.

"Get on with your food," said Nora. "It will be cold."

With grim pleasure she thought, Ah, if you only knew. You'll never find out. That's my power!

The conjuror ate in silence. Suddenly he made a grimace, pushed his plate away, and started to speak. As usual, he kept looking not directly at her, but a little above her, and his voice was melodious and soft. He described his day, telling her he had visited the king at Windsor, where he had been invited to amuse the little dukes, who wore velvet jackets and lace collars. He related all this with light vivid touches, mimicking the people he had seen, twinkling, cocking his head slightly.

"I produced a whole flock of white doves from my gibus," said Shock.

And the dwarf's little palms were clammy, and you're making it all up, reflected Nora in brackets.

"Those pigeons, you know, went flying around the queen. She shoo-flied them but kept smiling out of politeness."

Shock got up, swayed, lightly leaned on the table edge with two fingers, and said, as if completing his story: "I'm not feeling well, Nora. That was poison I drank. You shouldn't have been unfaithful to me."

His throat swelled convulsively, and, pressing a handkerchief to his lips, he left the dining room. Nora sprang up; the amber beads of her long necklace caught at the fruit knife upon her plate and brushed it off.

It's all an act, she thought bitterly. Wants to scare me, to torment me. No, my good man, it's no use. You shall see!

How vexing that Shock had somehow discovered her secret! But at least she would now have the opportunity to reveal all her feelings to him, to shout that she hated him, that she despised him furiously, that he was not a person, but a phantom of rubber, that she could not bear to live with him any longer, that—

The conjuror sat on the bed, all huddled up and gritting his teeth in anguish, but he managed a faint smile when Nora stormed into the bedroom.

"So you thought I'd believe you," she said, gasping. "Oh no, that's the end! I, too, know how to cheat. You repel me, oh, you're a laughingstock with your unsuccessful tricks—"

Shock, still smiling helplessly, attempted to get off the bed. His foot scraped against the carpet. Nora paused in an effort to think what else she could yell in the way of insult.

"Don't," uttered Shock with difficulty. "If there was something that I . . . please, forgive. . . ."

The vein in his forehead was tensed. He hunched up still more, his throat rattled, the moist lock on his brow shook, and the handkerchief at his mouth got all soaked with bile and blood.

"Stop playing the fool!" cried Nora and stamped her foot.

He managed to straighten up. His face was wax-pale. He threw the balled rag into a corner.

"Wait, Nora. . . . You don't understand. . . . This is my very last trick. . . . I won't do any other. . . ."

Again a spasm distorted his terrible, shiny face. He staggered, fell on the bed, threw back his head on the pillow.

She came near, she looked, knitting her brows. Shock lay with closed eyes and his clenched teeth creaked. When she bent over him, his eyelids quivered, he glanced at her vaguely, not recognizing his wife, but suddenly he did recognize her and his eyes flickered with a humid light of tenderness and pain.

At that instant Nora knew that she loved him more than anything in the world. Horror and pity overwhelmed her. She whirled about the room, poured out some water, left the glass on the washstand, dashed back to her husband, who had raised his head and was pressing the edge of the sheet to his lips, his whole body shuddering as he retched heavily, staring with unseeing eyes which death had already veiled. Then Nora with a wild gesture dashed into the next room, where there was a telephone, and there, for a long time, she joggled the holder, repeated the wrong number, rang again, sobbing for breath and hammering the telephone table with her fist; and finally, when the doctor's voice responded, Nora cried that her husband had poisoned himself, that he was dying; upon which she flooded the receiver with a storm of tears, and cradling it crookedly, ran back into the bedroom.

The conjuror, bright-faced and sleek, in white waistcoat and impeccably pressed black trousers, stood before the pier glass and, elbows parted, was meticulously working upon his tie. He saw Nora in the mirror, and without turning gave her an absentminded twinkle while whistling softly and continuing to knead with transparent fingertips the black ends of his silk bow.

7

———

Drowse, a tiny town in the north of England, looked, indeed, so somnolent that one suspected it might have been somehow mislaid among those misty, gentle-sloped fields where it had fallen asleep forever. It had a post office, a bicycle shop, two or three tobacconists with red and blue signs, an ancient gray church surrounded by tombstones over which stretched sleepily the shade of an enormous chestnut tree. The main street was lined with hedges, small gardens, and brick cottages diagonally girt with ivy. One of these had been rented to a certain F. R. Dobson whom nobody knew except his housekeeper and the local doctor, and he was no gossiper. Mr. Dobson, apparently, never went out. The housekeeper, a large stern woman, who had formerly been employed in an insane asylum, would answer the casual questions of neighbors by explaining that Mr. Dobson was an aged paralytic, doomed to vegetate in curtained silence. No wonder the inhabitants forgot him the same year that he arrived in Drowse: he became an un-noticeable presence whom people took for granted as they did the unknown bishop whose stone effigy had been standing so long in its niche above the church portal. The mysterious old man was thought to have a grandchild—a quiet fair-haired little boy who sometimes, at dusk, used to come out of the Dobson cottage with small, timid steps. This happened, however, so seldom that nobody could say for sure that it was always the same child, and, of course, twilight at Drowse was particularly blurry and blue, softening every outline. Thus the un-curious and sluggish Drowsians missed the fact that the supposed grandson of the supposed paralytic did not grow as the years went by and that his flaxen hair was nothing but an admirably made wig; for the Potato Elf started to go bald at the very beginning of his new ex-istence, and his head was soon so smooth and glossy that Ann, his housekeeper, thought at times what fun it would be to fit one's palm over that globe. Otherwise, he had not much changed: his tummy, perhaps, had grown plumper, and purple veins showed through on his dingier, fleshier nose which he powdered when dressed up as a little boy. Furthermore, Ann and his doctor knew that the heart attacks be-setting the dwarf would come to no good.

He lived peacefully and inconspicuously in his three rooms, sub-scribed to a circulating library at the rate of three or four books (mostly novels) per week, acquired a black yellow-eyed cat because he mortally feared mice (which bumped about somewhere behind the wardrobe as if rolling minute balls of wood), ate a lot, especially sweet-meats (sometimes jumping up in the middle of the night and pattering along the chilly floor, eerily small and shivery in his long nightshirt, to get, like a little boy, at the chocolate-coated biscuits in the pantry), and recalled less and less frequently his love affair and the first dreadful days he had spent in Drowse.

Nevertheless, in his desk, among wispy, neatly folded playbills, he still preserved a sheet of peach-colored notepaper with a dragon-shaped watermark, scribbled over in an angular, barely legible hand. Here is what it said:

Dear Mr. Dobson

  I received your first letter, as well as your second one, in which you ask me to come to D. All this, I am afraid, is an awful misunderstanding. Please try to forget and forgive me. Tomorrow my husband and I are leaving for the States and shall probably not be back for quite some time. I simply do not know what more I can write you, my poor Fred.

It was then that the first attack of angina pectoris occurred. A meek look of astonishment remained since then in his eyes. And during a number of days afterwards he would walk from room to room, swallowing his tears and gesturing in front of his face with one trembling tiny hand.

Presently, though, Fred began to forget. He grew fond of the coziness he had never known before—of the blue film of flame over the coals in the fireplace, of the dusty small vases on their own rounded small shelves, of the print between two casements: a St. Bernard dog, complete with barrelet, reviving a mountaineer on his bleak rock. Rarely did he recollect his past life. Only in dream did he sometimes see a starry sky come alive with the tremor of many trapezes while he was being clapped into a black trunk: through its walls he distinguished Shock's bland singsong voice but could not find the trap in the floor of the stage and suffocated in sticky darkness, while the conjuror's voice grew sadder and more remote and melted away, and Fred would wake up with a groan on his spacious bed, in his snug, dark room, with its faint fragrance of lavender, and would stare for a long time, gasping for breath and pressing his child's fist to his stumbling heart, at the pale blur of the window blind.

As the years passed, the yearning for a woman's love sighed in him fainter and fainter, as if Nora had drained him of all the ardor that had tormented him once. True, there were certain times, certain vague spring evenings, when the dwarf, having shyly put on short pants and the blond wig, left the house to plunge into crepuscular dimness, and there, stealing along some path in the fields, would suddenly stop as he looked with anguish at a dim pair of lovers locked in each other's arms near a hedge, under the protection of brambles in blossom. Presently that too passed, and he ceased seeing the world altogether. Only once in a while the doctor, a white-haired man with piercing black eyes, would come for a game of chess and, across the board, would consider with scientific delight those tiny soft hands, that little bulldoggish face, whose prominent brow would wrinkle as the dwarf pondered a move.

8

Eight years elapsed. It was Sunday morning. A jug of cocoa under a cozy in the guise of a parrot's head was awaiting Fred on the breakfast table. The sunny greenery of apple trees streamed through the window. Stout Ann was in the act of dusting the little pianola on which the dwarf occasionally played wobbly waltzes. Flies settled on the jar of orange marmalade and rubbed their front feet.

Fred came in, slightly sleep-rumpled, wearing carpet slippers and a little black dressing gown with yellow frogs. He sat down slitting his eyes and stroking his bald head. Ann left for church. Fred pulled open the illustrated section of a Sunday paper and, alternately drawing in and pouting his lips, examined at length prize pups, a Russian ballerina folding up in a swan's languishing agony, the top hat and mug of a financier who had bamboozled everyone . . . Under the table the cat, curving her back, rubbed herself against his bare ankle. He finished his breakfast; rose, yawning: he had had a very bad night, never yet had his heart caused him such pain, and now he felt too lazy to dress, although his feet were freezing. He transferred himself to the window-nook armchair and curled up in it. He sat there without a thought in his head, and near him the black cat stretched, opening tiny pink jaws.

The doorbell tinkled.

Doctor Knight, reflected Fred indifferently, and remembering that Ann was out, went to open the door himself.

Sunlight poured in. A tall lady all in black stood on the threshold. Fred recoiled, muttering and fumbling at his dressing gown. He dashed back into the inner rooms, losing one slipper on the way but ignoring it, his only concern being that whoever had come must not notice he was a dwarf. He stopped, panting, in the middle of the parlor. Oh, why hadn't he simply slammed shut the entrance door! And who on earth could be calling on him? A mistake, no doubt.

And then he heard distinctly the sound of approaching steps. He retreated to the bedroom; wanted to lock himself up, but there was no key. The second slipper remained on the rug in the parlor.

"This is dreadful," said Fred under his breath and listened.

The steps had entered the parlor. The dwarf emitted a little moan and made for the wardrobe, looking for a hiding place.

A voice that he certainly knew pronounced his name, and the door of the room opened:

"Fred, why are you afraid of me?"

The dwarf, barefooted, black-robed, his pate beaded with sweat, stood by the wardrobe, still holding on to the ring of its lock. He recalled with the utmost clarity the orange-gold fish in their glass bowl.

She had aged unhealthily. There were olive-brown shadows under her eyes. The little dark hairs above her upper lip had become more distinct than before; and from her black hat, from the severe folds of her black dress, there wafted something dusty and woeful.

"I never expected—" Fred slowly began, looking up at her warily.

Nora took him by the shoulders, turned him to the light, and with eager, sad eyes examined his features. The embarrassed dwarf blinked, deploring his wiglessness and marveling at Nora's excitement. He had ceased thinking of her so long ago that now he felt nothing except sadness and surprise. Nora, still holding him, shut her eyes, and then, lightly pushing the dwarf away, turned toward the window.

Fred cleared his throat and said: "I lost sight of you entirely. Tell me, how's Shock?"

"Still performing his tricks," replied Nora absently. "We returned to England only a short while ago."

Without removing her hat she sat down near the window and kept staring at him with odd intensity.

"It means that Shock—" hastily resumed the dwarf, feeling uneasy under her gaze.

"—Is the same as ever," said Nora, and, still not taking her glistening eyes from the dwarf, quickly peeled off and crumpled her glossy black gloves, which were white inside.

Can it be that she again—? abruptly wondered the dwarf. There rushed through his mind the fishbowl, the smell of eau de cologne, the green pompons on her slippers.

Nora got up. The black balls of her gloves rolled on the floor.

"It's not a big garden but it has apple trees," said Fred, and continued to wonder inwardly: Had there really been a moment when I—? Her skin is quite sallow. She has a mustache. And why is she so silent?

"I seldom go out, though," said he, rocking slightly back and forth in his seat and massaging his knees.

"Fred, do you know why I'm here?" asked Nora.

She rose and came up to him quite close. Fred with an apologetic grin tried to escape by slipping off his chair.

It was then that she told him in a very soft voice: "The fact is I had a son from you."

The dwarf froze, his gaze fixing a minuscule casement burning on the side of a dark blue cup. A timid smile of amazement flashed at the corners of his lips, then it spread, and lit up his cheeks with a purplish flush.

"My . . . son . . ."

And all at once he understood everything, all the meaning of life, of his long anguish, of the little bright window upon the cup.

He slowly raised his eyes. Nora sat sideways on a chair and was shaking with violent sobs. The glass head of her hatpin glittered like a teardrop. The cat, purring tenderly, rubbed itself against her legs.

He dashed up to her, he remembered a novel read a short while ago: "You have no cause," said Mr. Dobson, "no cause whatever for fearing that I may take him away from you. I am so happy!"

She glanced at him through a mist of tears. She was about to explain something, but gulped—saw the tender and joyful radiance with which the dwarf's countenance breathed—and explained nothing.

She hastened to pick up her crumpled gloves.

"Well, now you know. Nothing more is necessary. I must be going."

A sudden thought stabbed Fred. Acute shame joined the quivering joy. He inquired, fingering the tassel of his dressing gown.

"And . . . and what is he like? He is not—"

"Oh, on the contrary," replied Nora rapidly. "A big boy, like all boys," And again she burst into tears.

Fred lowered his eyes.

"I would like to see him."

Joyously he corrected himself: "Oh, I understand! He must not know that I am like this. But perhaps you might arrange—"

"Yes, by all means," said Nora, hurriedly, and almost sharply, as she stepped through the hall. "Yes, we'll arrange something. I must be on my way. It's a twenty-minute walk to the railway station."

She turned her head in the doorway and for the last time, avidly and mournfully, she examined Fred's features. Sunlight trembled on his bald head, his ears were of a translucent pink. He understood nothing in his amazement and bliss. And after she had gone, Fred remained standing for a long time in the hallway, as if afraid to spill his full heart with an imprudent movement. He kept trying to imagine his son, and all he could do was to imagine his own self dressed as a schoolboy and wearing a little blond wig. And by the act of transferring his own aspect onto his boy, he ceased to feel that he was a dwarf.

He saw himself entering a house, a hotel, a restaurant, to meet his son. In fancy, he stroked the boy's fair hair with poignant parental pride. . . . And then, with his son and Nora (silly goose—to fear he would snatch him away!), he saw himself walking down a street, and there—

Fred clapped his thighs. He had forgotten to ask Nora where and how he could reach her!

Here commenced a crazy, absurd sort of phase. He rushed to his bedroom, began to dress in a wild hurry. He put on the best things he had, an expensive starched shirt, practically new, striped trousers, a jacket made by Resartre of Paris years ago—and as he dressed, he kept chuckling, and breaking his fingernails in the chinks of tight commode drawers, and had to sit down once or twice to let his swelling and knocking heart rest; and again he went skipping about the room looking for the bowler he had not worn for years, and at last, on consulting a mirror in passing, he glimpsed the image of a stately elderly gentleman, in smart formal dress, and ran down the steps of the porch, dazzled by a new idea: to travel back with Nora—whom he would certainly manage to overtake—and to see his son that very evening!

A broad dusty road led straight to the station. It was more or less deserted on Sundays—but unexpectedly a boy with a cricket bat appeared at a corner. He was the first to notice the dwarf. In gleeful surprise he slapped himself on the top of his bright-colored cap as he watched Fred's receding back and the flicking of his mouse-gray spats.

And instantly, from God knows where, more boys appeared, and with gaping stealthiness started to follow the dwarf. He walked faster and faster, now and then looking at his watch, and chuckling excitedly. The sun made him feel a little queasy. Meanwhile, the number of boys increased, and chance passersby stopped to look in wonder. Somewhere afar church chimes rang forth: the drowsy town was coming to life—and all of a sudden it burst into uncontrollable, long-restrained laughter.

The Potato Elf, unable to master his eagerness, switched to a jog. One of the lads darted in front of him to have a look at his face; another yelled something in a rude hoarse voice. Fred, grimacing because of the dust, ran on, and abruptly it seemed to him that all those boys crowding in his wake were his sons, merry, rosy, well-built sons—and he smiled a bewildered smile as he trotted along, puffing and trying to forget the heart breaking his chest with a burning ram.

A cyclist, riding beside the dwarf on glittering wheels, pressed his fist to his mouth like a megaphone and urged the sprinter along as they do at a race. Women came out on their porches and, shading their eyes and laughing loudly, pointed out the running dwarf to one another. All the dogs of the town woke up. The parishioners in the stuffy church could not help listening to the barking, to the inciting halloos. And the crowd that kept up with the dwarf continued to grow around him. People thought it was all a capital stunt, circus publicity or the shooting of a picture.

Fred was beginning to stumble, there was a singing in his ears, the front stud of his collar dug into his throat, he could not breathe. Moans of mirth, shouts, the tramping of feet deafened him. Then through the fog of sweat he saw at last her black dress. She was slowly walking along a brick wall in a torrent of sun. She looked back, she stopped. The dwarf reached her and clutched at the folds of her skirt.

With a smile of happiness he glanced up at her, attempted to speak, but instead raised his eyebrows in surprise and collapsed in slow motion on the sidewalk. All around people noisily swarmed. Someone, realizing that this was no joke, bent over the dwarf, then whistled softly and bared his head. Nora looked listlessly at Fred's tiny body resembling a crumpled black glove. She was jostled. A hand grasped her elbow.

"Leave me alone," said Nora in a toneless voice. "I don't know anything. My son died a few days ago."

THE AURELIAN

1

Luring aside one of the trolley-car numbers, the street started at the corner of a crowded avenue. For a long time it crept on in obscurity, with no shopwindows or any such joys. Then came a small square (four benches, a bed of pansies) round which the trolley steered with rasping disapproval. Here the street changed its name, and a new life began. Along the right side, shops appeared: a fruiterer's, with vivid pyramids of oranges; a tobacconist's, with the picture of a voluptuous Turk; a delicatessen, with fat brown and gray coils of sausages; and then, all of a sudden, a butterfly store. At night, and especially when it was damp, with the asphalt shining like the back of a seal, passersby would stop for a second before that symbol of fair weather. The insects on exhibit were huge and gorgeous. People would say to themselves, "What colors—amazing!" and plod on through the drizzle. Eyed wings wide-open in wonder, shimmering blue satin, black magic—these lingered for a while floating in one's vision, until one boarded the trolley or bought a newspaper. And, just because they were together with the butterflies, a few other objects would remain in one's memory: a globe, pencils, and a monkey's skull on a pile of copybooks.

As the street blinked and ran on, there followed again a succession of ordinary shops—soap, coal, bread—with another pause at the corner where there was a small bar. The bartender, a dashing fellow in a starched collar and green sweater, was deft at shaving off with one stroke the foam topping the glass under the beer tap; he also had a well-earned reputation as a wit. Every night, at a round table by the window, the fruiterer, the baker, an unemployed man, and the bartender's first cousin played cards with great gusto. As the winner of the current stake immediately ordered four drinks, none of the players could ever get rich.

On Saturdays, at an adjacent table, there would sit a flabby elderly man with a florid face, lank hair, and a grayish mustache, carelessly clipped. When he appeared, the players greeted him noisily without looking up from their cards. He invariably ordered rum, filled his pipe, and gazed at the game with pink-rimmed watery eyes. The left eyelid drooped slightly.

Occasionally someone turned to him, and asked how his shop was doing; he would be slow to answer, and often did not answer at all. If the bartender's daughter, a pretty freckled girl in a polka-dotted frock, happened to pass close enough, he had a go at her elusive hip, and, whether the slap succeeded or not, his gloomy expression never changed, although the veins on his temple grew purple. Mine host very humorously called him "Herr Professor." "Well, how is the Herr Professor tonight?" he would ask, coming over to him, and the man would ponder for some time in silence and then, with a wet underlip pushing out from under the pipe like that of a feeding elephant, he would answer something neither funny nor polite. The bartender would counter briskly, which made the players at the next table, though seemingly absorbed in their cards, rock with ugly glee.

The man wore a roomy gray suit with great exaggeration of the vest motif, and when the cuckoo popped out of the clock he ponderously extracted a thick silver watch and gazed at it askance, holding it in the palm of his hand and squinting because of the smoke. Punctually at eleven he knocked out his pipe, paid for his rum, and, after extending a flaccid hand to anyone who might choose to shake it, silently left.

He walked awkwardly, with a slight limp. His legs seemed too thin for his body. Just before the window of his shop he turned into a passage, where there was a door on the right with a brass plate: PAUL PILGRAM. This door led into his tiny dingy apartment, which could also be reached by an inner corridor at the back of the shop. Eleanor was usually asleep when he came home on those festive nights. Half a dozen faded photographs of the same clumsy ship, taken from different angles, and of a palm tree that looked as bleak as if it were growing on Helgoland hung in black frames above the double bed. Muttering to himself, Pilgram limped away into bulbless darkness with a lighted candle, came back with his suspenders dangling, and kept muttering while sitting on the edge of the bed and slowly, painfully, taking off his shoes. His wife, half-waking, moaned into her pillow and offered to help him; and then with a threatening rumble in his voice, he would tell her to keep quiet, and repeated that guttural *"Ruhe!"* several times, more and more fiercely.

After the stroke which had almost killed him some time ago (like a mountain falling upon him from behind just as he had bent toward his shoestrings), he now undressed reluctantly, growling until he got safely into bed, and then growling again if the faucet happened to drip in the adjoining kitchen. Eleanor would roll out of bed and totter into the kitchen and totter back with a dazed sigh, her small face wax-pale and shiny, and the plastered corns on her feet showing from under her dismally long nightgown. They had married in 1905, almost a quarter of a century before, and were childless because Pilgram had always thought that children would be merely a hindrance to the realization of what had been in his youth a delightfully exciting plan but had now gradually become a dark, passionate obsession.

He slept on his back with an old-fashioned nightcap coming down on his forehead; it was to all appearances the solid and sonorous sleep that might be expected in an elderly German shopkeeper, and one could readily suppose that his quilted torpor was entirely devoid of visions; but actually this churlish, heavy man, who fed mainly on *Erbswurst* and boiled potatoes, placidly believing in his newspaper and quite ignorant of the world (insofar as his secret passion was not involved), dreamed of things that would have seemed utterly unintelligible to his wife or his neighbors; for Pilgram belonged, or rather was meant to belong (something—the place, the time, the man—had been ill-chosen), to a special breed of dreamers, such dreamers as used to be called in the old days "Aurelians"—perhaps on account of those chrysalids, those "jewels of nature," which they loved to find hanging on fences above the dusty nettles of country lanes.

On Sundays he drank his morning coffee in several sloppy sessions, and then went out for a walk with his wife, a slow silent stroll which Eleanor looked forward to all week. On workdays he opened his shop as early as possible because of the children who passed by on their way to school; for lately he had been keeping school supplies in addition to his basic stock. Some small boy, swinging his satchel and chewing a sandwich, would slouch past the tobacconist's (where a certain brand of cigarettes offered airplane pictures), past the delicatessen (which rebuked one for having eaten that sandwich long before lunchtime), and then, remembering he wanted an eraser, would enter the next shop. Pilgram would mumble something, sticking out his lower lip from under the stem of his pipe and, after a listless search, would plump down an open carton on the counter. The boy would feel and squeeze the virgin-pale India rubber, would not find the sort he favored, and would leave without even noticing the principal wares in the store.

These modern children! Pilgram would think with disgust and he recalled his own boyhood. His father—a sailor, a rover, a bit of a rogue—married late in life a sallow-skinned, light-eyed Dutch girl whom he brought from Java to Berlin, and opened a shop of exotic curios. Pilgram could not remember now when, exactly, butterflies had begun to oust the stuffed birds of paradise, the stale talismans, the fans with dragons, and the like; but as a boy he already feverishly swapped specimens with collectors, and after his parents died butterflies reigned supreme in the dim little shop. Up to 1914 there were enough amateurs and professionals about to keep things going in a mild, very mild, way; later on, however, it became necessary to make concessions, a display case with the biography of the silkworm furnishing a transition to school supplies, just as in the old days pictures ignominiously composed of sparkling wings had probably been a first step toward lepidopterology.

Now the window contained, apart from penholders, mainly showy insects, popular stars among butterflies, some of them set on plaster and framed—intended merely for ornamenting the home. In the shop itself, permeated with the pungent odor of a disinfectant, the real, the precious collections were kept. The whole place was littered with various cases, cartons, cigar boxes. Tall cabinets contained numerous glass-lidded drawers filled with ordered series of perfect specimens impeccably spread and labeled. A dusty old shield or something (last remnant of the original wares) stood in a dark corner. Now and then live stock would appear: loaded brown pupae with a symmetrical confluence of delicate lines and grooves on the thorax, showing how the rudimentary wings, feet, antennae, and proboscis were packed. If one touched such a pupa as it lay on its bed of moss, the tapering end of the segmented abdomen would start jerking this way and that like the swathed limbs of a baby. The pupae cost a reichsmark apiece and in due time yielded a limp, bedraggled, miraculously expanding moth. And sometimes other creatures would be temporarily on sale: just then there happened to be a dozen lizards, natives of Majorca, cold, black, blue-bellied things, which Pilgram fed on mealworms for the main course and grapes for dessert.

2
—————

He had spent all his life in Berlin and its suburbs; had never traveled farther than Peacock Island on a neighboring lake. He was a first-class entomologist. Dr. Rebel, of Vienna, had named a certain rare moth *Agrotis pilgrami*; and Pilgram himself had published several descriptions. His boxes contained most of the countries of the world, but all he had ever seen of it was the dull sand-and-pine scenery of an occasional Sunday trip; and he would be reminded of captures that had seemed to him so miraculous in his boyhood as he melancholically gazed at the familiar fauna about him, limited by a familiar landscape, to which it corresponded as hopelessly as he to his street. From a roadside shrub he would pick up a large turquoise-green caterpillar with a china-blue horn on the last ring; there it lay quite stiff on the palm of his hand, and presently, with a sigh, he would put it back on its twig as if it were some dead trinket.

Although once or twice he had had the chance to switch to a more profitable business—selling cloth, for instance, instead of moths—he stubbornly held on to his shop as the symbolic link between his dreary existence and the phantom of perfect happiness. What he craved for, with a fierce, almost morbid intensity, was *himself* to net the rarest butterflies of distant countries, to see them in flight with his own eyes, to stand waist-deep in lush grass and feel the follow-through of the swishing net and then the furious throbbing of wings through a clutched fold of the gauze.

Every year it seemed to him stranger that the year before he had not managed somehow to lay aside enough money for at least a fortnight's collecting trip abroad, but he had never been thrifty, business had always been slack, there was always a gap somewhere, and, even if luck did come his way now and then, something was sure to go wrong at the last moment. He had married counting heavily on a share in his father-in-law's business, but a month later the man had died, leaving nothing but debts. Just before World War I an unexpected deal brought a journey to Algeria so near that he even acquired a sun helmet. When all travel stopped, he still consoled himself with the hope that he might be sent to some exciting place as a soldier; but he was clumsy, sickly, not very young, and thus saw neither active service nor exotic lepidoptera. Then, after the war, when he had managed again to save a little money (for a week in Zermatt, this time), the inflation suddenly turned his meager hoard into something less than the price of a trolley-car ticket.

After that he gave up trying. He grew more and more depressed as his passion grew stronger. When some entomological acquaintance happened to drop in, Pilgram was only annoyed. That fellow, he would think, may be as learned as the late Dr. Staudinger, but he has no more imagination than a stamp collector. The glass-lidded trays over which both were bending gradually took up the whole counter, and the pipe in Pilgram's sucking lips kept emitting a wistful squeak. Pensively he gazed at the serried rows of delicate insects, all alike to you or me, and now and then he tapped on the glass with a stubby forefinger, stressing some special rarity. "That's a curiously dark aberration," the learned visitor might say. "Eisner got one like that at an auction in London, but it was not so dark, and it cost him fourteen pounds." Painfully sniffling with his extinguished pipe, Pilgram would raise the box to the light, which made the shadows of the butterflies slip from beneath them across the papered bottom; then he would put it down again and, working in his nails under the tight edges of the lid, would shake it loose with a jerk and smoothly remove it. "And Eisner's female was not so fresh," the visitor would add, and some eavesdroppers coming in for a copybook or a postage stamp might well wonder what on earth these two were talking about.

Grunting, Pilgram plucked at the gilded head of the black pin upon which the silky little creature was crucified, and took the specimen out of the box. Turning it this way and that, he peered at the label pinned under the body. "Yes—'Tatsienlu, East Tibet,' " he read. " 'Taken by the native collectors of Father Dejean' " (which sounded almost like "Prester John")—and he would stick the butterfly back again, right into the same pinhole. His motions seemed casual, even careless, but this was the unerring nonchalance of the specialist: the pin, with the precious insect, and Pilgram's fat fingers were the correlated parts of one and the same flawless machine. It might happen, however, that some open box, having been brushed by the elbow of the visitor, would stealthily begin to slide off the counter—to be stopped just in the nick of time by Pilgram, who would then calmly go on lighting his pipe; only much later, when busy elsewhere, he would suddenly produce a moan of retrospective anguish.

But not only averted crashes made him moan. Father Dejean, stout-hearted missionary climbing among the rhododendrons and snows, how enviable was thy lot! And Pilgram would stare at his boxes and puff and brood and reflect that he need not go so far: that there were thousands of hunting grounds all over Europe. Out of localities cited in entomological works he had built up a special world of his own, to which his science was a most detailed guidebook. In that world there were no casinos, no old churches, nothing that might attract a normal tourist. Digne in southern France, Ragusa in Dalmatia, Sarepta on the Volga, Abisko in Lapland—those were the famous sites dear to butterfly collectors, and this is where they had poked about, on and off, since the fifties of the last century (always greatly perplexing the local inhabitants). And as clearly as if it were a reminiscence Pilgram saw himself troubling the sleep of a little hotel by stamping and jumping about a room through the wide-open window of which, out of the black generous night, a whitish moth had dashed in and, in an audible bob dance, was kissing its shadow all over the ceiling.

In these impossible dreams of his he visited the Islands of the Blessed, where in the hot ravines that cut the lower slopes of the chestnut- and laurel-clad mountains there occurs a weird local race of the cabbage white; and also that other island, those railway banks near Vizzavona and the pine woods farther up, which are the haunts of the squat and dusky Corsican swallowtail. He visited the far North, the arctic bogs that produced such delicate downy butterflies. He knew the high alpine pastures, with those flat stones lying here and there among the slippery matted grass; for there is no greater delight than to lift such a stone and find beneath it a plump sleepy moth of a still undescribed species. He saw glazed Apollo butterflies, ocellated with red, float in the mountain draft across the mule track that ran between a steep cliff and an abyss of wild white waters. In Italian gardens in the summer dusk, the gravel crunched invitingly underfoot, and Pilgram gazed through the growing darkness at clusters of blossoms in front of which suddenly there appeared an oleander hawk, which passed from flower to flower, humming intently and stopping at the corolla, its wings vibrating so rapidly that nothing but a ghostly nimbus was visible about its streamlined body. And best of all, perhaps, were the white heathered hills near Madrid, the valleys of Andalusia, fertile and wooded Albarracin, whither a little bus driven by the forest guard's brother groaned up a twisted road.

He had more difficulty in imagining the tropics, but experienced still keener pangs when he did, for never would he catch the loftily flapping Brazilian morphos, so ample and radiant that they cast an azure reflection upon one's hand, never come upon those crowds of African butterflies closely stuck like innumerable fancy flags into the rich black mud and rising in a colored cloud when his shadow approached—a long, very long, shadow.

3
———————

"*Ja, ja, ja,*" he would mutter, nodding his heavy head, and holding the case before him as if it were a beloved portrait. The bell over the door would tinkle, his wife would come in with a wet umbrella and a shopping bag, and slowly he would turn his back to her as he inserted the case into the cabinet. So it went on, that obsession and that despair and that nightmarish impossibility to swindle destiny, until a certain first of April, of all dates. For more than a year he had had in his keeping a cabinet devoted solely to the genus of those small clear-winged moths that mimic wasps or mosquitoes. The widow of a great authority on that particular group had given Pilgram her husband's collection to sell on commission. He hastened to tell the silly woman that he would not be able to get more than 75 marks for it, although he knew very well that, according to catalogue prices, it was worth fifty times more, so that the amateur to whom he would sell the lot for, say, a thousand marks would consider it a good bargain. The amateur, however, did not appear, though Pilgram had written to all the wealthiest collectors. So he had locked up the cabinet, and stopped thinking about it.

That April morning a sunburned, bespectacled man in an old mackintosh and without any hat on his brown bald head sauntered in, and asked for some carbon paper. Pilgram slipped the small coins paid for the sticky violet stuff he so hated to handle into the slit of a small clay money pot and, sucking on his pipe, fixed his stare into space. The man cast a rapid glance round the shop, and remarked upon the extravagant brilliancy of an iridescent green insect with many tails. Pilgram mumbled something about Madagascar. "And that—that's not a butterfly, is it?" said the man, indicating another specimen. Pilgram slowly replied that he had a whole collection of that special kind. "*Ach, was!*" said the man. Pilgram scratched his bristly chin, and limped into a recess of the shop. He pulled out a glass-topped tray, and laid it on the counter. The man pored over those tiny vitreous creatures with bright orange feet and belted bodies. Pilgram pointed with the stem of his pipe to one of the rows, and simultaneously the man exclaimed: "Good God—*uralensis*!" and that ejaculation gave him away. Pilgram heaped case after case on the counter as it dawned upon him that the visitor knew perfectly well of the existence of this collection, had come for its sake, was as a matter of fact the rich amateur Sommer, to whom he had written and who had just returned from a trip to Venezuela; and finally, when the question was carelessly put—"Well, and what would the price be?"—Pilgram smiled.

He knew it was madness; he knew he was leaving a helpless Eleanor, debts, unpaid taxes, a store at which only trash was bought; he knew that the 950 marks he might get would permit him to travel for no longer than a few months; and still he accepted it all as a man who felt that tomorrow would bring dreary old age and that the good fortune which now beckoned would never again repeat its invitation.

When finally Sommer said that on the fourth he would give a definite answer, Pilgram decided that the dream of his life was about to break at last from its old crinkly cocoon. He spent several hours examining a map, choosing a route, estimating the time of appearance of this or that species, and suddenly something black and blinding welled before his eyes, and he stumbled about his shop for quite a while before he felt better. The fourth came and Sommer failed to turn up, and, after waiting all day, Pilgram retired to his bedroom and silently lay down. He refused his supper, and for several minutes, with his eyes closed, nagged his wife, thinking she was still standing near; then he heard her sobbing softly in the kitchen, and toyed with the idea of taking an axe and splitting her pale-haired head. Next day he stayed in bed, and Eleanor took his place in the shop and sold a box of watercolors. And after still another day, when the whole thing seemed merely delirium, Sommer, a carnation in his buttonhole and his mackintosh on his arm, entered the store. And when he took out a wad, and the banknotes rustled, Pilgram's nose began to bleed violently.

The delivery of the cabinet and a visit to the credulous old woman, to whom he reluctantly gave 50 marks, were his last business in town. The much more expensive visit to the travel agency already referred to his new existence, where only butterflies mattered. Eleanor, though not familiar with her husband's transactions, looked happy, feeling that he had made a good profit, but fearing to ask how much. That afternoon a neighbor dropped in to remind them that tomorrow was the wedding of his daughter. So next morning Eleanor busied herself with brightening up her silk dress and pressing her husband's best suit. She would go there about five, she thought, and he would follow later, after closing time. When he looked up at her with a puzzled frown and then flatly refused to go, it did not surprise her, for she had long become used to all sorts of disappointments. "There might be champagne," she said, when already standing in the doorway. No answer—

only the shuffling of boxes. She looked thoughtfully at the nice clean gloves on her hands, and went out.

Pilgram, having put the more valuable collections in order, looked at his watch and saw it was time to pack: his train left at 8:29. He locked the shop, dragged out of the corridor his father's old checkered suitcase, and packed the hunting implements first: a folding net, killing jars, pillboxes, a lantern for mothing at night on the sierras, and a few packages of pins. As an afterthought he put in a couple of spreading boards and a cork-bottomed box, though in general he intended to keep his captures in papers, as is usually done when going from place to place. Then he took the suitcase into the bedroom and threw in some thick socks and underwear. He added two or three things that might be sold in an extremity, such as, for instance, a silver tumbler and a bronze medal in a velvet case, which had belonged to his father-in-law.

Again he looked at his watch, and then decided it was time to start for the station. "Eleanor!" he called loudly, getting into his overcoat. As she did not reply, he looked into the kitchen. No, she was not there; and then vaguely he remembered something about a wedding. Hurriedly he got a scrap of paper and scribbled a few words in pencil. He left the note and the keys in a conspicuous place, and with a chill of excitement, a sinking feeling in the pit of the stomach, verified for the last time whether the money and tickets were in his wallet. *"Also los!"* said Pilgram, and gripped the suitcase.

But, as it was his first journey, he still kept worrying nervously whether there was anything he might have forgotten; then it occurred to him that he had no small change, and he remembered the clay money pot where there might be a few coins. Groaning and knocking the heavy suitcase against corners, he returned to his counter. In the twilight of the strangely still shop, eyed wings stared at him from all sides, and Pilgram perceived something almost appalling in the richness of the huge happiness that was leaning toward him like a mountain. Trying to avoid the knowing looks of those numberless eyes, he drew a deep breath and, catching sight of the hazy money pot, which seemed to hang in midair, reached quickly for it. The pot slipped from his moist grasp and broke on the floor with a dizzy spinning of twinkling coins; and Pilgram bent low to pick them up.

4
_____

Night came; a slippery polished moon sped, without the least friction, in between chinchilla clouds, and Eleanor, returning from the wedding supper, and still all atingle from the wine and the juicy jokes, recalled her own wedding day as she leisurely walked home. Somehow all the thoughts now passing through her brain kept turning so as to show their moon-bright, attractive side; she felt almost lighthearted as she entered the gateway and proceeded to open the door, and she caught herself thinking that it was surely a great thing to have an apartment of one's own, stuffy and dark though it might be. Smiling, she turned on the light in her bedroom, and saw at once that all the drawers had been pulled open: she hardly had time to imagine burglars, for there were those keys on the night table and a bit of paper propped against the alarm clock. The note was brief: *"Off to Spain. Don't touch anything till I write. Borrow from Sch. or W. Feed the lizards."*

The faucet was dripping in the kitchen. Unconsciously she picked up her silver bag where she had dropped it, and kept on sitting on the edge of the bed, quite straight and still, with her hands in her lap as if she were having her photograph taken. After a time someone got up, walked across the room, inspected the bolted window, came back again, while she watched with indifference, not realizing that it was she who was moving. The drops of water plopped in slow succession, and suddenly she felt terrified at being alone in the house. The man whom she had loved for his mute omniscience, stolid coarseness, grim perseverance in work, had stolen away. . . . She felt like howling, running to the police, showing her marriage certificate, insisting, pleading; but still she kept on sitting, her hair slightly ruffled, her hands in white gloves.

Yes, Pilgram had gone far, very far. Most probably he visited Granada and Murcia and Albarracin, and then traveled farther still, to Surinam or Taprobane; and one can hardly doubt that he saw all the glorious bugs he had longed to see—velvety black butterflies soaring over the jungles, and a tiny moth in Tasmania, and that Chinese "skipper" said to smell of crushed roses when alive, and the short-clubbed beauty that a Mr. Baron had just discovered in Mexico. So, in a certain sense, it is quite irrelevant that some time later, upon wandering into the shop, Eleanor saw the checkered suitcase, and then her husband, sprawling on the floor with his back to the counter, among scattered coins, his livid face knocked out of shape by death.

A DASHING FELLOW

OUR suitcase is carefully embellished with bright-colored stickers: "Nürnberg," "Stuttgart," "Köln"—and even "Lido" (but that one is fraudulent). We have a swarthy complexion, a network of purple-red veins, a black mustache, trimly clipped, and hairy nostrils. We breathe hard through our nose as we try to solve a crossword puzzle in an émigré paper. We are alone in a third-class compartment—alone and, therefore, bored.

Tonight we arrive in a voluptuous little town. Freedom of action! Fragrance of commercial travels! A golden hair on the sleeve of one's coat! Oh, woman, thy name is Goldie! That's how we called Mamma and, later, our wife Katya. Psychoanalytic fact: every man is Oedipus. During the last trip we were unfaithful to Katya three times, and that cost us 30 reichsmarks. Funny—they all look a fright in the place one lives in, but in a strange town they are as lovely as antique hetaerae. Even more delicious, however, might be the elegancies of a chance encounter: your profile reminds me of the girl for whose sake years ago . . . After one single night we shall part like ships. . . . Another possibility: she might turn out to be Russian. Allow me to introduce myself: Konstantin . . . Better omit the family name—or maybe invent one? Obolenski. Yes, relatives.

We do not know any famous Turkish general and can guess neither the father of aviation nor an American rodent. It is also not very amusing to look at the view. Fields. A road. Birches-smirches. Cottage and cabbage patch. Country lass, not bad, young.

Katya is the very type of a good wife. Lacks any sort of passion, cooks beautifully, washes her arms as far as the shoulders every morning, and is not overbright: therefore, not jealous. Given the sterling breadth of her pelvis one is surprised that for the second time now she has produced a stillborn babikins. Laborious years. Uphill all the way.

259

Absolut Marasmus in business. Sweating twenty times before persuading one customer. Then squeezing out the commission drop by drop. God, how one longs to tangle with a graceful gold-bright little devil in a fantastically lit hotel room! Mirrors, orgies, a couple of drinks. Another five hours of travel. Railroad riding, it is proclaimed, disposes one to this kind of thing. Am extremely disposed. After all, say what you will, but the mainspring of life is robust romance. Can't concentrate on business unless I take care first of my romantic interests. So here is the plan: starting point, the café which Lange told me about. Now if I don't find anything there—

Crossing gate, warehouse, big station. Our traveler let down the window and leaned upon it, elbows wide apart. Beyond a platform, steam was issuing from under some sleeping cars. One could vaguely make out the pigeons changing perches under the lofty glass dome. Hotdogs cried out in treble, beer in baritone. A girl, her bust enclosed in white wool, stood talking to a man, now joining her bare arms behind her back, swaying slightly and beating her buttocks with her handbag, now folding her arms on her chest and stepping with one foot upon the other, or else holding her handbag under her arm and with a small snapping sound thrusting nimble fingers under her glossy black belt; thus she stood, and laughed, and sometimes touched her companion in a valedictory gesture, only to resume at once her twisting and turning: a suntanned girl with a heaped-up hairdo that left her ears bare, and a quite ravishing scratch on her honey-hued upper arm. She does not look at us, but never mind, let us ogle her fixedly. In the beam of the gloating tense glance she starts to shimmer and seems about to dissolve. In a moment the background will show through her—a refuse bin, a poster, a bench; but here, unfortunately, our crystalline lens had to return to its normal condition, for everything shifted, the man jumped into the next carriage, the train jerked into motion, and the girl took a handkerchief out of her handbag. When, in the course of her receding glide, she came exactly in front of his window, Konstantin, Kostya, Kostenka, thrice kissed with gusto the palm of his hand, but his salute passed unnoticed: with rhythmical waves of her handkerchief, she floated away.

He shut the window and, on turning around, saw with pleased surprise that during his mesmeric activities the compartment had managed to fill up: three men with their newspapers and, in the far corner, a brunette with a powdered face. Her shiny coat was of gelatinlike translucency—resisting rain, maybe, but not a man's gaze. Decorous humor and correct eye-reach—that's our motto.

Ten minutes later he was deep in conversation with the passenger in the opposite window seat, a neatly dressed old gentleman; the prefatory theme had sailed by in the guise of a factory chimney; certain statistics came to be mentioned, and both men expressed themselves with melancholic irony regarding industrial trends; meanwhile the white-faced woman dismissed a sickly bouquet of forget-me-nots to the baggage rack, and having produced a magazine from her traveling bag became engrossed in the transparent process of reading: through it comes our caressive voice, our commonsensical speech. The second male passenger joined in: he was engagingly fat, wore checked knickerbockers stuck into green stockings and talked about pig breeding. What a good sign—she adjusts every part you look at. The third man, an arrogant recluse, hid behind his paper. At the next stop the industrialist and the expert on hogs got out, the recluse retired to the dining car, and the lady moved to the window seat.

Let us appraise her point by point. Funereal expression of eyes, lascivious lips. First-rate legs, artificial silk. What is better: the experience of a sexy thirty-year-old brunette, or the silly young bloom of a bright-curled romp? Today the former is better, and tomorrow we shall see. Next point: through the gelatin of her raincoat glimmers a beautiful nude, like a mermaid seen through the yellow waves of the Rhine. Spasmodically rising, she shed her coat, but revealed only a beige dress with a piqué collaret. Arrange it. That's right.

"May weather," affably said Konstantin, "and yet the trains are still heated."

Her left eyebrow went up, and she answered, "Yes, it *is* warm here, and I'm mortally tired. My contract is finished, I'm going home now. They all toasted me—the station buffet there is tops. I drank too much, but I never get tipsy, just a heaviness in my stomach. Life has grown hard, I receive more flowers than money, and a month's rest will be most welcome; after that I have a new contract, but of course, it's impossible to lay anything by. The potbellied chap who just left behaved obscenely. How he stared at me! I feel as if I have been on this train for a long, long time, and I am so very anxious to return to my cozy little apartment far from all that flurry and claptrap and rot."

"Allow me to offer you," said Kostya, "something to palliate the offense."

He pulled from under his backside a square pneumatic cushion, its rubber covered in speckled satin: he always had it under him during his flat, hard, hemorrhoidal trips.

"And what about yourself?" she inquired.

"We'll manage, we'll manage. I must ask you to rise a little. Excuse me. Now sit down. Soft, isn't it? That part is especially sensitive on the road."

"Thank you," she said. "Not all men are so considerate. I've lost quite a bit of flesh lately. Oh, how nice! Just like traveling second class."

"Galanterie, Gnädigste," said Kostenka, "is an innate property with us. Yes, I'm a foreigner. Russian. Here's an example: one day my father had gone for a walk on the grounds of his manor with an old pal, a well-known general. They happened to meet a peasant woman—a little old hag, you know, with a bundle of firewood on her back—and my father took off his hat. This surprised the general, and then my father said, 'Would Your Excellency really want a simple peasant to be more courteous than a member of the gentry?' "

"I know a Russian—I'm sure you've heard his name, too—let me see, what was it? Baretski . . . Baratski. . . . From Warsaw. He now owns a drugstore in Chemnitz. Baratski . . . Baritski. I'm sure you know him?"

"I do not. Russia is a big country. Our family estate was about as large as your Saxony. And all has been lost, all has been burnt down. The glow of the fire could be seen at a distance of seventy kilometers. My parents were butchered in my presence. I owe my life to a faithful retainer, a veteran of the Turkish campaign."

"How terrible," she said, "how very terrible!"

"Yes, but it inures one. I escaped, disguised as a country girl. In those days I made a very cute little maiden. Soldiers pestered me. Especially one beastly fellow . . . And thereby hangs a most comic tale."

He told his tale. *"Pfui!"* she uttered, smiling.

"Well, after that came the era of wanderings, and a multitude of trades. At one time I even used to shine shoes—and would see in my dreams the precise spot in the garden where the old butler, by torchlight, had buried our ancestral jewels. There was, I remember, a sword, studded with diamonds—"

"I'll be back in a minute," said the lady.

The resilient cushion had not yet had time to cool when she again sat down upon it and with mellow grace recrossed her legs.

"—and moreover two rubies, that big, then stocks in a golden casket, my father's epaulets, a string of black pearls—"

"Yes, many people are ruined at present," she remarked with a sigh, and continued, again raising that left eyebrow: "I too have experienced all sorts of hardships. I had a husband, it was a dreadful marriage, and I said to myself: enough! I'm going to live my own way. For almost a year now I'm not on speaking terms with my parents—old people, you know, don't understand the young—and it affects me deeply. Sometimes I pass by their house and sort of dream of dropping in—and my second husband is now, thank goodness, in Argentina, he writes me absolutely marvelous letters, but I will never return to him. There was another man, the director of a factory, a very sedate gentleman, he adored me, wanted me to bear him a child, and his wife was also such a dear, so warmhearted—much older than he—oh, we three were such friends, went boating on the lake in summer, but then they moved to Frankfurt. Or take actors—such good, gay people—and affairs with them are so *kameradschaftlich*, there's no pouncing upon you, at once, at once, at once. . . ."

In the meantime Kostya reflected: We know all those parents and directors. She's making up everything. Very attractive, though. Breasts like a pair of piggies, slim hips. Likes to tipple, apparently. Let's order some beer from the diner.

"Well, some time later, there was a lucky break, brought me heaps of money. I had four apartment houses in Berlin. But the man whom I trusted, my friend, my partner, deceived me. . . . Painful recollections. I lost a fortune but not my optimism, and now, again, thank God, despite the depression. . . . Apropos, let me show you something, madam."

The suitcase with the swanky stickers contained (among other meretricious articles) samples of a highly fashionable kind of vanity-bag looking glass; little things neither round, nor square, but *Phantasie*-shaped, say, like a daisy or a butterfly or a heart. Meanwhile came the beer. She examined the little mirrors and looked in them at herself; blinks of light shot across the compartment. She downed the beer like a trooper, and with the back of her hand removed the foam from her orange-red lips. Kostenka fondly replaced the samples in the valise and put it back on the shelf. All right, let's begin.

"Do you know—I keep looking at you, and imagining that we met once years ago. You resemble to an absurd degree a girl—she died of consumption—whom I loved so much that I almost shot myself. Yes, we Russians are sentimental eccentrics, but believe me we can love with the passion of a Rasputin and the naïveté of a child. You are lonely, and I am lonely. You are free, and I am free. Who, then, can forbid us to spend several pleasant hours in a sheltered love nest?"

Her silence was enticing. He left his seat and sat next to her. He leered, and rolled his eyes, and knocked his knees together, and rubbed his hands, as he gaped at her profile.

"What is your destination?" she asked.

Kostenka told her.

"And I am returning to—"

She named a city famous for its cheese production.

"All right, I'll accompany you, and tomorrow continue my journey. Though I dare not predict anything, madam, I have all grounds to believe that neither you nor I will regret it."

The smile, the eyebrow.

"You don't even know my name yet."

"Oh, who cares, who cares? Why should one have a name?"

"Here's mine," she said, and produced a visiting card: Sonja Bergmann.

"And I'm just Kostya. Kostya, and no nonsense. Call me Kostya, right?"

An enchanting woman! A nervous, supple, interesting woman! We'll be there in half an hour. Long live Life, Happiness, Ruddy Health! A long night of double-edged pleasures. See our complete collection of caresses! Amorous Hercules!

The person we nicknamed the recluse returned from the diner, and flirtation had to be suspended. She took several snapshots out of her handbag and proceeded to show them: "This girl's just a friend. Here's a very sweet boy, his brother works for the radio station. In this one I came out appallingly. That's my leg. And here—do you recognize this person? I've put spectacles on and a bowler—cute, isn't it?"

We are on the point of arriving. The little cushion has been returned with many thanks. Kostya deflated it and slipped it into his valise. The train began braking.

"Well, so long," said the lady.

Energetically and gaily he carried out both suitcases—hers, a small fiber one, and his, of a nobler make. The glass-topped station was shot through by three beams of dusty sunlight. The sleepy recluse and the forgotten forget-me-nots rode away.

"You're completely mad," she said with a laugh.

Before checking his bag, he extracted from it a pair of flat folding slippers. At the taxi stand there still remained one cab.

"Where are we going?" she asked. "To a restaurant?

"We'll fix something to eat at your place," said terribly impatient Kostya. "That will be much cozier. Get in. It's a better idea. I suppose he'll be able to change fifty marks? I've got only big bills. No, wait a sec, here's some small cash. Come on, come on, tell him where to go."

The inside of the cab smelt of kerosene. We must not spoil our fun with the small fry of osculatory contacts. Shall we get there soon?

What a dreary town. Soon? Urge becoming intolerable. That firm I know. Ah, we've arrived.

The taxi pulled up in front of an old, coal-black house with green shutters. They climbed to the fourth landing and there she stopped and said, "And what if there's somebody else there? How do you know that I'll let you in? What's that on your lip?"

"A cold sore," said Kostya, "just a cold sore. Hurry up. Open. Let's dismiss the whole world and its troubles. Quick. Open."

They entered. A hallway with a large wardrobe, a kitchen, and a small bedroom.

"No, please wait. I'm hungry. We shall first have supper. Give me that fifty-mark note, I'll take the occasion to change it for you."

"All right, but for God's sake, hurry," said Kostya, rummaging in his wallet. "There's no need to change anything. Here's a nice tenner."

"What would you like me to buy?"

"Oh, anything you want. I only beseech you to make haste."

She left. She locked him in, using both keys. Taking no chances. But what loot could one have found here? None. In the middle of the kitchen floor a dead cockroach lay on its back, brown legs stretched out. The bedroom contained one chair and a lace-covered wooden bed. Above it, the photograph of a man with fat cheeks and waved hair was nailed to the spotty wall. Kostya sat down on the chair and in a twinkle substituted the morocco slippers for his mahogany-red street shoes. Then he shed his Norfolk jacket, unbuttoned his lilac braces, and took off his starched collar. There was no toilet, so he quickly used the kitchen sink, then washed his hands and examined his lip. The doorbell rang.

He tiptoed fast to the door, placed his eye to the peephole, but could see nothing. The person behind the door rang again, and the copper ring was heard to knock. No matter—we can't let him in even if we wished to.

"Who's that?" asked Kostya insinuatingly through the door.

A cracked voice inquired, "Please, is Frau Bergmann back?"

"Not yet," replied Kostya. "Why?"

"Misfortune," said the voice and paused. Kostya waited.

The voice continued, "You don't know when she will be back in town? I was told she was expected to return today. You are Herr Seidler, I believe?"

"What's happened? I'll pass her the message."

A throat was cleared and the voice said as if over the telephone,

"Franz Loschmidt speaking. She does not know me, but tell her please—"

Another pause and an uncertain query: "Perhaps you can let me come in?"

"Never mind, never mind," said Kostya impatiently, "I'll tell her everything."

"Her father is dying, he won't live through the night: he has had a stroke in the shop. Tell her to come over at once. When do you think she'll be back?"

"Soon," answered Kostya, "soon. I'll tell her. Good-bye."

After a series of receding creaks the stairs became silent. Kostya made for the window. A gangling youth, death's apprentice, rain-cloaked, hatless, with a small close-cropped smoke-blue head, crossed the street and vanished around the corner. A few moments later from another direction appeared the lady with a well-filled net bag.

The door's upper lock clicked, then its lower one.

"Phew!" she said, entering. "What a load of things I bought!"

"Later, later," cried Kostya, "we'll sup later. Quick to the bedroom. Forget those parcels, I beseech you."

"I want to eat," she replied in a long-drawn-out voice.

She smacked his hand away, and went into the kitchen. Kostya followed her.

"Roast beef," she said. "White bread. Butter. Our celebrated cheese. Coffee. A pint of cognac. Goodness me, can't you wait a little? Let me go, it's indecent."

Kostya, however, pressed her against the table, she started to giggle helplessly, his fingernails kept catching in the knit silk of her green undies, and everything happened very ineffectually, uncomfortably, and prematurely.

"*Pfui!*" she uttered, smiling.

No, it was not worth the trouble. Thank you kindly for the treat. Wasting my strength. I'm no longer in the bloom of youth. Rather disgusting. Her perspiring nose, her faded mug. Might have washed her hands before fingering eatables. What's that on your lip? Impudence! Still to be seen, you know, who catches what from whom. Well, nothing to be done.

"Bought that cigar for me?" he inquired.

She was busy taking knives and forks out of the cupboard and did not hear.

"What about that cigar?" he repeated.

"Oh, sorry. I didn't know you smoked. Shall I run down to get one?"

"Never mind, I'll go myself," he replied gruffly and passed into the bedroom where he put on his shoes and coat. Through the open door he could see her moving gracelessly as she laid the table.

"The tobacconist's right on the corner," she sang out, and choosing a plate arranged upon it with loving care the cool, rosy slices of roast beef which she had not been able to afford since quite a time.

"Moreover, I'll get some pastry," said Konstantin, and went out. Pastry, and whipped cream, and a chunk of pineapple, and chocolates with brandy filling, he added mentally.

Once in the street, he looked up, seeking out her window (the one with the cactuses or the next?), then turned right, walked around the back of a furniture van, nearly got struck by the front wheel of a cyclist, and showed him his fist. Further on there was a small public garden and some kind of stone *Herzog*. He made another turn, and saw at the very end of the street, outlined against a thundercloud and lit up by a gaudy sunset, the brick tower of the church, past which, he recalled, they had driven. From there it was but a step to the station. A convenient train could be had in a quarter of an hour: in this respect, at least, luck was on his side. Expenses: bag-check, 30 pfennigs, taxi, 1.40, she, 10 marks (5 would have been enough). What else? Yes, the beer, 55 pfennigs, with tip. In all: 12 marks and 25 pfennigs. Idiotic. As to the bad news, she was sure to get it sooner or later. I spared her several sad minutes by a deathbed. Still, maybe, I should send her a message from here? But I've forgotten the house number. No, I remember: 27. Anyway, one may assume I forgot it—nobody is obliged to have such a good memory. I can imagine what a rumpus there would have been if I had told her at once! The old bitch. No, we like only small blonds—remember that once for all.

The train was crammed, the heat stifling. We feel out of sorts, but do not quite know if we are hungry or drowsy. But when we have fed and slept, life will regain its looks, and the American instruments will make music in the merry café described by our friend Lange. And then, sometime later, we die.

A BAD DAY

P ETER sat on the box of the open carriage, next to the coachman (he was not particularly fond of that seat, but the coachman and everybody at home thought he liked it extremely, and he on his part did not want to hurt people, so this is how he came to be sitting there, a sallow-faced, gray-eyed youngster in a smart sailor blouse). The pair of well-fed black horses, with a gloss on their fat croups and something extraordinarily feminine about their long manes, kept lashing their tails in sumptuous fashion as they progressed at a rippling trot, and it pained one to observe how avidly, despite that movement of tails and that twitching of tender ears—despite, too, the thick tarry odor of the repellent in use—dull gray deerflies, or some big gadfly with shimmery eyes bulging, would stick to the sleek coats.

Coachman Stepan, a taciturn elderly man wearing a sleeveless vest of black velvet over a crimson Russian shirt, had a dyed beard and a brown neck lined with thin cracks. Peter felt embarrassed to keep silent while sitting on the same box; therefore he fixed his gaze on the middle shaft, on the traces, trying to invent a keen question or a sound remark. From time to time this or that horse would half-raise its tail, under the tensed root of which a bulb of flesh would swell, squeezing out one tawny globe, then another, a third, after which the folds of black skin would close again and the tail droop.

In the victoria sat, with her legs crossed, Peter's sister, a dark-complexioned young lady (although only nineteen, she had already divorced one husband), in a bright frock, high-laced white boots with glistening black caps, and a wide-brimmed hat that cast a lacy shadow upon her face. Ever since morning she had been in a vile temper, and now, when Peter turned to her for the third time, she directed at him the point of her iridescent parasol and said: "Stop fidgeting please."

268

The first part of the way went through the woods. Splendid clouds gliding across the blue only increased the glitter and vivacity of the summer day. If one looked from below at the tops of the birches, their verdure reminded one of sun-soaked translucent grapes. On both sides of the road bushes exposed the pale underside of their leaves to the hot wind. Shine and shade speckled the depths of the forest: one could not separate the pattern of tree trunks from that of their interspaces. Here and there a patch of moss flashed its heavenly emerald. Floppy ferns ran past, almost brushing against the wheels.

There appeared in front a great wagon of hay, a greenish mountain flecked with tremulous light. Stepan reined in his steeds; the mountain inclined over to one side, the carriage to the other—there was barely room enough to pass on the narrow forest road—and one caught a tangy whiff of new-mown fields, and the ponderous creak of cart-wheels, and a glimpse of wilted scabiouses and daisies amid the hay, and then Stepan clicked his tongue, gave a shake to his reins, and the wagon was left behind. Presently the woods parted, the victoria turned onto the highway, and farther came harvested fields, the stridulation of grasshoppers in the ditches, and the humming of telegraph poles. In a moment the village of Voskresensk would show up, and a few minutes later it would be the end.

Plead sickness? Topple down from the box? glumly wondered Peter as the first isbas appeared.

His tightish white shorts hurt in the crotch, his brown shoes pinched dreadfully, he felt nasty qualms in his stomach. The afternoon awaiting him was oppressive, repulsive—and inevitable.

They were now driving through the village, and somewhere from behind the fences and log cabins a wooden echo responded to the harmonious plashing of hooves. On the clayey, grass-patched side of the road peasant boys were playing *gorodki*—pitching stout sticks at wooden pins which resoundingly flew up in the air. Peter recognized the stuffed hawk and silvered spheres that ornamented the garden of the local grocer. A dog dashed out of a gateway, in perfect silence—storing up voice, as it were—and only after flying across the ditch, and finally overtaking the carriage, did it peal forth its bark. Shakily strad-dling a shaggy nag, a peasant rode by, his elbows widely parted, his shirt, with a tear on the shoulder, ballooning in the wind.

At the end of the village, on a hillock thickly crested with limes, stood a red church and, next to it, a smaller mausoleum of white stone and pyramidal shape, thus resembling a cream paskha. The river came into view; with the green brocade of aquatic flora coating it at the bend. Close to the sloping highway stood a squat smithy, on the wall of which someone had chalked: "Long Live Serbia!" The sound of the hooves suddenly acquired a ringing, resilient tone—because of the boards of the bridge over which the carriage passed. A barefoot old angler stood leaning against the railing; a tin receptacle gleamed at his ankle. Presently the sound of the hooves turned to a soft thudding: the bridge, the fisherman, and the riverbend dropped back irremediably.

The victoria was now rolling along a dusty, fluffy road between two rows of stout-trunked birches. In an instant, yes, in an instant, from behind its park the green roof of the Kozlovs' manorhouse would loom. Peter knew by experience how awkward and revolting it would be. He was ready to give away his new Swift bicycle—and what else in the bargain?—well, the steel bow, say, and the Pugach pistol and all its supply of powder-stuffed corks, in order to be back again in the ancestral domain ten versts from here, and to spend the summer day as always, in solitary, marvelous games.

From the park came a dark, damp reek of mushrooms and firs. Then appeared a corner of the house and the brick-red sand in front of the stone porch.

"The children are in the garden," said Mrs. Kozlov, when Peter and his sister, having traversed several cool rooms redolent of carnations, reached the main veranda where a number of grown-ups were assembled. Peter said how-do-you-do to each, scraping, and making sure not to kiss a man's hand by mistake as had once happened. His sister kept her palm on the top of his head—something she never did at home. Then she settled in a wicker armchair and became unusually animated. Everybody started talking at once. Mrs. Kozlov took Peter by the wrist, led him down a short flight of steps between tubbed laurels and oleanders, and with an air of mystery pointed gardenward: "You will find them there," she said; "go and join them," whereupon she returned to her guests. Peter remained standing on the lower step.

A rotten beginning. He now had to walk across the garden terrace and penetrate into an avenue where, in spotted sunshine, voices throbbed and colors flickered. One had to accomplish that journey all alone, coming ever nearer, endlessly nearer, while entering gradually the visual field of many eyes.

It was the name-day of Mrs. Kozlov's eldest son, Vladimir, a lively and teasy lad of Peter's age. There was also Vladimir's brother Constantine, and their two sisters, Baby and Lola. From the adjacent estate a pony-drawn *sharabanchik* brought the two young Barons Korff and their sister Tanya, a pretty girl of eleven or twelve with an ivory-pale skin, bluish shadows under the eyes, and a black braid caught by a white bow above her delicate neck. In addition there were three schoolboys in their summer uniforms and Vasiliy Tuchkov, a robust, well-built, suntanned thirteen-year-old cousin of Peter's. The games were directed by Elenski, a university student, the tutor of the Kozlov boys. He was a fleshy, plump-chested young man with a shaven head. He wore a *kosovorotka*, a shirtlike affair with side buttons on the collarbone. A rimless pince-nez surmounted his nose, whose chiseled sharpness did not suit at all the soft ovality of his face. When finally Peter approached, he found Elenski and the children in the act of throwing javelins at a large target of painted straw nailed to a fir trunk.

Peter's last visit to the Kozlovs had been in St. Petersburg at Easter and on that occasion magic-lantern slides had been shown. Elenski read aloud Lermontov's poem about Mtsyri, a young monk who left his Caucasian retreat to roam among the mountains, and a fellow student handled the lantern. In the middle of a luminous circle on the damp sheet there would appear (stopping there after a spasmodic incursion) a colored picture: Mtsyri and the snow leopard attacking him. Elenski, interrupting the reading for a minute, would point out with a short stick first the young monk and then the leaping leopard, and as he did so, the stick borrowed the picture's colors which would then slip off his wand when Elenski removed it. Each illustration tarried for quite a time on the sheet as only some ten slides were assigned to the long-winded epic. Vasiliy Tuchkov now and then raised his hand in the dark, reached up to the ray, and five black fingers spread out on the sheet. Once or twice the assistant inserted a slide the wrong way, topsy-turvying the picture. Tuchkov roared with laughter, but Peter was embarrassed for the assistant and, in general, did his best to feign enormous interest. That time, too, he first met Tanya Korff and since then often thought about her, imagining himself saving her from highwaymen, with Vasiliy Tuchkov helping him and devotedly admiring his courage (it was rumored that Vasiliy had a real revolver at home, with a mother-of-pearl grip).

At present, his brown legs set wide, his left hand loosely placed on the chainlet of his cloth belt which had a small canvas purse on one side, Vasiliy was aiming the javelin at the target. He swung back his throwing arm, he hit the bull's-eye, and Elenski uttered a loud "bravo." Peter carefully pulled out the spear, quietly walked back to Vasiliy's former position, quietly took aim and also hit the white, red-ringed center; no one, however, witnessed this as the competition was over by now and busy preparations for another game had begun. A kind of low cabinet or whatnot had been dragged into the avenue and set up there on the sand. Its top had several round holes and a fat frog of metal with a wide-open mouth. A large leaden counter had to be cast in such a way as to pop into one of the holes or enter the gaping green mouth. The counter fell through the holes or the mouth into numbered compartments on the shelves below; the frog's mouth gave one five hundred points, each of the other holes one hundred or less depending on its distance from *la grenouille* (a Swiss governess had imported the game). The players took turns in throwing one by one several counters, and marks were laboriously written down on the sand. The whole affair was rather tedious, and between turns some of the players sought the bilberry jungle under the trees of the park. The berries were big, with a bloom dimming their blue, which revealed a bright violet luster if touched by beslavered fingers. Peter, squatting on his haunches and gently grunting, would accumulate the berries in his cupped hand and then transfer the entire handful to his mouth. That way it tasted particularly good. Sometimes a serrate little leaf got mixed up in one's mouth with the fruit. Vasiliy Tuchkov found a small caterpillar, with varicolored tufts of hair along its back in toothbrush arrangement, and calmly swallowed it to the general admiration. A woodpecker was tapping nearby; heavy bumblebees droned above the undergrowth and crawled into the pale bending corollas of boyar bellflowers. From the avenue came the clatter of cast counters and the stentorian, *r*-trilling voice of Elenski advising somebody to "keep trying." Tanya crouched next to Peter, and with her pale face expressing the greatest attention, her glistening purple lips parted, groped for the berries. Peter silently offered her his hand-cupped collection, she graciously accepted it, and he started to gather a new helping for her. Presently, however, came her turn to play, and she ran back to the avenue, lifting high her slim legs in white stockings.

The *grenouille* game was becoming a universal bore. Some dropped out, others played haphazardly; as to Vasiliy Tuchkov, he went and hurled a stone at the gaping frog, and everybody laughed, except Elenski and Peter. The *imeninnik* (name-dayer), handsome, charming, merry Vladimir, now demanded that they play at *palochkastukalochka* (knock-knock stick). The Korff boys joined in his request. Tanya skipped on one foot, applauding.

"No, no, children, impossible," said Elenski. "In half an hour or so we shall go to a picnic; it is a long drive, and colds are caught quickly if one is all hot from running."

"Oh, please, please," cried the children.

"Please," softly repeated Peter after the others, deciding he would manage to share a hiding place either with Vasiliy or Tanya.

"I am forced to grant the general request," said Elenski, who was prone to round out his utterings. "I do not see, however, the necessary implement." Vladimir sped off to borrow it from a flower bed.

Peter went up to a seesaw on which stood Tanya, Lola, and Vasiliy; the latter kept jumping and stamping, making the plank creak and jerk while the girls squealed, trying to keep their balance.

"I'm falling, I'm falling!" exclaimed Tanya, and both she and Lola jumped down on the grass.

"Would you like some more bilberries?" asked Peter.

She shook her head, then looked askance at Lola and, turning to Peter again, added: "She and I have decided to stop speaking to you."

"But why?" mumbled Peter, flushing painfully.

"Because you are a poseur," replied Tanya, and jumped back onto the seesaw. Peter pretended to be deeply engrossed in the examination of a frizzly-black molehill on the edge of the avenue.

In the meantime a panting Vladimir had brought the "necessary implement"—a green sharp little stick, of the sort used by gardeners to prop up peonies and dahlias but also very much like Elenski's wand at the magic-lantern show. It remained to be settled who would be the "knocker."

"One. Two. Three. Four," began Elenski in a comic narrative tone, while pointing the stick at every player in turn. "The rabbit. Peeped out. Of his door. A hunter. Alas" (Elenski paused and sneezed powerfully). "Happened to pass" (the narrator replaced his pince-nez). "And his gun. Went bang. Bang. And. The. Poor" (the syllables grew more and more stressed and spaced). "Hare. Died. There."

The "there" fell on Peter. But all the other children crowded around Elenski, clamoring for him to be the seeker. One could hear them exclaiming: "Please, please, it will be much more fun!"

"All right, I consent," replied Elenski, without even glancing at Peter.

At the point where the avenue joined the garden terrace, there stood a whitewashed, partly peeled bench with a barred back, also white and also peeling. It was on this bench that Elenski sat down with the green stick in his hands. He humped his fat shoulders, closed his eyes tight and started to count aloud to one hundred, giving time to the players to hide. Vasiliy and Tanya, as if acting in collusion, disappeared in the depths of the park. One of the uniformed schoolboys cannily placed himself behind a linden trunk, only three yards away from the bench. Peter, after a wistful glance at the speckled shade of the shrubbery, turned away and went in the opposite direction, toward the house: he planned to ambuscade on the veranda—not on the main one, of course, where the grown-ups were having tea to the sound of a brass-horned gramophone singing in Italian, but on a lateral porch giving on Elenski's bench. Luckily, it turned out to be empty. The various colors of the panes inset in its latticed casements were reflected beneath on the long narrow divans, upholstered in dove-gray with exaggerated roses, that lined the walls. There were also a bentwood rocking chair, a dog's bowl, licked clean, on the floor, and an oilcloth-covered table with nothing upon it save a lone-looking pair of old-person spectacles.

Peter crept up on the many-colored window and kneeled on a cushion under the white ledge. At some distance one saw a coral-pink Elenski sitting on a coral-pink bench under the ruby-black leaves of a linden. The rule was that the "seeker," when leaving his post to spy out the concealed players, should also leave his stick behind. Wariness and nice judgment of pace and place advised him not to stray too far, lest a player made a sudden dash from an unsighted point and reach the bench before the "seeker" could get back to it and give a rap of victory with the regained wand. Peter's plan was simple: as soon as Elenski, having finished counting, put the stick down on the bench, and set off toward the shrubbery with its most likely lurking spots, Peter would sprint from his veranda to the bench and give it the sacramental "knock-knock" with the unguarded stick. About half a minute had already elapsed. A light-blue Elenski sat hunched up under indigo-black foliage and tapped his toe on the silver-blue sand in rhythm with the count. How delightful it would have been to wait thus, and peer through this or that lozenge of stained glass, if only Tanya . . . Oh, why? What did I do to her?

The number of plain-glass panes was much inferior to that of the rest. A gray and white wagtail walked past across the sand-colored sand. There were bits of cobweb in the corners of the latticework. On the ledge a dead fly lay on its back. A bright-yellow Elenski rose from his golden bench and gave a warning knock. At the same instant, the door leading onto the veranda from the inside of the house opened, and out of the dusk of a room there came first a corpulent brown dachshund and then a gray bobhaired little old woman in a tight-belted black dress with a trefoil-shaped brooch on her chest and a chainlet around her neck connecting with the watch stuck into her belt. Very indolently, sideways, the dog descended the steps into the garden. As to the old lady she angrily snatched up the spectacles—for which she had come. All of a sudden she noticed the boy crawling off his seat.

"Priate-qui? Priate-qui?" (pryatki, hide-and-seek), she uttered with the farcical accent inflicted on Russian by old Frenchwomen after half a century of life in our country. *"Toute n'est caroche"* (*tut ne khorosho*, here not good), she continued, considering with kindly eyes Peter's face that expressed both embarrassment with his situation and entreaty not to speak too loud. *"Sichasse pocajou caroche messt"* (*seychas pokazhu khoroshee mesto*, right away I'll show a good place).

An emerald Elenski stood with arms akimbo on the pale green sand and kept glancing in all directions at once. Peter, fearing the creaky and fussy voice of the old governess might be heard outside, and fearing even more to offend her by a refusal, hastened to follow her, though quite conscious of the ludicrous turn things were taking. Holding him firmly by the hand she led him through one room after another, past a white piano, past a card table, past a little tricycle, and as the variety of sudden objects increased—elk antlers, bookcases, a decoy duck on a shelf—he felt she was taking him to the opposite side of the house and making it more and more difficult to explain, without hurting her, that the game she had interrupted was not so much a matter of hiding as of awaiting the moment when Elenski would retreat sufficiently far from the bench to allow one to run to it and knock upon it with the all-important stick!

After passing through a succession of rooms, they turned into a corridor, then went up a flight of stairs, then traversed a sunlit mangle room where a rosy-cheeked woman sat knitting on a trunk near the window: she looked up, smiled, and lowered her lashes again, her knitting needles never stopping. The old governess led Peter into the next room where stood a leathern couch and an empty bird's cage and where there was a dark niche between a huge mahogany wardrobe and a Dutch stove.

"Votte" ("Here you are"), said the old lady, and having pressed him with a light push into that hiding place, went back to the mangle room, where in her garbled Russian she continued a gossipy conversation with the comely knitter who kept inserting every now and then an automatic *"Skazhite pozhaluysta!"* ("Well, I never!").

For a while Peter remained kneeling politely in his absurd nook; presently he straightened up, but continued standing there and peering at the wallpaper with its blandly indifferent azure scroll, at the window, at the top of a poplar rippling in the sun. One could hear a clock hoarsely ticktocking and that sound reminded one of various dull and sad things.

A lot of time passed. The conversation in the next room began to move away and to lose itself in the distance. Now all was silent, except the clock. Peter emerged from his niche.

He ran down the stairs, tiptoed rapidly through the rooms (book-cases, elkhorns, tricycle, blue card table, piano) and was met at the open door leading to the veranda by a pattern of colored sun and by the old dog returning from the garden. Peter stole up to the window-panes and chose an unstained one. On the white bench lay the green wand. Elenski was invisible—he had walked off, no doubt, in his un-wary search, far beyond the lindens that lined the avenue.

Grinning from sheer excitement, Peter skipped down the steps and rushed toward the bench. He was still running, when he noted an odd irresponsiveness around him. However, at the same swift pace he reached the beach and knocked its seat thrice with the stick. A vain gesture. Nobody appeared. Flecks of sunlight pulsated on the sand. A ladybird was walking up a bench arm, the transparent tips of her care-lessly folded wings showing untidily from under her small spotted cupola.

Peter waited for a minute or two, stealing glances around, and finally realized that he had been forgotten, that the existence of a last, unfound, unflushed lurker had been overlooked, and that everybody had gone to the picnic without him. That picnic, incidentally, had been for him the only acceptable promise of the day: he had been looking forward after a fashion to it, to the absence of grown-ups there, to the fire built in a forest clearing, to the baked potatoes, to the bilberry tarts, to the iced tea in thermos bottles. The picnic was now snatched away, but one could reconcile oneself to that privation. What rankled was something else.

Peter swallowed hard and still holding the green stick wandered back to the house. Uncles, aunts, and their friends were playing cards on the main veranda; he distinguished the sound of his sister's laugh-ter—a nasty sound. He walked around the mansion, with the vague thought that somewhere near it there must be a lily pond and that he might leave on its brink his monogrammed handkerchief and his silver whistle on its white cord, while he himself would go, unnoticed, all the way home. Suddenly, near the pump behind a corner of the house he heard a familiar burst of voices. All were there—Elenski, Vasiliy, Tanya, her brothers and cousins; they clustered around a peasant who was showing a baby owl he had just found. The owlet, a fat little thing, brown, white-speckled, kept shifting this way and that its head or rather its facial disc, for one could not make out exactly where the head started and the body stopped.

Peter approached. Vasiliy Tuchkov glanced at him and said to Tanya with a chuckle:

"And here comes the poseur."

THE VISIT TO THE MUSEUM

SEVERAL years ago a friend of mine in Paris—a person with oddities, to put it mildly—learning that I was going to spend two or three days at Montisert, asked me to drop in at the local museum where there hung, he was told, a portrait of his grandfather by Leroy. Smiling and spreading out his hands, he related a rather vague story to which I confess I paid little attention, partly because I do not like other people's obtrusive affairs, but chiefly because I had always had doubts about my friend's capacity to remain this side of fantasy. It went more or less as follows: after the grandfather died in their St. Petersburg house back at the time of the Russo-Japanese War, the contents of his apartment in Paris were sold at auction. The portrait, after some obscure peregrinations, was acquired by the museum of Leroy's native town. My friend wished to know if the portrait was really there; if there, if it could be ransomed; and if it could, for what price. When I asked why he did not get in touch with the museum, he replied that he had written several times, but had never received an answer.

I made an inward resolution not to carry out the request—I could always tell him I had fallen ill or changed my itinerary. The very notion of seeing sights, whether they be museums or ancient buildings, is loathsome to me; besides, the good freak's commission seemed absolute nonsense. It so happened, however, that, while wandering about Montisert's empty streets in search of a stationery store, and cursing the spire of a long-necked cathedral, always the same one, that kept popping up at the end of every street, I was caught in a violent downpour which immediately went about accelerating the fall of the maple leaves, for the fair weather of a southern October was holding on by a mere thread. I dashed for cover and found myself on the steps of the museum.

It was a building of modest proportions, constructed of many-colored stones, with columns, a gilt inscription over the frescoes of the pediment, and a lion-legged stone bench on either side of the bronze door. One of its leaves stood open, and the interior seemed dark against the shimmer of the shower. I stood for a while on the steps, but, despite the overhanging roof, they were gradually growing speckled. I saw that the rain had set in for good, and so, having nothing better to do, I decided to go inside. No sooner had I trod on the smooth, resonant flagstones of the vestibule than the clatter of a moved stool came from a distant corner, and the custodian—a banal pensioner with an empty sleeve—rose to meet me, laying aside his newspaper and peering at me over his spectacles. I paid my franc and, trying not to look at some statues at the entrance (which were as traditional and as insignificant as the first number in a circus program), I entered the main hall.

Everything was as it should be: gray tints, the sleep of substance, matter dematerialized. There was the usual case of old, worn coins resting in the inclined velvet of their compartments. There was, on top of the case, a pair of owls, Eagle Owl and Long-eared, with their French names reading "Grand Duke" and "Middle Duke" if translated. Venerable minerals lay in their open graves of dusty papier-mâché; a photograph of an astonished gentleman with a pointed beard dominated an assortment of strange black lumps of various sizes. They bore a great resemblance to frozen frass, and I paused involuntarily over them, for I was quite at a loss to guess their nature, composition, and function. The custodian had been following me with felted steps, always keeping a respectful distance; now, however, he came up, with one hand behind his back and the ghost of the other in his pocket, and gulping, if one judged by his Adam's apple.

"What are they?" I asked.

"Science has not yet determined," he replied, undoubtedly having learned the phrase by rote. "They were found," he continued in the same phony tone, "in 1895, by Louis Pradier, Municipal Councillor and Knight of the Legion of Honor," and his trembling finger indicated the photograph.

"Well and good," I said, "but who decided, and why, that they merited a place in the museum?"

"And now I call your attention to this skull!" the old man cried energetically, obviously changing the subject.

"Still, I would be interested to know what they are made of," I interrupted.

"Science . . ." he began anew, but stopped short and looked crossly at his fingers, which were soiled with dust from the glass.

I proceeded to examine a Chinese vase, probably brought back by a naval officer; a group of porous fossils; a pale worm in clouded alcohol; a red-and-green map of Montisert in the seventeenth century; and a trio of rusted tools bound by a funereal ribbon—a spade, a mattock, and a pick. To dig in the past, I thought absentmindedly, but this time did not seek clarification from the custodian, who was following me noiselessly and meekly, weaving in and out among the display cases. Beyond the first hall there was another, apparently the last, and in its center a large sarcophagus stood like a dirty bathtub, while the walls were hung with paintings.

At once my eye was caught by the portrait of a man between two abominable landscapes (with cattle and "atmosphere"). I moved closer and, to my considerable amazement, found the very object whose existence had hitherto seemed to me but the figment of an unstable mind. The man, depicted in wretched oils, wore a frock coat, whiskers, and a large pince-nez on a cord; he bore a likeness to Offenbach, but, in spite of the work's vile conventionality, I had the feeling one could make out in his features the horizon of a resemblance, as it were, to my friend. In one corner, meticulously traced in carmine against a black background, was the signature *Leroy* in a hand as commonplace as the work itself.

I felt a vinegarish breath near my shoulder, and turned to meet the custodian's kindly gaze. "Tell me," I asked, "supposing someone wished to buy one of these paintings, whom should he see?"

"The treasures of the museum are the pride of the city," replied the old man, "and pride is not for sale."

Fearing his eloquence, I hastily concurred, but nevertheless asked for the name of the museum's director. He tried to distract me with the story of the sarcophagus, but I insisted. Finally he gave me the name of one M. Godard and explained where I could find him.

Frankly, I enjoyed the thought that the portrait existed. It is fun to be present at the coming true of a dream, even if it is not one's own. I decided to settle the matter without delay. When I get in the spirit, no one can hold me back. I left the museum with a brisk, resonant step, and found that the rain had stopped, blueness had spread across the sky, a woman in besplattered stockings was spinning along on a silver-shining bicycle, and only over the surrounding hills did clouds still hang. Once again the cathedral began playing hide-and-seek with me, but I outwitted it. Barely escaping the onrushing tires of a furious red bus packed with singing youths, I crossed the asphalt thoroughfare and a minute later was ringing at the garden gate of M. Godard. He turned out to be a thin, middle-aged gentleman in high collar and dickey, with a pearl in the knot of his tie, and a face very much resembling a Russian wolfhound; as if that were not enough, he was licking his chops in a most doglike manner, while sticking a stamp on an envelope, when I entered his small but lavishly furnished room with its malachite inkstand on the desk and a strangely familiar Chinese vase on the mantel. A pair of fencing foils hung crossed over the mirror, which reflected the narrow gray back of his head. Here and there photographs of a warship pleasantly broke up the blue flora of the wallpaper.

"What can I do for you?" he asked, throwing the letter he had just sealed into the wastebasket. This act seemed unusual to me; however, I did not see fit to interfere. I explained in brief my reason for coming, even naming the substantial sum with which my friend was willing to part, though he had asked me not to mention it, but wait instead for the museum's terms.

"All this is delightful," said M. Godard. "The only thing is, you are mistaken—there is no such picture in our museum."

"What do you mean there is no such picture? I have just seen it! *Portrait of a Russian Nobleman* by Gustave Leroy."

"We do have one Leroy," said M. Godard when he had leafed through an oilcloth notebook and his black fingernail had stopped at the entry in question. "However, it is not a portrait but a rural landscape: *The Return of the Herd*."

I repeated that I had seen the picture with my own eyes five minutes before and that no power on earth could make me doubt its existence.

"Agreed," said M. Godard, "but I am not crazy either. I have been curator of our museum for almost twenty years now and know this catalogue as well as I know the Lord's Prayer. It says here *Return of the Herd* and that means the herd is returning, and, unless perhaps your friend's grandfather is depicted as a shepherd, I cannot conceive of his portrait's existence in our museum."

"He is wearing a frock coat," I cried. "I swear he is wearing a frock coat!"

"And how did you like our museum in general?" M. Godard asked suspiciously. "Did you appreciate the sarcophagus?"

"Listen," I said (and I think there was already a tremor in my voice), "do me a favor—let's go there this minute, and let's make an agreement that if the portrait is there, you will sell it."

"And if not?" inquired M. Godard.

"I shall pay you the sum anyway."

"All right," he said. "Here, take this red-and-blue pencil and using the red—the red, please—put it in writing for me."

In my excitement I carried out his demand. Upon glancing at my signature, he deplored the difficult pronunciation of Russian names. Then he appended his own signature and, quickly folding the sheet, thrust it into his waistcoat pocket.

"Let's go," he said, freeing a cuff.

On the way he stepped into a shop and bought a bag of sticky-looking caramels which he began offering me insistently; when I flatly refused, he tried to shake out a couple of them into my hand. I pulled my hand away. Several caramels fell on the sidewalk; he stopped to pick them up and then overtook me at a trot. When we drew near the museum we saw the red tourist bus (now empty) parked outside.

"Aha," said M. Godard, pleased. "I see we have many visitors today."

He doffed his hat and, holding it in front of him, walked decorously up the steps.

All was not well at the museum. From within issued rowdy cries, lewd laughter, and even what seemed like the sound of a scuffle. We entered the first hall; there the elderly custodian was restraining two sacrilegists who wore some kind of festive emblems in their lapels and were altogether very purple-faced and full of pep as they tried to extract the municipal councillor's merds from beneath the glass. The rest of the youths, members of some rural athletic organization, were making noisy fun, some of the worm in alcohol, others of the skull. One joker was in rapture over the pipes of the steam radiator, which he pretended was an exhibit; another was taking aim at an owl with his fist and forefinger. There were about thirty of them in all, and their motion and voices created a condition of crush and thick noise.

M. Godard clapped his hands and pointed at a sign reading "VISITORS TO THE MUSEUM MUST BE DECENTLY ATTIRED." Then he pushed his way, with me following, into the second hall. The whole company immediately swarmed after us. I steered Godard to the portrait; he froze before it, chest inflated, and then stepped back a bit, as if admiring it, and his feminine heel trod on somebody's foot.

"Splendid picture," he exclaimed with genuine sincerity. "Well, let's not be petty about this. You were right, and there must be an error in the catalogue."

As he spoke, his fingers, moving as it were on their own, tore up our agreement into little bits which fell like snowflakes into a massive spittoon.

"Who's the old ape?" asked an individual in a striped jersey, and, as my friend's grandfather was depicted holding a glowing cigar, another funster took out a cigarette and prepared to borrow a light from the portrait.

"All right, let us settle on the price," I said, "and, in any case, let's get out of here."

"Make way, please!" shouted M. Godard, pushing aside the curious.

There was an exit, which I had not noticed previously, at the end of the hall and we thrust our way through to it.

"I can make no decision," M. Godard was shouting above the din. "Decisiveness is a good thing only when supported by law. I must first discuss the matter with the mayor, who has just died and has not yet been elected. I doubt that you will be able to purchase the portrait but nonetheless I would like to show you still other treasures of ours."

We found ourselves in a hall of considerable dimensions. Brown books, with a half-baked look and coarse, foxed pages, lay open under glass on a long table. Along the walls stood dummy soldiers in jack-boots with flared tops.

"Come, let's talk it over," I cried out in desperation, trying to direct M. Godard's evolutions to a plush-covered sofa in a corner. But in this I was prevented by the custodian. Flailing his one arm, he came running after us, pursued by a merry crowd of youths, one of whom had put on his head a copper helmet with a Rembrandtesque gleam.

"Take it off, take it off!" shouted M. Godard, and someone's shove made the helmet fly off the hooligan's head with a clatter.

"Let us move on," said M. Godard, tugging at my sleeve, and we passed into the section of Ancient Sculpture.

I lost my way for a moment among some enormous marble legs, and twice ran around a giant knee before I again caught sight of M. Godard, who was looking for me behind the white ankle of a neighboring giantess. Here a person in a bowler, who must have clambered up her, suddenly fell from a great height to the stone floor. One of his companions began helping him up, but they were both drunk, and, dismissing them with a wave of the hand, M. Godard rushed on to the next room, radiant with Oriental fabrics; there hounds raced across azure carpets, and a bow and quiver lay on a tiger skin.

Strangely, though, the expanse and motley only gave me a feeling of oppressiveness and imprecision, and, perhaps because new visitors kept dashing by or perhaps because I was impatient to leave the unnecessarily spreading museum and amid calm and freedom conclude my business negotiations with M. Godard, I began to experience a vague sense of alarm. Meanwhile we had transported ourselves into yet an-other hall, which must have been really enormous, judging by the fact that it housed the entire skeleton of a whale, resembling a frigate's frame; beyond were visible still other halls, with the oblique sheen of large paintings, full of storm clouds, among which floated the delicate idols of religious art in blue and pink vestments; and all this resolved itself in an abrupt turbulence of misty draperies, and chandeliers came aglitter and fish with translucent frills meandered through illuminated aquariums. Racing up a staircase, we saw, from the gallery above, a crowd of gray-haired people with umbrellas examining a gigantic mock-up of the universe.

At last, in a somber but magnificent room dedicated to the history of steam machines, I managed to halt my carefree guide for an instant. "Enough!" I shouted. "I'm leaving. We'll talk tomorrow."

He had already vanished. I turned and saw, scarcely an inch from me, the lofty wheels of a sweaty locomotive. For a long time I tried to find the way back among models of railroad stations. How strangely glowed the violet signals in the gloom beyond the fan of wet tracks, and what spasms shook my poor heart! Suddenly everything changed again: in front of me stretched an infinitely long passage, containing numerous office cabinets and elusive, scurrying people. Taking a sharp turn, I found myself amid a thousand musical instruments; the walls, all mirror, reflected an enfilade of grand pianos, while in the center there was a pool with a bronze Orpheus atop a green rock. The aquatic theme did not end here as, racing back, I ended up in the Sec-tion of Fountains and Brooks, and it was difficult to walk along the winding, slimy edges of those waters.

Now and then, on one side or the other, stone stairs, with puddles on the steps, which gave me a strange sensation of fear, would descend into misty abysses, whence issued whistles, the rattle of dishes, the clat-ter of typewriters, the ring of hammers, and many other sounds, as if, down there, were exposition halls of some kind or other, already clos-ing or not yet completed. Then I found myself in darkness and kept bumping into unknown furniture until I finally saw a red light and walked out onto a platform that clanged under me—and suddenly, be-yond it, there was a bright parlor, tastefully furnished in Empire style, but not a living soul, not a living soul. . . . By now I was indescribably terrified, but every time I turned and tried to retrace my steps along the passages, I found myself in hitherto unseen places—a greenhouse with hydrangeas and broken windowpanes with the darkness of artifi-cial night showing through beyond; or a deserted laboratory with dusty alembics on its tables. Finally I ran into a room of some sort

with coatracks monstrously loaded down with black coats and astrakhan furs; from beyond a door came a burst of applause, but when I
flung the door open, there was no theater, but only a soft opacity and
splendidly counterfeited fog with the perfectly convincing blotches of
indistinct streetlights. More than convincing! I advanced, and immediately a joyous and unmistakable sensation of reality at last replaced all
the unreal trash amid which I had just been dashing to and fro. The
stone beneath my feet was real sidewalk, powdered with wonderfully
fragrant, newly fallen snow, in which the infrequent pedestrians had already left fresh black tracks. At first the quiet and the snowy coolness
of the night, somehow strikingly familiar, gave me a pleasant feeling
after my feverish wanderings. Trustfully, I started to conjecture just
where I had come out, and why the snow, and what were those lights
exaggeratedly but indistinctly beaming here and there in the brown
darkness. I examined and, stooping, even touched a round spur stone
on the curb, then glanced at the palm of my hand, full of wet granular
cold, as if hoping to read an explanation there. I felt how lightly, how
naively I was clothed, but the distinct realization that I had escaped
from the museum's maze was still so strong that, for the first two or
three minutes, I experienced neither surprise nor fear. Continuing my
leisurely examination, I looked up at the house beside which I was
standing and was immediately struck by the sight of iron steps and railings that descended into the snow on their way to the cellar. There was
a twinge in my heart, and it was with a new, alarmed curiosity that I
glanced at the pavement, at its white cover along which stretched black
lines, at the brown sky across which there kept sweeping a mysterious
light, and at the massive parapet some distance away. I sensed that
there was a drop beyond it; something was creaking and gurgling
down there. Further on, beyond the murky cavity, stretched a chain of
fuzzy lights. Scuffling along the snow in my soaked shoes, I walked a
few paces, all the time glancing at the dark house on my right; only in
a single window did a lamp glow softly under its green-glass shade.
Here, a locked wooden gate. . . . There, what must be the shutters of
a sleeping shop. . . . And by the light of a streetlamp whose shape had
long been shouting to me its impossible message, I made out the ending of a sign—". . . INKA SAPOG" (". . . OE REPAIR")—but no, it was not
the snow that had obliterated the "hard sign" at the end. "No, no, in
a minute I shall wake up," I said aloud, and, trembling, my heart
pounding, I turned, walked on, stopped again. From somewhere came
the receding sound of hooves, the snow sat like a skullcap on a slightly
leaning spur stone and indistinctly showed white on the woodpile on
the other side of the fence, and already I knew, irrevocably, where I

was. Alas, it was not the Russia I remembered, but the factual Russia of today, forbidden to me, hopelessly slavish, and hopelessly my own native land. A semiphantom in a light foreign suit, I stood on the impassive snow of an October night, somewhere on the Moyka or the Fontanka Canal, or perhaps on the Obvodny, and I had to do something, go somewhere, run; desperately protect my fragile, illegal life. Oh, how many times in my sleep I had experienced a similar sensation! Now, though, it was reality. Everything was real—the air that seemed to mingle with scattered snowflakes, the still unfrozen canal, the floating fish house, and that peculiar squareness of the darkened and the yellow windows. A man in a fur cap, with a briefcase under his arm, came toward me out of the fog, gave me a startled glance, and turned to look again when he had passed me. I waited for him to disappear and then, with a tremendous haste, began pulling out everything I had in my pockets, ripping up papers, throwing them into the snow and stamping them down. There were some documents, a letter from my sister in Paris, five hundred francs, a handkerchief, cigarettes; however, in order to shed all the integument of exile, I would have to tear off and destroy my clothes, my linen, my shoes, everything, and remain ideally naked; and, even though I was already shivering from my anguish and from the cold, I did what I could.

But enough. I shall not recount how I was arrested, nor tell of my subsequent ordeals. Suffice it to say that it cost me incredible patience and effort to get back abroad, and that, ever since, I have forsworn carrying out commissions entrusted one by the insanity of others.

A BUSY MAN

T HE man who busies himself overmuch with the workings of
his own soul cannot help being confronted by a common,
melancholy, but rather curious phenomenon: namely, he witnesses the sudden death of an insignificant memory that a chance
occasion causes to be brought back from the humble and remote alms-
house where it had been completing quietly its obscure existence. It
blinks, it is still pulsating and reflecting light—but the next moment,
under your very eyes, it breathes one last time and turns up its poor
toes, having not withstood the too abrupt transit into the harsh glare
of the present. Henceforth all that remains at your disposal is the
shadow, the abridgment of that recollection, now devoid, alas, of the
original's bewitching convincingness. Grafitski, a gentle-tempered and
death-fearing person, remembered a boyhood dream which had contained a laconic prophecy; but he had ceased long ago to feel any organic link between himself and that memory, for at one of the first
summonses, it arrived looking wan, and died—and the dream he now
remembered was but the recollection of a recollection. When was it,
that dream? Exact date unknown. Grafitski answered, pushing away
the little glass pot with smears of yogurt and leaning his elbow on the
table. When? Come on—approximately? A long time ago. Presumably,
between the ages of ten and fifteen: during that period he often
thought about death—especially at night.

So here he is—a thirty-two-year-old, smallish, but broad-shouldered
man, with protruding transparent ears, half-actor, half-literatus, author of
topical jingles in the émigré papers over a not very witty pen name (unpleasantly reminding one of the "Caran d'Ache" adopted by an immortal cartoonist). Here he is. His face consists of horn-framed dark glasses,
with a blindman's glint in them, and of a soft-tufted wart on the left

cheek. His head is balding and through the straight strands of brushed-back dunnish hair one discerns the pale-pink chamois of his scalp.

What had he been thinking about just now? What was the recollection under which his jailed mind kept digging? The recollection of a dream. The warning addressed to him in a dream. A prediction, which up to now had in no way hampered his life, but which at present, at the inexorable approach of a certain deadline, was beginning to sound with an insistent, ever-increasing resonance.

"You must control yourself," cried Itski to Graf in a hysterical recitative. He cleared his throat and walked to the closed window.

An ever-increasing insistence. The figure 33—the theme of that dream—had got entangled with his unconscious, its curved claws like those of a bat, had got caught in his soul, and there was no way to unravel that subliminal snarl. According to tradition, Jesus Christ lived to the age of thirty-three and perhaps (mused Graf, immobilized next to the cross of the casement frame), perhaps a voice in that dream had indeed said: "You'll die at Christ's age"—and had displayed, illumined upon a screen, the thorns of two tremendous threes.

He opened the window. It was lighter without than within, but streetlamps had already started to glow. Smooth clouds blanketed the sky; and only westward, between ochery housetops, an interspace was banded with tender brightness. Farther up the street a fiery-eyed automobile had stopped, its straight tangerine tusks plunged in the watery gray of the asphalt. A blond butcher stood on the threshold of his shop and contemplated the sky.

As if crossing a stream from stone to stone, Graf's mind jumped from butcher to carcass and then to somebody who had been telling him that somebody else somewhere (in a morgue? at a medical school?) used to call a corpse fondly: the "smully" or "smullicans." "He's waiting around the corner, your smullicans." "Don't you worry: smully won't let you down."

"Allow me to sort out various possibilities," said Graf with a snigger as he looked down askance from his fifth floor at the black iron spikes of a palisade. "Number one (the most vexing): I dream of the house being attacked or on fire, I leap out of bed, and, thinking (we are fools in sleep) that I live at street level, I dive out of the window—into an abyss. Second possibility: in a different nightmare I swallow my tongue—that's known to have happened—the fat thing performs a back somersault in my mouth and I suffocate. Case number three: I'm roaming, say, through noisy streets—aha, that's Pushkin trying to imagine his way of death:

In combat, wanderings or waves,
Or will it be the nearby valley . . .

etc., but mark—he began with 'combat,' which means he did have a presentiment. Superstition may be masked wisdom. What can I do to stop thinking those thoughts? What can I do in my loneliness?"

He married in 1924, in Riga, coming from Pskov with a skimpy theatrical company. Was the coupleteer of the show—and when before his act he took off his spectacles to touch up with paint his deadish little face one saw that he had eyes of a smoky blue. His wife was a large, robust woman with short black hair, a glowing complexion, and a fat prickly nape. Her father sold furniture. Soon after marrying her Graf discovered that she was stupid and coarse, that she had bowlegs, and that for every two Russian words she used a dozen German ones. He realized that they must separate, but deferred the decision because of a kind of dreamy compassion he felt for her and so things dragged until 1926 when she deceived him with the owner of a delicatessen on Lachplesis Street. Graf moved from Riga to Berlin where he was promised a job in a filmmaking firm (which soon folded up). He led an indigent, disorganized, solitary life and spent hours in a cheap pub where he wrote his topical poems. This was the pattern of his life—a life that made little sense—the meager, vapid existence of a third-rate Russian émigré. But as is well known, consciousness is not determined by this or that way of life. In times of comparative ease as well as on such days when one goes hungry and one's clothes begin to rot, Grafitski lived not unhappily—at least before the approach of the fateful year. With perfect good sense he could be called a "busy man," for the subject of his occupation was his own soul—and in such cases, there can be no question of leisure or indeed any necessity for it. We are discussing the air holes of life, a dropped heartbeat, pity, the irruptions of past things—what fragrance is that? What does it remind me of? And why does no one notice that on the dullest street every house is different, and what a profusion there is, on buildings, on furniture, on every object, of seemingly useless ornaments—yes, useless, but full of disinterested, sacrificial enchantment.

Let us speak frankly. There is many a person whose soul has gone to sleep like a leg. Per contra, there exist people endowed with principles, ideals—sick souls gravely affected by problems of faith and morality; they are not artists of sensibility, but the soul is their mine where they dig and drill, working deeper and deeper with the coal-cutting machine of religious conscience and getting giddy from the black dust of sins, small sins, pseudo-sins. Graf did not belong to their group: he lacked any special sins and had no special principles. He busied himself with his individual self, as others study a certain painter, or collect certain mites, or decipher manuscripts rich in complex transpositions and insertions, with doodles, like hallucinations, in the margin, and temperamental deletions that burn the bridges between masses of imagery—bridges whose restoration is such wonderful fun.

His studies were now interrupted by alien considerations—this was unexpected and dreadfully painful—what should be done about it? After lingering by the window (and doing his best to find some defense against the ridiculous, trivial, but invincible idea that in a few days, on June the nineteenth, he would have attained the age mentioned in his boyhood dream), Graf quietly left his darkening room, in which all objects, buoyed up slightly by the waves of the crepuscule, no longer stood, but floated, like furniture during a great flood. It was still day—and somehow one's heart contracted from the tenderness of early lights. Graf noticed at once that not all was right, that a strange agitation was spreading around: people gathered at the corners of streets, made mysterious angular signals, walked over to the opposite side, and there again pointed at something afar and then stood motionless in eerie attitudes of torpor. In the twilight dimness, nouns were lost, only verbs remained—or at least the archaic forms of a few verbs. This kind of thing might mean a lot: for example, the end of the world. Suddenly with a numbing tingle in every part of his frame, he understood: There, there, across the deep vista between buildings, outlined softly against a clear golden background, under the lower rim of a long ashen cloud, very low, very far, and very slowly, and also ash-colored, also elongated, an airship was floating by. The exquisite, antique loveliness of its motion, mating with the intolerable beauty of the evening sky, tangerine lights, blue silhouettes of people, caused the contents of Graf's soul to brim over. He saw it as a celestial token, an old-fashioned apparition, reminding him that he was on the point of reaching the established limit of his life; he read in his mind the inexorable obituary: our valuable collaborator . . . so early in life . . . we who knew him so well . . . fresh humor . . . fresh grave. . . . And what was still more inconceivable: all around that obituary, to paraphrase Pushkin again, . . . *indifferent nature would be shining*—the flora of a newspaper, weeds of domestic news, burdocks of editorials.

On a quiet summer night he turned thirty-three. Alone in his room, clad in long underpants, striped like those of a convict, glassless and blinking, he celebrated his unbidden birthday. He had not invited anybody because he feared such contingencies as a broken pocket mirror or some talk about life's fragility, which the retentive mind of a guest would be sure to promote to the rank of an omen. Stay, stay, moment—thou art not as fair as Goethe's—but nevertheless stay. Here we have an unrepeatable individual in an unrepeatable medium: the storm-felled worn books on the shelves, the little glass pot of yogurt (said to lengthen life), the tufted brush for cleaning one's pipe, the stout album of an ashen tint in which Graf pasted everything, beginning with the clippings of his verse and finishing with a Russian tram ticket—these are the surroundings of Graf Ytski (a pen name he had thought up on a rainy night while waiting for the next ferry), a butterfly-eared, husky little man who sat on the edge of his bed holding the holey violet sock he had just taken off.

Henceforth he began to fear everything—the lift, a draft, builders' scaffolds, the traffic, demonstrators, a truck-mounted platform for the repairing of trolley wires, the colossal dome of the gashouse that might explode right when he passed by on his way to the post office, where, furthermore, a bold bandit in a homemade mask might go on a shooting spree. He realized the silliness of his state of mind but was unable to overcome it. In vain did he try to divert his attention, to think of something else: on the footboard at the back of every thought that went speeding by like a sledded carriage stood Smully, the ever-present groom. On the other hand the topical poems with which he continued diligently to supply the papers became more and more playful and artless (since nobody should note in them retrospectively the presentiment of nearing death), and those wooden couplets whose rhythm recalled the seesaw of the Russian toy featuring a muzhik and a bear, and in which "shrilly" rhymed with "Dzhugashvili"—those couplets, and not anything else, turned out to be actually the most substantial and fitty piece of his being.

Naturally, faith in the immortality of the soul is not forbidden; but there is one terrible question which nobody to my knowledge has set (mused Graf over a mug of beer): may not the soul's passage into the hereafter be attended with the possibility of random impediments and vicissitudes similar to the various mishaps surrounding a person's birth in this world? Cannot one help that passage to succeed by taking while still alive certain psychological or even physical measures? Which specifically? What must one foresee, what must one stock, what must one avoid? Should one regard religion (argued Graf, dallying in the deserted darkened pub where the chairs were already yawning and being put to bed on the tables)—religion, which covers the walls of life with sacred pictures—as something on the lines of that attempt to create a favorable setting (rather in the same way as, according to certain physicians, the photographs of professional babies, with nice, chubby cheeks, by adorning the bedroom of a pregnant woman act beneficially on the fruit of her womb)? But even if the necessary measures have been taken, even if we do know why Mr. X (who fed on this or that—milk, music—or whatever) safely crossed over into the hereafter, while Mr. Y (whose nourishment was slightly different) got stuck and perished—might there not exist other hazards capable of occurring at the very moment of passing over—and somehow getting in one's way, spoiling everything—for, mind you, even animals or plain people creep away when their hour approaches: do not hinder, do not hinder me in my difficult, perilous task, allow me to be delivered peacefully of my immortal soul.

All this depressed Graf, but meaner yet and more terrible was the thought of there not being any "hereafter" at all, that a man's life bursts as irremediably as the bubbles that dance and vanish in a tempestuous tub under the jaws of a rainpipe—Graf watched them from the veranda of the suburban café—it was raining hard, autumn had come, four months had elapsed since he had reached the fatidic age, death might hit any minute now—and those trips to the dismal pine barrens near Berlin were extremely risky. If, however, thought Graf, there is no hereafter, then away with it goes everything else that involves the idea of an independent soul, away goes the possibility of omens and presentiments; all right, let us be materialists, and therefore, I, a healthy individual with a healthy heredity shall, probably, live half a century more, and so why yield to neurotic illusions—they are only the result of a certain temporary instability of my social class, and the individual is immortal inasmuch as his class is immortal—and the great class of the bourgeoisie (continued Graf, now thinking aloud with disgusting animation), our great and powerful class shall conquer the hydra of the proletariat, for we, too, slave-owners, corn merchants, and their loyal troubadours, must step onto the platform of our class (more zip, please), we all, the bourgeois of all countries, the bourgeois of all lands . . . and nations, arise, our oil-mad (or gold-mad?) *kollektiv*, down with plebeian miscreations—and now any verbal adverb ending in *'iv'* will do as a rhyme; after that two more strophes and again: up, bourgeois of all lands and nations! long live our sacred *kapitál*! Tra-ta-ta (anything in '-ations'), our bourgeois *Internatsionál*! Is the result witty? Is it amusing?

Winter came. Graf borrowed 50 marks from a neighbor and used the money to eat his fill, since he was not prepared to allow fate the slightest loophole. That odd neighbor, who of his own (his own!) accord had offered financial assistance, was a newcomer occupying the two best rooms of the fifth floor, called Ivan Ivanovich Engel—a sort of stoutish gentleman with gray locks, resembling the accepted type of a composer or chess maestro, but in point of fact, representing some kind of foreign (very foreign, perhaps, Far Eastern or Celestial) firm. When they happened to meet in the corridor he smiled kindly, shyly, and poor Graf explained this sympathy by assuming his neighbor to be a businessman of no culture, remote from literature and other mountain resorts of the human spirit, and thus instinctively bearing for him, Grafitski the Dreamer, a delicious thrilling esteem. Anyway, Graf had too many troubles to pay much attention to his neighbor, but in a rather absentminded way he kept availing himself of the old gentleman's angelic nature—and on nights of unendurable nicotinelessness, for example, would knock at Mr. Engel's door and obtain a cigar—but did not really grow chummy with him and, indeed, never asked him in (except that time when the desk lamp burned out, and the landlady had chosen that evening for going to the cinema, and the neighbor brought a brand-new bulb and delicately screwed it in).

On Christmas Graf was invited by some literary friends to a *yolka* (Yule tree) party and through the motley talk told himself with a sinking heart that he saw those colored baubles for the last time. Once, in the middle of a serene February night, he kept looking too long at the firmament and suddenly felt unable to suffer the burden and pressure of human consciousness, that ominous and ludicrous luxury: a detestable spasm made him gasp for breath, and the monstrous star-stained sky swung into motion. Graf curtained the window and, holding one hand to his heart, knocked with the other at Ivan Engel's door. The latter, with a mild smile and a slight German accent, offered him some *valerianka*. It so happened, by the way, that when Graf entered, he caught Mr. Engel standing in the middle of his bedroom and distilling the calmative into a wineglass—no doubt for his own use: holding the glass in his right hand and raising high the left one with the dark-amber bottle, he silently moved his lips, counting twelve, thirteen, fourteen, and then very rapidly, as if running on tiptoe, fifteensixteenseventeen, and again slowly, to twenty. He wore a canary-yellow dressing gown; a pince-nez straddled the tip of his attentive nose.

And after another period of time came spring, and a smell of mastic pervaded the staircase. In the house just across the street somebody died, and for quite a while there was a funereal automobile standing there, of a glossy black, like a grand piano. Graf was tormented by nightmares. He thought he saw tokens in everything, the merest coincidence frightened him. The folly of chance is the logic of fate. How not to believe in fate, in the infallibility of its promptings, in the obstinacy of its purpose, when its black lines persistently show through the handwriting of life?

The more one heeds coincidences the more often they happen. Graf reached a point when having thrown away the newspaper sheet out of which he, an amateur of misprints, had cut out the phrase "after a song and painful illness," he saw a few days later that same sheet with its neat little window in the hands of a marketwoman who was wrapping up a head of cabbage for him; and the same evening, from beyond the remotest roofs a misty and malignant cloud began to swell, engulfing the first stars, and one suddenly felt such a suffocating heaviness as if carrying upstairs on one's back a huge iron-forged trunk—and presently, without warning, the sky lost its balance and the huge chest clattered down the steps. Graf hastened to close and curtain the casement, for as is well known, drafts and electric light attract thunderbolts. A flash shone through the blinds and to determine the distance of the lightning's fall he used the domestic method of counting: the thunderclap came at the count of six which meant six versts. The storm increased. Dry thunderstorms are the worst. The windowpanes shook and rumbled. Graf went to bed, but then imagined so vividly the lightning's striking the roof any moment now, passing through all seven floors and transforming him on the way into a convulsively contracted Negro, that he jumped out of bed with a pounding heart (through the blind the casement flashed, the black cross of its sash cast a fleeting shadow upon the wall) and, producing loud clanging sounds in the dark, he removed from the washstand and placed on the floor a heavy faïence basin (rigorously wiped) and stood in it, shivering, his bare toes squeaking against the earthenware, virtually all night, until dawn put a stop to the nonsense.

During the May thunderstorm Graf descended to the most humiliating depths of transcendental cowardice. In the morning a break occurred in his mood. He considered the merry bright-blue sky, the arborescent designs of dark humidity crossing the drying asphalt, and realized that only one more month remained till the nineteenth of June. On that day he would be thirty-four. Land! But would he be able to swim that distance? Could he hold out?

He hoped he could. Zestfully, he decided to take extraordinary measures to protect his life from the claims of fate. He stopped going out. He did not shave. He pretended to be ill; his landlady took care of his meals, and through her Mr. Engel would transmit to him an orange, a magazine, or laxative powder in a dainty little envelope. He smoked less and slept more. He worked out the crosswords in the émigré papers, breathed through his nose, and before going to bed was careful to spread a wet towel over his bedside rug in order to be at once awakened by its chill, if his body tried, in a somnambulistic trance, to sneak past the surveillance of thought.

Would he make it? June the first. June the second. June the third. On the tenth the neighbor inquired through the door if he was all right. The eleventh. The twelfth. The thirteenth. Like that world-famous Finnish runner who throws away, before the last lap, his nickel-plated watch which has helped him to compute his strong smooth course, so Graf, on seeing the end of the track, abruptly changed his mode of action. He shaved off his straw-colored beard, took a bath, and invited guests for the nineteenth.

He did not give in to the temptation of celebrating his birthday one day earlier, as slyly advised by the imps of the calendar (he was born in the previous century when there were twelve, not thirteen, days between the Old Style and the New, by which he lived now); but he did write to his mother in Pskov asking her to apprise him of the exact hour of his birth. Her reply, however, was rather evasive: "It happened at night. I remember being in great pain."

The nineteenth dawned. All morning, his neighbor could be heard walking up and down in his room, displaying unusual agitation, and even running out into the corridor whenever the front-door bell rang, as if he awaited some message. Graf did not invite him to the evening party—they hardly knew each other after all—but he did ask the landlady, for Graf's nature oddly united absentmindedness and calculation. In the late afternoon he went out, bought vodka, meat patties, smoked herring, black bread. . . . On his way home, as he was crossing the street, with the unruly provisions in his unsteady embrace, he noticed Mr. Engel illumined by the yellow sun, watching him from the balcony.

Around eight o'clock, at the very moment that Graf, after nicely laying the table, leaned out of the window, the following happened: at the corner of the street, where a small group of men had collected in front of the pub, loud angry cries rang out followed suddenly by the cracking of pistol shots. Graf had the impression that a stray bullet whistled past his face, almost smashing his glasses, and with an *"akh"* of terror, he drew back. From the hallway came the sound of the front-door bell. Trembling, Graf peeped out of his room, and simultaneously, Ivan Ivanovich Engel, in his canary-yellow dressing gown, swept into the hallway. It was a messenger with the telegram he had been awaiting all day. Engel opened it eagerly—and beamed with joy.

"Was dort für Skandale?" asked Graf, addressing the messenger, but the latter—baffled, no doubt, by his questioner's bad German—did not understand, and when Graf, very cautiously, looked out of the window again, the sidewalk in front of the pub was empty, the janitors sat on chairs near their porches, and a bare-calved housemaid was walking a pinkish toy poodle.

At about nine all the guests were there—three Russians and the German landlady. She brought five liqueur glasses and a cake of her own making. She was an ill-formed woman in a rustling violet dress, with prominent cheekbones, a freckled neck, and the wig of a comedy mother-in-law. Graf's gloomy friends, émigré men of letters, all of them elderly, ponderous people, with various ailments (the tale of which always comforted Graf), immediately got the landlady drunk, and got tight themselves without growing merrier. The conversation was, of course, conducted in Russian; the landlady did not understand a word of it, yet giggled, rolled in futile coquetry her poorly penciled eyes, and kept up a private soliloquy, but nobody listened to her. Graf every now and then consulted his wristwatch under the table, yearned for the nearest churchtower to strike midnight, drank orange juice, and took his pulse. By midnight the vodka gave out and the landlady, staggering and laughing her head off, fetched a bottle of cognac. "Well, your health, *staraya morda*" (old fright), one of the guests coldly addressed her, and she naively, trustfully, clinked glasses with him, and then stretched toward another drinker, but he brushed her away.

At sunrise Grafitski said good-bye to his guests. On the little table in the hallway there lay, he noticed, now torn open and discarded, the telegram that had so delighted his neighbor. Graf abstractly read it: "SOGLASEN PRODLENIE" ("EXTENSION AGREED"), then he returned to his room, introduced some order, and, yawning, replete with a strange sense of boredom (as if he had planned the length of his life according to the prediction, and now had to start its construction all over again), sat down in an armchair and flipped through a dilapidated book (somebody's birthday present)—a Russian anthology of good stories and puns, published in the Far East: "How's your son, the poet?" —"He's a sadist now." —"Meaning?" —"He writes only sad distichs." Gradually Graf dozed off in his chair and in his dream he saw Ivan Ivanovich Engel singing couplets in a garden of sorts and fanning his bright-yellow, curly-feathered wings, and when Graf woke up the lovely June sun was lighting little rainbows in the landlady's liqueur glasses, and everything was somehow soft and luminous and enigmatic—as if there was something he had not understood, not thought through to the end, and now it was already too late, another life had begun, the past had withered away, and death had quite, quite removed the meaningless memory, summoned by chance from the distant and humble home where it had been living out its obscure existence.

TERRA INCOGNITA

T H E sound of the waterfall grew more and more muffled, until it finally dissolved altogether, and we moved on through the wildwood of a hitherto unexplored region. We walked, and had been walking, for a long time already—in front, Gregson and I; our eight native porters behind, one after the other; last of all, whining and protesting at every step, came Cook. I knew that Gregson had recruited him on the advice of a local hunter. Cook had insisted that he was ready to do anything to get out of Zonraki, where they pass half the year brewing their *von-gho* and the other half drinking it. It remained unclear, however—or else I was already beginning to forget many things, as we walked on and on—exactly who this Cook was (a runaway sailor, perhaps?).

Gregson strode on beside me, sinewy, lanky, with bare, bony knees. He held a long-handled green butterfly net like a banner. The porters, big, glossy-brown Badonians with thick manes of hair and cobalt arabesques between their eyes, whom we had also engaged in Zonraki, walked with a strong, even step. Behind them straggled Cook, bloated, red-haired, with a drooping underlip, hands in pockets and carrying nothing. I recalled vaguely that at the outset of the expedition he had chattered a lot and made obscure jokes, in a manner he had, a mixture of insolence and servility, reminiscent of a Shakespearean clown; but soon his spirits fell and he grew glum and began to neglect his duties, which included interpreting, since Gregson's understanding of the Badonian dialect was still poor.

There was something languorous and velvety about the heat. A stifling fragrance came from the inflorescences of *Vallieria mirifica*, mother-of-pearl in color and resembling clusters of soap bubbles, that arched across the narrow, dry streambed along which we proceeded. The branches of porphyroferous trees intertwined with those of the

black-leafed limia to form a tunnel, penetrated here and there by a ray
of hazy light. Above, in the thick mass of vegetation, among brilliant
pendulous racemes and strange dark tangles of some kind, hoary monkeys snapped and chattered, while a cometlike bird flashed like Bengal
light, crying out in its small, shrill voice. I kept telling myself that my
head was heavy from the long march, the heat, the medley of colors,
and the forest din, but secretly I knew that I was ill. I surmised it to
be the local fever. I had resolved, however, to conceal my condition
from Gregson, and had assumed a cheerful, even merry air, when disaster struck.

"It's my fault," said Gregson. "I should never have got involved
with him."

We were now alone. Cook and all eight of the natives, with tent,
folding boat, supplies, and collections, had deserted us and vanished
noiselessly while we busied ourselves in the thick bush, chasing fascinating insects. I think we tried to catch up with the fugitives—I do not
recall clearly, but, in any case, we failed. We had to decide whether to
return to Zonraki or continue our projected itinerary, across as yet unknown country, toward the Gurano Hills. The unknown won out. We
moved on. I was already shivering all over and deafened by quinine,
but still went on collecting nameless plants, while Gregson, though
fully realizing the danger of our situation, continued catching butterflies and diptera as avidly as ever.

We had scarcely walked half a mile when suddenly Cook overtook
us. His shirt was torn—apparently by himself, deliberately—and he was
panting and gasping. Without a word Gregson drew his revolver and
prepared to shoot the scoundrel, but he threw himself at Gregson's
feet and, shielding his head with both arms, began to swear that the
natives had led him away by force and had wanted to eat him (which
was a lie, for the Badonians are not cannibals). I suspect that he had
easily incited them, stupid and timorous as they were, to abandon the
dubious journey, but had not taken into account that he could not
keep up with their powerful stride and, having fallen hopelessly behind, had returned to us. Because of him invaluable collections were
lost. He had to die. But Gregson put away the revolver and we moved
on, with Cook wheezing and stumbling behind.

The woods were gradually thinning. I was tormented by strange
hallucinations. I gazed at the weird tree trunks, around some of which
were coiled thick, flesh-colored snakes; suddenly I thought I saw, between the trunks, as though through my fingers, the mirror of a half-
open wardrobe with dim reflections, but then I took hold of myself,
looked more carefully, and found that it was only the deceptive glim-

mer of an acreana bush (a curly plant with large berries resembling plump prunes). After a while the trees parted altogether and the sky rose before us like a solid wall of blue. We were at the top of a steep incline. Below shimmered and steamed an enormous marsh, and, far beyond, one distinguished the tremulous silhouette of a mauve-colored range of hills.

"I swear to God we must turn back," said Cook in a sobbing voice. "I swear to God we'll perish in these swamps—I've got seven daughters and a dog at home. Let's turn back—we know the way. . . ."

He wrung his hands, and the sweat rolled from his fat, red-browed face. "Home, home," he kept repeating. "You've caught enough bugs. Let's go home!"

Gregson and I began to descend the stony slope. At first Cook remained standing above, a small white figure against the monstrously green background of forest; but suddenly he threw up his hands, uttered a cry, and started to slither down after us.

The slope narrowed, forming a rocky crest that reached out like a long promontory into the marshes; they sparkled through the steamy haze. The noonday sky, now freed of its leafy veils, hung oppressively over us with its blinding darkness—yes, its blinding darkness, for there is no other way to describe it. I tried not to look up; but in this sky, at the very verge of my field of vision, there floated, always keeping up with me, whitish phantoms of plaster, stucco curlicues and rosettes, like those used to adorn European ceilings; however, I had only to look directly at them and they would vanish, and again the tropical sky would boom, as it were, with even, dense blueness. We were still walking along the rocky promontory, but it kept tapering and betraying us. Around it grew golden marsh reeds, like a million bared swords gleaming in the sun. Here and there flashed elongated pools, and over them hung dark swarms of midges. A large swamp flower, presumably an orchid, stretched toward me its drooping, downy lip, which seemed smeared with egg yolk. Gregson swung his net—and sank to his hips in the brocaded ooze as a gigantic swallowtail, with a flap of its satin wing, sailed away from him over the reeds, toward the shimmer of pale emanations where the indistinct folds of a window curtain seemed to hang. *I must not,* I said to myself, *I must not.* . . . I shifted my gaze and walked on beside Gregson, now over rock, now across hissing and lip-smacking soil. I felt chills, in spite of the greenhouse heat. I foresaw that in a moment I would collapse altogether, that the contours and convexities of delirium, showing through the sky and through the golden reeds, would gain complete control of my consciousness. At times Gregson and Cook seemed to grow transparent, and I thought I saw, through them, wallpaper with an endlessly repeated design of reeds. I took hold of myself, strained to keep my eyes open, and moved on. Cook by now was crawling on all fours, yelling, and snatching at Gregson's legs, but the latter would shake him off and keep walking. I looked at Gregson, at his stubborn profile, and felt, to my horror, that I was forgetting who Gregson was, and why I was with him.

Meanwhile we kept sinking into the ooze more and more frequently, deeper and deeper; the insatiable mire would suck at us; and, wriggling, we would slip free. Cook kept falling down and crawling, covered with insect bites, all swollen and soaked, and, dear God, how he would squeal when disgusting bevies of minute, bright-green hydrotic snakes, attracted by our sweat, would take off in pursuit of us, tensing and uncoiling to sail two yards and then another two. I, however, was much more frightened by something else: now and then, on my left (always, for some reason, on my left), listing among the repetitious reeds, what seemed a large armchair but was actually a strange, cumbersome gray amphibian, whose name Gregson refused to tell me, would rise out of the swamp.

"A break," said Gregson abruptly, "let's take a break."

By a stroke of luck we managed to scramble onto an islet of rock, surrounded by the swamp vegetation. Gregson took off his knapsack and issued us some native patties, smelling of ipecacuanha, and a dozen acreana fruit. How thirsty I was, and how little help was the scanty, astringent juice of the acreana. . . .

"Look, how odd," Gregson said to me, not in English, but in some other language, so that Cook would not understand. "We must get through to the hills, but look, how odd—could the hills have been a mirage?—they are no longer visible."

I raised myself up from my pillow and leaned my elbow on the resilient surface of the rock. . . . Yes, it was true that the hills were no longer visible; there was only the quivering vapor hanging over the marsh. Once again everything around me assumed an ambiguous transparency. I leaned back and said softly to Gregson, "You probably can't see, but something keeps trying to come through."

"What are you talking about?" asked Gregson.

I realized that what I was saying was nonsense and stopped. My head was spinning and there was a humming in my ears; Gregson, down on one knee, rummaged through his knapsack, but found no medicine there, and my supply was exhausted. Cook sat in silence, morosely picking at a rock. Through a rent in his shirtsleeve there showed a strange tattoo on his arm: a crystal tumbler with a teaspoon, very well executed.

"Vallière is sick—haven't you got some tablets?" Gregson said to him. I did not hear the exact words, but I could guess the general sense of their talk, which would grow absurd and somehow spherical when I tried to listen more closely.

Cook turned slowly and the glassy tattoo slid off his skin to one side, remaining suspended in midair; then it floated off, floated off, and I pursued it with my frightened gaze, but, as I turned away, it lost itself in the vapor of the swamp, with a last faint gleam.

"Serves you right," muttered Cook. "It's just too bad. The same will happen to you and me. Just too bad. . . ."

In the course of the last few minutes—that is, ever since we had stopped to rest on the rocky islet—he seemed to have grown larger, had swelled, and there was now something mocking and dangerous about him. Gregson took off his sun helmet and, pulling out a dirty handkerchief, wiped his forehead, which was orange over the brows, and white above that. Then he put on his helmet again, leaned over to me, and said, "Pull yourself together, please" (or words to that effect). "We shall try to move on. The vapor is hiding the hills, but they are there. I am certain we have covered about half the swamp." (This is all very approximate.)

"Murderer," said Cook under his breath. The tattoo was now again on his forearm; not the entire glass, though, but one side of it—there was not quite enough room for the remainder, which quivered in space, casting reflections. "Murderer," Cook repeated with satisfaction, raising his inflamed eyes. "I told you we would get stuck here. Black dogs eat too much carrion. Mi, re, fa, sol."

"He's a clown," I softly informed Gregson, "a Shakespearean clown."

"Clow, clow, clow," Gregson answered, "clow, clow—clo, clo, clo. . . . Do you hear," he went on, shouting in my ear. "You must get up. We have to move on."

The rock was as white and as soft as a bed. I raised myself a little, but promptly fell back on the pillow.

"We shall have to carry him," said Gregson's faraway voice. "Give me a hand."

"Fiddlesticks," replied Cook (or so it sounded to me). "I suggest we enjoy some fresh meat before he dries up. Fa, sol, mi, re."

"He's sick, he's sick too," I cried to Gregson. "You're here with two lunatics. Go ahead alone. You'll make it. . . . Go."

"Fat chance we'll let him go," said Cook.

Meanwhile delirious visions, taking advantage of the general confusion, were quietly and firmly finding their places. The lines of a dim ceiling stretched and crossed in the sky. A large armchair rose, as if supported from below, out of the swamp. Glossy birds flew through the haze of the marsh and, as they settled, one turned into the wooden knob of a bedpost, another into a decanter. Gathering all my will-power, I focused my gaze and drove off this dangerous trash. Above the reeds flew real birds with long flame-colored tails. The air buzzed with insects. Gregson was waving away a varicolored fly, and at the same time trying to determine its species. Finally he could contain himself no longer and caught it in his net. His motions underwent curious changes, as if someone kept reshuffling them. I saw him in different poses simultaneously; he was divesting himself of himself, as if he were made of many glass Gregsons whose outlines did not coincide. Then he condensed again, and stood up firmly. He was shaking Cook by the shoulder.

"You are going to help me carry him," Gregson was saying distinctly. "If you were not a traitor, we would not be in this mess."

Cook remained silent, but slowly flushed purple.

"See here, Cook, you'll regret this," said Gregson. "I'm telling you for the last time—"

At this point occurred what had been ripening for a long time. Cook drove his head like a bull into Gregson's stomach. They both fell; Gregson had time to get his revolver out, but Cook managed to knock it out of his hand. Then they clutched each other and started rolling in their embrace, panting deafeningly. I looked at them, help-less. Cook's broad back would grow tense and the vertebrae would show through his shirt; but suddenly, instead of his back, a leg, also his, would appear, covered with coppery hairs, and with a blue vein running up the skin, and Gregson was rolling on top of him. Greg-son's helmet flew off and wobbled away, like half of an enormous card-board egg. From somewhere in the labyrinth of their bodies Cook's fingers wriggled out, clenching a rusty but sharp knife; the knife en-tered Gregson's back as if it were clay, but Gregson only gave a grunt, and they both rolled over several times; when I next saw my friend's back the handle and top half of the blade protruded, while his hands had locked around Cook's thick neck, which crunched as he squeezed, and Cook's legs were twitching. They made one last full revolution, and now only a quarter of the blade was visible—no, a fifth—no, now not even that much showed: it had entered completely. Gregson grew still after having piled on top of Cook, who had also become motionless.

I watched, and it seemed to me (fogged as my senses were by fever) that this was all a harmless game, that in a moment they would get up and, when they had caught their breath, would peacefully carry me off across the swamp toward the cool blue hills, to some shady place with babbling water. But suddenly, at this last stage of my mortal illness—for I knew that in a few minutes I would die—in these final minutes everything grew completely lucid: I realized that all that was taking place around me was not the trick of an inflamed imagination, not the veil of delirium, through which unwelcome glimpses of my supposedly real existence in a distant European city (the wallpaper, the armchair, the glass of lemonade) were trying to show. I realized that the obtrusive room was fictitious, since everything beyond death is, at best, fictitious: an imitation of life hastily knocked together, the furnished rooms of nonexistence. I realized that reality was here, here beneath that wonderful, frightening tropical sky, among those gleaming swordlike reeds, in that vapor hanging over them, and in the thick-lipped flowers clinging to the flat islet, where, beside me, lay two clinched corpses. And, having realized this, I found within me the strength to crawl over to them and pull the knife from the back of Gregson, my leader, my dear friend. He was dead, quite dead, and all the little bottles in his pockets were broken and crushed. Cook, too, was dead, and his ink-black tongue protruded from his mouth. I pried open Gregson's fingers and turned his body over. His lips were half-open and bloody; his face, which already seemed hardened, appeared badly shaven; the bluish whites of his eyes showed between the lids. For the last time I saw all this distinctly, consciously, with the seal of authenticity on everything— their skinned knees, the bright flies circling over them, the females of those flies already seeking a spot for oviposition. Fumbling with my enfeebled hands, I took a thick notebook out of my shirt pocket, but here I was overcome by weakness; I sat down and my head drooped. And yet I conquered this impatient fog of death and looked around. Blue air, heat, solitude. . . . And how sorry I felt for Gregson, who would never return home—I even remembered his wife and the old cook, and his parrots, and many other things. Then I thought about our discoveries, our precious finds, the rare, still undescribed plants and animals that now would never be named by us. I was alone. Hazier flashed the reeds, dimmer flamed the sky. My eyes followed an exquisite beetle that was crawling across a stone, but I had no strength left to catch it. Everything around me was fading, leaving bare the scenery of death —a few pieces of realistic furniture and four walls. My last motion was to open the book, which was damp with my sweat, for I absolutely had to make a note of something; but, alas, it slipped out of my hand. I groped all along the blanket, but it was no longer there.

THE REUNION

LEV had a brother, Serafim, who was older and fatter than he, although it was entirely possible that during the past nine years—no, wait . . . God, it was ten, more than ten—he had got thinner, who knows. In a few minutes we shall find out. Lev had left Russia and Serafim had remained, a matter of pure chance in both cases. In fact, you might say that it was Lev who had been leftish, while Serafim, a recent graduate of the Polytechnic Institute, thought of nothing but his chosen field and was wary of political air currents. . . . How strange, how very strange that in a few minutes he would come in. Was an embrace called for? So many years . . . A *"spets,"* a specialist. Ah, those words with the chewed-off endings, like discarded fishheads . . . *"spets"* . . .

There had been a phone call that morning, and an unfamiliar female voice had announced in German that he had arrived, and would like to drop in that evening, as he was leaving again the following day. This had come as a surprise, even though Lev already knew that his brother was in Berlin. Lev had a friend who had a friend, who in turn knew a man who worked at the USSR Trade Mission. Serafim had come on an assignment to arrange a purchase of something or other. Was he a Party member? More than ten years . . .

All those years they had been out of touch. Serafim knew absolutely nothing about his brother, and Lev knew next to nothing about Serafim. A couple of times Lev caught a glimpse of Serafim's name through the smokescreen grayness of the Soviet papers that he glanced through at the library. "And inasmuch as the fundamental prerequisite of industrialization," spouted Serafim, "is the consolidation of socialist elements in our economic system generally, radical progress in the village emerges as one of the particularly essential and immediate current tasks."

Lev, who had finished his studies with an excusable delay at the University of Prague (his thesis was about Slavophile influences in Russian literature), was now seeking his fortune in Berlin, without ever really being able to decide where that fortune lay: in dealing in various knickknacks, as Leshcheyev advised, or in a printer's job, as Fuchs suggested. Leshcheyev and Fuchs and their wives, by the way, were supposed to come over that evening (it was Russian Christmas). Lev had spent his last bit of cash on a secondhand Christmas tree, fifteen inches tall; a few crimson candles; a pound of zwieback; and half a pound of candy. His guests had promised to take care of the vodka and the wine. However, as soon as he received the conspiratorial, incredible message that his brother wanted to see him, Lev promptly called off the party. The Leshcheyevs were out, and he left word with the maid that something unexpected had come up. Of course, a face-to-face talk with his brother in stark privacy would already be sheer torture, but it would be even worse if . . . "This is my brother, he's here from Russia." "Pleased to meet you. Well, are they about ready to croak?" "Whom exactly are you referring to? I don't understand." Leshcheyev was particularly impassioned and intolerant. . . . No, the Christmas party had to be called off.

Now, at about eight in the evening, Lev was pacing his shabby but clean little room, bumping now against the table, now against the white headboard of the lean bed—a needy but neat little man, in a black suit worn shiny and a turndown collar that was too large for him. His face was beardless, snub-nosed, and not very distinguished, with smallish, slightly mad eyes. He wore spats to hide the holes in his socks. He had recently been separated from his wife, who had quite unexpectedly betrayed him, and with whom! A vulgarian, a nonentity. . . . Now he put away her portrait; otherwise he would have to answer his brother's questions ("Who's that?" "My ex-wife." "What do you mean, ex?"). He removed the Christmas tree too, setting it, with his landlady's permission, out on her balcony—otherwise, who knows, his brother might start making fun of émigré sentimentality. Why had he bought it in the first place? Tradition. Guests, candlelight. Turn off the lamp—let the little tree glow alone. Mirrorlike glints in Mrs. Leshcheyev's pretty eyes.

What would he talk about to his brother? Should he tell him, casually and lightheartedly, about his adventures in the south of Russia at the time of the civil war? Should he jokingly complain about his present (unbearable, stifling) poverty? Or pretend to be a broadminded man who was above émigré resentment, and understood . . . understood what? That Serafim could have preferred to my poverty, my purity, an active collaboration . . . and with whom, with whom! Or should he, instead, attack him, shame him, argue with him, even be acidly witty? "Grammatically, Leningrad can only mean the town of Nellie."

He pictured Serafim, his meaty, sloping shoulders, his huge rubbers, the puddles in the garden in front of their dacha, the death of their parents, the beginning of the Revolution. . . . They had never been particularly close—even when they were at school, each had his own friends, and their teachers were different. . . . In the summer of his seventeenth year Serafim had a rather unsavory affair with a lady from a neighboring dacha, a lawyer's wife. The lawyer's hysterical screams, the flying fists, the disarray of the not so young lady, with the catlike face, running down the garden avenue and, somewhere in the background, the disgraceful noise of shattering glass. One day, while swimming in a river, Serafim had nearly drowned. . . . These were Lev's more colorful recollections of his brother, and God knows they didn't amount to much. You often feel that you remember someone vividly and in detail, then you check the matter and it all turns out to be so inane, so meager, so shallow—a deceptive façade, a bogus enterprise on the part of your memory. Nevertheless, Serafim was still his brother. He ate a lot. He was orderly. What else? One evening, at the tea table . . .

The clock struck eight. Lev cast a nervous glance out the window. It was drizzling, and the streetlamps swam in the mist. The white remains of wet snow showed on the sidewalk. Warmed-over Christmas. Pale paper ribbons, left over from the German New Year, hung from a balcony across the street, quivering limply in the dark. The sudden peal of the front-door bell hit Lev like a flash of electricity somewhere in the region of his solar plexus.

He was even bigger and fatter than before. He pretended to be terribly out of breath. He took Lev's hand. Both of them were silent, with identical grins on their faces. A Russian wadded coat, with a small astrakhan collar that fastened with a hook; a gray hat that had been bought abroad.

"Over here," said Lev. "Take it off. Come, I'll put it here. Did you find the house right away?"

"Took the subway," said Serafim, panting. "Well, well. So that's how it is. . . ."

With an exaggerated sigh of relief he sat down in an armchair.

"There'll be some tea ready in a minute," Lev said in a bustling tone as he fussed with a spirit lamp on the sink.

"Foul weather," said Serafim, rubbing his palms together. Actually it was rather warm out.

The alcohol went into a copper sphere; when you turned a thumbscrew it oozed into a black groove. You had to release a tiny amount, turn the screw shut, and light a match. A soft, yellowish flame would appear, floating in the groove, then gradually die, whereupon you opened the valve again, and, with a loud report (under the iron base where a tall tin teapot bearing a large birthmark on its flank stood with the air of a victim) a very different, livid flame like a serrated blue crown burst into life. How and why all this happened Lev did not know, nor did the matter interest him. He blindly followed the landlady's instructions. At first Serafim watched the fuss with the spirit lamp over his shoulder, to the extent allowed by his corpulence; then he got up and came closer, and they talked for a while about the apparatus, Serafim explaining its operation and turning the thumbscrew gently back and forth.

"Well, how's life?" he asked, sinking once again into the tight armchair.

"Well—you can see for yourself," replied Lev. "Tea will be ready in a minute. If you're hungry I have some sausage."

Serafim declined, blew his nose thoroughly, and started discussing Berlin.

"They've outdone America," he said. "Just look at the traffic. The city has changed enormously. I was here, you know, in 'twenty-four."

"I was living in Prague at the time," said Lev.

"I see," said Serafim.

Silence. They both watched the teapot, as if they expected some miracle from it.

"It's going to boil soon," said Lev. "Have some of these caramels in the meantime."

Serafim did and his left cheek started working. Lev still could not bring himself to sit down: sitting meant getting set for a chat; he preferred to stand or keep loitering between bed and table, table and sink. Several fir needles lay scattered about the colorless carpet. Suddenly the faint hissing ceased.

"Prussak kaput," said Serafim.

"We'll fix that," Lev began in haste, "just one second."

But there was no alcohol left in the bottle. "Stupid situation. . . . You know, I'll go get some from the landlady."

He went out into the corridor and headed for her quarters.— Idiotic. He knocked on the door. No answer. Not an ounce of atten-

tion, a pound of contempt. Why did it come to mind, that schoolboy
tag (uttered when ignoring a tease)? He knocked again. Everything
was dark. She was out. He found his way to the kitchen. The kitchen
had been providently locked.

Lev stood for a while in the corridor, thinking not so much about
the alcohol as about what a relief it was to be alone for a minute and
what agony it would be to return to that tense room where a stranger
was securely ensconced. What might one discuss with him? That article
on Faraday in an old issue of *Die Natur*? No, that wouldn't do. When
he returned Serafim was standing by the bookshelf, examining the tattered, miserable-looking volumes.

"Stupid situation," said Lev. "It's really frustrating. Forgive me, for
heaven's sake. Maybe . . ."

(Maybe the water was just about to boil? No. Barely tepid.)

"Nonsense. To be frank, I'm not a great lover of tea. You read a
lot, don't you?"

(Should he go downstairs to the pub and get some beer? Not
enough money and no credit there. Damn it, he'd blown it all on the
candy and the tree.)

"Yes, I do read," he said aloud. "What a shame, what a damn
shame. If only the landlady . . ."

"Forget it," said Serafim, "we'll do without. So that's how it is.
Yes. And how are things in general? How's your health? Feeling all
right? One's health is the main thing. As for me, I don't do much
reading," he went on, looking askance at the bookshelf. "Never have
enough time. On the train the other day I happened to pick up—"

The phone rang in the corridor.

"Excuse me," said Lev. "Help yourself. Here's the zwieback, and
the caramels. I'll be right back." He hurried out.

"What's the matter with you, good sir?" said Leshcheyev's voice.
"What's going on here? What happened? Are you sick? What? I can't
hear you. Speak up."

"Some unexpected business," replied Lev. "Didn't you get my
message?"

"Message my foot. Come on. It's Christmas, the wine's been
bought, the wife has a present for you."

"I can't make it," said Lev, "I'm terribly sorry myself. . . ."

"You're a rum fellow! Listen, get out of whatever you're doing
there, and we'll be right over. The Fuchses are here too. Or else, I
have an even better idea—you get yourself over here. Eh? Olya, be
quiet, I can't hear. What's that?"

"I can't. I have my . . . I'm busy, that's all there is to it."

Leshcheyev emitted a national curse. "Good-bye," said Lev awkwardly into the already dead phone.

Now Serafim's attention had shifted from the books to a picture on the wall.

"Business call. Such a bore," said Lev with a grimace. "Please excuse me."

"You have a lot of business?" asked Serafim, without taking his eyes off the oleograph—a girl in red with a soot-black poodle.

"Well, I make a living—newspaper articles, various stuff," Lev answered vaguely. "And you—so you aren't here for long?"

"I'll probably leave tomorrow. I dropped in to see you for just a few minutes. Tonight I still have to—"

"Sit down, please, sit down. . . ."

Serafim sat down. They remained silent for a while. They were both thirsty.

"We were talking about books," said Serafim. "What with one thing and another I just don't have the time for them. On the train, though, I happened to pick something up, and read it for want of anything better to do. A German novel. Piffle, of course, but rather entertaining. About incest. It went like this. . . ."

He retold the story in detail. Lev kept nodding and looking at Serafim's substantial gray suit, and his ample smooth cheeks, and as he looked he thought: Was it really worth having a reunion with your brother after ten years to discuss some philistine tripe by Leonard Frank? It bores him to talk about it and I'm just as bored to listen. Now, let's see, there was something I wanted to say . . . Can't remember. What an agonizing evening.

"Yes, I think I've read it. Yes, that's a fashionable subject these days. Help yourself to some candy. I feel so guilty about the tea. You say you found Berlin greatly changed." (Wrong thing to say—they had already discussed that.)

"The Americanization," answered Serafim. "The traffic. The remarkable buildings."

There was a pause.

"I have something to ask you," said Lev spasmodically. "It's not quite your field, but in this magazine here . . . There were bits I didn't understand. This, for instance—these experiments of his."

Serafim took the magazine and began explaining. "What's so complicated about it? Before a magnetic field is formed—you know what a magnetic field is?—all right, before it is formed, there exists a so-called electric field. Its lines of force are situated in planes that pass through a so-called vibrator. Note that, according to Faraday's teach-ings, a magnetic line appears as a closed circle, while an electric one is always open. Give me a pencil—no, it's all right, I have one. . . . Thanks, thanks, I have one."

He went on explaining and sketching something for quite a time, while Lev nodded meekly. He spoke of Young, Maxwell, Hertz. A regular lecture. Then he asked for a glass of water.

"It's time for me to be going, you know," he said, licking his lips and setting the glass back on the table. "It's time." From somewhere in the region of his belly he extracted a thick watch. "Yes, it's time."

"Oh, come on, stay awhile longer," mumbled Lev, but Serafim shook his head and got up, tugging down his waistcoat. His gaze stopped once again on the oleograph of the girl in red with the black poodle.

"Do you recall its name?" he asked, with his first genuine smile of the evening.

"Whose name?"

"Oh, you know—Tikhotski used to visit us at the dacha with a girl and a poodle. What was the poodle's name?"

"Wait a minute," said Lev. "Wait a minute. Yes, that's right. I'll remember in a moment."

"It was black," said Serafim. "Very much like this one. . . . Where did you put my coat? Oh, there it is. Got it."

"It's slipped my mind too," said Lev. "Oh, what was the name?"

"Never mind. To hell with it. I'm off. Well . . . It was great to see you. . . ." He donned his coat adroitly in spite of his corpulence.

"I'll accompany you," said Lev, producing his frayed raincoat.

Awkwardly, they both cleared their throats at the same instant. Then they descended the stairs in silence and went out. It was drizzling.

"I'm taking the subway. What was that name, though? It was black and had pompons on its paws. My memory is getting incredibly bad."

"There was a *k* in it," replied Lev. "That much I'm sure of—it had a *k* in it."

They crossed the street.

"What soggy weather," said Serafim. "Well, well. . . . So we'll never remember? You say there was a *k*?"

They turned the corner. Streetlamp. Puddle. Dark post office building. Old beggar woman standing as usual by the stamp machine. She extended a hand with two matchboxes. The beam of the streetlamp touched her sunken cheek; a bright drop quivered under her nostril.

"It's really absurd," exclaimed Serafim. "I know it's there in one of my brain cells, but I can't reach it."

"What was the name . . . what was it?" Lev chimed in. "It really is absurd that we can't . . . Remember how it got lost once, and you and Tikhotski's girl wandered for hours in the woods searching for it. I'm sure there was a *k* and perhaps an *r* somewhere."

They reached the square. On its far side shone a pearl horseshoe on blue glass—the emblem of the subway. Stone steps led into the depths.

"She was a stunner, that girl," said Serafim. "Well, I give up. Take care of yourself. Sometime we'll get together again."

"It was something like Turk. . . . Trick . . . No, it won't come. It's hopeless. You also take care of yourself. Good luck."

Serafim gave a wave of his spread hand, and his broad back hunched over and vanished into the depths. Lev started walking back slowly, across the square, past the post office and the beggar woman. . . . Suddenly he stopped short. Somewhere in his memory there was a hint of motion, as if something very small had awakened and begun to stir. The word was still invisible, but its shadow had already crept out as from behind a corner, and he wanted to step on that shadow to keep it from retreating and disappearing again. Alas, he was too late. Everything vanished, but, at the instant his brain ceased straining, the thing stirred again, more perceptibly this time, and like a mouse emerging from a crack when the room is quiet, there appeared, lightly, silently, mysteriously, the live corpuscle of a word. . . . "Give me your paw, Joker." Joker! How simple it was. Joker. . . .

He looked back involuntarily, and thought how Serafim, sitting in his subterranean car, might have remembered too. What a wretched reunion.

Lev heaved a sigh, looked at his watch, and, seeing it was not yet too late, decided to head for the Leshcheyevs' house. He would clap his hands under their window, and maybe they would hear and let him in.

LIPS TO LIPS

*T*HE *violins were still weeping, performing, it seemed, a hymn of passion and love, but already Irina and the deeply moved Dolinin were rapidly walking toward the exit. They were lured by the spring night, by the mystery that had tensely stood up between them. Their two hearts were beating as one.*

"Give me your cloakroom ticket," uttered Dolinin (crossed out).

"Please, let me get your hat and manteau" (crossed out).

"Please," uttered Dolinin, *"let me get your things"* (*"and my"* inserted between *"your"* and *"things"*).

Dolinin went up to the cloakroom, and after producing his little ticket (corrected to *"both little tickets"*)—

Here Ilya Borisovich Tal grew pensive. It was awkward, most awkward, to dawdle there. Just now there had been an ecstatic surge, a sudden blaze of love between the lonely, elderly Dolinin and the stranger who happened to share his box, a girl in black, whereupon they decided to escape from the theater, far, far away from the décolletés and military uniforms. Somewhere beyond the theater the author dimly visualized the Kupecheskiy or Tsarskiy Park, locusts in bloom, precipices, a starry night. The author was terribly impatient to plunge with his hero and heroine into that starry night. Still one had to get one's coats, and that interfered with the glamour. Ilya Borisovich reread what he had written, puffed out his cheeks, stared at the crystal paperweight, and finally made up his mind to sacrifice glamour to realism. This did not prove simple. His leanings were strictly lyrical, descriptions of nature and emotions came to him with surprising facility, but on the other hand he had a lot of trouble with routine items, such as, for instance, the opening and closing of doors, or shaking hands when there were numerous characters in a room, and one person or two persons saluted many people. Furthermore Ilya Borisovich tussled constantly with pronouns, as for example "she," which had a teasing way of referring not only to the heroine but also to her mother or sister in the same sentence, so that in order to avoid repeating a proper name one was often compelled to put "that lady" or "her interlocutress" although no interlocution was taking place. Writing meant to him an unequal contest with indispensable objects; luxury goods appeared to be much more compliant, but even they rebelled now and then, got stuck, hampered one's freedom of movement—and now, having ponderously finished with the cloakroom fuss and being about to present his hero with an elegant cane, Ilya Borisovich naively delighted in the gleam of its rich knob, and did not foresee, alas, what claims that valuable article would make, how painfully it would demand mention, when Dolinin, his hands feeling the curves of a supple young body, would be carrying Irina across a vernal rill.

Dolinin was simply "elderly"; Ilya Borisovich Tal would soon be fifty-five. Dolinin was "colossally wealthy," without precise explanation of his source of income; Ilya Borisovich directed a company engaged in the installation of bathrooms (that year, incidentally, it had been appointed to panel with enameled tiles the cavernal walls of several underground stations) and was quite well-to-do. Dolinin lived in Russia—South Russia, probably—and first met Irina long before the Revolution. Ilya Borisovich lived in Berlin, whither he had migrated with wife and son in 1920. His literary output was of long standing, but not big: the obituary of a local merchant, famous for his liberal political views, in the *Kharkov Herald* (1910), two prose poems, *ibid.* (August 1914 and March 1917), and one book, consisting of that obituary and those two prose poems—a pretty volume that landed right in the raging middle of the civil war. Finally, upon reaching Berlin, Ilya Borisovich wrote a little étude, "Travelers by Sea and Land," which appeared in a humble émigré daily published in Chicago; but that newspaper soon vanished like smoke, while other periodicals did not return manuscripts and never discussed rejections. Then followed two years of creative silence: his wife's illness and death, the *Inflationszeit*, a thousand business undertakings. His son finished high school in Berlin and entered Freiburg University. And now, in 1925, at the onset of old age, this prosperous and on the whole very lonely person experienced such an attack of writer's itch, such a longing—oh, not for fame, but simply for some warmth and heed on the part of readerdom—that he resolved to let himself go, write a novel and have it published at his own cost.

Already by the time that its protagonist, the heavy-hearted, world-weary Dolinin, hearkened to the clarion of a new life and (after that almost fatal stop at the cloakroom) escorted his young companion into the April night, the novel had acquired a title: *Lips to Lips*. Dolinin had Irina move to his flat, but nothing had happened yet in the way of lovemaking, for he desired that she come to his bed of her own accord, exclaiming:

"Take me, take my purity, take my torment. Your loneliness is my loneliness, and however long or short your love may be, I am prepared for everything, because around us spring summons us to humanness and good, because the sky and the firmament radiate divine beauty, and because I love you."

"A powerful passage," observed Euphratski. "*Terra firma* meant, I dare say. Very powerful."

"And it is not boring?" asked Ilya Borisovich Tal, glancing over his horn-rimmed glasses. "Eh? Tell me frankly."

"I suppose he'll deflower her," mused Euphratski.

"Mimo, chitatel', mimo!" ("Wrong, reader, wrong!") answered Ilya Borisovich (misinterpreting Turgenev). He smiled rather smugly, gave his manuscript a resettling shake, crossed his fat-thighed legs more comfortably, and continued his reading.

He read his novel to Euphratski bit by bit, at the rate of production. Euphratski, who had once swooped upon him on the occasion of a concert with a charitable purpose, was an émigré journalist "with a name," or, rather, with a dozen pseudonyms. Hitherto Ilya Borisovich's acquaintances used to come from German industrial circles; now he attended émigré meetings, lectures, amateur theatricals, and had learned to recognize some of the belles-lettres brethren. He was on especially good terms with Euphratski and valued his opinion as coming from a stylist, although Euphratski's style belonged to the topical sort we all know. Ilya Borisovich frequently invited him, they sipped cognac and talked about Russian literature, or more exactly Ilya Borisovich did the talking, and the guest avidly collected comical scraps with which to entertain his own cronies later. True, Ilya Borisovich's tastes were on the heavyish side. He gave Pushkin his due, of course, but knew him mainly through the medium of three or four operas, and in general found him "olympically serene and incapable of stirring the reader." His knowledge of more recent poetry was limited to his remembering two poems, both with a political slant, "The Sea" by Veynberg (1830–1908) and the famous lines of Skitaletz (Stepan Petrov, born 1868) in which "dangled" (on the gallows) rhymes with "entangled" (in a revolutionary plot). Did Ilya Borisovich like to make mild fun of the "Decadents"? Yes, he did, but then, one must note that he frankly admitted his incomprehension of verse. Per contra, he was fond of discussing Russian fiction: he esteemed Lugovoy (a regional mediocrity of the 1900s), appreciated Korolenko, and considered that Artsybashev debauched young readers. In regard to the novels of modern émigré writers he would say, with the "empty-handed" Russian gesture of inutility, "Dull, dull!," which sent Euphratski into a kind of rapturous trance.

"An author should be soulful," Ilya Borisovich would reiterate, "and compassionate, and responsive, and fair. Maybe I'm a flea, a nonentity, but I have my credo. Let at least one word of my writings impregnate a reader's heart." And Euphratski would fix reptilian eyes upon him, foretasting with agonizing tenderness tomorrow's mimetic report, A's belly laugh, Z's ventriloquistic squeak.

At last came the day when the first draft of the novel was finished. To his friend's suggestion that they repair to a café, Ilya Borisovich replied in a mysterious and weighty tone of voice, "Impossible. I'm polishing my phrasing."

The polishing consisted of his launching an attack on the too frequently occurring adjective *molodaya*, "young" (feminine gender), replacing it here and there by "youthful," *yunaya*, which he pronounced with a provincial doubling of the consonant as if it were spelled *yunnaya*.

One day later. Twilight. Café on Kurfürstendamm. Settee of red plush. Two gentlemen. To a casual eye: businessmen. One—respectable-looking, even rather majestic, a nonsmoker, with an expression of trust and kindliness on his fleshy face; the other—lean, beetle-browed, with a pair of fastidious folds descending from his triangular nostrils to the lowered corners of his mouth from which protrudes obliquely a cigarette not yet lit. The first man's quiet voice: "I penned the end in one spurt. He dies, yes, he dies."

Silence. The red settee is nice and soft. Beyond the picture window a transluscent tram floats by like a bright fish in an aquarium tank.

Euphratski clicked his cigarette lighter, expulsed smoke from his nostrils, and said, "Tell me, Ilya Borisovich, why not have a literary magazine run it as a serial before it comes out in book form?"

"But, look, I've no pull with that crowd. They publish always the same people."

"Nonsense. I have a little plan. Let me think it over."

"I'd be happy. . . ." murmured Tal dreamily.

A few days later in I. B. Tal's room at the office. The unfolding of the little plan.

"Send your thing" (Euphratski narrowed his eyes and lowered his voice) "to *Arion*."

"*Arion*? What's that?" said I.B., nervously patting his manuscript.

"Nothing very frightening. It's the name of the best émigré review. You don't know it? Ay-ya-yay! The first number came out this spring, the second is expected in the fall. You should keep up with literature a bit closer, Ilya Borisovich!"

"But how to contact them? Just mail it?"

"That's right. Straight to the editor. It's published in Paris. Now don't tell me you've never heard Galatov's name?"

Guiltily Ilya Borisovich shrugged one fat shoulder. Euphratski, his face working wryly, explained: a writer, a master, new form of the novel, intricate construction, Galatov the Russian Joyce.

"Djoys," meekly repeated Ilya Borisovich after him.

"First of all have it typed," said Euphratski. "And for God's sake acquaint yourself with the magazine."

He acquainted himself. In one of the Russian bookshops of exile he was handed a plump pink volume. He bought it, thinking aloud, as it were: "Young venture. Must be encouraged."

"Finished, the young venture," said the bookseller. "One number was all that came out."

"You are not in touch," rejoined Ilya Borisovich with a smile. "I definitely know that the next number will be out in autumn."

Upon coming home, he took an ivory paperknife and neatly cut the magazine's pages. Therein he found an unintelligible piece of prose by Galatov, two or three short stories by vaguely familiar authors, a mist of poems, and an extremely capable article about German industrial problems signed Tigris.

Oh, they'll never accept it, reflected Ilya Borisovich with anguish. They all belong to one crew.

Nevertheless he located one Madame Lubansky ("stenographer and typist") in the advertisement columns of a Russian-language newspaper and, having summoned her to his apartment, started to dictate with tremendous feeling, boiling with agitation, raising his voice—and glancing ever and again at the lady to see her reaction to his novel. Her pencil kept flitting as she bent over her writing pad—a small, dark woman with a rash on her forehead—and Ilya Borisovich paced his study in circles, and the circles would tighten around her at the approach of this or that spectacular passage. Toward the end of the first chapter the room vibrated with his cries.

"And his entire yore seemed to him a horrible error," roared Ilya Borisovich, and then added, in his ordinary office voice, "Type this out for tomorrow, five copies, wide margins, I shall expect you here at the same hour."

That night, in bed, he kept thinking up what he would tell Galatov when sending the novel (". . . awaiting your stern judgment . . . my contributions have appeared in Russia and America. . . ."), and on the following morning—such is the enchanting obligingness of fate—Ilya Borisovich received this letter from Paris:

Dear Boris Grigorievich,

I learn from a common friend that you have completed a new opus. The editorial board of Arion *would be interested in seeing it, since we would like to have something "refreshing" for our next issue.*

How strange! Only the other day I found myself recalling your elegant miniatures in the Kharkov Herald!

"I'm remembered, I'm wanted," distractedly uttered Ilya Borisovich. Thereupon he rang up Euphratski, and throwing himself back in his armchair, sideways—with the uncouthness of triumph—leaning the hand that held the receiver upon his desk, while outlining an ample gesture with the other, and beaming all over, he drawled, "Well, oh-old boy, well, oh-old boy"—and suddenly the various bright objects upon the desk began to tremble and twin and dissolve in a moist mirage. He blinked, everything resumed its right place, and Euphratski's languid voice replied, "Oh, come! Brother writers. Ordinary good turn."

Five stacks of typed pages grew higher and higher. Dolinin, who with one thing and another had not yet possessed his fair companion, happened to discover that she was infatuated with another man, a young painter. Sometimes I.B. dictated in his office, and then the German typists in the other rooms, hearing that remote roar, wondered who on earth was being bawled out by the usually good-natured boss. Dolinin had a heart-to-heart talk with Irina, she told him she would never leave him, because she prized too highly his beautiful lonely soul, but, alas, she belonged physically to another, and Dolinin silently bowed. At last, the day came when he made a will in her favor, the day came when he shot himself (with a Mauser pistol), the day came when Ilya Borisovich, smiling blissfully, asked Madame Lubansky, who had brought the final portion of the typescript, how much he owed her, and attempted to overpay.

With ravishment he reread *Lips to Lips* and handed over one copy to Euphratski for corrections (some discreet editing had already been accomplished by Madame Lubansky at such points where chance omissions garbled her shorthand notes). All Euphratski did was to insert in one of the first lines a temperamental comma in red pencil. Ilya Borisovich religiously transported that comma to the copy destined for *Arion*, signed his novel with a pseudonym derived from "Anna" (the name of his dead wife), fastened every chapter with a trim clip, added a lengthy letter, slipped all this into a huge solid envelope, weighed it, went to the post office himself, and sent the novel by registered mail.

With the receipt tucked away in his wallet, Ilya Borisovich braced himself for weeks and weeks of tremulous waiting. Galatov's reply came, however, with miraculous promptness—on the fifth day.

> *Dear Ilya Grigorievich,*
>
> *The editors are more than entranced with the material you sent us. Seldom have we had the occasion to peruse pages upon which a "human soul" has been so clearly imprinted. Your novel moves the reader with a face's singular expression, to paraphrase Baratynski, the singer of the Finnish crags. It breathes "bitterness and tenderness." Some of the descriptions, such as for example that of the theater, in the very beginning, compete with analogous images in the works of our classical writers and in a certain sense gain the ascendancy. This I say with a full awareness of the "responsibility" attached to such a statement. Your novel would have been a genuine adornment of our review.*

As soon as Ilya Borisovich had somewhat recovered his composure, he walked over to the Tiergarten—instead of riding to his office—and sat there on a park bench, tracing arcs on the brown ground, thinking of his wife, and imagining how she would have rejoiced with him. After a while he went to see Euphratski. The latter lay in bed, smoking. They analyzed together every line of the letter. When they got to the last one, Ilya Borisovich meekly raised his eyes and asked, "Tell me, why do you think he put 'would have been' and not 'will be'? Doesn't he understand that I'm overjoyed to give them my novel? Or is it simply a stylistic device?"

"I'm afraid there's another reason," answered Euphratski. "No doubt it's a case of concealing something out of sheer pride. In point of fact the magazine is folding up—yes, that's what I've just learned. The émigré public consumes as you know all sorts of trash, and *Arion* is meant for the sophisticated reader. Well, that's the result."

"I've also heard rumors," said very much perturbed Ilya Borisovich, "but I thought it was slander spread by competitors, or mere stupidity. Can it be really possible that no second issue will ever come out? It is awful!"

"They have no funds. The review is a disinterested, idealistic enterprise. Such publications, alas, perish."

"But how, how can it be!" cried Ilya Borisovich, with a Russian splash-gesture of helpless dismay. "Haven't they approved my thing, don't they want to print it?"

"Yes, too bad," said Euphratski calmly. "By the way, tell me—" and he changed the subject.

That night Ilya Borisovich did some hard thinking, conferred with his inner self, and next morning phoned his friend to submit to him certain questions of a financial nature. Euphratski's replies were listless in tone but most accurate in sense. Ilya Borisovich pondered some more and on the following day made Euphratski an offer to be submitted to *Arion*. The offer was accepted, and Ilya Borisovich transferred to Paris a certain amount of money. In reply he got a letter with expressions of deep gratitude and a communication to the effect that the next issue of *Arion* would come out in a month's time. A postscript contained a courteous request:

> *Allow us to put, 'a novel by Ilya Annenski,' and not, as you suggest, 'I. Annenski,' otherwise there might be some confusion with the 'last swan of Tsarskoe Selo,' as Gumilyov calls him.*

Ilya Borisovich answered:

> *Yes, of course, I just did not know that there already existed an author writing under that name. I am delighted my work will be printed. Please have the kindness to send me five specimens of your journal as soon as it is out.*

(He had in view an old female cousin and two or three business acquaintances. His son did not read Russian.)

Here began the era in his life which the wits denoted by the term "apropos." Either in a Russian bookshop, or at a meeting of the Friends of Expatriate Arts, or else simply on the sidewalk of a West Berlin street, you were amiably accosted ("Ah! How goes it?") by a person you knew slightly, a pleasant and dignified gentleman wearing horn-rimmed glasses and carrying a cane, who would engage you in casual conversation about this and that, would imperceptibly pass from this and that to the subject of literature, and would suddenly say: "Apropos, here's what Galatov writes me. Yes—Galatov. Galatov the Russian Djoys."

You take the letter and scan it:

> . . . *editors are more than entranced* . . . *our classical writers* . . .
> *adornment of our review.*

"He got my patronymic wrong," adds Ilya Borisovich with a kindly chuckle. "You know how writers are: absentminded! The journal will come out in September, you will read my little work." And replacing the letter in his wallet, he takes leave of you and with a worried air hurries away.

Literary failures, hack journalists, special correspondents of forgotten newspapers derided him with savage volupty. Such hoots are emitted by delinquents torturing a cat; such a spark glows in the eyes of a no longer young, sexually unlucky fellow telling a particularly dirty story. Naturally, it was behind his back that they jeered, but they did so with the utmost *sans-gêne*, disregarding the superb acoustics of every locus of tattle. Being, however, as deaf to the world as a grouse in courtship, he probably did not catch one sound of all this. He blossomed, he walked his cane with a new, novelistic stance, he started writing to his son in Russian with an interlinear German translation of most of the words. At the office one knew already that I. B. Tal was not only an excellent person but also a *Schriftsteller*, and some of his business friends confided their love secrets to him as themes he might use. To him, sensing a certain warm zephyr, there began to flock in, through front hall or back door, the motley mendicancy of emigration. Public figures addressed him with respect. The fact could not be denied: Ilya Borisovich was indeed surrounded by esteem and fame. Not a single party in a cultured Russian milieu passed without his name being mentioned. *How* it was mentioned, with *what* kind of snicker, hardly matters: the thing, not the way, is important, says true wisdom.

At the end of the month Ilya Borisovich had to leave town on a tedious business trip and so he missed the advertisements in Russian-language newspapers regarding the coming publication of *Arion 2*. When he returned to Berlin, a large cubical package awaited him on the hallway table. Without taking his topcoat off, he instantaneously undid the parcel. Pink, plump, cool tomes. And, on the covers, ARION in purple-red letters. Six copies.

Ilya Borisovich attempted to open one; the book crackled deliciously but refused to unclose. Blind, newborn! He tried again, and caught a glimpse of alien, alien versicles. He swung the mass of uncut pages from right to left—and happened to spot the table of contents. His eye raced through names and titles, but *he* was not there, *he* was not there! The volume endeavored to shut, he applied force, and reached the end of the list. Nothing! How could that be, good God? Impossible! Must have been omitted by chance from the table, such things happen, they happen! He was now in his study, and seizing his white knife, he stuck it into the thick, foliated flesh of the book. First Galatov, of course, then poetry, then two stories, then again poetry, again prose, and farther on nothing but trivia—surveys, critiques, and so forth. Ilya Borisovich was overwhelmed all at once by a sense of fatigue and futility. Well, nothing to be done. Maybe they had too much material. They'll print it on the next number. Oh, that's for certain! But a new period of waiting— Well, I'll wait. Mechanically he kept sifting the soft pages between finger and thumb. Fancy paper. Well, I've been at least of some help. One can't insist on being printed instead of Galatov or— And here, abruptly, there jumped out and whirled and went tripping, tripping along, hand on hip, in a Russian dance, the dear, heart-warm words: ". . . her youthful, hardly formed bosom . . . violins were still weeping . . . both little tickets . . . the spring night welcomed them with a car—" and on the reverse page, as inevitably as the continuation of rails after a tunnel: "essing and passionate breath of wind—"

"How the deuce didn't I guess immediately!" ejaculated Ilya Borisovich.

It was entitled "Prologue to a novel." It was signed "A. Ilyin," with, in parentheses, "To be continued." A small bit, three pages and a half, but what a *nice* bit! Overture. Elegant. "Ilyin" is better than "Annenski." Might have been a mix-up even if they had put "Ilya Annenski." But why "Prologue" and not simply: *Lips to Lips*, Chapter One? Oh, that's quite unimportant.

He reread the piece thrice. Then he laid the magazine aside, paced his study, whistling negligently the while, as if nothing whatever had happened: well, yes, there's that book lying there—some book or other—who cares? Whereupon he rushed toward it and reread himself eight times in a row. Then he looked up "A. Ilyin, p. 205" in the table of contents, found p. 205, and, relishing every word, reread his "Prologue." He kept playing that way for quite a time.

The magazine replaced the letter. Ilya Borisovich constantly carried a copy of *Arion* under his arm, and upon running into any sort of acquaintance, opened the volume at a page that had grown accustomed to presenting itself. *Arion* was reviewed in the papers. The first of those reviews did not mention Ilyin at all. The second had: "Mr. Ilyin's 'Prologue to a novel' must surely be a joke of some kind." The third noted merely that Ilyin and another were newcomers to the magazine. Finally, a fourth reviewer (in a charming, modest little periodical appearing somewhere in Poland) wrote as follows: "Ilyin's piece attracts one by its sincerity. The author pictures the birth of love against a background of music. Among the indubitable qualities of the piece one should mention the good style of the narration." A new era started (after the "apropos" period and the book-carrying one): Ilya Borisovich would extract that review from his wallet.

He was happy. He purchased six more copies. He was happy. Silence was readily explained by inertia, detraction by enmity. He was happy. "To be continued." And then, one Sunday, came a telephone call from Euphratski: "Guess," he said, "who wants to speak to you? Galatov! Yes, he's in Berlin for a couple of days. I pass the receiver."

A voice never yet heard took over. A shimmering, urgeful, mellow, narcotic voice. A meeting was settled.

"Tomorrow at five at my place," said Ilya Borisovich, "what a pity you can't come tonight!"

"Very regrettable," rejoined the shimmering voice; "you see, I'm being dragged by friends to attend *The Black Panther*—terrible play— but it's such a long time since I've seen dear Elena Dmitrievna."

Elena Dmitrievna Garina, a handsome elderly actress, who had arrived from Riga to star in the repertoire of a Russian-language theater in Berlin. Beginning at half-past eight. After a solitary supper Ilya Borisovich suddenly glanced at his watch, smiled a sly smile, and took a taxi to the theater.

The "theater" was really a large hall meant for lectures, rather than plays. The performance had not yet started. An amateur poster featured Garina reclining on the skin of a panther shot by her lover, who was to shoot her later on. Russian speech crepitated in the cold vestibule. Ilya Borisovich relinquished into the hands of an old woman in black his cane, his bowler, and his topcoat, paid for a numbered jetton, which he slipped into his waistcoat pocket, and leisurely rubbing his hands looked around the vestibule. Close to him stood a group of three people: a young reporter whom Ilya Borisovich knew slightly, the young man's wife (an angular lady with a lorgnette), and a stranger in a flashy suit, with a pale complexion, a little black beard, beautiful ovine eyes, and a gold chainlet around his hairy wrist.

"But why, oh why," the lady was saying to him vivaciously, "why did you print it? 'Cause you know—"

"Now stop attacking that unfortunate fellow," replied her interlocutor in an iridescent baritone voice. "All right, he's a hopeless mediocrity, I grant you that, but evidently we had reasons—"

He added something in an undertone and the lady, with a click of her lorgnette, retorted in anger, "Excuse me, but in my opinion, if you print him only because he supports you financially—"

"*Doucement, doucement.* Don't proclaim our editorial secrets."

Here Ilya Borisovich caught the eye of the young reporter, the angular lady's husband, and the latter froze for an instant and then moaned with a start, and proceeded to push his wife away with his whole body, but she continued to speak at the top of her voice: "I'm not concerned with the wretched Ilyin, I'm concerned with matters of principle—"

"Sometimes, principles have to be sacrificed," coolly said the opal-voiced fop.

But Ilya Borisovich was no longer listening. He saw things through a haze, and being in a state of utter distress, not yet realizing fully the horror of the event, but instinctively striving to retreat as fast as possible from something shameful, odious, intolerable, he moved at first toward the vague spot where vague seats were being sold, but then abruptly turned back, almost collided with Euphratski who was hurrying toward him, and made for the cloakroom.

Old woman in black. Number 79. Down there. He was in a desperate hurry, had already swept his arm back to get into a last coat sleeve, but here Euphratski caught up with him, accompanied by the other, the other—

"Meet our editor," said Euphratski, while Galatov, rolling his eyes and trying not to let Ilya Borisovich regain his wits, kept catching the sleeve in a semblance of assistance and talking fast: "Innokentiy Borisovich, how are you? Very glad to make your acquaintance. Pleasant occasion. Allow me to help you."

"For God's sake, leave me alone," muttered Ilya Borisovich, struggling with the coat and with Galatov. "Go away. Disgusting. I can't. It's disgusting."

"Obvious misunderstanding," put in Galatov at top speed.

"Leave me alone," cried Ilya Borisovich, wrenched himself free, scooped up his bowler from the counter, and went out, still putting on his coat.

He kept whispering incoherently as he marched along the sidewalk; then he spread his hands: he had forgotten his cane!

Automatically he continued to walk, but presently with a quiet little stumble came to a stop as if the clockwork had run out.

He would go back for the thing once the performance had started. Must wait a few minutes.

Cars sped by, tramcars rang their bells, the night was clear, dry, spruced up with lights. He began to walk slowly toward the theater. He reflected that he was old, lonely, that his joys were few, and that old people must pay for their joys. He reflected that perhaps even tonight, and in any case, tomorrow, Galatov would come with explanations, exhortations, justifications. He knew that he must forgive everything, otherwise the "To be continued" would never materialize. And he also told himself that he would be fully recognized after his death, and he recollected, he gathered up in a tiny heap, all the crumbs of praise he had received lately, and slowly walked to and fro, and after a while went back for his cane.

ORACHE

THE vastest room in their St. Petersburg mansion was the library. There, before the drive to school, Peter would look in to say good morning to his father. Crepitations of steel and the scraping of soles: every morning his father fenced with Monsieur Mascara, a diminutive elderly Frenchman made of gutta-percha and black bristle. On Sundays Mascara came to teach Peter gymnastics and pugilism—and usually interrupted the lesson because of dyspepsia: through secret passages, through canyons of bookcases, through deep dim corridors, he retreated for half an hour to one of the water closets on the first floor. Peter, his thin hot wrists thrust into huge boxing gloves, waited, sprawling in a leather armchair, listening to the light buzz of silence, and blinking to ward off somnolence. The lamplight, which on winter mornings seemed always of a dull tawny tint, shone on the rosined linoleum, on the shelves lining the walls, on the defenseless spines of books huddling there in tight ranks, and on the black gallows of a pear-shaped punching ball. Beyond the plate-glass windows, soft slow snow kept densely falling with a kind of monotonous and sterile grace.

At school, recently, the geography teacher, Berezovski (author of a booklet "Chao-San, the Land of the Morning: Korea and Koreans, with thirteen illustrations and a map in the text"), fingering his dark little beard, informed the entire class, unexpectedly and malapropos, that Mascara was giving Peter and him private lessons in boxing. Everybody stared at Peter. Embarrassment caused Peter's face to glow brightly and even to become somewhat puffy. At the next recess, Shchukin, his strongest, roughest, and most backward classmate, came up to him and said with a grin: "Come on, show how you box." "Leave me alone," replied Peter gently. Shchukin emitted a nasal grunt and hit Peter in the underbelly. Peter resented this. With a straight left, as taught by Monsieur Mascara, he bloodied Shchukin's nose. A stunned pause, red spots on a handkerchief. Having recovered from his astonishment, Shchukin fell upon Peter and started to maul him. Though his whole body hurt, Peter felt satisfied. Blood from Shchukin's nose continued to flow throughout the lesson of Natural History, stopped during Sums, and retrickled at Sacred Studies. Peter watched with quiet interest.

That winter Peter's mother took Mara to Mentone. Mara was sure she was dying of consumption. The absence of his sister, a rather badgering young lady with a caustic tongue, did not displease Peter, but he could not get over his mother's departure; he missed her terribly, especially in the evenings. He never saw much of his father. His father was busy in a place known as the Parliament (where a couple of years earlier the ceiling had collapsed). There was also something called the Kadet Party, which had nothing to do with parties or cadets. Very often Peter would have to dine separately upstairs, with Miss Sheldon—who had black hair and blue eyes and wore a knit tie with transverse stripes over her voluminous blouse—while downstairs near the monstrously swollen hallstands fully fifty pairs of rubbers would accumulate; and if he passed from the vestibule to the side room with its silk-covered Turkish divan he could suddenly hear—when somewhere in the distance a footman opened a door—a cacophonic din, a zoolike hubbub, and the remote but clear voice of his father.

One gloomy November morning Dmitri Korff, who shared a school desk with Peter, took out of his piebald satchel and handed to him a cheap satirical magazine. On one of the first pages there was a cartoon—with green color predominating—depicting Peter's father and accompanied by a jingle. Glancing at the lines, Peter caught a fragment from the middle:

> *V syom stolknovenii neschastnom*
> *Kak dzentelmen on predlagal*
> *Revolver, sablyu il' kinzhal.*

> (In this unfortunate affray
> He offered like a gentleman
> Revolver, dagger, or épée.)

"Is it true?" asked Dmitri in a whisper (the lesson had just begun). "What do you mean—true?" whispered Peter back. "Pipe down, you two," broke in Aleksey Matveich, the teacher of Russian, a muzhik-looking man, with an impediment in his speech, a nondescript and untidy growth above a crooked lip, and celebrated legs in screwy trousers:

when he walked his feet tangled—he set the right one where the left should have landed and vice versa—but nevertheless his progress was extremely rapid. He now sat at his table and leafed through his little notebook; presently his eyes focused on a distant desk, from behind which, like a tree grown by the glance of a fakir, Shchukin was rising.

"What do you mean—true?" softly repeated Peter, holding the magazine in his lap and looking askance at Dmitri. Dmitri moved a little closer to him. Meanwhile, Shchukin, crop-headed, wearing a Russian blouse of black serge, was beginning for the third time, with a sort of hopeless zest: "*Mumu* . . . Turgenev's story *Mumu* . . ." "That bit about your father," answered Dmitri in a low voice. Aleksey Matveich banged the *Zhivoe Slovo* (a school anthology) against the table with such violence that a pen jumped and stuck its nib in the floor. "What's going on there? . . . What's this . . . you whisperers?" spoke the teacher, spitting out sibilant words incoherently: "Stand up, stand up. . . . Korff, Shishkov. . . . What is it you're doing there?" He advanced and nimbly snatched away the magazine. "So you're reading smut . . . sit down, sit down . . . smut." His booty he put into his briefcase.

Next, Peter was called to the blackboard. He was told to write out the first line of a poem which he was supposed to have learned by heart. He wrote:

> . . . *uzkoyu mezhoy*
> *Porosshey kashkoyu . . . ili bedoy . . .*

> (. . . along a narrow margin overgrown
> with clover . . . or ache . . .)

Here came a shout so jarring that Peter dropped his bit of chalk:

"What are you scrawling? Why *bedoy*, when it's *lebedoy*, orache—a clingy weed? Where are your thoughts roaming? Go back to your seat!"

"Well, is it true?" asked Dmitri in a well-timed whisper. Peter pretended he did not hear. He could not stop the shiver running through him; in his ears there kept echoing the verse about the "revolver, dagger, or épée"; he kept seeing before him the sharp-angled pale-green caricature of his father, with the green crossing the outline in one place and not reaching it in another—a negligence of the color print. Quite recently, before his ride to school, that crepitation of steel, that scrape of soles . . . his father and the fencing master, both wearing padded chest protectors and wire-mesh masks. . . . It had all been so habitual— the Frenchman's uvular cries, *rompez, battez!,* the robust movements of his father, the flicker and clink of the foils. . . . A pause: panting and smiling, he removed the convex mask from his damp pink face.

The lesson ended. Aleksey Matveich carried away the magazine. Chalk-pale, Peter kept sitting where he was, lifting and lowering the lid of his desk. His classmates, with deferential curiosity, clustered around him, pressing him for details. He knew nothing and tried himself to discover something from the shower of questions. What he could make out was that Tumanski, a fellow member of the Parliament, had aspersed his father's honor and his father had challenged him to a duel.

Two more lessons dragged by, then came the main recess, with snowball fights in the yard. For no reason at all Peter began stuffing his snowballs with frozen earth, something he had never done before. In the course of the next lesson Nussbaum, the German teacher, lost his temper and roared at Shchukin (who was having bad luck that day), and Peter felt a spasm in his throat and asked leave to go to the toilet—so as not to burst into tears in public. There, in solitary suspension near the washbowl, was the unbelievably soiled, unbelievably slimy towel—more exactly the corpse of a towel that had passed through many wet, hastily kneading hands. For a minute or so Peter looked at himself in the glass—the best method of keeping the face from dissolving in a grimace of crying.

He wondered if he should not leave for home before three o'clock, the regular time, but chased that thought away. Self-control, the motto is self-control! The storm in class had subsided. Shchukin, scarlet-eared but absolutely calm, was back in his place, sitting there with his arms folded crosswise.

One more lesson—and then the final bell, which differed in sustained hoarse emphasis from those that marked the earlier periods. Arctics, short fur coat, *shapska* with earflaps, were quickly slipped on, and Peter ran across the yard, penetrated into its tunnel-like exit, and jumped over the dogboard of the gate. No automobile had been sent to fetch him, so he had to take a hackney sleigh. The driver, lean-bottomed, flat-backed, perching slightly askew on his low seat, had an eccentric way of urging his horse on: he would pretend to draw the knout out of the leg of his long boot, or else his hand adumbrated a kind of beckoning gesture directed to no one in particular, and then the sleigh jerked, causing the pencil case to rattle in Peter's satchel, and it was all dully oppressive and increased his anxiety, and oversize, irregularly shaped, hastily modeled snowflakes fell upon the sleazy sleighrobe.

At home, since the departure of his mother and sister, afternoons were quiet. Peter went up the wide, gentle-graded staircase where on the second landing stood a table of green malachite with a vase for visiting cards, presided over by a replica of the Venus of Milo that his cousins had once rigged up in a plush-velveteen coat and a hat with sham cherries, whereupon she began to resemble Praskovia Stepanovna, an impoverished widow who would call every first of the month. Peter reached the upper floor and hallooed his governess's name. But Miss Sheldon had a guest for tea, the English governess of the Veretennikovs. Miss Sheldon sent Peter to prepare his school tasks for the next morning. Not forgetting first to wash his hands and drink his glass of milk. Her door closed. Peter, feeling smothered in cotton-woollish, ghastly anguish, dawdled in the nursery, then descended to the second floor and peeped into his father's study. The silence there was unendurable. Then a crisp sound broke it—the fall of an incurved chrysanthemum petal. On the monumental writing desk the familiar, discreetly gleaming objects were fixed in an orderly cosmic array, like planets: cabinet photographs, a marble egg, a majestic inkstand.

Peter passed into his mother's boudoir, and thence into its oriel and stood there for quite a while looking through an elongated casement. It was almost night by that time, at that latitude. Around the globes of lilac-tinted lights the snowflakes fluttered. Below, the black outlines of sleighs with the silhouettes of hunched-up passengers flowed hazily. Maybe next morning? It always takes place in the morning, very early.

He walked down to the first floor. A silent wilderness. In the library, with nervous haste, he switched on the light and the black shadows swept away. Having settled down in a nook near one of the bookcases, he tried to occupy his mind with the examination of the huge bound volumes of the *Zhivopisnoe obozrenie* (a Russian counterpart of *The Graphic*): Masculine beauty depends on a splendid beard and a sumptuous mustache. Since girlhood I suffered from blackheads. Concert accordion "Pleasure," with twenty voices and ten valves. A group of priests and a wooden church. A painting with the legend "Strangers": gentleman moping at his writing desk, lady with curly boa standing some distance away in the act of gloving her wide-fingered hand. I've already looked at this volume. He pulled out another and instantly was confronted by the picture of a duel between two Italian swordsmen: one lunges madly, the other sidesteps the thrust and pierces his opponent's throat. Peter slammed the heavy tome shut, and froze, holding his temples like a grown-up. Everything was frightening—the stillness, the motionless bookcases, the glossy dumbbells on an oaken table, the black boxes of the card index. With bent head he sped like the wind through murky rooms. Back again in the nursery, he lay down on a couch and remained lying there until Miss Sheldon remembered his existence. From the stairs came the sound of the dinner gong.

As Peter was on his way down, his father came out of his study, accompanied by Colonel Rozen, who had once been engaged to the long-dead young sister of Peter's father. Peter dared not glance at his father and when the latter's large palm, emitting familiar warmth, touched the side of his son's head, Peter blushed to the point of tears. It was impossible, unbearable, to think that this man, the best person on earth, was going to duel with some dim *Enigmanski*. Using what weapons? Pistols? Swords? Why does nobody talk about it? Do the servants know? The governess? Mother in Mentone? At table the colonel joked as he always did, abruptly, briefly, as if cracking nuts, but tonight Peter instead of laughing was suffused with blushes, which he tried to conceal by deliberately dropping his napkin so as to rally quietly under the table and regain there his normal complexion, but he would crawl out even redder than before and his father would raise his eyebrows— and merrily, unhurriedly, with characteristic evenness perform the rites of eating dinner, of carefully quaffing wine from a low golden cup with a handle. Colonel Rozen went on cracking jokes. Miss Sheldon, who had no Russian, kept silent, sternly protruding her chest; and whenever Peter hunched his back she would give him a nasty poke under the shoulder blades. For dessert there was pistachio parfait, which he loathed.

After dinner, his father and the colonel went up to the study. Peter looked so queer that his father asked: "What's the matter? Why are you sulking?" And miraculously Peter managed to answer distinctly: "No, I'm not sulking." Miss Sheldon led him bedward. As soon as the light was extinguished, he buried his face in the pillow. Onegin shed his cloak, Lenski plopped down on the boards like a black sack. One could see the point of the épée coming out at the back of the Italian's neck. Mascara liked to tell about the *rencontre* which he had had in his youth: half a centimeter lower—and the liver would have been pierced. And the homework for tomorrow has not been done, and the darkness in the bedroom is total, and he must get up early, very early, better not shut my eyes or I'll oversleep—the thing is sure to be scheduled for tomorrow. Oh, I'll skip school, I'll skip it, I'll say—sore throat. Mother will be back only at Christmas. Mentone, blue picture postcards. Must insert the latest one in my album. One corner has now gone in, the next—

Peter woke up as usual, around eight, as usual he heard a ringing sound: that was the servant responsible for the stoves—he had opened a damper. With his hair still wet after a hasty bath, Peter went downstairs and found his father boxing with Mascara as if it were an ordinary day. "Sore throat?" he said, repeating it after Peter. "Yes, a scrapy feeling," said Peter, speaking low. "Look here, are you telling the truth?" Peter felt that all further explanations were perilous: the floodgate was about to burst, liberating a disgraceful torrent. He silently turned away and presently was seated in the limousine with his satchel in his lap. He felt queasy. Everything was horrible and irremediable.

Somehow or other he managed to be late for the first lesson, and stood for a long time with his hand raised behind the glazed door of his class but was not permitted to enter and went roaming about in the hall, and then hoisted himself onto a window ledge with the vague idea of doing his tasks but did not get farther than:

> . . . *with clover and with clinging orache*

and for the thousandth time began imagining the way it would all happen—in the mist of a frosty dawn. How should he go about discovering the date agreed upon? How could he find out the details? Had he been in the last form—no, even in the last but one—he might have suggested: "Let me take your place."

Finally the bell rang. A noisy crowd filled the recreation hall. He heard Dmitri Korff's voice in sudden proximity: "Well, are you glad? Are you glad?" Peter looked at him with dull perplexity. "Andrey downstairs has a newspaper," said Dmitri excitedly. "Come, we have just got time, you'll see— But what's the matter? If I were you—"

In the vestibule, on his stool, sat Andrey the old porter, reading. He raised his eyes and smiled. "It is all here, all written down here," said Dmitri. Peter took the paper and made out through a trembling blur: "Yesterday in the early afternoon, on Krestovski Island, G. D. Shishkov and Count A. S. Tumanski fought a duel, the outcome of which was fortunately bloodless. Count Tumanski, who fired first, missed, whereupon his opponent discharged his pistol into the air. The seconds were—"

And then the floodgate broke. The porter and Dmitri Korff attempted to calm him, but he kept pushing them away, shaken by spasms, his face concealed, he could not breathe, never before had he known such tears, do not tell anyone, please, I am simply not very well, I have this pain—and again a tumult of sobs.

MUSIC

THE entrance hall overflowed with coats of both sexes; from the drawing room came a rapid succession of piano notes. Victor's reflection in the hall mirror straightened the knot of a reflected tie. Straining to reach up, the maid hung his overcoat, but it broke loose, taking down two others with it, and she had to begin all over again.

Already walking on tiptoe, Victor reached the drawing room, whereupon the music at once became louder and manlier. At the piano sat Wolf, a rare guest in that house. The rest—some thirty people in all—were listening in a variety of attitudes, some with chin propped on fist, others sending cigarette smoke up toward the ceiling, and the uncertain lighting lent a vaguely picturesque quality to their immobility. From afar, the lady of the house, with an eloquent smile, indicated to Victor an unoccupied seat, a pretzel-backed little armchair almost in the shadow of the grand piano. He responded with self-effacing gestures—it's all right, it's all right, I can stand; presently, however, he began moving in the suggested direction, cautiously sat down, and cautiously folded his arms. The performer's wife, her mouth half-open, her eyes blinking fast, was about to turn the page; now she has turned it. A black forest of ascending notes, a slope, a gap, then a separate group of little trapezists in flight. Wolf had long, fair eyelashes; his translucent ears were of a delicate crimson hue; he struck the keys with extraordinary velocity and vigor and, in the lacquered depths of the open keyboard lid, the doubles of his hands were engaged in a ghostly, intricate, even somewhat clownish mimicry.

To Victor any music he did not know—and all he knew was a dozen conventional tunes—could be likened to the patter of a conversation in a strange tongue: in vain you strive to define at least the limits of the words, but everything slips and merges, so that the laggard ear begins to feel boredom. Victor tried to concentrate on listening, but soon caught himself watching Wolf's hands and their spectral reflections. When the sounds grew into insistent thunder, the performer's neck would swell, his widespread fingers tensed, and he emitted a faint grunt. At one point his wife got ahead of him; he arrested the page with an instant slap of his open left palm, then with incredible speed himself flipped it over, and already both hands were fiercely kneading the compliant keyboard again. Victor made a detailed study of the man: sharp-tipped nose, jutting eyelids, scar left by a boil on his neck, hair resembling blond fluff, broad-shouldered cut of black jacket. For a moment Victor tried to attend to the music again, but scarcely had he focused on it when his attention dissolved. He slowly turned away, fishing out his cigarette case, and began to examine the other guests. Among the strange faces he discovered some familiar ones— nice, chubby Kocharovsky over there—should I nod to him? He did, but overshot his mark: it was another acquaintance, Shmakov, who acknowledged the nod: I heard he was leaving Berlin for Paris—must ask him about it. On a divan, flanked by two elderly ladies, corpulent, red-haired Anna Samoylovna, half-reclined with closed eyes, while her husband, a throat specialist, sat with his elbow propped on the arm of his chair. What is that glittering object he twirls in the fingers of his free hand? Ah yes, a pince-nez on a Chekhovian ribbon. Further, one shoulder in shadow, a hunchbacked, bearded man known to be a lover of music listened intently, an index finger stretched up against his temple. Victor could never remember his name and patronymic. Boris? No, that wasn't it. Borisovich? Not that either. More faces. Wonder if the Haruzins are here. Yes, there they are. Not looking my way. And in the next instant, immediately behind them, Victor saw his former wife.

At once he lowered his gaze, automatically tapping his cigarette to dislodge the ash that had not yet had time to form. From somewhere low down his heart rose like a fist to deliver an uppercut, drew back, struck again, then went into a fast, disorderly throb, contradicting the music and drowning it. Not knowing which way to look, he glanced askance at the pianist, but did not hear a sound: Wolf seemed to be pounding a silent keyboard. Victor's chest got so constricted that he had to straighten up and draw a deep breath; then, hastening back from a great distance, gasping for air, the music returned to life, and his heart resumed beating with a more regular rhythm.

They had separated two years before, in another town, where the sea boomed at night, and where they had lived since their marriage. With his eyes still cast down, he tried to ward off the thunder and rush of the past with trivial thoughts: for instance, that she must have observed him a few moments ago as, with long, noiseless, bobbing strides, he had tiptoed the whole length of the room to reach this chair. It was as if someone had caught him undressed or engaged in some idiotic occupation; and, while recalling how in his innocence he had glided and plunged under her gaze (hostile? derisive? curious?), he interrupted himself to consider if his hostess or anyone else in the room might be aware of the situation, and how had she got here, and whether she had come alone or with her new husband, and what he, Victor, ought to do: stay as he was or look her way? No, looking was still impossible; first he had to get used to her presence in this large but confining room—for the music had fenced them in and had become for them a kind of prison, where they were both fated to remain captive until the pianist ceased constructing and keeping up his vaults of sound.

What had he had time to observe in that brief glance of recognition a moment ago? So little: her averted eyes, her pale cheek, a lock of black hair, and, as a vague secondary character, beads or something around her neck. So little! Yet that careless sketch, that half-finished image already *was* his wife, and its momentary blend of gleam and shade already formed the unique entity which bore her name.

How long ago it all seemed! He had fallen madly in love with her one sultry evening, under a swooning sky, on the terrace of the tennis-club pavilion, and, a month later, on their wedding night, it rained so hard you could not hear the sea. What bliss it had been. Bliss—what a moist, lapping, and plashing word, so alive, so tame, smiling and crying all by itself. And the morning after: those glistening leaves in the garden, that almost noiseless sea, that languid, milky, silvery sea.

Something had to be done about his cigarette butt. He turned his head, and again his heart missed a beat. Someone had stirred, blocking his view of her almost totally, and was taking out a handkerchief as white as death; but presently the stranger's elbow would go and she would reappear, yes, in a moment she would reappear. No, I can't bear to look. There's an ashtray on the piano.

The barrier of sounds remained just as high and impenetrable. The spectral hands in their lacquered depths continued to go through the same contortions. "We'll be happy forever"—what melody in that phrase, what shimmer! She was velvet-soft all over, one longed to gather her up the way one could gather up a foal and its folded legs. Embrace her and fold her. And then what? What could one do to possess her completely? I love your liver, your kidneys, your blood cells. To this she would reply, "Don't be disgusting." They lived neither in luxury nor in poverty, and went swimming in the sea almost all year round. The jellyfish, washed up onto the shingly beach, trembled in the wind. The Crimean cliffs glistened in the spray. Once they saw fishermen carrying away the body of a drowned man; his bare feet, protruding from under the blanket, looked surprised. In the evenings she used to make cocoa.

He looked again. She was now sitting with downcast eyes, legs crossed, chin propped upon knuckles: she was very musical, Wolf must be playing some famous, beautiful piece. I won't be able to sleep for several nights, thought Victor as he contemplated her white neck and the soft angle of her knee. She wore a flimsy black dress, unfamiliar to him, and her necklace kept catching the light. No, I won't be able to sleep, and I shall have to stop coming here. It has all been in vain: two years of straining and struggling, my peace of mind almost regained—now I must start all over again, trying to forget everything, everything that had already been almost forgotten, plus this evening on top of it. It suddenly seemed to him that she was looking at him furtively and he turned away.

The music must be drawing to a close. When they come, those stormy, gasping chords, it usually signifies that the end is near. Another intriguing word, *end* . . . Rend, impend . . . Thunder rending the sky, dust clouds of impending doom. With the coming of spring she became strangely unresponsive. She spoke almost without moving her lips. He would ask "What is the matter with you?" "Nothing. Nothing in particular." Sometimes she would stare at him out of narrowed eyes, with an enigmatic expression. "What *is* the matter?" "Nothing." By nightfall she would be as good as dead. You could not do anything with her, for, despite her being a small, slender woman, she would grow heavy and unwieldy, and as if made of stone. "Won't you finally tell me what is the matter with you?" So it went for almost a month. Then, one morning—yes, it was the morning of her birthday—she said quite simply, as if she were talking about some trifle, "Let's separate for a while. We can't go on like this." The neighbors' little daughter burst into the room to show her kitten (the sole survivor of a litter that had been drowned). "Go away, go away, later." The little girl left. There was a long silence. After a while, slowly, silently, he began twisting her wrists—he longed to break all of her, to dislocate all her joints with loud cracks. She started to cry. Then he sat down at the table and pretended to read the newspaper. She went out into the garden, but soon returned. "I can't keep it back any longer. I have to tell you everything." And with an odd astonishment, as if discussing another woman, and being astonished at her, and inviting him to share her astonishment, she told it, told it all. The man in question was a burly, modest, and reserved fellow; he used to come for a game of whist, and liked to talk about artesian wells. The first time had been in the park, then at his place.

The rest is all very vague. I paced the beach till nightfall. Yes, the music does seem to be ending. When I slapped his face on the quay, he said, "You'll pay dearly for this," picked up his cap from the ground, and walked away. I did not say good-bye to her. How silly it would have been to think of killing her. Live on, live. Live as you are living now; as you are sitting now, sit like that forever. Come, look at me, I implore you, please, please look. I'll forgive you everything, because someday we must all die, and then we shall know everything, and everything will be forgiven—so why put it off? Look at me, look at me, turn your eyes, *my* eyes, my darling eyes. No. Finished.

The last many-clawed, ponderous chords—another, and just enough breath left for one more, and, after this concluding chord, with which the music seemed to have surrendered its soul entirely, the performer took aim and, with feline precision, struck one simple, quite separate little golden note. The musical barrier dissolved. Applause. Wolf said, "It's been a very long time since I last played this." Wolf's wife said, "It's been a long time, you know, since my husband last played this piece." Advancing upon him, crowding him, nudging him with his paunch, the throat specialist said to Wolf: "Marvelous! I have always maintained that's the best thing he ever wrote. I think that toward the end you modernize the color of sound just a bit too much. I don't know if I make myself clear, but, you see—"

Victor was looking in the direction of the door. There, a slightly built, black-haired lady with a helpless smile was taking leave of the hostess, who kept exclaiming in surprise, "I won't hear of it, we're all going to have tea now, and then we're going to hear a singer." But she kept on smiling helplessly and made her way to the door, and Victor realized that the music, which before had seemed a narrow dungeon where, shackled together by the resonant sounds, they had been compelled to sit face-to-face some twenty feet apart, had actually been incredible bliss, a magic glass dome that had embraced and imprisoned him and her, had made it possible for him to breathe the same air as she; and now everything had been broken and scattered, she was disappearing through the door, Wolf had shut the piano, and the enchanting captivity could not be restored.

She left. Nobody seemed to have noticed anything. He was greeted by a man named Boke who said in a gentle voice, "I kept watching you. What a reaction to music! You know, you looked so bored I felt sorry for you. Is it possible that you are so completely indifferent to it?"

"Why, no. I wasn't bored," Victor answered awkwardly. "It's just that I have no ear for music, and that makes me a poor judge. By the way, what was it he played?"

"What you will," said Boke in the apprehensive whisper of a rank outsider. " 'A Maiden's Prayer,' or the 'Kreutzer Sonata.' Whatever you will."

PERFECTION

"Now then, here we have two lines," he would say to David in a cheery, almost rapturous voice as if to have two lines were a rare fortune, something one could be proud of. David was gentle but dullish. Watching David's ears evolve a red glow, Ivanov foresaw he would often appear in David's dreams, thirty or forty years hence: human dreams do not easily forget old grudges.

Fair-haired and thin, wearing a yellow sleeveless jersey held close by a leather belt, with scarred naked knees and a wristwatch whose crystal was protected by a prison-window grating, David sat at the table in a most uncomfortable position, and kept tapping his teeth with the blunt end of his fountain pen. He was doing badly at school, and it had become necessary to engage a private tutor.

"Let us now turn to the second line," Ivanov continued with the same studied cheeriness. He had taken his degree in geography but his special knowledge could not be put to any use: dead riches, a highborn pauper's magnificent manor. How beautiful, for instance, are ancient charts! Viatic maps of the Romans, elongated, ornate, with snakelike marginal stripes representing canal-shaped seas; or those drawn in ancient Alexandria, with England and Ireland looking like two little sausages; or again, maps of medieval Christendom, crimson-and-grass-colored, with the paradisian Orient at the top and Jerusalem—the world's golden navel—in the center. Accounts of marvelous pilgrimages: that traveling monk comparing the Jordan to a little river in his native Chernigov, that envoy of the Tsar reaching a country where people strolled under yellow parasols, that merchant from Tver picking his way through a dense *"zhengel,"* his Russian for "jungle," full of monkeys, to a torrid land ruled by a naked prince. The islet of the known universe keeps growing: new hesitant contours emerge from the fabulous mists, slowly the globe disrobes—and lo, out of the remoteness beyond the seas, looms South America's shoulder and from their four corners blow fat-cheeked winds, one of them wearing spectacles.

But let us forget the maps. Ivanov had many other joys and eccentricities. He was lanky, swarthy, none too young, with a permanent shadow cast on his face by a black beard that had once been permitted to grow for a long time, and had then been shaven off (at a barbershop in Serbia, his first stage of expatriation): the slightest indulgence made that shadow revive and begin to bristle. Throughout a dozen years of émigré life, mostly in Berlin, he had remained faithful to starched collars and cuffs; his deteriorating shirts had an outdated tongue in front to be buttoned to the top of his long underpants. Of late he had been obliged to wear constantly his old formal black suit with braid piping along the lapels (all his other clothes having rotted away); and occasionally, on an overcast day, in a forbearing light, it seemed to him that he was dressed with sober good taste. Some sort of flannel entrails were trying to escape from his necktie, and he was forced to trim off parts of them, but could not bring himself to excise them altogether.

He would set out for his lesson with David at around three in the afternoon, with a somewhat unhinged, bouncing gait, his head held high. He would inhale avidly the young air of the early summer, rolling his large Adam's apple, which in the course of the morning had already fledged. On one occasion a youth in leather leggings attracted Ivanov's absent gaze from the opposite sidewalk by means of a soft whistle, and, throwing up his own chin, kept it up for a distance of a few steps: thou shouldst correct thy fellow man's oddities. Ivanov, however, misinterpreted that didactic mimicry and, assuming that something was being pointed out to him overhead, looked trustingly even higher than was his wont—and, indeed, three lovely cloudlets, holding each other by the hand, were drifting diagonally across the sky; the third one fell slowly behind, and its outline, and the outline of the friendly hand still stretched out to it, slowly lost their graceful significance.

During those first warm days everything seemed beautiful and touching: the leggy little girls playing hopscotch on the sidewalk, the old men on the benches, the green confetti that sumptuous lindens scattered every time the air stretched its invisible limbs. He felt lonesome and stifled in black. He would take off his hat and stand still for a moment looking around. Sometimes, as he looked at a chimney sweep (that indifferent carrier of other people's luck, whom women in passing touched with superstitious fingers), or at an airplane overtaking a cloud, Ivanov daydreamed about the many things that he would

never get to know closer, about professions that he would never practice, about a parachute, opening like a colossal corolla, or the fleeting,
speckled world of automobile racers, about various images of happiness, about the pleasures of very rich people amid very picturesque
natural surroundings. His thought fluttered and walked up and down
the glass pane which for as long as he lived would prevent him from
having direct contact with the world. He had a passionate desire to experience everything, to attain and touch everything, to let the dappled
voices, the bird calls, filter through his being and to enter for a moment into a passerby's soul as one enters the cool shade of a tree. His
mind would be preoccupied with unsolvable problems: How and
where do chimney sweeps wash after work? Has anything changed
about that forest road in Russia that a moment ago he had recalled so
vividly?

When, at last, late as usual, he went up in the elevator, he would
have a sensation of slowly growing, stretching upward, and, after his
head had reached the sixth floor, of pulling up his legs like a swimmer. Then, having reverted to normal length, he would enter David's
bright room.

During lessons David liked to fiddle with things but otherwise remained fairly attentive. He had been raised abroad and spoke Russian
with difficulty and boredom, and, when faced with the necessity of
expressing something important, or when talking to his mother, the
Russian wife of a Berlin businessman, would immediately switch to
German. Ivanov, whose knowledge of the local language was poor, ex-
pounded mathematics in Russian, while the textbook was, of course,
in German, and this produced a certain amount of confusion. As he
watched the boy's ears, edged with fair down, he tried to imagine the
degree of tedium and detestation he must arouse in David, and this distressed him. He saw himself from the outside—a blotchy complexion,
a *feu du rasoir* rash, a shiny black jacket, stains on its sleeve cuffs—and
caught his own falsely animated tone, the throat-clearing noises he
made, and even that sound which could not reach David—the blundering but dutiful beat of his long-ailing heart. The lesson came to an end,
the boy would hurry to show him something, such as an automobile
catalogue, or a camera, or a cute little screw found in the street—and
then Ivanov did his best to give proof of intelligent participation—but,
alas, he never had been on intimate terms with the secret fraternity of
man-made things that goes under the name technology, and this or
that inexact observation of his would make David fix him with puzzled
pale-gray eyes and quickly take back the object which seemed to be
whimpering in Ivanov's hands.

And yet David was not untender. His indifference to the unusual could be explained—for I, too, reflected Ivanov, must have appeared to be a stolid and dryish lad, I who never shared with anyone my loves, my fancies and fears. All that my childhood expressed was an excited little monologue addressed to itself. One might construct the following syllogism: a child is the most perfect type of humanity; David is a child; David is perfect. With such adorable eyes as he has, a boy cannot possibly keep thinking only about the prices of various mechanical gadgets or about how to save enough trading stamps to obtain fifty pfennigs' worth of free merchandise at the store. He must be saving up something else too: bright childish impressions whose paint remains on the fingertips of the mind. He keeps silent about it just as I kept silent. But if several decades later—say, in 1970 (how they resemble telephone numbers, those distant years!), he will happen to see again that picture now hanging above his bed—Bonzo devouring a tennis ball— what a jolt he will feel, what light, what amazement at his own existence. Ivanov was not entirely wrong, David's eyes, indeed, were not devoid of a certain dreaminess; but it was the dreaminess of concealed mischief.

Enters David's mother. She has yellow hair and a high-strung temperament. The day before she was studying Spanish; today she subsists on orange juice. "I would like to speak to you. Stay seated, please. Go away, David. The lesson is over? David, go. This is what I want to say. His vacation is coming soon. It would be appropriate to take him to the seaside. Regrettably, I shan't be able to go myself. Would you be willing to take him along? I trust you, and he listens to you. Above all, I want him to speak Russian more often. Actually, he's nothing but a little *Sportsmann* as are all modern kids. Well, how do you look at it?"

With doubt. But Ivanov did not voice his doubt. He had last seen the sea in 1912, eighteen years ago when he was a university student. The resort was Hungerburg in the province of Estland. Pines, sand, silvery-pale water far away—oh, how long it took one to reach it, and then how long it took it to reach up to one's knees! It would be the same Baltic Sea, but a different shore. However, the last time I went swimming was not at Hungerburg but in the river Luga. Muzhiks came running out of the water, frog-legged, hands crossed over their private parts: *pudor agrestis*. Their teeth chattered as they pulled on their shirts over their wet bodies. Nice to go bathing in the river toward evening, especially under a warm rain that makes silent circles, each spreading and encroaching upon the next, all over the water. But I like to feel underfoot the presence of the bottom. How hard to put on again one's socks and shoes without muddying the soles of one's feet! Water in one's ear: keep hopping on one foot until it spills out like a tickly tear.

The day of departure soon came. "You will be frightfully hot in those clothes," remarked David's mother by way of farewell as she glanced at Ivanov's black suit (worn in mourning for his other defunct things). The train was crowded, and his new, soft collar (a slight compromise, a summer treat) turned gradually into a tight clammy compress. Happy David, his hair neatly trimmed, with one small central tuft playing in the wind, his open-necked shirt aflutter, stood, at the corridor window, peering out, and on curves the semicircles of the front cars would become visible, with the heads of passengers who leaned on the lowered frames. Then the train, its bell ringing, its elbows working ever so rapidly, straightened out again to enter a beech forest.

The house was located at the rear of the little seaside town, a plain two-storied house with red-currant shrubs in the yard, which a fence separated from the dusty road. A tawny-bearded fisherman sat on a log, slitting his eyes in the low sun as he tarred his net. His wife led them upstairs. Terra-cotta floors, dwarf furniture. On the wall, a fair-sized fragment of an airplane propeller: "My husband used to work at the airport." Ivanov unpacked his scanty linen, his razor, and a dilapidated volume of Pushkin's works in the Panafidin edition. David freed from its net a varicolored ball that went jumping about and from sheer exuberance only just missed knocking a horned shell off its shelf. The landlady brought tea and some flounder. David was in a hurry. He could not wait to get a look at the sea. The sun had already begun to set.

When they came down to the beach after a fifteen-minute walk, Ivanov instantly became conscious of an acute discomfort in his chest, a sudden tightness followed by a sudden void, and out on the smooth, smoke-blue sea a small boat looked black and appallingly alone. Its imprint began to appear on whatever he looked at, then dissolved in the air. Because now the dust of twilight dimmed everything around, it seemed to him that his eyesight was dulled, while his legs felt strangely weakened by the squeaky touch of the sand. From somewhere came the playing of an orchestra, and its every sound, muted by distance, seemed to be corked up; breathing was difficult. David chose a spot on the beach and ordered a wicker cabana for next day. The way back was uphill; Ivanov's heart now drifted away, then hurried back to perform anyhow what was expected of it, only to escape again, and through all this pain and anxiety the nettles along the fences smelled of Hungerburg.

David's white pajamas. For reasons of economy Ivanov slept naked.

At first the earthen cold of the clean sheets made him feel even worse, but then repose brought relief. The moon groped its way to the wash-stand, selected there one facet of a tumbler, and started to crawl up the wall. On that and on the following nights, Ivanov thought vaguely of several matters at once, imagining among other things that the boy who slept in the bed next to his was his own son. Ten years before, in Serbia, the only woman he had ever loved—another man's wife—had become pregnant by him. She suffered a miscarriage and died the next night, deliring and praying. He would have had a son, a little fellow about David's age. When in the morning David prepared to pull on his swimming trunks, Ivanov was touched by the way his café-au-lait tan (already acquired on a Berlin lakeside) abruptly gave way to a childish whiteness below the waist. He was about to forbid the boy to go from house to beach with nothing on but those trunks, and was a little taken aback, and did not immediately give in, when David began to ar-gue, with the whining intonations of German astonishment, that he had done so at another resort and that everyone did it. As to Ivanov, he languished on the beach in the sorrowful image of a city dweller. The sun, the sparkling blue, made him seasick. A hot tingling ran over the top of his head under his fedora, he felt as if he were being roasted alive, but he would not even dispense with his jacket, not only because as is the case with many Russians, it would embarrass him to "appear in his braces in the presence of ladies," but also because his shirt was too badly frayed. On the third day he suddenly gathered up his cour-age and, glancing furtively around from under his brows, took off his shoes. He settled at the bottom of a crater dug by David, with a news-paper sheet spread under his elbow, and listened to the tight snapping of the gaudy flags, or else peered over the sandy brink with a kind of tender envy at a thousand brown corpses felled in various attitudes by the sun; one girl was especially magnificent, as if cast in metal, tanned to the point of blackness, with amazingly light eyes and with finger-nails as pale as a monkey's. Looking at her he tried to imagine what it felt like to be so sun-baked.

On obtaining permission for a dip, David would noisily swim off while Ivanov walked to the edge of the surf to watch his charge and to jump back whenever a wave spreading farther than its predecessors threatened to douse his trousers. He recalled a fellow student in Rus-sia, a close friend of his, who had the knack of pitching pebbles so as to have them glance off the water's surface two, three, four times, but when he tried to demonstrate it to David, the projectile pierced the surface with a loud plop, and David laughed, and made a nice flat stone perform not four but at least six skips.

A few days later, during a spell of absentmindedness (his eyes had strayed, and it was too late when he caught up with them), Ivanov read a postcard that David had begun writing to his mother and had left lying on the window ledge. David wrote that his tutor was probably ill for he never went swimming. That very day Ivanov took extraordinary measures: he acquired a black bathing suit and, on reaching the beach, hid in the cabana, undressed gingerly, and pulled on the cheap shop-smelling stockinet garment. He had a moment of melancholy embarrassment when, pale-skinned and hairy-legged, he emerged into the sunlight. David, however, looked at him with approval. "Well!" exclaimed Ivanov with devil-may-care jauntiness, "here we go!" He went in up to his knees, splashed some water on his head, then walked on with outspread arms, and the higher the water rose, the deadlier became the spasm that contracted his heart. At last, closing his ears with his thumbs, and covering his eyes with the rest of his fingers, he immersed himself in a crouching position. The stabbing chill compelled him to get promptly out of the water. He lay down on the sand, shivering and filled to the brim of his being with ghastly, unresolvable anguish. After a while the sun warmed him, he revived, but from then on forswore sea bathing. He felt too lazy to dress; when he closed his eyes tightly, optical spots glided against a red background, Martian canals kept intersecting, and, the moment he parted his lids, the wet silver of the sun started to palpitate between his lashes.

The inevitable took place. By evening, all those parts of his body that had been exposed turned into a symmetrical archipelago of fiery pain. "Today, instead of going to the beach, we shall take a walk in the woods," he said to the boy on the morrow. *"Ach, nein,"* wailed David. "Too much sun is bad for the health," said Ivanov. "Oh, please!" insisted David in great dismay. But Ivanov stood his ground.

The forest was dense. Geometrid moths, matching the bark in coloration, flew off the tree trunks. Silent David walked reluctantly. "We should cherish the woods," Ivanov said in an attempt to divert his pupil. "It was the first habitat of man. One fine day man left the jungle of primitive intimations for the sunlit glade of reason. Those bilberries appear to be ripe, you have my permission to taste them. Why do you sulk? Try to understand: one should vary one's pleasures. And one should not overindulge in sea bathing. How often it happens that a careless bather dies of sun stroke or heart failure!"

Ivanov rubbed his unbearably burning and itching back against a tree trunk and continued pensively: "While admiring nature at a given locality, I cannot help thinking of countries that I shall never see. Try to imagine, David, that this is not Pomerania but a Malayan forest.

Look about you: you'll presently see the rarest of birds fly past, Prince Albert's paradise bird, whose head is adorned with a pair of long plumes consisting of blue oriflammes." *"Ach, quatsch,"* responded David dejectedly.

"In Russian you ought to say *'erundá.'* Of course, it's nonsense, we are not in the mountains of New Guinea. But the point is that with a bit of imagination—if, God forbid, you were someday to go blind or be imprisoned, or were merely forced to perform, in appalling poverty, some hopeless, distasteful task, you might remember this walk we are taking today in an ordinary forest as if it had been—how shall I say?—fairy-tale ecstasy."

At sundown dark-pink clouds fluffed out above the sea. With the dulling of the sky they seemed to rust, and a fisherman said it would rain tomorrow, but the morning turned out to be marvelous and David kept urging his tutor to hurry, but Ivanov was not feeling well; he longed to stay in bed and think of remote and vague semievents illumined by memory on only one side, of some pleasant smoke-gray things that might have happened once upon a time, or drifted past quite close to him in life's field of vision, or else had appeared to him in a recent dream. But it was impossible to concentrate on them, they all somehow slipped away to one side, half-turning to him with a kind of friendly and mysterious slyness but gliding away relentlessly, as do those transparent little knots that swim diagonally in the vitreous humor of the eye. Alas, he had to get up, to pull on his socks, so full of holes that they resembled lace mittens. Before leaving the house he put on David's dark-yellow sunglasses—and the sun swooned amid a sky dying a turquoise death, and the morning light upon the porch steps acquired a sunset tinge. David, his naked back amber-colored, ran ahead, and when Ivanov called to him, he shrugged his shoulders in irritation. "Do not run away," Ivanov said wearily. His horizon was narrowed by the glasses, he was afraid of a sudden automobile.

The street sloped sleepily toward the sea. Little by little his eyes became used to the glasses, and he ceased to wonder at the sunny day's khaki uniform. At the turn of the street he suddenly half-remembered something—something extraordinarily comforting and strange—but it immediately dissolved, and the turbulent sea air constricted his chest. The dusky flags flapped excitedly, pointing all in the same direction, though nothing was happening there yet. Here is the sand, here is the dull splash of the sea. His ears felt plugged up, and when he inhaled through the nose a rumble started in his head, and something bumped into a membranous dead end. I've lived neither very long nor very well, reflected Ivanov. Still it would be a shame to complain; this alien world is beautiful, and I would feel happy right now if only I could recall that wonderful, wonderful—what? What was it?

He lowered himself onto the sand. David began busily repairing with a spade the sand wall where it had crumbled slightly. "Is it hot or cool today?" asked Ivanov. "Somehow I cannot decide." Presently David threw down the spade and said, "I'll go for a swim." "Sit still for a moment," said Ivanov. "I must gather my thoughts. The sea will not run away." "*Please* let me go!" pleaded David.

Ivanov raised himself on one elbow and surveyed the waves. They were large and humpbacked; nobody was bathing at that spot; only much farther to the left a dozen orange-capped heads bobbed and were carried off to one side in unison. "Those waves," said Ivanov with a sigh, and then added: "You may paddle a little, but don't go beyond a *sazhen*. A *sazhen* equals about two meters."

He sank his head, propping one cheek, grieving, computing indefinite measures of life, of pity, of happiness. His shoes were already full of sand, he took them off with slow hands, then was again lost in thought, and again those evasive little knots began to swim across his field of vision—and how he longed, how he longed to recall— A sudden scream. Ivanov stood up.

Amid yellow-blue waves, far from the shore, flitted David's face, and his open mouth was like a dark hole. He emitted a spluttering yell, and vanished. A hand appeared for a moment and vanished too. Ivanov threw off his jacket. "I'm coming," he shouted. "I'm coming. Hold on!" He splashed through the water, lost his footing, his ice-cold trousers stuck to his shins. It seemed to him that David's head came up again for an instant. Then a wave surged, knocking off Ivanov's hat, blinding him; he wanted to take off his glasses, but his agitation, the cold, the numbing weakness, prevented him from doing so. He realized that in its retreat the wave had dragged him a long way from the shore. He started to swim trying to catch sight of David. He felt enclosed in a tight painfully cold sack, his heart was straining unbearably. All at once a rapid something passed through him, a flash of fingers rippling over piano keys—and *this* was the very thing he had been trying to recall throughout the morning. He came out on a stretch of sand. Sand, sea, and air were of an odd, faded, opaque tint, and everything was perfectly still. Vaguely he reflected that twilight must have come, and that David had perished a long time ago, and he felt what he knew from earthly life—the poignant heat of tears. Trembling and bending toward the ashen sand, he wrapped himself tighter in the black cloak with the snake-shaped brass fastening that he had seen on a student friend, a long, long time ago, on an autumn day—and he felt so sorry for David's mother, and wondered what would he tell her. It is not my fault, I did all I could to save him, but I am a poor swimmer, and I have a bad heart, and he drowned. But there was something amiss about these thoughts, and when he looked around once more and saw himself in the desolate mist all alone with no David beside him, he understood that if David was not with him, David was not dead.

Only then were the clouded glasses removed. The dull mist immediately broke, blossomed with marvelous colors, all kinds of sounds burst forth—the rote of the sea, the clapping of the wind, human cries—and there was David standing, up to his ankles in bright water, not knowing what to do, shaking with fear, not daring to explain that he had not been drowning, that he had struggled in jest—and farther out people were diving, groping through the water, then looking at each other with bulging eyes, and diving anew, and returning empty-handed, while others shouted to them from the shore, advising them to search a little to the left; and a fellow with a Red Cross armband was running along the beach, and three men in sweaters were pushing into the water a boat grinding against the shingle; and a bewildered David was being led away by a fat woman in a pince-nez, the wife of a veterinarian, who had been expected to arrive on Friday but had had to postpone his vacation, and the Baltic Sea sparkled from end to end, and, in the thinned-out forest, across a green country road, there lay, still breathing, freshly cut aspens; and a youth, smeared with soot, gradually turned white as he washed under the kitchen tap, and black parakeets flew above the eternal snows of the New Zealand mountains; and a fisherman, squinting in the sun, was solemnly predicting that not until the ninth day would the waves surrender the corpse.

THE ADMIRALTY SPIRE

Y OU will please pardon me, dear Madam, but I am a rude and straightforward person, so I'll come right out with it: do not labor under any delusion: this is far from being a fan letter. On the contrary, as you will realize yourself in a minute, it is a rather odd little epistle that, who knows, might serve as a lesson of sorts not only for you but for other impetuous lady novelists as well. I hasten, first of all, to introduce myself, so that my visual image may show through like a watermark; this is much more honest than to encourage by silence the incorrect conclusions that the eye involuntarily draws from the calligraphy of penned lines. No, in spite of my slender handwriting and the youthful flourish of my commas, I am stout and middle-aged; true, my corpulence is not flabby, but has piquancy, zest, waspishness. It is far removed, Madam, from the turndown collars of the poet Apukhtin, the fat pet of ladies. But that will do. You, as a writer, have already collected these clues to fill in the rest of me. *Bonjour, Madame*. And now let's get down to business.

The other day at a Russian library, relegated by illiterate fate to a murky Berlin alleyway, I took out three or four new items, and among them your novel *The Admiralty Spire*. Neat title—if for no other reason than that it is, isn't it, an iambic tetrameter, *admiraltéyskaya iglá*, and a famous Pushkinian line to boot. But it was the very neatness of that title that boded no good. Besides, I am generally wary of books published in the backwoods of our expatriation, such as Riga or Reval. Nevertheless, as I was saying, I did take your novel.

Ah, my dear Madam, ah, "Mr." Serge Solntsev, how easy it is to guess that the author's name is a pseudonym, that the author is not a man! Every sentence of yours buttons to the left. Your predilection for such expressions as "time passed" or "cuddled up *frileusement* in Mother's shawl," the inevitable appearance of an episodic ensign (straight from imitations of *War and Peace*) who pronounces the letter *r* as a hard *g*, and, finally, footnotes with translations of French clichés, afford sufficient indication of your literary skill. But all this is only half the trouble.

Imagine the following: suppose I once took a walk through a marvelous landscape, where turbulent waters tumble and bindweed chokes the columns of desolate ruins, and then, many years later, in a stranger's house, I come across a snapshot showing me in a swaggering pose in front of what is obviously a pasteboard pillar; in the background there is the whitish smear of a daubed-in cascade, and somebody has inked a mustache on me. Where did the thing come from? Take away this horror! The dinning waters I remember were real, and, what is more, no one took a picture of me there.

Shall I interpret the parable for you? Shall I tell you that I had the same feeling, only nastier and sillier, on reading your nimble handiwork, your terrible *Spire*? As my index finger burst the uncut pages open and my eyes raced along the lines, I could only blink from the bewildering shock.

Do you wish to know what happened? Glad to oblige. As you lay massively in your hammock and recklessly allowed your pen to flow like a fountain (a near pun), you, Madam, wrote the story of my first love. Yes, a bewildering shock, and, as I too am a massive person, bewilderment is accompanied by shortness of breath. By now you and I are both puffing, for, doubtless, you are also dumbfounded by the sudden appearance of the hero that you invented. No, that was a slip—the trimmings are yours, I'll concede, and so are the stuffing and the sauce, but the game (another near pun), the game, Madam, is not yours but mine, with my buckshot in its wing. I am amazed—where and how could a lady unknown to me have kidnapped my past? Must I admit the possibility that you are acquainted with Katya—that you are close friends, even—and that she blabbed the whole business, as she whiled away summer crepuscles under the Baltic pines with you, the voracious novelist? But how did you dare, where did you find the gall not only to use Katya's tale, but, on top of that, to distort it so irreparably?

Since the day of our last meeting there has been a lapse of sixteen years—the age of a bride, an old dog, or the Soviet republic. Incidentally, let us note the first, but not the worst by far, of your innumerable and sloppy mistakes: Katya and I are not coevals. I was going on eighteen, and she on twenty. Relying on a tried and true method, you have your heroine strip before a full-length mirror whereupon you proceed to describe her loose hair, ash-blond of course, and her young curves.

According to you her cornflower eyes would turn violet in pensive moments—a botanical miracle! You shaded them with the black fringe of lashes which, if I may make a contribution of my own, seemed longer toward the outer corners, giving her eyes a very special, though illusory, slant. Katya's figure was graceful, but she cultivated a slight stoop, and would lift her shoulders as she entered a room. You make her a stately maiden with contralto tones in her voice.

Sheer torture. I had a mind to copy out your images, all of which ring false, and scathingly juxtapose my infallible observations, but the result would have been "nightmarish nonsense," as the real Katya would have said, for the Logos allotted me does not possess sufficient precision or power to get disentangled from you. On the contrary, I myself get bogged down in the sticky snares of your conventional descriptions, and have no strength left to liberate Katya from your pen. Nevertheless, like Hamlet, I will argue, and, in the end, will out-argue you.

The theme of your concoction is love: a slightly decadent love with the February Revolution for backdrop, but still, love. Katya has been renamed Olga by you, and I have become Leonid. Well and good. Our first encounter, at the house of friends on Christmas Eve; our meetings at the Yusupov Skating Rink; her room, its indigo wallpaper, its mahogany furniture, and its only ornament, a porcelain ballerina with lifted leg—this is all right, this is all true. Except that you managed to give it all a taint of pretentious fabrication. As he takes his seat at the Parisiana Cinema on Nevsky Avenue, Leonid, a student of the Imperial Lyceum, puts his gloves in his three-cornered hat, while a couple of pages later he is already wearing civilian clothes: he doffs his bowler, and the reader is faced by an elegant young man, with his hair parted à l'anglaise exactly in the middle of his small, lacquered-looking head, and a purple handkerchief drooping out of his breast pocket. I do in fact remember dressing like the film actor Max Linder, and recall the generous spurts of Vezhetal lotion cooling my scalp, and Monsieur Pierre taking aim with his comb and flipping my hair over with a lino-type swing, and then, as he yanked off the sheet, yelling to a middle-aged, mustachioed fellow, "Boy! Bross off the 'air!" Today my memory reacts with irony to the breast-pocket handkerchief and white spats of those days, but, on the other hand, can in no way reconcile the remembered torments of adolescent shaving with your Leonid's "smooth opaque pallor." And I shall leave on your conscience his Lermontovian lusterless eyes and aristocratic profile, as it is impossible to discern much today because of an unexpected increase in fleshiness.

Good Lord, keep me from bogging down in the prose of this lady writer, whom I do not know and do not wish to know, but who has encroached with astonishing insolence on another person's past! How dare you write, "The pretty Christmas tree with its *chatoyant* lights seemed to augur to them joy jubilant"? You have extinguished the whole tree with your breath, for one adjective placed after the noun for the sake of elegance is enough to kill the best of recollections. Before the disaster, i.e., before your book, one such recollection of mine was the rippling, fragmentary light in Katya's eyes, and the cherry reflection on her cheek from the glossy little dollhouse of plasmic paper hanging on a branch as, brushing aside the bristly foliage, she stretched to pinch out the flame of a candle that had gone berserk. What do I have left of all this? Nothing—just a nauseating whiff of literary combustion.

Your version gives the impression that Katya and I inhabited a kind of exquisitely cultured beau monde. You have your parallax wrong, dear lady. That upper-class milieu—the fashionable set, if you will—to which Katya belonged, had backward tastes, to put it mildly. Chekhov was considered an "impressionist," the society rhymster Grand Duke Constantine a major poet, and the arch-Christian Alexander Blok a wicked Jew who wrote futuristic sonnets about dying swans and lilac liqueurs. Handwritten copies of album verse, French and English, made the rounds, and were recopied in turn, not without distortions, while the author's name imperceptibly vanished, so that those outpourings quite accidentally assumed a glamorous anonymity; and, generally speaking, it is amusing to juxtapose their meanderings with the clandestine copying of seditious jingles practiced in lower circles. A good indication of how undeservedly these male and female monologues about love were considered most modern examples of foreign lyricism is the fact that the darling among them was a piece by poor Louis Bouilhet, who wrote in the middle of last century. Reveling in the rolling cadences, Katya would declaim his alexandrines, and scold me for finding fault with a certain highly sonorous strophe in which, after having referred to his passion as a violin bow, the author compares his mistress to a guitar.

Apropos of guitars, Madam, you write that "in the evening the young people would gather and Olga would sit at a table and sing in a rich contralto." Oh, well—one more death, one more victim of your sumptuous prose. Yet how I cherished the echoes of modish *tziganshchina* that inclined Katya to singing, and me to composing verse! Well do I know that this was no longer authentic Gypsy art such as that which enchanted Pushkin and, later, Apollon Grigoriev, but a barely breathing, jaded, and doomed muse; everything contributed to her ruin: the gramophone, the war, and various so-called *tzigane* songs. It was for good reason that Blok, in one of his customary spells of providence, wrote down whatever words he remembered from Gypsy lyrics, as if hastening to save at least this before it was too late.

Should I tell you what those husky murmurs and plaints meant to us? Should I reveal to you the image of a distant, strange world where:

> *Pendulous willow boughs slumber*
> *Drooping low over the pond,*

where, deep in the lilac bushes,

> *The nightingale sobs out her passion,*

and where all the senses are dominated by the memory of lost love, that wicked ruler of pseudo-Gypsy romanticism? Katya and I also would have liked to reminisce, but, since we had nothing yet to reminisce about, we would counterfeit the remoteness of time and push back into it our immediate happiness. We transformed everything we saw into monuments to our still nonexistent past by trying to look at a garden path, at the moon, at the weeping willows, with the same eyes with which *now*—when fully conscious of irreparable losses—we might have looked at that old, waterlogged raft on the pond, at that moon above the black cow shed. I even suppose that, thanks to a vague inspiration, we were preparing in advance for certain things, training ourselves to remember, imagining a distant past and practicing nostalgia, so that subsequently, when that past really existed for us, we would know how to cope with it, and not perish under its burden.

But what do you care about all this? When you describe my summer sojourn at the ancestral estate you dub "Glinskoye," you chase me into the woods and there compel me to write verse "redolent of youth and faith in life." This was all not quite so. While the others played tennis (using a single red ball and some Doherty racquets, heavy and saggy, found in the attic) or croquet on a ridiculously overgrown lawn with a dandelion in front of every hoop, Katya and I would make for the kitchen garden, and, squatting there, gorge ourselves on two species of strawberry—the bright-crimson "Victoria" (*sadovaya zemlyanika*) and the Russian hautbois (*klubnika*), purplish berries often slimed by frogs; and there was also our favorite "Ananas" variety, unripe-looking, yet wonderfully sweet. Without straightening our backs, we moved, grunting, along the furrows, and the tendons behind our knees ached, and our insides filled with a rubious weight. The hot sun bore down, and that sun, and the strawberries, and Katya's frock of tussore silk with darkening blotches under the arms, and the patina of tan on the back of her neck—all of it blended into a sense of oppressive delight; and what bliss it was, without rising, still picking berries, to clasp Katya's warm shoulder and hear her soft laughter and little grunts of greed and the crunch of her joints as she rummaged under the leaves. Forgive me if I pass directly from that orchard, floating by with the blinding gleam of its hothouses and the swaying of hairy poppies along its avenues, to the water closet where, in the pose of Rodin's *Thinker*, my head still hot from the sun, I composed my verse. It was dismal in all senses of the word, that verse; it contained the trills of nightingales from *tzigane* songs and bits of Blok, and helpless echoes of Verlaine: *Souvenir, Souvenir, que me veux-tu? L'automne* . . . —even though autumn was still far off, and my happiness shouted with its marvelous voice nearby, probably over there, by the bowling alley, behind the old lilac bushes under which lay piles of kitchen refuse, and hens walked about. In the evenings, on the veranda, the gramophone's gaping mouth, as red as the lining of a Russian general's coat, would pour forth uncontrollable Gypsy passion; or, to the tune of "Under a Cloud the Moon's Hidden," a menacing voice would mimic the Kaiser: "Give me a nib and a holder, to write ultimatums it's time." And on the garden terrace a game of *Gorodki* (townlets) was going on: Katya's father, his collar unbuttoned, one foot advanced in its soft house boot, would take aim with a cudgel as if he were firing a rifle and then hurl it with force (but wide of the mark) at the "townlet" of skittles while the setting sun, with the tip of its final ray, brushed across the palisade of pine trunks, leaving on each a fiery band. And when night finally fell, and the house was asleep, Katya and I would look at the dark house from the park where we kept huddled on a hard, cold, invisible bench until our bones ached, and it all seemed to us like something that had already once happened long ago: the outline of the house against the pale-green sky, the sleepy movements of the foliage, our prolonged, blind kisses.

In your elegant description, with profuse dots, of that summer, you naturally do not forget for a minute—as we used to forget—that since February of that year the nation was "under the rule of the Provisional Government," and you oblige Katya and me to follow revolutionary events with keen concern, that is, to conduct (for dozens of pages) political and mystical conversations that—I assure you—we never had. In the first place, I would have been embarrassed to speak, with the righteous pathos you lend me, of Russia's destiny and, in the second place, Katya and I were too absorbed in each other to pay much attention to the Revolution. I need but say that my most vivid impression in that respect was a mere trifle: one day, on Million Street in St. Petersburg, a truck packed with jolly rioters made a clumsy but accurate swerve so as to deliberately squash a passing cat, which remained lying there, as a perfectly flat, neatly ironed, black rag (only the tail still belonged to a cat—it stood upright, and the tip, I think, still moved). At the time this struck me with some deep occult meaning, but I have since had occasion to see a bus, in a bucolic Spanish village, flatten by exactly the same method an exactly similar cat, so I have become disenchanted with hidden meanings. You, on the other hand, have not only exaggerated my poetic talent beyond recognition, but have made me a prophet besides, for only a prophet could have talked, in the fall of 1917, about the green pulp of Lenin's deceased brain, or the "inner" emigration of intellectuals in Soviet Russia.

No, that fall and that winter we talked of other matters. I was in anguish. The most awful things were happening to our romance. You give a simple explanation: "Olga began to understand that she was sensual rather than passionate, while for Leonid it was the opposite. Their risky caresses understandably inebriated her, but deep inside there always remained a little unmelted piece"—and so on, in the same vulgar, pretentious spirit. What do you understand of our love? So far, I have deliberately avoided direct discussion of it; but now, if I were not afraid of contagion by your style, I would describe in greater detail both its fire and its underlying melancholy. Yes, there was the summer, and the foliage's omnipresent rustle, and the headlong pedaling along all of the park's winding paths, to see who would be the first to race from different directions to the *rond-point*, where the red sand was covered by the writhing serpentine tracks of our rock-hard tires, and each live, everyday detail of that final Russian summer screamed at us in desperation, "I am real! I am now!" As long as all of this sunny euphoria managed to stay on the surface, the innate sadness of our love went no further than the devotion to a nonexistent past. But when Katya and I once again found ourselves in Petersburg, and it had already snowed more than once, and the wooden paving blocks were already filmed with that yellowish layer—a mixture of snow and horse dung—without which I cannot picture a Russian city, the flaw emerged, and we were left with nothing but torment.

I can see her now, in her black sealskin coat, with a big, flat muff and gray fur-trimmed boots, walking on her slender legs, as if on stilts, along a very slippery sidewalk; or in a dark, high-necked dress, sitting on a blue divan, her face heavily powdered after much crying. As I walked to her house in the evenings and returned after midnight, I would recognize amid the granite night, under a frosty sky, dove-gray with starlight, the imperturbable and immutable landmarks of my itinerary—always those same huge Petersburg objects, lone edifices of legendary times, adorning the nocturnal wastes and half-turning away from the traveler as all beauty does: it sees you not, it is pensive, and listless, its mind is elsewhere. I would talk to myself, exhorting fate, Katya, the stars, the columns of a huge, mute, abstracted cathedral; and when a desultory exchange of fire began in the dark streets, it would occur to me casually, and not without a sense of pleasure, that I might be picked off by a stray bullet and die right there, reclining on dim snow, in my elegant fur coat, my bowler askew, among scattered white paperbacks of Gumilyov's or Mandelshtam's new collections of verse that I had dropped and that were barely visible against the snow. Or else, sobbing and moaning as I walked, I would try to persuade myself that it was I who had stopped loving Katya, as I hastened to gather up all I could recall of her mendacity, her presumption, her vacuity, the pretty patch masking a pimple, the artificial *grasseyement* that would appear in her speech when she needlessly switched to French, her invulnerable weakness for titled poetasters, and the ill-tempered, dull expression of her eyes when, for the hundredth time, I tried to make her tell me with whom she had spent the previous evening. And when it was all gathered and weighed in the balance, I would perceive with anguish that my love, burdened as it was with all that trash, had settled and lodged only deeper, and that not even draft horses with iron muscles could haul it out of the morass. And the following evening again, I would make my way through the sailor-manned identity checks on the street corners (documents were demanded that allowed me access at least to the threshold of Katya's soul, and were invalid beyond that point); I would once again go to gaze at Katya, who, at the first pitiful word of mine, would turn into a large, rigid doll who would lower her convex eyelids and respond in china-doll language. When, one memorable night, I demanded that she give me a final, super-truthful reply, Katya simply said nothing, and, instead, remained lying motionless on the couch, her mirrorlike eyes reflecting the flame of the candle which on that night of historical turbulence substituted for electric light, and, after hearing her silence through to the end, I got up and left. Three days later, I had my valet take a note to her, in which I wrote that I would commit suicide if I could not see her just once more. So one glorious morning, with a rosy round sun and creaking snow, we met on Post Office Street; I silently kissed her hand, and for a quarter of an hour, without a single word interrupting our silence, we strolled to and fro, while nearby, on the corner of the Horse

Guards Boulevard, stood smoking, with feigned nonchalance, a perfectly respectable-looking man in an astrakhan cap. As she and I silently walked to and fro, a little boy passed, pulling by its string a baized hand sled with a tattered fringe, and a drainpipe suddenly gave a rattle and disgorged a chunk of ice, while the man on the corner kept smoking; then, at precisely the same spot where we had met, I just as silently kissed her hand, which slipped back into its muff forever.

> *Farewell, my anguish and my ardor,*
> *Farewell, my dream, farewell, my pain!*
> *Along the paths of the old garden*
> *We two shall never pass again.*

Yes, yes: farewell, as the *tzigane* song has it. In spite of everything you were beautiful, impenetrably beautiful, and so adorable that I could cry, ignoring your myopic soul, and the trivality of your opinions, and a thousand minor betrayals; while I, with my overambitious verse, the heavy and hazy array of my feelings, and my breathless, stuttering speech, in spite of all my love for you, must have been contemptible and repulsive. And there is no need for me to tell you what torments I went through afterwards, how I looked and looked at the snapshot in which, with a gleam on your lip and a glint in your hair, you are looking past me. Katya, why have you made such a mess of it now?

Come, let us have a calm, heart-to-heart talk. With a lugubrious hiss the air has now been let out of the arrogant rubber fatman who, tightly inflated, clowned around at the beginning of this letter; and you, my dear, are really not a corpulent lady novelist in her novelistic hammock but the same old Katya, with Katya's calculated dash of demeanor, Katya of the narrow shoulders, a comely, discreetly made-up lady who, out of silly coquetry, has concocted a worthless book. To think that you did not even spare our parting! Leonid's letter, in which he threatens to shoot Olga, and which she discusses with her future husband; that future husband, in the role of undercover agent, standing on a street corner, ready to rush to the rescue if Leonid should draw the revolver that he is clutching in his coat pocket, as he passionately entreats Olga not to go, and keeps interrupting with his sobs her level-headed words: what a disgusting, senseless fabrication! And at the end of the book you have me join the White Army and get caught by the Reds during a reconnaissance, and, with the names of two traitresses—Russia, Olga—on my lips, die valiantly, felled by the bullet of a "Hebrew-dark" commissar. How intensely I must have loved you if I still see you as you were sixteen years ago, make agonizing efforts to free our past from its humiliating captivity, and save your image from the rack and disgrace of your own pen! I honestly do not know, though, if I am succeeding. My letter smacks strangely of those rhymed epistles that you would rattle off by heart—remember?

> *The sight of my handwriting may surprise you*

—but I shall refrain from closing, as Apukhtin does, with the invitation:

> *The sea awaits you here, as vast as love*
> *And love, vast as the sea!*

—I shall refrain, because, in the first place, there is no sea here, and, in the second, I have not the least desire to see you. For, after your book, Katya, I am afraid of you. Truly there was no point in rejoicing and suffering as we rejoiced and suffered only to find one's past besmirched in a lady's novel. Listen—stop writing books! At least let this flop serve as a lesson. "At least," for I have the right to wish that you will be stunned by horror upon realizing what you have perpetrated. And do you know what else I long for? Perhaps, perhaps (this is a very small and sickly "perhaps," but I grasp at it and hence do not sign this letter)—perhaps, after all, Katya, in spite of everything, a rare coincidence has occurred, and it is not you that wrote that tripe, and your equivocal but enchanting image has not been mutilated. In that case, please forgive me, colleague Solntsev.

THE LEONARDO

T HE objects that are being summoned assemble, draw near
from different spots; in doing so, some of them have to overcome not only the distance of space but that of time: which
nomad, you may wonder, is more bothersome to cope with, this one
or that, the young poplar, say, that once grew in the vicinity but was
cut down long ago, or the singled-out courtyard which still exists
today but is situated far away from here? Hurry up, please.

Here comes the ovate little poplar, all punctated with April greenery, and takes its stand where told, namely by the tall brick wall, imported in one piece from another city. Facing it, there grows up a
dreary and dirty tenement house, with mean little balconies pulled out
one by one like drawers. Other bits of scenery are distributed about
the yard: a barrel, a second barrel, the delicate shade of leaves, an urn
of sorts, and a stone cross propped at the foot of the wall. All this is
only sketched and much has to be added and finished, and yet two live
people—Gustav and his brother Anton—already come out on their
tiny balcony, while rolling before him a little pushcart with a suitcase
and a heap of books, Romantovski, the new lodger, enters the yard.

As seen from the yard, and especially on a bright day, the rooms of
the house seem filled up with dense blackness (night is always with us,
in this or that place, inside, during one part of twenty-four hours, outside, during the other). Romantovski looked up at the black open windows, at the two frog-eyed men watching him from their balcony, and
shouldering his bag—with a forward lurch as if someone had banged
him on the back of the head—plunged into the doorway. There remained, sunlit: the pushcart with the books, one barrel, another barrel,
the nictating young poplar and an inscription in tar on the brick wall:
VOTE FOR (illegible). Presumably it had been scrawled by the brothers
before the elections.

Now this is the way we'll arrange the world: every man shall sweat, every man shall eat. There will be work, there will be belly-cheer, there will be a clean, warm, sunny—

(Romantovski became the occupant of the adjacent one. It was even drabber than theirs. But under the bed he discovered a small rubber doll. He concluded that his predecessor had been a family man.)

Despite the world's not having yet conclusively and totally turned into solid matter and still retaining sundry regions of an intangible and hallowed nature, the brothers felt snug and confident. The elder one, Gustav, had a furniture-moving job; the younger happened to be temporarily unemployed, but did not lose heart. Gustav had an evenly ruddy complexion, bristling fair eyebrows, and an ample, cupboardlike torso always clothed in a pullover of coarse gray wool. He wore elastic bands to hold his shirtsleeves at the joints of his fat arms, so as to keep his wrists free and prevent sloppiness. Anton's face was pockmarked, he trimmed his mustache in the shape of a dark trapezoid, and wore a dark red sweater over his spare wiry frame. But when they both leaned their elbows on the balcony railings, their backsides were exactly the same, big and triumphant, with identically checkered cloth enclosing tightly their prominent buttocks.

Repeat: the world shall be sweaty and well fed. Idlers, parasites, and musicians are not admitted. While one's heart pumps blood one should *live*, damn it! For two years now Gustav had been saving money to marry Anna, acquire a sideboard, a carpet.

She would come every other evening, that plump-armed buxom woman, with freckles on the broad bridge of her nose, a leaden shadow under her eyes, and spaced teeth one of which, moreover, had been knocked out. The brothers and she would swill beer. She had a way of clasping her bare arms behind her nape, displaying the gleaming-wet red tufts of her armpits. With head thrown back, she opened her mouth so generously that one could survey her entire palate and uvula, which resembled the tail end of a boiled chicken. The anatomy of her mirth was greatly to the liking of the two brothers. They tickled her with zest.

In the daytime, while his brother worked, Anton sat in a friendly pub or sprawled among the dandelions on the cool, still vividly green grass along the canal bank and observed with envy exuberant roughs loading coals on a barge, or else stared stupidly at the empty blue of the sleep-inducing sky. But presently in the well-oiled life of the brothers some obstruction occurred.

From the very moment he had appeared, rolling his pushcart into the yard, Romantovski had provoked a mixture of irritation and curiosity in the two brothers. Their infallible flair let them sense that here was someone different from other people. Normally, one would not discern anything special in him at a casual glance, but the brothers did. For example, he walked differently: at every step he rose on a buoyant toe in a peculiar manner, stepping and flying up as if the mere act of treading allowed him a chance to perceive something uncommon over the common heads. He was what is termed a "slank," very lean, with a pale sharp-nosed face and appallingly restless eyes. Out of the much too short sleeves of his double-breasted jacket his long wrists protruded with a kind of annoying and nonsensical obviousness ("here we are: what should we do?"). He went out and came home at unpredictable hours. On one of the first mornings Anton caught sight of him near a bookstand: he was pricing, or had actually bought something, because the vendor nimbly beat one dusty volume against another and carried them to his nook behind the stand. Additional eccentricities were noted: his light remained on practically until dawn; he was oddly unsociable.

We hear Anton's voice: "That fine gentleman shows off. We should give him a closer look."

"I'll sell him the pipe," said Gustav.

The misty origins of the pipe. Anna had brought it over one day, but the brothers recognized only cigarillos. An expensive pipe, not yet blackened. It had a little steel tube inserted in its stem. With it came a suede case.

"Who's there? What do you want?" asked Romantovski through the door.

"Neighbors, neighbors," answered Gustav in a deep voice.

And the neighbors entered, avidly looking around. A stump of sausage lay on the table next to an uneven pile of books; one of them was opened on a picture of ships with numerous sails and, flying above, in one corner, an infant with puffed-out cheeks.

"Let's get acquainted," rumbled the brothers. "Folks live side by side, one can say, but never meet somehow or other."

The top of the commode was shared by an alcohol burner and an orange.

"Delighted," said Romantovski softly. He sat down on the edge of the bed, and with bent forehead, its V-vein inflamed, started to lace his shoes.

"You were resting," said Gustav with ominous courtesy. "We come at the wrong time?"

Not a word, not a word, did the lodger say in reply; instead he straightened up suddenly, turned to the window, raised his finger, and froze.

The brothers looked but found nothing unusual about that window; it framed a cloud, the tip of the poplar, and part of the brick wall.

"Why, don't you see anything?" asked Romantovski.

Red sweater and gray went up to the window and actually leaned out, becoming identical twins. Nothing. And both had the sudden feeling that something was wrong, very wrong! They wheeled around. He stood near the chest of drawers in an odd attitude.

"I must have been mistaken," said Romantovski, not looking at them. "Something seemed to have flown by. I saw once an airplane fall."

"That happens," assented Gustav. "Listen, we dropped in with a purpose. Would you care to buy this? Brand new. And there's a nice sheath."

"Sheath? Is that so? Only, you know, I smoke very seldom."

"Well, you'll smoke oftener. We sell it cheap. Three-fifty."

"Three-fifty. I see."

He fingered the pipe, biting his nether lip and pondering something. His eyes did not really look at the pipe, they moved to and fro.

Meanwhile the brothers began to swell, to grow, they filled up the whole room, the whole house, and then grew out of it. In comparison to them the young poplar was, by then, no bigger than one of those toy treelets, made of dyed cotton wool, that are so unstable on their round green supports. The dollhouse, a thing of dusty pasteboard with mica windowpanes, barely reached up to the brothers' knees. Gigantic, imperiously reeking of sweat and beer, with beefy voices and senseless speeches, with fecal matter replacing the human brain, they provoke a tremor of ignoble fear. I don't know why they push against me; I implore you, do leave me alone. I'm not touching you, so don't you touch me either; I'll give in, only do leave me alone.

"All right, but I don't have enough change," said Romantovski in a low voice. "Now if you can give me six-fifty—"

They could, and went away, grinning. Gustav examined the ten-mark bill against the light and put it away in an iron money box.

Nevertheless, they did not leave their room neighbor in peace. It just maddened them that despite their having got acquainted with him, a man should remain as inaccessible as before. He avoided running into them: one had to waylay and trap him in order to glance fleetingly into his evasive eyes. Having discovered the nocturnal life of Romantovski's lamp, Anton could not bear it any longer. He crept up barefoot to the door (from under which showed a taut thread of golden light) and knocked.

Romantovski did not respond.

"Sleep, sleep," said Anton, slapping the door with his palm.

The light peered silently through the chink. Anton shook the door handle. The golden thread snapped.

Thenceforth both brothers (but especially Anton, thanks to his lacking a job) established a watch over their neighbor's insomnia. The enemy, however, was astute and endowed with a fine hearing. No matter how quietly one advanced toward his door, his light went out instantly, as if it never had been there; and only if one stood in the cold corridor for a goodish length of time, holding one's breath, could one hope to see the return of the sensitive lamp beam. Thus beetles faint and recover.

The task of detection turned out to be most exhausting. Finally, the brothers chanced to catch him on the stairs and jostled him.

"Suppose it's my habit to read at night. What business of yours is it? Let me pass, please."

When he turned away, Gustav knocked off his hat in jest. Romantovski picked it up without a word.

A few days later, choosing a moment at nightfall—he was on his way back from the W.C. and failed to dart back into his room quickly enough—the brothers crowded around him. There were only two of them, yet they managed to form a crowd. They invited him to their room.

"There will be some beer," said Gustav with a wink.

He tried to refuse.

"Oh, come along!" cried the brothers; they grabbed him under the arms and swept him off (while at it, they could feel how thin he was—that weakness, that slenderness below the shoulder offered an irresistible temptation—ah, to give a good squeeze so as to make him crunch, ah, hard to control oneself, let us, at least, dig into him on the move, just once, lightly . . .).

"You are hurting me," said Romantovski. "Leave me alone, I can walk by myself."

The promised beer, the large mouth of Gustav's fiancée, a heavy smell in the room. They tried to make him drunk. Collarless, with a copper stud under his conspicuous and defenseless Adam's apple, long-faced and pale, with quivering eyelashes, he sat in a complicated pose, partly doubled up, partly bent out, and when he got up from his chair he seemed to unwind like a spiral. However, they forced him to fold up again and, upon their suggestion, Anna sat in his lap. He kept glancing askance at the swell of her instep in the harness of a tight shoe, but mastered his dull anguish as best he could, not daring to get rid of the inert red-haired creature.

There was a minute when it seemed to them that he was broken, that he had become one of them. In fact, Gustav said, "You see, you were silly to look down on our company. We find offensive the way you have of keeping mum. What do you read all night?"

"Old, old tales," replied Romantovski in such a tone of voice that the brothers suddenly felt very bored. The boredom was suffocating and grim, but drink prevented the storm from bursting out, and, on the contrary, weighed the eyelids down. Anna slipped off Romantovski's knee, brushing the table with a drowsy hip; empty bottles swayed like ninepins, one collapsed. The brothers stooped, toppled, yawned, still looking through sleepy tears at their guest. He, vibrating and diffusing rays, stretched out, thinned, and gradually vanished.

This cannot go on. He poisons the life of honest folks. Why, it can well happen that he will move at the end of the month—intact, whole, never taken to pieces, proudly strutting about. It is not enough that he moves and breathes differently from other people; the trouble is that we just cannot put our finger upon the difference, cannot catch the tip of the ear by which to pull out the rabbit. Hateful is everything that cannot be palpated, measured, counted.

A series of trivial torments began. On Monday they managed to sprinkle his bedclothes with potato flour, which is said to provoke a maddening itch. On Tuesday they ambushed him at the corner of their street (he was carrying books hugged to his breast) and hustled him so neatly that his load landed in the puddle they had picked out for it. On Wednesday they painted the toilet seat with carpenter's glue. By Thursday the brothers' imagination was exhausted.

He said nothing, nothing whatever. On Friday, he overtook Anton, with his flying step, at the gate of the yard, and offered him an illustrated weekly—maybe you'd like to look at it? This unexpected courtesy perplexed the brothers and made them glow still hotter.

Gustav ordered his fiancée to stir up Romantovski, which would give one the opportunity to pick a quarrel with him. You involuntarily tend to set a football rolling before kicking it. Frolicsome animals also prefer a mobile object. And though Anna, no doubt, greatly repelled Romantovski with those bug-brown freckles on her milky skin, the vacant look in her light eyes, and the little promontories of wet gums between her teeth, he found fit to conceal his distaste, fearing to infuriate Anna's lover by spurning her.

Since he went all the same to the cinema once a week, he took her with him on Saturday in the hope that this attention would be enough. Unnoticed, at a discreet distance, both wearing new caps and orange-red shoes, the brothers stole after the pair, and on those dubious streets, in that dusty dusk, there were hundreds of their likes but only one Romantovski.

In the small elongated movie house, night had started to flicker, a self-manufactured lunar night, when the brothers, furtively hunching, seated themselves in the back row. They sensed the darkly delicious presence of Romantovski somewhere in front. On the way to the cinema, Anna failed to worm anything out of her disagreeable companion, nor did she quite understand what exactly Gustav wanted of him. As they walked, the mere sight of his lean figure and melancholy profile made her want to yawn. But once the picture started, she forgot about him, pressing an insensate shoulder against him. Specters conversed in trumpet tones on the newfangled speaking screen. The baron tasted his wine and carefully put his glass down—with the sound of a dropped cannonball.

And after a while the sleuths were pursuing the baron. Who would have recognized in him the master crook? He was hunted passionately, frenziedly. Automobiles sped with bursts of thunder. In a nightclub they fought with bottles, chairs, tables. A mother was putting an enchanting child to bed.

When it was all over, and Romantovski, with a little stumble, followed her out into the cool darkness, Anna exclaimed, "Oh, that was wonderful!"

He cleared his throat and said after a pause, "Let's not exaggerate. In real life, it is all considerably duller."

"It's you who's dull," she retorted crossly, and presently chuckled softly as she recalled the pretty child.

Behind them, gliding along at the same distance as before, came the brothers. Both were gloomy. Both were pumping themselves up with gloomy violence. Gloomily, Anton said, "That's not done, after all—going out walking with another's bride."

"And especially on Saturday night," said Gustav.

A passerby, coming abreast of them, happened to glance at their faces—and could not help walking faster.

The night wind chased rustling rubbish along the fences. It was a dark and desolate part of Berlin. Far to the left of the road, above the canal, blinked scattered lights. On the right were vacant lots from which a few hastily silhouetted houses had turned their black backs away. After a little while the brothers accelerated their step.

"My mother and sister live in the country," Anna was telling him in a rather cozy undertone amid the velvety night. "As soon as I get married, I hope to visit them with him. Last summer my sister—"

Romantovski suddenly looked back.

"—won a lottery prize," continued Anna, mechanically looking back too.

Gustav emitted a sonorous whistle.

"Why, it's them!" exclaimed Anna, and joyfully burst out laughing. "Ah, the rascals!"

"Good evening, good evening," said Gustav hastily, in a panting voice. "What are you doing here, you ass, with my girl?"

"I'm not doing anything. We have just been—"

"Now, now," said Anton and, drawing back his elbow, hit Romantovski crisply in the lower ribs.

"Please, don't use your fists. You know perfectly well that—"

"Leave him alone, fellows," said Anna with a soft snigger.

"Must teach him a lesson," said Gustav, warming up and forefeeling with a poignant glow how he too would follow his brother's example and feel those cartilages, that crumpy backbone.

"Apropos, a funny thing happened to me one day," Romantovski started to say, talking fast, but here Gustav began to jam and twist the huge lumps of his knuckles into his victim's side, causing utterly indescribable pain. In lurching back Romantovski slipped and nearly fell: to fall would have meant perishing then and there.

"Let him go," said Anna.

He turned and, holding his side, walked off along the dark rustling fences. The brothers followed, all but treading upon his heels. Gustav rumbled in the anguish of blood lust, and that rumble might turn any moment into a pounce.

Far away before him a bright twinkle promised safety; it meant a lighted street, and although what could be seen was probably one lone lamp, that slit in the blackness seemed a marvelous festive blaze, a blissful region of radiance, full of rescued men. He knew that if he started to run it would be the end, since he could not get there sufficiently fast; he should go at a quiet and smooth walk, then he might cover that distance, keeping silent the while and trying not to press his hand against his burning ribs. So he strode on, with his usual springy step, and the impression was that he did so on purpose, to mock nonflyers, and that next moment he might take off.

Anna's voice: "Gustav, don't tangle with him. You know quite well you won't be able to stop. Remember what you did once to that bricklayer."

"Hold your tongue, old bitch, don't teach him what must be done." (That's Anton's voice.)

Now at last, the region of light—where one could distinguish a chestnut's foliage, and what looked like a Morris pillar, and farther still, to the left, a bridge—that breathlessly waiting imploring light, at last, at last, was not so very remote. . . . And still one should not run. And though he knew he was making a fatal mistake, all at once, beyond the control of his will, he flew up and, with a sob, dashed forward.

He ran and seemed, as he ran, to be laughing exultingly. Gustav overtook him in a couple of leaps. Both fell, and amid the fierce rasping and crunching there occurred a special sound—smooth and moist, once, and a second time, up to the hilt—and then Anna instantly fled into the darkness, holding her hat in her hand.

Gustav stood up. Romantovski was lying on the ground and speaking in Polish. Abruptly his voice broke off.

"And now let's be gone," said Gustav. "I stuck him."

"Take it out," said Anton, "take it out of him."

"I did," said Gustav. "God, how I stuck him."

They scurried off, though not toward the light, but across dark vacant lots. After skirting the cemetery they reached a back alley, exchanged glances, and slowed down to a normal walk.

Upon coming home, they immediately fell asleep. Anton dreamed he was sitting on the grass and watching a barge drift by. Gustav did not dream of anything.

Early next morning police agents arrived; they searched the murdered man's room and briefly questioned Anton, who had come out into the passage. Gustav stayed in bed, replete and somnolent, his face the color of Westphalian ham, in contrast to the whitish tufts of his eyebrows.

Presently, the police left and Anton returned. He was in an unusual state of elation, choking with laughter, flexing his knees, noiselessly hitting his palm with his fist.

"What fun!" he said. "Do you know who the fellow was? A leonardo!"

In their lingo a leonardo (from the name of the painter) meant a maker of counterfeit bills. And Anton related what he had managed to find out: the fellow, it appeared, belonged to a gang and had just got out of jail. Before that he had been designing fake paper money; an accomplice had knifed him, no doubt.

Gustav shook with mirth too, but then his expression changed suddenly.

"He slipped us his slither, the rogue!" cried Gustav and ran, naked, to the wardrobe where he kept his money box.

"Doesn't matter, we'll pass it," said his brother. "A nonexpert won't see the difference."

"Yes, but what a rogue!" Gustav kept repeating.

My poor Romantovski! And I who believed with them that you were indeed someone exceptional. I believed, let me confess, that you were a remarkable poet whom poverty obliged to dwell in that sinister district. I believed, on the strength of certain indices, that every night, by working on a line of verse or nursing a growing idea, you celebrated an invulnerable victory over the brothers. My poor Romantovski! It is all over now. Alas, the objects I had assembled wander away. The young poplar dims and takes off—to return where it had been fetched from. The brick wall dissolves. The house draws in its little balconies one by one, then turns, and floats away. Everything floats away. Harmony and meaning vanish. The world irks me again with its variegated void.

IN MEMORY OF L. I. SHIGAEV

LEONID IVANOVICH SHIGAEV is dead. . . . The suspension dots, customary in Russian obituaries, must represent the footprints of words that have departed on tiptoe, in reverent single file, leaving their tracks on the marble. . . . However, I would like to violate this sepulchral silence. Please allow me to . . . Just a few fragmentary, chaotic, basically uncalled-for . . . But no matter. He and I met about eleven years ago, in a year that for me was disastrous. I was virtually perishing. Picture to yourself a young, still very young, helpless and lonely person, with a perpetually inflamed soul (it feared the least contact, it was like raw flesh) and unable to cope with the pangs of an unhappy love affair. . . . I shall take the liberty of dwelling on this point for a moment.

There was nothing exceptional about that thin, bobhaired German girl, but when I used to look at her, at her suntanned cheek, at her rich fair hair, whose shiny, golden-yellow and olive-gold strands sloped so roundly in profile from crown to nape, I felt like howling with tenderness, a tenderness that just would not fit inside me simply and comfortably, but remained wedged in the door and would not bulge in or out—bulky, brittle-cornered, and of no use to anyone, least of all to that lass. In short, I discovered that once a week, at her house, she betrayed me with a respectable paterfamilias, who, incidentally, was so infernally meticulous that he would bring his own shoe trees with him. It all ended with the circuslike whump of a monstrous box on the ear with which I knocked down the traitress, who rolled up in a ball where she had collapsed, her eyes glistening at me through her spread fingers—all in all quite flattered, I think. Automatically, I searched for something to throw at her, saw the china sugar bowl I had given her for Easter, took the thing under my arm and went out, slamming the door.

A footnote: this is but one of the conceivable versions of my parting with her; I had considered many of these impossible possibilities while still in the first heat of my drunken delirium, imagining now the gross gratification of a good slap; now the firing of an old Parabellum pistol, at her and at myself, at her and at the paterfamilias, only at her, only at myself; then, finally, a glacial irony, noble sadness, silence—oh, things can go in so many ways, and I have long since forgotten how they actually went.

My landlord at the time, an athletic Berliner, suffered permanently from furunculosis: the back of his neck showed a square of disgustingly pink sticking plaster with three neat apertures—for ventilation, maybe, or for the release of the pus. I worked in an émigré publishing house for a couple of languid-looking individuals who in reality were such cunning crooks that plain people upon observing them got spasms in the chest, as when one steps onto a cloud-piercing summit. As I began coming late ("systematically late" as they called it) and missing work, or arriving in such condition that it was necessary to send me home, our relationship became unbearable, and finally, thanks to a joint effort—with the enthusiastic collaboration of the bookkeeper and of some stranger who had come in with a manuscript—I was thrown out.

My poor, my pitiful youth! I vividly visualize the ghastly little room that I rented for five dollars a month, the ghastly flowerets of the wallpaper, the ghastly lamp hanging from its cord, with a naked bulb whose manic light glowed sometimes till morn. I was so miserable there, so indecently, luxuriously miserable, that the walls to this day must be saturated with misfortune and fever, and it is unthinkable that some happy chap could have lived there after me, whistling, humming. Ten years have elapsed, and even now I can still imagine myself then, a pale youth seated in front of the shimmery mirror, with his livid forehead and black beard, dressed only in a torn shirt, guzzling cheap booze and clinking glasses with his reflection. What times those were! Not only was I of no use to anyone in the world, but I could not even imagine a set of circumstances in which someone might care a whit about me.

By dint of prolonged, persistent, solitary drinking I drove myself to the most vulgar of visions, the most Russian of all hallucinations: I began seeing devils. I saw them every evening as soon as I emerged from my diurnal dreamery to dispel with my wretched lamp the twilight that was already engulfing us. Yes, even more clearly than I now see the perpetual tremor of my hand, I saw the precious intruders and after some time I even became accustomed to their presence, as they kept pretty much to themselves. They were smallish but rather plump, the size of an overweight toad—peaceful, limp, black-skinned, more or less warty little monsters. They crawled rather than walked, but, with all their feigned clumsiness, they proved uncapturable. I remember buying a dog whip and, as soon as enough of them had gathered on my desk, I tried to give them a good lashing, but they miraculously avoided the blow; I struck again, and one of them, the nearest, only blinked, screwing up his eyes crookedly, like a tense dog that someone wishes to threaten away from some tempting bit of ordure. The others dispersed, dragging their hind legs. But they all stealthily clustered together again while I wiped up the ink spilled on the desk and picked up a prostrate portrait. Generally speaking, their densest habitat was the vicinity of my writing table; they materialized from somewhere underneath and, in leisurely fashion, their sticky bellies crepitating and smacking against the wood, made their way up the desk legs, in a parody of climbing sailors. I tried smearing their route with Vaseline but this did not help, and only when I happened to select some particularly appetizing little rotter, intently clambering upward, and swatted him with the whip or with my shoe, only then did he fall on the floor with a fat-toad thud; but a minute later there he was again, on his way up from a different corner, his violet tongue hanging out from the strain, and once over the top he would join his comrades. They were numerous, and at first they all seemed alike to me: dark little creatures with puffy, basically rather good-natured faces; they sat in groups of five or six on the desk, on various papers, on a volume of Pushkin, glancing at me with indifference. One of them might scratch behind his ear with his foot, the long claw making a coarse scraping sound, and then freeze motionless, forgetting his leg in midair. Another would doze, uncomfortably crowding his neighbor, who, for that matter, was not blameless either: the reciprocal inconsiderateness of amphibians, capable of growing torpid in intricate attitudes. Gradually I began distinguishing them, and I think I even gave them names depending on their resemblance to acquaintances of mine or to various animals. One could make out larger and smaller specimens (although they were all of quite portable size), some were more repulsive, others more acceptable in aspect, some had lumps or tumors, others were perfectly smooth. A few had a habit of spitting at each other. Once they brought a new boy, an albino, of a cinereous tint, with eyes like beads of red caviar; he was very sleepy and glum, and gradually crawled away. With an effort of will I would manage to vanquish the spell for a moment. It was an agonizing effort, for I had to repel and hold away a horrible iron weight, for which my entire being served as a magnet: I had but to loosen my grip, to give in ever so slightly, and the phantasma would take shape again, becoming precise, growing stereoscopic, and I would experience a deceptive sense of relief—the relief of despair, alas—when I once again yielded to the hallucination, and once again the clammy mass of thick-skinned clods sat before me on the desk, looking at me sleepily and yet somehow expectantly. I tried not only the whip, but also a famous time-honored method, on which I now find myself embarrassed to enlarge, especially since I must have used it in some wrong, very wrong way. Still, the first time it did work: a certain sacramental sign with bunched fingers, pertaining to a particular religious cult, was unhurriedly performed by me at a height of a few inches above the compact group of devils and grazed them like a red-hot iron, with a succulent hiss, both pleasant and nasty; whereupon, squirming from their burns, my rascals disparted and dropped with ripe plops to the floor. But, when I repeated the experiment with a new gathering, the effect proved weaker and after that they stopped reacting altogether, that is, they very quickly developed a certain immunity . . . but enough about that. With a laugh—what else did I have left?—I would utter *"T'foo!"* (the only expletive, by the way, borrowed by the Russian language from the lexicon of devils; see also the German *"Teufel"*), and, without undressing, go to bed (on top of the covers, of course, as I was afraid of encountering unwanted bedfellows). Thus the days passed, if one can call them days—these were not days, but a timeless fog—and when I came to I found myself rolling on the floor, grappling with my hefty landlord among the shambles of the furniture. With a desperate lunge I freed myself and flew out of the room and thence onto the stairs, and the next thing I knew I was walking down the street, trembling, disheveled, a vile bit of alien plaster sticking to my fingers, with an aching body and a ringing head, but almost totally sober.

That was when L.I. took me under his wing. "What's the matter, old man?" (We already knew each other slightly; he had been compiling a Russian-German pocket dictionary of technical terms and used to visit the office where I worked.) "Wait a minute, old man, just look at yourself." Right there on the corner (he was coming out of a delicatessen shop with his supper in his briefcase) I burst into tears, and, without a word, L.I. took me to his place, installed me on the sofa, fed me liverwurst and beef-tea, and spread over me a quilted overcoat with a worn astrakhan collar. I shivered and sobbed, and presently fell asleep.

In short, I remained in his little apartment, and lived like that for a couple of weeks, after which I rented a room next door, and we continued seeing each other daily. And yet, who would think we had anything in common? We were different in every respect! He was nearly

twice my age, dependable, debonair, portly, dressed generally in a cutaway coat, cleanly and thriftily, like the majority of our orderly, elderly
émigré bachelors: it was worth seeing, and especially hearing, how me-
thodically he brushed his trousers in the morning: the sound of that
brushing is now so intimately associated with him, so prominent in my
recollection of him—especially the rhythm of the process, the pauses
between spells of scraping, when he would stop to examine a suspicious place, scratch at it with his fingernail, or hold it up to the light.
Oh, those "inexpressibles" (as he called them), that let the sky's azure
shine through at the knee, his inexpressibles, inexpressibly spiritualized
by that ascension!

His room was characterized by the naive neatness of poverty. He
would imprint his address and telephone number on his letters with
a rubber stamp (a rubber stamp!). He knew how to make *botviniya*,
a cold soup of beet tops. He was capable of demonstrating for hours
on end some little trinket he considered a work of genius, a curious
cuff link or cigarette lighter sold to him by a smooth-talking hawker
(note that L.I. himself did not smoke), or his pets, three diminutive
turtles with hideous cronelike necks; one of them perished in my presence when it crashed down from a round table along the edge of
which it used to keep moving, like a hurrying cripple, under the impression that it was following a straight course, leading far, far away.
Another thing that I just remembered with such clarity: on the wall
above his bed, which was as smooth as a prisoner's cot, hung two
lithographs: a view of the Neva from the *Columna Rostrata* side and
a portrait of Alexander I. He had happened to acquire them in a moment of yearning for the Empire, a nostalgia he distinguished from the
yearning for one's native land.

L.I. totally lacked any sense of humor, and was totally indifferent to
art, literature, and what is commonly known as nature. If the talk did
happen to turn, say, to poetry, his contribution would be limited to a
statement like "No, say what you will, but Lermontov is somehow
closer to us than Pushkin." And when I pestered him to quote even a
single line of Lermontov, he made an obvious effort to recall something out of Rubinstein's opera *The Demon*, or else answered,
"Haven't reread him in a long while, 'all these are deeds of bygone
days,' and, anyway, my dear Victor, just let me alone." Incidentally, he
did not realize that he was quoting from Pushkin's *Ruslan and
Ludmila*.

In the summer, on Sundays, he would invariably go on a trip out
of town. He knew the outskirts of Berlin in astonishing detail and
prided himself on his knowledge of "wonderful spots" unfamiliar to

others. This was a pure, self-sufficient delight, related, perhaps, to the delights of collectors, to the orgies indulged in by amateurs of old catalogues; otherwise it was incomprehensible why he needed it all: painstakingly preparing the route, juggling various means of transportation (there by train, then back to this point by steamer, thence by bus, and this is how much it costs, and nobody, not even the Germans themselves, knows it is so cheap). But when he and I finally stood in the woods it turned out that he could not tell the difference between a bee and a bumblebee, or between alder and hazel, and perceived his surroundings quite conventionally and collectively: greenery, fine weather, the feathered tribe, little bugs. He was even offended if I, who had grown up in the country, remarked, for the sake of a bit of fun, on the differences between the flora around us and a forest in central Russia: he felt that there existed no significant difference, and that sentimental associations alone mattered.

He liked to stretch out on the grass in a shady spot, prop himself up on his right elbow, and discourse lengthily on the international situation or tell stories about his brother Peter, apparently quite a dashing fellow—ladies' man, musician, brawler—who, back in prehistoric times, drowned one summer night in the Dnieper—a very glamorous end. In dear old L.I.'s account, though, it all turned out so dull, so thorough, so well rounded out, that when, during a rest in the woods, he would suddenly ask with a kind smile: "Did I ever tell you about the time Pete took a ride on the village priest's she-goat?" I felt like crying out, "Yes, yes, you did, please spare me!"

What would I not give to hear his uninteresting yarns now, to see his absentminded, kindly eyes, that bald pate, rosy from the heat, those graying temples. What, then, was the secret of his charm, if everything about him was so dull? Why was everybody so fond of him, why did they all cling to him? What did he do in order to be so well liked? I don't know. I don't know the answer. I only know that I felt uneasy during his morning absences when he would leave for his Institute of Social Sciences (where he spent the time poring over bound volumes of *Die Ökonomische Welt*, from which he would copy in a neat, minute hand, excerpts that in his opinion were significant and noteworthy in the utmost), or for a private lesson of Russian, which he eternally taught to an elderly couple and the elderly couple's son-in-law; his association with them led him to make many incorrect conclusions about the German way of life—on which the members of our intelligentsia (the most unobservant race in the world) consider themselves authorities. Yes, I would feel uneasy, as though I had a premonition of what has since happened to him in Prague: heart failure in the street. How happy he was, though, to get that job in Prague, how he beamed! I have an exceptionally clear recollection of the day we saw him off. Just think, a man gets the opportunity to lecture on his favorite subject! He left me a pile of old magazines (nothing grows old and dusty as fast as a Soviet magazine), his shoe trees (shoe trees were destined to pursue me), and a brand-new fountain pen (as a memento). He showed great concern for me as he left, and I know that afterwards, when our correspondence somehow wilted and ceased, and life again crashed into deep darkness—a darkness howling with thousands of voices, from which it is unlikely I will ever escape—L.I., I know, kept thinking about me, questioning people, and trying to help indirectly. He left on a beautiful summer day; tears welled persistently in the eyes of some of those seeing him off; a myopic Jewish girl with white gloves and a lorgnette brought a whole sheaf of poppies and cornflowers; L.I. inexpertly sniffed them, smiling. Did it occur to me that I might be seeing him for the last time?

Of course it did. That is exactly what occurred to me: yes, I am seeing you for the last time; this, in fact is what I always think, about everything, about everyone. My life is a perpetual good-bye to objects and people, that often do not pay the least attention to my bitter, brief, insane salutation.

THE CIRCLE

I N T H E second place, because he was possessed by a sudden mad hankering after Russia. In the third place, finally, because he regretted those years of youth and everything associated with it—the fierce resentment, the uncouthness, the ardency, and the dazzlingly green mornings when the coppice deafened you with its golden orioles. As he sat in the café and kept diluting with syphoned soda the paling sweetness of his cassis, he recalled the past with a constriction of the heart, with melancholy—what kind of melancholy?—well, a kind not yet sufficiently investigated. All that distant past rose with his breast, raised by a sigh, and slowly his father ascended from the grave, squaring his shoulders: Ilya Ilyich Bychkov, *le maître d'école chez nous au village,* in flowing black tie, picturesquely knotted, and pongee jacket, whose buttons began, in the old fashion, high on the breast-bone but stopped also at a high point, letting the diverging coat flaps reveal the watch chain across the waistcoat; his complexion was reddish, his head bald yet covered with a tender down resembling the velvet of a deer's vernal antlers; there were lots of little folds along his cheeks, and a fleshy wart next to the nose producing the effect of an additional volute described by the fat nostril. In his high school and college days, Innokentiy used to travel from town on holidays to visit his father at Leshino. Diving still deeper, he could remember the demolition of the old school at the end of the village, the clearing of the ground for its successor, the foundation-stone ceremony, the religious service in the wind, Count Konstantin Godunov-Cherdyntsev throwing the traditional gold coin, the coin sticking edgewise in the clay. The new building was of a grainy granitic gray on its outside; its inside, for several years and then for another long spell (that is, when it joined the staff of memory) sunnily smelled of glue; the classes were graced with glossy educational appliances such as enlarged portraits of insects injurious to field or forest; but Innokentiy found even more irritating the stuffed birds provided by Godunov-Cherdyntsev. Flirting with the common people! Yes, he saw himself as a stern plebeian: hatred (or so it seemed) suffocated him when as a youth he used to look across the river at the great manorial park, heavy with ancient privileges and imperial grants, casting the reflection of its black amassments onto the green water (with the creamy blur of a racemosa blooming here and there among the fir trees).

The new school was built on the threshold of this century, at a time when Godunov-Cherdyntsev had returned from his fifth expedition to central Asia and was spending the summer at Leshino, his estate in the Government of St. Petersburg, with his young wife (at forty he was twice as old as she). To what a depth one has plunged, good God! In a melting crystalline mist, as if it were all taking place under water, Innokentiy saw himself as a boy of three or four entering the manor house and floating through marvelous rooms, with his father moving on tiptoe, a damp nosegay of lilies of the valley bunched in his fist so tight that they squeaked—and everything around seemed moist too, a luminous, squeaking, quivering haze, which was all one could distinguish—but in later years it turned into a shameful recollection, his father's flowers, tiptoeing progress, and sweating temples darkly symbolizing grateful servility, especially after Innokentiy was told by an old peasant that Ilya Ilyich had been disentangled by "our good master" from a trivial but tacky political affair, for which he would have been banished to the backwoods of the empire had the Count not interceded.

Tanya used to say that they had relatives not only in the animal kingdom but also among plants and minerals. And, indeed, Russian and foreign naturalists had described under the specific name of *"godunovi"* a new pheasant, a new antelope, a new rhododendron, and there was even a whole Godunov Range (he himself described only insects). Those discoveries of his, his outstanding contributions to zoology, and a thousand perils, for disregarding which he was famous, could not, however, make people indulgent to his high descent and great wealth. Furthermore, let us not forget that certain sections of our intelligentsia had always held nonapplied scientific research in contempt, and therefore Godunov was rebuked for showing more interest in "Sinkiang bugs" than in the plight of the Russian peasant. Young Innokentiy readily believed the tales (actually idiotic) told about the Count's traveling concubines, his Chinese-style inhumanity, and the secret errands he discharged for the Tsar—to spite the English. The reality of his image remained dim: an ungloved hand throwing a gold piece (and, in the still earlier recollection, that visit to the manor house, the lord of which got confused by the child with a Kalmuck, dressed in sky blue, met on the way through a reception hall). Then Godunov departed again, to Samarkand or to Vernyi (towns from which he usually started his fabulous strolls), and was gone a long time. Meanwhile his family summered in the south, apparently preferring their Crimean country place to their Petropolitan one. Their winters were spent in the capital. There, on the quay, stood their house, a two-floor private residence, painted an olive hue. Innokentiy sometimes happened to walk by; his memory retained the feminine forms of a statue showing its dimpled sugar-white buttock through the patterned gauze on a whole-glassed window. Olive-brown atlantes with strongly arched ribs supported a balcony: the strain of their stone muscles and their agonizingly twisted mouths struck our hotheaded uppergrader as an allegory of the enslaved proletariat. Once or twice, on that quay, in the beginning of the gusty Neva spring, he glimpsed the little Godunov girl with her fox terrier and governess; they positively whirled by, yet were so vividly outlined: Tanya wore boots laced up to the knee and a short navy-blue coat with knobbed brass buttons, and as she marched rapidly past, she slapped the pleats of her short navy-blue skirt—with what? I think with the dog leash she carried—and the Ladoga wind tossed the ribbons of her sailor cap, and a little behind her sped her governess, karakul-jacketed, her waist flexed, one arm thrown out, the hand encased in a muff of tight-curled black fur.

He lodged at his aunt's, a seamstress, in an Okhta tenement. He was morose, unsociable, applied ponderous groaning efforts to his studies while limiting his ambition to a passing mark, but to everybody's astonishment finished school brilliantly and at the age of eighteen entered St. Petersburg University as a medical student—at which point his father's worship of Godunov-Cherdyntsev mysteriously increased. He spent one summer as a private tutor with a family in Tver. By May of the following year, 1914, he was back in the village of Leshino—and discovered not without dismay that the manor across the river had come alive.

More about that river, about its steep bank, about its old bathhouse. This was a wooden structure standing on piles; a stepped path, with a toad on every other step, led down to it, and not everyone could have found the beginning of that clayey descent in the alder thicket at the back of the church. His constant companion in riparian pastimes was Vasiliy, the blacksmith's son, a youth of indeterminable age (he could not say himself whether he was fifteen or a full twenty), sturdily built, ungainly, in skimpy patched trousers, with huge bare feet dirty carrot in color, and as gloomy in temper as was Innokentiy at the time. The pinewood piles cast concertina-shaped reflections that wound and unwound on the water. Gurgling and smacking sounds came from under the rotten planks of the bathhouse. In a round, earth-soiled tin box depicting a horn of plenty—it had once contained cheap fruit drops—worms wriggled listlessly. Vasiliy, taking care that the point of the hook would not stick through, pulled a plump segment of worm over it, leaving the rest to hang free; then seasoned the rascal with sacramental spittle and proceeded to lower the lead-weighted line over the outer railing of the bathhouse. Evening had come. Something resembling a broad fan of violet-pink plumes or an aerial mountain range with lateral spurs spanned the sky, and the bats were already flitting, with the overstressed soundlessness and evil speed of membraned beings. The fish had begun to bite, and scorning the use of a rod, simply holding the tensing and jerking line between finger and thumb, Vasiliy tugged at it ever so slightly to test the solidity of the underwater spasms—and suddenly landed a roach or a gudgeon. Casually, and even with a kind of devil-may-care crackling snap, he would wrench the hook out of the toothless round little mouth and place the frenzied creature (rosy blood oozing from a torn gill) in a glass jar where already a chevin was swimming, its lower lip stuck out. Angling was especially good in warm overcast weather when rain, invisible in the air, covered the water with mutually intersecting widening circles, among which appeared here and there a circle of different origin, with a sudden center: the jump of a fish that vanished at once or the fall of a leaf that immediately sailed away with the current. And how delicious it was to go bathing beneath that tepid drizzle, on the blending line of two homogeneous but differently shaped elements—the thick river water and the slender celestial one! Innokentiy took his dip intelligently and indulged afterwards in a long rubdown with a towel. The peasant boys, per contra, kept floundering till complete exhaustion; finally, shivering, with chattering teeth and a turbid snot trail from nostril to lip, they would hop on one foot to pull their pants up to their wet thighs.

That summer Innokentiy was gloomier than ever and scarcely spoke to his father, limiting himself to mumbles and "hms." Ilya Ilyich, on his part, experienced an odd embarrassment in his son's presence—mainly because he assumed, with terror and tenderness, that Innokentiy lived wholeheartedly in the pure world of the underground as he had himself at that age. Schoolmaster Bychkov's room: motes of dust in a slanting sunbeam; lit by that beam, a small table he had made

with his own hands, varnishing the top and adorning it with a pyro-
graphic design; on the table, a photograph of his wife in a velvet
frame—so young, in such a nice dress, with a little pelerine and a
corset-belt, charmingly oval-faced (that ovality coincided with the idea
of feminine beauty in the 1890s); next to the photograph a crystal paperweight with a mother-of-pearl Crimean view inside, and a cockerel
of cloth for wiping pens; and on the wall above, between two casement
windows, a portrait of Leo Tolstoy, entirely composed of the text of
one of his stories printed in microscopic type. Innokentiy slept on a
leathern couch in an adjacent smaller chamber. After a long day in the
open air he slept soundly; sometimes, however, a dream image would
take an erotic turn, the force of its thrill would carry him out of the
sleep circle, and for several moments he would remain lying as he was,
squeamishness preventing him from moving.

In the morning he would go to the woods, a medical manual under
his arm and both hands thrust under the tasseled cord girting his white
Russian blouse. His university cap, worn askew in conformance to left-
wing custom, allowed locks of brown hair to fall on his bumpy forehead. His eyebrows were knitted in a permanent frown. He might
have been quite good-looking had his lips been less blubbery. Once in
the forest, he seated himself on a thick birch bole which had been
felled not long before by a thunderstorm (and still quivered with all its
leaves from the shock), and smoked, and obstructed with his book the
trickle of hurrying ants or lost himself in dark meditation. A lonely, im-
pressionable, and touchy youth, he felt overkeenly the social side of
things. He loathed the entire surroundings of the Godunovs' country
life, such as their menials—"menials," he repeated, wrinkling his nose
in voluptuous disgust. In their number he included the plump chauffeur, with his freckles, corduroy livery, orange-brown leggings, and
starched collar propping a fold of his russet neck that used to flush
purple when, in the carriage shed, he cranked up the no less revolting
convertible upholstered in glossy red leather; and the senile flunky
with gray side-whiskers who was employed to bite off the tails of newborn fox terriers; and the English tutor who could be seen striding
across the village, hatless, raincoated, white-trousered—which had the
village boys allude wittily to underpants and bare-headed religious pro-
cessions; and the peasant girls, hired to weed the avenues of the park
morning after morning under the supervision of one of the gardeners,
a deaf little hunchback in a pink shirt, who in conclusion would sweep
the sand near the porch with particular zest and ancient devotion.
Innokentiy with the book still under his arm—which hindered his

crossing his arms, something he would have liked to do—stood leaning against a tree in the park and considered sullenly various items,
such as the shiny roof of the white manor which was not yet astir.

The first time he saw them that summer was in late May (Old Style)
from the top of a hill. A cavalcade appeared on the road curving
around its base: Tanya in front, astraddle, boylike, on a bright bay;
next Count Godunov-Cherdyntsev himself, an insignificant-looking
person riding an oddly small mouse-gray pacer; behind them the
breeched Englishman; then some cousin or other; and coming last,
Tanya's brother, a boy of thirteen or so, who suddenly spurred his
mount, overtook everybody, and dashed up the steep bit to the village,
working his elbows jockey-fashion.

After that there followed several other chance encounters and
finally—all right, here we go. Ready? On a hot day in mid-June—

On a hot day in mid-June the mowers went swinging along on
both sides of the path leading to the manor, and each mower's shirt
stuck in alternate rhythm now to the right shoulder blade, now to the
left. "May God assist you!" said Ilya Ilyich in a passerby's traditional
salute to men at work. He wore his best hat, a panama, and carried a
bouquet of mauve bog orchids. Innokentiy walked alongside in silence, his mouth in circular motion (he was cracking sunflower seeds
between his teeth and munching at the same time). They were nearing
the manor park. At one end of the tennis court the deaf pink dwarf
gardener, now wearing a workman's apron, soaked a brush in a pail
and, bent in two, walked backward as he traced a thick creamy line on
the ground. "May God assist you," said Ilya Ilyich in passing.

The table was laid in the main avenue; Russian dappled sunlight
played on the tablecloth. The housekeeper, wearing a gorget, her
steely hair smoothly combed back, was already in the act of ladling out
chocolate which the footmen were serving in dark-blue cups. At close
range the Count looked his age: there were ashy streaks in his yellowish beard, and wrinkles fanned out from eye to temple; he had placed
his foot on the edge of a garden bench and was making a fox terrier
jump: the dog jumped not only very high, trying to hap the already
wet ball he was holding, but actually contrived, while hanging in midair, to jerk itself still higher by an additional twist of its entire body.
Countess Elizaveta Godunov, a tall rosy woman in a big wavery hat,
was coming up from the garden with another lady to whom she was vivaciously talking, and making the Russian two-hand splash gesture of
uncertain dismay. Ilya Ilyich stood with his bouquet and bowed. In
this varicolored haze (as perceived by Innokentiy, who, despite having
briefly rehearsed on the eve an attitude of democratic scorn, was over-

come by the greatest embarrassment) there flickered young people, running children, somebody's black shawl embroidered with gaudy poppies, a second fox terrier, and above all, above all, those eyes gliding through shine and shade, those features still indistinct but already threatening him with fatal fascination, the face of Tanya whose birthday was being fêted.

Everybody was now seated. He found himself at the shade end of the long table, at which end convives did not indulge so much in mutual conversation as keep looking, all their heads turned in the same direction, at the brighter end where there was loud talk, and laughter, and a magnificent pink cake with a satiny glaze and sixteen candles, and the exclamations of children, and the barking of both dogs that had all but jumped onto the table—while here at this end the garlands of linden shade linked up people of the meanest rank: Ilya Ilyich, smiling in a sort of daze; an ethereal but ugly damsel whose shyness expressed itself in onion sweat; a decrepit French governess with nasty eyes who held in her lap under the table a tiny invisible creature that now and then emitted a tinkle; and so forth. Innokentiy's direct neighbor happened to be the estate steward's brother, a blockhead, a bore, and a stutterer; Innokentiy talked to him only because silence would have been worse, so that despite the paralyzing nature of the conversation, he desperately tried to keep it up; later, however, when he became a frequent visitor, and chanced to run into the poor fellow, Innokentiy never spoke to him, shunning him as a kind of snare or shameful memory.

Rotating in slow descent, the winged fruit of a linden lit on the tablecloth.

At the nobility's end Godunov-Cherdyntsev raised his voice, speaking across the table to a very old lady in a lacy gown, and as he spoke encircled with one arm the graceful waist of his daughter who stood near and kept tossing up a rubber ball on her palm. For quite a time Innokentiy tussled with a luscious morsel of cake that had come to rest beyond the edge of his plate. Finally, following an awkward poke, the damned raspberry stuff rolled and tumbled under the table (where we shall leave it). His father either smiled vacantly or licked his mustache. Somebody asked him to pass the biscuits; he burst into happy laughter and passed them. All at once, right above Innokentiy's ear, there came a rapid gasping voice: unsmilingly, and still holding that ball, Tanya was asking him to join her and her cousins; all hot and confused, he struggled to rise from table, pushing against his neighbor in the process of disengaging his right leg from under the shared garden bench.

When speaking of her, people exclaimed, "What a pretty girl!" She had light-gray eyes, velvet-black eyebrows, a largish, pale, tender mouth, sharp incisors, and—when she was unwell or out of humor—one could distinguish the dark little hairs above her lip. She was inordinately fond of all summer games, tennis, badminton, croquet, doing everything deftly, with a kind of charming concentration—and, of course, that was the end of the artless afternoons of fishing with Vasiliy, who was greatly perplexed by the change and would pop up in the vicinity of the school toward evening, beckoning Innokentiy with a hesitating grin and holding up at face level a canful of worms. At such moments Innokentiy shuddered inwardly as he sensed his betrayal of the people's cause. Meanwhile he derived not much joy from the company of his new friends. It so happened that he was not really admitted to the center of their existence, being kept on its green periphery, taking part in open-air amusements, but never being invited into the house. This infuriated him; he longed to be asked for lunch or dinner just to have the pleasure of haughtily refusing; and, in general, he remained constantly on the alert, sullen, suntanned, and shaggy, the muscles of his clenched jaws twitching—and feeling that every word Tanya said to her playmates cast an insulting little shadow in his direction, and, good God, how he hated them all, her boy cousins, her girl-friends, the frolicsome dogs. Abruptly, everything dimmed in noiseless disorder and vanished, and there he was, in the deep blackness of an August night, sitting on a bench at the bottom of the park and waiting, his breast prickly because of his having stuffed between shirt and skin the note which, as in an old novel, a barefooted little girl had brought him from the manor. The laconic style of the assignation led him to suspect a humiliating practical joke, yet he succumbed to the summons—and rightly so: a light crunch of footfalls detached itself from the even rustle of the night. Her arrival, her incoherent speech, her nearness struck him as miraculous; the sudden intimate touch of her cold nimble fingers amazed his chastity. A huge, rapidly ascending moon burned through the trees. Shedding torrents of tears and blindly nuzzling him with salt-tasting lips, Tanya told him that on the following day her mother was taking her to the Crimea, that everything was finished, and—oh, how could he have been so obtuse! "Don't go anywhere, Tanya!" he pleaded, but a gust of wind drowned his words, and she sobbed even more violently. When she had hurried away he remained on the bench without moving, listening to the hum in his ears, and presently walked back in the direction of the bridge along the country road that seemed to stir in the dark, and then came the war years—ambulance work, his father's death—and after that, a general disintegration of things, but gradually life picked up again, and by

1920 he was already the assistant of Professor Behr at a spa in Bohemia, and three or four years later worked, under the same lung specialist, in Savoy, where one day, somewhere near Chamonix, Innokentiy happened to meet a young Soviet geologist; they got into conversation, and the latter mentioned that it was here, half a century ago, that Fedchenko, the great explorer of Fergana, had died the death of an ordinary tourist; how strange (the geologist added) that it should always turn out that way: death gets so used to pursuing fearless men in wild mountains and deserts that it also keeps coming at them in jest, without any special intent to harm, in all other circumstances, and to its own surprise catches them napping. Thus perished Fedchenko, and Severtsev, and Godunov-Cherdyntsev, as well as many foreigners of classic fame—Speke, Dumont d'Urville. And after several years more spent in medical research, far from the cares and concerns of political expatriation, Innokentiy happened to be in Paris for a few hours for a business interview with a colleague, and was already running downstairs, gloving one hand, when, on one of the landings, a tall stoop-shouldered lady emerged from the lift—and he at once recognized Countess Elizaveta Godunov-Cherdyntsev. "Of course I remember you, how could I not remember?" she said, gazing not at his face but over his shoulder as if somebody were standing behind him (she had a slight squint). "Well, come in, my dear," she continued, recovering from a momentary trance, and with the point of her shoe turned back a corner of the thick doormat, replete with dust, to get the key. Innokentiy entered after her, tormented by the fact that he could not recall what he had been told exactly about the how and the when of her husband's death.

And a few moments later Tanya came home, all her features fixed more clearly now by the etching needle of years, with a smaller face and kinder eyes; she immediately lit a cigarette, laughing, and without the least embarrassment recalling that distant summer, while he kept marveling that neither Tanya nor her mother mentioned the dead explorer and spoke so simply about the past, instead of bursting into the awful sobs that he, a stranger, kept fighting back—or were those two displaying, perhaps, the self-control peculiar to their class? They were soon joined by a pale dark-haired little girl about ten years of age: "This is my daughter, come here, darling," said Tanya, putting her cigarette butt, now stained with lipstick, into a seashell that served as an ashtray. Then her husband, Ivan Ivanovich Kutaysov, came home, and the Countess, meeting him in the next room, was heard to identify their visitor, in her domestic French brought over from Russia, as *"le fils du maître d'école chez nous au village,"* which reminded Innokentiy of Tanya saying once in his presence to a girlfriend of hers whom she wanted to notice his very shapely hands: *"Regarde ses mains";* and now, listening to the melodious, beautifully idiomatic Russian in which the child replied to Tanya's questions, he caught himself thinking, malevolently and quite absurdly, Aha, there is no longer the money to teach the kids foreign languages!—for it did not occur to him at that moment that in those émigré times, in the case of a Paris-born child going to a French school, this Russian language represented *the* idlest and best luxury.

The Leshino topic was falling apart; Tanya, getting it all wrong, insisted that he used to teach her the pre-Revolution songs of radical students, such as the one about "the despot who feasts in his rich palace hall while destiny's hand has already begun to trace the dread words on the wall." "In other words, our first *stengazeta*" (Soviet wall gazette), remarked Kutaysov, a great wit. Tanya's brother was mentioned: he lived in Berlin, and the Countess started to talk about him. Suddenly Innokentiy grasped a wonderful fact: nothing is lost, nothing whatever; memory accumulates treasures, stored-up secrets grow in darkness and dust, and one day a transient visitor at a lending library wants a book that has not once been asked for in twenty-two years. He got up from his seat, made his adieus, was not detained overeffusively. How strange that his knees should be trembling. That was really a shattering experience. He crossed the square, entered a café, ordered a drink, briefly rose to remove his own squashed hat from under him. What a dreadful feeling of uneasiness. He felt that way for several reasons. In the first place, because Tanya had remained as enchanting and as invulnerable as she had been in the past.

A RUSSIAN BEAUTY

OLGA, of whom we are about to speak, was born in the year 1900, in a wealthy, carefree family of nobles. A pale little girl in a white sailor suit, with a side parting in her chestnut hair and such merry eyes that everyone kissed her there, she was deemed a beauty since childhood. The purity of her profile, the expression of her closed lips, the silkiness of her tresses that reached to the small of her back—all this was enchanting indeed.

Her childhood passed festively, securely, and gaily, as was the custom in our country since the days of old. A sunbeam falling on the cover of a *Bibliothèque Rose* volume at the family estate, the classical hoarfrost of the Saint Petersburg public gardens. . . . A supply of memories, such as these, comprised her sole dowry when she left Russia in the spring of 1919. Everything happened in full accord with the style of the period. Her mother died of typhus, her brother was executed by the firing squad. All these are ready-made formulae, of course, the usual dreary small talk, but it all did happen, there is no other way of saying it, and it's no use turning up your nose.

Well, then, in 1919 we have a grown-up young lady, with a pale, broad face that overdid things in terms of the regularity of its features, but just the same very lovely. Tall, with soft breasts, she always wears a black jumper and a scarf around her white neck and holds an English cigarette in her slender-fingered hand with a prominent little bone just above the wrist.

Yet there was a time in her life, at the end of 1916 or so, when at a summer resort near the family estate there was no schoolboy who did not plan to shoot himself because of her, there was no university student who would not . . . In a word, there had been a special magic about her, which, had it lasted, would have caused . . . would have wreaked . . . But somehow, nothing came of it. Things failed to develop, or else happened to no purpose. There were flowers that she was too lazy to put in a vase, there were strolls in the twilight now with this one, now with another, followed by the blind alley of a kiss.

She spoke French fluently, pronouncing *les gens* (the servants) as if rhyming with *agence* and splitting *août* (August) in two syllables (*a-ou*). She naively translated the Russian *grabezhi* (robberies) as *les grabuges* (quarrels) and used some archaic French locutions that had somehow survived in old Russian families, but she rolled her *r*'s most convincingly even though she had never been to France. Over the dresser in her Berlin room a postcard of Serov's portrait of the Tsar was fastened with a pin with a fake turquoise head. She was religious, but at times a fit of giggles would overcome her in church. She wrote verse with that terrifying facility typical of young Russian girls of her generation: patriotic verse, humorous verse, any kind of verse at all.

For about six years, that is until 1926, she resided in a boarding-house on the Augsburgerstrasse (not far from the clock), together with her father, a broad-shouldered, beetle-browed old man with a yellow-ish mustache, and with tight, narrow trousers on his spindly legs. He had a job with some optimistic firm, was noted for his decency and kindness, and was never one to turn down a drink.

In Berlin, Olga gradually acquired a large group of friends, all of them young Russians. A certain jaunty tone was established. "Let's go to the cinemonkey," or "That was a heely deely German *Diele*, dance hall." All sorts of popular sayings, cant phrases, imitations of imitations were much in demand. "These cutlets are grim." "I wonder who's kissing her now?" Or, in a hoarse, choking voice: *"Mes-sieurs les officiers . . ."*

At the Zotovs', in their overheated rooms, she languidly danced the fox-trot to the sound of the gramophone, shifting the elongated calf of her leg not without grace and holding away from her the cigarette she had just finished smoking, and when her eyes located the ashtray that revolved with the music she would shove the butt into it, without missing a step. How charmingly, how meaningfully she could raise the wineglass to her lips, secretly drinking to the health of a third party as she looked through her lashes at the one who had confided in her. How she loved to sit in the corner of the sofa, discussing with this person or that somebody else's affairs of the heart, the oscillation of chances, the probability of a declaration—all this indirectly, by hints— and how understandingly her eyes would smile, pure, wide-open eyes with barely noticeable freckles on the thin, faintly bluish skin under-neath and around them. But as for herself, no one fell in love with her, and this was why she long remembered the boor who pawed her at a charity ball and afterwards wept on her bare shoulder. He was challenged to a duel by the little Baron R., but refused to fight. The word "boor," by the way, was used by Olga on any and every occasion. "Such boors," she would sing out in chest tones, languidly and affectionately. "What a boor . . ." "Aren't they boors?"

But presently her life darkened. Something was finished, people were already getting up to leave. How quickly! Her father died, she moved to another street. She stopped seeing her friends, knitted the little bonnets in fashion, and gave cheap French lessons at some ladies' club or other. In this way her life dragged on to the age of thirty.

She was still the same beauty, with that enchanting slant of the widely spaced eyes and with that rarest line of lips into which the geometry of the smile seems to be already inscribed. But her hair lost its shine and was poorly cut. Her black tailored suit was in its fourth year. Her hands, with their glistening but untidy fingernails, were roped with veins and were shaking from nervousness and from her wretched continuous smoking. And we'd best pass over in silence the state of her stockings. . . .

Now, when the silken insides of her handbag were in tatters (at least there was always the hope of finding a stray coin); now, when she was so tired; now, when putting on her only pair of shoes she had to force herself not to think of their soles, just as when, swallowing her pride, she entered the tobacconist's, she forbade herself to think of how much she already owed there; now that there was no longer the least hope of returning to Russia, and hatred had become so habitual that it almost ceased to be a sin; now that the sun was getting behind the chimney, Olga would occasionally be tormented by the luxury of certain advertisements, written in the saliva of Tantalus, imagining herself wealthy, wearing that dress, sketched with the aid of three or four insolent lines, on that ship-deck, under that palm tree, at the balustrade of that white terrace. And then there was also another thing or two that she missed.

One day, almost knocking her off her feet, her one-time friend Vera rushed like a whirlwind out of a telephone booth, in a hurry as always, loaded with parcels, with a shaggy-eyed terrier whose leash immediately became wound twice around her skirt. She pounced upon Olga, imploring her to come and stay at their summer villa, saying that it was fate itself, that it was wonderful and how have you been and are there many suitors. "No, my dear, I'm no longer that age," answered Olga, "and besides. . . ." She added a little detail and Vera burst out laughing, letting her parcels sink almost to the ground. "No, seriously," said Olga, with a smile. Vera continued coaxing her, pulling at the terrier, turning this way and that. Olga, starting all at once to speak through her nose, borrowed some money from her.

Vera adored arranging things, be it a party with punch, a visa, or a wedding. Now she avidly took up arranging Olga's fate. "The matchmaker within you has been aroused," joked her husband, an elderly Balt (shaven head, monocle). Olga arrived on a bright August day. She was immediately dressed in one of Vera's frocks, her hairdo and make-up were changed. She swore languidly, but yielded, and how festively the floorboards creaked in the merry little villa! How the little mirrors, suspended in the green orchard to frighten off birds, flashed and sparkled!

A Russified German named Forstmann, a well-off athletic widower, author of books on hunting, came to spend a week. He had long been asking Vera to find him a bride, "a real Russian beauty." He had a massive, strong nose with a fine pink vein on its high bridge. He was polite, silent, at times even morose, but knew how to form, instantly and while no one noticed, an eternal friendship with a dog or with a child. With his arrival Olga became difficult. Listless and irritable, she did all the wrong things and she knew that they were wrong. When the conversation turned to old Russia (Vera tried to make her show off her past), it seemed to her that everything she said was a lie and that everyone understood that it was a lie, and therefore she stubbornly refused to say the things that Vera was trying to extract from her and in general would not cooperate in any way.

On the veranda, they would slam their cards down hard. Everyone would go off together for a stroll through the woods, but Forstmann conversed mostly with Vera's husband, and, recalling some pranks of their youth, the two of them would turn red with laughter, lag behind, and collapse on the moss. On the eve of Forstmann's departure they were playing cards on the veranda, as they usually did in the evening. Suddenly, Olga felt an impossible spasm in her throat. She still managed to smile and to leave without undue haste. Vera knocked on her door but she did not open. In the middle of the night, having swatted a multitude of sleepy flies and smoked continuously to the point where she was no longer able to inhale, irritated, depressed, hating herself and everyone, Olga went into the garden. There, the crickets stridulated, the branches swayed, an occasional apple fell with a taut thud, and the moon performed calisthenics on the whitewashed wall of the chicken coop.

Early in the morning, she came out again and sat down on the porch step that was already hot. Forstmann, wearing a dark blue bathrobe, sat next to her and, clearing his throat, asked if she would consent to become his spouse—that was the very word he used: "spouse." When they came to breakfast, Vera, her husband, and his maiden cousin, in utter silence, were performing nonexistent dances, each in a different corner, and Olga drawled out in an affectionate voice "What boors!" and next summer she died in childbirth.

That's all. Of course, there may be some sort of sequel, but it is not known to me. In such cases, instead of getting bogged down in guesswork, I repeat the words of the merry king in my favorite fairy tale: Which arrow flies forever? The arrow that has hit its mark.

BREAKING THE NEWS

EUGENIA ISAKOVNA MINTS was an elderly émigré widow, who always wore black. Her only son had died on the previous day. She had not yet been told.

It was a March day in 1935, and after a rainy dawn, one horizontal section of Berlin was reflected in the other—variegated zigzags intermingling with flatter textures, et cetera. The Chernobylskis, old friends of Eugenia Isakovna, had received the telegram from Paris around seven a.m., and a couple of hours later a letter had come by airmail. The head of the factory office where Misha had worked announced that the poor young man had fallen into an elevator shaft from the top floor, and had remained in agony for forty minutes: although unconscious, he kept moaning horribly and uninterruptedly, till the very end.

In the meantime Eugenia Isakovna got up, dressed, flung with a crosswise flick a black woolen shawl over her sharp thin shoulders and made herself some coffee in the kitchen. The deep, genuine fragrance of her coffee was something she prided herself upon in relation to Frau Doktor Schwarz, her landlady, "a stingy, uncultured beast": it had now been a whole week since Eugenia Isakovna had stopped speaking to her—and that was not their first quarrel by far—but, as she told her friends, she did not care to move elsewhere for a number of reasons, often enumerated and never tedious. A manifest advantage that she had over this or that person with whom she might decide to break off relations lay in her being able simply to switch off her hearing aid, a portable gadget resembling a small black handbag.

As she carried the pot of coffee back to her room across the hallway, she noticed the flutter of a postcard, which, upon having been pushed by the mailman through a special slit, settled on the floor. It was from her son, of whose death the Chernobylskis had just learned by more advanced postal means, in consequence of which the lines (virtually inexistent) that she now read, standing with the coffeepot in one hand, on the threshold of her sizable but inept room, could have been compared by an objective observer to the still visible beams of an already extinguished star. *My darling Moolik* (her son's pet-name for her since childhood), *I continue to be plunged up to the neck in work and when evening comes I literally fall off my feet, and I never go anywhere*—

Two streets away, in a similar grotesque apartment crammed with alien bagatelles, Chernobylski, not having gone downtown today, paced from one room to another, a large, fat, bald man, with huge arching eyebrows and a diminutive mouth. He wore a dark suit but was collarless (the hard collar with inserted tie hung yokelike on the back of a chair in the dining room) and he gestured helplessly as he paced and spoke: "How shall I tell her? What gradual preparation can there be when one has to yell? Good God, what a calamity. Her heart will not bear it, it will burst, her poor heart!"

His wife wept, smoked, scraped her head through her sparse gray hair, telephoned the Lipshteyns, Lenochka, Dr. Orshanski—and could not make herself go to Eugenia Isakovna first. Their lodger, a woman pianist with a pince-nez, big-bosomed, very compassionate and experienced, advised the Chernobylskis not to hurry too much with the telling—"All the same there will be that blow, so let it be later."

"But on the other hand," cried Chernobylski hysterically, "neither can one postpone it! Clearly one cannot! She is the mother, she may want to go to Paris—who knows? I don't—or she may want him to be brought here. Poor, poor Mishuk, poor boy, not yet thirty, all life before him! And to think that it was I who helped him, found him a job, to think that, if it had not been for that lousy Paris—"

"Now, now, Boris Lvovich," soberly countered the lady lodger, "who could foresee? What have you to do with it? It is comical— In general, I must say, incidentally, that I don't understand how he could fall. You understand how?"

Having finished her coffee and rinsed her cup in the kitchen (while not paying any attention *whatsoever* to the presence of Frau Schwarz), Eugenia Isakovna, with black net bag, handbag, and umbrella, went out. The rain, after hesitating a little, had stopped. She closed her umbrella and proceeded to walk along the shining sidewalk, still holding herself quite straight, on very thin legs in black stockings, the left sagging slightly. One also noted that her feet seemed disproportionately large and that she set them down somewhat draggingly, with toes turned out. When not connected with her hearing aid she was ideally deaf, and very deaf when connected. What she took for the hum of the town was the hum of her blood, and against this customary background, without ruffling it, there moved the surrounding world—rubbery pedestrians, cotton-wool dogs, mute tramcars—and overhead crept the ever-so-slightly rustling clouds through which, in this or that place, blabbed, as it were, a bit of blue. Amid the general silence, she passed, impassive, rather satisfied on the whole, black-coated, bewitched and limited by her deafness, and kept an eye on things, and reflected on various matters. She reflected that tomorrow, a holiday, So-and-so would drop in; that she ought to get the same little pink *gaufrettes* as last time, and also *marmelad* (candied fruit jellies) at the Russian store, and maybe a dozen dainties in that small pastry shop where one can always be sure that everything is fresh. A tall bowler-hatted man coming toward her seemed to her from a distance (quite some distance, in fact) frightfully like Vladimir Markovich Vilner, Ida's first husband, who had died alone, in a sleeping-car, of heart failure, so sad, and as she went by a watchmaker's she remembered that it was time to call for Misha's wristwatch, which he had broken in Paris and had sent her by *okaziya* (i.e., "taking the opportunity of somebody's traveling that way"). She went in. Noiselessly, slipperily, never brushing against anything, pendulums swung, all different, all in discord. She took her purselike gadget out of her larger, ordinary handbag, introduced with a quick movement that had been shy once the insert into her ear, and the familiar faraway voice of the watchmaker replied—began to vibrate—then faded away, then jumped at her with a crash: "*Freitag . . . Freitag—*"

"All right, I hear you, next Friday."

Upon leaving the shop, she again cut herself off from the world. Her faded eyes with yellowish stains about the iris (as if its color had run) acquired once more a serene, even gay, expression. She went along streets which she had not only learned to know well during the half-dozen years since her escape from Russia, but which had now become as full of fond entertainment as those of Moscow or Kharkov. She kept casting casual looks of approval on kids, on small dogs, and presently she yawned as she went, affected by the resilient air of early spring. An awfully unfortunate man, with an unfortunate nose, in an awful old fedora, passed by: a friend of some friends of hers who always mentioned him, and by now she knew everything about him—that he had a deranged daughter, and a despicable son-in-law, and diabetes. Having reached a certain fruit stall (discovered by her last spring) she bought a bunch of wonderful bananas; then she waited quite a time for her turn in a grocery, with her eyes never leaving the profile of an impudent woman, who had come later than she but nevertheless had squeezed nearer than she to the counter: there came a moment when the profile opened like a nutcracker—but here Eugenia Isakovna took the necessary measures. In the pastry shop she carefully chose her cakes, leaning forward, straining on tiptoe like a little girl, and moving hither and thither a hesitant index—with a hole in the black wool of the glove. Hardly had she left and grown engrossed in a display of men's shirts next door than her elbow was grasped by Madame Shuf, a vivacious lady with a somewhat exaggerated make-up; whereupon Eugenia Isakovna, staring away into space, nimbly adjusted her complicated machine, and only then, with the world become audible, gave her friend a welcoming smile. It was noisy and windy; Madame Shuf stooped and exerted herself, red mouth all askew, as she endeavored to aim the point of her voice straight into the black hearing aid: "Do you have—news—from Paris?"

"Oh I do, even most regularly," answered Eugenia Isakovna softly, and added, "Why don't you come to see me, why do you never ring me up?"—and a gust of pain rippled her gaze because well-meaning Madame Shuf shrieked back too piercingly.

They parted. Madame Shuf, who did not know anything yet, went home, while her husband, in his office, was uttering *akh*s and *tsk*s, and shaking his head with the receiver pressed to it, as he listened to what Chernobylski was telling him over the telephone.

"My wife has already gone to her," said Chernobylski, "and in a moment I'll go there also, though kill me if I know how to begin but my wife is after all a woman, maybe she'll somehow manage to pave the way."

Shuf suggested they write on bits of paper, and give her to read, gradual communications: "Sick." "Very sick." "Very, very sick."

"*Akh*, I also thought about that, but it doesn't make it easier. What a calamity, eh? Young, healthy, exceptionally endowed. And to think that it was *I* who got that job for him, *I* who helped him with his living expenses! What? Oh, I understand all that perfectly, but still these thoughts drive me crazy. Okay, we're sure to meet there."

Fiercely and agonizingly baring his teeth and throwing back his fat face, he finally got his collar fastened. He sighed as he started to go. He had already turned into her street when he saw her from behind walking quietly and trustfully in front of him, with a net bag full of her purchases. Not daring to overtake her, he slowed down. God grant she does not turn! Those dutifully moving feet, that narrow back, still suspecting nothing. Ah, it shall bend!

She noticed him only on the staircase. Chernobylski remained silent as he saw her ear was still bare.

"Why, how nice to drop in, Boris Lvovich. No, don't bother—I've been carrying my load long enough to bring it upstairs too; but hold this umbrella if you like, and then I'll unlock the door."

They entered. Madame Chernobylski and the warmhearted pianist had been waiting there for quite a long time. Now the execution would start.

Eugenia Isakovna liked visitors and her friends often called on her, so that now she had no reason to be astonished; she was only pleased, and without delay started fussing hospitably. They found it hard to arrest her attention while she dashed this way and that, changing her course at an abrupt angle (the plan that spread its glow within her was to fix a real lunch). At last the musician caught her in the corridor by the end of her shawl and the others heard the woman shouting to her that nobody, nobody would stay for lunch. So Eugenia Isakovna got out the fruit knives, arranged the *gaufrettes* in one little glass vase, bonbons in another. . . . She was made to sit down practically by force. The Chernobylskis, their lodger, and a Miss Osipov who by that time had somehow managed to appear—a tiny creature, almost a dwarf—all sat down, too, at the oval table. In this way a certain array, a certain order had, at least, been attained.

"For God's sake, begin, Boris," pleaded his wife, concealing her eyes from Eugenia Isakovna, who had begun to examine more carefully the faces around her, without interrupting, however, the smooth flow of her amiable, pathetic, completely defenseless words.

"Nu, chto ya mogu!" ("Well, what can I!") cried Chernobylski, and spasmodically rising started to walk around the room.

The doorbell rang, and the solemn landlady, in her best dress, let in Ida and Ida's sister: their awful white faces expressed a kind of concentrated avidity.

"She doesn't know yet," Chernobylski told them; he undid all three buttons of his jacket and immediately buttoned it up again.

Eugenia Isakovna, her eyebrows twitching but her lips still retaining their smile, stroked the hands of her new visitors and reseated herself, invitingly turning her little apparatus, which stood before her on the tablecloth, now toward this guest, now toward that, but the sounds slanted, the sounds crumbled. All of a sudden the Shufs came in, then lame Lipshteyn with his mother, then the Orshanskis, and

Lenochka, and (by sheer chance) aged Madame Tomkin—and they all talked among themselves, but were careful to keep their voices away from her, though actually they collected around her in grim, oppressive groups, and somebody had already walked away to the window and was shaking and heaving there, and Dr. Orshanski, who sat next to her at the table, attentively examined a *gaufrette*, matching it, like a domino, with another, and Eugenia Isakovna, her smile now gone and replaced by something akin to rancor, continued to push her hearing aid toward her visitors—and sobbing Chernobylski roared from a distant corner: "What's there to explain—dead, dead, dead!" but she was already afraid to look in his direction.

TORPID SMOKE

WHEN the streetlamps hanging in the dusk came on, practically in unison, all the way to Bayerischer Platz, every object in the unlit room shifted slightly under the influence of the outdoor rays, which started by taking a picture of the lace curtain's design. He had been lying supine (a long-limbed flat-chested youth with a pince-nez glimmering in the semiobscurity) for about three hours, apart from a brief interval for supper, which had passed in merciful silence: his father and sister, after yet another quarrel, had kept reading at table. Drugged by the oppressive, protracted feeling so familiar to him, he lay and looked through his lashes, and every line, every rim, or shadow of a rim, turned into a sea horizon or a strip of distant land. As soon as his eye got used to the mechanics of these metamorphoses, they began to occur of their own accord (thus small stones continue to come alive, quite uselessly, behind the wizard's back), and now, in this or that place of the room's cosmos, an illusionary perspective was formed, a remote mirage enchanting in its graphic transparency and isolation: a stretch of water, say, and a black promontory with the minuscule silhouette of an araucaria.

At intervals scraps of indistinct, laconic speech came from the adjacent parlor (the cavernal centerpiece of one of those bourgeois flats which Russian émigré families used to rent in Berlin at the time), separated from his room by sliding doors, through whose ripply matte glass the tall lamp beyond shone yellow, while lower down there showed through, as if in deep water, the fuzzy dark back of a chair placed in that position to foil the propensity of the door leaves to crawl apart in a series of jerks. In that parlor (probably on the divan at its farthest end) his sister sat with her boyfriend, and, to judge by the mysterious pauses, resolving at last in a slight cough or a tender questioning laugh, the two were kissing. Other sounds could be heard

396

from the street: the noise of a car would curl up like a wispy column to be capitaled by a honk at the crossing; or, vice versa, the honk would come first, followed by an approaching rumble in which the shudder of the door leaves participated as best it could.

And in the same way as the luminosity of the water and its every throb pass through a medusa, so everything traversed his inner being, and that sense of fluidity became transfigured into something like second sight. As he lay flat on his couch, he felt carried sideways by the flow of shadows and, simultaneously, he escorted distant foot-passengers, and visualized now the sidewalk's surface right under his eyes (with the exhaustive accuracy of a dog's sight), now the design of bare branches against a sky still retaining some color, or else the alternation of shop windows: a hairdresser's dummy, hardly surpassing the queen of hearts in anatomic development; a picture framer's display, with purple heathscapes and the inevitable *Inconnue de la Seine*, so popular in the Reich, among numerous portraits of President Hindenburg; and then a lampshade shop with all bulbs aglow, so that one could not help wondering which of them was the workaday lamp belonging to the shop itself.

All at once it occurred to him, as he reclined mummylike in the dark, that it was all rather awkward—his sister might think that he was not at home, or that he was eavesdropping. To move was, however, incredibly difficult; difficult, because the very form of his being had now lost all distinctive marks, all fixed boundaries. For example, the lane on the other side of the house might be his own arm, while the long skeletal cloud that stretched across the whole sky with a chill of stars in the east might be his backbone. Neither the striped obscurity in his room nor the glass of the parlor door, which was transmuted into nighttime seas shining with golden undulations, offered him a dependable method of measuring and marking himself off; that method he found only when in a burst of agility the tactile tip of his tongue, performing a sudden twist in his mouth (as if dashing to check, half-awake, if all was well), palpated and started to worry a bit of soft foreign matter, a shred of boiled beef firmly lodged in his teeth; whereupon he reflected how many times, in some nineteen years, it had changed, that invisible but tangible householdry of teeth, which the tongue would get used to until a filling came out, leaving a great pit that presently would be refurnished.

He was now prompted to move not so much by the shamelessly frank silence behind the door as by the urge to seek out a nice, pointed little tool, to aid the solitary blind toiler. He stretched, raised his head, and switched on the light near his couch, thus entirely restoring his corporeal image. He perceived himself (the pince-nez, the thin, dark mustache, the bad skin on his forehead) with that utter revulsion he always experienced on coming back to his body out of the languorous mist, promising—what? What shape would the force oppressing and teasing his spirit finally take? Where did it originate, this thing growing in me? Most of my day had been the same as usual—university, public library—but later, when I had to trudge to the Osipovs on Father's errand, there was that wet roof of some pub on the edge of a vacant lot, and the chimney smoke hugged the roof, creeping low, heavy with damp, sated with it, sleepy, refusing to rise, refusing to detach itself from beloved decay, and right then came that thrill, right then.

Under the table lamp gleamed an oilcloth-bound exercise book, and next to it, on the ink-mottled blotter, lay a razor blade, its apertures encircled with rust. The light also fell on a safety pin. He unbent it, and following his tongue's rather fussy directions, removed the mote of meat, swallowed it—better than any dainties; after which the contented organ calmed down.

Suddenly a mermaid's hand was applied from the outside to the ripply glass of the door; then the leaves parted spasmodically and his sister thrust in her shaggy head.

"Grisha dear," she said, "be an angel, do get some cigarettes from Father."

He did not respond, and the bright slits of her furry eyes narrowed (she saw very poorly without her horn-rimmed glasses) as she tried to make out whether or not he was asleep on the couch.

"Get them for me, Grishenka," she repeated, still more entreatingly. "Oh, please! I don't want to go to him after what happened yesterday."

"Maybe I don't want to either," he said.

"Hurry, hurry," tenderly uttered his sister, "come on, Grisha dear!"

"All right, lay off," he said at last, and carefully reuniting the two halves of the door, she dissolved in the glass.

He examined again his lamp-lit island, remembering hopefully that he had put somewhere a pack of cigarettes which one evening a friend had happened to leave behind. The shiny safety pin had disappeared, while the exercise book now lay otherwise and was half-open (as a person changes position in sleep). Perhaps, between my books. The light just reached their spines on the shelves above the desk. Here was haphazard trash (predominantly), and manuals of political economy (I wanted something quite different, but Father won out); there were also some favorite books that at one time or another had done his heart good: Gumilyov's collection of poems *Shatyor* (*Tent*), Pasternak's

Sestra moya Zhizn' (*Life, My Sister*), Gazdanov's *Vecher u Kler* (*Evening at Claire's*), Radiguet's *Le Bal du Comte d'Orgel*, Sirin's *Zashchita Luzhina* (*Luzhin's Defense*), Ilf and Petrov's *Dvenadtsat' Stul'ev* (*Twelve Chairs*), Hoffmann, Hölderlin, Baratynski, and an old Russian guidebook. Again that gentle mysterious shock. He listened. Would the thrill be repeated? His mind was in a state of extreme tension, logical thought was eclipsed, and when he came out of his trance, it took him some time to recall why he was standing near the shelves and fingering books. The blue-and-white package that he had stuck between Professor Sombart and Dostoyevski proved to be empty. Well, it had to be done, no getting out of it. There was, however, another possibility.

In worn bedroom slippers and sagging pants, listlessly, almost noiselessly, dragging his feet, he passed from his room to the hallway and groped for the switch. On the console under the looking glass, next to the guest's smart beige cap, there remained a crumpled piece of soft paper: the wrappings of liberated roses. He rummaged in his father's overcoat, penetrating with squeamish fingers into the insensate world of a strange pocket, but did not find there the spare pack he had hoped to obtain, knowing as he did his father's heavyish providence. Nothing to be done, I must go to him.

Here, that is at some indeterminate point of his somnambulic itinerary, he again stepped into a zone of mist, and this time the renewed vibration within him possessed such power, and, especially, was so much more vivid than all external perceptions, that he did not immediately identify as his proper confines and countenance the stoop-shouldered youth with the pale, unshaven cheek and the red ear who glided soundlessly by in the mirror. He overtook his own self and entered the dining room.

There, at the table which long since, before going to bed, the maid had laid for late-evening tea, sat his father: one finger was grating in his black, gray-streaked beard; between the finger and thumb of his other hand he held aloft a pince-nez by its springy clips; he sat studying a large plan of Berlin badly worn at the folds. A few days ago, at the house of some friends, there had been a passionate, Russian-style argument about which was the shortest way to walk from a certain street to another, neither of which, incidentally, did any of the arguers ever frequent; and now, to judge by the expression of displeased astonishment on his father's inclined face, with those two pink figure-eights on the sides of his nose, the old man had turned out to be wrong.

"What is it?" he asked, glancing up at his son (with the secret hope, perhaps, that I would sit down, divest the teapot of its cozy, pour a cup for him, for myself). "Cigarettes?" he went on in the same interrogatory tone, having noticed the direction in which his son gazed; the latter had started to go behind his father's back to reach for the box, which stood on the far side of the table, but his father was already handing it across so that there ensued a moment of muddle.

"Is he gone?" came the third question.

"No," said the son, taking a silky handful of cigarettes.

On his way out of the dining room he noticed his father turn his whole torso in his chair to face the wall clock as if it had said something, and then begin turning back—but there the door I was closing closed, and I did not see that bit to the end. I did not see it to the end, I had other things on my mind, yet that too, and the distant seas of a moment ago, and my sister's flushed little face, and the indistinct rumble on the circular rim of the transparent night—everything, somehow or other, helped to form what now had at last taken shape. With terrifying clarity, as if my soul were lit up by a noiseless explosion, I glimpsed a future recollection; it dawned upon me that exactly as I recalled such images of the past as the way my dead mother had of making a weepy face and clutching her temples when mealtime squabbles became too loud, so one day I would have to recall, with merciless, irreparable sharpness, the hurt look of my father's shoulders as he leaned over that torn map, morose, wearing his warm indoor jacket powdered with ashes and dandruff; and all this mingled creatively with the recent vision of blue smoke clinging to dead leaves on a wet roof.

Through a chink between the door leaves, unseen, avid fingers took away what he held, and now he was lying again on his couch, but the former languor had vanished. Enormous, alive, a metrical line extended and bent; at the bend a rhyme was coming deliciously and hotly alight, and as it glowed forth, there appeared, like a shadow on the wall when you climb upstairs with a candle, the mobile silhouette of another verse.

Drunk with the italianate music of Russian alliteration, with the longing to live, the new temptation of obsolete words (modern *bereg* reverting to *breg*, a farther "shore," *holod* to *hlad*, a more classic "chill," *veter* to *vetr*, a better Boreas), puerile, perishable poems, which, by the time the next were printed, would have been certain to wither as had withered one after the other all the previous ones written down in the black exercise book; but no matter: at this moment I trust the ravishing promises of the still breathing, still revolving verse, my face is wet with tears, my heart is bursting with happiness, and I know that this happiness is the greatest thing existing on earth.

RECRUITING

H E WAS old, he was ill, and nobody in the world needed him. In the matter of poverty Vasiliy Ivanovich had reached the point where a man no longer asks himself on what he will live tomorrow, but merely wonders what he had lived on the day before. In the way of private attachments, nothing on this earth meant much to him apart from his illness. His elder, unmarried sister, with whom had he had migrated from Russia to Berlin in the 1920s, had died ten years ago. He no longer missed her, having got used instead to a void shaped in her image. That day, however, in the tram, as he was returning from the Russian cemetery where he had attended Professor D.'s funeral, he pondered with sterile dismay the state of abandon into which her grave had fallen: the paint of the cross had peeled here and there, the name was barely distinguishable from the linden's shade that glided across it, erasing it. Professor D.'s funeral was attended by a dozen or so resigned old émigrés, linked up by death's shame and its vulgar equality. They stood, as happens in such cases, both singly and together, in a kind of grief-stricken expectation, while the humble ritual, punctuated by the secular stir of the boughs overhead, ran its course. The sun's heat was unbearable, especially on an empty stomach; yet, for the sake of decency, he had worn an overcoat to conceal the meek disgrace of his suit. And even though he had known Professor D. rather well, and tried to hold squarely and firmly before his mind's eye the kindly image of the deceased, in this warm, joyous July wind, which was already rippling and curling it, and tearing it out of his grasp, his thoughts nevertheless kept slipping off into that corner of his memory where, with her inalterable habits, his sister was matter-of-factly returning from the dead, heavy and corpulent like him, with spectacles of identical prescription on her quite masculine, massive, red, seemingly varnished nose, and dressed in a gray jacket

401

such as Russian ladies active in social politics wear to this day: a splendid, splendid soul, living, at first sight, wisely, ably, and briskly but, strangely enough, revealing wonderful vistas of melancholy which only he noticed, and for which, in the final analysis, he loved her as much as he did.

In the impersonal Berlin crush of the tram, there was another old refugee staying around to the very last, a nonpracticing lawyer, who was also returning from the cemetery and was also of little use to anyone except me. Vasiliy Ivanovich, who knew him only slightly, tried to decide whether or not to start a conversation with him if the shifting jumble of the tram's contents happened to unite them; the other, meanwhile, remained glued to the window, observing the evolutions of the streets with an ironic expression on his badly neglected face. Finally (and *that* was the very moment I caught, after which I never let the recruit out of my sight), V.I. got off, and, since he was heavy and clumsy, the conductor helped him clamber down onto the oblong stone island of the stop. Once on the ground, he accepted from above, with unhurried gratitude, his own arm, which the conductor had still been holding by the sleeve. Then he slowly shifted his feet, turned, and, looking warily around, made for the asphalt with the intention of crossing the perilous street toward a public garden.

He crossed safely. A little while ago, in the churchyard, when the tremulous old priest proposed, according to the ritual, that the choir sing to the eternal memory of the deceased, it took V.I. such a long time and such effort to kneel that the singing was over by the time his knees communicated with the ground, whereupon he could not rise again; old Tihotsky helped him up as the tram conductor had just helped him down. These twin impressions increased a sense of unusual fatigue, which, no doubt, already smacked of the ultimate glebe, yet was pleasant in its own way; and, having decided that in any case it was still too early to head for the apartment of the good, dull people who boarded him, V.I. pointed out a bench to himself with his cane and slowly, not yielding to the force of gravity until the last instant, finally sat down in surrender.

I would like to understand, though, whence comes this happiness, this swell of happiness, that immediately transforms one's soul into something immense, transparent, and precious. After all, just think, here is a sick old man with the mark of death already on him; he has lost all his loved ones: his wife, who, when they were still in Russia, left him for Dr. Malinovski, the well-known reactionary; the newspaper where V.I. had worked; his reader, friend, and namesake, dear Vasiliy

Ivanovich Maler, tortured to death by the Reds in the civil war years; his brother, who died of cancer in Kharbin; and his sister.

Once again he thought with dismay about the blurred cross of her grave, which was already creeping over into nature's camp; it must have been seven years or so since he had stopped taking care of it and let it go free. With striking vividness V.I. suddenly pictured a man his sister had once loved—the only man she had ever loved—a Garshin-like character, a half-mad, consumptive, fascinating man, with a coal-black beard and Gypsy eyes, who unexpectedly shot himself because of another woman: that blood on his dickey, those small feet in smart shoes. Then, with no connection at all, he saw his sister as a schoolgirl, with her new little head, shorn after she had had typhoid fever, explaining to him, as they sat on the ottoman, a complex system of tactile perception she had evolved, so that her life turned into a constant preoccupation with maintaining a mysterious equilibrium between objects: touch a wall in passing, a gliding stroke with the left palm, then the right, as if immersing one's hands in the sensation of the object, so that they be clean, at peace with the world and reflected in it; subsequently she was interested mainly in feminist questions, organized women's pharmacies of some kind or other, and had an insane terror of ghosts, because, as she said, she did not believe in God.

Thus, having lost this sister, whom he had loved with special tenderness for the tears she shed at night; back from the cemetery, where the ridiculous rigmarole with spadefuls of earth had revived those recollections; heavy, feeble, and awkward to such an extent that he could not get up off his knees or descend from the platform of the tram (the charitable conductor had to stoop with downstretched hands—and one of the other passengers helped too, I think); tired, lonely, fat, ashamed, with all the nuances of old-fashioned modesty, of his mended linen, his decaying trousers, his whole unkempt, unloved, shabbily furnished corpulence, V.I. nevertheless found himself filled with an almost indecent kind of joy of unknown origin, which, more than once in the course of his long and rather arduous life, had surprised him by its sudden onset. He sat quite still, his hands resting (with only an occasional spreading out of the fingers) on the crook of his cane and his broad thighs parted so that the rounded base of his belly, framed in the opening of his unbuttoned overcoat, reposed on the edge of the bench. Bees were ministering to the blooming linden tree overhead; from its dense festive foliage floated a clouded, melleous aroma, while underneath, in its shadow, along the sidewalk, lay the bright yellow debris of lime flowers, resembling ground-up horse dung. A wet red hose lay across the entire lawn in the center of the small public garden and, a little way off, radiant water gushed from it, with a ghostly iridescence in the aura of its spray. Between some hawthorn bushes and a chalet-style public toilet a dove-gray street was visible; there, a Morris pillar covered with posters stood like a fat harlequin, and tram after tram passed with a clatter and whine.

This little street garden, these roses, this greenery—he had seen them a thousand times, in all their uncomplicated transformations, yet it all sparkled through and through with vitality, novelty, participation in one's destiny, whenever he and I experienced such fits of happiness. A man with the local Russian newspaper sat down on the same dark-blue, sun-warmed, hospitable, indifferent bench. It is difficult for me to describe this man; then again, it would be useless, since a self-portrait is seldom successful, because of a certain tension that always remains in the expression of the eyes—the hypnotic spell of the indispensable mirror. Why did I decide that the man next to whom I had sat down was named Vasiliy Ivanovich? Well, because that blend of name and patronymic is like an armchair, and he was broad and soft, with a large cozy face, and sat, with his hands resting on his cane, comfortably and motionlessly; only the pupils of his eyes shifted to and fro, behind their lenses, from a cloud traveling in one direction to a truck traveling in the other, or from a female sparrow feeding her fledgling on the gravel to the intermittent, jerky motion of a little wooden automobile pulled on a string by a child who had forgotten all about it (there—it fell on its side, but nevertheless kept progressing). Professor D.'s obituary occupied a prominent place in the paper, and that is how, in my hurry to give V.I.'s morning some sort of setting as gloomy and typical as possible, I happened to arrange for him that trip to the funeral, even though the paper said there would be a special announcement of the date; but, I repeat, I was in a hurry, and I did wish he had really been to the cemetery, for he was exactly the type you see at Russian ceremonies abroad, standing to one side as it were, but emphasizing by this the habitual nature of his presence; and, since something about the soft features of his full clean-shaven face reminded me of a Moscow sociopolitical lady named Anna Aksakov, whom I remembered since childhood (she was a distant relative of mine), almost inadvertently but already with irrepressible detail, I made her his sister, and it all happened with vertiginous speed, because at all costs I had to have somebody like him for an episode in a novel with which I have been struggling for more than two years. What did I care if this fat old gentleman, whom I first saw being lowered from the tram, and who was now sitting beside me, was perhaps not Russian at all? I was so pleased with him! He was so capacious! By an odd combination of emotions I felt I was infecting that stranger with the blazing creative happiness that sends a chill over an artist's skin. I wished that, despite his age, his indigence, the tumor in his stomach, V.I. might share the terrible power of my bliss, redeeming its unlawfulness with his complicity, so that it would cease being a unique sensation, a most rare variety of madness, a monstrous sunbow spanning my whole inner being, and be accessible to two people at least, becoming their topic of conversation and thus acquiring rights to routine existence, of which my wild, savage, stifling happiness is otherwise deprived. Vasiliy Ivanovich (I persisted in this appellation) took off his black fedora, as if not in order to refresh his head but with the precise intention of greeting my thoughts. He slowly stroked the crown of his head; the shadows of the linden leaves passed across the veins of his large hand and fell anew on his grayish hair. Just as slowly, he turned his head toward me, glanced at my émigré paper, at my face which was made up to look like that of a reader, turned away majestically, and put his hat on again.

But he was already mine. Presently, with an effort, he got up, straightened, transferred his cane from one hand to the other, took a short, tentative step, and then calmly moved off, forever, if I am not mistaken. Yet he carried off with him, like the plague, an extraordinary disease, for he was sacramentally bound to me, being doomed to appear for a moment in the far end of a certain chapter, at the turning of a certain sentence.

My representative, the man with the Russian newspaper, was now alone on the bench and, as he had moved over into the shade where V.I. had just been sitting, the same cool linden pattern that had anointed his predecessor now rippled across his forehead.

A SLICE OF LIFE

IN THE next room Pavel Romanovich was roaring with laughter, as he related how his wife had left him.

I could not endure the sound of that horrible hilarity, and without even consulting my mirror, just as I was—in the rumpled dress of a slatternly after-lunch siesta, and no doubt still bearing the pillow's imprint on my cheek—I made for the next room (the dining room of my landlord) and came upon the following scene: my landlord, a person called Plekhanov (totally unrelated to the socialist philosopher), sat listening with an air of encouragement—all the time filling the tubes of Russian cigarettes by means of a tobacco injector—while Pavel Romanovich kept walking around the table, his face a regular nightmare, its pallor seeming to spread to his otherwise wholesome-looking close-shaven head: a very Russian kind of cleanliness, habitually making one think of neat engineer troops, but at the present moment reminding me of something evil, something as frightening as a convict's skull.

He had come, actually, looking for my brother—who had just gone, but this did not really matter to him: his grief had to speak, and so he found a ready listener in this rather unattractive person whom I hardly knew. He laughed, but his eyes did not participate in his guffaws, as he talked of his wife's collecting things all over their flat, of her taking away by some oversight his favorite eyeglasses, of the fact that all her relatives were in the know ahead of him, of his wondering—

"Yes, here's a nice point," he went on, now addressing directly Plekhanov, a God-fearing widower (for his speech until then had been more or less a harangue in sheer space), "a nice, interesting point: how will it be in the hereafter—will she cohabitate there with me or with that swine?"

"Let us go to my room," I said in my most crystalline tone of voice—and only then did he notice my presence: I had stood, leaning

406

forlornly against a corner of the dark sideboard, with which seemed to fuse my diminutive figure in its black dress—yes, I wear mourning, for everybody, for everything, for my own self, for Russia, for the fetuses scraped out of me. He and I passed into the tiny room I rented: it could scarcely accommodate a rather absurdly wide couch covered in silk, and next to it the little low table bearing a lamp whose base was a veritable bomb of thick glass filled with water—and in this atmosphere of my private coziness Pavel Romanovich became at once a different man.

He sat down in silence, rubbing his inflamed eyes. I curled up beside him, patted the cushions around us, and lapsed into thought, cheek-propped feminine thought, as I considered him, his turquoise head, his big strong shoulders which a military tunic would have suited so much better than that double-breasted jacket. I gazed at him and marveled how I could have been swept off my feet by this short, stocky fellow with insignificant features (except for the teeth—oh my, what fine teeth!); yet I was crazy about him barely two years ago at the beginning of émigré life in Berlin when he was only just planning to marry his goddess—and how very crazy I was, how I wept because of him, how haunted my dreams were by that slender chainlet of steel around his hairy wrist!

He fished out of his hip pocket his massive, "battlefield" (as he termed it) cigarette case. Against its lid, despondently nodding his head, he tapped the tube end of his Russian cigarette several times, more times than he usually did.

"Yes, Maria Vasilevna," he said at last through his teeth as he lit up, raising high his triangular eyebrows. "Yes, nobody could have foreseen such a thing. I had faith in that woman, absolute faith."

After his recent fit of sustained loquacity, everything seemed uncannily quiet. One heard the rain beating against the windowsill, the clicking of Plekhanov's tobacco injector, the whimpering of a neurotic old dog locked up in my brother's room across the corridor. I do not know why—either because the weather was so very gray, or perhaps because the kind of misfortune that had befallen Pavel Romanovich should demand some reaction from the surrounding world (dissolution, eclipse)—but I had the impression that it was late in the evening, though actually it was only three p.m., and I was still supposed to travel to the other end of Berlin on an errand my charming brother could have well done himself.

Pavel Romanovich spoke again, this time in sibilant tones: "That stinking old bitch," he said, "she and she alone pimped them together. I always found her disgusting and didn't conceal it from Lenochka.

What a bitch! You've seen her, I think—around sixty, dyed a rich roan, fat, so fat that she looks round-backed. It's a big pity that Nicholas is out. Let him call me as soon as he returns. I am, as you know, a simple, plain-spoken man and I've been telling Lenochka for ages that her mother is an evil bitch. Now here's what I have in mind: perhaps your brother might help me to rig up a letter to the old hag—a sort of formal statement explaining that I knew and realize perfectly well whose instigation it was, who nudged my wife—yes, something on those lines, but most politely worded, of course."

I said nothing. Here he was, visiting me for the first time (his visits to Nick did not count), for the first time he sat on my *Kautsch*, and shed cigarette ashes on my polychrome cushions; yet the event, which would formerly have given me divine pleasure, now did not gladden me one bit. Good people had been reporting a long while ago that his marriage had been a flop, that his wife had turned out to be a cheap, skittish fool—and far-sighted rumor had long been giving her a lover in the very person of the freak who had now fallen for her cowish beauty. The news of that wrecked marriage did not, therefore, come to me as a surprise; in fact I may have vaguely expected that someday Pavel Romanovich would be deposited at my feet by a wave of the storm. But no matter how deep I rummaged within myself, I failed to find one crumb of joy; on the contrary, my heart was, oh, so heavy, I simply cannot say how heavy. All my romances, by some kind of collusion between their heroes, have invariably followed a prearranged pattern of mediocrity and tragedy, or more precisely, the tragic slant was imposed by their very mediocrity. I am ashamed to recall the way they started, and appalled by the nastiness of their denouements, while the middle part, the part that should have been the essence and core of this or that affair, has remained in my mind as a kind of listless shuffle seen through oozy water or sticky fog. My infatuation with Pavel Romanovich had had at least the delightful advantage of staying cool and lovely in contrast to all the rest; but that infatuation too, so remote, so deeply buried in the past, was borrowing now from the present, in reverse order, a tinge of misfortune, failure, even plain mortification, just because I was forced to hear this man's complaining of his wife, of his mother-in-law.

"I do hope," he said, "Nicky comes back soon. I have still another plan in reserve, and, I think, it's quite a good one. And in the meantime I'd better toddle along."

And still I said nothing, in great sadness looking at him, my lips masked by the fringe of my black shawl. He stood for a moment by the windowpane, on which in tumbling motion, knocking and buzzing, a fly went up, up, and presently slid down again. Then he passed his finger across the spines of the books on my shelf. Like most people who read little, he had a sneaking affection for dictionaries, and now he pulled out a thick-bottomed pink volume with the seed head of a dandelion and a red-curled girl on the cover.

"Khoroshaya shtooka," he said—crammed back the *shtooka* (thing), and suddenly broke into tears. I had him sit down close to me on the couch, he swayed to one side with his sobs increasing, and ended by burying his face in my lap. I stroked lightly his hot emery-papery scalp and rosy robust nape which I find so attractive in males. Gradually his spasms abated. He bit me softly through my skirt, and sat up.

"Know what?" said Pavel Romanovich and while speaking he sonorously clacked together the concave palms of his horizontally placed hands (I could not help smiling as I remembered an uncle of mine, a Volga landowner, who used to render that way the sound of a procession of dignified cows letting their pies plop). "Know what, my dear? Let us move to my flat. I can't stand the thought of being there alone. We'll have supper there, take a few swigs of vodka, then go to the movies—what do you say?"

I could not decline his offer, though I knew that I would regret it. While telephoning to cancel my visit to Nick's former place of employment (he needed the rubber overshoes he had left there), I saw myself in the looking glass of the hallway as resembling a forlorn little nun with a stern waxy face; but a minute later, as I was in the act of prettying up and putting on my hat, I plunged as it were into the depth of my great, black, experienced eyes, and found therein a gleam of something far from nunnish—even through my voilette they blazed, good God, how they blazed!

In the tram, on the way to his place, Pavel Romanovich became distant and gloomy again: I was telling him about Nick's new job in the ecclesiastical library, but his gaze kept shifting, he was obviously not listening. We arrived. The disorder in the three smallish rooms which he had occupied with his Lenochka was simply incredible—as if his and her things had had a thorough fight. In order to amuse Pavel Romanovich I started to play the soubrette, I put on a diminutive apron that had been forgotten in a corner of the kitchen, I introduced peace in the disarray of the furniture, I laid the table most neatly—so that Pavel Romanovich slapped his hands together once more and decided to make some borscht (he was quite proud of his cooking abilities).

After two or three ponies of vodka, his mood became inordinately energetic and pseudoefficient, as if there really existed a certain project

that had to be attended to now. I am at a loss to decide whether he
had got self-infected by the theatrical solemnity with which a stalwart
expert in drinking is able to decorate the intake of Russian liquor, or
whether he really believed that he and I had begun, when still in my
room, to plan and discuss something or other—but there he was, filling his fountain pen and with a significant air bringing out what he
called the dossier: letters from his wife received by him last spring in
Bremen where he had gone on behalf of the émigré insurance company for which he worked. From these letters he began to cite passages
proving she loved *him* and not the other chap. In between he kept repeating brisk little formulas such as "That's that," "Okey-dokey,"
"Let's see now"—and went on drinking. His argument reduced itself
to the idea that if Lenochka wrote "I caress you mentally, Baboono-
vich dear," she could not be in love with another man, and if she
thought she was, her error should be patiently explained to her. After
a few more drinks his manner changed, his expression grew somber
and coarse. For no reason at all, he took off his shoes and his socks,
and then started to sob and walked sobbing, from one end of his flat
to the other, absolutely ignoring my presence and ferociously kicking
aside with a strong bare foot the chair into which he kept barging. En
passant, he managed to finish the decanter, and presently entered a
third phase, the final part of that drunken syllogism which had already
united, in keeping with strict dialectical rules, an initial show of bright
efficiency and a central period of utter gloom. At the present stage, it
appeared that he and I had established something (what exactly, remained rather blurry) that displayed her lover as the lowest of villains,
and the plan consisted in my going to see her on my own initiative,
as it were, to "warn" her. It was also to be understood that Pavel
Romanovich remained absolutely opposed to any intrusion or pressure
and that his own suggestions bore the stamp of angelic disinterested-
ness. Before I could disentangle my wits, already tightly enveloped in
the web of his thick whisper (while he was hastily putting on his
shoes), I found myself getting his wife on the phone and only when I
heard her high, stupidly resonant voice did I suddenly realize that I
was drunk and behaving like an idiot. I slammed down the receiver,
but he started to kiss my cold hands which I kept clenching—and I
called her again, was identified without enthusiasm, said I had to see
her on a piece of urgent business, and after some slight hesitation she
agreed to have me come over at once. By that time—that is by the
time he and I had started to go, our plan, it transpired, had ripened in
every detail and was amazingly simple. I was to tell Lenochka that
Pavel Romanovich had to convey to her something of exceptional

importance—in no way, in no way whatever, related to their broken marriage (this he forcibly stressed, with a tactician's special appetite) and that he would be awaiting her in the bar just across her street.

It took me ages, dim ages, to climb the staircase, and for some reason I was terribly tormented by the thought that at our last meeting I wore the same hat and the same black fox. Lenochka, on the other hand, came out to me smartly dressed. Her hair seemed to have just been curled, but curled badly, and in general she had grown plainer, and about her chicly painted mouth there were puffy little pouches owing to which all that chic was rather lost.

"I do not believe one minute," she said, surveying me with curiosity, "that it is all that important, but if he thinks we haven't done arguing, fine, I agree to come, but I want it to be before witnesses, I'm scared to remain alone with him, I've had enough of that, thank you very much."

When we entered the pub, Pavel Romanovich sat leaning on his elbow at a table next to the bar; he rubbed with his minimus his red naked eyes, while imparting at length, in monotone, some "slice of life," as he liked to put it, to a total stranger seated at the same table, a German, enormously tall, with sleekly parted hair but a black-downed nape and badly bitten fingernails.

"However," Pavel Romanovich was saying in Russian, "my father did not wish to get into trouble with the authorities and therefore decided to build a fence around it. Okay, that was settled. Our house was about as far from theirs as—" He looked around, nodded absentmindedly to his wife, and continued in a perfectly relaxed manner: "—as far as from here to the tramway, so that they could not have any claims. But you must agree, that spending the entire autumn in Vilna without electricity is no joking matter. Well, then, most reluctantly—"

I found it impossible to understand what he was talking about. The German listened dutifully, with half-opened mouth: his knowledge of Russian was scanty, the sheer process of trying to understand afforded him pleasure. Lenochka, who was sitting so close to me that I sensed her disagreeable warmth, began to rummage in her bag.

"My father's illness," went on Pavel Romanovich, "contributed to his decision. If you really lived there, as you say, then you remember, of course, that street. It is dark there by night, and not infrequently one happens to read—"

"Pavlik," said Lenochka, "here's your pince-nez. I took it away in my bag by mistake."

"It is dark there by night," repeated Pavel Romanovich, opening as he spoke the spectacle case that she had tossed to him across the table.

He put on his eyeglasses, produced a revolver, and started to shoot at his wife.

With a great howl she fell under the table dragging me after her while the German stumbled over us and joined us in our fall so that the three of us sort of got mixed up on the floor; but I had time to see a waiter rush up to the aggressor from behind and with monstrous relish and force hit him on the head with an iron ashtray. After this there was as usual in such cases the slow tidying up of the shattered world, with the participation of gapers, policemen, ambulancers. Extravagantly groaning, Lenochka (a bullet had merely gone through her fat suntanned shoulder) was driven away to the hospital, but somehow I did not see how they led Pavel Romanovich away. By the time everything was over—that is by the time everything had reoccupied its right place: streetlamps, houses, stars—I found myself walking on a deserted sidewalk in the company of our German survivor: that huge handsome man, hatless, in a voluminous raincoat floated beside me and at first I thought he was seeing me home but then it dawned upon me that we were heading for *his* place. We stopped in front of his house, and he explained to me—slowly, weightily but not without a certain shade of poetry, and for some reason in bad French—that he could not take me to his room because he lived with a chum who replaced for him a father, a brother, and a wife. His excuses struck me as so insulting that I ordered him to call a taxi at once and take me to my lodgings. He smiled a frightened smile and closed the door in my face, and there I was walking along a street which despite the rain's having stopped hours ago, was still wet and conveyed an air of deep humiliation—yes, there I was walking all alone as was my due to walk from the beginning of time, and before my eyes Pavel Romanovich kept rising, rising and rubbing off the blood and the ash from his poor head.

SPRING IN FIALTA

S PRING in Fialta is cloudy and dull. Everything is damp: the piebald trunks of the plane trees, the juniper shrubs, the railings,
the gravel. Far away, in a watery vista between the jagged edges
of pale bluish houses, which have tottered up from their knees to climb
the slope (a cypress indicating the way), the blurred Mount St. George
is more than ever remote from its likeness on the picture postcards
which since 1910, say (those straw hats, those youthful cabmen), have
been courting the tourist from the sorry-go-round of their prop,
among amethyst-toothed lumps of rock and the mantelpiece dreams of
seashells. The air is windless and warm, with a faint tang of burning.
The sea, its salt drowned in a solution of rain, is less glaucous than gray
with waves too sluggish to break into foam.

It was on such a day in the early thirties that I found myself, all my
senses wide open, on one of Fialta's steep little streets, taking in everything at once, that marine rococo on the stand, and the coral crucifixes
in a shop window, and the dejected poster of a visiting circus, one corner of its drenched paper detached from the wall, and a yellow bit of
unripe orange peel on the old, slate-blue sidewalk, which retained here
and there a fading memory of ancient mosaic design. I am fond of
Fialta; I am fond of it because I feel in the hollow of those violaceous
syllables the sweet dark dampness of the most rumpled of small flowers, and because the altolike name of a lovely Crimean town is echoed
by its viola; and also because there is something in the very somnolence of its humid Lent that especially anoints one's soul. So I was
happy to be there again, to trudge uphill in inverse direction to the rivulet of the gutter, hatless, my head wet, my skin already suffused with
warmth although I wore only a light mackintosh over my shirt.

I had come on the Capparabella express, which, with that reckless
gusto peculiar to trains in mountainous country, had done its thunder-

ing best to collect throughout the night as many tunnels as possible. A day or two, just as long as a breathing spell in the midst of a business trip would allow me, was all I expected to stay. I had left my wife and children at home, and that was an island of happiness always present in the clear north of my being, always floating beside me, and even through me, I dare say, but yet keeping on the outside of me most of the time.

A pantless infant of the male sex, with a taut mud-gray little belly, jerkily stepped down from a doorstep and waddled off, bowlegged, trying to carry three oranges at once, but continuously dropping the variable third, until he fell himself, and then a girl of twelve or so, with a string of heavy beads around her dusky neck and wearing a skirt as long as that of a Gypsy, promptly took away the whole lot with her more nimble and more numerous hands. Nearby, on the wet terrace of a café, a waiter was wiping the slabs of tables; a melancholy brigand hawking local lollipops, elaborate-looking things with a lunar gloss, had placed a hopelessly full basket on the cracked balustrade, over which the two were conversing. Either the drizzle had stopped or Fialta had got so used to it that she herself did not know whether she was breathing moist air or warm rain. Thumb-filling his pipe from a rubber pouch as he walked, a plus-foured Englishman of the solid exportable sort came from under an arch and entered a pharmacy, where large pale sponges in a blue vase were dying a thirsty death behind their glass. What luscious elation I felt rippling through my veins, how gratefully my whole being responded to the flutters and effluvia of that gray day saturated with a vernal essence which itself it seemed slow in perceiving! My nerves were unusually receptive after a sleepless night; I assimilated everything: the whistling of a thrush in the almond trees beyond the chapel, the peace of the crumbling houses, the pulse of the distant sea, panting in the mist, all this together with the jealous green of bottle glass bristling along the top of a wall and the fast colors of a circus advertisement featuring a feathered Indian on a rearing horse in the act of lassoing a boldly endemic zebra, while some thoroughly fooled elephants sat brooding upon their star-spangled thrones.

Presently the same Englishman overtook me. As I absorbed him along with the rest, I happened to notice the sudden side-roll of his big blue eye straining at its crimson canthus, and the way he rapidly moistened his lips—because of the dryness of those sponges, I thought; but then I followed the direction of his glance, and saw Nina.

Every time I had met her during the fifteen years of our—well, I fail to find the precise term for our kind of relationship—she had not seemed to recognize me at once; and this time too she remained quite still for a moment, on the opposite sidewalk, half turning toward me in sympathetic incertitude mixed with curiosity, only her yellow scarf already on the move like those dogs that recognize you before their owners do—and then she uttered a cry, her hands up, all her ten fingers dancing, and in the middle of the street, with merely the frank impulsiveness of an old friendship (just as she would rapidly make the sign of the cross over me every time we parted), she kissed me thrice with more mouth than meaning, and then walked beside me, hanging on to me, adjusting her stride to mine, hampered by her narrow brown skirt perfunctorily slit down the side.

"Oh, yes, Ferdie is here too," she replied and immediately in her turn inquired nicely after Elena.

"Must be loafing somewhere around with Segur," she went on in reference to her husband. "And I have some shopping to do; we leave after lunch. Wait a moment, where are you leading me, Victor dear?"

Back into the past, back into the past, as I did every time I met her, repeating the whole accumulation of the plot from the very beginning up to the last increment—thus in Russian fairy tales the already told is bunched up again at every new turn of the story. This time we had met in warm and misty Fialta, and I could not have celebrated the occasion with greater art, could not have adorned with brighter vignettes the list of fate's former services, even if I had known that this was to be the last one; the last one, I maintain, for I cannot imagine any heavenly firm of brokers that might consent to arrange me a meeting with her beyond the grave.

My introductory scene with Nina had been laid in Russia quite a long time ago, around 1917 I should say, judging by certain left-wing theater rumblings backstage. It was at some birthday party at my aunt's on her country estate, near Luga, in the deepest folds of winter (how well I remember the first sign of nearing the place: a red barn in a white wilderness). I had just graduated from the Imperial Lyceum; Nina was already engaged: although she was of my age and of that of the century, she looked twenty at least, and this in spite or perhaps because of her neat slender build, whereas at thirty-two that very slightness of hers made her look younger. Her fiancé was a guardsman on leave from the front, a handsome heavy fellow, incredibly well bred and stolid, who weighed every word on the scales of the most exact common sense and spoke in a velvety baritone, which grew even smoother when he addressed her; his decency and devotion probably got on her nerves; and he is now a successful if somewhat lonesome engineer in a most distant tropical country.

Windows light up and stretch their luminous lengths upon the dark billowy snow, making room for the reflection of the fan-shaped light above the front door between them. Each of the two side pillars is fluffily fringed with white, which rather spoils the lines of what might have been a perfect ex libris for the book of our two lives. I cannot recall why we had all wandered out of the sonorous hall into the still darkness, peopled only with firs, snow-swollen to twice their size; did the watchmen invite us to look at a sullen red glow in the sky, portent of nearing arson? Possibly. Did we go to admire an equestrian statue of ice sculptured near the pond by the Swiss tutor of my cousins? Quite as likely. My memory revives only on the way back to the brightly symmetrical mansion toward which we tramped in single file along a narrow furrow between snowbanks, with that crunch-crunch-crunch which is the only comment that a taciturn winter night makes upon humans. I walked last; three singing steps ahead of me walked a small bent shape; the firs gravely showed their burdened paws. I slipped and dropped the dead flashlight someone had forced upon me; it was devilishly hard to retrieve; and instantly attracted by my curses, with an eager, low laugh in anticipation of fun, Nina dimly veered toward me. I call her Nina, but I could hardly have known her name yet, hardly could we have had time, she and I, for any preliminary; "Who's that?" she asked with interest—and I was already kissing her neck, smooth and quite fiery hot from the long fox fur of her coat collar, which kept getting into my way until she clasped my shoulder, and with the candor so peculiar to her gently fitted her generous, dutiful lips to mine.

But suddenly parting us by its explosion of gaiety, the theme of a snowball fight started in the dark, and someone, fleeing, falling, crunching, laughing, and panting, climbed a drift, tried to run, and uttered a horrible groan: deep snow had performed the amputation of an arctic. And soon after, we all dispersed to our respective homes, without my having talked with Nina, nor made any plans about the future, about those fifteen itinerant years that had already set out toward the dim horizon, loaded with the parts of our unassembled meetings; and as I watched her in the maze of gestures and shadows of gestures of which the rest of that evening consisted (probably parlor games—with Nina persistently in the other camp), I was astonished, I remember, not so much by her inattention to me after that warmth in the snow as by the innocent naturalness of that inattention, for I did not yet know that had I said a word it would have changed at once into a wonderful sunburst of kindness, a cheerful, compassionate attitude with all possible cooperation, as if woman's love were springwater containing salubrious salts which at the least notice she ever so willingly gave anyone to drink.

"Let me see, where did we last meet," I began (addressing the Fialta version of Nina) in order to bring to her small face with prominent cheekbones and dark-red lips a certain expression I knew; and sure enough, the shake of her head and the puckered brow seemed less to imply forgetfulness than to deplore the flatness of an old joke; or to be more exact, it was as if all those cities where fate had fixed our various rendezvous without ever attending them personally, all those platforms and stairs and three-walled rooms and dark back alleys, were trite settings remaining after some other lives all brought to a close long before and were so little related to the acting out of our own aimless destiny that it was almost bad taste to mention them.

I accompanied her into a shop under the arcades; there, in the twilight beyond a beaded curtain, she fingered some red leather purses stuffed with tissue paper, peering at the price tags, as if wishing to learn their museum names. She wanted, she said, exactly that shape but in fawn, and when after ten minutes of frantic rustling the old Dalmatian found such a freak by a miracle that has puzzled me ever since, Nina, who was about to pick some money out of my hand, changed her mind and went through the streaming beads without having bought anything.

Outside it was just as milky dull as before; the same smell of burning, stirring my Tartar memories, drifted from the bare windows of the pale houses; a small swarm of gnats was busy darning the air above a mimosa, which bloomed listlessly, her sleeves trailing to the very ground; two workmen in broad-brimmed hats were lunching on cheese and garlic, their backs against a circus billboard, which depicted a red hussar and an orange tiger of sorts; curious—in his effort to make the beast as ferocious as possible, the artist had gone so far that he had come back from the other side, for the tiger's face looked positively human.

"*Au fond,* I wanted a comb," said Nina with belated regret.

How familiar to me were her hesitations, second thoughts, third thoughts mirroring first ones, ephemeral worries between trains. She had always either just arrived or was about to leave, and of this I find it hard to think without feeling humiliated by the variety of intricate routes one feverishly follows in order to keep that final appointment which the most confirmed dawdler knows to be unavoidable. Had I to submit before judges of our earthly existence a specimen of her average pose, I would have perhaps placed her leaning upon a counter at Cook's, left calf crossing right shin, left toe tapping floor, sharp elbows and coin-spilling bag on the counter, while the employee, pencil in hand, pondered with her over the plan of an eternal sleeping car.

After the exodus from Russia, I saw her—and that was the second time—in Berlin at the house of some friends. I was about to get married; she had just broken with her fiancé. As I entered that room I caught sight of her at once and, having glanced at the other guests, I instinctively determined which of the men knew more about her than I. She was sitting in the corner of a couch, her feet pulled up, her small comfortable body folded in the form of a Z; an ashtray stood aslant on the couch near one of her heels; and, having squinted at me and listened to my name, she removed her stalklike cigarette holder from her lips and proceeded to utter slowly and joyfully, "Well, of all people—" and at once it became clear to everyone, beginning with her, that we had long been on intimate terms: unquestionably, she had forgotten all about the actual kiss, but somehow because of that trivial occurrence she found herself recollecting a vague sketch of warm, pleasant friendship, which in reality had never existed between us. Thus the whole cast of our relationship was fraudulently based upon an imaginary amity—which had nothing to do with her random good will. Our meeting proved quite insignificant in regard to the words we said, but already no barriers divided us; and when that night I happened to be seated beside her at supper, I shamelessly tested the extent of her secret patience.

Then she vanished again; and a year later my wife and I were seeing my brother off to Posen, and when the train had gone, and we were moving toward the exit along the other side of the platform, suddenly near a car of the Paris express I saw Nina, her face buried in the bouquet she held, in the midst of a group of people whom she had befriended without my knowledge and who stood in a circle gaping at her as idlers gape at a street row, a lost child, or the victim of an accident. Brightly she signaled to me with her flowers; I introduced her to Elena, and in that life-quickening atmosphere of a big railway station where everything is something trembling on the brink of something else, thus to be clutched and cherished, the exchange of a few words was enough to enable two totally dissimilar women to start calling each other by their pet names the very next time they met. That day, in the blue shade of the Paris car, Ferdinand was first mentioned: I learned with a ridiculous pang that she was about to marry him. Doors were beginning to slam; she quickly but piously kissed her friends, climbed into the vestibule, disappeared; and then I saw her through the glass settling herself in her compartment, having suddenly forgotten about us or passed into another world, and we all, our hands in our pockets, seemed to be spying upon an utterly unsuspecting life moving in that aquarium dimness, until she grew aware of us and drummed on the windowpane, then raised her eyes, fumbling at the frame as if hanging a picture, but nothing happened; some fellow passenger helped her, and she leaned out, audible and real, beaming with pleasure; one of us, keeping up with the stealthily gliding car, handed her a magazine and a Tauchnitz (she read English only when traveling); all was slipping away with beautiful smoothness, and I held a platform ticket crumpled beyond recognition, while a song of the last century (connected, it has been rumored, with some Parisian drama of love) kept ringing and ringing in my head, having emerged, God knows why, from the music box of memory, a sobbing ballad which often used to be sung by an old maiden aunt of mine, with a face as yellow as Russian church wax, but whom nature had given such a powerful, ecstatically full voice that it seemed to swallow her up in the glory of a fiery cloud as soon as she would begin:

> *On dit que tu te maries,*
> *tu sais que j'en vais mourir*

and that melody, the pain, the offense, the link between hymen and death evoked by the rhythm, and the voice itself of the dead singer, which accompanied the recollection as the sole owner of the song, gave me no rest for several hours after Nina's departure and even later arose at increasing intervals like the last flat little waves sent to the beach by a passing ship, lapping ever more infrequently and dreamily, or like the bronze agony of a vibrating belfry after the bell ringer has already reseated himself in the cheerful circle of his family. And another year or two later, I was in Paris on business; and one morning on the landing of a hotel, where I had been looking up a film actor fellow, there she was again, clad in a gray tailored suit, waiting for the elevator to take her down, a key dangling from her fingers. "Ferdinand has gone fencing," she said conversationally; her eyes rested on the lower part of my face as if she were lip reading, and after a moment of reflection (her amatory comprehension was matchless), she turned and rapidly swaying on slender ankles led me along the sea-blue carpeted passage. A chair at the door of her room supported a tray with the remains of breakfast—a honey-stained knife, crumbs on the gray porcelain; but the room had already been done, and because of our sudden draft a wave of muslin embroidered with white dahlias got sucked in, with a shudder and knock, between the responsive halves of the French window, and only when the door had been locked did they let go that curtain with something like a blissful sigh; and a little later I stepped out on the diminutive cast-iron balcony beyond to inhale a combined smell of dry maple leaves and gasoline—the dregs of the hazy blue morning street; and as I did not yet realize the presence of that growing morbid pathos which was to embitter so my subsequent meetings with Nina, I was probably quite as collected and carefree as she was, when from the hotel I accompanied her to some office or other to trace a suitcase she had lost, and thence to the café where her husband was holding session with his court of the moment.

I will not mention the name (and what bits of it I happen to give here appear in decorous disguise) of that man, that Franco-Hungarian writer. . . . I would rather not dwell upon him at all, but I cannot help it—he is surging up from under my pen. Today one does not hear much about him; and this is good, for it proves that I was right in resisting his evil spell, right in experiencing a creepy chill down my spine whenever this or that new book of his touched my hand. The fame of his likes circulates briskly but soon grows heavy and stale; and as for history it will limit his life story to the dash between two dates. Lean and arrogant, with some poisonous pun ever ready to fork out and quiver at you, and with a strange look of expectancy in his dull brown veiled eyes, this false wag had, I daresay, an irresistible effect on small rodents. Having mastered the art of verbal invention to perfection, he particularly prided himself on being a weaver of words, a title he valued higher than that of a writer; personally, I never could understand what was the good of thinking up books, of penning things that had not really happened in some way or other; and I remember once saying to him as I braved the mockery of his encouraging nods that, were I a writer, I should allow only my heart to have imagination, and for the rest rely upon memory, that long-drawn sunset shadow of one's personal truth.

I had known his books before I knew him; a faint disgust was already replacing the aesthetic pleasure which I had suffered his first novel to give me. At the beginning of his career, it had been possible perhaps to distinguish some human landscape, some old garden, some dream-familiar disposition of trees through the stained glass of his prodigious prose . . . but with every new book the tints grew still more dense, the gules and purpure still more ominous; and today one can no longer see anything at all through that blazoned, ghastly rich glass, and it seems that were one to break it, nothing but a perfectly black void would face one's shivering soul. But how dangerous he was in his prime, what venom he squirted, with what whips he lashed when provoked! The tornado of his passing satire left a barren waste where felled oaks lay in a row, and the dust still twisted, and the unfortunate author of some adverse review, howling with pain, spun like a top in the dust.

At the time we met, his *Passage à niveau* was being acclaimed in Paris; he was, as they say, "surrounded," and Nina (whose adaptability was an amazing substitute for the culture she lacked) had already assumed if not the part of a muse at least that of a soul mate and subtle adviser, following Ferdinand's creative convolutions and loyally sharing his artistic tastes; for although it is wildly improbable that she had ever waded through a single volume of his, she had a magic knack of gleaning all the best passages from the shop talk of literary friends.

An orchestra of women was playing when we entered the café; first I noted the ostrich thigh of a harp reflected in one of the mirror-faced pillars, and then I saw the composite table (small ones drawn together to form a long one) at which, with his back to the plush wall, Ferdinand was presiding; and for a moment his whole attitude, the position of his parted hands, and the faces of his table companions all turned toward him reminded me in a grotesque, nightmarish way of something I did not quite grasp, but when I did so in retrospect, the suggested comparison struck me as hardly less sacrilegious than the nature of his art itself. He wore a white turtleneck sweater under a tweed coat; his glossy hair was combed back from the temples, and above it cigarette smoke hung like a halo; his bony, pharaohlike face was motionless: the eyes alone roved this way and that, full of dim satisfaction. Having forsaken the two or three obvious haunts where naive amateurs of Montparnassian life would have expected to find him, he had started patronizing this perfectly bourgeois establishment because of his peculiar sense of humor, which made him derive ghoulish fun from the pitiful *spécialité de la maison*—this orchestra composed of half a dozen weary-looking, self-conscious ladies interlacing mild harmonies on a crammed platform and not knowing, as he put it, what to do with their motherly bosoms, quite superfluous in the world of music. After each number he would be convulsed by a fit of epileptic applause, which the ladies had stopped acknowledging and which was already arousing, I thought, certain doubts in the minds of the proprietor of the café and its fundamental customers, but which seemed highly diverting to Ferdinand's friends. Among these I recall: an artist with an impeccably bald though slightly chipped head, which under various pretexts he constantly painted into his eye-and-guitar canvases; a poet, whose special gag was the ability to represent, if you asked him, Adam's Fall by means of five matches; a humble businessman who financed surrealist ventures (and paid for the aperitifs) if permitted to print in a corner eulogistic allusions to the actress he kept; a pianist, presentable insofar as the face was concerned, but with a dreadful expression of the fingers; a jaunty but linguistically impotent Soviet writer fresh from Moscow, with an old pipe and a new wristwatch, who was completely and ridiculously unaware of the sort of company he was in; there were several other gentlemen present who have become confused in my memory, and doubtless two or three of the lot had been intimate with Nina. She was the only woman at the table; there she stooped, eagerly sucking at a straw, the level of her lemonade sinking with a kind of childish celerity, and only when the last drop had gurgled and squeaked, and she had pushed away the straw with her tongue, only then did I finally catch her eye, which I had been obstinately seeking, still not being able to cope with the fact that she had had time to forget what had occurred earlier in the morning—to forget it so thoroughly that upon meeting my glance, she replied with a blank questioning smile, and only after peering more closely did she remember suddenly what kind of answering smile I was expecting. Meanwhile, Ferdinand (the ladies having temporarily left the platform after pushing away their instruments like so many pieces of furniture) was juicily drawing his cronies' attention to the figure of an elderly luncher in a far corner of the café, who had, as some Frenchmen for some reason or other have, a little red ribbon or something on his coat lapel and whose gray beard combined with his mustaches to form a cozy yellowish nest for his sloppily munching mouth. Somehow the trappings of old age always amused Ferdie.

I did not stay long in Paris, but that week proved sufficient to engender between him and me that fake chumminess the imposing of which he had such a talent for. Subsequently I even turned out to be of some use to him: my firm acquired the film rights of one of his more intelligible stories, and then he had a good time pestering me with telegrams. As the years passed, we found ourselves every now and then beaming at each other in some place, but I never felt at ease in his presence, and that day in Fialta too I experienced a familiar depression upon learning that he was on the prowl nearby; one thing, however, considerably cheered me up: the flop of his recent play.

And here he was coming toward us, garbed in an absolutely waterproof coat with belt and pocket flaps, a camera across his shoulder, double rubber soles to his shoes, sucking with an imperturbability that was meant to be funny a long stick of moonstone candy, that specialty of Fialta's. Beside him walked the dapper, doll-like, rosy Segur, a lover of art and a perfect fool; I never could discover for what purpose Ferdinand needed him; and I still hear Nina exclaiming with a moaning tenderness that did not commit her to anything: "Oh, he is such a darling, Segur!" They approached; Ferdinand and I greeted each other lustily, trying to crowd into handshake and backslap as much fervor as possible, knowing by experience that actually that was all but pretending it was only a preface; and it always happened like that: after every separation we met to the accompaniment of strings being excitedly tuned, in a bustle of geniality, in the hubbub of sentiments taking their seats; but the ushers would close the doors, and after that no one was admitted.

Segur complained to me about the weather, and at first I did not understand what he was talking about; even if the moist, gray, greenhouse essence of Fialta might be called "weather," it was just as much outside of anything that could serve us as a topic of conversation as was, for instance, Nina's slender elbow, which I was holding between finger and thumb, or a bit of tinfoil someone had dropped, shining in the middle of the cobbled street in the distance.

We four moved on, vague purchases still looming ahead. "God, what an Indian!" Ferdinand suddenly exclaimed with fierce relish, violently nudging me and pointing at a poster. Farther on, near a fountain, he gave his stick of candy to a native child, a swarthy girl with beads round her pretty neck; we stopped to wait for him: he crouched saying something to her, addressing her sooty-black lowered eyelashes, and then he caught up with us, grinning and making one of those remarks with which he loved to spice his speech. Then his attention was drawn by an unfortunate object exhibited in a souvenir shop: a dreadful marble imitation of Mount St. George showing a black tunnel at its base, which turned out to be the mouth of an inkwell, and with a compartment for pens in the semblance of railroad tracks. Open-mouthed, quivering, all agog with sardonic triumph, he turned that dusty, cumbersome, and perfectly irresponsible thing in his hands, paid without bargaining, and with his mouth still open came out carrying the monster. Like some autocrat who surrounds himself with hunchbacks and dwarfs, he would become attached to this or that hideous object; this infatuation might last from five minutes to several days or even longer if the thing happened to be animate.

Nina wistfully alluded to lunch, and seizing the opportunity when Ferdinand and Segur stopped at a post office, I hastened to lead her away. I still wonder what exactly she meant to me, that small dark woman of the narrow shoulders and "lyrical limbs" (to quote the expression of a mincing émigré poet, one of the few men who had sighed platonically after her), and still less do I understand what was the purpose of fate in bringing us constantly together. I did not see her for quite a long while after my sojourn in Paris, and then one day when I came home from my office I found her having tea with my wife and examining on her silk-hosed hand, with her wedding ring gleaming through, the texture of some stockings bought cheap in Tauentzien-strasse. Once I was shown her photograph in a fashion magazine full of autumn leaves and gloves and windswept golf links. On a certain Christmas she sent me a picture postcard with snow and stars. On a Riviera beach she almost escaped my notice behind her dark glasses and terra-cotta tan. Another day, having dropped in on an ill-timed errand at the house of some strangers where a party was in progress, I saw her scarf and fur coat among alien scarecrows on a coatrack. In a bookshop she nodded to me from a page of one of her husband's stories, a page referring to an episodic servant girl, but smuggling in Nina in spite of the author's intention: "Her face," he wrote, "was rather nature's snapshot than a meticulous portrait, so that when . . . tried to imagine it, all he could visualize were fleeting glimpses of disconnected features: the downy outline of her pommettes in the sun, the amber-tinted brown darkness of quick eyes, lips shaped into a friendly smile which was always ready to change into an ardent kiss."

Again and again she hurriedly appeared in the margins of my life, without influencing in the least its basic text. One summer morning (Friday—because housemaids were thumping out carpets in the sun-dusted yard), my family was away in the country and I was lolling and smoking in bed when I heard the bell ring with tremendous violence—and there she was in the hall having burst in to leave (incidentally) a hairpin and (mainly) a trunk illuminated with hotel labels, which a fortnight later was retrieved for her by a nice Austrian boy, who (according to intangible but sure symptoms) belonged to the same very cosmopolitan association of which I was a member. Occasionally, in the middle of a conversation her name would be mentioned, and she would run down the steps of a chance sentence, without turning her head. While traveling in the Pyrenees, I spent a week at the château belonging to people with whom she and Ferdinand happened to be staying, and I shall never forget my first night there: how I waited, how certain I was that without my having to tell her she would steal to my room, how she did not come, and the din thousands of crickets made in the delirious depth of the rocky garden dripping with moon-light, the mad bubbling brooks, and my struggle between blissful southern fatigue after a long day of hunting on the screes and the wild thirst for her stealthy coming, low laugh, pink ankles above the swan's-down trimming of high-heeled slippers, but the night raved on, and she did not come, and when next day, in the course of a general ramble in the mountains, I told her of my waiting, she clasped her hands in dismay—and at once with a rapid glance estimated whether the backs of the gesticulating Ferd and his friend had sufficiently receded. I remember talking to her on the telephone across half of Europe (on her husband's business) and not recognizing at first her eager barking voice; and I remember once dreaming of her: I dreamt that my eldest girl had run in to tell me the doorman was sorely in trouble—and when I had gone down to him, I saw lying on a trunk, a roll of burlap under her head, pale-lipped and wrapped in a woolen kerchief, Nina fast asleep, as miserable refugees sleep in godforsaken railway stations. And regardless of what happened to me or to her, in between, we never discussed anything, as we never thought of each other during the intervals in our destiny, so that when we met the pace of life altered at once, all its atoms were recombined, and we lived in another, lighter time-medium, which was measured not by the lengthy separations but by those few meetings of which a short, supposedly frivolous life was thus artificially formed. And with each new meeting I grew more and more apprehensive; no—I did not experience any inner emotional collapse, the shadow of tragedy did not haunt our revels, my married life remained unimpaired, while on the other hand her eclectic husband ignored her casual affairs although deriving some profit from them in the way of pleasant and useful connections. I grew apprehensive because something lovely, delicate, and unrepeatable was being wasted: something which I abused by snapping off poor bright bits in gross haste while neglecting the modest but true core which perhaps it kept offering me in a pitiful whisper. I was apprehensive because, in the long run, I was somehow accepting Nina's life, the lies, the futility, the gibberish of that life. Even in the absence of any sentimental discord, I felt myself bound to seek for a rational, if not moral, interpretation of my existence, and this meant choosing between the world in which I sat for my portrait, with my wife, my young daughters, the Doberman pinscher (idyllic garlands, a signet ring, a slender cane), between that happy, wise, and good world . . . and what? Was there any practical chance of life together with Nina, life I could barely imagine, for it would be penetrated, I knew, with a passionate, intolerable bitterness and every moment of it would be aware of a past, teeming with protean partners. No, the thing was absurd. And moreover was she not chained to her husband by something stronger than love—the staunch friendship between two convicts? Absurd! But then what should I have done with you, Nina, how should I have disposed of the store of sadness that had gradually accumulated as a result of our seemingly carefree, but really hopeless meetings?

Fialta consists of the old town and of the new one; here and there, past and present are interlaced, struggling either to disentangle themselves or to thrust each other out; each one has its own methods: the newcomer fights honestly—importing palm trees, setting up smart tourist agencies, painting with creamy lines the red smoothness of tennis courts; whereas the sneaky old-timer creeps out from behind a corner in the shape of some little street on crutches or the steps of stairs leading nowhere. On our way to the hotel, we passed a half-built white villa, full of litter within, on a wall of which again the same elephants, their monstrous baby knees wide apart, sat on huge, gaudy drums; in ethereal bundles the equestrienne (already with a penciled mustache) was resting on a broad-backed steed; and a tomato-nosed clown was walking a tightrope, balancing an umbrella ornamented with those recurrent stars—a vague symbolic recollection of the heavenly fatherland of circus performers. Here, in the Riviera part of Fialta, the wet gravel crunched in a more luxurious manner, and the lazy sighing of the sea was more audible. In the backyard of the hotel, a kitchen boy armed with a knife was pursuing a hen which was clucking madly as it raced for its life. A bootblack offered me his ancient throne with a toothless smile. Under the plane trees stood a motorcycle of German make, a mud-bespattered limousine, and a yellow long-bodied Icarus that looked like a giant scarab ("That's ours—Segur's, I mean," said Nina, adding, "Why don't you come with us, Victor?" although she knew very well that I could not come); in the lacquer of its elytra a gouache of sky and branches was engulfed; in the metal of one of the bomb-shaped lamps we ourselves were momentarily reflected, lean filmland pedestrians passing along the convex surface; and then, after a few steps, I glanced back and foresaw, in an almost optical sense, as it were, what really happened an hour or so later: the three of them wearing motoring helmets, getting in, smiling and waving to me, transparent to me like ghosts, with the color of the world shining through them, and then they were moving, receding, diminishing (Nina's last ten-fingered farewell); but actually the automobile was still standing quite motionless, smooth and whole like an egg, and Nina under my outstretched arm was entering a laurel-flanked doorway, and as we sat down we could see through the window Ferdinand and Segur, who had come by another way, slowly approaching.

There was no one on the veranda where we lunched except the Englishman I had recently observed; in front of him, a long glass containing a bright crimson drink threw an oval reflection on the tablecloth. In his eyes, I noticed the same bloodshot desire, but now it was in no sense related to Nina; that avid look was not directed at her at all, but was fixed on the upper right-hand corner of the broad window near which he was sitting.

Having pulled the gloves off her small thin hands, Nina, for the last time in her life, was eating the shellfish of which she was so fond. Ferdinand also busied himself with food, and I took advantage of his hunger to begin a conversation which gave me the semblance of power over him: to be specific, I mentioned his recent failure. After a brief period of fashionable religious conversion, during which grace descended upon him and he undertook some rather ambiguous pilgrimages, which ended in a decidedly scandalous adventure, he had turned his dull eyes toward barbarous Moscow. Now, frankly speaking, I have always been irritated by the complacent conviction that a ripple of stream consciousness, a few healthy obscenities, and a dash of communism in any old slop pail will alchemically and automatically produce ultramodern literature; and I will contend until I am shot that art as soon as it is brought into contact with politics inevitably sinks to the level of any ideological trash. In Ferdinand's case, it is true, all this was rather irrelevant: the muscles of his muse were exceptionally strong, to say nothing of the fact that he didn't care a damn for the plight of the underdog; but because of certain obscurely mischievous undercurrents of that sort, his art had become still more repulsive. Except for a few snobs none had understood the play; I had not seen it myself, but could well imagine that elaborate Kremlinesque night along the impossible spirals of which he spun various wheels of dismembered symbols; and now, not without pleasure, I asked him whether he had read a recent bit of criticism about himself.

"Criticism!" he exclaimed. "Fine criticism! Every slick jackanapes sees fit to read me a lecture. Ignorance of my work is their bliss. My books are touched gingerly, as one touches something that may go bang. Criticism! They are examined from every point of view except the essential one. It is as if a naturalist, in describing the equine genus, started to jaw about saddles or Mme. de V." (he named a well-known literary hostess who indeed strongly resembled a grinning horse). "I would like some of that pigeon's blood too," he continued in the same loud, ripping voice, addressing the waiter, who understood his desire only after he had looked in the direction of the long-nailed finger which unceremoniously pointed at the Englishman's glass. For some reason or other, Segur mentioned Ruby Rose, the lady who painted flowers on her breast, and the conversation took on a less insulting character. Meanwhile the big Englishman suddenly made up his mind, got up on a chair, stepped from there onto the windowsill, and stretched up till he reached that coveted corner of the frame where rested a compact furry moth, which he deftly slipped into a pillbox.

". . . rather like Wouwerman's white horse," said Ferdinand, in regard to something he was discussing with Segur.

"Tu es très hippique ce matin," remarked the latter.

Soon they both left to telephone. Ferdinand was particularly fond of long-distance calls, and particularly good at endowing them, no matter what the distance, with a friendly warmth when it was necessary, as for instance now, to make sure of free lodgings.

From afar came the sounds of music—a trumpet, a zither. Nina and I set out to wander again. The circus on its way to Fialta had apparently sent out runners: an advertising pageant was tramping by; but we did not catch its head, as it had turned uphill into a side alley: the gilded back of some carriage was receding, a man in a burnoose led a camel, a file of four mediocre Indians carried placards on poles, and behind them, by special permission, a tourist's small son in a sailor suit sat reverently on a tiny pony.

We wandered by a café where the tables were now almost dry but still empty; the waiter was examining (I hope he adopted it later) a horrible foundling, the absurd inkstand affair, stowed by Ferdinand on the banisters in passing. At the next corner we were attracted by an old stone stairway, and we climbed up, and I kept looking at the sharp angle of Nina's step as she ascended, raising her skirt, its narrowness requiring the same gesture as formerly length had done; she diffused a familiar warmth, and going up beside her, I recalled the last time we had come together. It had been in a Paris house, with many people around, and my dear friend Jules Darboux, wishing to do me a refined aesthetic favor, had touched my sleeve and said, "I want you to meet—" and led me to Nina, who sat in the corner of a couch, her body folded Z-wise, with an ashtray at her heel, and she took a long turquoise cigarette holder from her lips and joyfully, slowly exclaimed, "Well, of all people—" and then all evening my heart felt like breaking, as I passed from group to group with a sticky glass in my fist, now and then looking at her from a distance (she did not look . . .), and listened to scraps of conversation, and overheard one man saying to another, "Funny, how they all smell alike, burnt leaf through whatever perfume they use, those angular dark-haired girls," and as it often happens, a trivial remark related to some unknown topic coiled and clung to one's own intimate recollection, a parasite of its sadness.

At the top of the steps, we found ourselves on a rough kind of terrace. From here one could see the delicate outline of the dove-colored Mount St. George with a cluster of bone-white flecks (some hamlet) on one of its slopes; the smoke of an indiscernible train undulated along its rounded base—and suddenly disappeared; still lower, above the jumble of roofs, one could perceive a solitary cypress, resembling the moist-twirled black tip of a watercolor brush; to the right, one caught a glimpse of the sea, which was gray, with silver wrinkles. At our feet lay a rusty old key, and on the wall of the half-ruined house adjoining the terrace, the ends of some wire still remained hanging. . . . I reflected that formerly there had been life here, a family had enjoyed the coolness at nightfall, clumsy children had colored pictures by the light of a lamp. . . . We lingered there as if listening to something; Nina, who stood on higher ground, put a hand on my shoulder and smiled, and carefully, so as not to crumple her smile, kissed me. With an unbearable force, I relived (or so it now seems to me) all that had ever been between us beginning with a similar kiss; and I said (substituting for our cheap, formal "thou" that strangely full and expressive "you" to which the circumnavigator, enriched all around, returns), "Look here—what if I love you?" Nina glanced at me, I repeated those words, I wanted to add . . . but something like a bat passed swiftly across her face, a quick, queer, almost ugly expression, and she, who would utter coarse words with perfect simplicity, became embarrassed; I also felt awkward. . . . "Never mind, I was only joking," I hastened to say, lightly encircling her waist. From somewhere a firm bouquet of small, dark, unselfishly smelling violets appeared in her hands, and before she returned to her husband and car, we stood for a little while longer by the stone parapet, and our romance was even more hopeless than it had ever been. But the stone was as warm as flesh, and suddenly I understood something I had been seeing without understanding—why a piece of tinfoil had sparkled so on the pavement, why the gleam of a glass had trembled on a tablecloth, why the sea was ashimmer: somehow, by imperceptible degrees, the white sky above Fialta had got saturated with sunshine, and now it was sunpervaded throughout, and this brimming white radiance grew broader and broader, all dissolved in it, all vanished, all passed, and I stood on the station platform of Mlech with a freshly bought newspaper, which told me that the yellow car I had seen under the plane trees had suffered a crash beyond Fialta, having run at full speed into the truck of a traveling circus entering the town, a crash from which Ferdinand and his friend, those invulnerable rogues, those salamanders of fate, those basilisks of good fortune, had escaped with local and temporary injury to their scales, while Nina, in spite of her long-standing, faithful imitation of them, had turned out after all to be mortal.

CLOUD, CASTLE, LAKE

O NE of my representatives—a modest, mild bachelor, very efficient—happened to win a pleasure trip at a charity ball given by Russian refugees. That was in 1936 or 1937. The Berlin summer was in full flood (it was the second week of damp and cold, so that it was a pity to look at everything which had turned green in vain, and only the sparrows kept cheerful); he did not care to go anywhere, but when he tried to sell his ticket at the office of the Bureau of Pleasantrips he was told that to do so he would have to have special permission from the Ministry of Transportation; when he tried them, it turned out that first he would have to draw up a complicated petition at a notary's on stamped paper; and besides, a so-called "certificate of nonabsence from the city for the summertime" had to be obtained from the police.

So he sighed a little, and decided to go. He borrowed an aluminum flask from friends, repaired his soles, bought a belt and a fancy-style flannel shirt—one of those cowardly things which shrink in the first wash. Incidentally, it was too large for that likable little man, his hair always neatly trimmed, his eyes so intelligent and kind. I cannot remember his name at the moment. I think it was Vasiliy Ivanovich.

He slept badly the night before the departure. And why? Because he had to get up unusually early, and hence took along into his dreams the delicate face of the watch ticking on his night table; but mainly because that very night, for no reason at all, he began to imagine that this trip, thrust upon him by a feminine fate in a low-cut gown, this trip which he had accepted so reluctantly, would bring him some wonderful, tremulous happiness. This happiness would have something in common with his childhood, and with the excitement aroused in him by Russian lyrical poetry, and with some evening skyline once seen in a dream, and with that lady, another man's wife, whom he had hope-

430

lessly loved for seven years—but it would be even fuller and more significant than all that. And besides, he felt that the really good life must be oriented toward something or someone.

The morning was dull, but steam-warm and close, with an inner sun, and it was quite pleasant to rattle in a streetcar to the distant railway station where the gathering place was: several people, alas, were taking part in the excursion. Who would they be, these drowsy beings, drowsy as seem all creatures still unknown to us? By Window Number 6, at seven a.m., as was indicated in the directions appended to the ticket, he saw them (they were already waiting; he had managed to be late by about three minutes).

A lanky blond young man in Tyrolese garb stood out at once. He was burned the color of a cockscomb, had huge brick-red knees with golden hairs, and his nose looked lacquered. He was the leader furnished by the Bureau, and as soon as the newcomer had joined the group (which consisted of four women and as many men) he led it off toward a train lurking behind other trains, carrying his monstrous knapsack with terrifying ease, and firmly clanking with his hobnailed boots.

Everyone found a place in an empty car, unmistakably third-class, and Vasiliy Ivanovich, having sat down by himself and put a peppermint into his mouth, opened a little volume of Tyutchev, whom he had long intended to reread; but he was requested to put the book aside and join the group. An elderly bespectacled post-office clerk, with skull, chin, and upper lip a bristly blue as if he had shaved off some extraordinarily luxuriant and tough growth especially for this trip, immediately announced that he had been to Russia and knew some Russian—for instance, *patzlui*—and, recalling philanderings in Tsaritsyn, winked in such a manner that his fat wife sketched out in the air the outline of a backhand box on the ear. The company was getting noisy. Four employees of the same building firm were tossing each other heavy-weight jokes: a middle-aged man, Schultz; a younger man, Schultz also, and two fidgety young women with big mouths and big rumps. The red-headed, rather burlesque widow in a sport skirt knew something too about Russia (the Riga beaches). There was also a dark young man by the name of Schramm, with lusterless eyes and a vague velvety vileness about his person and manners, who constantly switched the conversation to this or that attractive aspect of the excursion, and who gave the first signal for rapturous appreciation; he was, as it turned out later, a special stimulator from the Bureau of Pleasantrips.

The locomotive, working rapidly with its elbows, hurried through a pine forest, then—with relief—among fields. Only dimly realizing as yet all the absurdity and horror of the situation, and perhaps attempting to persuade himself that everything was very nice, Vasiliy Ivanovich contrived to enjoy the fleeting gifts of the road. And indeed, how enticing it all is, what charm the world acquires when it is wound up and moving like a merry-go-round! The sun crept toward a corner of the window and suddenly spilled over the yellow bench. The badly pressed shadow of the car sped madly along the grassy bank, where flowers blended into colored streaks. A crossing: a cyclist was waiting, one foot resting on the ground. Trees appeared in groups and singly, revolving coolly and blandly, displaying the latest fashions. The blue dampness of a ravine. A memory of love, disguised as a meadow. Wispy clouds—greyhounds of heaven.

We both, Vasiliy Ivanovich and I, have always been impressed by the anonymity of all the parts of a landscape, so dangerous for the soul, the impossibility of ever finding out where that path you see leads—and look, what a tempting thicket! It happened that on a distant slope or in a gap in the trees there would appear and, as it were, stop for an instant, like air retained in the lungs, a spot so enchanting—a lawn, a terrace—such perfect expression of tender well-meaning beauty—that it seemed that if one could stop the train and go thither, forever, to you, my love . . . But a thousand beech trunks were already madly leaping by, whirling in a sizzling sun pool, and again the chance for happiness was gone.

At the stations, Vasiliy Ivanovich would look at the configuration of some entirely insignificant objects—a smear on the platform, a cherry stone, a cigarette butt—and would say to himself that never, never would he remember these three little things here in that particular interrelation, this pattern, which he now could see with such deathless precision; or again, looking at a group of children waiting for a train, he would try with all his might to single out at least one remarkable destiny—in the form of a violin or a crown, a propeller or a lyre—and would gaze until the whole party of village schoolboys appeared as in an old photograph, now reproduced with a little white cross above the face of the last boy on the right: the hero's childhood.

But one could look out of the window only by snatches. All had been given sheet music with verses from the Bureau:

> Stop that worrying and moping,
> Take a knotted stick and rise,
> Come a-tramping in the open
> With the good, the hearty guys!

Tramp your country's grass and stubble,
With the good, the hearty guys,
Kill the hermit and his trouble
And to hell with doubts and sighs!

In a paradise of heather
Where the field mouse screams and dies,
Let us march and sweat together
With the steel-and-leather guys!

This was to be sung in chorus: Vasiliy Ivanovich, who not only could not sing but could not even pronounce German words clearly, took advantage of the drowning roar of mingling voices and merely opened his mouth while swaying slightly, as if he were really singing— but the leader, at a sign from the subtle Schramm, suddenly stopped the general singing and, squinting askance at Vasiliy Ivanovich, de-manded that he sing solo. Vasiliy Ivanovich cleared his throat, timidly began, and after a minute of solitary torment all joined in; but he did not dare thereafter to drop out.

He had with him his favorite cucumber from the Russian store, a loaf of bread, and three eggs. When evening came, and the low crim-son sun entered wholly the soiled seasick car, stunned by its own din, all were invited to hand over their provisions, in order to divide them evenly—this was particularly easy, as all except Vasiliy Ivanovich had the same things. The cucumber amused everybody, was pronounced inedible, and was thrown out of the window. In view of the insuffi-ciency of his contribution, Vasiliy Ivanovich got a smaller portion of sausage.

He was made to play cards. They pulled him about, questioned him, verified whether he could show the route of the trip on a map—in a word, all busied themselves with him, at first good-naturedly, then with malevolence, which grew with the approach of night. Both girls were called Greta; the red-headed widow somehow resembled the rooster-leader; Schramm, Schultz, and the other Schultz, the post-office clerk and his wife, all gradually melted to-gether, merged together, forming one collective, wobbly, many-handed being, from which one could not escape. It pressed upon him from all sides. But suddenly at some station all climbed out, and it was already dark, although in the west there still hung a very long, very pink cloud, and farther along the track, with a soul-piercing light, the star of a lamp trembled through the slow smoke of the engine, and crickets chirped in the dark, and from somewhere there came the odor of jasmine and hay, my love.

They spent the night in a tumble-down inn. A mature bedbug is awful, but there is a certain grace in the motions of silky silverfish. The post-office clerk was separated from his wife, who was put with the widow; he was given to Vasiliy Ivanovich for the night. The two beds took up the whole room. Quilt on top, chamber pot below. The clerk said that somehow he did not feel sleepy, and began to talk of his Russian adventures, rather more circumstantially than in the train. He was a great bully of a man, thorough and obstinate, clad in long cotton drawers, with mother-of-pearl claws on his dirty toes, and bear's fur between fat breasts. A moth dashed about the ceiling, hobnobbing with its shadow. "In Tsaritsyn," the clerk was saying, "there are now three schools, a German, a Czech, and a Chinese one. At any rate, that is what my brother-in-law says; he went there to build tractors."

Next day, from early morning to five o'clock in the afternoon, they raised dust along a highway, which undulated from hill to hill; then they took a green road through a dense fir wood. Vasiliy Ivanovich, as the least burdened, was given an enormous round loaf of bread to carry under his arm. How I hate you, our daily! But still his precious, experienced eyes noted what was necessary. Against the background of fir-tree gloom a dry needle was hanging vertically on an invisible thread.

Again they piled into a train, and again the small partitionless car was empty. The other Schultz began to teach Vasiliy Ivanovich how to play the mandolin. There was much laughter. When they got tired of that, they thought up a capital game, which was supervised by Schramm. It consisted of the following: the women would lie down on the benches they chose, under which the men were already hidden, and when from under one of the benches there would emerge a ruddy face with ears, or a big outspread hand, with a skirt-lifting curve of the fingers (which would provoke much squealing), then it would be revealed who was paired off with whom. Three times Vasiliy Ivanovich lay down in filthy darkness, and three times it turned out that there was no one on the bench when he crawled out from under. He was acknowledged the loser and was forced to eat a cigarette butt.

They spent the night on straw mattresses in a barn, and early in the morning set out again on foot. Firs, ravines, foamy streams. From the heat, from the songs which one had constantly to bawl, Vasiliy Ivanovich became so exhausted that during the midday halt he fell asleep at once, and awoke only when they began to slap at imaginary horseflies on him. But after another hour of marching, that very happiness of which he had once half dreamt was suddenly discovered.

It was a pure, blue lake, with an unusual expression of its water. In the middle, a large cloud was reflected in its entirety. On the other side, on a hill thickly covered with verdure (and the darker the verdure, the more poetic it is), towered, arising from dactyl to dactyl, an ancient black castle. Of course, there are plenty of such views in Central Europe, but just this one—in the inexpressible and unique harmoniousness of its three principal parts, in its smile, in some mysterious innocence it had, my love! my obedient one!—was something so unique, and so familiar, and so long-promised, and it so *understood* the beholder that Vasiliy Ivanovich even pressed his hand to his heart, as if to see whether his heart was there in order to give it away.

At some distance, Schramm, poking into the air with the leader's alpenstock, was calling the attention of the excursionists to something or other; they had settled themselves around on the grass in poses seen in amateur snapshots, while the leader sat on a stump, his behind to the lake, and was having a snack. Quietly, concealing himself in his own shadow, Vasiliy Ivanovich followed the shore, and came to a kind of inn. A dog still quite young greeted him; it crept on its belly, its jaws laughing, its tail fervently beating the ground. Vasiliy Ivanovich accompanied the dog into the house, a piebald two-storied dwelling with a winking window beneath a convex tiled eyelid; and he found the owner, a tall old man vaguely resembling a Russian war veteran, who spoke German so poorly and with such a soft drawl that Vasiliy Ivanovich changed to his own tongue, but the man understood as in a dream and continued in the language of his environment, his family.

Upstairs was a room for travelers. "You know, I shall take it for the rest of my life," Vasiliy Ivanovich is reported to have said as soon as he had entered it. The room itself had nothing remarkable about it. On the contrary, it was a most ordinary room, with a red floor, daisies daubed on the white walls, and a small mirror half filled with the yellow infusion of the reflected flowers—but from the window one could clearly see the lake with its cloud and its castle, in a motionless and perfect correlation of happiness. Without reasoning, without considering, only entirely surrendering to an attraction the truth of which consisted in its own strength, a strength which he had never experienced before, Vasiliy Ivanovich in one radiant second realized that here in this little room with that view, beautiful to the verge of tears, life would at last be what he had always wished it to be. What exactly it would be like, what would take place here, that of course he did not know, but all around him were help, promise, and consolation—so that there could not be any doubt that he must live here. In a moment he figured out how he would manage it so as not to have to return to Berlin again, how to get the few possessions that he had—books, the blue suit, her photograph. How simple it was turning out! As my representative, he was earning enough for the modest life of a refugee Russian.

"My friends," he cried, having run down again to the meadow by the shore, "my friends, good-bye. I shall remain for good in that house over there. We can't travel together any longer. I shall go no farther. I am not going anywhere. Good-bye!"

"How is that?" said the leader in a queer voice, after a short pause, during which the smile on the lips of Vasiliy Ivanovich slowly faded, while the people who had been sitting on the grass half rose and stared at him with stony eyes.

"But why?" he faltered. "It is here that . . ."

"Silence!" the post-office clerk suddenly bellowed with extraordinary force. "Come to your senses, you drunken swine!"

"Wait a moment, gentlemen," said the leader, and, having passed his tongue over his lips, he turned to Vasiliy Ivanovich.

"You probably have been drinking," he said quietly. "Or have gone out of your mind. You are taking a pleasure trip with us. Tomorrow, according to the appointed itinerary—look at your ticket—we are all returning to Berlin. There can be no question of anyone—in this case you—refusing to continue this communal journey. We were singing today a certain song—try and remember what it said. That's enough now! Come, children, we are going on."

"There will be beer at Ewald," said Schramm in a caressing voice. "Five hours by train. Hikes. A hunting lodge. Coal mines. Lots of interesting things."

"I shall complain," wailed Vasiliy Ivanovich. "Give me back my bag. I have the right to remain where I want. Oh, but this is nothing less than an invitation to a beheading"—he told me he cried when they seized him by the arms.

"If necessary we shall carry you," said the leader grimly, "but that is not likely to be pleasant. I am responsible for each of you, and shall bring back each of you, alive or dead."

Swept along a forest road as in a hideous fairy tale, squeezed, twisted, Vasiliy Ivanovich could not even turn around, and only felt how the radiance behind his back receded, fractured by trees, and then it was no longer there, and all around the dark firs fretted but could not interfere. As soon as everyone had got into the car and the train had pulled off, they began to beat him—they beat him a long time, and with a good deal of inventiveness. It occurred to them, among other things, to use a corkscrew on his palms; then on his feet. The post-office clerk, who had been to Russia, fashioned a knout out of a stick and a belt, and began to use it with devilish dexterity. Atta boy! The other men relied more on their iron heels, whereas the women were satisfied to pinch and slap. All had a wonderful time.

After returning to Berlin, he called on me, was much changed, sat down quietly, putting his hands on his knees, told his story; kept on repeating that he must resign his position, begged me to let him go, insisted that he could not continue, that he had not the strength to belong to mankind any longer. Of course, I let him go.

TYRANTS DESTROYED

1

T HE growth of his power and fame was matched, in my imagination, by the degree of the punishment I would have liked to inflict on him. Thus, at first, I would have been content with an electoral defeat, a cooling of public enthusiasm. Later I already required his imprisonment; still later, his exile to some distant, flat island with a single palm tree, which, like a black asterisk, refers one to the bottom of an eternal hell made of solitude, disgrace, and helplessness. Now, at last, nothing but his death could satisfy me.

As in the graphs that visually demonstrate his ascension, indicating the number of his adherents by the gradual increase in size of a little figure that becomes biggish and then enormous, my hatred of him, its arms folded like those of his image, ominously swelled in the center of the space that was my soul, until it had nearly filled it, leaving me only a narrow rim of curved light (resembling more the corona of madness than the halo of martyrdom), though I foresee an utter eclipse still to come.

His first portraits, in the papers and shop windows and on the posters—which also kept growing in our abundantly irrigated, crying, and bleeding country—looked rather blurred: this was when I still had doubts about the deadly outcome of my hatred. Something human, certain possibilities of his failing, his cracking, his falling ill, heaven knows what, came feebly shivering through some of his photographs in the random variety of not yet standardized poses and in a vacillating gaze which had not yet found its historical expression. Little by little, though, his countenance consolidated: his cheeks and cheekbones, in the official portrait photographs, became overlaid with a godly gloss, the olive oil of public affection, the varnish of a completed masterpiece; it became impossible to imagine that nose being blown, or that finger poking on the inside of that lip to extricate a food particle lodged behind a rotten incisor. Experimental variety was followed by a canonized uniformity that established the now familiar, stony, and lusterless look of his neither intelligent nor cruel, but somehow unbearably eerie eyes. Established, too, was the solid fleshiness of his chin, the bronze of his jowls, and a feature that had already become the common property of all the cartoonists in the world and almost automatically brought off the trick of resemblance—a thick wrinkle across his whole forehead—the fatty sediment of thought, of course, rather than thought's scar. I am forced to believe that his face has been rubbed with all sorts of patent balsams, else I cannot comprehend its metallic good quality, for I once knew it when it was sickly, bloated, and illshaven, so that one heard the scrape of bristles against his dirty starch collar when he turned his head. And the glasses—what became of the glasses that he wore as a youth?

2

Not only have I never been fascinated by politics, but I have hardly ever read a single editorial or even a short report on a party congress. Sociological problems have never intrigued me, and to this day I cannot picture myself taking part in a conspiracy or simply sitting in a smoke-filled room among politically excited, tensely serious people, discussing methods of struggle in the light of recent developments. I don't give a hoot for the welfare of mankind, and not only do I not believe in any majority being automatically right, but I tend to reexamine the question whether it is proper to strive for a state of affairs where literally everyone is half-fed and half-schooled. I further know that my fatherland, enslaved by him at the present time, is destined, in the distant future, to undergo many other upheavals, independent of any acts on *this* tyrant's part. Nevertheless, he must be killed.

3

When the gods used to assume earthly form and, clad in violet-tinted raiment, demurely but powerfully stepping with muscular feet in still dustless sandals, appeared to field laborers or mountain shepherds, their divinity was not in the least diminished for it; on the contrary, the charm of humanness enwafting them was a most eloquent reconfirmation of their celestial essence. But when a limited, coarse, little-educated man—at first glance a third-rate fanatic and in reality a pigheaded, brutal, and gloomy vulgarian full of morbid ambition—when such a man dresses up in godly garb, one feels like apologizing to the gods. It would be useless to try and convince me that actually he has nothing to do with it, that what elevated him to an iron-and-concrete throne, and now keeps him there, is the implacable evolution of dark, zoological, Zoorlandic ideas that have caught my fatherland's fancy. An idea selects only the helve; man is free to complete the axe—and use it.

Then again, let me repeat that I am no good at distinguishing what is good or bad for a state, and why it is that blood runs off it like water off a goose. Amid everybody and everything it is only one individual that interests me. That is my ailment, my obsession, and at the same time a thing that somehow belongs to me and that is entrusted to me alone for judgment. Since my early years—and I am no longer young—evil in people has struck me as particularly loathsome, unbearable to the point of suffocation and calling for immediate derision and destruction, while on the other hand I hardly noticed good in people, so much did it always seem to me the normal, indispensable condition, something granted and inalienable as, for example, the capacity to breathe is implied by the fact of being alive. With passing years I developed an extremely fine flair for evil, but my attitude toward good underwent a slight change, as I came to understand that its commonness, which had conditioned my indifference, was indeed so *uncommon* that I could not be sure at all of always finding it close to hand should the need arise. This is why I have led a hard, lonely life, always indigent, in shabby lodgings; yet I invariably had the obscure sensation of my real home being just around the corner, waiting for me, so that I could enter it as soon as I had finished with a thousand imaginary matters that cluttered my existence. Good God how I detested dull rectangular minds, how unfair I could be to a kindly person in whom I had happened to notice something comic, such as stinginess or respect for the well-to-do! And now I have before me not merely a weak solution of evil, such as can be obtained from any man, but a most highly concentrated, undiluted evil, in a huge vessel filled to the neck and sealed.

4

He transformed my wildflowery country into a vast kitchen garden, where special care is lavished on turnips, cabbages, and beets; thus all the nation's passions were reduced to the passion for the fat vegetable in the good earth. A kitchen garden next to a factory with the inevitable accompaniment of a locomotive maneuvering somewhere in the background; the hopeless, drab sky of city outskirts, and everything the imagination associates with the scene: a fence, a rusted can among thistles, broken glass, excrements, a black, buzzing burst of flies under one's feet—this is the present-day image of my country. An image of the utmost dejection, but then dejection is in favor here, and a slogan *he* once tossed off (into the trash pit of stupidity)—"one half of our land must be cultivated, and the other asphalted"—is repeated by imbeciles as if it were a supreme expression of human happiness. There would be some excuse if he fed us the shoddy maxims he had once gleaned from reading sophists of the most banal kind, but he feeds us the chaff of those truths, and the manner of thinking required of us is based not simply on false wisdom, but on its rubble and stumblings. For me, however, the crux of the matter is not here either, for it stands to reason that even if the idea of which we are slaves were supremely inspired, exquisite, refreshingly moist, and sunny through and through, slavery would still be slavery inasmuch as the idea was inflicted on us. No, the point is that, as his power grew, I began to notice that the obligations of citizens, admonitions, restrictions, decrees, and all the other forms of pressure put on us were coming to resemble the man himself more and more closely, displaying an unmistakable relation to certain traits of his character and details of his past, so that on the basis of those admonitions and decrees one could reconstruct his personality like an octopus by its tentacles—that personality of his that I was one of the few to know well. In other words, everything around him began taking on his appearance. Legislation began to show a ludicrous likeness to his gait and gestures. Greengrocers began stocking a remarkable abundance of cucumbers, which he had so greedily consumed in his youth. The schools' curriculum now includes Gypsy wrestling, which, in rare moments of cold playfulness, he used to practice on the floor with my brother twenty-five years ago. Newspaper articles and the novels of sycophantic writers have taken on that abruptness of style, that supposedly lapidary quality (basically senseless, for every minted phrase repeats in a different key one and the same official truism), that force of language cum weakness of thinking, and all those other stylistic affectations that are characteristic of him. I soon had the feeling that he, he as I remembered him, was penetrating everywhere, infecting with his presence the way of thinking and the everyday life of every person, so that his mediocrity, his tediousness, his gray habitude, were becoming the very life of my country. And finally the law he established—the implacable power of the majority, the incessant sacrifice to the idol of the majority—lost all sociological meaning, for *he* is the majority.

5
———

He was a comrade of my brother Gregory, who had a feverish, poetic passion for extreme forms of organized society (forms that had long been alarming the meek constitution we then had) in the final years of his short life: he drowned at twenty-three, bathing one summer evening in a wide, very wide river, so that when I now recall my brother the first thing that comes to my mind is a shiny spread of water, an islet overgrown with alder (that he never reached but toward which he always swims through the trembling haze of my memory), and a long, black cloud crossing another, opulently fluffed-up and orange-colored one, all that is left of a Saturday-morning thunderstorm in the clear, turquoise Sunday's-eve sky, where a star will shine through in a moment, where there will never be any star. At any time I was much too engrossed in the history of painting and in my dissertation on its cave origins to frequent watchfully the group of young people that had inveigled my brother; for that matter, as I recall, there was no definite group, but simply several youths who had drifted together, different in many respects but, for the time being, loosely bound by a common attraction to rebellious adventure. The present, however, always exercises such a perverse influence on reminiscence that now I involuntarily single *him* out against the indistinct background, awarding him (neither the closest nor the most vociferous of Gregory's companions) the kind of somber, concentrated will deeply conscious of its sullen self, which in the end molds a giftless person into a triumphant monster.

I remember him waiting for my brother in the gloomy dining room of our humble provincial house; perching on the first chair he saw, he immediately began to read a rumpled newspaper extracted from a pocket of his black jacket, and his face, half-hidden by the armature of smoke-colored glasses, assumed a disgusted and weepy expression, as if he had hit upon some scurrilous stuff. I remember that his sloppily laced town boots were always dirty, as if he had just walked many miles along a cart road between unnoticed meadows. His cropped hair ended in a bristly wedge on his forehead (nothing foretold yet his present Caesar-like baldness). The nails of his large, humid hands were so closely bitten that it was painful to see the tight little cushions at the tips of his hideous fingers. He gave off a goatish smell. He was hard up, and indiscriminate as to sleeping quarters.

When my brother arrived (and in my recollection Gregory is always tardy, always comes in out of breath, as if hastening terribly to live but arriving late all the same—and thus it was that life finally left him behind), he greeted Gregory without smiling, getting up abruptly and giving his hand with an odd jerk, a kind of preliminary retraction of the elbow; it seemed that if one did not snatch his hand in time it would bounce back, with a springy click, into its detachable cuff. If some member of our family entered, he limited himself to a surly nod; per contra, he would demonstratively shake hands with the cook, who, taken by surprise and not having time to wipe her palm before the clasp, wiped it afterwards, in a retake of the scene, as it were. My mother died not long before his first visits, while my father's attitude toward him was as absentminded as it was toward everyone and everything—toward us, toward life's adversities, toward the presence of grubby dogs to whom Gregory offered shelter, and even, it seems, toward his patients. On the other hand, two elderly aunts of mine were openly wary of the "eccentric" (if anyone ever was the opposite of eccentric it was he) as, for that matter, they were of Gregory's other pals.

Now, twenty-five years later, I often have occasion to hear his voice, his bestial roar, diffused by the thunders of radio; back then, however, I recall he always spoke softly, even with a certain huskiness, a certain susurrous lisp. Only that famous vile bit of breathlessness of his, at the end of a sentence, was already there, yes, already there. When he stood, head and arms lowered, before my brother, who was greeting him with affectionate exclamations, still trying to catch at least an elbow of his, or his bony shoulder, he seemed curiously short-legged, owing, probably, to the length of his jacket, which came down to midhip; and one could not determine whether the mournfulness of his posture was caused by glum shyness or by a straining of the faculties before uttering some tragic message. Later it seemed to me that he had at last uttered it and done with it, when, on that dreadful summer evening, he came from the river carrying what looked like a heap of clothes but was only Gregory's shirt and canvas pants; now, however,

I think that the message he seemed to be always pregnant with was not that one after all, but the muffled news of his own monstrous future.

Sometimes, through a half-open door, I could hear his abnormally halting speech in a talk with my brother; or he would be sitting at the tea table, breaking a pretzel, his night-bird eyes turned away from the light of the kerosene lamp. He had a strange and unpleasant way of rinsing his mouth with his milk before he swallowed it, and when he bit into the pretzel he cautiously twisted his mouth; his teeth were bad, and to deceive the fiery pain of a bared nerve by a brief whiff of coolness, he would repeatedly suck in the air, with a sidewise whistle. Once, I remember, my father soaked a bit of cotton wool for him with some brown drops containing opium and, chuckling aimlessly, recommended that he see a dentist. "The whole is stronger than its parts," he answered with awkward gruffness, "ergo I will vanquish my tooth." I am no longer certain, though, whether I heard those wooden words personally, or whether they were subsequently repeated to me as a pronouncement by the "eccentric"; only, as I have already said, he was nothing of the sort, for how can an animal faith in one's blear guiding star be regarded as something peculiar and rare? But, believe it or not, he impressed people with his mediocrity as others do with their talent.

6

———

Sometimes his innate mournfulness was broken by spasms of nasty, jagged joviality, and then I would hear his laughter, as jarring and unexpected as the yowl of a cat, to whose velvet silence you grow so accustomed that its nocturnal voice seems a demented, demonic thing. Shrieking thus, he would be drawn by his companions into games and tussles; it turned out then that he had the arms of a weakling, but legs strong as steel. On one occasion a particularly prankish boy put a toad in his pocket, whereupon he, being afraid to go after it with his fingers, started tearing off the weighted jacket and in that state, his face darkly flushed, disheveled, with nothing but a dickey over his torn undershirt, he fell prey to a heartless hunchbacked girl, whose massive braid and ink-blue eyes were so attractive to many that she was willingly forgiven a resemblance to a black chess knight.

I know about his amorous tendencies and system of courtship from that very girl, now, unfortunately, deceased, like the majority of those who knew him well in his youth (as if death were an ally of his, removing from his path dangerous witnesses to his past). To this vivacious hunchback he would write either in a didactic tone, with excursions—of a popular-educational type—into history (which he knew from political pamphlets), or else complain in obscure and soggy terms about another woman (also with a physical defect of some kind, I believe), who remained unknown to me, and with whom at one time he had shared bed and board in the most dismal part of the city. Today I would give a lot to search out and interrogate that anonymous person, but she, too, no doubt, is safely dead. A curious feature of his missives was their noisome wordiness: he hinted at the machinations of mysterious enemies; polemicized at length with some poetaster, whose verselets he had read in a calendar—oh, if it were possible to resurrect those precious exercise-book pages, filled with his minuscule, myopic handwriting! Alas, I do not recall a single phrase from them (at the time I was not very interested, even if I did listen and chuckle), and only very indistinctly do I see, in the depths of memory, the bow on that braid, the thin clavicle, and the quick, dusky hand in the garnet bracelet crumpling his letters; and I also catch the cooing note of perfidious feminine laughter.

7

The difference between dreaming of a reordered world and dreaming of reordering it oneself as one sees fit is a profound and fatal one; yet none of his friends, including my brother, apparently made any distinction between their abstract rebellion and *his* merciless lust for power. A month after my brother's death he vanished, transferring his activity to the northern provinces (my brother's group withered and fell apart and, as far as I know, none of its other participants went into politics), and soon there were rumors that the work being done there, both in its aims and methods, had grown diametrically opposed to all that had been said, thought, and hoped in that initial young circle. When I recall his aspect in those days, I find it amazing that no one noticed the long, angular shadow of treason that he dragged behind him wherever he went, tucking its fringe under the furniture when he sat down, and letting it interfere strangely with the banister's own shadow on the wall of the staircase, down which he was seen to the door by the light of a portable kerosene lamp. Or is it our dark present time that was cast forward there?

I do not know if they liked him, but in any case my brother and the others mistook his moroseness for the intensity of spiritual force. The cruelty of his ideas seemed a natural consequence of enigmatic calamities he had suffered; and his whole unprepossessive shell presupposed, as it were, a clean, bright kernel. I may as well confess that I myself once had the fleeting impression that he was capable of mercy; only subsequently did I determine its true shade. Those who are fond of cheap paradoxes took note long ago of the sentimentality of executioners; and indeed, the sidewalk in front of butcher shops is always dampish.

8

The first days after the tragedy he kept turning up, and several times spent the night in our place. That death did not evoke any visible signs of grief in him. He behaved as always, which did not shock us in the least, since his usual state was already mournful: and as usual he would sit in some corner, reading something uninteresting and behaving, in short, as, in a house where a great misfortune has occurred, people do who are neither close intimates nor complete strangers. Now, moreover, his constant presence and sullen silence could pass for grim commiseration—the commiseration, you see, of a strong reticent man, inconspicuous but ever-present—a very pillar of sympathy—about whom you later learn that he himself was seriously ill at the time he spent those sleepless nights on a chair among tear-blinded members of the household. In his case, however, this was all a dreadful misconception: if he did feel drawn to our house at the time, it was solely because nowhere did he breathe so naturally as in the sphere of gloom and despair, when uncleared dishes litter the table and nonsmokers ask for cigarettes.

I vividly remember setting out with him to perform one of the minor formalities, one of the excruciatingly dim bits of business with which death (having, as it always has, an element of red tape about it) tries to entangle survivors for as long as possible. Probably someone said to me, "There, *he* will go with you," and he came, discreetly clearing his throat. It was on that occasion (we were walking along a houseless street, fluffy with dust, past fences and piles of lumber) that I did something the memory of which traverses me from top to toe like an electrical jolt of insufferable shame: driven by God knows what feeling—perhaps not so much by gratitude as by condolence for another's condolence—in a surge of nervousness and ill-timed emotion, I clasped and squeezed his hand (which caused us both to stumble slightly). It all lasted an instant, and yet, if I had then embraced him and pressed my lips to his horrible golden bristles, I could not have felt any greater torment now. Now, after twenty-five years, I wonder: the two of us were walking alone through a deserted neighborhood, and in my pocket I had Gregory's loaded revolver, which, for some reason or other, I kept meaning to hide; I could perfectly well have dispatched him with a shot at point-blank range, and then there would have been nothing of what there is today—no rain-drenched holidays, no gigantic festivities with millions of my fellow citizens marching by with shovels, hoes, and rakes on their slavish shoulders; no loudspeakers, deafeningly multiplying the same inescapable voice; no secret mourning in every other family, no assortment of tortures, no torpor of the mind, no colossal portraits—nothing. Oh if it were possible to claw into the past, drag a missed opportunity by its hair back into the present, resurrect that dusty street, the vacant lots, the weight in my hip pocket, the youth walking at my side!

9

I am dull and fat, like Prince Hamlet. What can I do? Between me, a humble teacher of drawing in a provincial high school, and him, sitting behind a multitude of steel and oaken doors in an unknown chamber of the capital's main jail, transformed for him into a castle (for this tyrant calls himself "prisoner of the will of the people that elected him"), there is an unimaginable distance. Someone was telling me, after having locked himself in the basement with me, about an old widow, a distant relative of his, who succeeded in growing an eighty-pound turnip, thus meriting an audience with the exalted one. She was conducted through one marble corridor after another, and an endless succession of doors was unlocked in front of her and locked behind her, until she found herself in a white, starkly lit hall, whose entire furnishings consisted of two gilt chairs. Here she was told to stand and wait. In due time she heard numerous footfalls from behind the door, and, with respectful bows, deferring to each other, half a dozen of his bodyguards came in. With frightened eyes she searched for *him* among them; their eyes were directed not at her but somewhere beyond her head; then, turning, she saw that behind her, through another, unnoticed door, he himself had noiselessly entered and, having stopped and placed a hand on the back of one of the two chairs, was scrutinizing the guest of the State with a habitual air of encouragement. Then he seated himself and suggested that she describe in her own words her glorious achievement (here an attendant brought in and placed on the second chair a clay replica of her vegetable), and, for ten unforgettable minutes, she narrated how she had planted the turnip; how she had tugged and tugged without being able to get it out of the ground, even though she thought she saw her deceased husband tugging with her; how she had had to call first her son, then her nephew and even a couple of firemen who were resting in the hayloft; and how, finally, backing in tandem arrangement, they had extracted the monster. Evidently he was overwhelmed by her vivid narrative; "Now that's genuine poetry," he said, addressing his retinue. "Here's somebody the poet fellows ought to learn from." And, crossly ordering that the likeness be cast in bronze, he left. I, however, do not grow turnips, so I cannot find a way to him; and, even if I did, how would I carry my treasured weapon to his lair?

On occasion he appears before the people, and, even though no one is allowed near him, and everyone has to hold up the heavy staff of an issued banner so that hands are kept busy, and everyone is watched by a guard of incalculable proportions (to say nothing of the secret agents and the secret agents watching the secret agents), someone very adroit and resolute might have the good fortune to find a loophole, one transparent instant, some tiny chink of fate through which to rush forward. I mentally considered, one by one, all kinds of destructive means, from the classic dagger to plebeian dynamite, but it was all in vain, and it is with good reason that I frequently dream I am repeatedly squeezing the trigger of a weapon that is disintegrating in my hand, whilst the bullets trickle out of the barrel, or bounce like harmless peas off the chest of my grinning foe while he begins unhurriedly to crush my rib cage.

10
————

Yesterday I invited several people, unacquainted among themselves but united by one and the same sacred task, which had so transfigured them that one could notice among them an inexpressible resemblance, such as occurs, for instance, among elderly Freemasons. They were people of various professions—a tailor, a masseur, a physician, a barber, a baker—but all exhibited the same dignified deportment, the same economy of gestures. And no wonder! One made his clothes, and that meant measuring his lean, yet broad-hipped body, with its odd, womanish pelvis and round back, and respectfully reaching into his armpits, and, together with him, looking into a mirror garlanded with gilt ivy; the second and third had penetrated even further: they had seen him naked, had kneaded his muscles and listened to his heart, by whose beat, it is said, our clocks will soon be set, so that his pulse, in the most literal sense, will become a basic unit of time; the fourth shaved him, with crepitating strokes, down on the cheeks and on the neck, using a blade that to me is enticingly sharp-looking; the fifth, and last, baked his bread, putting, the idiot, through sheer force of habit raisins instead of arsenic into his favorite loaf. I wanted to palpate these people, so as to partake at least in that way of their mysterious rites, of their diabolical manipulations; it seemed to me that their hands were imbued with his smell, that through those people he, too, was present. It was all very nice, very prim at that party. We talked about things that did not concern him, and I knew that if I mentioned his name there would flash in the eyes of each of them the same sacerdotal alarm. And when I suddenly found myself wearing a suit cut by my neighbor on the right, and eating my vis-à-vis' pastry, which I washed down with a special kind of mineral water prescribed by my neighbor on the left, I was overcome by a dreadful, dream-significant feeling, which immediately awakened me—in my poor-man's room, with a poor-man's moon in the curtainless window.

I am grateful to the night for even such a dream: of late I have been racked by insomnia. It is as if his agents were accustoming me beforehand to the most popular of the tortures inflicted on present-day criminals. I write "present-day" because, since he came to power, there has appeared a completely new breed, as it were, of political criminals (the other, penal, kind actually no longer exists, as the pettiest theft swells into embezzlement which, in turn, is considered an attempt to undermine the regime), exquisitely frail creatures, with a most diaphanous skin and protruding eyes emitting bright rays. This is a rare and highly valued breed, like a young okapi or the smallest species of lemur; they are hunted passionately, self-obliviously, and every captured specimen is hailed by public applause, even though the hunt actually involves no particular difficulty or danger, for they are quite tame, those strange, transparent beasts.

Timorous rumor has it that he himself is not loath to pay an occasional visit to the torture chamber, but there is probably no truth in this: the postmaster general does not distribute the mail himself, nor is the secretary of the navy necessarily a crack swimmer. I am in general repelled by the homey, gossipy tone with which meek ill-wishers speak of him, getting sidetracked into a special kind of primitive joke, as, in olden times, the common people would make up stories about the Devil, dressing up their superstitious fear in buffoonish humor. Vulgar, hastily adapted anecdotes (dating back, say, to Celtic prototypes), or secret information "from a usually reliable source" (as to who, for instance, is in favor and who is not) always smack of the servants' quarters. There are even worse examples, though: when my friend N., whose parents were executed only three years ago (to say nothing of the disgraceful persecution N. himself underwent), remarks, upon his return from an official festivity where he has heard and seen him, "You know, though, in spite of everything, there is a certain strength about that man," I feel like punching N. in the mug.

11
———

In the published letters of his "Sunset Years" a universally acclaimed foreign writer mentions that everything now leaves him cold, disenchanted, indifferent, everything with one exception: the vital, romantic thrill that he experiences to this day at the thought of how squalid his youthful years were compared with the sumptuous fulfillment of his later life, and of the snowy gleam of its summit, which he has now reached. That initial insignificance, that penumbra of poetry and pain, in which the young artist is on a par with a million such insignificant fellow beings, now lures him and fills him with excitement and gratitude—to his destiny, to his craft—and to his own creative will. Visits to places where he had once lived in want, and reunions with his coevals, elderly men of no note whatsoever, hold for him such a complex wealth of enchantment that the detailed study of these sensations will last him for his soul's future leisure in the hereafter.

Thus, when I try to imagine what our lugubrious ruler feels upon contact with *his* past, I clearly understand, first, that the real human being is a poet and, second, that he, our ruler, is the incarnate negation of a poet. And yet the foreign papers, especially those whose names have vesperal connotations and which know how easily "tales" can be transformed into "sales," are fond of stressing the legendary quality of his destiny, guiding their crowd of readers into the enormous black house where he was born, and where supposedly to this day live similar paupers, endlessly hanging out the wash (paupers do a great deal of washing); and they also print a photo, obtained God knows how, of his progenitress (father unknown), a thickset broad-nosed woman with a fringe who worked in an alehouse at the city gate. So few eyewitnesses of his boyhood and youth remain, and those who are still around respond with such circumspection (alas, no one has questioned *me*) that a journalist needs a great gift for invention to portray today's ruler excelling at warlike games as a boy or, as a youth, reading books till cockcrow. His demagogic luck is construed to be the elemental force of destiny, and, naturally, a great deal of attention is devoted to that overcast winter day when, upon his election to parliament, he and his gang arrested the parliament (after which the army, bleating meekly, went over at once to his side).

Not much of a myth, but still a myth (in this nuance the journalist was not mistaken), a myth that is a closed circle and a discrete whole, ready to begin living its own, insular life, and it is *already* impossible to replace it with the real truth, even though its hero is still alive: impossible, since he, the only one who could know the truth, is useless as a witness, and this not because he is prejudiced or dishonest, but because, like a runaway slave, he "doesn't remember"! Oh, he remembers his old enemies, of course, and two or three books he has read, and how the man thrashed him for falling off a woodpile and crushing to death a couple of chicks: that is, a certain crude mechanism of memory does function in him, but, if the gods were to propose that he synthesize himself out of his memories, with the condition that the synthesized image be rewarded with immortality, the result would be a dim embryo, an infant born prematurely, a blind and deaf dwarf, in no sense capable of immortality.

Should he visit the house where he lived when he was poor, no thrill would ripple his skin—not even a thrill of malevolent vanity. But I did visit his former abode! Not the multiplex edifice where he is supposed to have been born, and where there is now a museum dedicated to him (old posters, a flag grimy with gutter mud, in the place of honor, under a bell jar, a button: all that it was possible to preserve of his niggardly youth), but those vile furnished rooms where he spent several months during the period he and my brother were close. The former proprietor had long since died, roomers had never been registered, so that no trace was left of his erstwhile sojourn. And the thought that I alone in the world (for he has forgotten those lodgings of his—there have been so many) *knew* about this filled me with a special satisfaction, as if, by touching that dead furniture and looking at the neighboring roof through the window, I felt my hand closing on the key to his life.

12

I have just had yet another visitor: a very seedy old man, who was evidently in a state of extreme agitation: his tight-skinned, glossy-backed hands were trembling, a stale senile tear dampened the pink lining of his eyelids, and a pallid sequence of involuntary expressions, from a foolish smile to a crooked crease of pain, passed across his face. With the pen I lent him he traced on a scrap of paper the digits of a crucial year, day, and month: the date—nearly half a century past—of the ruler's birth. He rested his gaze on me, pen raised, as if not daring to continue, or simply using a semblance of hesitation to emphasize the little trick he was about to play. I answered with a nod of encouragement and impatience, whereupon he wrote another date, preceding the first by nine months, underlined it twice, parted his lips as if for a burst of triumphant laughter, but, instead, suddenly covered his face with his hands. "Come on, get to the point," I said, giving this indifferent actor's shoulder a shake. Quickly regaining his composure, he rummaged in his pocket and handed me a thick, stiff photograph, which, over the years, had acquired an opaque milky tint. It showed a husky young man in a soldier's uniform; his peaked cap lay on a chair, on whose back, with wooden ease, he rested his hand, while behind him you could make out the balustrade and the urn of a conventional backdrop. With the help of two or three connective glances I ascertained that between my guest's features and the shadowless, flat face of the soldier (adorned with a thin mustache, and topped by a brush cut, which made the forehead look smaller) there was little resemblance, but that nevertheless the soldier and he were the same person. In the snapshot he was about twenty, the snapshot itself was some fifty years old, and it was easy to fill this interval with the trite account of one of those third-rate lives, the imprint of which one reads (with an agonizing sense of superiority, sometimes unjustified) on the faces of old ragmen, public-garden attendants, and embittered invalids in the uniforms of old wars. I was about to pump him as to how it felt to live with such a secret, how he could carry the weight of that monstrous paternity, and incessantly see and hear his offspring's public presence—but then I noticed that the mazy and issueless design of the wallpaper was showing through his body; I stretched out my hand to detain my guest, but the dodderer dissolved, shivering from the chill of vanishment.

And yet he exists, this father (or existed until quite recently), and if only fate did not bestow on him a salutary ignorance as to the identity of his momentary bedmate, God knows what torment is at large among us, not daring to speak out, and perhaps made even more acute by the fact that the hapless fellow is not fully certain of his paternity, for the wench was a loose one, and in consequence there might be several like him in the world, indefatigably calculating dates, blundering in the hell of too many figures and too meager memories, ignobly dreaming of extracting profit from the shadows of the past, fearing instant punishment (for some error, or blasphemy, for the too odious truth), feeling rather proud in their heart of hearts (after all, he is the Ruler!), losing their mind between supputation and supposition—horrible, horrible!

13

————

Time passes, and meanwhile I get bogged down in wild, oppressive fancies. In fact, it astonishes me, for I know of a good number of resolute and even daring actions that I have to my credit, nor am I in the least afraid of the perilous consequences that an assassination attempt would have for me; on the contrary, while I have no clear idea at all of how the act itself will occur, I can make out distinctly the tussle that will immediately follow—the human tornado seizing me, the puppet-like jerkiness of my motions amid avid hands, the crack of clothes being ripped, the blinding red of the blows, and finally (should I emerge from this tussle alive) the iron grip of jailers, imprisonment, a swift trial, the torture chamber, the scaffold, all this to the thundering accompaniment of my mighty happiness. I do not expect that my fellow citizens will immediately perceive their own liberation; I can even allow that the regime might get harsher out of sheer inertia. There is nothing about me of the civic hero who dies for his people. I die only for myself, for the sake of my own world of good and truth—the good and the true, which are now distorted and violated within me and outside me, and if they are as precious to someone else as they are to me, all the better; if not, if my fatherland needs men of a different stamp than I, I willingly accept my uselessness, but will still perform my task.

My life is too much engrossed and submerged by my hatred to be in the least pleasant, and I do not fear the black nausea and agony of death, especially since I anticipate a degree of bliss, a level of supernatural being undreamt of either by barbarians or by modern followers of old religions. Thus, my mind is lucid and my hand free—and yet I don't know, I don't know how to go about killing him.

I sometimes think that perhaps it is so because murder, the intent to kill, is after all insufferably trite, and the imagination, reviewing methods of homicide and types of weapons, performs a degrading task, the sham of which is the more keenly felt, the more righteous the force that impels one. Or else, maybe I could not kill him out of squeamishness, as some people, while they feel a fierce aversion to anything that crawls, are unable so much as to crush a garden worm underfoot because for them it would be like stamping on the dust-begrimed extremities of their own innards. But whatever explanations I conjure up for my irresoluteness, it would be foolish to hide from myself the fact that I must destroy him. O Hamlet, O moony oaf!

14

He has just given a speech at the groundbreaking ceremony for a new, multistoried greenhouse, and, while he was at it, he touched on the equality of men and the equality of wheat ears in the field, using Latin or dog-Latin, for the sake of poetry, *arista*, *aristifer*, and even "aristize" (meaning "to ear")—I do not know what corny schoolman counseled him to adopt this questionable method, but, in recompense, I now understand why, of late, magazine verse contains such archaisms as:

> *How sapient the veterinarian*
> *Who physics the lactific kine.*

For two hours the enormous voice thundered throughout our city, erupting with varying degrees of force from this or that window, so that, if you walk along a street (which, by the way, is deemed a dangerous discourtesy: sit and listen), you have the impression that he accompanies you, crashing down from the rooftops, squirming on all fours between your legs, and sweeping up again to peck at your head, cackling, cawing, and quacking in a caricature of human speech, and you have no place to hide from the Voice, and the same thing is going on in every city and village of my successfully stunned country. Apparently no one except me has noticed an interesting feature of his frenzied oratory, namely the pause he makes after a particularly effective sentence, rather like a drunk who stands in the middle of the street, in the independent but unsatisfied solitude characteristic of drunks, and while declaiming fragments of an abusive monologue, most emphatic in its wrath, passion, and conviction, but obscure as to meaning and aim, stops frequently to collect his strength, ponder the next passage, let what he has said sink in; then, having waited out the pause, he repeats verbatim what he has just disgorged, but in a tone of voice suggesting that he has thought of a new argument, another absolutely new and irrefutable idea.

When the Ruler at last ran dry, and the faceless, cheekless trumpets played our agrarian anthem, I not only did not feel relieved, but, on the contrary, had a sense of anguish and loss: while he was speaking I could at least keep watch over him, could know where he was and what he was doing; now he has again dissolved into the air, which I breathe but which has no tangible point of focus.

I can understand the smooth-haired women of our mountain tribes when, abandoned by a lover, every morning, with a persistent pressure of their brown fingers on the turquoise head of a pin, they prick the navel of a clay figurine representing the fugitive. Many times, of late, I have summoned all the force of my mind to imagine at a given moment the flow of his cares and thoughts, in order to duplicate the rhythm of his existence, making it yield and come crashing down, like a suspension bridge whose own oscillations have coincided with the cadenced step of a detachment of soldiers crossing it. The soldiers will also perish—so shall I, losing my reason the instant that I catch the rhythm, while he falls dead in his distant castle; however, no matter what the method of tyrannicide, I would not survive. When I wake up in the morning, at half past eight or so, I strain to conjure up his awakening: he gets up neither early nor late, at an average hour, just as he calls himself—even officially, I think—an "average man." At nine both he and I breakfast frugally on a glass of milk and a bun, and, if on a given day I am not busy at the school, I continue my pursuit of his thoughts. He reads through several newspapers, and I read them with

him, searching for something that might catch his attention, even
though I know he was aware the evening before of the general content
of my morning paper, of its leading articles, its summaries and national
news, so that this perusal can give him no particular cause for administrative meditation. After which his assistants come with reports and
queries. Together with him, I learn how rail communications are feeling today, how heavy industry is sweating along, and how many cent-
ners per hectare the winter wheat crop yielded this year. After looking
through several petitions for clemency and tracing on them his invariable refusal—a penciled X—the symbol of his heart's illiteracy—he
takes his usual walk before lunch: as in the case of many not overbright
people devoid of imagination, walking is his favorite exercise; he walks
in his walled garden, formerly a large prison yard. I am also familiar
with the menu of his unpretentious lunch, after which I share my siesta
with him and ponder plans for making his power flourish further, or
new measures for suppressing sedition. In the afternoon we inspect a
new building, a fortress, a forum, and other forms of governmental
prosperity, and I approve with him an inventor's new kind of venti-
lator. I skip dinner, usually a gala affair with various functionaries in
attendance, but, on the other hand, by nightfall my thoughts have re-
doubled their force and I issue orders to newspaper editors, listen to
accounts of evening meetings, and, alone in my darkening room, whisper, gesticulate, and ever more insanely hope that at least one of my
thoughts may fall in step with a thought of his—and then, I know, the
bridge will snap, like a violin string. But the ill luck familiar to overly
eager gamblers haunts me, the right card never comes, even though I
must have achieved a certain secret liaison with him, for around eleven
o'clock, when he goes to bed, my entire being senses a collapse, a void,
a weakening, and a melancholy relief. Presently he sleeps, he sleeps,
and, since, on his convict's cot, not a single praedormitory thought
troubles him, I too am left at liberty, and only occasionally, without
the least hope of success, try to compose his dreams, combining fragments of his past with impressions of the present; probably, though, he
does not dream and I work in vain, and never, never, will the night be
rent by a royal death rattle, leading history to comment: "The dictator
died in his sleep."

15

How can I get rid of him? I cannot stand it any longer. Everything is full of him, everything I love has been besmirched, everything has become his likeness, his mirror image, and, in the features of passersby and in the eyes of my wretched schoolchildren, his countenance shows ever clearer and more hopelessly. Not only the posters that I am obliged to have them copy in color do nothing but interpret the pattern of his personality, but even the simple white cube I give the younger classes to draw seems to me his portrait—perhaps his best portrait. O cubic monster, how can I eradicate you?

16

And suddenly I realized I had a way! It was on a frosty, motionless morning, with a pale pink sky and lumps of ice lodged in the drainpipes' jaws; there was a doomful stillness everywhere: in an hour the town would awake, and how it would awake! That day his fiftieth birthday was to be celebrated, and already people, looking against the snow like black quarter notes, were creeping out into the streets, so as to gather on schedule at the points where they would be marshaled into different marching groups determined by their trades. At the risk of losing my meager pay, I was not making ready to join any festive procession; I had something else, a little more important, on my mind. Standing by the window, I could hear the first distant fanfares and the radio barker's inducements at the crossroads, and I found comfort in the thought that I, and I alone, could interrupt all this. Yes, the solution had been found: the assassination of the tyrant now turned out to be something so simple and quick that I could accomplish it without leaving my room. The only weapons available for the purpose were either an old but very well preserved revolver, or a hook over the window that must have served at one time to support a drapery rod. This last was even better, as I had my doubts about the performance of the twenty-five-year-old cartridge.

By killing myself I would kill him, as he was totally inside me, fattened on the intensity of my hatred. Along with him I would kill the world he had created, all the stupidity, cowardice, and cruelty of that world, which, together with him, had grown huge within me, ousting, to the last sun-bathed landscape, to the last memory of childhood, all the treasures I had collected. Conscious now of my power, I reveled in it, unhurriedly preparing for self-destruction, going through my belongings, correcting this chronicle of mine. And then, abruptly, the incredible intensification of all the senses that had overwhelmed me underwent a strange, almost alchemic metamorphosis. The festivities were spreading outside my window, the sun transformed the blue snowdrifts into sparkling down, and one could see playing over distant roofs, a new kind of fireworks (invented recently by a peasant genius) whose colors blazed even in broad daylight. The general jubilation; the Ruler's gem-bright likeness flashing pyrotechnically in the heavens; the gay hues of the procession winding across the river's snowy cover; the delightful pasteboard symbols of the fatherland's welfare; the slogans, designed with variety and elegance, that bobbed above the marchers' shoulders; the jaunty primitive music; the orgy of banners; the contented faces of the young yokels and the national costumes of the hefty wenches—all of it caused a crimson wave of tenderness to surge within me, and I understood my sin against our great and merciful Master. Is it not he who manured our fields, who directed the poor to be shod, he whom we must thank for every second of our civic being? Tears of repentance, hot, good tears, gushed from my eyes onto the windowsill when I thought how I had been repudiating the kindness of the Master, how blindly I had reneged the beauty of what he had created, the social order, the way of life, the splendid walnut-finished new fences, and how I plotted to lay hands on myself, daring, thus, to endanger the life of one of his subjects! The festivities, as I have said, were spreading; I stood at the window, my whole being drenched with tears and convulsed with laughter, listening to the verses of our foremost poet, declaimed on the radio by an actor's juicy voice, replete with baritone modulations:

> Now then, citizens,
> You remember how long
> Our land wilted without a Father?
> Thus, without hops, no matter how strong
> One's thirst, it is rather
> Difficult, isn't it,
> To make both the beer and the drinking song!
> Just imagine, we lacked potatoes,
> No turnips, no beets could we get:

> *Thus the poem, now blooming, wasted*
> *In the bulbs of the alphabet!*
> *A well-trodden road we had taken,*
> *Bitter toadstools we ate,*
> *Until by great thumps was shaken*
> *History's gate!*
> *Until in his trim white tunic*
> *Which upon us its radiance cast,*
> *With his wonderful smile the Ruler*
> *Came before his subjects at last!*

Yes, "radiance," yes, "toadstools," yes, "wonderful," that's right. I, a little man, I, the blind beggar who today has gained his sight, fall on my knees and repent before you. Execute me—no, even better, pardon me, for the block is your pardon, and your pardon the block, illuminating with an aching benignant light the whole of my iniquity. You are our pride, our glory, our banner! O magnificent, gentle giant, who intently and lovingly watches over us, I swear to serve you from this day on, I swear to be like all your other nurslings, I swear to be yours indivisibly, and so forth, and so forth, and so forth.

17

Laughter, actually, saved me. Having experienced all the degrees of hatred and despair, I achieved those heights from which one obtains a bird's-eye view of the ludicrous. A roar of hearty mirth cured me, as it did, in a children's storybook, the gentleman "in whose throat an abscess burst at the sight of a poodle's hilarious tricks." Rereading my chronicle, I see that, in my efforts to make him terrifying, I have only made him ridiculous, thereby destroying him—an old, proven method. Modest as I am in evaluating my muddled composition, something nevertheless tells me that it is not the work of an ordinary pen. Far from having literary aspirations, and yet full of words forged over the years in my enraged silence, I have made my point with sincerity and fullness of feeling where another would have made it with artistry and inventiveness. This is an incantation, an exorcism, so that henceforth any man can exorcise bondage. I believe in miracles. I believe that in some way, unknown to me, this chronicle will reach other men, neither tomorrow nor the next day, but at a distant time when the world has a day or so of leisure for archaeological diggings, on the eve of new annoyances, no less amusing than the present ones. And, who knows—I may be right not to rule out the thought that my chance labor may prove immortal, and may accompany the ages, now persecuted, now exalted, often dangerous, and always useful. While I, a "boneless shadow," *un fantôme sans os*, will be content if the fruit of my forgotten insomnious nights serves for a long time as a kind of secret remedy against future tyrants, tigroid monsters, half-witted torturers of man.

LIK

T HERE is a play of the 1920s, called *L'Abîme* (*The Abyss*),
by the well-known French author Suire. It has already passed
from the stage straight into the Lesser Lethe (the one, that is,
that serves the theater—a stream, incidentally, not quite as hopeless as
the main river, and containing a weaker solution of oblivion, so that
angling producers may still fish something out many years later). This
play—essentially idiotic, even ideally idiotic, or, putting it another
way, ideally constructed on the solid conventions of traditional drama-
turgy—deals with the torments of a middle-aged, rich, and religious
French lady suddenly inflamed by a sinful passion for a young Russian
named Igor, who has turned up at her château and fallen in love with
her daughter Angélique. An old friend of the family, a strong-willed,
sullen bigot, conveniently knocked together by the author out of mysticism and lechery, is jealous of the heroine's interest in Igor, while she
in turn is jealous of the latter's attentions to Angélique; in a word, it is
all very compelling and true to life, every speech bears the trademark of
a respectable tradition, and it goes without saying that there is not a
single jolt of talent to disrupt the ordered course of action, swelling
where it ought to swell, and interrupted when necessary by a lyric
scene or a shamelessly explanatory dialogue between two old retainers.

The apple of discord is usually an early, sour fruit, and should be
cooked. Thus the young man of the play threatens to be somewhat
colorless, and it is in a vain attempt to touch him up a little that the
author has made him a Russian, with all the obvious consequences of
such trickery. According to Suire's optimistic intention, he is an émigré
Russian aristocrat, recently adopted by an old lady, the Russian wife of
a neighboring landowner. One night, at the height of a thunderstorm,
Igor comes knocking at our door, enters, riding crop in hand, and an-
nounces in agitation that the pinewood is burning on his benefactress's

461

estate, and that our pinery is also in danger. This affects us less strongly than the visitor's youthful glamour, and we are inclined to sink onto a hassock, toying pensively with our necklace, whereupon our bigot friend observes that the reflection of flames is at times more dangerous than the conflagration itself. A solid, high-quality plot, as you can see, for it is clear at once that the Russian will become a regular caller and, in fact, Act Two is all sunny weather and bright summer clothes.

Judging by the printed text of the play, Igor expresses himself (at least in the first scenes, before the author tires of this) not incorrectly but, as it were, a bit hesitantly, every so often interposing a questioning "I think that is how you say it in French?" Later, though, when the turbulent flow of the drama leaves the author no time for such trifles, all foreign peculiarities of speech are discarded and the young Russian spontaneously acquires the rich vocabulary of a native Frenchman; it is only toward the end, during the lull before the final burst of action, that the playwright remembers with a start the nationality of Igor, whereupon the latter casually addresses these words to the old man-servant: *"J'étais trop jeune pour prendre part à la . . . comment dit-on . . . velika voïna . . . grande, grande guerre. . . ."* In all fairness to the author, it is true that, except for this *"velika voïna"* and one modest *"dosvidania,"* he does not abuse his acquaintance with the Russian language, contenting himself with the stage direction "Slavic singsong lends a certain charm to Igor's speech."

In Paris, where the play had great success, Igor was played by François Coulot, and played not badly but for some reason with a strong Italian accent, which he evidently wanted to pass off as Russian, and which did not surprise a single Parisian critic. Afterwards, when the play trickled down into the provinces, this role fell by chance to a real Russian actor, Lik (stage name of Lavrentiy Ivanovich Kruzhev-nitsyn), a lean, fair-haired fellow with coffee-dark eyes, who had previously won some fame, thanks to a film in which he did an excellent job in the bit part of a stutterer.

It was hard to say, though, if Lik (the word means "countenance" in Russian and Middle English) possessed genuine theatrical talent or was a man of many indistinct callings who had chosen one of them at random but could just as well have been a painter, jeweler, or rat-catcher. Such a person resembles a room with a number of different doors, among which there is perhaps one that does lead straight into some great garden, into the moonlit depths of a marvelous human night, where the soul discovers the treasure intended for it alone. But, be that as it may, Lik had failed to open *that* door, taking instead the Thespian path, which he followed without enthusiasm, with the absent manner of a man looking for signposts that do not exist but that perhaps have appeared to him in a dream, or can be distinguished in the undeveloped photograph of some other locality that he will never, never visit. On the conventional plane of earthly habitus, he was in his thirties, and so was the century. In elderly people stranded not only outside the border of their country but outside that of their own lives, nostalgia evolves into an extraordinarily complex organ, which functions continuously, and its secretion compensates for all that has been lost; or else it becomes a fatal tumor on the soul that makes it painful to breathe, sleep, and associate with carefree foreigners. In Lik, this memory of Russia remained in the embryonic state, confined to misty childhood recollections, such as the resinous fragrance of the first spring day in the country, or the special shape of the snowflake on the wool of his hood. His parents were dead. He lived alone. There was always something sleazy about the loves and friendships that came his way. Nobody wrote gossipy letters to him, nobody took a greater interest in his worries than he did himself, and there was no one to go and complain to about the undeserved precariousness of his very being when he learned from two doctors, a Frenchman and a Russian, that (like many protagonists) he had an incurable heart ailment—while the streets were virtually swarming with robust oldsters. There seemed to be a certain connection between this illness of his and his fondness for fine, expensive things; he might, for example, spend his last 200 francs on a scarf or a fountain pen, but it always, always happened that the scarf would soon get soiled, the pen broken, despite the meticulous, even pious, care he took of things.

In relation to the other members of the company, which he had joined as casually as a fur doffed by a woman lands on this or that quite anonymous chair, he remained as much a stranger as he had been at the first rehearsal. He had immediately had the feeling of being superfluous, of having usurped someone else's place. The director of the company was invariably friendly toward him, but Lik's hypersensitive soul constantly imagined the possibility of a row—as if at any moment he might be unmasked and accused of something unbearably shameful. The very constancy of the director's attitude he interpreted as the utmost indifference to his work, as though everyone had long since reconciled himself to its hopelessly poor quality—and he was being tolerated merely because there was no convenient pretext for his dismissal.

It seemed to him—and perhaps this was actually so—that to these loud, sleek French actors, interconnected by a network of personal and professional passions, he was as much a chance object as the old bicycle that one of the characters deftly disassembled in the second act; hence, when someone gave him a particularly hearty greeting or offered him a cigarette, he would think that there was some misunderstanding, which would, alas, be resolved in a moment. Because of his illness he avoided drinking, but his absence from friendly gatherings, instead of being attributed to lack of sociability (leading to accusations of haughtiness and thus endowing him with, at least, some semblance of a personality), simply went unnoticed, as if there was no question of its being otherwise; and when they did happen to invite him somewhere, it was always in a vaguely interrogative manner ("Coming with us, or . . . ?")—a manner particularly painful to one who is yearning to be persuaded to come. He understood little of the jokes, allusions, and nicknames that the others bandied about with cryptic gaiety. He almost wished some of the joking were at his expense, but even this failed to happen. At the same time, he rather liked some of his colleagues. The actor who played the bigot was in real life a pleasant fat fellow, who had recently purchased a sports car, about which he would talk to you with genuine inspiration. And the ingénue was most charming, too—dark-haired and slender, with her splendidly bright, carefully made-up eyes—but in daytime hopelessly oblivious of her evening confessions on the stage in the garrulous embrace of her Russian fiancé, to whom she so candidly clung. Lik liked to tell himself that only on the stage did she live her true life, being subject the rest of the time to periodic fits of insanity, during which she no longer recognized him and called herself by a different name. With the leading lady he never exchanged a single word apart from their lines, and when this thickset, tense, handsome woman walked past him in the wings, her jowls shaking, he had the feeling that he was but a piece of scenery, apt to fall flat on the floor if someone brushed against him. It is indeed difficult to say whether it was all as poor Lik imagined or whether these perfectly harmless, self-centered people left him alone simply because he did not seek their company, and did not start a conversation with him just as passengers who have established contact among themselves do not address the foreigner absorbed in his book in a corner of the compartment. But even if Lik did attempt in rare moments of self-confidence to convince himself of the irrationality of his vague torments, the memory of similar torments was too recent, and they were too often repeated in new circumstances, for him to be able to overcome them now. Loneliness as a situation can be corrected, but as a state of mind it is an incurable illness.

He played his part conscientiously, and, at least as far as accent was concerned, more successfully than his predecessor, since Lik spoke

French with a Russian lilt, drawing out and softening his sentences, dropping the stress before their close, and filtering off with excessive care the spray of auxiliary expressions that so nimbly and rapidly fly off a Frenchman's tongue. His part was so small, so inconsequential, in spite of its dramatic impact on the actions of the other characters, that it was not worth pondering over; yet he would ponder, especially at the outset of the tour, and not so much out of love for his art as because the disparity between the insignificance of the role itself and the importance of the complex drama of which he was the prime cause struck him as being a paradox that somehow humiliated him personally. However, although he soon cooled to the possibility of improvements suggested to him by both art and vanity (two things that often coincide), he would hurry onstage with unchanged, mysterious delight, as though, every time, he anticipated some special reward—in no way connected, of course, with the customary dose of neutral applause. Neither did this reward consist in the performer's inner satisfaction. Rather, it lurked in certain extraordinary furrows and folds that he discerned in the life of the play itself, banal and hopelessly pedestrian as it was, for, like any piece acted out by live people, it gained, God knows whence, an individual soul, and attempted for a couple of hours to exist, to evolve its own heat and energy, bearing no relation to its author's pitiful conception or the mediocrity of the players, but awakening, as life awakes in water warmed by sunlight. For instance, Lik might hope, one vague and lovely night, in the midst of the usual performance, to tread, as it were, on a quicksandy spot; something would give, and he would sink forever in a newborn element, unlike anything known—independently developing the play's threadbare themes in ways altogether new. He would pass irrevocably into this element, marry Angélique, go riding over the crisp heather, receive all the material wealth hinted at in the play, go to live in that castle, and, moreover, find himself in a world of ineffable tenderness—a bluish, delicate world where fabulous adventures of the senses occur, and unheard-of metamorphoses of the mind. As he thought about all this, Lik imagined for some reason that when he died of heart failure—and he would die soon—the attack would certainly come onstage, as it had been with poor Molière, barking out his dog Latin among the doctors; but that he would not notice his death, crossing over instead into the actual world of a chance play, now blooming anew because of his arrival, while his smiling corpse lay on the boards, the toe of one foot protruding from beneath the folds of the lowered curtain.

At the end of the summer, *The Abyss* and two other plays in the repertory were running at a Mediterranean town. Lik appeared only in

The Abyss, so between the first performance and the second (only two were scheduled) he had a week of free time, which he did not quite know how to use. What is more, the southern climate did not agree with him; he went through the first performance in a blur of greenhouse delirium, with a hot drop of greasepaint now hanging from the tip of his nose, now scalding his upper lip, and when, during the first intermission, he went out on the terrace separating the back of the theater from an Anglican church, he suddenly felt he would not last out the performance, but would dissolve on the stage amid many-colored exhalations, through which, at the final mortal instant, would flash the blissful ray of another—yes, another life. Nevertheless, he made it to the end somehow or other, even if he did see double from the sweat in his eyes, while the smooth contact of his young partner's cool bare arms agonizingly accentuated the melting state of his palms. He returned to his boardinghouse quite shattered, with aching shoulders and a reverberating pain in the back of his head. In the dark garden, everything was in bloom and smelled of candy, and there was a continuous trilling of crickets, which he mistook (as all Russians do) for cicadas.

His illuminated room was antiseptically white compared to the southern darkness framed in the open window. He crushed a red-bellied drunken mosquito on the wall, then sat for a long time on the edge of the bed, afraid to lie down, afraid of the palpitations. The proximity of the sea whose presence he divined beyond the lemon grove oppressed him, as if this ample, viscously glistening space, with only a membrane of moonlight stretched tight across its surface, was akin to the equally taut vessel of his drumming heart, and, like it, was agonizingly bare, with nothing to separate it from the sky, from the shuffling of human feet and the unbearable pressure of the music playing in a nearby bar. He glanced at the expensive watch on his wrist and noticed with a pang that he had lost the crystal; yes, his cuff had brushed against a stone parapet as he had stumbled uphill a while ago. The watch was still alive, defenseless and naked, like a live organ exposed by the surgeon's knife.

He passed his days in a quest for shade and a longing for coolness. There was something infernal in the glimpses of sea and beach, where bronzed demons basked on the torrid shingle. The sunny side of the narrow streets was so strictly forbidden to him that he would have had to solve intricate route-finding problems if there had been purpose in his wanderings. He had, however, nowhere to go. He strolled aimlessly along the shop fronts, which displayed, among other objects, some rather amusing bracelets of what looked like pink amber, as well as decidedly attractive leather bookmarks and wallets tooled with gilt. He would sink into a chair beneath the orange awning of a café, then go home and lie on his bed—stark naked, dreadfully thin and white—and think about the same things he thought about incessantly.

He reflected that he had been condemned to live on the outskirts of life, that it had always been thus and always would be, and that, therefore, if death did not present him with an exit into true reality, he would simply never come to know life. He also reflected that if his parents were alive instead of having died at the dawn of émigré existence, the fifteen years of his adult life might have passed in the warmth of a family; that, had his destiny been less mobile, he would have finished one of the three gymnasiums he had happened to attend at random points of middle, median, mediocre Europe, and would now have a good, solid job among good, solid people. But, strain his imagination as he might, he could not picture either that job or those people, just as he could not explain to himself why he had studied as a youth at a screen-acting school, instead of taking up music or numismatics, window-washing or bookkeeping. And, as always, from each point of its circumference his thought would follow a radius back to the dark center, to the presentiment of nearing death, for which he, who had accumulated no spiritual treasures, was hardly an interesting prey. Nonetheless, she had apparently determined to give him precedence.

One evening, as he was reclining in a canvas chair on the veranda, he was importuned by one of the pension guests, a loquacious old Russian (who had managed on two occasions already to recount to Lik the story of his life, first in one direction, from the present toward the past, and then in the other, against the grain, resulting in two different lives, one successful, the other not), who, settling himself comfortably and fingering his chin, said: "A friend of mine has turned up here; that is, a 'friend,' *c'est beaucoup dire*—I met him a couple of times in Brussels, that's all. Now, alas, he's a completely derelict character. Yesterday—yes, I think it was yesterday—I happened to mention your name, and he says, 'Why, of course I know him—in fact, we're even relatives.' "

"Relatives?" asked Lik with surprise. "I almost never had any relatives. What's his name?"

"A certain Koldunov—Oleg Petrovich Koldunov. . . . Petrovich, isn't it? Know him?"

"It just can't be!" cried Lik, covering his face with his hands.

"Yes. Imagine!" said the other.

"It can't be," repeated Lik. "You see, I always thought— This is awful! You didn't give him my address, did you?"

"I did. I understand, though. One feels disgusted and sorry at the same time. Kicked out of everywhere, embittered, has a family, and so on."

"Listen, do me a favor. Can't you tell him I've left."

"If I see him, I'll tell him. But . . . well, I just happened to run into him down at the port. My, what lovely yachts they have down there. That's what I call fortunate people. You live on the water, and sail wherever you feel like. Champagne, girlies, everything all polished . . ."

And the old fellow smacked his lips and shook his head.

What a mad thing to happen, Lik thought all evening. What a mess. . . . He did not know what had given him the idea that Oleg Koldunov was no longer among the living. It was one of those axioms that the rational mind no longer keeps on active duty, relegating it to the remotest depths of consciousness, so that now, with Koldunov's resurrection, he had to admit the possibility of two parallel lines crossing after all; yet it was agonizingly difficult to get rid of the old concept, embedded in his brain—as if the extraction of this single false notion might vitiate the entire order of his other notions and concepts. And now he simply could not recall what data had led him to conclude that Koldunov had perished, and why, in the past twenty years, there had been such a strengthening in the chain of dim initial information out of which Koldunov's doom had been wrought.

Their mothers had been cousins. Oleg Koldunov was two years his elder; for four years they had gone to the same provincial gymnasium, and the memory of those years had always been so hateful to Lik that he preferred not to recall his boyhood. Indeed, his Russia was perhaps so thickly clouded over for the very reason that he did not cherish any personal recollections. Dreams, however, would still occur even now, for there was no control over them. Sometimes Koldunov would appear in person, in his own image, in the surroundings of boyhood, hastily assembled by the director of dreams out of such accessories as a classroom, desks, a blackboard, and its dry, weightless sponge. Besides these down-to-earth dreams there were also romantic, even decadent ones—devoid, that is, of Koldunov's obvious presence but coded by him, saturated with his oppressive spirit or filled with rumors about him, with situations and shadows of situations somehow expressing his essence. And this excruciating Koldunovian decor, against which the action of a chance dream would develop, was far worse than the straightforward dream visitations of Koldunov as Lik remembered him—a coarse, muscular high school boy, with cropped hair and a disagreeably handsome face. The regularity of his strong features was spoiled by eyes that were set too close together and equipped with heavy, leathery lids (no wonder they had dubbed him "The Crocodile," for indeed there was a certain turbid muddy-Nile quality in his glance).

Koldunov had been a hopelessly poor student; his was that peculiarly Russian hopelessness of the seemingly bewitched dunce as he sinks, in a vertical position, through the transparent strata of several repeated classes, so that the youngest boys gradually reach his level, numb with fear, and then, a year later, leave him behind with relief. Koldunov was remarkable for his insolence, uncleanliness, and savage physical strength; after one had a tussle with him, the room would always reek of the menagerie. Lik, on the other hand, was a frail, sensitive, vulnerably proud boy, and therefore represented an ideal, inexhaustible prey. Koldunov would come flowing over him wordlessly, and industriously torture the squashed but always squirming victim on the floor. Koldunov's enormous, splayed palm would go into an obscene, scooping motion as it penetrated the convulsive, panic-stricken depths it sought. Thereupon he would leave Lik, whose back was covered with chalk dust and whose tormented ears were aflame, in peace for an hour or two, content to repeat some obscenely meaningless phrase, insulting to Lik. Then, when the urge returned, Koldunov would sigh, almost reluctantly, before piling on him again, digging his hornlike nails into Lik's ribs or sitting down for a rest on the victim's face. He had a thorough knowledge of all the bully's devices for causing the sharpest pain without leaving marks, and therefore enjoyed the servile respect of his schoolmates. At the same time he nurtured a vaguely sentimental affection for his habitual patient, making a point of strolling with his arm around the other's shoulders during the class breaks, his heavy, distrait paw palpating the thin collarbone, while Lik tried in vain to preserve an air of independence and dignity. Thus Lik's school days were an utterly absurd and unbearable torment. He was embarrassed to complain to anyone, and his nighttime thoughts of how he would finally kill Koldunov merely drained his spirit of all strength. Fortunately, they almost never met outside of school, although Lik's mother would have liked to establish closer ties with her cousin, who was much richer than she and kept her own horses. Then the Revolution began rearranging the furniture, and Lik found himself in a different city, while fifteen-year-old Oleg, already sporting a mustache and completely brutified, disappeared in the general confusion, and a blissful lull began. It was soon replaced, however, by new, more subtle tortures at the hands of the initial rackmaster's minor successors.

Sad to say, on the rare occasions when Lik spoke of his past, he would publicly recall the presumed deceased with that artificial smile with which we reward a distant time ("Those were the happy days") that sleeps with a full belly in a corner of its evil-smelling cage. Now, however, when Koldunov proved to be alive, no matter what adult arguments Lik invoked, he could not conquer the same sensation of helplessness—metamorphosed by reality but all the more manifest—that oppressed him in dreams when from behind a curtain, smirking, fiddling with his belt buckle, stepped the lord of the dream, a dark, dreadful schoolboy. And, even though Lik understood perfectly well that the real, live Koldunov would not harm him now, the possibility of meeting him seemed ominous, fateful, dimly linked to the whole system of evil, with its premonitions of torment and abuse, so familiar to him.

After his conversation with the old man, Lik decided to stay at home as little as possible. Only three days remained before the last performance, so it was not worth the trouble to move to a different boardinghouse; but he could, for instance, take daylong trips across the Italian border or into the mountains, since the weather had grown much cooler, with a drizzling rain and a brisk wind. Early next morning, walking along a narrow path between flower-hung walls, he saw coming toward him a short, husky man, whose dress in itself differed little from the usual uniform of the Mediterranean vacationer—beret, open-necked shirt, espadrilles—but somehow suggested not so much the license of the season as the compulsion of poverty. In the first instant, Lik was struck most of all by the fact that the monstrous figure that filled his memory with its bulk proved to be in reality hardly taller than himself.

"Lavrentiy, Lavrusha, don't you recognize me?" Koldunov drawled dramatically, stopping in the middle of the path.

The large features of that sallow face with a rough shadow on its cheeks and upper lip, that glimpse of bad teeth, that large, insolent Roman nose, that bleary, questioning gaze—all of it was Koldunovian, indisputably so, even if dimmed by time. But, as Lik looked, this resemblance noiselessly disintegrated, and before him stood a disreputable stranger with the massive face of a Caesar, though a very shabby one.

"Let's kiss like good Russians," Koldunov said grimly, and pressed his cold, salty cheek for an instant against Lik's childish lips.

"I recognized you immediately," babbled Lik. "Just yesterday I heard about you from What's-His-Name . . . Gavrilyuk."

"Dubious character," interrupted Koldunov. "*Méfie-toi*. Well, well—so here is my Lavrusha. Remarkable! I'm glad. Glad to meet you again. That's fate for you! Remember, Lavrusha, how we used to catch gobies together? As clear as if it happened yesterday. One of my fondest memories. Yes."

Lik knew perfectly well that he had never fished with Koldunov, but confusion, ennui, and timidity prevented him from accusing this stranger of appropriating a nonexistent past. He suddenly felt wiggly and overdressed.

"How many times," continued Koldunov, examining with interest Lik's pale-gray trousers, "how many times during the past years . . . Oh, yes, I thought of you. Yes, indeed! And where, thought I, is my Lavrusha? I've told my wife about you. She was once a pretty woman. And what line of work are you in?"

"I'm an actor," sighed Lik.

"Allow me an indiscretion," said Koldunov in a confidential tone. "I'm told that in the United States there is a secret society that considers the word 'money' improper, and if payment must be made, they wrap the dollars in toilet paper. True, only the rich belong—the poor have no time for it. Now, here's what I'm driving at," and, his brows raised questioningly, Koldunov made a vulgar, palpating motion with two fingers and thumb—the feel of hard cash.

"Alas, no!" Lik exclaimed innocently. "Most of the year I'm unemployed, and the pay is miserable."

"I know how it is and understand perfectly," said Koldunov with a smile. "In any case . . . Oh, yes—in any case, there's a project I'd like to discuss with you sometime. You could make a nice little profit. Are you doing anything right now?"

"Well, you see, as a matter of fact, I'm going to Bordighera for the whole day, by bus. . . . And tomorrow . . ."

"What a shame—if you had told me, there's a Russian chauffeur I know here, with a smart private car, and I would have shown you the whole Riviera. You ninny! All right, all right. I'll walk you to the bus stop."

"And anyway I'm leaving for good soon," Lik put in.

"Tell me, how's the family? . . . How's Aunt Natasha?" Koldunov asked absently as they walked along a crowded little street that led down to the seafront. "I see, I see," he nodded at Lik's reply. Suddenly a guilty, demented look passed fleetingly across his evil face. "Listen, Lavrusha," he said, pushing him involuntarily and bringing his face close to Lik's on the narrow sidewalk. "Meeting you is an omen for me. It is a sign that all is not lost yet, and I must admit that just the other day I was thinking that all *was* lost. Do you understand what I am saying?"

"Oh, everybody has such thoughts now and then," said Lik.

They reached the promenade. The sea was opaque and corrugated under the overcast sky, and, here and there near the parapet, the foam had splashed onto the pavement. There was no one about except for a solitary lady in slacks sitting on a bench with an open book in her lap.

"Here, give me five francs and I'll buy you some cigarettes for the trip," Koldunov said rapidly. Taking the money, he added in a different, easy tone, "Look, that's the little wife over there—keep her company for a minute, and I'll be right back."

Lik went up to the blond lady and said with an actor's automatism, "Your husband will be right back and forgot to introduce me. I'm a cousin of his."

At the same moment he was sprinkled by the cool dust of a breaker. The lady looked up at Lik with blue, English eyes, unhurriedly closed her red book, and left without a word.

"Just a joke," said Koldunov, as he reappeared, out of breath. "Voilà. I'll take a few for myself. Yes, I'm afraid my little woman has no time to sit on a bench and look at the sea. I implore you, promise me that we'll meet again. Remember the omen! Tomorrow, after tomorrow, whenever you want. Promise me! Wait, I'll give you my address."

He took Lik's brand-new gilt-and-leather notebook, sat down, bent forward his sweaty, swollen-veined forehead, joined his knees, and not only wrote his address, reading it over with agonizing care, redotting an *i* and underlining a word, but also sketched a street map: so, so, then so. Evidently he had done this more than once, and more than once people had stood him up, using the forgotten address as an excuse; hence he wrote with great diligence and force—a force that was almost incantational.

The bus arrived. "So, I'll expect you!" shouted Koldunov, helping Lik aboard. Then he turned, full of energy and hope, and walked resolutely off along the promenade as if he had some pressing, important business, though it was perfectly obvious that he was an idler, a drunkard, and a boor.

The following day, a Wednesday, Lik took a trip to the mountains, and then spent the greater part of Thursday lying in his room with a bad headache. The performance was that evening, the departure tomorrow. At about six in the afternoon he went out to pick up his watch at the jeweler's and buy some nice white shoes—an innovation he had long wanted to sport in the second act. Separating the bead curtain, he emerged from the shop, shoebox under arm, and ran straight into Koldunov.

Koldunov's greeting lacked the former ardor, and had a slightly derisive note instead. "Oho! You won't wriggle out of it this time," he said, taking Lik firmly by the elbow. "Come on, let's go. You'll see how I live and work."

"I have a performance tonight," Lik objected, "and I'm leaving tomorrow!"

"That's just the point, my friend, that's just the point. Seize the opportunity! Take advantage of it! There will never be another chance. The card is trumped! Come on. Get going."

Repeating disconnected words and imitating with all his unattractive being the senseless joy of a man who has reached the borderline, and perhaps even gone beyond it (a poor imitation, Lik thought vaguely), Koldunov walked briskly, prodding on his weak companion. The entire company of actors was sitting on the terrace of a corner café, and, noticing Lik, greeted him with a peripatetic smile that really did not belong to any one member of the group, but skittered across the lips of each like an independent spot of reflected sunlight.

Koldunov led Lik up a crooked little street, mottled here and there by jaundiced, crooked sunlight. Lik had never visited this squalid, old quarter. The tall, bare façades of the narrow houses seemed to lean over the pavement from either side, with their tops almost meeting; sometimes they coalesced completely, forming an arch. Repulsive infants were puttering about by the doorways; black, foul-smelling water ran down the sidewalk gutter. Suddenly changing direction, Koldunov shoved him into a shop and, flaunting the cheapest French slang (in the manner of many Russian paupers), bought two bottles of wine with Lik's money. It was evident that he was long since in debt here, and now there was a desperate glee in his whole bearing and in his menacing exclamations of greeting, which brought no response whatever from either the shopkeeper or the shopkeeper's mother-in-law, and this made Lik even more uncomfortable. They walked on, turning into an alley, and although it had seemed that the vile street they had just ascended represented the utmost limit of squalor, filth, and congestion, this passage, with limp wash hanging overhead, managed to embody an even greater dejection. At the corner of a lopsided little square, Koldunov said that he would go in first, and, leaving Lik, headed for the black cavity of an open door. Simultaneously a fair-haired little boy came dashing out of it, but, seeing the advancing Koldunov, ran back, brushing against a pail which reacted with a harsh clink. "Wait, Vasyuk!" shouted Koldunov, and lumbered into his murky abode. As soon as he entered, a frenzied female voice issued from within, yelling something in what seemed a habitually over-wrought tone, but then the scream ceased abruptly, and a minute later Koldunov peeped out and grimly beckoned to Lik.

Lik crossed the threshold and immediately found himself in a low-ceilinged, dark room, whose bare walls, as if distorted by some awful pressure from above, formed incomprehensible curves and corners. The place was crammed with the dingy stage properties of indigence. The boy of a moment ago sat on the sagging connubial bed; a huge fair-haired woman with thick bare feet emerged from a corner and, without a smile on her bloated pale face (whose every feature, even the eyes, seemed smudged, by fatigue, or melancholy, or God knows what), wordlessly greeted Lik.

"Get acquainted, get acquainted," Koldunov muttered in derisive encouragement, and immediately set about uncorking the wine. His wife put some bread and a plate of tomatoes on the table. She was so silent that Lik began to doubt whether it had been this woman who had screamed a moment ago.

She sat down on a bench in the back of the room, busying herself with something, cleaning something . . . with a knife over a spread newspaper, it seemed—Lik was afraid to look too closely—while the boy, his eyes glistening, moved over to the wall and, maneuvering cautiously, slipped out into the street. There was a multitude of flies in the room, and with maniacal persistence they haunted the table and settled on Lik's forehead.

"All right, let's have a drink," said Koldunov.

"I can't—I'm not allowed to," Lik was about to object, but instead, obeying the oppressive influence he knew well from his nightmares, he took a swallow—and went into a fit of coughing.

"That's better," said Koldunov with a sigh, wiping his trembling lips with the back of his hand. "You see," he continued, filling Lik's glass and his own, "here's the situation. This is going to be a business talk! Allow me to tell you in brief. At the beginning of summer, I worked for a month or so with some other Russians here, collecting beach garbage. But, as you well know, I am an outspoken man who likes the truth, and when a scoundrel turns up, I come right out and say, 'You're a scoundrel,' and, if necessary, I punch him in the mouth. Well, one day . . ."

And Koldunov began telling, circumstantially, with painstaking repetitions, a dull, wretched episode, and one had the feeling that for a long time his life had consisted of such episodes; that humiliation and failure, heavy cycles of ignoble idleness and ignoble toil, culminating in the inevitable row, had long since become a profession with him. Lik, meanwhile, began to feel drunk after the first glass, but nevertheless went on sipping, with concealed revulsion. A kind of tickling fog permeated every part of his body, but he dared not stop, as if his refusal of wine would lead to a shameful punishment. Leaning on one elbow, Koldunov talked uninterruptedly, stroking the edge of the table with one hand and occasionally slapping it to stress some particularly somber word. His head, the color of yellowish clay (he was almost completely bald), the bags under his eyes, the enigmatically malignant expression of his mobile nostrils—all of this had completely lost any connection with the image of the strong, handsome schoolboy who used to torment Lik, but the coefficient of nightmare remained unchanged.

"There you are, friend. . . . This is no longer important," said Koldunov in a different, less narrative tone. "Actually, I had this little tale all ready for you last time, when it occurred to me that fate—I'm an old fatalist—had given a certain meaning to our meeting, that you had come as a savior, so to speak. But now it turns out that, in the first place, you—forgive me—are as stingy as a Jew and, in the second place . . . Who knows, maybe you really are not in a position to make me a loan. . . . Have no fear, have no fear. . . . This topic is closed! Moreover, it would have only been a question of a small sum to get me back not on my feet—that would be a luxury—but merely on all fours. Because I'm sick of sprawling with my face in the muck. I'm not going to ask anything of you; it's not my style to beg. All I want is your opinion, about something. It's merely a philosophical question. Ladies need not listen. How do you explain all this? You see, if a definite explanation exists, then fine, I'm willing to put up with the muck, since that means there is something logical and justified in all this, perhaps something useful to me or to others, I don't know. Here, explain this to me: I am a human being—you certainly cannot deny that, can you? All right. I am a human being, and the same blood runs in my veins as in yours. Believe it or not, I was my late mama's only and beloved. As a boy, I played pranks; as a youth, I went to war, and the ball started rolling—God, how it rolled! What went wrong? No, you tell *me*—what went wrong? I just want to know what went wrong, then I'll be satisfied. Why has life systematically baited me? Why have I been assigned the part of some kind of miserable scoundrel who is spat on by everybody, gypped, bullied, thrown into jail? Here's an example for you: When they were taking me away after a certain incident in Lyon—and I might add that I was absolutely in the right, and am now very sorry I did not finish him off—well, as the police were taking me away, ignoring my protests, you know what they did? They stuck a little hook right here in the live flesh of my neck—what kind of treatment is that, I ask you?—and off the cop led me to the police station, and I floated along like a sleepwalker, because every additional motion made me black out with pain. Well, can you explain why they don't do this to other people and then, all of a sudden, do it to me? Why did my first wife run away with a Circassian? Why did seven people nearly beat me to death in Antwerp in '32, in a small room? And look at all this—what's the reason for it?—these rags, these walls, that Katya over there? . . . The story of my life interests me, and has so for a long while! This isn't any Jack London or Dostoyevski story for you! I live in a corrupt country—all right. I am willing to put up with the French. All right! But we must find some explanation, gentlemen! I was talking with a guy once, and he asks me, 'Why don't you go back to Russia?' Why not, after all? The difference is very small! There they'd persecute me just the same, knock my teeth in, stick me in the cooler, and then invite me to be shot—and at least that would be honest. You see, I'm even willing to respect them—God knows, they are honest murderers—while here these crooks will think up such tortures for you, it's almost enough to make you feel nostalgic for the good old Russian bullet. Hey, why aren't you looking at me—you, you, you—or don't you understand what I'm saying?"

"No, I understand everything," said Lik. "Only please excuse me. I don't feel well, I must be going. I have to be at the theater soon."

"Oh, no. Wait just a minute. I understand a few things myself. You're a strange fellow. . . . Come on, make me an offer of some kind. . . . Try! Maybe you'll shower me with gold after all, eh? Listen, you know what? I'll sell you a gun—it'll be very useful to you on the stage: bang, and down goes the hero. It's not even worth a hundred francs, but I need more than a hundred—I'll let you have it for a thousand. Want it?"

"No, I don't," said Lik listlessly. "And I really have no money. I've been through it all myself, the hunger and so forth. . . . No, I won't have any more, I feel sick."

"You keep drinking, you son of a bitch, and you won't feel sick. All right, forget it. I just did it to see what you'd say—I won't be bought anyway. Only, please answer my question. Who was it decided I should suffer, and then condemned my child to the same lousy Russian fate? Just a minute, though—suppose I, too, want to sit down in my dressing gown and listen to the radio? What went wrong, eh? Take you, for instance—what makes you better than me? You go swaggering around, living in hotels, smooching with actresses. . . . What's the reason for it? Come on, explain it to me."

Lik said, "I turned out to have—I happened to have . . . Oh, I don't know . . . a modest dramatic talent, I suppose you could say."

"Talent?" shouted Koldunov. "I'll show you talent! I'll show you such talent that you'll start cooking applesauce in your pants! You're a dirty rat, chum. That's your only talent. I must say that's a good one!" (Koldunov started shaking in very primitive mimicry of side-splitting laughter.) "So, according to you, I'm the lowest, filthiest vermin and deserve my rotten end? Splendid, simply splendid. Everything is explained—eureka, eureka! The card is trumped, the nail is in, the beast is butchered!"

"Oleg Petrovich is upset—maybe you ought to be going now," Koldunov's wife suddenly said from her corner, with a strong Estonian accent. There was not the least trace of emotion in her voice, causing her remark to sound wooden and senseless. Koldunov slowly turned in his chair, without altering the position of his hand, which lay as if lifeless on the table, and fixed his wife with an enraptured gaze.

"I am not detaining anyone," he spoke softly and cheerfully. "And I'll be thankful not to be detained by others. Or told what to do. So long, mister," he added, not looking at Lik, who for some reason found it necessary to say: "I'll write from Paris, without fail. . . ."

"So he's going to write, is he?" said Koldunov softly, apparently still addressing his wife. With some trouble Lik extricated himself from the chair and started in her direction, but swerved and bumped into the bed.

"Go away, it's all right," she said calmly, and then, with a polite smile, Lik stumbled out of the house.

His first sensation was one of relief. He had escaped from the orbit of that drunken, moralizing moron. Then came a mounting horror: he was sick to his stomach, and his arms and legs belonged to different people. How was he to perform that night? The worst of all, though, was that his whole body, which seemed to consist of ripples and dots, sensed the approach of a heart attack. It was as if an invisible stake were pointing at him and he might impale himself any moment. This was why he must follow a weaving course, even stopping and backing slightly now and then. Nevertheless, his mind remained rather lucid, he knew that only thirty-six minutes remained before the start of the performance, and he knew the way home. . . . It would be a better idea, though, to go down to the embankment, to sit by the sea until he felt better. This will pass, this will pass, if only I don't die. . . . He also grasped the fact that the sun had just set, that the sky was already more luminous and more tender than the earth. What unnecessary, offensive nonsense. He walked, calculating every step, but sometimes he would err and passersby would turn to look at him. Happily, he did not encounter many of them, since it was the hallowed dinner hour, and when he reached the seafront, he found it quite deserted; the lights burned on the pier, casting long reflections on the tinted water, and these bright dots and inverted exclamation marks seemed to be shining translucently in his own head. He sat down on a bench, hurting his coccyx as he did so, and shut his eyes. But then everything began to spin; his heart was reflected as a terrifying globe on the dark inner side of his eyelids. It continued to swell agonizingly, and, to put a stop to this, he opened his eyes and tried to hook his gaze on things—on the evening star, on that black buoy in the sea, on a darkened eucalyptus tree at the end of the promenade. I know all this, he thought, I understand all this, and, in the twilight, the eucalyptus strangely resembles a big Russian birch. Can this be the end? Such an idiotic end. . . . I feel worse and worse. . . . What's happening to me? . . . Oh, my God!

About ten minutes passed, no more. His watch ticked on, trying tactfully not to look at him. The thought of death coincided precisely with the thought that in half an hour he would walk out onto the bright stage and say the first words of his part, *"Je vous prie d'excuser, Madame, cette invasion nocturne."* And these words, clearly and elegantly engraved in his memory, seemed far more real than the lapping and splashing of the weary waves, or the sound of two gay female voices coming from behind the stone wall of a nearby villa, or the recent talk of Koldunov, or even the pounding of his own heart. His feeling of sickness suddenly reached such a panicky pitch that he got up and walked along the parapet, dazedly stroking it and peering at the colored inks of the evening sea. "In any case," Lik said aloud, "I have to cool off. . . . Instant cure. . . . Either I'll die or it'll help." He slid down the sloping edge of the sidewalk, where the parapet stopped, and crunched across the pebbly beach. There was nobody on the shore except for a shabbily dressed man, who happened to be lying supine near a boulder, his feet spread wide apart. Something about the outline of his legs and shoulders for some reason reminded Lik of Koldunov. Swaying a little and already stooping, Lik walked self-consciously to the edge of the water, and was about to scoop some up in his hands and douse his head; but the water was alive, moving, and threatening to soak his feet. Perhaps I have enough coordination left to take off my shoes and socks, he thought, and in the same instant remembered the carton box containing his new shoes. He had forgotten it at Koldunov's!

And as soon as he remembered it, this image proved so stimulating that immediately everything was simplified, and this saved Lik, in the same way as a situation is sometimes saved by its rational formulation. He must get those shoes at once, there was just time enough to get them, and as soon as this was accomplished, he would step onstage in them. (All perfectly clear and logical.) Forgetting the pressure in his chest, the foggy feeling, the nausea, Lik climbed back up to the promenade, and in a sonorously recorded voice hailed the empty taxi that was just leaving the curb by the villa across the way. Its brakes responded with a lacerating moan. He gave the chauffeur the address from his notebook, telling him to go as fast as possible, even though the entire trip—there and from there to the theater—would not take more than five minutes.

The taxi approached Koldunov's place from the direction of the square. A crowd had gathered, and it was only by dint of persistent threats with its horn that the driver managed to squeeze through. Koldunov's wife was sitting on a chair by the public fountain. Her forehead and left cheek glistened with blood, her hair was matted, and she sat quite straight and motionless, surrounded by the curious, while, next to her, also motionless, stood her boy, in a bloodstained shirt, covering his face with his fist, a kind of tableau. A policeman, mistaking Lik for a doctor, escorted him into the room. The dead man lay on the floor amid broken crockery, his face blasted by a gunshot in the mouth, his widespread feet in new, white—

"Those are mine," said Lik in French.

MADEMOISELLE O

1

I HAVE often noticed that after I had bestowed on the characters of my novels some treasured item of my past, it would pine away in the artificial world where I had so abruptly placed it. Although it lingered on in my mind, its personal warmth, its retrospective appeal had gone and, presently, it became more closely identified with my novel than with my former self, where it had seemed to be so safe from the intrusion of the artist. Houses have crumbled in my memory as soundlessly as they did in the mute films of yore; and the portrait of my old French governess, whom I once lent to a boy in one of my books, is fading fast, now that it is engulfed in the description of a childhood entirely unrelated to my own. The man in me revolts against the fictionist and here is my desperate attempt to save what is left of poor Mademoiselle.

A large woman, a very stout woman, Mademoiselle rolled into our existence in 1905 when I was six and my brother five. There she is. I see so plainly her abundant dark hair, brushed up high and covertly graying; the three wrinkles on her austere forehead; her beetling brows; the steely eyes behind the black-rimmed pince-nez; that vestigial mustache; that blotchy complexion, which in moments of wrath develops an additional flush in the region of the third, and amplest, chin so regally spread over the frilled mountain of her blouse. And now she sits down, or rather she tackles the job of sitting down, the jelly of her jowl quaking, her prodigious posterior, with the three buttons on the side, lowering itself warily; then, at the last second, she surrenders her bulk to the wicker armchair, which out of sheer fright bursts into a salvo of crackling.

The winter she came was the only one of my childhood that I spent in the country. It was a year of strikes, riots, and police-inspired massacres; and I suppose my father wished to tuck his family away from the city, in our quiet country place, where his popularity with the peasants might mitigate, as he correctly surmised, the risk of agrarian troubles. It was also a particularly severe winter, producing as much snow as Mademoiselle might have expected to find in the Hyperborean gloom of remote Muscovy. When she alighted at the little station, from which she still had to travel half a dozen miles by sleigh to our country home, I was not there to greet her; but I do so now as I try to imagine what she saw and felt at that last stage of her fabulous and ill-timed journey. Her Russian vocabulary consisted, I know, of one short word, the same solitary word that years later she was to take back to Switzerland, where she had been born of French parents. This word, which in her pronunciation may be phonetically rendered as "giddy-eh" (actually it is *gde*, with *e* as in "yet"), meant "Where?" And that was a good deal. Uttered by her like the raucous cry of some lost bird, it accumulated such interrogatory force that it sufficed for all her needs. "Giddy-eh? Giddy-eh?" she would wail, not only to find out her whereabouts but also to express an abyss of misery: the fact that she was a stranger, shipwrecked, penniless, ailing, in search of the blessed land where at last she would be understood.

I can visualize her, by proxy, as she stands in the middle of the station platform, where she has just alighted, and vainly my ghostly envoy offers her an arm that she cannot see. The door of the waiting room opens with a shuddering whine peculiar to nights of intense frost; a cloud of hot air rushes out, almost as profuse as the steam from the great stack of the panting engine; and now our coachman Zakhar takes over—a burly man in sheepskin with the leather outside, his huge gloves protruding from his scarlet sash into which he has stuffed them. I hear the snow crunching under his felt boots while he busies himself with the luggage, the jingling harness, and then his own nose, which he eases by means of a dexterous flip of finger and thumb as he trudges back round the sleigh. Slowly, with grim misgivings, Mademoiselle climbs in, clutching at her helper in mortal fear lest the sleigh move off before her vast form is securely encased. Finally, she settles down with a grunt and thrusts her fists into her skimpy plush muff. At the juicy smack of their driver's lips the horses strain their quarters, shift hooves, strain again; and then Mademoiselle gives a backward jerk of her torso as the heavy sleigh is wrenched out of its world of steel, fur, flesh, to enter a frictionless medium where it skims along a spectral road that it seems barely to touch.

For one moment, thanks to the sudden radiance of a lone lamp where the station square ends, a grossly exaggerated shadow, also holding a muff, races beside the sleigh, climbs a billow of snow, and is gone, leaving Mademoiselle to be swallowed up by what she will later allude to, with awe and gusto, as *"la steppe."* There, in the limitless gloom, the changeable twinkle of remote village lights seems to her to be the yellow eyes of wolves. She is cold, she is frozen stiff, frozen "to the center of her brain," for she soars with the wildest hyperbole when not clinging to the safest old saw. Every now and then, she looks back to make sure that a second sleigh, bearing her trunk and hatbox, is following—always at the same distance, like those companionable phantoms of ships in polar waters which explorers have described. And let me not leave out the moon—for surely there must be a moon, the full, incredibly clear disc that goes so well with Russian lusty frosts. So there it comes, steering out of a flock of small dappled clouds, which it tinges with a vague iridescence; and, as it sails higher, it glazes the runner tracks left on the road, where every sparkling lump of snow is emphasized by a swollen shadow.

Very lovely, very lonesome. But what am I doing there in that stereoscopic dreamland? Somehow those two sleighs have slipped away; they have left my imaginary double behind on the blue-white road. No, even the vibration in my ears is not their receding bells, but my own blood singing. All is still, spellbound, enthralled by that great heavenly O shining above the Russian wilderness of my past. The snow is real, though, and as I bend to it and scoop up a handful, forty-five years crumble to glittering frost-dust between my fingers.

2

A kerosene lamp is steered into the gloaming. Gently it floats and comes down; the hand of memory, now in a footman's white cotton glove, places it in the center of a round table. The flame is nicely adjusted, and a rosy, silk-flounced lamp shade crowns the light. Revealed: a warm, bright room in a snow-muffled house—soon to be termed *"le château"*—built by my great-grandfather, who, being afraid of fires, had the staircase made of iron, so that when the house did get burnt to the ground, sometime after the Soviet Revolution, those fretted steps remained standing there, all alone but still leading up.

Some more about that room, please. The oval mirror. Hanging on taut cords, its pure brow inclined, it strives to retain the falling furniture and a slope of bright floor that keep slipping from its embrace. The chandelier pendants. These emit a delicate tinkling whenever anything is moved in an upstairs room. Colored pencils. That tiny heap of emerald pencil dust on the oilcloth where a penknife had just done its recurrent duty. We are sitting at the table, my brother and I and Miss Robinson, who now and then looks at her watch: roads must be dreadful with all that snow; and anyway many professional hardships lie in wait for the vague French person who will replace her.

Now the colored pencils in more detail. The green one, by a mere whirl of the wrist, could be made to produce a ruffled tree, or the chimney smoke of a house where spinach was cooking. The blue one drew a simple line across the page—and the horizon of all seas was there. A nondescript blunt one kept getting into one's way. The brown one was always broken, and so was the red, but sometimes, just after it had snapped, one could still make it serve by holding it so that the loose tip was propped, none too securely, by a jutting splinter. The little purple fellow, a special favorite of mine, had got worn down so short as to become scarcely manageable. The white one alone, that lanky albino among pencils, kept its original length, or at least did so until I discovered that, far from being a fraud leaving no mark on the page, it was the ideal tool since I could imagine whatever I wished while I scrawled.

Alas, these pencils, too, have been distributed among the characters in my books to keep fictitious children busy; they are not quite my own now. Somewhere, in the apartment house of a chapter, in the hired room of a paragraph, I have also placed that tilted mirror, and the lamp, and the chandelier-drops. Few things are left; many have been squandered. Have I given away Box (son and husband of Loulou, the housekeeper's pet), that old brown dachshund fast asleep on the sofa? No, I think he is still mine. His grizzled muzzle, with the wart at the puckered corner of the mouth, is tucked into the curve of his hock, and from time to time a deep sigh distends his ribs. He is so old and his sleep is so thickly padded with dreams (about chewable slippers and a few last smells) that he does not stir when faint bells jingle outside. Then a pneumatic door heaves and clangs in the vestibule. She has come after all: I had so hoped she would not.

3

Another dog, the sweet-tempered sire of a ferocious family, a Great Dane not allowed in the house, played a pleasant part in an adventure that took place on one of the following days, if not the very day after. It so happened that my brother and I were left completely in charge of the newcomer. As I reconstruct it now, my mother had probably gone for a few hours to St. Petersburg (a distance of some fifty miles) where my father was deeply involved in the grave political events of that winter. She was pregnant and very nervous. Miss Robinson, instead of staying to break in Mademoiselle, had gone too—or perhaps my little sister, aged three, had inherited her. In order to prove that this was no way of treating us, I immediately formed the project of repeating the exciting performance of a year before, when we escaped from poor Miss Hunt in gay, populous Wiesbaden, a paradise of multicolored dead leaves. This time the countryside all around was a wilderness of snow, and it is hard to imagine what exactly could have been the goal of the journey I planned. We had just returned from our first afternoon walk with Mademoiselle and were throbbing with frustration and hatred. To keep up with an unfamiliar tongue (all we knew in the way of French were a few household words), and on top of it to be crossed in all our fond habits, was more than we could bear. The *bonne promenade* she had promised us had turned out to be a tedious stroll around the house where the snow had been cleared and the icy ground sprinkled with sand. She had had us wear things we never used to wear, even on the frostiest day—horrible gaiters and hoods that hampered our every movement. She had restrained us when we were tempted to explore the creamy, smooth swellings of snow that had been flower beds in summer. She had not allowed us to walk under the organ-pipe-like system of huge icicles that hung from the eaves and gloriously burned in the low sun. As soon as we came back from that walk, we left Mademoiselle puffing on the steps of the vestibule and dashed indoors, giving her the impression that we were about to conceal ourselves in some remote room. Actually, we trotted on till we reached the other side of the house, and then, through a veranda, emerged into the garden again. The above-mentioned Great Dane was in the act of fussily adjusting himself to a nearby snowdrift, but while deciding which hind leg to lift he noticed us and at once joined us at a joyful gallop.

The three of us followed a fairly easy trail and, after plodding through deeper snow, reached the road that led to the village. Meanwhile the sun had set. Dusk came with uncanny suddenness. My brother declared he was cold and tired, but I urged him on and finally made him ride the dog (the only member of the party to be still enjoying himself). We had gone more than two miles and the moon was fantastically shiny, and my brother, in perfect silence, had begun to fall every now and then from his mount, when a servant with a lantern overtook us and led us home. "Giddy-eh, giddy-eh?" Mademoiselle was frantically shouting from the porch. I brushed past her without a word. My brother burst into tears, and gave himself up. The Great Dane, whose name was Turka, returned to his interrupted affairs in connection with serviceable and informative snowdrifts around the house.

4

In our childhood we know a lot about hands since they live and hover at the level of our stature; Mademoiselle's were unpleasant because of the froggy gloss on their tight skin besprinkled with brown ecchymotic spots. Before her time no stranger had ever stroked my face. Mademoiselle, as soon as she came, had taken me completely aback by patting my cheek in sign of spontaneous affection. All her mannerisms come back to me when I think of her hands. Her trick of peeling rather than sharpening a pencil, the point held toward her stupendous and sterile bosom swathed in green wool. The way she had of inserting her little finger into her ear and vibrating it very rapidly. The ritual observed every time she gave me a fresh copybook. Always panting a little, her mouth slightly open and emitting in quick succession a series of asthmatic puffs, she would open the copybook to make a margin in it; that is, she would sharply imprint a vertical line with her thumbnail, fold in the edge of the page, press, release, smooth it out with the heel of her hand, after which the book would be briskly twisted around and placed before me ready for use. A new pen followed; she would moisten the glistening nib with susurrous lips before dipping it into the baptismal ink font. Then, delighting in every limb of every limpid letter (especially so because the preceding copybook had ended in utter sloppiness), with exquisite care I would inscribe the word *Dictée* while Mademoiselle hunted through her collection of spelling tests for a good, hard passage.

5

Meanwhile the setting has changed. Hoarfrost and snow have been removed by a silent property man. The summer afternoon is alive with
steep clouds breasting the blue. Eyed shadows move on the garden
paths. Presently, lessons are over and Mademoiselle is reading to us on
the veranda where the mats and plaited chairs develop a spicy, biscuity
smell in the heat. On the white windowsills, on the long window seats
covered with faded calico, the sun breaks into geometrical gems after
passing through rhomboids and squares of stained glass. This is the
time when Mademoiselle is at her very best.

What a number of volumes she read through to us on that veranda!
Her slender voice sped on and on, never weakening, without the
slightest hitch or hesitation, an admirable reading machine wholly independent of her sick bronchial tubes. We got it all: *Les Malheurs de
Sophie, Le Tour du Monde en Quatre-Vingts Jours, La Petite Chose, Les
Misérables, Le Comte de Monte Cristo,* many others. There she sat, distilling her reading voice from the still prison of her person. Apart from
the lips, one of her chins, the smallest but true one, was the only mobile detail of her Buddha-like bulk. The black-rimmed pince-nez reflected eternity. Occasionally a fly would settle on her stern forehead
and its three wrinkles would instantly leap up all together like three
runners over three hurdles. But nothing whatever changed in the expression of her face—the face I so often tried to depict in my sketch-
book, for its impassive and simple symmetry offered a far greater
temptation to my stealthy pencil than the bowl of flowers or the decoy
duck on the table before me, which I was supposedly drawing.

Presently my attention would wander still farther, and it was then,
perhaps, that the rare purity of her rhythmic voice accomplished its
true purpose. I looked at a cloud and years later was able to visualize
its exact shape. The gardener was pottering among the peonies. A
wagtail took a few steps, stopped as if it had remembered something—
and then walked on, enacting its name. Coming from nowhere, a
comma butterfly settled on the threshold, basked in the sun with its
angular fulvous wings spread, suddenly closed them just to show the
tiny initial chalked on their underside, and as suddenly darted away.
But the most constant source of enchantment during those readings
came from the harlequin pattern of colored panes inset in a whitewashed framework on either side of the veranda. The garden when

viewed through these magic glasses grew strangely still and aloof. If one looked through blue glass, the sand turned to cinders while inky trees swam in a tropical sky. The yellow created an amber world infused with an extra strong brew of sunshine. The red made the foliage drip ruby dark upon a coral-tinted footpath. The green soaked greenery in a greener green. And when, after such richness, one turned to a small square of normal, savorless glass, with its lone mosquito or lame daddy longlegs, it was like taking a draft of water when one is not thirsty, and one saw a matter-of-fact white bench under familiar trees. But of all the windows this is the pane through which in later years parched nostalgia longed to peer.

Mademoiselle never found out how potent had been the even flow of her voice. The subsequent claims she put forward were quite different. "Ah," she sighed, *"comme on s'aimait!"* ("didn't we love each other!") "Those good old days in the château! The dead wax doll we once buried under the oak!" (No—a wool-stuffed golliwogg.) "And that time you and Serge ran away and left me stumbling and howling in the depths of the forest!" (Exaggerated.) *"Ah, la fessée que je vous ai flanquée!"* ("My, what a spanking I gave you!") (She did try to slap me once but the attempt was never repeated.) "*Votre tante, la Princesse,* whom you struck with your little fist because she had been rude to me!" (Do not remember.) "And the way you whispered to me your childish troubles!" (Never!) "And the cozy nook in my room where you loved to snuggle because you felt so warm and secure!"

Mademoiselle's room, both in the country and in town, was a weird place to me—a kind of hothouse sheltering a thick-leaved plant imbued with a heavy, queerly acrid odor. Although next to ours, when we were small, it did not seem to belong to our pleasant, well-aired home. In that sickening mist, reeking, among other effluvia, of the brown smell of oxidized apple peel, the lamp burned low, and strange objects glimmered upon the writing desk: a lacquered box with licorice sticks, black segments of which she would hack off with her penknife and put to melt under her tongue; a picture postcard of a lake and a castle with mother-of-pearl spangles for windows; a bumpy ball of tightly rolled bits of silver paper that came from all those chocolates she used to consume at night; photographs of the nephew who had died, of his mother who had signed her picture *Mater Dolorosa*, and of a certain Monsieur de Marante who had been forced by his family to marry a rich widow.

Lording it over the rest was one in a noble frame incrusted with garnets; it showed, in three-quarter view, a slim young brunette clad in a close-fitting dress, with brave eyes and abundant hair. "A braid as thick as my arm and reaching down to my ankles!" was Mademoiselle's melodramatic comment. For this had been she—but in vain did my eyes probe her familiar form to try and extract the graceful creature it had engulfed. Such discoveries as my awed brother and I did make merely increased the difficulties of that task; and the grown-ups who during the day beheld a densely clothed Mademoiselle never saw what we children saw when, roused from her sleep by one of us shrieking himself out of a bad dream, disheveled, candle in hand, a gleam of gilt lace on the blood-red dressing gown that could not quite wrap her quaking mass, the ghastly Jézabel of Racine's absurd play stomped barefooted into our bedroom.

All my life I have been a poor go-to-sleeper. No matter how great my weariness, the wrench of parting with consciousness is unspeakably repulsive to me. I loathe Somnus, that black-masked headsman binding me to the block; and if in the course of years I have got so used to my nightly ordeal as almost to swagger while the familiar axe is coming out of its great velvet-lined case, initially I had no such comfort or defense: I had nothing—save a door left slightly ajar into Mademoiselle's room. Its vertical line of meek light was something I could cling to, since in absolute darkness my head would swim, just as the soul dissolves in the blackness of sleep.

Saturday night used to be a pleasurable prospect because that was the night Mademoiselle indulged in the luxury of a weekly bath, thus granting a longer lease to my tenuous gleam. But then a subtler torture set in. The nursery bathroom in our St. Petersburg house was at the end of a Z-shaped corridor some twenty heartbeats' distance from my bed, and between dreading Mademoiselle's return from the bathroom to her lighted bedroom and envying my brother's stolid snore, I could never really put my additional time to profit by deftly getting to sleep while a chink in the dark still bespoke a speck of myself in nothingness. At length they would come, those inexorable steps, plodding along the passage and causing some little glass object, which had been secretly sharing my vigil, to tinkle in dismay on its shelf.

Now she has entered her room. A brisk interchange of light values tells me that the candle on her bed table takes over the job of the lamp on her desk. My line of light is still there, but it has grown old and wan, and flickers whenever Mademoiselle makes her bed creak by moving. For I still hear her. Now it is a silvery rustle spelling "Suchard"; now the *trk-trk-trk* of a fruit knife cutting the pages of *La Revue des Deux Mondes*. I hear her panting slightly. And all the time I am in acute distress, desperately trying to coax sleep, opening my eyes every few seconds to check the faded gleam, and imagining paradise as a place where a sleepless neighbor reads an endless book by the light of an eternal candle.

The inevitable happens: the pince-nez case shuts with a snap, the review shuffles onto the marble of the bed table, and gustily Mademoiselle's pursed lips blow; the first attempt fails, a groggy flame squirms and ducks; then comes a second lunge, and light collapses. In that pitchy blackness I lose my bearings, my bed seems to be slowly drifting, panic makes me sit up and stare; finally my dark-adapted eyes sift out, among entoptic floaters, certain more precious blurrings that roam in aimless amnesia until, half-remembering, they settle down as the dim folds of window curtains behind which streetlights are remotely alive.

How utterly foreign to the troubles of the night were those exciting St. Petersburg mornings when the fierce and tender, damp and dazzling arctic spring bundled away broken ice down the sea-bright Neva! It made the roofs shine. It painted the slush in the streets a rich purplish-blue shade which I have never seen anywhere since. Mademoiselle, her coat of imitation seal majestically swelling on her bosom, sat in the back seat of the landau with my brother next to her and me facing them—joined to them by the valley of the lap rug; and as I looked up I could see, strung on ropes from housefront to housefront high above the street, great, tensely smooth, semitransparent banners billowing, their three wide bands—pale red, pale blue, and merely pale—deprived by the sun and the flying cloud shadows of any too blunt connection with a national holiday, but undoubtedly celebrating now, in the city of memory, the essence of that spring day, the swish of the mud, the ruffled exotic bird with one bloodshot eye on Mademoiselle's hat.

6

_____

She spent seven years with us, lessons getting rarer and rarer and her temper worse and worse. Still, she seemed like a rock of grim permanence when compared to the ebb and flow of English governesses and Russian tutors passing through our large household. She was on bad terms with all of them. Seldom less than a dozen people sat down for meals and when, on birthdays, this number rose to thirty or more, the question of place at table became a particularly burning one for Mademoiselle. Uncles and aunts and cousins would arrive on such days from neighboring estates, and the village doctor would come in his dogcart, and the village schoolmaster would be heard blowing his nose in the cool hall, where he passed from mirror to mirror with a greenish, damp, creaking bouquet of lilies of the valley or a sky-colored, brittle one of cornflowers in his fist.

If Mademoiselle found herself seated too far at the end of the table, and especially if she lost precedence to a certain poor relative who was almost as fat as she (*"Je suis une sylphide à côté d'elle,"* Mademoiselle would say with a shrug of contempt), then her sense of injury caused her lips to twitch in a would-be ironical smile—and when a naive neighbor would smile back, she would rapidly shake her head, as if coming out of some very deep meditation, with the remark: *"Excusez-moi, je souriais à mes tristes pensées."*

And as though nature had not wished to spare her anything that makes one supersensitive, she was hard of hearing. Sometimes at table we boys would suddenly become aware of two big tears crawling down Mademoiselle's ample cheeks. "Don't mind me," she would say in a small voice, and she kept on eating till the unwiped tears blinded her; then, with a heartbroken hiccup she would rise and blunder out of the dining room. Little by little the truth would come out. The general talk had turned, say, on the subject of the warship my uncle commanded, and she had perceived in this a sly dig at her Switzerland that had no navy. Or else it was because she fancied that whenever French was spoken, the game consisted in deliberately preventing her from directing and bejeweling the conversation. Poor lady, she was always in such a nervous hurry to seize control of intelligible table talk before it bolted back into Russian that no wonder she bungled her cue.

"And your Parliament, Sir, how is it getting along?" she would suddenly burst out brightly from her end of the table, challenging my father, who, after a harassing day, was not exactly eager to discuss troubles of the State with a singularly unreal person who neither knew nor cared anything about them. Thinking that someone had referred to music, "But Silence, too, may be beautiful," she would bubble. "Why, one evening, in a desolate valley of the Alps, I actually *heard* Silence." Sallies like these, especially when growing deafness led her to answer questions none had put, resulted in a painful hush, instead of touching off the rockets of a sprightly *causerie*.

And, really, her French was so lovely! Ought one to have minded the shallowness of her culture, the bitterness of her temper, the banality of her mind, when that pearly language of hers purled and scintillated, as innocent of sense as the alliterative sins of Racine's pious verse? My father's library, not her limited lore, taught me to appreciate authentic poetry; nevertheless, something of her tongue's limpidity and luster has had a singularly bracing effect upon me, like those sparkling salts that are used to purify the blood. This is why it makes me so sad to imagine now the anguish Mademoiselle must have felt at seeing how lost, how little valued was the nightingale voice which came from her elephantine body. She stayed with us long, much too long, obstinately hoping for some miracle that would transform her into a kind of Madame de Rambouillet holding a gilt-and-satin *salon* of poets, princes, and statesmen under her brilliant spell.

She would have gone on hoping had it not been for one Lenski, a young Russian tutor, with mild myopic eyes and strong political opinions, who had been engaged to coach us in various subjects and participate in our sports. He had had several predecessors, none of whom Mademoiselle had liked, but he, as she put it, was *"le comble."* While venerating my father, Lenski could not quite stomach certain aspects of our household, such as footmen and French, which last he considered an aristocratic convention of no use in a liberal's home. On the other hand, Mademoiselle decided that if Lenski answered her pointblank questions only with short grunts (which he tried to Germanize for want of a better language) it was not because he could not understand French, but because he wished to insult her in front of everybody.

I can hear and see Mademoiselle requesting him in dulcet tones, but with an ominous quiver of her upper lip, to pass her the bread; and, likewise, I can hear and see Lenski Frenchlessly and unflinchingly going on with his soup; finally, with a slashing *"Pardon, Monsieur,"* Mademoiselle would swoop right across his plate, snatch up the breadbasket, and recoil again with a *"Merci!"* so charged with irony that Lenski's downy ears would turn the hue of geraniums. "The brute! The cad! The Nihilist!" she would sob later in her room—which was no longer next to ours though still on the same floor.

If Lenski happened to come tripping downstairs while, with an asthmatic pause every ten steps or so, she was working her way up (for the little hydraulic elevator of our house in St. Petersburg would constantly, and rather insultingly, refuse to function), Mademoiselle maintained that he had viciously bumped into her, pushed her, knocked her down, and we already could see him trampling her prostrate body. More and more frequently she would leave the table, and the dessert she would have missed was diplomatically sent up in her wake. From her remote room she would write a sixteen-page letter to my mother, who, upon hurrying upstairs, would find her dramatically packing her trunk. And then, one day, she was allowed to go on with her packing.

7
————

She returned to Switzerland. World War I came, then the Revolution. In the early twenties, long after our correspondence had fizzled out, by a fluke move of life in exile I chanced to visit Lausanne with a college friend of mine, so I thought I might as well look up Mademoiselle, if she were still alive.

She was. Stouter than ever, quite gray and almost totally deaf, she welcomed me with a tumultuous outburst of affection. Instead of the Château de Chillon picture, there was now one of a garish troika. She spoke as warmly of her life in Russia as if it were her own lost homeland. Indeed, I found in the neighborhood quite a colony of such old Swiss governesses. Clustering together in a constant seething of competitive reminiscences, they formed a small island in an environment that had grown alien to them. Mademoiselle's bosom friend was now mummylike Mlle. Golay, my mother's former governess, still prim and pessimistic at eighty-five; she had remained in our family long after my mother had married, and her return to Switzerland had preceded only by a couple of years that of Mademoiselle, with whom she had not been on speaking terms when both had been living under our roof. One is always at home in one's past, which partly explains those pathetic ladies' posthumous love for another country, which they never had really known and in which none of them had been very content.

As no conversation was possible because of Mademoiselle's deafness, my friend and I decided to bring her next day the appliance which we gathered she could not afford. She adjusted the clumsy thing improperly at first, but no sooner had she done so than she turned to me with a dazzled look of moist wonder and bliss in her eyes. She swore she could hear every word, every murmur of mine. She could not for, having my doubts, I had not spoken. If I had, I would have told her to thank my friend, who had paid for the instrument. Was it, then, silence she heard, that Alpine Silence she had talked about in the past? In that past, she had been lying to herself; now she was lying to me.

Before leaving for Basle and Berlin, I happened to be walking along the lake in the cold, misty night. At one spot a lone light dimly diluted the darkness. In its nimbus the mist seemed transformed into a visible drizzle. *"Il pleut toujours en Suisse"* was one of those casual comments which, formerly, had made Mademoiselle weep. Below, a wide ripple, almost a wave, and something vaguely white attracted my eye. As I came quite close to the lapping water, I saw what it was—an aged swan, a large, uncouth, dodolike creature, making ridiculous efforts to hoist himself into a moored boat. He could not do it. The heavy, impotent flapping of his wings, their slippery sound against the rocking and plashing boat, the gluey glistening of the dark swell where it caught the light—all seemed for a moment laden with that strange significance which sometimes in dreams is attached to a finger pressed to mute lips and then pointed at something the dreamer has no time to distinguish before waking with a start. But although I soon forgot that dismal night, it was, oddly enough, that night, that compound image—shudder and swan and swell—which first came to my mind when a couple of years later I learned that Mademoiselle had died.

She had spent all her life in feeling miserable; this misery was her native element; its fluctuations, its varying depths, alone gave her the impression of moving and living. What bothers me is that a sense of misery, and nothing else, is not enough to make a permanent soul. My enormous and morose Mademoiselle is all right on earth but impossible in eternity. Have I really salvaged her from fiction? Just before the rhythm I hear falters and fades, I catch myself wondering whether, during the years I knew her, I had not kept utterly missing something in her that was far more she than her chins or her ways or even her French—something perhaps akin to that last glimpse of her, to the radiant deceit she had used in order to have me depart pleased with my own kindness, or to that swan whose agony was so much closer to artistic truth than a drooping dancer's pale arms; something, in short, that I could appreciate only after the things and beings that I had most loved in the security of my childhood had been turned to ashes or shot through the heart.

VASILIY SHISHKOV

T HE little I remember about him is centered within the confines of last spring: the spring of 1939. I had been to some "Evening of Russian Émigré Literature"—one of those boring affairs so current in Paris since the early twenties. As I was quickly descending the stairs (an intermission having given me the opportunity to escape), I seemed to hear the gallop of eager pursuit behind me; I looked back, and this is when I saw him for the first time. From a couple of steps above me where he had come to a stop, he said: "My name is Vasiliy Shishkov. I am a poet."

Then he came down to my level—a solidly built young man of an eminently Russian type, thick-lipped and gray-eyed, with a deep voice and a capacious, comfortable handshake.

"I want to consult you about something," he continued. "A meeting between us would be desirable."

I am a person not spoiled by such desires. My assent all but brimmed with tender emotion. We decided he would see me next day at my shabby hotel (grandly named Royal Versailles). Very punctually I came down into the simulacrum of a lounge which was comparatively quiet at that hour, if one discounted the convulsive exertions of the lift, and the conversation conducted in their accustomed corner by four German refugees who were discussing certain intricacies of the *carte d'identité* system. One of them apparently thought that his plight was not as bad as that of the others, and the others argued that it was exactly the same. Then a fifth appeared and greeted his compatriots for some reason in French: facetiousness? swank? the lure of a new language? He had just bought a hat; they all started trying it on.

Shishkov entered. With a serious expression on his face and something equally serious in the thrust of his shoulder, he overcame the rusty reluctance of the revolving door and barely had time to look

around before he saw me. Here I noted with pleasure that he es-
chewed the conventional grin which I fear so greatly—and to which I
myself am prone. I had some difficulty in drawing together two overstuffed armchairs—and again I found most pleasing that instead of
sketching a mechanical gesture of cooperation, he remained standing
at ease, his hands in the pockets of his ancient trench coat, waiting for
me to arrange our seats. As soon as we had settled down, he produced
a tawny notebook.

"First of all," said Shishkov, fixing me with nice, furry eyes, "a person must produce his credentials—am I right? At the police station I
would have shown my identity card, and to you, Gospodin Nabokov,
I must show this—a cahier of verse."

I leafed through it. The firm handwriting, slightly inclined to the
left, emanated health and talent. Alas, once my glance went zigzagging
down the lines, I felt a pang of disappointment. The poetry was
dreadful—flat, flashy, ominously pretentious. Its utter mediocrity was
stressed by the fraudulent chic of alliterations and the meretricious
richness of illiterate rhymes. Sufficient to say that such pairs were
formed as, for example, *teatr–gladiator*, *mustang–tank*, *Madonna–
belladonna*. As to the themes, they were best left alone: the author
sang with unvarying gusto anything that his lyre came across. Reading
his poems one after the other was torture for a nervous person, but
since my conscientiousness happened to be reinforced by the author's
watching closely over me and controlling both the direction of my
gaze and the action of my fingers, I found myself obliged to stop for
a few moments at every consecutive page.

"Well, what's the verdict?" he asked when I had finished: "Not too
awful?"

I considered him. His somewhat glossy face with enlarged pores expressed no ominous premonition whatever. I replied that his poetry
was hopelessly bad. Shishkov clicked his tongue, thrust the notebook
back into the pocket of his trench coat, and said: "Those credentials
are not mine. I mean, I did write that stuff myself, and yet it is all
forged. The entire lot of thirty poems was composed this morning,
and to tell the truth, I found rather nasty the task of parodying the
product of metromania. In return, I now have learned that you are
merciless—which means that you can be trusted. Here is my real passport." (Shishkov handed me another, much more tattered, notebook.)
"Read just one poem at random, it will be enough for both you and
me. By the way, to avoid any misapprehension, let me warn you that
I do not care for your novels; they irritate me as would a harsh light
or the loud conversation of strangers when one longs not to talk, but

to think. Yet, at the same time, in a purely physiological way—if I may put it like that—you possess some secret of writing, the secret of certain basic colors, something exceptionally rare and important, which, alas, you apply to little purpose, within the narrow limits of your general abilities—driving about, so to speak, all over the place in a powerful racing car for which you have absolutely no use, but which keeps you thinking where could one thunder off next. However, as you possess that secret, people must reckon with you—and this is why I should like to enlist your support in a certain matter; but first take, please, a look at my poems."

(I must admit that the unexpected and uncalled-for lecture on the character of my literary work struck me as considerably more impudent than the harmless bit of deception my visitor had devised. I write for the sake of concrete pleasure and publish my writings for the sake of much less concrete money, and though the latter point should imply, in one way or another, the existence of a consumer, it always seems to me that the farther my published books, in the course of their natural evolution, retreat from their self-contained source, the more abstract and insignificant become the fortuitous events of their career. As to the so-called Readers' Judgment, I feel, at that trial, not as the defendant, but, at best, as a distant relative of one of the least important witnesses. In other words a reviewer's praise seems to me an odd kind of *sans-gêne*, and his abuse, a vain lunge at a specter. At the moment, I was trying to decide whether Shishkov tumbled his candid opinion into the lap of every proud writer he met or whether it was only with me that he was so blunt because he believed I deserved it. I concluded that just as the doggerel trick had been a result of his somewhat childish but genuine thirst for truth, so the voicing of his views about me was prompted by the urge of widening to the utmost the frame of mutual frankness.)

I vaguely feared that the genuine product might reveal traces of the defects monstrously exaggerated in the parody, but my fears proved unfounded. The poems were very good—I hope to discuss them some other time in much greater detail. Recently, I was instrumental in getting one published in an émigré magazine, and lovers of poetry noticed its originality.* To the poet that was so strangely gourmand in regard to another's opinion, I incontinently expressed mine, adding, as a corrective, that the poem in question contained some tiny fluctuations of style such as, for instance, the not quite idiomatic *v soldatskih mundirah*; here *mundir* (uniform) should rather be *forma* when refer-

*See note, page 656.

ring as it did to the lower ranks. The line, however, was much too good to be tampered with.

"You know what," said Shishkov, "since you agree with me that my poems are not trifles, let me leave that book in your keeping. One never knows what may happen; strange, very strange thoughts occur to me, and— Well, anyway, everything now turns out admirably. You see, my object in visiting you was to ask you to take part in a new magazine I am planning to launch. Saturday there will be a gathering at my place and everything must be decided. Naturally, I cherish no illusions concerning your capacity for being carried away by the problems of the modern world, but I think the idea of that journal might interest you from a stylistic point of view. So, please, come. Incidentally, we expect" (Shishkov named an extremely famous Russian writer) "and some other prominent people. You have to understand—I have reached a certain limit, I absolutely must take the strain off, or else I'll go mad. I'll be thirty soon; last year I came here, to Paris, after an utterly sterile adolescence in the Balkans and then in Austria. I am working here as a bookbinder but I have been a typesetter and even a librarian—in short I have always rubbed against books. Yet, I repeat, my life has been sterile, and, of late, I'm bursting with the urge to do something—a most agonizing sensation—for you must see yourself, from another angle, perhaps, but still you *must* see, how much suffering, imbecility, and filth surround us; yet people of my generation notice nothing, do nothing, though action is simply as necessary as, say, breath or bread. And mind you, I speak not of big, burning questions that have bored everybody to death, but of a trillion trivia which people do not perceive, although they, those trifles, are the embryos of most obvious monsters. Just the other day, for example, a mother, having lost patience, drowned her two-year-old daughter in the bathtub and then took a bath in the same water, because it was hot, and hot water should not be squandered. Good God, how far this is from the old peasant woman, in one of Turgenev's turgid little tales, who had just lost her son and shocked the fine lady who visited her in her isba by calmly finishing a bowl of cabbage soup 'because it had been salted'! I shan't mind in the least if you regard as absurd the fact that the tremendous number of similar trifles, every day, everywhere, of various degrees of importance and of different shapes—tailed germs, punctiform, cubic—can trouble a man so badly that he suffocates and loses his appetite—but, maybe, you will come all the same."

I have combined here our conversation at the Royal Versailles with excerpts from a diffuse letter that Shishkov sent me next day by way of corroboration. On the following Saturday I was a little late for the meeting, so that when I entered his *chambre garnie* which was as modest as it was tidy, all were assembled, excepting the famous writer. Among those present, I knew by sight the editor of a defunct publication; the others—an ample female (a translatress, I believe, or perhaps a theosophist) with a gloomy little husband resembling a black breloque; her old mother; two seedy gentlemen in the kind of ill-fitting suits that the émigré cartoonist Mad gives to his characters; and an energetic-looking blond fellow, our host's chum—were unknown to me. Upon observing that Shishkov kept cocking an anxious ear—observing, too, how resolutely and joyfully he clapped the table and rose, before realizing that the doorbell he had heard pertained to another apartment—I ardently hoped for the celebrity's arrival, but the old boy never turned up.

"Ladies and gentlemen," said Shishkov and began to develop, quite eloquently and engagingly, his plans for a monthly, which would be entitled *A Survey of Pain and Vulgarity* and would mainly consist of a collection of relevant newspaper items for the month, with the stipulation that they be arranged not chronologically but in an "ascending" and "artistically unobtrusive" sequence. The one-time editor quoted certain figures and declared he was perfectly sure that a Russian émigré review of that sort would never sell. The husband of the ample literary lady removed his pince-nez and, while massaging the bridge of his nose, said with horrible haws and hems that if the intention was to fight human misery, it might be much more practical to distribute among the poor the sum of money needed for the review; and since it was from him one expected that money, a chill came over the listeners. After that, the host's friend repeated—in brisker but baser terms—what Shishkov had already stated. My opinion was also asked. The expression on Shishkov's face was so tragic that I did my best to champion his project. We dispersed rather early. As he was accompanying us to the landing, Shishkov slipped and, a little longer than was required to encourage the general laughter, remained sitting on the floor with a cheerful smile and impossible eyes.

A fortnight later he again came to see me, and again the four German refugees were discussing passport problems, and presently a fifth entered and cheerfully said: *"Bonjour, Monsieur Weiss, bonjour, Monsieur Meyer."* To my questions, Shishkov replied, rather absently and as it were reluctantly, that the idea of his journal had been found unrealizable, and that he had stopped thinking about it.

"Here's what I wanted to tell you," he began after an uneasy silence: "I have been trying and trying to come to a decision and now I think I have hit upon something, more or less. *Why* I am in this terrible state would hardly interest you; I explained what I could in my letter but that concerned mainly the business in hand, the magazine. The question is more extensive, the question is more hopeless. I have been trying to decide what to do—how to stop things, how to get out. Beat it to Africa, to the colonies? But it is hardly worth starting the Herculean task of obtaining the necessary papers only to find myself pondering in the midst of date palms and scorpions the same things I ponder under the Paris rain. Try making my way back to Russia? No, the frying pan is enough. Retire to a monastery? But religion is boring and alien to me and relates no more than a chimera to what is to me the reality of the spirit. Commit suicide? But capital punishment is something I find too repulsive to be able to act as my own executioner, and, furthermore, I dread certain consequences undreamt of in Hamlet's philosophy. Thus there remains but one issue: to disappear, to dissolve."

He inquired further whether his manuscript was safe, and shortly afterwards left, broad-shouldered yet a little stooped, trench-coated, hatless, the back of his neck needing a haircut—an extraordinarily attractive, pure, melancholy human being, to whom I did not know what to say, what assistance to render.

In late May I left for another part of France and upon returning to Paris at the end of August happened to run into Shishkov's friend. He told me a bizarre story: some time after my departure, "Vasya" had vanished, abandoning his meager belongings. The police could discover nothing—beyond the fact that *le sieur Chichkoff* had long since allowed his *karta*, as the Russians call it, to run out.

That is all. With the kind of incident that opens a mystery story my narrative closes. I got from his friend, or rather chance acquaintance, bits of scant information about Shishkov's life and these I jotted down—they may prove useful someday. But where the deuce did he go? And, generally speaking, what did he have in mind when he said he intended "to disappear, to dissolve"? Cannot it actually be that in a wildly literal sense, unacceptable to one's reason, he meant disappearing in his art, dissolving in his verse, thus leaving of himself, of his nebulous person, nothing but verse? One wonders if he did not overestimate

The transparence and soundness
Of such an unusual coffin.

ULTIMA THULE

D O Y O U remember the day you and I were lunching (partaking of nourishment) a couple of years before your death? Assuming, of course, that memory can live without its headdress? Let us imagine—just an "apropositional" thought—some totally new handbook of epistolary samples. To a lady who has lost her right hand: I kiss your ellipsis. To a deceased: Respecterfully yours. But enough of these sheepish vignettes. If you don't remember, then I remember for you: the memory of you can pass, grammatically speaking at least, for your memory, and I am perfectly willing to grant for the sake of an ornate phrase that if, after your death, I and the world still endure, it is only because you recollect the world and me. I address you now for the following reason. I address you now on the following occasion. I address you now simply to chat with you about Falter. What a fate! What a mystery! What a handwriting! When I tire of trying to persuade myself that he is a half-wit or a *kvak* (as you used to Russianize the English synonym for "charlatan"), he strikes me as a person who . . . who, because he survived the bomb of truth that exploded in him . . . became a god! Beside him, how paltry seem all the bygone clairvoyants: the dust raised by the herd at sunset, the dream within a dream (when you dream you have awakened), the crack students in this our institute of learning hermetically closed to outsiders; for Falter stands *outside* our world, in the true reality. Reality!—that is the pouter-pigeon throat of the snake that fascinates me. Remember the time we lunched at the hotel managed by Falter near the luxuriant, many-terraced Italian border, where the asphalt is infinitely exalted by the wisteria, and the air smells of rubber and paradise? Adam Falter was still one of us then, and, if nothing about him presaged . . . what shall I call it?—say, seerhood—nevertheless his whole strong cast (the caromlike coordination of his bodily movements, as though he had

500

ball bearings for cartilages, his precision, his aquiline aloofness) now, in retrospect, explains why he survived the shock: the original figure was large enough to withstand the subtraction.

Oh, my love, how your presence smiles from that fabled bay—and nevermore!—oh, I bite my knuckles so as not to start shaking with sobs, but there is no holding them back; down I slide with locked brakes, making "hoo" and "boohoo" sounds, and it is all such humiliating physical nonsense: the hot blinking, the feeling of suffocation, the dirty handkerchief, the convulsive yawning alternating with the tears—I just can't, can't live without you. I blow my nose, swallow, and then all over again try to persuade the chair which I clutch, the desk which I pound, that I can't boohoo without you. Are you able to hear me? That's from a banal questionnaire, which ghosts do not answer, but how willingly our death-cell-mates respond for them; "I know!" (pointing skyward at random), "I'll be glad to tell you!" Your darling head, the hollow of your temple, the forget-me-not gray of an eye squinting at an incipient kiss, the placid expression of your ears when you would lift up your hair . . . how can I reconcile myself to your disappearance, to this gaping hole, into which slides everything—my whole life, wet gravel, objects, and habits—and what tombal railings can prevent me from tumbling, with silent relish, into this abyss? Vertigo of the soul. Remember how, right after you died, I hurried out of the sanatorium, not walking but sort of stamping and even dancing with pain (life having got jammed in the door like a finger), alone on that winding road among the exaggeratedly scaly pines and the prickly shields of agaves, in a green armored world that quietly drew in its feet so as not to catch the disease. Ah, yes—everything around me kept warily, attentively silent, and only when I looked at something did that something give a start and begin ostentatiously to move, rustle, or buzz, pretending not to notice me. "Indifferent nature," says Pushkin. Nonsense! A continuous shying-away would be a more accurate description.

What a shame, though. You were such a darling. And, holding on to you from within by a little button, our child went with you. But, my poor sir, one does not make a child to a woman when she has tuberculosis of the throat. Involuntary translation from French into Hadean. You died in your sixth month and took the remaining twelve weeks with you, not paying off your debt in full, as it were. How much I wanted her to bear me a child, the red-nosed widower informed the walls. *Êtes-vous tout à fait certain, docteur, que la science ne connaît pas de ces cas exceptionnels où l'enfant naît dans la tombe?* And the dream I had: that garlicky doctor (who was at the same time Falter, or was it

Alexander Vasilievich?) replying with exceptional readiness, that yes, of course it sometimes did happen, and that such children (i.e., the post-humously born) were known as cadaverkins.

As to you, never once since you died have you appeared in my dreams. Perhaps the authorities intercept you, or you yourself avoid such prison visits with me. At first, base ignoramus that I was, I feared—superstitiously, humiliatingly—the small cracklings that a room always emits at night, but that were now reflected within me by terri-fying flashes which made my clucking heart scuttle away faster with low-spread wings. Even worse, however, was the nighttime waiting, when I would lie in bed, trying not to think how you might suddenly give me an answering knock if I thought about it, but this only meant complicating the mental parenthesization, placing brackets within braces (thinking about trying not to think), and the fear within them grew and grew. Oh, how awful was the dry tap of the phantasmal fin-gernail inside the tabletop, and how little it resembled, of course, the intonation of your soul, of your life. A vulgar ghost with the tricks of a woodpecker, a disincarnate humorist, a corny cobold taking advan-tage of my stark-naked grief! In the daytime, on the other hand, I was fearless, and would challenge you to manifest your responsiveness in any way you liked, as I sat on the pebbles of the beach, where once your golden legs had been extended; and, as before, a wave would ar-rive, all out of breath, but, as it had nothing to report, it would dis-perse in apologetic salaams. Pebbles like cuckoo eggs, a piece of tile shaped like a pistol clip, a fragment of topaz-colored glass, something quite dry resembling a whisk of bast, my tears, a microscopic bead, an empty cigarette package with a yellow-bearded sailor in the center of a life buoy, a stone like a Pompeian's foot, some creature's small bone or a spatula, a kerosene can, a shiver of garnet-red glass, a nutshell, a nondescript rusty thingum related to nothing, a shard of porcelain, of which the companion fragments must inevitably exist somewhere—and I imagined an eternal torment, a convict's task, that would serve as the best punishment for such as I, whose thoughts had ranged too far dur-ing their life span: namely, to find and gather all these parts, so as to re-create that gravy boat or soup tureen—hunchbacked wanderings along wild, misty shores. And, after all, if one is supremely lucky, one might restore the dish on the first morning instead of the trillionth—and there it is, that most agonizing question of *luck*, of Fortune's Wheel, of the right lottery ticket, without which a given soul might be denied eternal felicity beyond the grave.

On these early spring days the narrow strip of shingle is unadorned and forlorn, but strollers would pass along the promenade above, and this person or that, no doubt, must have said, on observing my shoulder blades, "There's Sineusov, the artist—lost his wife the other day." And I would probably have sat like that forever, picking at the desiccated jetsam, watching the stumbling foam, noting the sham tenderness of elongated serial cloudlets all along the horizon and the wine-dark washes of warmth in the chill blue-green of the sea, if someone indeed had not recognized me from the sidewalk.

However (as I fumble among the torn silks of phrase), let me return to Falter. As you have by now remembered, we went there once, on a torrid day, crawling like two ants up a flower-basket ribbon, because I was curious to take a look at my former tutor (whose lessons were limited to witty polemics with the compilers of my manuals), a resilient-looking, well-groomed man with a large white nose and a glossy parting in his hair; and it was along this straight line that he later traveled to business success, while his father, Ilya Falter, was only the senior chef at Ménard's in St. Petersburg: *il y a pauvre Ilya*, turning on *povar*, which is "man cook" in Russian. My angel, oh my angel, perhaps our whole earthly existence is now but a pun to you, or a grotesque rhyme, something like "dental" and "transcendental" (remember?), and the true meaning of reality, of that piercing term, purged of all our strange, dreamy, masquerade interpretations, now sounds so pure and sweet that you, angel, find it amusing that we could have taken the dream seriously (although you and I did have an inkling of why everything disintegrated at one furtive touch—words, conventions of everyday life, systems, persons—so, you know, I think laughter is some chance little ape of truth astray in our world).

I was now seeing him after an interval of twenty years; and how right I had been, when approaching the hotel, to construe all of its classical ornaments—the cedar of Lebanon, the eucalyptus, the banana tree, the terra-cotta tennis court, the enclosure for cars beyond the lawn—as a ceremonial of fortunate fate, as a symbol of the corrections that the former image of Falter now required! During our years of separation (quite painless for us both) he had changed from a poor, wiry student with animated night-dark eyes and a beautiful, strong, sinistral handwriting into a dignified, rather corpulent gentleman, though the liveliness of his glance and the beauty of his large hands were undiminished—only I would never have recognized him from the back, for, instead of the thick, sleek hair and shaven nape, there was now a nimbus of black fluff encircling a sun-browned bald spot akin to a tonsure. With his silk shirt, the color of stewed rutabaga, his checked tie, his wide pearl-gray pants, and his piebald shoes, he struck me as being dressed up for a fancy-dress ball; but his large nose was the same as ever, and with it he infallibly caught the light scent of the past when I came up, slapped him on his muscular shoulder, and posed him my riddle. You were standing a little way off, your bare ankles pressed together on their high cobalt-blue heels, examining with restrained but mischievous interest the furnishings of the enormous hall, empty at that hour—the hippopotamus hide of the armchairs, the austere bar, the British magazines on the glass-topped table, the frescoes, of studied simplicity, depicting scanty-breasted bronzed girls against a golden background, one of whom, with parallel strands of stylized hair falling along her cheek, had for some reason gone down on one knee. Could we conceive that the master of all this splendor would ever cease to see it? My angel. . . . Meanwhile, taking my hands in his, squeezing them, puckering the skin between his brows and fixing me with dark, narrowed eyes, he was observing that life-suspending pause observed by those who are about to sneeze but are not quite sure if they will succeed . . . but he succeeded, the past burst into light, and he loudly pronounced my nickname. He kissed your hand, without bending his head, and then, in a benevolent fuss, obviously enjoying the fact that I, a person who had seen better days, had now found him in the full glory of the life he had himself created by the power of his sculptitory will, he seated us on the terrace, ordered cocktails and lunch, introduced us to his brother-in-law, Mr. L., a cultured man in a dark business suit that contrasted oddly with Falter's exotic foppishness. We drank, we ate, we talked about the past as about someone gravely ill, I managed to balance a knife on the back of a fork, you petted the wonderful nervous dog that feared its master, and after a minute of silence, in the midst of which Falter suddenly uttered a distinct "Yes," as if concluding a diagnostic deliberation, we parted, making each other promises that neither he nor I had the least intention of keeping.

You didn't find anything remarkable about him, did you? And to be sure—that type has been done to death: throughout a drab youth supported his alcoholic father by giving lessons, and then slowly, obstinately, buoyantly achieved prosperity; for, in addition to the not very profitable hotel, he had flourishing interests in the wine business. But, as I understood later, you were wrong when you said that it was all somewhat dull and that energetic, successful fellows like him always reek of sweat. Actually, I am madly envious now of the early Falter's basic trait: the precision and power of his "volitional substance," as— you remember?—poor Adolf put it in a quite different context. Whether sitting in a trench or in an office, whether catching a train or getting up on a dark morning in an unheated room, whether arranging business connections or pursuing someone in friendship or enmity,

Adam Falter not only was always in possession of all his faculties, not only lived every moment cocked like a pistol, but was always certain of unfailingly achieving today's aim, and tomorrow's, and the whole gradual progression of his aims, at the same time working economically, for he did not aim high, and knew his limitations exactly. His greatest service to himself was that he deliberately disregarded his talents, and banked on the ordinary, the commonplace; for he was endowed with strange, mysteriously fascinating gifts, which some other, less circumspect person might have tried to put to practical use. Perhaps only in the very beginning of life had he sometimes been unable to control himself, intermixing the humdrum coaching of a schoolboy in a humdrum subject with unusually elegant manifestations of mathematical thought, which left a certain chill of poetry hanging about my schoolroom after he had hurried away to his next lesson. I think with envy that if my nerves were as strong as his, my soul as resilient, my willpower as condensed, he would have imparted to me nowadays the essence of the superhuman discovery he recently made—that is, he would not have feared that the information would crush me; I, on the other hand, would have been sufficiently persistent to make him tell me everything to the end.

A slightly husky voice hailed me discreetly from the promenade, but, as more than a year had passed since our luncheon with Falter, I did not immediately recognize his humble brother-in-law in the person who now cast a shadow on my stones. Out of mechanical politeness I went up to join him on the sidewalk, and he expressed his deepest et cetera: he had happened to stop by at my *pension*, he said, and the good people there had not only informed him of your death, but also indicated to him from afar my figure upon the deserted beach, a figure that had become a kind of local curiosity (for a moment I felt ashamed that the round back of my grief should be visible from every terrace).

"We met at Adam Ilyich's," he said, showing the stumps of his incisors and taking his place in my limp consciousness. I must have proceeded to ask him something about Falter.

"Oh, so you haven't heard?" the prattler said in surprise, and it was then that I learned the whole story.

It happened that the previous spring Falter had gone on business to a particularly viny Riviera town, and, as usual, stopped at a quiet little hotel, whose proprietor was a debtor of his of long standing. One must picture this hotel, tucked up in the feathered armpit of a hill overgrown with mimosa, and the little lane, not fully built up yet, with its half-dozen tiny villas, where radio sets sang in the small human space between the stardust and the sleeping oleanders, while crickets zinked the night with their stridulation in the vacant lot under Falter's open third-story window. After having passed a hygienic evening in a small bordello on the Boulevard de la Mutualité, he returned at about eleven to the hotel, in an excellent mood, clear of head and light of loin, and immediately went up to his room. The star-ashed brow of night; her expression of gentle insanity; the swarming of lights in the old town; an amusing mathematical problem about which he had corresponded the year before with a Swedish scholar; the dry, sweet smell that seemed to loll, without thought or task, here and there in the hollows of the darkness; the metaphysical taste of a wine, well bought and well sold; the news, recently received from a remote, unattractive country, of the death of a half-sister, whose image had long since wilted in his memory—all of this, I imagine, was floating through Falter's mind as he walked up the street and then mounted to his room; and while taken separately none of these reflections and impressions was in the least new or unusual for this hard-nosed, not quite ordinary, but superficial man (for, on the basis of our human core, we are divided into professionals and amateurs; Falter, like me, was an amateur), in their totality they formed perhaps the most favorable medium for the flash, the unearthly lightning, as catastrophic as a sweepstakes win, monstrously fortuitous, in no way foretold by the normal function of his reason, that struck him that night in that hotel.

About half an hour had passed since his return when the collective slumber of the small white building, with its barely rippling crapelike mosquito netting and wall flowers, was abruptly—no, not interrupted, but rent, split, blasted by sounds that remained unforgettable to the hearers, my darling—those sounds, those dreadful sounds. They were not the porcine squeals of a mollycoddle being dispatched by hasty villains in a ditch, not the roar of a wounded soldier whom a savage surgeon relieves of a monstrous leg—no, they were worse, far worse. . . . And if, said later the innkeeper, Monsieur Paon, one were going to make comparisons, those sounds resembled most of all the paroxysmal, almost exultant screams of a woman in the throes of infinitely painful childbirth—a woman, however, with a man's voice and a giant in her womb. It was hard to identify the dominant note amid the storm rending that human throat—whether it was pain, fear, or the clarion of madness, or again, and most likely of all, the expression of an unfathomable sensation, whose very unknowability imparted to the exultation bursting from Falter's room something that aroused in the hearers a panical desire to put an immediate stop to it. The newlyweds who were toiling in the nearest bed paused, diverting their eyes in parallel and holding their breath; the Dutchman living downstairs scuttled out into the garden, which already contained the housekeeper and the white shimmer of eighteen maids (only two, really, multiplied by their darting to and fro). The hotel keeper, who, according to his own account, had retained full presence of mind, rushed upstairs and ascertained that the door behind which continued the hurricane of howling, so mighty that it seemed to thrust one back, was locked from within and would yield neither to thump nor entreaty. Roaring Falter, insofar as one could assume it was indeed he that roared (his open window was dark, and the intolerable sounds issuing from within did not bear the imprint of anyone's personality), spread out far beyond the limits of the hotel, and neighbors gathered in the surrounding darkness, and one rascal had five cards in his hand, all trumps. By now it was completely incomprehensible how anyone's vocal cords could endure the strain: according to one account, Falter screamed for at least fifteen minutes; according to another and probably more accurate one, for about five without interruption. Suddenly (while the landlord was deciding whether to break down the door with a joint effort, place a ladder outside, or call the police) the screams, having attained the ultimate limits of agony, horror, amazement, and of that other quite undefinable something, turned into a medley of moans and then stopped altogether. It grew so quiet that at first those present conversed in whispers.

Cautiously, the landlord again knocked at the door, and from behind it came sighs and unsteady footfalls. Presently one heard someone fumbling at the lock, as though he did not know how to open it. A weak, soft fist began smacking feebly from within. Then Monsieur Paon did what he could actually have done much sooner—he found another key and opened the door.

"One would like some light," Falter said softly in the dark. Thinking for an instant that Falter had broken the lamp during his fit, the landlord automatically checked the switch, but the light obediently came on, and Falter, blinking in sickly surprise, turned his eyes from the hand that had engendered light to the newly filled glass bulb, as if seeing for the first time how it was done.

A strange, repulsive change had come over his entire exterior: he looked as if his skeleton had been removed. His sweaty and now somehow flabby face, with its hanging lip and pink eyes, expressed not only a dull fatigue, but also relief, an animal relief as after the pangs of monster-bearing. Naked to the waist, wearing only his pajama bottoms, he stood with lowered face, rubbing the back of one hand with the palm of the other. To the natural questions of Monsieur Paon and the hotel guests he gave no answer; he merely puffed out his cheeks,

pushed aside those who had surrounded him, came out on the landing, and began urinating copiously right on the stairs. Then he went
back, lay down on his bed, and fell asleep.

In the morning the hotel keeper called up Mrs. L., Falter's sister, to
warn her that her brother had gone mad, and he was bundled off
home, listless and half-asleep. The family doctor suggested it was just
a slight stroke and prescribed the correspondent treatment. But Falter
did not get better. After a time, it is true, he began walking about
freely, and even whistling at times, and uttering loud insults, and grabbing food the doctor had forbidden. However, the change remained.
He was like a man who had lost everything: respect for life, all interest
in money and business, all customary and traditional feelings, everyday
habits, manners, absolutely everything. It was unsafe to let him go
anywhere alone, for, with a curiosity quite superficial and quickly forgotten but offensive to others, he would address chance passersby, to
discuss the origin of a scar on someone's face or a statement, not addressed to him, that he had overheard in a conversation between
strangers. He would take an orange from a fruit stand as he passed,
and eat it unpeeled, responding with an indifferent half-smile to the
jabber of the fruit-woman who had run after him. When he grew tired
or bored he would squat on the sidewalk Turkish fashion and, for
something to do, try to catch girls' heels in his fist like flies. Once he
appropriated several hats, five felts and two panamas, which he had
painstakingly collected in various cafés, and there were difficulties with
the police.

His case attracted the attention of a well-known Italian psychiatrist, who happened to have a patient at Falter's hotel. This Dr.
Bonomini, a youngish man, was studying, as he himself would willingly explain, "the dynamics of the psyche," and sought to demonstrate in his works, whose popularity was not confined to learned
circles, that all psychic disorders could be explained by subliminal
memories of calamities that befell the patient's forebears, and that if,
for example, the subject were afflicted by megalomania, to cure him
completely it sufficed to determine which of his great-grandfathers was
a power-hungry failure, and explain to the great-grandson that the ancestor being dead had found eternal peace, although in complex cases
it was actually necessary to resort to theatrical representation, in costumes of the period, depicting the specific demise of the ancestor
whose role was assigned to the patient. These *tableaux vivants* grew so
fashionable that Bonomini was obliged to explain to the public in print
the dangers of staging them without his direct control.

Having questioned Falter's sister, Bonomini established that the

Falters did not know much about their forebears; true, Ilya Falter had been addicted to drink; but since, according to Bonomini's theory, "the patient's illness reflects only the distant past," as, for instance, a folk epic "sublimates" only remote occurrences, the details about Falter *père* were useless to him. Nevertheless he offered to try to help the patient, hoping by means of clever questioning to make Falter himself produce the explanation for his condition, after which the necessary ancestors could become deducible of their own accord; that an explanation did exist was confirmed by the fact that when Falter's intimates succeeded in penetrating his silence he would succinctly and dismissively allude to something quite out of the ordinary that he had experienced on that enigmatic night.

One day Bonomini closeted himself with Falter in the latter's room, and, like the knower of human hearts he was, with his horn-rimmed glasses and that hankie in his breast pocket, managed apparently to get out of him an exhaustive reply about the cause of his nocturnal howls. Hypnotism probably played its part in the business, for at the subsequent inquest Falter insisted that he had blabbed against his will, and that it rankled. He added, however, that never mind, sooner or later he would have made the experiment anyway, but that now he would definitely never repeat it. Be that as it may, the poor author of *The Heroics of Insanity* became the prey of Falter's Medusa. Since the intimate encounter between doctor and patient seemed to be lasting abnormally long, Eleonora L., Falter's sister, who had been knitting a gray shawl on the terrace, and for a long time already had not heard the psychiatrist's release-inducing, high-spirited, or falsely cajoling little tenor, which at first had been more or less audible through the half-open French window, entered her brother's room, and found him examining with dull curiosity the alpine sanatoriums in a brochure that had probably been brought by the doctor, while the doctor himself sprawled half on a chair and half on the carpet, with a gap of linen showing between waistcoat and trousers, his short legs spread wide and his pale café-au-lait face thrown back, felled, as was later determined, by heart failure. To the questions of the officiously meddling police Falter replied absently and tersely; but, when he finally grew tired of this pestering, he pointed out that, having accidentally solved "the riddle of the universe," he had yielded to artful exhortation and shared that solution with his inquisitive interlocutor, whereupon the latter had died of astonishment. The local newspapers caught up the story, embellished it properly, and the person of Falter, in the guise of a Tibetan sage, for several days nourished the not overparticular news columns.

But, as you know, during those days I did not read the papers: you were dying then. Now, however, having heard the story of Falter in detail, I experienced a certain very strong and perhaps slightly shame-faced desire.

You understand, of course. In the condition I was in, people with-out imagination—i.e., deprived of its support and inquiry—turn to the advertisements of wonder-workers; to chiromancers in comedy tur-bans, who combine the magic business with a trade in rat poison or rubber sheaths; to fat, swarthy women fortune-tellers; but particularly to spiritualists, who fake a still unidentified force by giving it the milky features of phantoms and getting them to manifest themselves in silly physical ways. But I have my share of imagination, and therefore two possibilities existed: the first was my work, my art, the consolation of my art; the second consisted of taking the plunge and believing that a person like Falter, rather average when you come down to it, despite a shrewd mind's parlor games, and even a little vulgar, had actually and conclusively learned that at which no seer, no sorcerer had ever arrived.

My art? You remember him, don't you, that strange Swede or Dane—or Icelander, for all I know—anyway, that lanky, orange-tanned blond fellow with the eyelashes of an old horse, who introduced him-self to me as "a well-known writer," and, for a price that gladdened you (you were already confined to your bed and unable to speak, but would write me funny trifles with colored chalk on slate—for instance, that the things you liked most in life were "verse, wildflowers, and for-eign currency"), commissioned me to make a series of illustrations for the epic poem *Ultima Thule*, which he had just composed in his lan-guage. Of course there could be no question of my acquainting myself thoroughly with his manuscript, since French, in which we agonizingly communicated, was known to him mostly by hearsay, and he was un-able to translate his imagery for me. I managed to understand only that his hero was some Northern king, unhappy and unsociable; that his kingdom, amid the sea mists, on a melancholy and remote island, was plagued by political intrigues of some kind, assassinations, insur-rections, and that a white horse which had lost its rider was flying along the misty heath. . . . He was pleased with my first *blanc et noir* sample, and we decided on the subjects of the other drawings. As he did not turn up in a week as he had promised, I called his hotel, and learned that he had left for America.

I concealed my employer's disappearance from you, but did not go on with the drawings; then again, you were already so ill that I did not feel like thinking about my golden pen and traceries in India ink. But when you died, when the early mornings and late evenings became especially unbearable, then, with a pitiful, feverish eagerness, the awareness of which would bring tears to my own eyes, I would continue the work for which I knew no one would come, and for that very reason that task seemed to me appropriate—its spectral, intangible nature, the lack of aim or reward would lead me away to a realm akin to the one in which, for me, you exist, my ghostly goal, my darling, such a darling earthly creation, for which no one will ever come anywhere; and since everything kept distracting me, fobbing upon me the paint of temporality instead of the graphic design of eternity, tormenting me with your tracks on the beach, with the stones on the beach, with your blue shadow on the loathsome bright beach, I decided to return to our lodging in Paris and settle down to work seriously. *Ultima Thule*, that island born in the desolate, gray sea of my heartache for you, now attracted me as the home of my least expressible thoughts.

However, before leaving the Riviera, I absolutely had to see Falter. This was the second solace I had invented for myself. I managed to convince myself that he was not simply a lunatic after all, that not only did he believe in the discovery he had made, but that this very discovery was the source of his madness, and not vice versa. I learned that he had moved to an apartment next to my *pension*. I also learned that his health was flagging; that when the flame of life had gone out in him it had left his body without supervision and without incentive; that he would probably die soon. I learned, finally, and this was especially important to me, that lately, in spite of his failing strength, he had grown unusually talkative and for days on end would treat his visitors (and alas, a different kind of curiosity-seeker than I got through to him) to speeches in which he caviled at the mechanics of human thought, oddly meandering speeches, exposing nothing, but almost Socratic in rhythm and sting. I offered to visit him, but his brother-in-law replied that the poor fellow enjoyed any diversion, and had the strength to reach my house.

And so they arrived—that is, the brother-in-law in his inevitable shabby black suit, his wife Eleonora (a tall, taciturn woman, whose clear-cut sturdiness recalled the former frame of her brother, and now served as a kind of living lesson to him, an adjacent moralistic picture), and Falter himself, whose appearance shocked me, even though I was prepared to see him changed. How can I express it? Mr. L. had said that he looked as if his bones had been removed; I, on the other hand, had the impression that his soul had been extracted but his mind intensified tenfold in recompense. By this I mean that one look at Falter was sufficient to understand that one need not expect from him any of the human feelings common in everyday life, that Falter had utterly lost the knack of loving anyone, of feeling pity, if only for himself, of experiencing kindness and, on occasion, compassion for the soul of another, of habitually serving, as best he could, the cause of good, if only that of his own standard, just as he had lost the knack of shaking hands or using his handkerchief. And yet he did not strike one as a madman—oh, no, quite the contrary! In his oddly bloated features, in his unpleasant, satiated gaze, even in his flat feet, shod no longer in fashionable Oxfords but in cheap espadrilles, one could sense some concentrated power, and this power was not in the least interested in the flabbiness and inevitable decay of the flesh that it squeamishly controlled.

His attitude toward me now was not that of our last brief encounter, but that which I remembered from the days of our youth, when he would come to coach me. No doubt he was perfectly aware that, chronologically, a quarter of a century had passed since those days, and yet as though along with his soul he had lost his sense of time (without which the *soul* cannot live), he obviously regarded me—a matter not so much of words, but of his whole manner—as if it had all been yesterday; yet he had no sympathy, no warmth whatever for me—nothing, not even a speck of it.

They seated him in an armchair, and he spread his limbs strangely, as a chimpanzee might do when his keeper makes him parody a Sybarite in a recumbent position. His sister settled down to her knitting, and during the whole course of the conversation did not once raise her short-haired gray head. Her husband took two newspapers—a local one, and one from Marseilles—out of his pocket, and was also silent. Only when Falter, noticing a large photograph of you that happened to be standing right in his line of sight, asked where were you hiding, did Mr. L. say, in the loud, artificial voice people use to address the deaf, and without looking up from his newspaper: "Come, you know perfectly well she is dead."

"Ah, yes," remarked Falter with inhuman unconcern, and, addressing me, added, "Oh well, may the kingdom of heaven be hers—isn't that what one is supposed to say in society?"

Then the following conversation began between us; total recall, rather than shorthand notes, now allows me to transcribe it exactly.

"I wanted to see you, Falter," I said (actually addressing him by first name and patronymic, but, in narration, his timeless image does not tolerate any conjunction of the man with a definite country and a genetic past), "I wanted to see you in order to have a frank talk with you. I wonder if you would consider it possible to ask your relatives to leave us alone."

"They do not count," abruptly observed Falter.

"When I say 'frank,' " I went on, "I presuppose the reciprocal possibility of asking no matter what questions, and the readiness to answer them. But since it is I who shall ask the questions, and expect answers from you, everything depends upon your consent to be straightforward; you do not need that assurance from me."

"To a straightforward question I shall give a straightforward answer," said Falter.

"In that case allow me to come right to the point. We shall ask Mr. and Mrs. L. to step outside for a moment, and you will tell me verbatim what you told the Italian doctor."

"Well, I'll be damned," said Falter.

"You cannot refuse me this. In the first place, the information won't kill me—this I guarantee you; I may look tired and seedy but don't you worry, I still have enough strength left. In the second place, I promise to keep your secret to myself, and even to shoot myself, if you like, immediately after learning it. You see, I allow that my loquacity may bother you even more than my death. Well, do you agree?"

"I refuse absolutely," replied Falter, and swept away a book from the table next to him to make room for his elbow.

"For the sake of somehow starting our talk, I shall temporarily accept your refusal. Let us proceed *ab ovo*. Now then, Falter, I understand that the essence of things has been revealed to you."

"Yes, period," said Falter.

"Agreed—you will not tell me about it; nevertheless, I draw two important deductions: things do have an essence, and this essence can be revealed to the mind."

Falter smiled. "Only do not call them deductions, mister. They are but flag stops. Logical reasoning may be a most convenient means of mental communication for covering short distances, but the curvature of the earth, alas, is reflected even in logic: an ideally rational progression of thought will finally bring you back to the point of departure where you return aware of the simplicity of genius, with a delightful sensation that you have embraced truth, while actually you have merely embraced your own self. Why set out on that journey, then? Be content with the formula: the essence of things has been revealed—wherein, incidentally, a blunder of yours is already present; I cannot explain it to you, since the least hint at an explanation would be a lethal glimpse. As long as the proposition remains static, one does not notice the blunder. But anything you might term a deduction already exposes the flaw: logical development inexorably becomes an envelopment."

"All right, for the present I shall be content with that much. Now allow me a question. When a hypothesis enters a scientist's mind, he checks it by calculation and experiment, that is, by the mimicry and the pantomime of truth. Its plausibility infects others, and the hypothesis is accepted as the true explanation for the given phenomenon, until someone finds its faults. I believe the whole of science consists of such exiled or retired ideas: and yet at one time each of them boasted high rank; now only a name or a pension is left. But in your case, Falter, I suspect that you have found some different method of discovery and test. May I call it 'revelation' in the theological sense?"

"You may not," said Falter.

"Wait a minute. Right now I am interested not so much in the method of discovery as in your conviction that the result is true. In other words, either you have a method of checking the result, or the awareness of its truth is inherent in it."

"You see," answered Falter, "in Indochina, at the lottery drawings, the numbers are extracted by a monkey. I happen to be that monkey. Another metaphor: in a country of honest men a yawl was moored at the shore, and it did not belong to anyone; but no one knew that it did not belong to anyone; and its assumed appurtenance to someone rendered it invisible to all. I happened to get into it. But perhaps it would be simplest of all if I said that in a moment of playfulness, not mathematical playfulness, necessarily—mathematics, I warn you, is but a perpetual game of leapfrog over its own shoulders as it keeps breeding—I kept combining various ideas, and finally found the right combination and exploded, like Berthold Schwartz. Somehow I survived; perhaps another in my place might have survived, too. However, after the incident with my charming doctor I do not have the least desire to be bothered by the police again."

"You're warming up, Falter. But let's get back to the point: what exactly makes you certain that it is the truth? That monkey is not really a party to the cast lots."

"Truths, and shadows of truths," said Falter, "in the sense of species, of course, not specimens, are so rare in the world, and available ones are either so trivial or tainted, that—how shall I put it?—that the *recoil* upon perceiving Truth, the instant reaction of one's whole being, remains an unfamiliar, little-studied phenomenon. Oh, well, sometimes in children—when a boy wakes up or regains his senses after a bout with scarlet fever and there is an electric discharge of reality, relative reality, no doubt, for you, humans, possess no other. Take any truism, that is, the corpse of a relative truth. Now analyze the physical sensation evoked in you by the words 'black is darker than brown,' or 'ice is cold.' Your thought is too lazy even to make a polite pretense of raising its rump from its bench, as if the same teacher were to enter your classroom a hundred times in the course of one lesson in old Russia. But, in my childhood, one day of great frost, I licked the shiny lock of a wicket. Let us dismiss the physical pain, or the pride of discovery, if it is a pleasant one—all that is not the real reaction to truth. You see, its impact is so little known that one cannot even find an exact word for it. All your nerves simultaneously answer 'yes!'—something like that. Let us also set aside a kind of astonishment, which is merely the unaccustomed assimilation of the *thingness* of truth, not of Truth itself. If you tell me that So-and-so is a thief, then I combine at once in my mind a number of suddenly illuminated trifles that I had myself observed, yet I have time to marvel that a man who had seemed so upright turned out to be a crook, but unconsciously I have already absorbed the truth, so that my astonishment itself promptly assumes an inverted form (how could one have ever thought honest such an obvious crook?); in other words, the sensitive point of truth lies exactly halfway between the first surprise and the second."

"Right. This is all fairly clear."

"On the other hand, surprise carried to stunning, unimaginable dimensions," Falter went on, "can have extremely painful effects, and it is still nothing compared to the shock of Truth itself. And *that* can no longer be 'absorbed.' It was by chance that it did not kill me, just as it was by chance that it struck me. I doubt one could think of checking a sensation of such intensity. A check can, however, be made ex post facto, though I personally have no need for the complexities of the verification. Take any commonplace truth—for instance, that two angles equal to a third are equal to each other; does the postulate also include anything about ice being hot or rocks occurring in Canada? In other words, a given truthlet, to coin a diminutive, does not contain any other related truthlets and, even less, such ones that belong to different kinds or levels of knowledge or thought. What, then, would you say about a Truth with a capital *T* that comprises in itself the explanation and the proof of all possible mental affirmations? One can believe in the poetry of a wildflower or the power of money, but neither belief predetermines faith in homeopathy or in the necessity to exterminate antelope on the islands of Lake Victoria Nyanza; but in any case, having learned what I have—if this can be called learning—I received a key to absolutely all the doors and treasure chests in the world; only I

have no need to use it, since every thought about its practical significance automatically, by its very nature, grades into the whole series of
hinged lids. I may doubt my physical ability to imagine to the very end
all the consequences of my discovery, and namely, to what degree I
have not yet gone insane, or, inversely, how far behind I have left all
that is meant by insanity; but I certainly cannot doubt that, as you put
it, 'essence has been revealed to me.' Some water, please."

"Here you are. But let me see, Falter—did I understand you correctly? Are you really henceforth a candidate for omniscience? Excuse
me, but I don't have that impression. I can allow that you know something fundamental, but your words contain no concrete indications of
absolute wisdom."

"Saving my strength," said Falter. "Anyway, I never affirmed that I
know everything now—Arabic, for example, or how many times in
your life you have shaved, or who set the type for the newspaper which
that fool over there is reading. I only say that I know everything I
might want to know. Anyone could say that—couldn't he?—after having leafed through an encyclopedia; only, the encyclopedia whose exact
title I have learned (there, by the way—I am giving you a more elegant
definition: I know the title of things) is literally all-inclusive, and
therein lies the difference between me and the most versatile scholar
on earth. You see, I have learned—and here I am leading you to the
very edge of the Riviera precipice, ladies don't look—I have learned
one very simple thing about the world. It is by itself so obvious, so
amusingly obvious, that only my wretched humanity can consider it
monstrous. When in a moment I say 'congruent' I shall mean something infinitely removed from all the congruencies known to you, just
as the nature itself of my discovery has nothing in common with the
nature of any physical or philosophical conjectures. Now the main
thing in me that is congruent with the main thing in the universe
could not be affected by the bodily spasm that has thus shattered me.
At the same time the possible knowledge of all things, consequent to
the knowledge of the fundamental one, did not dispose in me of a sufficiently solid apparatus. I am training myself by willpower not to leave
the vivarium, to observe the rules of your mentality as if nothing had
happened; in other words, I act like a beggar, a versifier, who has received a million in foreign currency, but goes on living in his basement, for he knows that the least concession to luxury would ruin his
liver."

"But the treasure is in your possession, Falter—that's what hurts.
Let us drop the discussion of your attitude toward it, and talk about
the thing itself. I repeat—I have taken note of your refusal to let me

peek at your Medusa, and am further willing to refrain from the most evident inferences, since, as you hint, any logical conclusion is a confinement of thought in itself. I propose to you a different method for our questions and answers: I shall not ask you about the contents of your treasure; but, after all, you will not give away its secret by telling me if, say, it lies in the East, or if there is even one topaz in it, or if even one man has ever passed in its proximity. At the same time, if you answer 'yes' or 'no' to a question, I not only promise to avoid choosing that particular line for a further series of related questions, but pledge to end the conversation altogether."

"Theoretically, you are luring me into a clumsy trap," said Falter, shaking slightly, as another might do when laughing. "Actually, it would be a trap only if you were capable of asking me at least one such question. There is very little chance of that. Therefore, if you enjoy pointless amusement, fire away."

I thought a moment and said, "Falter, allow me to begin like the traditional tourist—with an inspection of an ancient church, familiar to him from pictures. Let me ask you: does God exist?"

"Cold," said Falter.

I did not understand and repeated the question.

"Forget it," snapped Falter. "I said 'cold,' as they say in the game, when one must find a hidden object. If you are looking under a chair or under the shadow of a chair, and the object cannot be in that place, because it happens to be somewhere else, then the question of there existing a chair or its shadow has nothing whatever to do with the game. To say that perhaps the chair exists but the object is not there is the same as saying that perhaps the object is there but the chair does not exist, which means that you end up again in the circle so dear to human thought."

"You must agree, though, Falter, that if as you say the thing sought is not anywhere near to the concept of God, and if that thing is, according to your terminology, a kind of universal 'title,' then the concept of God does not appear on the title page; hence, there exists no true necessity for such a concept, and since there is no need for God, no God exists."

"Then you did not understand what I said about the relationship between a possible place and the impossibility of finding the object in it. All right, I shall put it more clearly. By the very act of your mentioning a given concept you placed your own self in the position of an enigma, as if the seeker himself were to hide. And by persisting in your question, you not only hide, but also believe that by sharing with the sought-for object the quality of 'hiddenness' you bring it closer to you.

How can I answer you whether God exists when the matter under discussion is perhaps sweet peas or a soccer linesman's flag? You are looking in the wrong place and in the wrong way, *cher monsieur*, that is all the answer I can give you. And if it seems to you that from this answer you can draw the least conclusion about the uselessness or necessity of God, it is just because you are looking in the wrong place and in the wrong way. Wasn't it you, though, that promised not to follow logical patterns of thought?"

"Now I too am going to trap you, Falter. Let's see how you'll manage to avoid a direct statement. One cannot, then, seek the title of the world in the hieroglyphics of deism?"

"Pardon me," replied Falter, "by means of ornate language and grammatical trickery Moustache-Bleue is merely disguising the expected *non* as an expected *oui*. At the moment all I do is deny. I deny the expediency of the search for Truth in the realm of common theology, and, to save your mind empty labor, I hasten to add that the epithet I have used is a dead end: do not turn into it. I shall have to terminate the discussion *for lack of an interlocutor* if you exclaim 'Aha, then there is *another*, "uncommon," truth!'—for this would mean that you have hidden yourself so well as to have lost yourself."

"All right. I shall believe you. Let us grant that theology muddies the issue. Is that right, Falter?"

"This is the house that Jack built," said Falter.

"All right, we dismiss this false trail as well. Even though you could probably explain to me why it is false (for there is something queer and elusive here, something that irritates you), and then your reluctance to reply would be clear to me."

"I could," said Falter, "but it would be equivalent to revealing the gist of the matter, that is, exactly what you are not going to get out of me."

"You repeat yourself, Falter. Don't tell me you will be just as evasive if, for instance, I ask you: can one expect an afterlife?"

"Does it interest you very much?"

"Just as much as it does you, Falter. Whatever you may know about death, we are both mortal."

"In the first place," said Falter, "I call your attention to the following curious catch: any man is mortal; you are a man; therefore, it is also possible that *you are not mortal*. Why? Because a specified man (you or I) for that very reason ceases to be *any man*. Yet both of us are indeed mortal, but I am mortal in a different way than you."

"Don't spite my poor logic, but give me a plain answer: is there even a glimmer of one's identity beyond the grave, or does it all end in ideal darkness?"

"Bon," said Falter, as is the habit of Russian émigrés in France. "You want to know whether Gospodin Sineusov will forever reside within the snugness of Gospodin Sineusov, otherwise Moustache-Bleue, or whether everything will abruptly vanish. There are two ideas here, aren't there? Round-the-clock lighting and the black inane. Actually, despite the difference in metaphysical color, they greatly resemble each other. And they move in parallel. They even move at considerable speed. Long live the totalizator! Hey, hey, look through your turf glasses, they're racing each other, and you would very much like to know which will arrive first at the post of truth, but in asking me to give you a yes or no for either one or the other, you want me to catch one of them at full speed by the neck—and those devils have awfully slippery necks—but even if I were to grab one of them for you, I would merely interrupt the competition, or the winner would be the other, the one I did not snatch, an utterly meaningless result inasmuch as no rivalry would any longer exist. If you ask, however, which of the two runs faster, I shall retort with another question: what runs faster, strong desire or strong fear?"

"Same pace, I suppose."

"That's just it. For look what happens in the case of the poor little human mind. Either it has no way to express what awaits you—I mean, us—after death, and then total unconsciousness is excluded, for *that* is quite accessible to our imagination—every one of us has experienced the total darkness of dreamless sleep; or, on the contrary, death *can* be imagined, and then one's reason naturally adopts not the notion of eternal life, an unknown entity, incongruent with anything terrestrial, but precisely that which seems more probable—the familiar darkness of stupor. Indeed, how can a man who trusts in his reason admit, for instance, that someone who is dead drunk and dies while sound asleep from a chance external cause—thus losing by chance what he no longer really possessed—again acquires the ability to reason and feel thanks to the mere extension, consolidation, and perfection of his unfortunate condition? Hence, if you were to ask me only one thing: do I know, in human terms, what lies beyond death—that is, if you attempted to avert the absurdity in which must peter out the competition between two opposite, but basically similar concepts—a negative reply on my part would logically make you conclude that your life cannot end in nothingness, while from an affirmative you would draw the opposite conclusion. In either case, as you see, you would remain in exactly the same situation as before, since a dry 'no' would prove to you that I know no more than you about the given subject, while a moist 'yes' would suggest that you accept the existence of an international heaven which your reason cannot fail to doubt."

"You are simply evading a straightforward answer, but allow me to observe nevertheless that on the subject of death you do not give me the answer 'cold.' "

"There you go again," sighed Falter. "Didn't I just explain to you that any deduction whatsoever conforms to the curvature of thought? It is correct, as long as you remain in the sphere of earthly dimensions, but when you attempt to go beyond, your error grows in proportion to the distance you cover. And that's not all: your mind will construe any answer of mine exclusively from a utilitarian viewpoint, for you are unable to conceive death otherwise than in the image of your own gravestone, and this in turn would distort to such an extent the sense of my answer as to turn it into a lie, ipso facto. So let us observe decorum even when dealing with the transcendental. I cannot express myself more clearly—and you ought to be grateful for any evasiveness. You have an inkling, I gather, that there is a little hitch in the very formulation of the question, a hitch, incidentally, that is more terrible than the fear itself of death. It's particularly strong in you, isn't it?"

"Yes, Falter. The terror I feel at the thought of my future unconsciousness is equal only to the revulsion caused in me by a mental foreview of my decomposing body."

"Well put. Probably other symptoms of this sublunary malady are present as well? A dull pang in the heart, suddenly, in the middle of the night, like the flash of a wild creature among domestic emotions and pet thoughts: 'Someday I also must die.' It happens to you, doesn't it? Hatred for the world, which will very cheerfully carry on without you. A basic sensation that all things in the world are trifles and phantasmata compared to your mortal agony, and therefore to your life, for, you say to yourself, life itself is the agony before death. Yes, oh yes, I can imagine perfectly well that sickness from which you all suffer to a lesser or greater degree, and I can say one thing: I fail to understand how people can live under such conditions."

"There, Falter, we seem to be getting somewhere. Apparently, then, if I admitted that, in moments of happiness, of rapture, when my soul is laid bare, I suddenly feel that there is no extinction beyond the grave; that in an adjacent locked room, from under whose door comes a frosty draft, there is being prepared a peacock-eyed radiance, a pyramid of delights akin to the Christmas tree of my childhood; that everything—life, patria, April, the sound of a spring or that of a dear voice—is but a muddled preface, and that the main text still lies ahead—if I can feel that way, Falter, is it not possible to live, to live— tell me it's possible, and I'll not ask you anything more."

"In that case," said Falter, shaking again in soundless mirth, "I understand you even less. Skip the preface, and it's in the bag!"

" *Un bon mouvement*, Falter—tell me your secret."

"What are you trying to do, catch me off guard? You're crafty, I see. No, that is out of the question. In the first days—yes, in the first days I thought it might be possible to share my secret. A grown man, unless he is a bull like me, would not stand it—all right; but I wondered if one could not bring up a new generation of the *initiated*, that is, turn my attention to children. As you see, I did not immediately overcome the infection of local dialects. In practice, however, what would happen? In the first place, one can hardly imagine pledging kiddies to a vow of priestly silence lest any of them with one dreamy word commit manslaughter. In the second place, as soon as the child grows up, the information once imparted to him, accepted on faith, and allowed to sleep in a remote corner of his consciousness may give a start and awake, with tragic consequences. Even if my secret does not always destroy a mature member of the species, it is unthinkable that it should spare a youth. For who is not familiar with that period of life when all kinds of things—the starry sky above a Caucasian spa, a book read in the toilet, one's own conjectures about the cosmos, the delicious panic of solipsism—are in themselves enough to provoke a frenzy in all the senses of an adolescent human being? There is no reason for me to become an executioner; I have no intention of annihilating enemy regiments through a megaphone; in short, there is no one for me to confide in."

"I asked you two questions, Falter, and you have twice proved to me the impossibility of an answer. It seems to me useless to ask you about anything else—say, about the limits of the universe, or the origin of life. You would probably suggest that I be content with a speckled minute on a second-rate planet, served by a second-rate sun, or else you would again reduce everything to a riddle: is the word 'heterologous' heterologous itself."

"Probably," agreed Falter, giving a lengthy yawn.

His brother-in-law quietly scooped his watch out of his waistcoat and glanced at his wife.

"Here's the odd thing, though, Falter. How does superhuman knowledge of the ultimate truth combine in you with the adroitness of a banal sophist who knows nothing? Admit it, all your absurd quibbling was nothing more than an elaborate sneer."

"Oh well, that is my only defense," said Falter, squinting at his sister, who was nimbly extracting a long gray woolen scarf from the sleeve of the overcoat already being offered to him by his brother-in-law. "Otherwise, you know, you might have teased it out of me. However," he added, inserting the wrong arm, and then the right one in the sleeve, and simultaneously moving away from the helping shoves of his assistants, "however, even if I did browbeat you a little, let me console you: amid all the piffle and prate I inadvertently gave myself away—only two or three words, but in them flashed a fringe of absolute insight—luckily, though, you paid no attention."

He was led away, and thus ended our rather diabolical dialogue. Not only had Falter told me nothing, he had not even allowed me to get close, and no doubt his last pronouncement was as much of a mockery as all the preceding ones. The following day his brother-in-law's dull voice informed me on the telephone that Falter charged 100 francs for a visit; I asked why on earth had I not been warned of this, and he promptly replied that if the interview were to be repeated, two conversations would cost me only 150. The purchase of Truth, even at a discount, did not tempt me, and, after sending him the sum of that unexpected debt, I forced myself not to think about Falter any more. Yesterday, though. . . . Yes, yesterday I received a note from Falter himself, from the hospital: he wrote, in a clear hand, that he would die on Tuesday, and that in parting he ventured to inform me that—here followed two lines which had been painstakingly and, it seemed, ironically, blacked out. I replied that I was grateful for his thoughtfulness and that I wished him interesting posthumous impressions and a pleasant eternity.

But all this brings me no nearer to you, my angel. Just in case, I am keeping all the windows and doors of life wide open, even though I sense that you will not condescend to the time-honored ways of apparitions. Most terrifying of all is the thought that, inasmuch as you glow henceforth within me, I must safeguard my life. My transitory bodily frame is perhaps the only guarantee of your ideal existence: when I vanish, it will vanish as well. Alas, with a pauper's passion I am doomed to use physical nature in order to finish recounting you to myself, and then to rely on my own ellipsis. . . .

SOLUS REX

A
S ALWAYS happened, the king was awakened by the clash between the predawn watch and the midmorning one (*morn-
dammer wagh* and *erldag wagh*). The former, unduly punctual,
would leave its post at the prescribed minute, while the latter would be
late by a constant number of seconds, not because of negligence, but
probably because somebody's gouty timepiece was habitually slow.
Therefore those departing and those arriving always met at one and
the same place—the narrow footpath directly under the king's bedroom window, between the rear wall of the palace and a tangled
growth of dense but meagerly blooming honeysuckle, under which
was scattered all manner of trash: chicken feathers, broken earthenware, and large, red-cheeked tin cans that had contained "Pomona," a
national brand of preserved fruit. The meeting would invariably be accompanied by the muffled sound of a brief, good-natured tussle (and
it was this that awakened the king), as one of the predawn sentries, being of a roguish bent, would pretend he did not want to surrender the
slate bearing the password to one of the midmorning men, an irritable
and stupid old codger, veteran of the Swirhulm campaign. Then all
would grow still again, and the only audible sound would be the businesslike, now and then accelerating, crepitation of rain, which would
systematically fall for precisely 306 days out of 365 or -6, so that the
weather's peripeties had long since ceased to trouble anyone (here the
wind addressed the honeysuckle).

The king made a right turn out of his sleep and propped a big
white fist under his cheek, on which the blazon embroidered on the
pillowcase had left a chessboard impression. Between the inside edges
of the brown, loosely drawn curtains, in the single but broad window,
there seeped a beam of soapy light, and the king at once remembered
an imminent duty (his presence at the inauguration of a new bridge

across the Egel) whose disagreeable image seemed inscribed with geometric inevitability into that pale trigon of day. He was not interested in bridges, canals, or shipbuilding, and even though after five years—yes, exactly five years (826 days)—of nebulous reign he really ought to have acquired the habit of attending diligently to a multitude of matters that filled him with loathing because of their organic sketchiness in his mind (where very different things, in no way related to his royal office, were infinitely and unquenchably perfect), he felt depressingly aggravated every time he was obliged to have contact not only with anything that demanded a false smile from his deliberate ignorance, but also with that which was nothing more than a veneer of conventional standards on a senseless or perhaps even nonexistent object. If the inauguration of the bridge, the plans for which he did not even remember though he had no doubt approved them, struck him as merely a vulgar festival, it was also because nobody ever bothered to inquire whether he was interested in that intricate fruit of technology, suspended in midair, and yet today he would have to ride slowly across in a lustrous convertible with a toothy grille, and this was torture; and then there was that other engineer about whom people had been telling him ever since he had happened to mention (just like that, simply to get rid of someone or something) that he would enjoy doing some climbing, if only the island had a single decent mountain (the old, long-dead coastal volcano did not count, and, furthermore, a lighthouse—which, incidentally, did not work either—had been built on its summit). This engineer, whose dubious fame thrived in the drawing rooms of court ladies and courtesans, attracted by his honey-brown complexion and insinuating speech, had proposed elevating the central part of the insular plain and transforming it into a mountain massif, by means of subterranean inflation. The inhabitants of the chosen locality would be allowed to remain in their dwellings while the soil was being puffed up. Poltroons who preferred to withdraw from the test area where their little brick houses huddled and amazed red cows mooed, sensing the change in altitude, would be punished by their having to spend much more time on their return along the newly formed escarpments than they had on their recent retreat over the doomed flatland. Slowly the meadows swelled; boulders moved their round backs; a lethargic stream tumbled out of bed and, to its own surprise, turned into an alpine waterfall; trees traveled in file cloudward and many of them (the firs, for instance) enjoyed the ride; the villagers, leaning on their porch railings, waved their handkerchiefs and admired the pneumatic development of landscape. So the mountain would grow and grow, until the engineer ordered that the monstrous pumps be stopped. The king, however, did not wait for the stoppage, but dozed off again, with barely time to regret that, constantly resisting as he did the Councilors' readiness to support the realization of every harebrained scheme (while, on the other hand, his most natural, most human rights were constricted by rigid laws), he had not given permission for the experiment, and now it was too late, the inventor had committed suicide after patenting a gallow tree for indoor use (thus, anyway, the spirit of slumber retold it to the slumberer).

The king slept on till half past seven and, at the habitual minute, his mind jolted into action and was already on its way to meet Frey when Frey entered the bedroom. That decrepit, asthmatic *konwacher* invariably emitted in motion a queer supplementary sound, as if he were in a great hurry, although haste was apparently not in his line, seeing he had not yet got around to dying. He lowered a silver basin onto a taboret with a heart design cut out in its seat, as he had already been doing for half a century, under two kings; today he was waking a third, for whose predecessors this vanilla-scented and seemingly witch-charmed water had probably served an ablutionary purpose. Now, however, it was quite superfluous; and yet every morning the basin and taboret appeared, along with a towel that had been folded five years before. Continuing to emit his special sound, the old valet admitted the daylight in its entirety. The king always wondered why Frey did not open the curtains first, instead of groping in the penumbra to move the taboret with its useless utensil toward the bed. But speaking to Frey was out of the question because of his deafness, that went so well with the snow-owl white of his hair: he was cut off from the world by the cotton wool of old age, and, as he went out with a bow to the bed, the wall clock in the bedroom began to ticktack more distinctly, as if it had been given a recharge of time.

The bedroom now came into focus, with the dragon-shaped crack traversing its ceiling and the huge clothes tree standing like an oak in the corner. An admirable ironing board stood leaning against the wall. A thing for yanking one's riding boot off by the heel, an obsolete appliance in the shape of a huge cast-iron stag beetle, lurked under the border of an armchair robed in a white furniture cover. An oak wardrobe, obese, blind, and drugged by naphthalene, stood next to an ovoid wickerwork receptacle for soiled linen, set on end there by some unknown Columbus. Various objects hung at random on the bluish walls: a clock (it had already tattled about its presence), a medicine cabinet, an old barometer that indicated remembered rather than real weather, a pencil sketch of a lake with reeds and a departing duck, a myopic photograph of a leather-legginged gentleman astride a blurry-tailed horse held by a solemn groom in front of a porch, the same porch with strained-faced servants assembled on its steps, some fluffy flowers pressed under dusty glass in a circular frame. . . . The paucity of the furnishings and their utter irrelevance to the needs and the tenderness of whoever used this spacious bedroom (once, it seems, inhabited by the *Husmuder*, as the wife of the preceding king had been dubbed) gave it an oddly untenanted appearance, and if it were not for the intrusive basin and the iron bed, on the edge of which sat a man in a nightshirt with a frilly collar, his strong bare feet resting upon the floor, it was impossible to imagine that anyone spent his nights here. His toes groped for and found a pair of morocco slippers and, donning a dressing gown as gray as the morning, the king walked across the creaking floorboards to the felt-padded door. When he subsequently recalled that morning, it seemed to him that, upon arising, he had experienced, both in mind and in muscles, an unaccustomed heaviness, the fateful burden of the coming day, so that the awful misfortune which that day brought (and which beneath the mask of trivial boredom stood *already* on guard at the Egel bridge), absurd and unforeseeable as it was, thereafter seemed to him a kind of resolvent. We are inclined to attribute to the immediate past (I just had it in my hands, I put it right there, and now it's not there) lineaments relating it to the unexpected present, which in fact is but a bounder pluming himself on a purchased escutcheon. We, the slaves of linked events, endeavor to close the gap with a spectral ring in the chain. As we look back, we feel certain that the road we see behind us is the very one that has brought us to the tomb or the fountainhead near which we find ourselves. Life's erratic leaps and lapses can be endured by the mind only when signs of resilience and quagginess are discoverable in anterior events. Such, incidentally, were the thoughts that occurred to the no longer independent artist Dmitri Nikolaevich Sineusov, and evening had come, and in vertically arranged ruby letters glowed the word RENAULT.

The king set out in search of breakfast. He never knew in which of the five possible chambers situated along the cold stone gallery, with cobwebs in the corners of its ogival windows, his coffee would be waiting. Opening the doors one by one, he kept trying to locate the little set table, and finally found it where it happened least frequently: under a large, opulently dark portrait of his predecessor. King Gafon was portrayed at the age at which he remembered him, but features, posture, and bodily structure were endowed with a magnificence that had never been characteristic of that stoop-shouldered, fidgety, and sloppy old man with a peasant crone's wrinkles above his hairless and somewhat crooked upper lip. The words of the family arms, "see and rule" (*sassed ud halsem*), used to be changed by wags, when referring to him, to "armchair and filbert brandy" (*sasse ud hazel*). He reigned thirty-odd years, arousing neither particular love nor particular hatred in anyone, believing equally in the power of good and the power of money, docile in his acquiescence to the parliamentary majority, whose vapid humanitarian aspirations appealed to his sentimental soul, and generously rewarding from a secret treasury the activities of those deputies whose devotion to the crown assured its stability. Kingcraft had long since become for him the flywheel of a mechanical habit, and the benighted submissiveness of the country, where the *Peplerhus* (parliament) faintly shone like a bleary and crackling rushlight, appeared as a similar form of regular rotation. And if the very last years of his reign were poisoned nevertheless by bitter sedition, coming as a belch after a long and carefree dinner, not he was to blame, but the person and behavior of the crown prince. Indeed, in the heat of vexation good burghers found that the one-time scourge of the learned world, the now forgotten Professor ven Skunk, did not err much when he affirmed that childbearing was but an illness, and that every babe was an "externalized," self-existent parental tumor, often malignant.

The present king (pre-accessionally, let us designate him as K in chess notation) was the old man's nephew, and in the beginning no one dreamed that the nephew would accede to a throne rightfully promised to King Gafon's son, Prince Adulf, whose utterly indecent folkname (based on a felicitous assonance) must, for the sake of decorum, be translated "Prince Fig." K grew up in a remote palace under the eye of a morose and ambitious grandee and his horsey, masculine wife, so he barely knew his cousin and started seeing him a little more often only at the age of twenty, when Adulf was near forty.

We have before us a well-fed, easygoing fellow, with a stout neck, a broad pelvis, a big-cheeked, evenly pink face, and fine, bulging eyes. His nasty little mustache, resembling a pair of blue-black feathers, somehow did not match his fat lips, which always looked greasy, as if he had just finished sucking on a chicken bone. His dark, thick, unpleasantly smelling, and also greasy hair lent a foppish something, uncommon in Thule, to his large, solidly planted head. He had a penchant for showy clothes and was at the same time as unwashed as a *papugh* (seminarian). He was well versed in music, sculpture, and graphics, but could spend hours in the company of dull, vulgar persons. He wept profusely while listening to the melting violin of the great Perelmon, and shed the same tears while picking up the shards of a favorite cup. He was ready to help anyone in any way, if at that moment he was not occupied with other matters; and, blissfully wheezing, poking, and nibbling at life, he constantly contrived, in regard to third parties whose existence he did not bother about, to cause sorrows far exceeding in depth that of his own soul—sorrows pertaining to another, *the* other, world.

In his twentieth year K entered the University of Ultimare, situated at four hundred miles of purple heather from the capital, on the shore of the gray sea, and there learned something about the crown prince's morals, and would have heard much more if he did not avoid talks and discussions that might overburden his already none too easy anonymity. The Count, his guardian, who came to visit him once a week (sometimes arriving in the sidecar of a motorcycle driven by his energetic wife), continually emphasized how nasty, disgraceful, and dangerous it would be if any of the students or professors learned that this lanky, gloomy youth, who excelled as much at his studies as at *vanbol* on the two-hundred-year-old-court behind the library building, was not at all a notary's son, but a king's nephew. Whether it was submission to one of those many whims, enigmatic in their stupidity, with which someone unknown and mightier than the king and the *Peplerhus* together for some reason troubled the shabby, monotonous, northern life, faithful to half-forgotten covenants, of that *"île triste et lointaine"*; or whether the peeved grandee had his own private scheme, his farsighted calculation (the rearing of kings was supposed to be kept secret), we do not know; nor was there any reason to speculate about this, since, anyway, the unusual student was busy with other matters. Books, wallball, skiing (winters then used to be snowy), but, most of all, nights of special meditation by the hearth, and, a little later, his romance with Belinda—all sufficiently filled up his existence to leave him unconcerned with the vulgar little intrigues of metapolitics. Moreover, while diligently studying the annals of the fatherland, it never occurred to him that within him slumbered the very blood that had coursed through the veins of preceding kings; or that actual life rushing past was also "history"—history that had issued from the tunnel of the ages into pallid sunlight. Either because his subject of concentration ended a whole century before the reign of Gafon, or because the magic involuntarily evolved by the most sober chroniclers seemed more precious to him than his own testimony, the bookman in him overcame the eyewitness, and later on, when he tried to reestablish connection with the present, he had to content himself with knocking together provisional passages, which only served to deform the familiar remoteness of legend (that bridge on the Egel, that blood-spattered bridge!).

It was, then, before the beginning of his second college year that K, having come to the capital for a brief vacation and taken modest lodgings at the so-called Cabinet Members' Club, met, at the very first court reception, the crown prince, a boisterous, plump, indecently young-looking *charmeur*, defying one not to recognize his charm. The meeting took place in the presence of the old king, who sat in a high-backed armchair by a stained-glass window, quickly and nimbly devouring those tiny olive-black plums that were more a delicacy than a medicine for him. Even though Adulf seemed at first not to notice his young relative and continued to address two stooge-courtiers, the prince nevertheless started on a subject carefully calculated to fascinate the newcomer, to whom he offered a three-quarter view of himself: paunch-proud, hands thrust deep into the pockets of his wrinkled check trousers, he stood rocking slightly from heels to toes.

"For instance," he said in the triumphant voice he reserved for public occasions, "take our entire history, and you will see, gentlemen, that the root of power has always been construed among us as having originated in magic, with obedience conceivable only when, in the mind of the obeyer, it could be identified with the infallible effect of a spell. In other words, the king was either sorcerer or himself bewitched, sometimes by the people, sometimes by the Councilors, sometimes by a political foe who would whisk the crown off his head like a hat from a hatrack. Recall the hoariest antiquity and the rule of the *mossmons*" (high priests, "bog people"), "the worship of luminescent peat, that sort of thing; or take those . . . those first pagan kings—Gildras and, yes, Ofodras, and that other one, I forget what he was called, anyway, the fellow who threw his goblet into the sea, after which, for three days and nights, fishermen scooped up seawater transformed into wine. . . . *Solg ud digh vor je sage vel, ud jem gotelm quolm osje musikel*" ("Sweet and rich was the wave of the sea and lassies drank it from seashells"—the prince was quoting Uperhulm's ballad). "And the first friars, who arrived in a skiff equipped with a cross instead of a sail, and all that business of the 'Fontal Rock'—for it was only because they guessed the weak spot of our people that they managed to introduce the crazy Roman creed. What is more," continued the prince, suddenly moderating the crescendos of his voice, for a dignitary of the clergy was now standing a short distance away, "if the so-called church never really engorged on the body of our state, and, in the last two centuries, entirely lost its political significance, it is precisely because the elementary and rather monotonous miracles that it was able to produce very soon became a bore"—the cleric moved away, and the prince's voice regained its freedom—"and could not compete with the natural sorcery, *la magie innée et naturelle* of our fatherland. Take the subsequent, unquestionably historical kings and the beginning of our dynasty. When Rogfrid the First mounted, or rather scrambled up onto the wobbly throne that he himself called a sea-tossed barrel, and the country was in the throes of such insurrection and chaos that his aspiration to kinghood seemed a childish dream, do you recall the first thing he does upon acceding to power? He immediately mints kruns, half-kruns, and grosken depicting a sexdigitate hand. Why a hand? Why the six fingers? Not one historian has been able to figure it out, and it is doubtful that Rogfrid even knew himself. The fact remains, however, that this magical measure promptly pacified the country. Later, under his grandson, when the Danes attempted to impose upon us their protégé, and he landed with immense forces, what happened? Suddenly, with the utmost simplicity, the anti-government party—I forget what it was called, anyway, the traitors, without whom the whole plot would not have come into existence—sent a messenger to the invader with a polite announcement that they were henceforth unable to support him; because, you see, 'the ling' "—that is, the heather of the plain across which the turncoat army was to pass to join with the foreign forces—" 'had entwined the stirrups and shins of treachery, thus preventing further advance,' which apparently is to be taken literally, and not interpreted in the spirit of those stale allegories on which schoolboys are nourished. Then again—ah, yes, a splendid example—Queen Ilda, we must not omit Queen Ilda of the white breast and the abundant amours, who would resolve all state problems by means of incantations, and so successfully that any individual who did not meet her approval would lose his reason; you know yourselves that to this day insane asylums are known among the populace as *ildehams*. And when that populace begins to take part in legislative and administrative matters, it is absurdly clear that magic is on the people's side. I assure you, for instance, that if poor King Edaric found himself unable to take his seat at the reception for the elected officers, it was certainly not a question of piles. And so on and so forth—" (the prince was beginning to have enough of the topic he had selected) "—the life of our country, like some amphibian, keeps its head up amid simple nordic reality, while submerging its belly in fable, in rich, vivifying sorcery. It's not for nothing that every one of our mossy stones, every old tree has participated at least once in some magical occurrence or other. Here's a young student, he is reading History, I am sure he will confirm my opinion."

As he listened seriously and trustingly to Adulf's reasoning, K was astounded to what extent it coincided with his own views. True, the textbook selection of examples adduced by the talkative crown prince seemed to K a bit crude; did not the whole point lie not in the striking manifestations of witchcraft but in the delicate shadings of a fantastic something, which profoundly, and at the same time mistily, colored the island's history? He was, however, unconditionally in agreement with the basic premise, and that was the answer he gave, lowering his head and nodding to himself. Only much later did he realize that the co-incidence of ideas which had so astonished him had been the consequence of an almost unconscious cunning on the part of their promulgator, who undeniably had a special kind of instinct that allowed him to guess the most effective bait for any fresh listener.

When the king had finished his plums he beckoned to his nephew and, having no idea what to talk to him about, asked how many students there were at the university. K lost countenance—he did not know the number, and was not alert enough to name one at random. "Five hundred? One thousand?" persisted the king, with a note of juvenile eagerness in his voice. "I'm sure there must be more," he added in a conciliatory tone, not having received an intelligible answer; then, after a reflective pause, he went on to inquire whether his nephew enjoyed riding. Here the crown prince butted in with his usual luscious unconstraint, inviting his cousin for an outing together the following Thursday.

"Astonishing, how much he has come to resemble my poor sister," said the king with a mechanical sigh, taking off his glasses and returning them to the breast pocket of his brown frogged jacket. "I am too poor to give you a horse," he continued, "but I have a fine little riding whip. Gotsen" (addressing the Lord Chamberlain), "where is that fine little riding whip with the doggie's head? Look for it afterwards and give it to him . . . an interesting little object, historical value and all that. Well, I'm delighted to give it to you, but a horse is beyond my means—all I have is a pair of nags, and I'm keeping them for my hearse. Don't be vexed—I'm not rich." (*"Il ment,"* said the crown prince under his breath and walked off, humming.)

On the day of the outing the weather was cold and restless, a nacreous sky skimmed overhead, the sallow bushes curtseyed in the ravines, the horsehooves plapped as they scattered the slush of thick puddles in chocolate ruts, crows croaked; and then, beyond the bridge, the riders left the road and set off at a trot across the dark heather, above which a slim, already yellowing birch rose here and there. The crown prince proved to be an excellent horseman, although he had evidently never attended a riding school, for his seat was indifferent. His heavy, broad, corduroy-and-chamois-encased bottom, bouncing up and down in the saddle, and his rounded, sloping shoulders aroused in his companion an odd, vague kind of pity, which vanished completely whenever K glanced at the prince's rosy face, radiating health and sufficiency, and heard his urgeful speech.

The riding whip had come the previous day but had not been taken: the prince (who, by the way, had set the fashion of using bad French at court) had called it with scorn *"ce machin ridicule"* and contended that it belonged to the groom's little boy, who must have forgotten it on the king's porch. *"Et mon bonhomme de père, tu sais, a une vraie passion pour les objets trouvés."*

"I've been thinking how much truth there is in what you were saying. Books say nothing about it at all."

"About what?" asked the prince, laboriously trying to reconstruct which stray theory he had been expounding lately in front of his cousin.

"Oh, you remember! The magical origin of power, and the fact—"

"Yes, I do, I do," hastily interrupted the prince and forthwith found the best way to have done with the faded topic: "I didn't finish then because there were too many ears around. You see, our whole misfortune lies today in the government's strange ennui, in national inertia, in the dreary bickering of *Peplerhus* members. All this is so because the very force of the spells, both popular and royal, has somehow evaporated, and our ancestral sorcery has been reduced to mere hocus-pocus. But let's not discuss these depressing matters now, let's turn to more cheerful ones. Say, you must have heard a good deal about me at college? I can imagine! Tell me, what did they talk about? Why are you silent? They called me a libertine, didn't they?"

"I kept away from malicious chatter," said K, "but there was indeed some gossip to that effect."

"Well, hearsay is the poetry of truth. You are still a boy—quite a pretty boy to boot—so there are many things you won't understand right now. I shall offer you only this observation: all people are basically naughty, but when it is done under the rose, when, for instance, you hasten to gorge yourself on jam in a dark corner, or send your imagination on God knows what errands, all that doesn't count; nobody considers it a crime. Yet when a person frankly and assiduously satisfies the appetites inflicted upon him by his imperious body, then, oh then, people begin to denounce intemperance! And another consideration: if, in my case, that legitimate satisfaction were limited simply to one and the same unvarying method, popular opinion would become resigned, or at most would reproach me for changing my mistresses too often. But God, what a ruckus they raise because I do not stick to the code of debauchery but gather my honey wherever I find it! And mark, I am fond of everything—whether a tulip or a plain little grass stalk—because you see," concluded the prince, smiling and slitting his eyes, "I really seek only the fractions of beauty, leaving the integers to the good burghers, and those fractions can be found in a ballet girl as well as in a docker, in a middle-aged Venus as well as in a young horseman."

"Yes," said K, "I understand. You are an artist, a sculptor, you worship form. . . ."

The prince reined in his horse and guffawed.

"Oh, well, it isn't exactly a matter of sculpture—*à moins que tu ne confondes la galanterie avec la Galatée*—which, however, is pardonable at your age. No, no—it's all much less complicated. Only don't be so bashful with me, I won't bite you, I simply can't stand lads *qui se tiennent toujours sur leurs gardes*. If you don't have anything more interesting in view, we can return via Grenlog and dine on the lakeside, and then we'll think up something."

"No, I'm afraid I—well—I have something to take care of— It so happens that tonight I—"

"Oh, well, I'm not forcing you," the prince said affably, and a little farther, by the mill, they said good-bye.

As many very shy people would have done in his place, K, when forcing himself to face that ride, foresaw an especially trying ordeal for the very reason of Adulf's passing for a jovial talker: with a mild, minor-mode person it would have been easier to establish the tone of the outing beforehand. As he prepared himself for it, K tried to imagine all the awkward moments that might result from the necessity of raising his normal mood to Adulf's sparkling level. Moreover he felt obligated by their first meeting, by the fact that he had imprudently concurred with the opinions of someone who therefore could rightfully expect that both men would get along just as nicely on subsequent occasions. In making a detailed inventory of his potential blunders and, above all, in fancying with the utmost clarity the tension, the leaden load in his jaws, the desperate boredom he would feel (because of his innate capacity, on all occasions, for watching askance his projected self)—in tabulating all this, including futile efforts to merge with his other self and find interesting such things as were supposed to be interesting, K also pursued a secondary, practical aim: to disarm the future, whose only force is surprise. In this he nearly succeeded. Fate, constrained by its own evil choice, was apparently content with the innocuous items he had left beyond the field of prevision: the pale sky, the heath-country wind, a creaking saddle, an impatiently responsive horse, the unflagging monologue of his self-complacent companion, all fused into a fairly endurable sensation, particularly since K had mentally set a certain time limit for the ride. It was only a matter of seeing it through. But when the prince, with a novel proposal, threatened to extend this limit into the unknown, all of whose possibilities had once again to be agonizingly appraised (and here "something interesting" was again being forced upon K, requiring an expression of happy anticipation), this additional period of time—superfluous! unforeseen!—was intolerable; and so, at the risk of seeming impolite, he had used the pretext of a nonexistent impediment. True, as soon as he turned his horse, he regretted this discourtesy just as acutely as, a moment ago, he had been concerned for his freedom. Consequently, all the nastiness expected from the future deteriorated into a doubtful echo of the past. He thought for a moment if he should not overtake the prince and consolidate the foundation of friendship through a belated, but hence doubly precious, acquiescence to a new ordeal. But his fastidious apprehension of offending a kind, cheerful man did not outweigh his fear of obviously being unable to match that kindness and cheerfulness. Thus it happened that fate outwitted him after all, and, by means of a last furtive pinprick, rendered valueless that which he was prepared to consider a victory.

A few days later he received another invitation from the prince, asking that he "drop in" any evening of the following week. K could not refuse. Moreover, a sense of relief that the other was not offended treacherously smoothed the way.

He was ushered into a large yellow room, as hot as a greenhouse, where a score of people, fairly evenly divided by sex, sat on divans, hassocks, and a deep rug. For a fraction of a second the host seemed vaguely perplexed by his cousin's arrival, as if he had forgotten that he had invited him, or thought he had asked him for a different day. However, this momentary expression immediately gave way to a grin of welcome, after which the prince ignored his cousin, and neither, for that matter, was any attention paid to K by the other guests, evidently close friends of the prince: extraordinarily thin, smooth-haired young women, half a dozen middle-aged gentlemen with clean-shaven, bronzed faces, and several young men in the open-necked silk shirts that were fashionable at the time. Among them K suddenly recognized the famous young acrobat Ondrik Guldving, a sullen blond boy with a bizarre gentleness of gesture and gait, as if the expressiveness of his body, so remarkable in the arena, were muffled by clothes. To K this acrobat served as a key to the entire constellation of the gathering; and, even if the observer was ridiculously inexperienced and chaste, he immediately sensed that those gauze-dim, delectably elongated girls,

their limbs folded with varied abandon, who were making not conversation but mirages of conversation (consisting of slow half-smiles and
"hms" of interrogation or response through the smoke of cigarettes
inserted in precious holders), belonged to that essentially deaf-and-
dumb world that in former days had been known as "demi-monde"
(all curtains drawn, no *other* world known). The fact that, interspersed
among them, were ladies one saw at court balls did not change things
in the least. The male group was likewise somehow homogeneous,
despite its comprising representatives of the nobility, artists with dirty
fingernails, and young roughs of the stevedore type. And precisely
because the observer was inexperienced and chaste, he immediately
had doubts about his initial, involuntary impression and accused himself of common prejudice, of trusting slavishly the trite talk of the
town. He decided that everything was in order, i.e., that his world was
in no way disrupted by the inclusion of this new province, and that
everything about it was simple and comprehensible: a fun-loving, independent person had freely selected his friends.

The quietly carefree and even somehow childish rhythm of this
gathering was particularly reassuring to K. The mechanical smoking,
the various dainties on gold-veined little plates, the comradely cycles of
motion (somebody found some sheet music for somebody; a girl tried
on another girl's necklace), the simplicity, the serenity, all of it denoted
in its own way that kindliness which K, who himself did not possess it,
recognized in all of life's phenomena, be it the smile of a bonbon in
its goffered bonnet, or the echo of an old friendship divined in another's small talk. With a frown of concentration, occasionally releasing a
series of agitated groans, which would end in a grunt of vexation, the
prince was busy trying to drive six tiny balls into the center of a
pocket-size maze of glass. A redhead in a green dress and sandals on
her bare feet kept repeating, with comic mournfulness, that he would
never succeed; but he persisted for a long time, jiggling the recalcitrant
gimmick, stamping his foot, and starting all over again. Finally he
tossed it on a sofa, where some of the others promptly started on it.
Then a man with handsome features, distorted by a tic, sat down at the
piano, struck the keys with disorderly vigor in parody of somebody's
way of playing, and right away rose again, whereupon he and the
prince began arguing about the talent of a third party, probably the author of the truncated melody, and the redhead, scratching a graceful
thigh through her dress, started explaining to the prince the injured
party's position in a complicated musical feud. Abruptly the prince
consulted his watch and turned to the blond young acrobat who was
drinking orangeade in a corner: "Ondrik," he said with a worried air,

"I think it is time." Ondrick somberly licked his lips, put down his glass, and came over. With fat fingers, the prince undid Ondrik's fly, extracted the entire pink mass of his private parts, selected the chief one, and started to rub regularly its glossy shaft.

"At first," related K, "I thought that I had lost my mind, that I was hallucinating." Most of all he was shocked by the natural quality of the procedure. Nausea welled within him, and he left. Once in the street, he even ran for a while.

The only person with whom he felt able to share his indignation was his guardian. Although he had no affection for the not very attractive Count, he resolved to consult him as the sole familiar he had. He asked the Count in despair how could it be that a man of Adulf's morals, a man, moreover, no longer young, and therefore unlikely to change, would become the ruler of the country. By the light in which he had suddenly seen the crown prince, he also perceived that besides hideous ribaldry, and despite a taste for the arts, Adulf was really a savage, a self-taught oaf, lacking real culture, who had appropriated a handful of its beads, had learned how to flaunt the glitter of his adaptive mind, and of course did not worry in the least about the problems of his impending reign. K kept asking was it not crazy nonsense, the delirium of dreams, to imagine such a person king; but in setting those questions he hardly expected matter-of-fact replies: it was the rhetoric of young disenchantment. Nevertheless, as he went on expressing his perplexity, in abrupt brittle phrases (he was not born eloquent), K overtook reality and had a glimpse of its face. Admittedly, he at once fell back again, but that glimpse imprinted itself in his soul, revealing to him in a flash what perils awaited a state doomed to become the plaything of a prurient ruffian.

The Count heard him out attentively, now and then turning on him the gaze of his lashless vulturine eyes: they reflected a strange satisfaction. A calculating and cool mentor, he replied most cautiously, as if not quite agreeing with K, calming him down by saying that what he had happened to catch sight of was acting upon his judgment with undue force; that the only purpose of the hygiene established by the prince was not to allow a young friend to waste his strength on wenching; and that Adulf had qualities which might show themselves upon his ascension. At the end of the interview the Count offered to have K meet a certain wise person, the well-known economist Gumm. Here the Count pursued a double purpose: on one hand, he freed himself of all responsibility for what might follow, and remained aloof, which would do very nicely in case of some mishap; and on the other hand, he was passing K over to an experienced conspirator, thus beginning the realization of a plan that the evil and wily Count had been nursing, it seems, for quite a time.

Meet Gumm, meet economist Gumm, a round-tummied little old man in a woolen waistcoat, with blue spectacles pushed up high on his pink forehead, bouncy, trim, giggly Gumm. Their meetings increased in frequency, and at the end of his second year at college, K even sojourned for about a week in Gumm's house. By that time K had discovered enough things about the crown prince's behavior not to regret that first explosion of indignation. Not so much from Gumm himself, who seemed always to be rolling somewhither, as from his relatives and entourage, K learned about the measures which had already been tried to subdue the prince. At first, people had attempted to inform the old king about his son's frolics, so as to obtain parental restraint. Indeed, when this or that person, after gaining, through the thorns of protocol, access to the king's *kabinet*, depicted frankly those stunts to His Majesty, the old man, flushing purple and nervously pulling together the skirts of his dressing gown, displayed greater wrath than one might have hoped for. He shouted that he would put an end to it, that the cup of endurance (wherein his morning coffee stormily splashed) was overflowing, that he was happy to hear a candid report, that he would banish the lecherous cur for six months to a *suyphellhus* (monastery ship, floating hermitage), that he would— And when the audience had come to a close, and the pleased official was about to bow his way out, the old king, still puffing, but already pacified, would take him aside, with a businesslike confidential air (though actually they were alone in the study), and say, "Yes, yes, I understand all that, all that is so, but listen—quite between us—tell me, if we look at it reasonably—after all my Adulf is a bachelor, a gay dog, he's fond of a little sport—is it necessary to get all worked up? Remember, we also were boys once." That last consideration sounded rather silly, for the king's distant youth had flowed with milky tranquillity, and afterwards, the late queen, his wife, treated him with unusual severity till he was sixty. She was, incidentally, a remarkably obstinate, stupid, and pettyminded woman with a constant propensity for innocent but extremely absurd fantasies; and very possibly it was owing to her that the habitus of the court and, to a certain extent, of the state acquired those peculiar, difficult-to-define features, oddly blending stagnation and caprice, improvidence and the primness of nonviolent insanity, that so much tormented the present king.

The second, chronologically speaking, form of opposition was considerably deeper: it consisted of rallying and fortifying public resources. One could scarcely rely on the conscious participation of the plebeian class: among the insular plowmen, weavers, bakers, carpenters, corn-mongers, fisherfolk, and so forth, the transformation of any crown prince into any king was accepted as meekly as a change in the weather: the rustic gazed at the auroral gleam amid the cumulated clouds, shook his head—and that was all; in his dark lichenian brain a traditional place was always reserved for traditional disaster, national or natural. The meagerness and sluggishness of economics, the frozen level of prices, which had long since lost vital sensitivity (through which there is formed all at once a connection between an empty head and an empty stomach), the grim constancy of inconsiderable but just sufficient harvests, the secret pact between greens and grain, which had agreed, it seemed, to supplement each other and thus hold agronomy in equipoise—all this, according to Gumm (see *The Basis and Anabasis of Economics*) kept the people in languid submission; and if some sort of sorcery prevailed here, then so much the worse for the victims of its viscous spells. Furthermore—and the enlightened found therein a source of especial sadness—Prince Fig enjoyed a kind of smutty popu-larity among the lower classes and the petty bourgeoisie (between whom the distinction was so wobbly that one could regularly observe such puzzling phenomena as the return of a shopkeeper's prosperous son to the humble manual trade of his grandfather). The hearty laugh-ter invariably accompanying talk about Fig's pranks prevented them from being condemned: the mask of mirth stuck to one's mouth, and that mimicry of approval could no longer be distinguished from the real thing. The more lewdly Fig romped, the louder folks guffawed, the mightier and merrier red fists thumped on the deal tables of pubs. A characteristic detail: one day when the prince, passing on horseback, a cigar between his teeth, through a backwoodsy hamlet, noticed a comely little girl to whom he offered a ride, and notwith-standing her parents' horror (which respect barely helped to restrain), swept her away, while her old granddad kept running along the road until he toppled into a ditch, the whole village, as agents reported, ex-pressed their admiration by roars of laughter, congratulated the family, reveled in surmise, and did not stint in mischievous inquiries when the child returned after an hour's absence, holding a hundred-krun note in one hand, and, in the other, a fledgling that had fallen out of its nest in a desolate grove where she had picked it up on her way back to the village.

In military circles displeasure with the prince was based not so much on considerations of general morals and national prestige as on direct resentment suscitated by his attitude toward flaming punch and booming guns. King Gafon himself, in contrast to his pugnacious predecessor, was a "deeply civilian" old party; nonetheless the army put up with it, his complete noncomprehension of military matters being redeemed by the timorous esteem in which he held them; per contra, the Guard could not forgive his son's open sneer. War games, parades, puff-cheeked music, regimental banquets with the observation of colorful customs, and various other conscientious recreations on the part of the small insular army produced nothing but scornful ennui in Adulf's eminently artistic soul. Yet the army's unrest did not go further than desultory murmurs, plus, maybe, the making of midnight oaths (to the gleam of tapers, goblets, and swords)—to be forgotten next morning. Thus the initiative belonged to the enlightened minds of the public, which sad to say were not numerous; the anti-Adulfian opposition included, however, certain statesmen, newspaper editors, and jurists—all respectable, tough-sinewed old fellows, wielding plenty of secret or manifest influence. In other words, public opinion rose to the occasion, and the ambition to curb the crown prince as his iniquity progressed became considered a sign of decency and intelligence. It only remained to find a weapon. Alas, this precisely was lacking. There existed the press, there existed a parliament, but by the code of the constitution the least disrespectful poke at a member of the royal family must result in the newspaper's being banned or the chamber's dissolved. A single attempt to stir up the nation failed. We are referring to the celebrated trial of Dr. Onze.

That trial presented something unparalleled even in the unparalleled annals of Thulean justice. A man renowned for his virtue, a lecturer and writer on civic and philosophical questions, a personality so highly regarded, endowed with such strictness of views and principles, in a word, such a dazzlingly unstained character that, in comparison, the reputation of anyone else appeared spotty, was accused of various crimes against morals, defended himself with the clumsiness of despair, and finally acknowledged his guilt. So far there was nothing very unusual about it: goodness knows into what furuncles the mamillae of merit may turn under scrutiny! The unusual and subtle part of the matter lay in the fact that the indictment and the evidence formed practically a replica of all that could be imputed to the crown prince. One could not help being amazed by the precision of details obtained in order to insert a full-length portrait in the prepared frame without touching up or omitting anything. Much of it was so new, and individualized so precisely the commonplaces of long-coarsened rumor, that at first the masses did not realize *who* had sat for the picture. Very soon, however, the daily reports in the papers began to stir up quite exceptional interest among such readers as had caught on, and people who used to pay up to twenty kruns to attend the trial now did not spare five hundred or more.

The initial idea had been generated in the womb of the *prokuratura* (magistracy). The oldest judge in the capital took a fancy to it. All one needed was to find a person sufficiently upright not to be confused with the prototype of the affair, sufficiently clever not to act as a clown or a cretin before the tribunal, and, in particular, sufficiently dedicated to the case to sacrifice everything to it, endure a monstrous mud bath, and exchange his career for hard labor. Candidates for that role were not available: the conspirators, most of them well-to-do family men, liked every part except the one without which the play could not be staged. The situation already looked hopeless—when one day, at a meeting of the plotters, appeared Dr. Onze dressed entirely in black and, without sitting down, declared that he put himself completely at their disposal. A natural impatience to grasp the occasion hardly allowed them time to marvel; for at first blush it surely must have been difficult to understand how the rarefied life of a thinker could be compatible with the willingness to be pilloried for the sake of political intrigue. Actually, his was not such an uncommon case. Being constantly occupied with spiritual problems, and constantly adapting the laws of the most rigid principles to the most fragile abstractions, Dr. Onze did not find it possible to refuse a personal application of the same method when presented with the opportunity of performing a deed that was disinterested and probably senseless (and therefore still abstract, owing to the utmost purity of its nature). Furthermore, one should remember that Dr. Onze was giving up his chair, the mollitude of his book-lined study, the continuation of his latest opus—in brief, everything that a philosopher has the right to treasure. Let us mention that he was in indifferent health; let us emphasize the fact that before submitting the case to a close examination he had been obliged to devote three nights to delving in rather special works dealing with problems of which an ascetic could know little; and let us add that not long before he took his decision, he had become engaged to a senescent virgin after years of unexpressed love, during which time her fiancé of long standing fought phthisis in distant Switzerland until he expired, hence freeing her of her pact with compassion.

The case started by that truly heroic female's suing Dr. Onze for allegedly luring her to his secret *garçonnière*, "a den of luxury and libertinism." A similar claim (the only difference being that the apartment surreptitiously taken and fitted by the conspirators was not the one which the prince used to rent at one time for special pleasures but faced it on the opposite side of the street—which immediately established the mirror-image idea characteristic of the entire trial) had been filed against Fig by a not overbright maiden, who did not happen to know that her seducer was the heir to the throne, i.e., a person who in no circumstances could be arraigned. There followed the testimony of numerous witnesses (some of them altruistic adherents, others paid agents: there had not been quite enough of the first); their declarations had been brilliantly composed by a committee of experts, among whom one noted a distinguished historian, two major literati, and several experienced jurists. In these declarations the activity of the crown prince developed gradually, in the correct chronological order, but with some calendric abridgment compared to the time it had taken the prince to exasperate the public so badly. Group fornication, ultraurningism, abduction of youngsters, and many other amusements were described to the accused in the form of detailed questions to which he replied much more briefly. Having studied the whole affair with the methodical diligence peculiar to his mentality, Dr. Onze, who had never considered theatrical art (in fact, he did not go to the theater), now, by means of a savant's approach, unconsciously achieved a splendid impersonation of the kind of criminal whose denial of the charge (an attitude which in the present case was meant to let the prosecution get into its stride) finds nourishment in contradictory statements and assistance in bewildered stubbornness.

Everything proceeded as planned; alas, it soon became clear that the conspirators had no idea what really to hope for. For the eyes of the people to open? But the people knew all along Fig's nominal value. For moral revulsion to turn into civic revolt? But nothing indicated the way to such a metamorphosis. Or maybe the whole scheme was to be but a link in a long chain of progressively more efficient disclosures? But then the boldness and bite of the affair, by the very fact of their lending it an unrepeatable character of exclusiveness, could not help breaking, between the first link and the next, a chain that demanded above all some gradual form of malleation.

The publication of all the details of the case only helped to enrich the papers: their circulation grew to such an extent that in the resulting lush shade certain alert people (as for example Sien) managed to create new organs which pursued this or that object, but whose success was guaranteed because of their reports on the trial. The honestly indignant citizens were vastly outnumbered by the lip-smackers and the curious. Plain folks read and laughed. In those public proceedings they saw a marvelously entertaining gag thought up by rascals. The crown prince's image acquired in their minds the aspect of a punchinello whose varnished pate gets, perhaps, thumped by the stick of a mangy devil, but who remains the pet of the gapers, the star of the show-box. On the other hand, the personality of sublime Dr. Onze not only failed to be recognized as such but provoked happy hoots of malice (echoed disgracefully by the yellow press), the populace having mistaken his position for a wretched readiness to please on the part of a bribed highbrow. In a word, the pornographic popularity which had always surrounded the prince was only augmented, and even the most ironic conjectures as to how he must feel reading about his own escapades bore the mark of that good nature with which we involuntarily encourage another chap's showy recklessness.

The nobility, the Councilors, the court, and "courtierist" members of the *Peplerhus* were caught napping. They tamely decided to lie in wait and thus lost invaluable political tempo. True, a few days before the verdict, members of the royalist party succeeded, by intricate or merely crooked means, in getting a law passed forbidding the newspapers to report on "divorce cases or other hearings apt to contain scandalous items"; but as, constitutionally, no law could be enforced until forty days had elapsed since its acceptance (a period termed "parturiency of Themis"), the papers had ample time to cover the trial to the very end.

Prince Adulf himself regarded the business with complete indifference, which, moreover, was so naturally expressed that one wondered if he understood about whom they really were talking. Since every scrap of the affair must have been familiar to him, one is forced to conclude that either he had suffered an amnesic shock or that his self-control was superb. Once only his intimates thought they saw a shadow of vexation flit across his large face: "What a pity," he cried, "why didn't that *polisson* invite me to his parties? *Que de plaisirs perdus!*" As to the king, he also looked unconcerned, but to judge by the way he cleared his throat while filing away the newspaper in a drawer and removing his reading glasses, and also by the frequency of his secret sessions with this or that Councilor summoned at an unseasonable hour, one gathered that he was strongly perturbed. It was said that during the days of the trial he offered several times, with feigned casualness, to lend his son the royal yacht so that Adulf might undertake "a little round-the-world voyage," but Adulf only laughed and kissed him on his bald spot. "Really, my dear boy," insisted the old king, "it's so delightful being at sea! You might take musicians with you, a barrel of wine!" *"Hélas!"* answered the prince, "a see-sawing sea line compromises my solar plexus."

The trial entered its final stage. The defense alluded to the accused's "youth," to his "hot blood," to the "temptations" attending a bachelor's life—all of which was a rather coarse parody of the king's overindulgence. The prosecutor made a speech of savage force—and overshot the mark by demanding the death penalty. The defendant's last word introduced an utterly unexpected note. Exhausted by lengthy tension, harrowed by having been forced to wallow in another's filth, and involuntarily staggered by the prosecutor's blast, the luckless scholar lost his nerve and, after a few incoherent mumblings, suddenly started, in a new, hysterically clear voice, to tell how one night in his youth, having drunk his first glass of hazel brandy, he accepted to go with a classmate to a brothel, and how he did not get there only because he fainted in the street. This unforeseen avowal convulsed the public with long laughter, while the prosecutor, losing his head, attempted to stop the defendant's mouth by physical means. Then the jury retired for a silent smoke to the room allotted to them, and presently came back to announce the verdict. It was suggested that Dr. Onze be sentenced to eleven years' hard labor.

The sentence was wordily approved by the press. At secret visits his friends shook hands with the martyr, as they took farewell of him. . . . But here, good old Gafon, for the first time in his life, unexpectedly for everybody including, maybe, his own self, acted rather wittily: he took advantage of an incontestable prerogative and granted Onze a full pardon.

Thus both the first and second modes of pressure upon the prince practically came to nothing. There remained a third, a most decisive and certain, way. All the talks in Gumm's entourage tended exclusively toward the realization of that third measure, though its actual name, apparently, nobody pronounced: Death enjoys a sufficient number of euphemisms. K, upon getting involved in the tangled circumstances of a plot, did not quite make out what was happening, and the reason of that blindness lay not solely in youthful inexperience; it depended upon his considering himself, instinctively, though quite erroneously, to be the main instigator (whereas, of course, he was no more than an honorary walk-on actor—or an honorary hostage) and therefore refusing to believe that the enterprise he had initiated could end in bloodshed; indeed, no enterprise really existed, since he vaguely felt that by the very act of surmounting his disgust in studying his cousin's life he was accomplishing something sufficiently important and needful; and when with the passing of time he got a little bored with that study and with constant talks about the same thing, he still kept participating in them, dutifully stuck to the tedious topic, and continued to think he was performing his duty by collaborating with some kind of force that remained obscure to him but that finally would transform, by a stroke of its wand, an impossible prince into an acceptable heir apparent. Even if it occurred to him to welcome the possibility of simply forcing Adulf to forgo his claim to the throne (and the vagaries of figurative speech used by the plotters might have chanced to imply such an interpretation), he, strangely enough, never brought that thought to the end, i.e., to himself as the next in line. For almost two years, in the margin of college work, he constantly associated with rotund Gumm and his friends, and imperceptibly found himself caught in a very dense and delicate web; and perhaps the enforced boredom he felt more and more keenly should not be reduced to the mere incapacity—otherwise characteristic of his nature—to keep concerned with things that gradually grew the integument of habit (through which he no longer distinguished the radiance of their passionate revival); but perhaps it was the deliberately changed voice of a subliminal warning. Meanwhile the business that had been commenced long before his participation in it neared its gory denouement.

On a cold summer evening he was invited to a secret assembly; he went, for the invitation hinted at nothing unusual. Later he recalled, it is true, how unwillingly, with what a burdensome sense of compulsion, he set out for the meeting; but with similar feelings he had gone to meetings before. In a large room, unheated, and, as it were, fictitiously furnished (wallpaper, fireplace, sideboard with dusty drinking horn on one shelf—all looked like stage properties), there sat a score of men, more than half of whom K did not know. Here for the first time he saw Dr. Onze: that marble-white calvity depressed along its middle, those thick blond eyelashes, the little freckles above the brows, the rufous shade on the cheekbones, the tightly compressed lips, the frock coat of a fanatic, and the eyes of a fish. A frozen expression of meek, lambent melancholy did not embellish his unfortunate features. He was addressed with pointed respect. Everyone knew that after the trial his fiancée had broken with him, explaining that she irrationally went on seeing on the wretched man's face the traces of soily vice to which he had confessed in assuming another's character. She retired to a distant village, where she became wholly absorbed in teaching; and Dr. Onze himself, soon after the event prefaced by that assembly, sought reclusion in a smallish monastery.

Among those present, K also noted the celebrated jurist Schliss, several *frad* (liberal) members of the *Peplerhus*, the son of the minister of public education. . . . And on an uncomfortable leathern divan sat three lanky and somber army officers.

He found a cane-seated free chair next to the window on whose ledge sat a small man who kept apart from the others. He had a plebeian type of face and fiddled with the postal department cap in his hands. K was close enough to observe his coarse-shod huge feet, which did not go at all with his puny figure, so that one obtained something like a photograph taken at point-blank range. Only later did K learn that this man was Sien.

At first it seemed to K that the people collected in the room were engaged in the kind of talk which had long grown familiar to him. Something within him (again, that innermost friend!) even *longed*, with a sort of childish eagerness, that this meeting would not differ from all previous ones. But Gumm's strange, somehow sickening gesture when in passing he put his hand on K's shoulder and nodded mysteriously—this, as well as the slow, guarded sound of voices, and the expression of those three officers' eyes, caused K to prick up his ears. Hardly two minutes passed before he knew that what they were coldly working out here, in this bogus room, was the already decided assassination of the crown prince.

He felt the breath of fate near his temples and the same, almost physical, nausea he had once experienced after that soirée at his cousin's. By the look which the silent pygmy in the embrasure gave him (a look of curiosity mixed with sarcasm), K realized that his confusion had not passed unnoticed. He got up, and then everyone turned toward him, and the bristly-haired, heavy man who was speaking at that minute (K had long ceased to hear the words) stopped short. K went up to Gumm, whose triangular eyebrows rose expectantly. "I must be going," said K, "I'm not feeling well. I think I had better go." He bowed; a few persons politely stood up; the man on the window ledge lit his pipe, smiling. As K advanced toward the exit, he had the nightmare sensation that, maybe, the door was a still-life painting, that its handle was *en trompe-l'oeil*, and could not be turned. But all at once the door became real, and, escorted by a youth, who had softly come out of some other room in his bedslippers with a bundle of keys, K proceeded to go down a long and dark staircase.

THE ASSISTANT PRODUCER

M EANING? Well, because sometimes life is merely that—an Assistant Producer. Tonight we shall go to the movies. Back to the thirties, and down the twenties, and round the corner to the old Europe Picture Palace. She was a celebrated singer. Not opera, not even *Cavalleria Rusticana*, not anything like that. "La Slavska"—that is what the French called her. Style: one-tenth *tzigane*, one-seventh Russian peasant girl (she had been that herself originally), and five-ninths popular—and by popular I mean a hodgepodge of artificial folklore, military melodrama, and official patriotism. The fraction left unfilled seems sufficient to represent the physical splendor of her prodigious voice.

Coming from what was, geographically at least, the very heart of Russia, it eventually reached the big cities, Moscow, St. Petersburg, and the Tsar's milieu where that sort of style was greatly appreciated. In Feodor Chaliapin's dressing room there hung a photograph of her: Russian headgear with pearls, hand propping cheek, dazzling teeth between fleshy lips, and a great clumsy scrawl right across: "For you, Fedyusha." Stars of snow, each revealing, before the edges melted, its complex symmetry, would gently come to rest on the shoulders and sleeves and mustaches and caps—all waiting in a queue for the box office to open. Up to her very death she treasured above all—or pretended to do so—a fancy medal and a huge brooch that had been given her by the Tsarina. They came from the firm of jewelers which used to do such profitable business by presenting the Imperial couple on every festive occasion with this or that emblem (each year increasing in worth) of massive Tsardom: some great lump of amethyst with a ruby-studded bronze troika stranded on top like Noah's Ark on Mount Ararat, or a sphere of crystal the size of a watermelon surmounted by a gold eagle with square diamond eyes very much like those of Rasputin (many years later some of the less symbolic ones were exhibited at a World's Fair by the Soviets as samples of their own thriving Art).

Had things gone on as they were seeming to go, she might have been still singing tonight in a central-heated Hall of Nobility or at Tsarskoye, and I should be turning off her broadcast voice in some remote corner of steppe-mother Siberia. But destiny took the wrong turning; and when the Revolution happened, followed by the War of the Reds and the Whites, her wily peasant soul chose the more practical party.

Ghostly multitudes of ghostly Cossacks on ghost-horseback are seen charging through the fading name of the assistant producer. Then dapper General Golubkov is disclosed idly scanning the battlefield through a pair of opera glasses. When movies and we were young, we used to be shown what the sights divulged neatly framed in two connected circles. Not now. What we do see next is General Golubkov, all indolence suddenly gone, leaping into the saddle, looming sky-high for an instant on his rearing steed, and then rocketing into a crazy attack.

But the unexpected is the infra-red in the spectrum of Art: instead of the conditional *ra-ta-ta* reflex of machine gunnery, a woman's voice is heard singing afar. Nearer, still nearer, and finally all-pervading. A gorgeous contralto voice expanding into whatever the musical director found in his files in the way of Russian lilt. Who is this leading the infra-Reds? A woman. The singing spirit of that particular, especially well-trained battalion. Marching in front, trampling the alfalfa, and pouring out her Volga-Volga song. Dapper and daring *djighit* Golubkov (now we know what he had descried), although wounded in several spots, manages to snatch her up on the gallop, and, lusciously struggling, she is borne away.

Strangely enough, that vile script was enacted in reality. I myself have known at least two reliable witnesses of the event; and the sentries of history have let it pass unchallenged. Very soon we find her maddening the officers' mess with her dark buxom beauty and wild, wild songs. She was a Belle Dame with a good deal of Merci, and there was a punch about her that Louise von Lenz or the Green Lady lacked. She it was who sweetened the general retreat of the Whites, which began shortly after her magic appearance at General Golubkov's camp. We get a gloomy glimpse of ravens, or crows, or whatever birds proved available, wheeling in the dusk and slowly descending upon a plain littered with bodies somewhere in Ventura County. A White soldier's dead hand is still clutching a medallion with his mother's face. A Red soldier nearby has on his shattered breast a letter from home with the same old woman blinking through the dissolving lines.

And then, in traditional contrast, pat comes a mighty burst of music and song with a rhythmic clapping of hands and stamping of booted feet and we see General Golubkov's staff in full revelry—a lithe Georgian dancing with a dagger, the self-conscious samovar reflecting distorted faces, the Slavska throwing her head back with a throaty laugh, and the fat man of the corps, horribly drunk, braided collar undone, greasy lips pursed for a bestial kiss, leaning across the table (close-up of an overturned glass) to hug—nothingness, for wiry and perfectly sober General Golubkov has deftly removed her and now, as they both stand facing the gang, says in a cold, clear voice: "Gentlemen, I want to present you my bride"—and in the stunned silence that follows, a stray bullet from outside chances to shatter the dawn-blue windowpane, after which a roar of applause greets the glamorous couple.

There is little doubt that her capture had not been wholly a fortuitous occurrence. Indeterminism is banned from the studio. It is even less doubtful that when the great exodus began and they, as many others, meandered via Sirkedji to Motzstrasse and rue Vaugirard, the General and his wife already formed one team, one song, one cipher. Quite naturally he became an efficient member of the W.W. (White Warriors Union), traveling about, organizing military courses for Russian boys, arranging relief concerts, unearthing barracks for the destitute, settling local disputes, and doing all this in a most unobtrusive manner. I suppose it was useful in some ways, that W.W. Unfortunately for its spiritual welfare, it was quite incapable of cutting itself off from monarchist groups abroad and did not feel, as the émigré intelligentsia felt, the dreadful vulgarity, the Ur-Hitlerism of those ludicrous but vicious organizations. When well-meaning Americans ask me whether I know charming Colonel So-and-so or grand old Count de Kickoffsky, I have not the heart to tell them the dismal truth.

But there was also another type of person connected with the W.W. I am thinking of those adventurous souls who helped the cause by crossing the frontier through some snow-muffled fir forest, to potter about their native land in the various disguises worked out, oddly enough, by the social revolutionaries of yore, and quietly bring back to the little café in Paris called "Esh-Bubliki," or to the little *Kneipe* in Berlin that had no special name, the kind of useful trifles which spies are supposed to bring back to their employers. Some of those men had become abstrusely entangled with the spying departments of other nations and would give an amusing jump if you came from behind and tapped them on the shoulder. A few went a-scouting for the fun of the thing. One or two perhaps really believed that in some mystical way they were preparing the resurrection of a sacred, if somewhat musty, past.

2
———

We are now going to witness a most weirdly monotonous series of events. The first president of the W.W. to die was the leader of the whole White movement and by far the best man of the lot; and certain dark symptoms attending his sudden illness suggested a poisoner's shadow. The next president, a huge, strong fellow with a voice of thunder and a head like a cannonball, was kidnapped by persons unknown; and there are reasons to believe that he died from an overdose of chloroform. The third president—but my reel is going too fast. Actually it took seven years to remove the first two—not because this sort of thing cannot be done more briskly, but because there were particular circumstances that necessitated some very precise timing, so as to coordinate one's steady ascent with the spacing of sudden vacancies. Let us explain.

Golubkov was not only a very versatile spy (a triple agent to be exact); he was also an exceedingly ambitious little fellow. Why the vision of presiding over an organization that was but a sunset behind a cemetery happened to be so dear to him is a conundrum only for those who have no hobbies or passions. He wanted it very badly—that is all. What is less intelligible is the faith he had in being able to safeguard his puny existence in the crush between the formidable parties whose dangerous money and dangerous help he received. I want all your attention now, for it would be a pity to miss the subtleties of the situation.

The Soviets could not be much disturbed by the highly improbable prospect of a phantom White Army ever being able to resume war operations against their consolidated bulk; but they could be very much irritated by the fact that scraps of information about forts and factories, gathered by elusive W.W. meddlers, were automatically falling into grateful German hands. The Germans were little interested in the recondite color variations of émigré politics, but what did annoy them was the blunt patriotism of a W.W. president every now and then obstructing on ethical grounds the smooth flow of friendly collaboration.

Thus, General Golubkov was a godsend. The Soviets firmly expected that under his rule all W.W. spies would be well known to them—and shrewdly supplied with false information for eager German consumption. The Germans were equally sure that through him they would be guaranteed a good cropping of their own absolutely trustworthy agents distributed among the usual W.W. ones. Neither side had any illusions concerning Golubkov's loyalty, but each assumed that it would turn to its own profit the fluctuations of double-crossing. The dreams of simple Russian folk, hardworking families in remote parts of the Russian diaspora, plying their humble but honest trades, as they would in Saratov or Tver, bearing fragile children, and naively believing that the W.W. was a kind of King Arthur's Round Table that stood for all that had been, and would be, sweet and decent and strong in fairy-tale Russia—these dreams may well strike the film pruners as an excrescence upon the main theme.

When the W.W. was founded, General Golubkov's candidacy (purely theoretical, of course, for nobody expected the leader to die) was very far down the list—not because his legendary gallantry was insufficiently appreciated by his fellow officers, but because he happened to be the youngest general in the army. Toward the time of the next president's election Golubkov had already disclosed such tremendous capacities as an organizer that he felt he could safely cross out quite a few intermediate names in the list, incidentally sparing the lives of their bearers. After the second general had been removed, many of the W.W. members were convinced that General Fedchenko, the next candidate, would surrender in favor of the younger and more efficient man the rights that his age, reputation, and academic distinction entitled him to enjoy. The old gentleman, however, though doubtful of the enjoyment, thought it cowardly to avoid a job that had cost two men their lives. So Golubkov set his teeth and started to dig again.

Physically he lacked attraction. There was nothing of your popular Russian general about him, nothing of that good, burly, popeyed, thick-necked sort. He was lean, frail, with sharp features, a clipped mustache, and the kind of haircut that is called by Russians "hedgehog": short, wiry, upright, and compact. There was a thin silver bracelet round his hairy wrist, and he offered you neat homemade Russian cigarettes or English prune-flavored "Kapstens," as he pronounced it, snugly arranged in an old roomy cigarette case of black leather that had accompanied him through the presumable smoke of numberless battles. He was extremely polite and extremely inconspicuous.

Whenever the Slavska "received," which she would do at the homes of her various Maecenases (a Baltic baron of sorts, a Dr. Bachrach whose first wife had been a famous Carmen, or a Russian merchant of the old school who, in inflation-mad Berlin, was having a wonderful time buying up blocks of houses for ten pounds sterling apiece), her silent husband would unobtrusively thread his way among the visitors, bringing you a sausage-and-cucumber sandwich or a tiny frosty-pale glass of vodka; and while the Slavska sang (on those informal occasions she used to sing seated with her fist at her cheek and her elbow cupped in the palm of her other hand) he would stand apart, leaning against something, or would tiptoe toward a distant ashtray which he would gently place on the fat arm of your chair.

I consider that, artistically, he overstressed his effacement, unwittingly introducing a hired-lackey note—which now seems singularly appropriate; but he of course was trying to base his existence upon the principle of contrast and would get a marvelous thrill from exactly knowing by certain sweet signs—a bent head, a rolling eye—that So-and-so at the far end of the room was drawing a newcomer's attention to the fascinating fact that such a dim, modest man was the hero of incredible exploits in a legendary war (taking towns single-handed and that sort of thing).

3

German film companies, which kept sprouting like poisonous mushrooms in those days (just before the child of light learned to talk), found cheap labor in hiring those among the Russian émigrés whose only hope and profession was their past—that is, a set of totally unreal people—to represent "real" audiences in pictures. The dovetailing of one phantasm into another produced upon a sensitive person the impression of living in a Hall of Mirrors, or rather a prison of mirrors, and not even knowing which was the glass and which was yourself.

Indeed, when I recall the halls where the Slavska sang, both in Berlin and in Paris, and the type of people one saw there, I feel as if I were Technicoloring and sonorizing some very ancient motion picture where life had been a gray vibration and funerals a scamper, and where only the sea had been tinted (a sickly blue), while some hand machine imitated offstage the hiss of the asynchronous surf. A certain shady character, the terror of relief organizations, a bald-headed man with mad eyes, slowly floats across my field of vision with his legs bent in a sitting position, like an elderly fetus, and then miraculously fits into a back-row seat. Our friend the Count is also here, complete with high collar and dingy spats. A venerable but worldly priest, with his cross gently heaving on his ample chest, sits in the front row and looks straight ahead.

The items of these right-wing festivals that the Slavska's name evokes in my mind were of the same unreal nature as was her audience. A variety artist with a fake Slav name, one of those guitar virtuosos that come as a cheap first in music hall programs, would be most welcome here; and the flashy ornaments on his glass-paneled instrument, and his sky-blue silk pants, would go well with the rest of the show. Then some bearded old rascal in a shabby cutaway coat, former member of the Holy Russ First, would take the chair and vividly describe what the Israel-sons and the Phreemasons (two secret Semitic tribes) were doing to the Russian people.

And now, ladies and gentlemen, we have the great pleasure and honor— There she would stand against a dreadful background of palms and national flags, and moisten her rich painted lips with her pale tongue, and leisurely clasp her kid-gloved hands on her corseted stomach, while her constant accompanist, marble-faced Joseph Levinsky, who had followed her, in the shadow of her song, to the Tsar's private concert hall and to Comrade Lunacharsky's salon, and to nondescript places in Constantinople, produced his brief introductory series of stepping-stone notes.

Sometimes, if the house was of the right sort, she would sing the national anthem before launching upon her limited but ever welcome repertoire. Inevitably there would be that lugubrious "Old Road to Kaluga" (with a thunderstruck pine tree at the forty-ninth verst), and the one that begins, in the German translation printed beneath the Russian text, *"Du bist im Schnee begraben, mein Russland,"* and the ancient folklore ballad (written by a private person in the eighties) about the robber chieftain and his lovely Persian princess, whom he threw into the Volga when his crew accused him of going soft.

Her artistic taste was nowhere, her technique haphazard, her general style atrocious; but the kind of people for whom music and sentiment are one, or who like songs to be mediums for the spirits of circumstances under which they had been first apprehended in an individual past, gratefully found in the tremendous sonorities of her voice both a nostalgic solace and a patriotic kick. She was considered especially effective when a strain of wild recklessness rang through her song. Had this abandon been less blatantly shammed it might still have saved her from utter vulgarity. The small, hard thing that was her soul stuck out of her song, and the most her temperament could attain was but an eddy, not a free torrent. When nowadays in some Russian household the gramophone is put on, and I hear her canned contralto, it is with something of a shudder that I recall the meretricious imitation she gave of reaching her vocal climax, the anatomy of her mouth fully displayed in a last passionate cry, her blue-black hair beautifully waved, her crossed hands pressed to the beribboned medal on her bosom as she acknowledged the orgy of applause, her broad dusky body rigid even when she bowed, crammed as it was into strong silver satin which made her look like a matron of snow or a mermaid of honor.

4

_____

You will see her next (if the censor does not find what follows offensive to piety) kneeling in the honey-colored haze of a crowded Russian church, lustily sobbing side by side with the wife or widow (she knew exactly which) of the general whose kidnapping had been so nicely arranged by her husband and so deftly performed by those big, efficient, anonymous men that the boss had sent down to Paris.

You will see her also on another day, two or three years later, while she is singing in a certain *appartement*, rue George Sand, surrounded by admiring friends—and look, her eyes narrow slightly, her singing smile fades, as her husband, who had been detained by the final details of the business in hand, now quietly slips in and with a soft gesture rebukes a grizzled colonel's attempt to offer him his own seat; and through the unconscious flow of a song delivered for the ten-thousandth time she peers at him (she is slightly nearsighted like Anna Karenin) trying to discern some definite sign, and then, as she drowns and his painted boats sail away, and the last telltale circular ripple on the Volga River, Samara County, dissolves into dull eternity (for this is the very last song that she ever will sing), her husband comes up to her and says in a voice that no clapping of human hands can muffle: "Masha, the tree will be felled tomorrow!"

That bit about the tree was the only dramatic treat that Golubkov allowed himself during his dove-gray career. We shall condone the outburst if we remember that this was the ultimate General blocking his way and that next day's event would automatically bring on his own election. There had been lately some mild jesting among their friends (Russian humor being a wee bird satisfied with a crumb) about the amusing little quarrel that those two big children were having, she petulantly demanding the removal of the huge old poplar that darkened her studio window at their suburban summer house, and he contending that the sturdy old fellow was her greenest admirer (sidesplitting, this) and so ought to be spared. Note too the good-natured roguishness of the fat lady in the ermine cape as she taunts the gallant General for giving in so soon, and the Slavska's radiant smile and outstretched jelly-cold arms.

Next day, late in the afternoon, General Golubkov escorted his wife to her dressmaker, sat there for a while reading the *Paris-Soir*, and then was sent back to fetch one of the dresses she wanted loosened and had forgotten to bring. At suitable intervals she gave a passable imitation of telephoning home and volubly directing his search. The dressmaker, an Armenian lady, and a seamstress, little Princess Tumanov, were much entertained in the adjacent room by the variety of her rustic oaths (which helped her not to dry up in a part that her imagination alone could not improvise). This threadbare alibi was not intended for the patching up of past tenses in case anything went wrong—for nothing could go wrong; it was merely meant to provide a man whom none would ever dream of suspecting with a routine account of his movements when people would want to know who had seen General Fedchenko last. After enough imaginary wardrobes had been ransacked Golubkov was seen to return with the dress (which long ago, of course, had been placed in the car). He went on reading his paper while his wife kept trying things on.

5

The thirty-five minutes or so during which he was gone proved quite a comfortable margin. About the time she started fooling with that dead telephone, he had already picked up the General at an unfrequented corner and was driving him to an imaginary appointment the circumstances of which had been so framed in advance as to make its secrecy natural and its attendance a duty. A few minutes later he pulled up and they both got out. "This is not the right street," said General Fedchenko. "No," said General Golubkov, "but it is a convenient one to park my car on. I should not like to leave it right in front of the café. We shall take a shortcut through that lane. It is only two minutes' walk." "Good, let us walk," said the old man and cleared his throat.

In that particular quarter of Paris the streets are called after various philosophers, and the lane they were following had been named by some well-read city father rue Pierre Labime. It gently steered you past a dark church and some scaffolding into a vague region of shuttered private houses standing somewhat aloof within their own grounds behind iron railings on which moribund maple leaves would pause in their flight between bare branch and wet pavement. Along the left side of that lane there was a long wall with crossword puzzles of brick showing here and there through its rough grayness; and in that wall there was at one spot a little green door.

As they approached it, General Golubkov produced his battle-scarred cigarette case and presently stopped to light up. General Fedchenko, a courteous nonsmoker, stopped too. There was a gusty wind ruffling the dusk, and the first match went out. "I still think—" said General Fedchenko in reference to some petty business they had been discussing lately, "I still think," he said (to say something as he stood near that little green door), "that if Father Fedor insists on paying for all those lodgings out of his own funds, the least we can do is to supply the fuel." The second match went out too. The back of a passerby hazily receding in the distance at last disappeared. General Golubkov cursed the wind at the top of his voice, and as this was the all-clear signal the green door opened and three pairs of hands with incredible speed and skill whisked the old man out of sight. The door slammed. General Golubkov lighted his cigarette and briskly walked back the way he had come.

The old man was never seen again. The quiet foreigners who had rented a certain quiet house for one quiet month had been innocent Dutchmen or Danes. It was but an optical trick. There is no green door, but only a gray one, which no human strength can burst open. I have vainly searched through admirable encyclopedias: there is no philosopher called Pierre Labime.

But I have seen the toad in her eyes. We have a saying in Russian: *vsevo dvoe i est; smert' da sovest'*—which may be rendered thus: "There are only two things that really exist—one's death and one's conscience." The lovely thing about humanity is that at times one may be unaware of doing right, but one is always aware of doing wrong. A very horrible criminal, whose wife had been even a worse one, once told me in the days when I was a priest that what had troubled him all through was the inner shame of being stopped by a still deeper shame from discussing with her the puzzle: whether perhaps in her heart of hearts she despised him or whether he secretly wondered if perhaps in his heart of hearts he despised her. And that is why I know perfectly well the kind of face General Golubkov and his wife had when the two were at last alone.

6

Not for very long, however. About ten p.m. General L., the W.W. Secretary, was informed by General R. that Mrs. Fedchenko was extremely worried by her husband's unaccountable absence. Only then did General L. remember that about lunchtime the President had told him in a rather casual way (but that was the old gentleman's manner) that he had some business in town in the late afternoon and that if he was not back by eight p.m. would General L. please read a note left in the middle drawer of the President's desk. The two generals now rushed to the office, stopped short, rushed back for the keys General L. had forgotten, rushed again, and finally found the note. It read: *"An odd feeling obsesses me of which later I may be ashamed. I have an appointment at five-thirty p.m. in a café 45 rue Descartes. I am to meet an informer from the other side. I suspect a trap. The whole thing has been arranged by General Golubkov, who is taking me there in his car."*

We shall skip what General L. said and what General R. replied—but apparently they were slow thinkers and proceeded to lose some more time in a muddled telephone talk with an indignant café owner. It was almost midnight when the Slavska, clad in a flowery dressing gown and trying to look very sleepy, let them in. She was unwilling to disturb her husband, who, she said, was already asleep. She wanted to know what it was all about and had perhaps something happened to General Fedchenko. "He has vanished," said honest General L. The Slavska said, "Akh!" and crashed in a dead swoon, almost wrecking the parlor in the process. The stage had not lost quite so much as most of her admirers thought.

Somehow or other the two generals managed not to impart to General Golubkov anything about the little note, so that when he accompanied them to the W.W. headquarters he was under the impression that they really wanted to discuss with him whether to ring up the police at once or first go for advice to eighty-eight-year-old Admiral Gromoboyev, who for some obscure reason was considered the Solomon of the W.W.

"What does this mean?" said General L., handing the fatal note to Golubkov. "Peruse it, please."

Golubkov perused—and knew at once that all was lost. We shall not bend over the abyss of his feelings. He handed the note back with a shrug of his thin shoulders.

"If this has been really written by the General," he said, "and I must admit it looks very similar to his hand, then all I can say is that somebody has been impersonating me. However, I have grounds to believe that Admiral Gromoboyev will be able to exonerate me. I suggest we go there at once."

"Yes," said General L., "we had better go now, although it is very late."

General Golubkov swished himself into his raincoat and went out first. General R. helped General L. to retrieve his muffler. It had half slipped down from one of those vestibule chairs which are doomed to accommodate things, not people. General L. sighed and put on his old felt hat, using both hands for this gentle action. He moved to the door. "One moment, General," said General R. in a low voice. "I want to ask you something. As one officer to another, are you absolutely sure that . . . well, that General Golubkov is speaking the truth?"

"That's what we shall find out," answered General L., who was one of those people who believe that so long as a sentence is a sentence it is bound to mean something.

They delicately touched each other's elbows in the doorway. Finally the slightly older man accepted the privilege and made a jaunty exit. Then they both paused on the landing, for the staircase struck them as being very still. "General!" cried General L. in a downward direction. Then they looked at each other. Then hurriedly, clumsily, they stomped down the ugly steps, and emerged, and stopped under a black drizzle, and looked this way and that, and then at each other again.

She was arrested early on the following morning. Never once during the inquest did she depart from her attitude of grief-stricken innocence. The French police displayed a queer listlessness in dealing with possible clues, as if they assumed that the disappearance of Russian generals was a kind of curious local custom, an Oriental phenomenon, a dissolving process which perhaps ought not to occur but which could not be prevented. One had, however, the impression that the *Sûreté* knew more about the workings of the vanishing trick than diplomatic wisdom found fit to discuss. Newspapers abroad treated the whole matter in a good-natured but bantering and slightly bored manner. On the whole, "L'affaire Slavska" did not make good headlines—Russian émigrés were decidedly out of focus. By an amusing coincidence both a German press agency and a Soviet one laconically stated that a pair of White Russian generals in Paris had absconded with the White Army funds.

7

The trial was strangely inconclusive and muddled, witnesses did not shine, and the final conviction of the Slavska on a charge of kidnapping was debatable on legal grounds. Irrelevant trifles kept obscuring the main issue. The wrong people remembered the right things and vice versa. There was a bill signed by a certain Gaston Coulot, farmer, *"pour un arbre abattu."* General L. and General R. had a dreadful time at the hands of a sadistic barrister. A Parisian *clochard*, one of those colorful ripe-nosed unshaven beings (an easy part, that) who keep all their earthly belongings in their voluminous pockets and wrap their feet in layers of bursting newspapers when the last sock is gone and are seen comfortably seated, with widespread legs and a bottle of wine against the crumbling wall of some building that has never been completed, gave a lurid account of having observed from a certain vantage point an old man being roughly handled. Two Russian women, one of whom had been treated some time before for acute hysteria, said they saw on the day of the crime General Golubkov and General Fedchenko driving in the former's car. A Russian violinist while sitting in the diner of a German train—but it is useless to retell all those lame rumors.

We get a few last glimpses of the Slavska in prison. Meekly knitting in a corner. Writing to Mrs. Fedchenko tear-stained letters in which she said that they were sisters now, because both their husbands had been captured by the Bolsheviks. Begging to be allowed the use of a lipstick. Sobbing and praying in the arms of a pale young Russian nun who had come to tell her of a vision she had had which disclosed the innocence of General Golubkov. Clamoring for the New Testament which the police were keeping—keeping mainly from the experts who had so nicely begun deciphering certain notes scribbled in the margin of St. John's Gospel. Some time after the outbreak of World War II, she developed an obscure internal trouble and when, one summer morning, three German officers arrived at the prison hospital and desired to see her, at once they were told she was dead—which possibly was the truth.

One wonders if in some way or other her husband managed to inform her of his whereabouts, or if he thought it safer to leave her in the lurch. Where did he go, poor *perdu*? The mirrors of possibility cannot replace the eyehole of knowledge. Perhaps he found a haven in Germany and was given there some small administrative job in the Baedecker Training School for Young Spies. Perhaps he returned to the land where he had taken towns single-handedly. Perhaps he did not. Perhaps he was summoned by whoever his arch-boss was and told with that slight foreign accent and special brand of blandness that we all know: "I am afraid, my friend, you are not needed any more"—and as X turns to go, Dr. Puppenmeister's delicate index presses a button at the edge of his impassive writing desk and a trap yawns under X, who plunges to his death (he who knows "too much"), or breaks his funny bone by crashing right through into the living room of the elderly couple below.

Anyhow, the show is over. You help your girl into her coat and join the slow exit-bound stream of your likes. Safety doors open into unexpected side portions of night, diverting proximal trickles. If, like me, you prefer for reasons of orientation to go out the way you came in, you will pass again by those posters that seemed so attractive a couple of hours ago. The Russian cavalryman in his half-Polish uniform bends from his polo-pony to scoop up red-booted romance, her black hair tumbling from under her astrakhan cap. The Arc de Triomphe rubs shoulders with a dim-domed Kremlin. The monocled agent of a Foreign Power is handed a bundle of secret papers by General Golubkov. . . . Quick, children, let us get out of here into the sober night, into the shuffling peace of familiar sidewalks, into the solid world of good freckled boys and the spirit of comradeship. Welcome reality! This tangible cigarette will be very refreshing after all that trashy excitement. See, the thin dapper man walking in front of us lights up too after tapping a "Lookee" against his old leathern cigarette case.

"THAT IN ALEPPO ONCE . . ."

DEAR V.—Among other things, this is to tell you that at last I am here, in the country whither so many sunsets have led. One of the first persons I saw was our good old Gleb Alexandrovich Gekko gloomily crossing Columbus Avenue in quest of the *petit café du coin* which none of us three will ever visit again. He seemed to think that somehow or other you were betraying our national literature, and he gave me your address with a deprecatory shake of his gray head, as if you did not deserve the treat of hearing from me.

I have a story for you. Which reminds me—I mean putting it like this reminds me—of the days when we wrote our first udder-warm bubbling verse, and all things, a rose, a puddle, a lighted window, cried out to us: "I'm a rhyme!" Yes, this is a most useful universe. We play, we die: *ig-rhyme, umi-rhyme*. And the sonorous souls of Russian verbs lend a meaning to the wild gesticulation of trees or to some discarded newspaper sliding and pausing, and shuffling again, with abortive flaps and apterous jerks along an endless windswept embankment. But just now I am not a poet. I come to you like that gushing lady in Chekhov who was dying to be described.

I married, let me see, about a month after you left France and a few weeks before the gentle Germans roared into Paris. Although I can produce documentary proofs of matrimony, I am positive now that my wife never existed. You may know her name from some other source, but that does not matter: it is the name of an illusion. Therefore, I am able to speak of her with as much detachment as I would of a character in a story (one of your stories, to be precise).

It was love at first touch rather than at first sight, for I had met her several times before without experiencing any special emotions; but one night, as I was seeing her home, something quaint she had said

560

made me stoop with a laugh and lightly kiss her on the hair—and of course we all know of that blinding blast which is caused by merely picking up a small doll from the floor of a carefully abandoned house: the soldier involved hears nothing; for him it is but an ecstatic soundless and boundless expansion of what had been during his life a pinpoint of light in the dark center of his being. And really, the reason we think of death in celestial terms is that the visible firmament, especially at night (above our blacked-out Paris with the gaunt arches of its boulevard Exelmans and the ceaseless alpine gurgle of desolate latrines), is the most adequate and ever-present symbol of that vast silent explosion.

But I cannot discern her. She remains as nebulous as my best poem—the one you made such gruesome fun of in the *Literaturnïe Zapiski*. When I want to imagine her, I have to cling mentally to a tiny brown birthmark on her downy forearm, as one concentrates upon a punctuation mark in an illegible sentence. Perhaps, had she used a greater amount of make-up or used it more constantly, I might have visualized her face today, or at least the delicate transverse furrows of dry, hot rouged lips; but I fail, I fail—although I still feel their elusive touch now and then in the blindman's buff of my senses, in that sobbing sort of dream when she and I clumsily clutch at each other through a heartbreaking mist and I cannot see the color of her eyes for the blank luster of brimming tears drowning their irises.

She was much younger than I—not as much younger as was Nathalie of the lovely bare shoulders and long earrings in relation to swarthy Pushkin; but still there was a sufficient margin for that kind of retrospective romanticism which finds pleasure in imitating the destiny of a unique genius (down to the jealousy, down to the filth, down to the stab of seeing her almond-shaped eyes turn to her blond Cassio behind her peacock-feathered fan) even if one cannot imitate his verse. She liked mine though, and would scarcely have yawned as the other was wont to do every time her husband's poem happened to exceed the length of a sonnet. If she has remained a phantom to me, I may have been one to her: I suppose she had been solely attracted by the obscurity of my poetry; then tore a hole through its veil and saw a stranger's unlovable face.

As you know, I had been for some time planning to follow the example of your fortunate flight. She described to me an uncle of hers who lived, she said, in New York: he had taught riding at a southern college and had wound up by marrying a wealthy American woman; they had a little daughter born deaf. She said she had lost their address long ago, but a few days later it miraculously turned up, and we wrote a dramatic letter to which we never received any reply. This did not much matter, as I had already obtained a sound affidavit from Professor Lomchenko of Chicago; but little else had been done in the way of getting the necessary papers, when the invasion began, whereas I foresaw that if we stayed on in Paris some helpful compatriot of mine would sooner or later point out to the interested party sundry passages in one of my books where I argued that, with all her many black sins, Germany was still bound to remain forever and ever the laughingstock of the world.

So we started upon our disastrous honeymoon. Crushed and jolted amid the apocalyptic exodus, waiting for unscheduled trains that were bound for unknown destinations, walking through the stale stage setting of abstract towns, living in a permanent twilight of physical exhaustion, we fled; and the farther we fled, the clearer it became that what was driving us on was something more than a booted and buckled fool with his assortment of variously propelled junk—something of which he was a mere symbol, something monstrous and impalpable, a timeless and faceless mass of immemorial horror that still keeps coming at me from behind even here, in the green vacuum of Central Park.

Oh, she bore it gamely enough—with a kind of dazed cheerfulness. Once, however, quite suddenly she started to sob in a sympathetic railway carriage. "The dog," she said, "the dog we left. I cannot forget the poor dog." The honesty of her grief shocked me, as we had never had any dog. "I know," she said, "but I tried to imagine we had actually bought that setter. And just think, he would be now whining behind a locked door." There had never been any talk of buying a setter.

I should also not like to forget a certain stretch of highroad and the sight of a family of refugees (two women, a child) whose old father, or grandfather, had died on the way. The sky was a chaos of black and flesh-colored clouds with an ugly sunburst beyond a hooded hill, and the dead man was lying on his back under a dusty plane tree. With a stick and their hands the women had tried to dig a roadside grave, but the soil was too hard; they had given it up and were sitting side by side, among the anemic poppies, a little apart from the corpse and its upturned beard. But the little boy was still scratching and scraping and tugging until he tumbled a flat stone and forgot the object of his solemn exertions as he crouched on his haunches, his thin, eloquent neck showing all its vertebrae to the headsman, and watched with surprise and delight thousands of minute brown ants seething, zigzagging, dispersing, heading for places of safety in the Gard, and the Aude, and the Drôme, and the Var, and the Basses-Pyrénées—we two paused only in Pau.

Spain proved too difficult and we decided to move on to Nice. At a place called Faugères (a ten-minute stop) I squeezed out of the train to buy some food. When a couple of minutes later I came back, the train was gone, and the muddled old man responsible for the atrocious void that faced me (coal dust glittering in the heat between naked indifferent rails, and a lone piece of orange peel) brutally told me that, anyway, I had had no right to get out.

In a better world I could have had my wife located and told what to do (I had both tickets and most of the money); as it was, my nightmare struggle with the telephone proved futile, so I dismissed the whole series of diminutive voices barking at me from afar, sent two or three telegrams which are probably on their way only now, and late in the evening took the next local to Montpellier, farther than which her train would not stumble. Not finding her there, I had to choose between two alternatives: going on because she might have boarded the Marseilles train which I had just missed, or going back because she might have returned to Faugères. I forget now what tangle of reasoning led me to Marseilles and Nice.

Beyond such routine action as forwarding false data to a few unlikely places, the police did nothing to help: one man bellowed at me for being a nuisance; another sidetracked the question by doubting the authenticity of my marriage certificate because it was stamped on what he contended to be the wrong side; a third, a fat *commissaire* with liquid brown eyes, confessed that he wrote poetry in his spare time. I looked up various acquaintances among the numerous Russians domiciled or stranded in Nice. I heard those among them who chanced to have Jewish blood talk of their doomed kinsmen crammed into hellbound trains; and my own plight, by contrast, acquired a commonplace air of irreality while I sat in some crowded café with the milky blue sea in front of me and a shell-hollow murmur behind telling and retelling the tale of massacre and misery, and the gray paradise beyond the ocean, and the ways and whims of harsh consuls.

A week after my arrival an indolent plainclothesman called upon me and took me down a crooked and smelly street to a black-stained house with the word "hotel" almost erased by dirt and time; there, he said, my wife had been found. The girl he produced was an absolute stranger, of course; but my friend Holmes kept on trying for some time to make her and me confess we were married, while her taciturn and muscular bedfellow stood by and listened, his bare arms crossed on his striped chest.

When at length I got rid of those people and had wandered back to my neighborhood, I happened to pass by a compact queue waiting at the entrance of a food store; and there, at the very end, was my wife, straining on tiptoe to catch a glimpse of what exactly was being sold. I think the first thing she said to me was that she hoped it was oranges.

Her tale seemed a trifle hazy, but perfectly banal. She had returned to Faugères and gone straight to the Commissariat instead of making inquiries at the station, where I had left a message for her. A party of refugees suggested that she join them; she spent the night in a bicycle shop with no bicycles, on the floor, together with three elderly women who lay, she said, like three logs in a row. Next day she realized that she had not enough money to reach Nice. Eventually she borrowed some from one of the log-women. She got into the wrong train, however, and traveled to a town the name of which she could not remember. She had arrived at Nice two days ago and had found some friends at the Russian church. They had told her I was somewhere around, looking for her, and would surely turn up soon.

Sometime later, as I sat on the edge of the only chair in my garret and held her by her slender young hips (she was combing her soft hair and tossing her head back with every stroke), her dim smile changed all at once into an odd quiver and she placed one hand on my shoulder, staring down at me as if I were a reflection in a pool, which she had noticed for the first time.

"I've been lying to you, dear," she said. "*Ya lgunia*. I stayed for several nights in Montpellier with a brute of a man I met on the train. I did not want it at all. He sold hair lotions."

The time, the place, the torture. Her fan, her gloves, her mask. I spent that night and many others getting it out of her bit by bit, but not getting it all. I was under the strange delusion that first I must find out every detail, reconstruct every minute, and only then decide whether I could bear it. But the limit of desired knowledge was unattainable, nor could I ever foretell the approximate point after which I might imagine myself satiated, because of course the denominator of every fraction of knowledge was potentially as infinite as the number of intervals between the fractions themselves.

Oh, the first time she had been too tired to mind, and the next had not minded because she was sure I had deserted her; and she apparently considered that such explanations ought to be a kind of consolation prize for me instead of the nonsense and agony they really were. It went on like that for eons, she breaking down every now and then, but soon rallying again, answering my unprintable questions in a breathless whisper or trying with a pitiful smile to wriggle into the semisecurity of irrelevant commentaries, and I crushing and crushing the mad molar till my jaw almost burst with pain, a flaming pain which seemed somehow preferable to the dull, humming ache of humble endurance.

And mark, in between the periods of this inquest, we were trying to get from reluctant authorities certain papers which in their turn would make it lawful to apply for a third kind which would serve as a stepping-stone toward a permit enabling the holder to apply for yet other papers which might or might not give him the means of discovering how and why it had happened. For even if I could imagine the accursed recurrent scene, I failed to link up its sharp-angled grotesque shadows with the dim limbs of my wife as she shook and rattled and dissolved in my violent grasp.

So nothing remained but to torture each other, to wait for hours on end in the Prefecture, filling forms, conferring with friends who had already probed the innermost viscera of all visas, pleading with secretaries, and filling forms again, with the result that her lusty and versatile traveling salesman became blended in a ghastly mix-up with rat-whiskered snarling officials, rotting bundles of obsolete records, the reek of violet ink, bribes slipped under gangrenous blotting paper, fat flies tickling moist necks with their rapid cold padded feet, new-laid clumsy concave photographs of your six subhuman doubles, the tragic eyes and patient politeness of petitioners born in Slutzk, Starodub, or Bobruisk, the funnels and pulleys of the Holy Inquisition, the awful smile of the bald man with the glasses, who had been told that his passport could not be found.

I confess that one evening, after a particularly abominable day, I sank down on a stone bench weeping and cursing a mock world where millions of lives were being juggled by the clammy hands of consuls and *commissaires*. I noticed she was crying too, and then I told her that nothing would really have mattered the way it mattered now, had she not gone and done what she did.

"You will think me crazy," she said with a vehemence that, for a second, almost made a real person of her, "but I didn't—I swear that I didn't. Perhaps I live several lives at once. Perhaps I wanted to test you. Perhaps this bench is a dream and we are in Saratov or on some star."

It would be tedious to niggle the different stages through which I passed before accepting finally the first version of her delay. I did not talk to her and was a good deal alone. She would glimmer and fade, and reappear with some trifle she thought I would appreciate—a handful of cherries, three precious cigarettes, or the like—treating me with the unruffled mute sweetness of a nurse that trips from and to a gruff convalescent. I ceased visiting most of our mutual friends because they had lost all interest in my passport affairs and seemed to have turned vaguely inimical. I composed several poems. I drank all the wine I could get. I clasped her one day to my groaning breast, and we went for a week to Caboule and lay on the round pink pebbles of the narrow beach. Strange to say, the happier our new relations seemed, the stronger I felt an undercurrent of poignant sadness, but I kept telling myself that this was an intrinsic feature of all true bliss.

In the meantime, something had shifted in the moving pattern of our fates and at last I emerged from a dark and hot office with a couple of plump *visas de sortie* cupped in my trembling hands. Into these the U.S.A. serum was duly injected, and I dashed to Marseilles and managed to get tickets for the very next boat. I returned and tramped up the stairs. I saw a rose in a glass on the table—the sugar pink of its obvious beauty, the parasitic air bubbles clinging to its stem. Her two spare dresses were gone, her comb was gone, her checkered coat was gone, and so was the mauve hairband with a mauve bow that had been her hat. There was no note pinned to the pillow, nothing at all in the room to enlighten me, for of course the rose was merely what French rhymesters call *une cheville*.

I went to the Veretennikovs, who could tell me nothing; to the Hellmans, who refused to say anything; and to the Elagins, who were not sure whether to tell me or not. Finally the old lady—and you know what Anna Vladimirovna is like at crucial moments—asked for her rubber-tipped cane, heavily but energetically dislodged her bulk from her favorite armchair, and took me into the garden. There she informed me that, being twice my age, she had the right to say I was a bully and a cad.

You must imagine the scene: the tiny graveled garden with its blue Arabian Nights jar and solitary cypress; the cracked terrace where the old lady's father had dozed with a rug on his knees when he retired from his Novgorod governorship to spend a few last evenings in Nice; the pale-green sky; a whiff of vanilla in the deepening dusk; the crickets emitting their metallic trill pitched at two octaves above middle C; and Anna Vladimirovna, the folds of her cheeks jerkily dangling as she flung at me a motherly but quite undeserved insult.

During several preceding weeks, my dear V., every time she had visited by herself the three or four families we both knew, my ghostly wife had filled the eager ears of all those kind people with an extraordinary story. To wit: that she had madly fallen in love with a young Frenchman who could give her a turreted home and a crested name; that she had implored me for a divorce and I had refused; that in fact I had said

I would rather shoot her and myself than sail to New York alone; that she had said her father in a similar case had acted like a gentleman; that I had answered I did not give a hoot for her *cocu de père*.

There were loads of other preposterous details of the kind—but they all hung together in such a remarkable fashion that no wonder the old lady made me swear I would not seek to pursue the lovers with a cocked pistol. They had gone, she said, to a château in Lozère. I inquired whether she had ever set eyes upon the man. No, but she had been shown his picture. As I was about to leave, Anna Vladimirovna, who had slightly relaxed and had even given me her five fingers to kiss, suddenly flared up again, struck the gravel with her cane, and said in her deep strong voice: "But one thing I shall never forgive you—her dog, that poor beast which you hanged with your own hands before leaving Paris."

Whether the gentleman of leisure had changed into a traveling salesman, or whether the metamorphosis had been reversed, or whether again he was neither the one nor the other, but the nondescript Russian who had courted her before our marriage—all this was absolutely inessential. She had gone. That was the end. I should have been a fool had I begun the nightmare business of searching and waiting for her all over again.

On the fourth morning of a long and dismal sea voyage, I met on the deck a solemn but pleasant old doctor with whom I had played chess in Paris. He asked me whether my wife was very much incommoded by the rough seas. I answered that I had sailed alone; whereupon he looked taken aback and then said he had seen her a couple of days before going on board, namely in Marseilles, walking, rather aimlessly he thought, along the embankment. She said that I would presently join her with bag and tickets.

This is, I gather, the point of the whole story—although if you write it, you had better not make him a doctor, as that kind of thing has been overdone. It was at that moment that I suddenly knew for certain that she had never existed at all. I shall tell you another thing. When I arrived I hastened to satisfy a certain morbid curiosity: I went to the address she had given me once; it proved to be an anonymous gap between two office buildings; I looked for her uncle's name in the directory; it was not there; I made some inquiries, and Gekko, who knows everything, informed me that the man and his horsey wife existed all right, but had moved to San Francisco after their deaf little girl had died.

Viewing the past graphically, I see our mangled romance engulfed in a deep valley of mist between the crags of two matter-of-fact mountains: life had been real before, life will be real from now on, I hope. Not tomorrow, though. Perhaps after tomorrow. You, happy mortal, with your lovely family (how is Ines? how are the twins?) and your diversified work (how are the lichens?), can hardly be expected to puzzle out my misfortune in terms of human communion, but you may clarify things for me through the prism of your art.

Yet the pity of it. Curse your art, I am hideously unhappy. She keeps on walking to and fro where the brown nets are spread to dry on the hot stone slabs and the dappled light of the water plays on the side of a moored fishing boat. Somewhere, somehow, I have made some fatal mistake. There are tiny pale bits of broken fish scales glistening here and there in the brown meshes. It may all end in *Aleppo* if I am not careful. Spare me, V.: you would load your dice with an unbearable implication if you took that for a title.

A FORGOTTEN POET

I N 1899, in the ponderous, comfortable padded St. Petersburg
       of those days, a prominent cultural organization, the Society for
       the Advancement of Russian Literature, decided to honor in a
grand way the memory of the poet Konstantin Perov, who had died
half a century before at the ardent age of four-and-twenty. He had
been styled the Russian Rimbaud and, although the French boy surpassed him in genius, such a comparison is not wholly unjustified.
When only eighteen he composed his remarkable *Georgian Nights*, a
long, rambling "dream epic," certain passages of which rip the veil of
its traditional Oriental setting to produce that heavenly draft which
suddenly locates the sensorial effect of true poetry right between one's
shoulder blades.

This was followed three years later by a volume of poems: he had
got hold of some German philosopher or other, and several of these
pieces are distressing because of the grotesque attempt at combining
an authentic lyrical spasm with a metaphysical explanation of the universe; but the rest are still as vivid and unusual as they were in the days
when that queer youth dislocated the Russian vocabulary and twisted
the necks of accepted epithets in order to make poetry splutter and
scream instead of twittering. Most readers like best those poems of his
where the ideas of emancipation, so characteristic of the Russian fifties,
are expressed in a glorious storm of obscure eloquence, which, as one
critic put it, "does not show you the enemy but makes you fairly burst
with the longing to fight." Personally I prefer the purer and at the
same time bumpier lyrics such as "The Gypsy" or "The Bat."

Perov was the son of a small landowner of whom the only thing
known is that he tried planting tea on his estate near Luga. Young
Konstantin (to use a biographical intonation) spent most of his time in
St. Petersburg vaguely attending the university, then vaguely looking

for a clerical job—little indeed is known of his activities beyond such trivialities as can be deduced from the general trends of his set. A passage in the correspondence of the famous poet Nekrasov, who happened to meet him once in a bookshop, conveys the image of a sulky, unbalanced, "clumsy and fierce" young man with "the eyes of a child and the shoulders of a furniture mover."

He is also mentioned in a police report as "conversing in low tones with two other students" in a coffeehouse on Nevsky Avenue. And his sister, who married a merchant from Riga, is said to have deplored the poet's emotional adventures with seamstresses and washerwomen. In the autumn of 1849 he visited his father with the special intent of obtaining money for a trip to Spain. His father, a man of simple reactions, slapped him on the face; and a few days later the poor boy was drowned while bathing in the neighboring river. His clothes and a half-eaten apple were found lying under a birch tree, but the body was never recovered.

His fame was sluggish: a passage from the *Georgian Nights*, always the same one, in all anthologies; a violent article by the radical critic Dobrolubov, in 1859, lauding the revolutionary innuendoes of his weakest poems; a general notion in the eighties that a reactionary atmosphere had thwarted and finally destroyed a fine if somewhat inarticulate talent—this was about all.

In the nineties, because of a healthier interest in poetry, coinciding as it sometimes does with a sturdy and dull political era, a flurry of rediscovery started around Perov's rhymes while, on the other hand, the liberal-minded were not averse to following Dobrolubov's cue. The subscription for a monument in one of the public parks proved a perfect success. A leading publisher collected all the scraps of information available in regard to Perov's life and issued his complete works in one fairly plump volume. The monthlies contributed several scholarly surveys. The commemorative meeting in one of the best halls of the capital attracted a crowd.

2

———

A few minutes before the start, while the speakers were still assembled in a committee room behind the stage, the door opened gustily and there entered a sturdy old man, clad in a frock coat that had seen—on his or on somebody else's shoulders—better times. Without paying the slightest heed to the admonishments of a couple of ribbon-badged university students who, in their capacity of attendants, were attempting to restrain him, he proceeded with perfect dignity toward the committee, bowed, and said, "I am Perov."

A friend of mine, almost twice my age and now the only surviving witness of the event, tells me that the chairman (who as a newspaper editor had a great deal of experience in the matter of extravagant intruders) said without even looking up, "Kick him out." Nobody did—perhaps because one is apt to show a certain courtesy to an old gentleman who is supposedly very drunk. He sat down at the table and, selecting the mildest-looking person, Slavsky, a translator of Longfellow, Heine, and Sully-Prudhomme (and later a member of the terrorist group), asked in a matter-of-fact tone whether the "monument money" had already been collected, and if so, when could he have it.

All the accounts agree on the singularly quiet way in which he made his claim. He did not press his point. He merely stated it as if absolutely unconscious of any possibility of his being disbelieved. What impressed one was that at the very beginning of that weird affair, in that secluded room, among those distinguished men, there he was with his patriarchal beard, faded brown eyes, and potato nose, sedately inquiring about the benefits from the proceedings without even bothering to produce such proofs as might have been faked by an ordinary impostor.

"Are you a relative?" asked someone.

"My name is Konstantin Konstantinovich Perov," said the old man patiently. "I am given to understand that a descendant of my family is in the hall, but that is neither here nor there."

"How old are you?" asked Slavsky.

"I am seventy-four," he replied, "and the victim of several poor crops in succession."

"You are surely aware," remarked the actor Yermakov, "that the poet whose memory we are celebrating tonight was drowned in the river Oredezh exactly fifty years ago."

"Vzdor" ("Nonsense"), retorted the old man. "I staged that business for reasons of my own."

"And now, my dear fellow," said the chairman, "I really think you must go."

They dismissed him from their consciousness and flocked out onto the severely lighted platform where another committee table, draped in solemn red cloth, with the necessary number of chairs behind it, had been hypnotizing the audience for some time with the glint of its traditional decanter. To the left of this, one could admire the oil painting loaned by the Sheremetevski Art Gallery: it represented Perov at twenty-two, a swarthy young man with romantic hair and an open shirt collar. The picture stand was piously camouflaged by means of leaves and flowers. A lectern with another decanter loomed in front and a grand piano was waiting in the wings to be rolled in later for the musical part of the program.

The hall was well packed with literary people, enlightened lawyers, schoolteachers, scholars, eager university students of both sexes, and the like. A few humble agents of the secret police had been delegated to attend the meeting in inconspicuous spots of the hall, as the government knew by experience that the most staid cultural assemblies had a queer knack of slipping into an orgy of revolutionary propaganda. The fact that one of Perov's first poems contained a veiled but benevolent allusion to the insurrection of 1825 suggested taking certain precautions: one never could tell what might happen after a public mouthing of such lines as "the gloomy sough of Siberian larches communicates with the underground ore" ("*sibirskikh pikht oogrewmyi shorokh s podzemnoy snositsa roodoy*").

As one of the accounts has it, "soon one became aware that something vaguely resembling a Dostoyevskian row [the author is thinking of a famous slapstick chapter in *The Possessed*] was creating an atmosphere of awkwardness and suspense." This was due to the fact that the old gentleman deliberately followed the seven members of the jubilee committee onto the platform and then attempted to sit down with them at the table. The chairman, being mainly intent upon avoiding a scuffle in full view of the audience, did his best to make him desist. Under the public disguise of a polite smile he whispered to the patriarch that he would have him ejected from the hall if he did not let go the back of the chair which Slavsky, with a nonchalant air but with a grip of iron, was covertly wresting from under the old man's gnarled hand. The old man refused but lost his hold and was left without a seat. He glanced around, noticed the piano stool in the wings, and coolly pulled it onto the stage just a fraction of a second before the hands of a screened attendant tried to snatch it back. He seated himself at some distance from the table and immediately became exhibit number one.

Here the committee made the fatal mistake of again dismissing his presence from their minds: they were, let it be repeated, particularly anxious to avoid a scene; and moreover, the blue hydrangea next to the picture stand half concealed the obnoxious party from their physical vision. Unfortunately, the old gentleman was most conspicuous to the audience, as he sat there on his unseemly pedestal (with its rotatory potentialities hinted at by a recurrent creaking), opening his spectacle case and breathing fishlike upon his glasses, perfectly calm and comfortable, his venerable head, shabby black clothes, and elastic-sided boots simultaneously suggesting the needy Russian professor and the prosperous Russian undertaker.

The chairman went up to the lectern and launched upon his introductory speech. Whisperings rippled all over the audience, for people were naturally curious to know who the old fellow was. Firmly bespectacled, with his hands on his knees, he peered sideways at the portrait, then turned away from it and inspected the front row. Answering glances could not help shuttling between the shiny dome of his head and the curly head of the portrait, for during the chairman's long speech the details of the intrusion spread, and the imagination of some started to toy with the idea that a poet belonging to an almost legendary period, snugly relegated to it by textbooks, an anachronistic creature, a live fossil in the nets of an ignorant fisherman, a kind of Rip van Winkle, was actually attending in his drab dotage the reunion dedicated to the glory of his youth.

". . . let the name of Perov," said the chairman, ending his speech, "be never forgotten by thinking Russia. Tyutchev has said that Pushkin will always be remembered by our country as a first love. In regard to Perov we may say that he was Russia's first experience in freedom. To a superficial observer this freedom may seem limited to Perov's phenomenal lavishness of poetical images which appeal more to the artist than to the citizen. But we, representatives of a more sober generation, are inclined to decipher for ourselves a deeper, more vital, more human, and more social sense in such lines of his as

> *When the last snow hides in the shade of the cemetery wall*
> *and the coat of my neighbor's black horse*
> *shows a swift blue sheen in the swift April sun,*
> *and the puddles are as many heavens cupped in the Negro-hands*
>   *of the Earth,*
> *then my heart goes out in its tattered cloak*
> *to visit the poor, the blind, the foolish,*
> *the round backs slaving for the round bellies,*
> *all those whose eyes dulled by care or lust do not see*
> *the holes in the snow, the blue horse, the miraculous puddle.*

A burst of applause greeted this, but all of a sudden there was a break in the clapping, and then disharmonious gusts of laughter; for, as the chairman, still vibrating with the words he had just uttered, went back to the table, the bearded stranger got up and acknowledged the applause by means of jerky nods and awkward wavings of the hand, his expression combining formal gratitude with a certain impatience. Slavsky and a couple of attendants made a desperate attempt to bundle him away, but from the depth of the audience there arose the cries of "Shame, shame!" and *"Astavte starika!"* ("Leave the old man alone!")

I find in one of the accounts the suggestion that there were accomplices among the audience, but I think that mass compassion, which may come as unexpectedly as mass vindictiveness, is sufficient to explain the turn things were taking. In spite of having to cope with three men the *"starik"* managed to retain a remarkable dignity of demeanor, and when his halfhearted assailants retired and he retrieved the piano stool that had been knocked down during the struggle, there was a murmur of satisfaction. However, the regrettable fact remained that the atmosphere of the meeting was hopelessly impaired. The younger and rowdier members of the audience were beginning to enjoy themselves hugely. The chairman, his nostrils quivering, poured himself out a tumbler of water. Two secret agents were cautiously exchanging glances from two different points of the house.

3
———

The speech of the chairman was followed by the treasurer's account of the sums received from various institutions and private persons for the erection of a Perov monument in one of the suburban parks. The old man unhurriedly produced a bit of paper and a stubby pencil and, propping the paper on his knee, began to check the figures which were being mentioned. Then the granddaughter of Perov's sister appeared for a moment on the stage. The organizers had had some trouble with this item of the program since the person in question, a fat, popeyed, wax-pale young woman, was being treated for melancholia in a home for mental patients. With twisted mouth and all dressed up in pathetic pink, she was shown to the audience for a moment and then whisked back into the firm hands of a buxom woman delegated by the home.

When Yermakov, who in those days was the darling of theatergoers, a kind of *beau ténor* in terms of the drama, began delivering in his chocolate-cream voice the Prince's speech from the *Georgian Nights*, it became clear that even his best fans were more interested in the reactions of the old man than in the beauty of the delivery. At the lines

> *If metal is immortal, then somewhere*
> *there lies the burnished button that I lost*
> *upon my seventh birthday in a garden.*
> *Find me that button and my soul will know*
> *that every soul is saved and stored and treasured*

a chink appeared for the first time in his composure and he slowly unfolded a large handkerchief and lustily blew his nose—a sound which sent Yermakov's heavily adumbrated, diamond-bright eye squinting like that of a timorous steed.

The handkerchief was returned to the folds of the coat and only several seconds *after* this did it become noticeable to the people in the first row that tears were trickling from under his glasses. He did not attempt to wipe them, though once or twice his hand did go up to his spectacles with claw-wise spread fingers, but it dropped again, as if by any such gesture (and this was the culminating point of the whole delicate masterpiece) he was afraid to attract attention to his tears. The tremendous applause that followed the recitation was certainly more a tribute to the old man's performance than to the poem in Yermakov's rendering. Then, as soon as the applause petered out, he stood up and marched toward the edge of the platform.

There was no attempt on the part of the committee to stop him, and this for two reasons. First, the chairman, driven to exasperation by the old man's conspicuous behavior, had gone out for a moment and given a certain order. In the second place, a medley of strange doubts was beginning to unnerve some of the organizers, so that there was a complete hush when the old man placed his elbows on the reading stand.

"And this is fame," he said in such a husky voice that from the back rows there came cries of *"Gromche, gromche!"* ("Louder, louder!")

"I am saying that this is fame," he repeated, grimly peering over his spectacles at the audience. "A score of frivolous poems, words made to joggle and jingle, and a man's name is remembered as if he had been of some use to humanity! No, gentlemen, do not delude yourselves. Our empire and the throne of our father the Tsar still stand as they stood, akin to frozen thunder in their invulnerable might, and the misguided youth who scribbled rebellious verse half a century ago is now a law-abiding old man respected by honest citizens. An old man, let me add, who needs your protection. I am the victim of the elements: the land I had plowed with my sweat, the lambs I had personally suckled, the wheat I had seen waving its golden arms—"

It was then that two enormous policemen quickly and painlessly removed the old man. The audience had a glimpse of his being rushed out—his dickey protruding one way, his beard the other, a cuff dangling from his wrist, but still that gravity and that pride in his eyes.

When reporting the celebration, the leading dailies referred only in passing to the "regrettable incident" that had marred it. But the disreputable *St. Petersburg Record*, a lurid and reactionary rag edited by the brothers Kherstov for the benefit of the lower middle class and of a blissfully semiliterate substratum of working people, blazed forth with a series of articles maintaining that the "regrettable incident" was nothing less than the reappearance of the authentic Perov.

4
———

In the meantime, the old man had been collected by the very wealthy and vulgarly eccentric merchant Gromov, whose household was full of vagabond monks, quack doctors, and "pogromystics." The *Record* printed interviews with the impostor. In these the latter said dreadful things about the "lackeys of the revolutionary party" who had cheated him of his identity and robbed him of his money. This money he proposed to obtain by law from the publishers of Perov's complete works. A drunken scholar attached to the Gromov household pointed out the (unfortunately rather striking) similarity between the old man's features and those of the portrait.

There appeared a detailed but most implausible account of his having staged a suicide in order to lead a Christian life in the bosom of Saint Russia. He had been everything: a peddler, a bird catcher, a ferryman on the Volga, and had wound up by acquiring a bit of land in a remote province. I have seen a copy of a sordid-looking booklet, *The Death and Resurrection of Konstantin Perov*, which used to be sold on the streets by shivering beggars, together with the *Adventures of the Marquis de Sade* and the *Memoirs of an Amazon*.

My best find, however, in looking through old files, is a smudgy photograph of the bearded impostor perched upon the marble of the unfinished Perov monument in a leafless park. He is seen standing very straight with his arms folded; he wears a round fur cap and a new pair of galoshes but no overcoat; a little crowd of his backers is gathered at his feet, and their little white faces stare into the camera with that special navel-eyed, self-complacent expression peculiar to old pictures of lynching parties.

Given this atmosphere of florid hooliganism and reactionary smugness (so closely linked up with governmental ideas in Russia, no matter whether the Tsar be called Alexander, Nicholas, or Joe), the intelligentsia could hardly bear to visualize the disaster of identifying the pure, ardent, revolutionary-minded Perov as represented by his poems with a vulgar old man wallowing in a painted pigsty. The tragic part was that while neither Gromov nor the Kherstov brothers really believed the purveyor of their fun was the true Perov, many honest, cultivated people had become obsessed by the impossible thought that what they had ejected was Truth and Justice.

As a recently published letter from Slavsky to Korolenko has it: "One shudders to think that a gift of destiny unparalleled in history, the Lazarus-like resurrection of a great poet of the past, may be ungratefully ignored—nay, even more, deemed a fiendish deceit on the part of a man whose only crime has been half a century of silence and a few minutes of wild talk." The wording is muddled but the gist is clear: intellectual Russia was less afraid of falling victim to a hoax than of sponsoring a hideous blunder. But there was something she was still more afraid of, and that was the destruction of an ideal; for your radical is ready to upset everything in the world except any such trivial bauble, no matter how doubtful and dusty, that for some reason radicalism has enshrined.

It is rumored that at a certain secret session of the Society for the Advancement of Russian Literature the numerous insulting epistles that the old man kept sending in were carefully compared by experts with a very old letter written by the poet in his teens. It had been discovered in a certain private archive, was believed to be the only sample of Perov's hand, and none except the scholars who pored over its faded ink knew of its existence. Neither do we know what their findings were.

It is further rumored that a lump of money was amassed and that the old man was approached without the knowledge of his disgraceful companions. Apparently, a substantial monthly pension was to be granted him under the condition that he return at once to his farm and stay there in decorous silence and oblivion. Apparently, too, the offer was accepted, for he vanished as jerkily as he had appeared, while

Gromov consoled himself for the loss of his pet by adopting a shady hypnotizer of French extraction who a year or two later was to enjoy some success at the Court.

The monument was duly unveiled and became a great favorite with the local pigeons. The sales of the collected works fizzled out genteelly in the middle of a fourth edition. Finally, a few years later, in the region where Perov had been born, the oldest though not necessarily the brightest inhabitant told a lady journalist that he remembered his father telling him of finding a skeleton in a reedy part of the river.

5

This would have been all had not the Revolution come, turning up slabs of rich earth together with the white rootlets of little plants and fat mauve worms which otherwise would have remained buried. When, in the early twenties, in the dark, hungry, but morbidly active city, various odd cultural institutions sprouted (such as bookshops where famous but destitute writers sold their own books, and so on), somebody or other earned a couple of months' living by arranging a little Perov museum, and this led to yet another resurrection.

The exhibits? All of them except one (the letter). A secondhand past in a shabby hall. The oval-shaped eyes and brown locks of the precious Sheremetevsky portrait (with a crack in the region of the open collar suggesting a tentative beheading); a battered volume of the *Georgian Nights* that was thought to have belonged to Nekrasov; an indifferent photograph of the village school built on the spot where the poet's father had owned a house and an orchard. An old glove that some visitor to the museum had forgotten. Several editions of Perov's works distributed in such a way as to occupy the greatest possible space.

And because all these poor relics still refused to form a happy family, several period articles had been added, such as the dressing gown that a famous radical critic had worn in his rococo study, and the chains he had worn in his wooden Siberian prison. But there again, since neither this nor the portraits of various writers of the time were bulky enough, a model of the first railway train to run in Russia (in the forties, between St. Petersburg and Tsarskoye Selo) had been installed in the middle of that dismal room.

The old man, now well over ninety but still articulate in speech and reasonably erect in carriage, would show you around the place as if he were your host instead of being the janitor. One had the odd impression that presently he would lead you into the next (nonexisting) room, where supper would be served. All that he really possessed, however, was a stove behind a screen and the bench on which he slept; but if you bought one of the books exhibited for sale at the entrance he would autograph it for you as a matter of course.

Then one morning he was found dead on his bench by the woman who brought him his food. Three quarrelsome families lived for a while in the museum, and soon nothing remained of its contents. And as if some great hand with a great rasping sound had torn out a great bunch of pages from a number of books, or as if some frivolous story writer had bottled an imp of fiction in the vessel of truth, or as if . . .

But no matter. Somehow or other, in the next twenty years or so, Russia lost all contact with Perov's poetry. Young Soviet citizens know as little about his works as they do about mine. No doubt a time will come when he will be republished and readmired; still, one cannot help feeling that, as things stand, people are missing a great deal. One wonders also what future historians will make of the old man and his extraordinary contention. But that, of course, is a matter of secondary importance.

TIME AND EBB

I N THE first floriferous days of convalescence after a severe illness, which nobody, least of all the patient himself, expected a ninety-year-old organism to survive, I was admonished by my dear friends Norman and Nura Stone to prolong the lull in my scientific studies and relax in the midst of some innocent occupation such as brazzle or solitaire.

The first is out of the question, since tracking the name of an Asiatic town or the title of a Spanish novel through a maze of jumbled syllables on the last page of the evening newsbook (a feat which my youngest great-granddaughter performs with the utmost zest) strikes me as far more strenuous than toying with animal tissues. Solitaire, on the other hand, is worthy of consideration, especially if one is sensitive to its mental counterpart; for is not the setting down of one's reminiscences a game of the same order, wherein events and emotions are dealt to oneself in leisurely retrospection?

Arthur Freeman is reported to have said of memoirists that they are men who have too little imagination to write fiction and too bad a memory to write the truth. In this twilight of self-expression I too must float. Like other old men before me, I have discovered that the near in time is annoyingly confused, whereas at the end of the tunnel there are color and light. I can discern the features of every month in 1944 or 1945, but seasons are utterly blurred when I pick out 1997 or 2012. I cannot remember the name of the eminent scientist who attacked my latest paper, as I have also forgotten those other names which my equally eminent defenders called him. I am unable to tell offhand what year the Embryological Section of the Association of Nature Lovers of Reykjavik elected me a corresponding member, or when, exactly, the American Academy of Science awarded me its choicest prize. (I remember, though, the keen pleasure which both these honors gave me.) Thus a man looking through a tremendous telescope does not see the cirri of an Indian summer above his charmed orchard, but does see, as my regretted colleague, the late Professor Alexander Ivanchenko, twice saw, the swarming of hesperozoa in a humid valley of the planet Venus.

No doubt the "numberless nebulous pictures" bequeathed us by the drab, flat, and strangely melancholic photography of the past century exaggerate the impression of unreality which that century makes upon those who do not remember it; but the fact remains that the beings that peopled the world in the days of my childhood seem to the present generation more remote than the nineteenth century seemed to them. They were still up to their waists in its prudery and prejudice. They clung to tradition as a vine still clings to a dead tree. They had their meals at large tables around which they grouped themselves in a stiff sitting position on hard wooden chairs. Clothes consisted of a number of parts, each of which, moreover, contained the reduced and useless remnants of this or that older fashion (a townsman dressing of a morning had to squeeze something like thirty buttons into as many buttonholes besides tying three knots and checking the contents of fifteen pockets).

In their letters they addressed perfect strangers by what was—insofar as words have sense—the equivalent of "beloved master" and prefaced a theoretically immortal signature with a mumble expressing idiotic devotion to a person whose very existence was to the writer a matter of complete unconcern. They were atavistically prone to endow the community with qualities and rights which they refused to the individual. Economics obsessed them almost as much as theologies had obsessed their ancestors. They were superficial, careless, and shortsighted. More than other generations, they tended to overlook outstanding men, leaving to us the honor of discovering their classics (thus Richard Sinatra remained, while he lived, an anonymous "ranger" dreaming under a Telluride pine or reading his prodigious verse to the squirrels of San Isabel Forest, whereas everybody knew another Sinatra, a minor writer, also of Oriental descent).

Elementary allobiotic phenomena led their so-called spiritualists to the silliest forms of transcendental surmise and made so-called common sense shrug its broad shoulders in equally silly ignorance. Our denominations of time would have seemed to them "telephone" numbers. They played with electricity in various ways without having the slightest notion of what it really was—and no wonder the chance revelation of its true nature came as a most hideous surprise (I was a man by that time and can well remember old Professor Andrews sobbing his heart out on the campus in the midst of a dumbfounded crowd).

But in spite of all the ridiculous customs and complications in which it was entangled, the world of my young days was a gallant and tough little world that countered adversity with a bit of dry humor and would calmly set out for remote battlefields in order to suppress the savage vulgarity of Hitler or Alamillo. And if I let myself go, many would be the bright, and kind, and dreamy, and lovely things which impassioned memory would find in the past—and then woe to the present age, for there is no knowing what a still vigorous old man might do to it if he tucked up his sleeves. But enough of this. History is not my field, so perhaps I had better turn to the personal lest I be told, as Mr. Saskatchewanov is told by the most charming character in present-day fiction (corroborated by my great-granddaughter, who reads more than I do), that "ev'ry cricket ought keep to its picket"—and not intrude on the rightful domain of other "gads and summersmiths."

2

I was born in Paris. My mother died when I was still an infant, so that I can only recall her as a vague patch of delicious lachrymal warmth just beyond the limit of iconographic memory. My father taught music and was a composer himself (I still treasure an ancient program where his name stands next to that of a great Russian); he saw me through my college stage and died of an obscure blood disease at the time of the South American War.

I was in my seventh year when he and I, and the sweetest grandmother a child has ever been blessed with, left Europe, where indescribable tortures were being inflicted by a degenerate nation upon the race to which I belong. A woman in Portugal gave me the hugest orange I had ever seen. From the stern of the liner two small cannon covered its portentously tortuous wake. A party of dolphins performed solemn somersaults. My grandmother read me a tale about a mermaid who had acquired a pair of feet. The inquisitive breeze would join in the reading and roughly finger the pages so as to discover what was going to happen next. That is about all I remember of the voyage.

Upon reaching New York, travelers in space used to be as much impressed as travelers in time would have been by the old-fashioned "skyscrapers"; this was a misnomer, since their association with the sky, especially at the ethereal close of a greenhouse day, far from suggesting any grating contact, was indescribably delicate and serene: to my childish eyes looking across the vast expanse of park land that used to grace the center of the city, they appeared remote and lilac-colored, and strangely aquatic, mingling as they did their first cautious lights with the colors of the sunset and revealing, with a kind of dreamy candor, the pulsating inside of their semitransparent structure.

Negro children sat quietly upon the artificial rocks. The trees had their Latin binomials displayed upon their trunks, just as the drivers of the squat, gaudy, scaraboid motorcabs (generically allied in my mind to certain equally gaudy automatic machines upon the musical constipation of which the insertion of a small coin used to act as a miraculous laxative) had their stale photographic pictures affixed to their backs; for we lived in the era of Identification and Tabulation; saw the personalities of men and things in terms of names and nicknames and did not believe in the existence of anything that was nameless.

In a recent and still popular play dealing with the quaint America of the Flying Forties, a good deal of glamour is infused into the part of the soda jerk, but the side-whiskers and the starched shirtfront are absurdly anachronistic, nor was there in my day such a continuous and violent revolving of tall mushroom seats as is indulged in by the performers. We imbibed our humble mixtures (through straws that were really much shorter than those employed on the stage) in an atmosphere of gloomy greed. I remember the shallow enchantment and the minor poetry of the proceedings: the copious froth engendered above the sunken lump of frozen synthetic cream, or the liquid brown mud of "fudge" sauce poured over its polar pate. Brass and glass surfaces, sterile reflections of electric lamps, the whirr and shimmer of a caged propeller, a Global War poster depicting Uncle Sam and his Rooseveltian tired blue eyes or else a dapper uniformed girl with a hypertrophied nether lip (that pout, that sullen kiss-trap, that transient fashion in feminine charm—1939–1950), and the unforgettable tonality of mixed traffic noises coming from the street—these patterns and melodic figures, for the conscious analysis of which time is alone responsible, somehow connected the "drugstore" with a world where men tormented metals and where metals hit back.

I attended a school in New York; then we moved to Boston; and then we moved again. We seem always to have been shifting quarters—and some homes were duller than others; but no matter how small the town, I was sure to find a place where bicycle tires were repaired, and a place where ice cream was sold, and a place where cinematographic pictures were shown.

Mountain gorges seemed to have been ransacked for echoes; these were subjected to a special treatment on a basis of honey and rubber until their condensed accents could be synchronized with the labial movements of serial photographs on a moon-white screen in a velvet-dark hall. With a blow of his fist a man sent a fellow creature crashing into a tower of crates. An incredibly smooth-skinned girl raised a linear eyebrow. A door slammed with the kind of ill-fitting thud that comes to us from the far bank of a river where woodsmen are at work.

3
————

I am also old enough to remember the coach trains: as a babe I worshipped them; as a boy I turned away to improved editions of speed. With their haggard windows and dim lights they still lumber sometimes through my dreams. Their hue might have passed for the ripeness of distance, for a blending succession of conquered miles, had it not surrendered its plum-bloom to the action of coal dust so as to match the walls of workshops and slums which preceded a city as inevitably as a rule of grammar and a blot precede the acquisition of conventional knowledge. Dwarf dunce caps were stored at one end of the car and could flabbily cup (with the transmission of a diaphanous chill to the fingers) the grottolike water of an obedient little fountain which reared its head at one's touch.

Old men resembling the hoary ferryman of still more ancient fairy tales chanted out their intermittent "nextations" and checked the tickets of the travelers, among whom there were sure to be, if the journey was reasonably long, a great number of sprawling, dead-tired soldiers and one live, drunken soldier, tremendously peripatetic and with only his pallor to connect him with death. He always occurred singly but he was always there, a freak, a young creature of clay, in the midst of what some very modern history textbooks glibly call Hamilton's period—after the indifferent scholar who put that period into shape for the benefit of the brainless.

Somehow or other my brilliant but unpractical father never could adapt himself to academic conditions sufficiently to stay very long in this or that place. I can visualize all of them, but one college town remains especially vivid: there is no need to name it if I say that three lawns from us, in a leafy lane, stood the house which is now the Mecca of a nation. I remember the sun-splashed garden chairs under the apple tree, and a bright copper-colored setter, and a fat, freckled boy with a book in his lap, and a handy-looking apple that I picked up in the shadow of a hedge.

And I doubt whether the tourists who nowadays visit the birthplace of the greatest man of his time and peer at the period furniture self-consciously huddled beyond the plush ropes of enshrined immortality can feel anything of that proud contact with the past which I owe to a chance incident. For whatever happens, and no matter how many index cards librarians may fill with the titles of my published papers, I shall go down to posterity as the man who had once thrown an apple at Barrett.

To those who have been born since the staggering discoveries of the seventies, and who thus have seen nothing in the nature of flying things save perhaps a kite or a toy balloon (still permitted, I understand, in several states in spite of Dr. de Sutton's recent articles on the subject), it is not easy to imagine airplanes, particularly because old photographic pictures of those splendid machines in full flight lack the life which only art could have been capable of retaining—and oddly enough no great painter ever chose them as a special subject into which to inject his genius and thus preserve their image from deterioration.

I suppose I am old-fashioned in my attitude toward many aspects of life that happen to be outside my particular branch of science; and possibly the personality of the very old man I am may seem divided, like those little European towns one half of which is in France and the other in Russia. I know this and proceed warily. Far from me is the intention to promote any yearning and morbid regret in regard to flying machines, but at the same time I cannot suppress the romantic undertone which is inherent to the symphonic entirety of the past as I feel it.

In those distant days when no spot on earth was more than sixty hours' flying time from one's local airport, a boy would know planes from propeller spinner to rudder trim tab, and could distinguish the species not only by the shape of the wing tip or the jutting of a cockpit, but even by the pattern of exhaust flames in the darkness; thus vying in the recognition of characters with those mad nature-sleuths—the post-Linnean systematists. A sectional diagram of wing and fuselage construction would give him a stab of creative delight, and the models he wrought of balsa and pine and paper clips provided such increasing excitement during the making that, by comparison, their completion seemed almost insipid, as if the spirit of the thing had flown away at the moment its shape had become fixed.

Attainment and science, retainment and art—the two couples keep to themselves, but when they do meet, nothing else in the world matters. And so I shall tiptoe away, taking leave of my childhood at its most typical point, in its most plastic posture: arrested by a deep drone that vibrates and gathers in volume overhead, stock-still, oblivious of the meek bicycle it straddles, one foot on the pedal, the toe of the other touching the asphalted earth, eyes, chin, and ribs lifted to the naked sky where a warplane comes with unearthly speed which only the expanse of its medium renders unhurried as ventral view changes to rear view, and wings and hum dissolve in the distance. Admirable monsters, great flying machines, they have gone, they have vanished like that flock of swans which passed with a mighty swish of multitudinous wings one spring night above Knights Lake in Maine, from the unknown into the unknown: swans of a species never determined by science, never seen before, never seen since—and then nothing but a lone star remained in the sky, like an asterisk leading to an undiscoverable footnote.

CONVERSATION PIECE, 1945

I HAPPEN to have a disreputable namesake, complete from nickname to surname, a man whom I have never seen in the flesh but whose vulgar personality I have been able to deduce from his chance intrusions into the castle of my life. The tangle began in Prague, where I happened to be living in the middle twenties. A letter came to me there from a small library apparently attached to some sort of White Army organization which, like myself, had moved out of Russia. In exasperated tones, it demanded that I return at once a copy of the *Protocols of the Wise Men of Zion*. This book, which in the old days had been wistfully appreciated by the Tsar, was a fake memorandum the secret police had paid a semiliterate crook to compile; its sole object was the promotion of pogroms. The librarian, who signed himself "Sinepuzov" (a surname meaning "blue belly," which affects a Russian imagination in much the same way as Winterbottom does an English one), insisted that I had been keeping what he chose to call "this popular and valuable work" for more than a year. He referred to previous requests addressed to me in Belgrade, Berlin, and Brussels, through which towns my namesake apparently had been drifting.

I visualized the fellow as a young, very White émigré, of the automatically reactionary type, whose education had been interrupted by the Revolution and who was successfully making up for lost time along traditional lines. He obviously was a great traveler; so was I—our only point in common. A Russian woman in Strasbourg asked me whether the man who had married her niece in Liège was my brother. One spring day, in Nice, a poker-faced girl with long earrings called at my hotel, asked to see me, took one look at me, apologized, and went away. In Paris, I received a telegram which jerkily ran, "NE VIENS PAS ALPHONSE DE RETOUR SOUPCONNE SOIS PRUDENT JE T'ADORE ANGOISSEE," and I admit deriving a certain grim satisfaction from the vision of my frivolous double inevitably bursting in, flowers in hand, upon Alphonse and his wife. A few years later, when I was lecturing in Zurich, I was suddenly arrested on a charge of smashing *three* mirrors in a restaurant—a kind of triptych featuring my namesake drunk (the first mirror), very drunk (the second), and roaring drunk (the third). Finally, in 1938, a French consul rudely refused to stamp my tattered sea-green Nansen passport because, he said, I had entered the country once before without a permit. In the fat dossier which was eventually produced, I caught a glimpse of my namesake's face. He had a clipped mustache and a crew haircut, the bastard.

When, soon after that, I came over to the United States and settled down in Boston, I felt sure I had shaken off my absurd shadow. Then—last month, to be precise—there came a telephone call.

In a hard and glittering voice, a woman said she was Mrs. Sybil Hall, a close friend of Mrs. Sharp, who had written to her suggesting that she *contact* me. I did know a Mrs. Sharp and didn't stop to think that both my Mrs. Sharp and myself might not be the right ones. Golden-voiced Mrs. Hall said she was having a little meeting at her apartment Friday night and would I come, because she was sure from what she had heard about me that I would be very, very much interested in the discussion. Although meetings of any kind are loathsome to me, I was prompted to accept the invitation by the thought that if I did not I might in some way disappoint Mrs. Sharp, a nice, maroon-trousered, short-haired old lady whom I had met on Cape Cod, where she shared a cottage with a younger woman; both ladies are mediocre leftist artists of independent means, and completely amiable.

Owing to a misadventure, which had nothing to do with the subject of the present account, I arrived much later than I intended at Mrs. Hall's apartment house. An ancient elevator attendant, oddly resembling Richard Wagner, gloomily took me up, and Mrs. Hall's unsmiling maid, her long arms hanging down her sides, waited while I removed my overcoat and rubbers in the hall. Here the chief decorative note was a certain type of ornamental vase manufactured in China, and possibly of great antiquity—in this case a tall, sickly-colored brute of a thing—which always makes me abominably unhappy.

As I crossed a self-conscious, small room that fairly brimmed with symbols of what advertisement writers call "gracious living" and was being ushered—theoretically, for the maid had dropped away—into a large, mellow, bourgeois salon, it gradually dawned upon me that this was exactly the sort of place where one would expect to be introduced to some old fool who had had caviar in the Kremlin or to some wooden Soviet Russian, and that my acquaintance Mrs. Sharp, who had for some reason always resented my contempt for the Party line and for the Communist and his Master's Voice, had decided, poor soul, that such an experience might have a beneficial influence upon my sacrilegious mind.

From a group of a dozen people, my hostess emerged in the form of a long-limbed, flat-chested woman with lipstick on her prominent front teeth. She introduced me rapidly to the guest of honor and her other guests, and the discussion, which had been interrupted by my entrance, was at once resumed. The guest of honor was answering questions. He was a fragile-looking man with sleek, dark hair and a glistening brow, and he was so brightly illumined by the long-stalked lamp at his shoulder that one could distinguish the specks of dandruff on the collar of his dinner jacket and admire the whiteness of his clasped hands, one of which I had found to be incredibly limp and moist. He was the type of fellow whose weak chin, hollow cheeks, and unhappy Adam's apple reveal, a couple of hours after shaving, when the humble talcum powder has worn off, a complex system of pink blotches overlaid with a stipple of bluish gray. He wore a crested ring, and for some odd reason I recalled a swarthy Russian girl in New York who was so troubled by the possibility of being mistaken for her notion of a Jewess that she used to wear a cross upon her throat, although she had as little religion as brains. The speaker's English was admirably fluent, but the hard *"djair"* in his pronunciation of "Germany" and the persistently recurring epithet "wonderful," the first syllable of which sounded like *"wan,"* proclaimed his Teutonic origin. He was, or had been, or was to become, a professor of German, or music, or both, somewhere in the Middle West, but I did not catch his name and so shall call him Dr. Shoe.

"*Naturally* he was mad!" exclaimed Dr. Shoe in answer to something one of the ladies had asked. "Look, only a madman could have messed up the war the way he did. And I certainly hope, as you do, that before long, if he should turn out to be alive, he will be safely interned in a sanatorium somewhere in a neutral country. He has earned it. It was madness to attack Russia instead of invading England. It was madness to think that the war with Japan would prevent Roosevelt from participating energetically in European affairs. The worst madman is the one who fails to consider the possibility of somebody else's being mad too."

"One cannot help feeling," said a fat little lady called, I think, Mrs. Mulberry, "that thousands of our boys who have been killed in the Pacific would still be alive if all those planes and tanks we gave England and Russia had been used to destroy Japan."

"Exactly," said Dr. Shoe. "And that was Adolf Hitler's mistake. Being mad, he failed to take into account the scheming of irresponsible politicians. Being mad, he believed that other governments would act in accordance with the principles of mercy and common sense."

"I always think of Prometheus," said Mrs. Hall. "Prometheus, who stole fire and was blinded by the angry gods."

An old lady in a bright blue dress, who sat knitting in a corner, asked Dr. Shoe to explain why the Germans had not risen against Hitler.

Dr. Shoe lowered his eyelids for a moment. "The answer is a terrible one," he said with an effort. "As you know, I am German myself, of pure Bavarian stock, though a loyal citizen of this country. And nevertheless, I am going to say something very terrible about my former countrymen. Germans"—the soft-lashed eyes were half-closed again—"Germans are dreamers."

By this time, of course, I had fully realized that Mrs. Hall's Mrs. Sharp was as totally distinct from my Mrs. Sharp as I was from my namesake. The nightmare into which I had been propelled would probably have struck him as a cozy evening with kindred souls, and Dr. Shoe might have seemed to him a most intelligent and brilliant *causeur*. Timidity, and perhaps morbid curiosity, kept me from leaving the room. Moreover, when I get excited, I stammer so badly that any attempt on my part to tell Dr. Shoe what I thought of him would have sounded like the explosions of a motorcycle which refuses to start on a frosty night in an intolerant suburban lane. I looked around, trying to convince myself that these were real people and not a Punch-and-Judy show.

None of the women were pretty; all had reached or overreached forty-five. All, one could be certain, belonged to book clubs, bridge clubs, babble clubs, and to the great, cold sorority of inevitable death. All looked cheerfully sterile. Possibly some of them had had children, but how they had produced them was now a forgotten mystery; many had found substitutes for creative power in various aesthetic pursuits, such as, for instance, the beautifying of committee rooms. As I glanced at the one sitting next to me, an intense-looking lady with a freckled neck, I knew that, while patchily listening to Dr. Shoe, she was, in all probability, worrying about a bit of decoration having to do with some social event or wartime entertainment the exact nature of which I could not determine. But I did know how badly she needed that additional touch. Something in the middle of the table, she was thinking. I need something that would make people gasp—perhaps a great big huge bowl of artificial fruit. Not the wax kind, of course. Something nicely marbleized.

It is most regrettable that I did not fix the ladies' names in my mind when I was introduced to them. Two willowy, interchangeable maiden ladies on hard chairs had names beginning with *W*, and, of the others, one was certainly called Miss Bissing. This I had heard distinctly, but could not later connect with any particular face or facelike object. There was only one other man besides Dr. Shoe and myself. He turned out to be a compatriot of mine, a Colonel Malikov or Melnikov; in Mrs. Hall's rendering it had sounded more like "Milwaukee." While some soft, pale drinks were being passed around, he leaned toward me with a leathery, creaking sound, as if he wore a harness under his shabby blue suit, and informed me in a hoarse Russian whisper that he had had the honor of knowing my esteemed uncle, whom I at once visualized as a ruddy but unpalatable apple on my namesake's family tree. Dr. Shoe, however, was becoming eloquent again, and the Colonel straightened up, revealing a broken yellow tusk in his retreating smile and promising me by means of discreet gestures that we would have a good talk later on.

"The tragedy of Germany," said Dr. Shoe as he carefully folded the paper napkin with which he had wiped his thin lips, "is also the tragedy of cultured America. I have spoken at numerous women's clubs and other educational centers, and everywhere I have noted how deeply this European war, now mercifully ended, was loathed by refined, sensitive souls. I have also noted how eagerly cultured Americans revert in memory to happier days, to their traveling experiences abroad, to some unforgettable month or still more unforgettable year they once spent in the country of art, music, philosophy, and good humor. They remember the dear friends they had there, and their season of education and well-being in the bosom of a German nobleman's family, the exquisite cleanness of everything, the songs at the close of a perfect day, the wonderful little towns, and all that world of kindliness and romance they found in Munich or Dresden."

"*My* Dresden is no more," said Mrs. Mulberry. "Our bombs have destroyed it and everything it stands for."

"British ones, in this particular case," said Dr. Shoe gently. "But, of course, war is war, although I admit one finds it difficult to imagine German bombers deliberately selecting for their target some sacred historical spot in Pennsylvania or Virginia. Yes, war is terrible. In fact, it becomes almost intolerably so when it is forced upon two nations that have so many things in common. It may strike you as a paradox, but really, when one thinks of the soldiers slaughtered in Europe, one says to oneself that they are at least spared the terrible misgivings which we civilians must suffer in silence."

"I think that is very true," remarked Mrs. Hall, slowly nodding her head.

"What about those stories?" asked an old lady who was knitting. "Those stories the papers keep printing about the German atrocities. I suppose all that is mostly propaganda?"

Dr. Shoe smiled a tired smile. "I was expecting that question," he said with a touch of sadness in his voice. "Unfortunately, propaganda, exaggeration, faked photographs, and so on are the tools of modern war. I should not be surprised if the Germans themselves had made up stories about the cruelty of the American troops to innocent civilians. Just think of all the nonsense which was invented about the so-called German atrocities in the First World War—those horrible legends about Belgian women being seduced, and so on. Well, immediately after the war, in the summer of 1920, if I am not mistaken, a special committee of German democrats thoroughly investigated the whole matter, and we all know how pedantically thorough and precise German experts can be. Well, they did not find one scintilla of evidence to prove that Germans had not acted like soldiers and gentlemen."

One of the Misses W. ironically remarked that foreign correspondents must make a living. Her remark was witty. Everybody appreciated her ironical and witty remark.

"On the other hand," continued Dr. Shoe when the ripples had subsided, "let us forget propaganda for a moment and turn to dull facts. Allow me to draw you a little picture from the past, a rather sad little picture, but perhaps a necessary one. I will ask you to imagine German boys proudly entering some Polish or Russian town they had conquered. They sang as they marched. They did not know that their Führer was mad; they innocently believed that they were bringing hope and happiness and wonderful order to the fallen town. They could not know that owing to subsequent mistakes and delusions on the part of Adolf Hitler, their conquest would eventually lead to the enemy's making a flaming battlefield of the very cities to which they, those German boys, thought they were bringing everlasting peace. As they bravely marched through the streets in all their finery, with their wonderful war machines and their banners, they smiled at everybody and everything because they were pathetically good-natured and well-meaning. They innocently expected the same friendly attitude on the part of the population. Then, gradually, they realized that the streets through which they so boyishly, so confidently, marched were lined with silent and motionless crowds of Jews, who glared at them with hatred and who insulted each passing soldier, not by words—they were too clever for that—but by black looks and ill-concealed sneers."

"I know that kind of look," said Mrs. Hall grimly.

"But *they* did not," said Dr. Shoe in plaintive tones. "That is the point. They were puzzled. They did not understand, and they were hurt. So what did they do? At first they tried to fight that hatred with patient explanations and little tokens of kindness. But the wall of hatred surrounding them only got thicker. Finally they were forced to imprison the leaders of the vicious and arrogant coalition. What else could they do?"

"I happen to know an old Russian Jew," said Mrs. Mulberry. "Oh, just a business acquaintance of Mr. Mulberry's. Well, he confessed to me once that he would gladly strangle with his own hands the very first German soldier he met. I was so shocked that I just stood there and did not know what to answer."

"I would have," said a stout woman who sat with her knees wide apart. "As a matter of fact, one hears much too much about punishing the Germans. They, too, are human beings. And any sensitive person will agree with what you say about their not being responsible for those so-called atrocities, most of which have probably been invented by the Jews. I get mad when I hear people still jabbering about furnaces and torture houses which, if they existed at all, were operated by only a few men as insane as Hitler."

"Well, I am afraid one must be understanding," said Dr. Shoe, with his impossible smile, "and take into account the workings of the vivid Semitic imagination which controls the American press. And one must remember, too, that there were many purely sanitary measures which the orderly German troops had to adopt in dealing with the corpses of the elderly who had died in camp, and, in some cases, in disposing of the victims of typhus epidemics. I am quite free from any racial prejudices myself, and I can't see how these age-old racial problems have anything to do with the attitude to be adopted toward Germany now that she has surrendered. Especially when I remember the way the British treat natives in their colonies."

"Or how the Jewish Bolsheviks used to treat the Russian people—*ai-ai-ai!*" remarked Colonel Melnikov.

"Which is no more the case, is it?" asked Mrs. Hall.

"No, no," said the Colonel. "The great Russian people has waked up and my country is again a great country. We had three great leaders. We had Ivan, whom his enemies called Terrible, then we had Peter the Great, and now we have Joseph Stalin. I am a White Russian and have served in the Imperial Guards, but also I am a Russian patriot and a Russian Christian. Today, in every word that comes out of Russia, I feel the power, I feel the splendor of old Mother Russia. She is again a country of soldiers, religion, and true Slavs. Also, I know that when the Red Army entered German towns, not a single hair fell from German shoulders."

"Head," said Mrs. Hall.

"Yes," said the Colonel. "Not a single head from their shoulders."

"We all admire your countrymen," said Mrs. Mulberry. "But what about Communism spreading to Germany?"

"If I may be permitted to offer a suggestion," said Dr. Shoe, "I would like to point out that if we are not careful, there will be no Germany. The main problem which this country will have to face is to prevent the victors from enslaving the German nation and sending the young and hale and the lame and old—intellectuals and civilians—to work like convicts in the vast area of the East. This is against all the principles of democracy and war. If you tell me that the Germans did the same thing to the nations they conquered, I will remind you of three things: first, that the German State was not a democracy and couldn't be expected to act like one; secondly, that most, if not all, of the so-called slaves came of their own free will; and in the third place— and this is the most important point—that they were well fed, well clothed, and lived in civilized surroundings which, in spite of all our natural enthusiasm for the immense population and geography of Russia, Germans are not likely to find in the country of the Soviets.

"Neither must we forget," continued Dr. Shoe, with a dramatic rise in his voice, "that Nazism was really not a German but an alien organization oppressing the German people. Adolf Hitler was an Austrian, Ley a Jew, Rosenberg half-French, half-Tartar. The German nation has suffered under this non-German yoke just as much as other European countries have suffered from the effects of the war waged on their soil. To civilians, who not only have been crippled and killed but whose treasured possessions and wonderful homes have been annihilated by bombs, it matters little whether those bombs were dropped by a German or an Allied plane. Germans, Austrians, Italians, Rumanians, Greeks, and all the other peoples of Europe are now members of one tragic brotherhood, all are equal in misery and hope, all should be treated alike, and let us leave the task of finding and judging the guilty to future historians, to unbiased old scholars in the immortal centers of European culture, in the serene universities of Heidelberg, Bonn, Jena, Leipzig, München. Let the phoenix of Europe spread its eagle wings again, and God bless America."

There was a reverent pause while Dr. Shoe tremulously lighted a cigarette, and then Mrs. Hall, pressing the palms of her hands together in a charming, girlish gesture, begged him to round out the meeting with some lovely music. He sighed, got up, trod upon my foot in passing, apologetically touched my knee with the tips of his fingers, and, having sat down before the piano, bowed his head and remained motionless for several audibly silent seconds. Then, slowly and very gently, he laid his cigarette on an ashtray, removed the ashtray from the piano into Mrs. Hall's helpful hands, and bent his head again. At last he said, with a little catch in his voice, "First of all, I will play 'The Star-Spangled Banner.' "

Feeling that this was more than I could stand—in fact, having reached a point where I was beginning to feel physically sick—I got up and hurriedly left the room. As I was approaching the closet where I had seen the maid store my things, Mrs. Hall overtook me, together with a billow of distant music.

"Must you leave?" she said. "Must you really leave?"

I found my overcoat, dropped the hanger, and stamped into my rubbers.

"You are either murderers or fools," I said, "or both, and that man is a filthy German agent."

As I have already mentioned, I am afflicted with a bad stammer at crucial moments and therefore the sentence did not come out as smooth as it is on paper. But it worked. Before she could gather herself to answer, I had slammed the door behind me and was carrying my overcoat downstairs as one carries a child out of a house on fire. I was in the street when I noticed that the hat I was about to put on did not belong to me.

It was a well-worn fedora, of a deeper shade of gray than my own and with a narrower brim. The head it was meant for was smaller than mine. The inside of the hat carried the label "Werner Bros. Chicago" and smelled of another man's hairbrush and hair lotion. It could not belong to Colonel Melnikov, who was as bald as a bowling ball, and I assumed that Mrs. Hall's husband was either dead or kept his hats in another place. It was a disgusting object to carry about, but the night was rainy and cold, and I used the thing as a kind of rudimentary umbrella. As soon as I got home, I started writing a letter to the Federal Bureau of Investigation, but did not get very far. My inability to catch and retain names seriously impaired the quality of the information I was trying to impart, and since I had to explain my presence at the meeting, a lot of diffuse and vaguely suspicious matter concerning my own namesake had to be dragged in. Worst of all, the whole affair assumed a dreamlike, grotesque aspect when related in detail, whereas all I really had to say was that a person from some unknown address in the Middle West, a person whose name I did not even know, had been talking sympathetically about the German people to a group of silly old women in a private house. Indeed, judging by the expression of that same sympathy continuously cropping up in the writings of certain well-known columnists, the whole thing might be perfectly legal, for all I knew.

Early the next morning I opened the door in answer to a ring, and there was Dr. Shoe, bareheaded, raincoated, silently offering me my hat, with a cautious half-smile on his blue-and-pink face. I took the hat and mumbled some thanks. This he mistook for an invitation to come in. I could not remember where I had put his fedora, and the feverish search I had to conduct, more or less in his presence, soon became ludicrous.

"Look here," I said. "I shall mail, I shall send, I shall forward you that hat when I find it, or a check, if I don't."

"But I'm leaving this afternoon," he said gently, "and moreover, I would like to have a little explanation of the strange remark you addressed to my very dear friend Mrs. Hall."

He waited patiently while I tried to tell him as neatly as I could that the police, the authorities, would explain that to her.

"You do not understand," he said at length. "Mrs. Hall is a very well-known society lady and has numerous connections in official circles. Thank God we live in a great country, where everybody can speak his mind without being insulted for expressing a private opinion."

I told him to go away.

When my final splutter had petered out, he said, "I go away, but please remember, in this country—" and he shook his bent finger at me sidewise, German fashion, in facetious reproof.

Before I could decide where to hit him, he had glided out. I was trembling all over. My inefficiency, which at times has amused me and even pleased me in a subtle way, now appeared atrocious and base. All of a sudden I caught sight of Dr. Shoe's hat on a heap of old magazines under the little telephone table in my hall. I hurried to a front window, opened it, and, as Dr. Shoe emerged four stories below, tossed the hat in his direction. It described a parabola and made a pancake landing in the middle of the street. There it turned a somersault, missed a puddle by a matter of inches, and lay gaping, wrong side up. Dr. Shoe, without looking up, waved his hand in acknowledgment, retrieved the hat, satisfied himself that it was not too muddy, put it on, and walked away, jauntily wiggling his hips. I have often wondered why is it that a thin German always manages to look so plump behind when wearing a raincoat.

All that remains to be told is that a week later I received a letter the peculiar Russian of which can hardly be appreciated in translation.

"*Esteemed Sir,*" it read. "*You have been pursuing me all my life. Good friends of mine, after reading your books, have turned away from me thinking that I was the author of those depraved, decadent writings. In 1941, and again in 1943, I was arrested in France by the Germans for things I never had said or thought. Now in America, not content with having caused me all sorts of troubles in other countries, you have the arrogance to impersonate me and to appear in a drunken condition at the house of a highly respected person. This I will not tolerate. I could have you jailed and branded as an impostor, but I suppose you would not like that, and so I suggest that by way of indemnity . . .*"

The sum he demanded was really a most modest one.

SIGNS AND SYMBOLS

1

————

F OR the fourth time in as many years they were confronted with the problem of what birthday present to bring a young man who was incurably deranged in his mind. He had no desires. Man-made objects were to him either hives of evil, vibrant with a malignant activity that he alone could perceive, or gross comforts for which no use could be found in his abstract world. After eliminating a number of articles that might offend him or frighten him (anything in the gadget line for instance was taboo), his parents chose a dainty and innocent trifle: a basket with ten different fruit jellies in ten little jars.

At the time of his birth they had been married already for a long time; a score of years had elapsed, and now they were quite old. Her drab gray hair was done anyhow. She wore cheap black dresses. Unlike other women of her age (such as Mrs. Sol, their next-door neighbor, whose face was all pink and mauve with paint and whose hat was a cluster of brookside flowers), she presented a naked white countenance to the fault-finding light of spring days. Her husband, who in the old country had been a fairly successful businessman, was now wholly dependent on his brother Isaac, a real American of almost forty years standing. They seldom saw him and had nicknamed him "the Prince."

That Friday everything went wrong. The underground train lost its life current between two stations, and for a quarter of an hour one could hear nothing but the dutiful beating of one's heart and the rustling of newspapers. The bus they had to take next kept them waiting for ages; and when it did come, it was crammed with garrulous high school children. It was raining hard as they walked up the brown path leading to the sanatorium. There they waited again; and instead of their boy shuffling into the room as he usually did (his poor face botched with acne, ill-shaven, sullen, and confused), a nurse they knew, and did not care for, appeared at last and brightly explained that he had again attempted to take his life. He was all right, she said, but a visit might disturb him. The place was so miserably understaffed, and things got mislaid or mixed up so easily, that they decided not to leave their present in the office but to bring it to him next time they came.

She waited for her husband to open his umbrella and then took his arm. He kept clearing his throat in a special resonant way he had when he was upset. They reached the bus-stop shelter on the other side of the street and he closed his umbrella. A few feet away, under a swaying and dripping tree, a tiny half-dead unfledged bird was helplessly twitching in a puddle.

During the long ride to the subway station, she and her husband did not exchange a word; and every time she glanced at his old hands (swollen veins, brown-spotted skin), clasped and twitching upon the handle of his umbrella, she felt the mounting pressure of tears. As she looked around trying to hook her mind onto something, it gave her a kind of soft shock, a mixture of compassion and wonder, to notice that one of the passengers, a girl with dark hair and grubby red toenails, was weeping on the shoulder of an older woman. Whom did that woman resemble? She resembled Rebecca Borisovna, whose daughter had married one of the Soloveichiks—in Minsk, years ago.

The last time he had tried to do it, his method had been, in the doctor's words, a masterpiece of inventiveness; he would have succeeded, had not an envious fellow patient thought he was learning to fly—and stopped him. What he really wanted to do was to tear a hole in his world and escape.

The system of his delusions had been the subject of an elaborate paper in a scientific monthly, but long before that she and her husband had puzzled it out for themselves. "Referential mania," Herman Brink had called it. In these very rare cases the patient imagines that everything happening around him is a veiled reference to his personality and existence. He excludes real people from the conspiracy—because he considers himself to be so much more intelligent than other men. Phenomenal nature shadows him wherever he goes. Clouds in the staring sky transmit to one another, by means of slow signs, incredibly detailed information regarding him. His inmost thoughts are discussed at nightfall, in manual alphabet, by darkly gesticulating trees. Pebbles or stains or sun flecks form patterns representing in some awful way messages which he must intercept. Everything is a cipher and of everything he is the theme. Some of the spies are detached observers, such as glass surfaces and still pools; others, such as coats in store windows, are prejudiced witnesses, lynchers at heart; others again (running water, storms) are hysterical to the point of insanity, have a distorted opinion

of him, and grotesquely misinterpret his actions. He must be always on
his guard and devote every minute and module of life to the decoding
of the undulation of things. The very air he exhales is indexed and filed
away. If only the interest he provokes were limited to his immediate
surroundings—but alas it is not! With distance the torrents of wild
scandal increase in volume and volubility. The silhouettes of his blood
corpuscles, magnified a million times, flit over vast plains; and still farther, great mountains of unbearable solidity and height sum up in
terms of granite and groaning firs the ultimate truth of his being.

2

When they emerged from the thunder and foul air of the subway, the
last dregs of the day were mixed with the streetlights. She wanted to
buy some fish for supper, so she handed him the basket of jelly jars,
telling him to go home. He walked up to the third landing and then
remembered he had given her his keys earlier in the day.

In silence he sat down on the steps and in silence rose when some
ten minutes later she came, heavily trudging upstairs, wanly smiling,
shaking her head in deprecation of her silliness. They entered their
two-room flat and he at once went to the mirror. Straining the corners
of his mouth apart by means of his thumbs, with a horrible masklike
grimace, he removed his new hopelessly uncomfortable dental plate
and severed the long tusks of saliva connecting him to it. He read his
Russian-language newspaper while she laid the table. Still reading, he
ate the pale victuals that needed no teeth. She knew his moods and
was also silent.

When he had gone to bed, she remained in the living room with
her pack of soiled cards and her old albums. Across the narrow yard
where the rain tinkled in the dark against some battered ash cans, windows were blandly alight and in one of them a black-trousered man
with his bare elbows raised could be seen lying supine on an untidy
bed. She pulled the blind down and examined the photographs. As a
baby he looked more surprised than most babies. From a fold in the album, a German maid they had had in Leipzig and her fat-faced fiancé
fell out. Minsk, the Revolution, Leipzig, Berlin, Leipzig, a slanting
housefront badly out of focus. Four years old, in a park: moodily,
shyly, with puckered forehead, looking away from an eager squirrel as

he would from any other stranger. Aunt Rosa, a fussy, angular, wild-eyed old lady, who had lived in a tremulous world of bad news, bankruptcies, train accidents, cancerous growths—until the Germans put her to death, together with all the people she had worried about. Age six—that was when he drew wonderful birds with human hands and feet, and suffered from insomnia like a grown-up man. His cousin, now a famous chess player. He again, aged about eight, already difficult to understand, afraid of the wallpaper in the passage, afraid of a certain picture in a book which merely showed an idyllic landscape with rocks on a hillside and an old cart wheel hanging from the branch of a leafless tree. Aged ten: the year they left Europe. The shame, the pity, the humiliating difficulties, the ugly, vicious, backward children he was with in that special school. And then came a time in his life, coinciding with a long convalescence after pneumonia, when those little phobias of his which his parents had stubbornly regarded as the eccentricities of a prodigiously gifted child hardened as it were into a dense tangle of logically interacting illusions, making him totally inaccessible to normal minds.

This, and much more, she accepted—for after all living did mean accepting the loss of one joy after another, not even joys in her case—mere possibilities of improvement. She thought of the endless waves of pain that for some reason or other she and her husband had to endure; of the invisible giants hurting her boy in some unimaginable fashion; of the incalculable amount of tenderness contained in the world; of the fate of this tenderness, which is either crushed, or wasted, or transformed into madness; of neglected children humming to themselves in unswept corners; of beautiful weeds that cannot hide from the farmer and helplessly have to watch the shadow of his simian stoop leave mangled flowers in its wake, as the monstrous darkness approaches.

3

———————

It was past midnight when from the living room she heard her husband moan; and presently he staggered in, wearing over his nightgown the old overcoat with astrakhan collar which he much preferred to the nice blue bathrobe he had.

"I can't sleep," he cried.

"Why," she asked, "why can't you sleep? You were so tired."

"I can't sleep because I am dying," he said and lay down on the couch.

"Is it your stomach? Do you want me to call Dr. Solov?"

"No doctors, no doctors," he moaned. "To the devil with doctors! We must get him out of there quick. Otherwise we'll be responsible. Responsible!" he repeated and hurled himself into a sitting position, both feet on the floor, thumping his forehead with his clenched fist.

"All right," she said quietly, "we shall bring him home tomorrow morning."

"I would like some tea," said her husband, and retired to the bathroom.

Bending with difficulty, she retrieved some playing cards and a photograph or two that had slipped from the couch to the floor: knave of hearts, nine of spades, ace of spades, Elsa and her bestial beau.

He returned in high spirits, saying in a loud voice: "I have it all figured out. We will give him the bedroom. Each of us will spend part of the night near him and the other part on this couch. By turns. We will have the doctor see him at least twice a week. It does not matter what the Prince says. He won't have to say much anyway because it will come out cheaper."

The telephone rang. It was an unusual hour for their telephone to ring. His left slipper had come off and he groped for it with his heel and toe as he stood in the middle of the room, and childishly, toothlessly, gaped at his wife. Having more English than he did, it was she who attended to calls.

"Can I speak to Charlie," said a girl's dull little voice.

"What number you want? No. That is not the right number."

The receiver was gently cradled. Her hand went to her old tired heart.

"It frightened me," she said.

He smiled a quick smile and immediately resumed his excited monologue. They would fetch him as soon as it was day. Knives would have to be kept in a locked drawer. Even at his worst he presented no danger to other people.

The telephone rang a second time. The same toneless anxious young voice asked for Charlie.

"You have the incorrect number. I will tell you what you are doing: you are turning the letter O instead of the zero."

They sat down to their unexpected festive midnight tea. The birthday present stood on the table. He sipped noisily; his face was flushed;

every now and then he imparted a circular motion to his raised glass so as to make the sugar dissolve more thoroughly. The vein on the side of his bald head where there was a large birthmark stood out conspicuously and, although he had shaved that morning, a silvery bristle showed on his chin. While she poured him another glass of tea, he put on his spectacles and reexamined with pleasure the luminous yellow, green, red little jars. His clumsy moist lips spelled out their eloquent labels: apricot, grape, beech plum, quince. He had got to crab apple, when the telephone rang again.

FIRST LOVE

I

IN THE early years of this century, a travel agency on Nevski Avenue displayed a three-foot-long model of an oak-brown international sleeping car. In delicate verisimilitude it completely outranked the painted tin of my clockwork trains. Unfortunately it was not for sale. One could make out the blue upholstery inside, the embossed leather lining of the compartment walls, their polished panels, inset mirrors, tulip-shaped reading lamps, and other maddening details. Spacious windows alternated with narrower ones, single or geminate, and some of these were of frosted glass. In a few of the compartments, the beds had been made.

The then great and glamorous Nord Express (it was never the same after World War I), consisting solely of such international cars and running but twice a week, connected St. Petersburg with Paris. I would have said: directly with Paris, had passengers not been obliged to change from one train to a superficially similar one at the Russo-German frontier (Verzhbolovo-Eydtkuhnen), where the ample and lazy Russian sixty-and-a-half-inch gauge was replaced by the fifty-six-and-a-half-inch standard of Europe and coal succeeded birch logs.

In the far end of my mind I can unravel, I think, at least five such journeys to Paris, with the Riviera or Biarritz as their ultimate destination. In 1909, the year I now single out, my two small sisters had been left at home with nurses and aunts. Wearing gloves and a traveling cap, my father sat reading a book in the compartment he shared with our tutor. My brother and I were separated from them by a washroom. My mother and her maid occupied a compartment adjacent to ours. The odd one of our party, my father's valet, Osip (whom, a decade later, the pedantic Bolsheviks were to shoot, because he appropriated our bicycles instead of turning them over to the nation), had a stranger for companion.

In April of that year, Peary had reached the North Pole. In May, Chaliapin had sung in Paris. In June, bothered by rumors of new and better zeppelins, the United States War Department had told reporters of plans for an aerial navy. In July, Blériot had flown from Calais to Dover (with a little additional loop when he lost his bearings). It was late August now. The firs and marshes of northwestern Russia sped by, and on the following day gave way to German pine barrens and heather.

At a collapsible table, my mother and I played a card game called *durachki*. Although it was still broad daylight, our cards, a glass, and on a different plane the locks of a suitcase were reflected in the window. Through forest and field, and in sudden ravines, and among scuttling cottages, those discarnate gamblers kept steadily playing on for steadily sparkling stakes.

"Ne budet-li, ti ved' ustal?" ("Haven't you had enough, aren't you tired?") my mother would ask, and then would be lost in thought as she slowly shuffled the cards. The door of the compartment was open and I could see the corridor window, where the wires—six thin black wires—were doing their best to slant up, to ascend skyward, despite the lightning blows dealt them by one telegraph pole after another; but just as all six, in a triumphant swoop of pathetic elation, were about to reach the top of the window, a particularly vicious blow would bring them down, as low as they had ever been, and they would have to start all over again.

When, on such journeys as these, the train changed its pace to a dignified amble and all but grazed housefronts and shop signs, as we passed through some big German town, I used to feel a twofold excitement, which terminal stations could not provide. I saw a city with its toylike trams, linden trees, and brick walls enter the compartment, hobnob with the mirrors, and fill to the brim the windows on the corridor side. This informal contact between train and city was one part of the thrill. The other was putting myself in the place of some passerby who, I imagined, was moved as I would be moved myself to see the long, romantic, auburn cars, with their intervestibular connecting curtains as black as bat wings and their metal lettering copper-bright in the low sun, unhurriedly negotiate an iron bridge across an everyday thoroughfare and then turn, with all windows suddenly ablaze, around a last block of houses.

There were drawbacks to those optical amalgamations. The wide-windowed dining car, a vista of chaste bottles of mineral water, miter-folded napkins, and dummy chocolate bars (whose wrappers—Cailler, Kohler, and so forth—enclosed nothing but wood) would be perceived at first as a cool haven beyond a consecution of reeling blue corridors; but as the meal progressed toward its fatal last course, one would keep catching the car in the act of being recklessly sheathed, lurching waiters and all, in the landscape, while the landscape itself went through a complex system of motion, the daytime moon stubbornly keeping abreast of one's plate, the distant meadows opening fanwise, the near trees sweeping up on invisible swings toward the track, a parallel rail line all at once committing suicide by anastomosis, a bank of nictitating grass rising, rising, rising, until the little witness of mixed velocities was made to disgorge his portion of *omelette aux confitures de fraises*.

It was at night, however, that the *Compagnie Internationale des Wagons-Lits et des Grands Express Européens* lived up to the magic of its name. From my bed under my brother's bunk (Was he asleep? Was he there at all?), in the semidarkness of our compartment, I watched things, and parts of things, and shadows, and sections of shadows cautiously moving about and getting nowhere. The woodwork gently creaked and crackled. Near the door that led to the toilet, a dim garment on a peg and, higher up, the tassel of the blue, bivalved night-light swung rhythmically. It was hard to correlate those halting approaches, that hooded stealth, with the headlong rush of the outside night, which I knew *was* rushing by, spark-streaked, illegible.

I would put myself to sleep by the simple act of identifying myself with the engine driver. A sense of drowsy well-being invaded my veins as soon as I had everything nicely arranged—the carefree passengers in their rooms enjoying the ride I was giving them, smoking, exchanging knowing smiles, nodding, dozing; the waiters and cooks and train guards (whom I had to place somewhere) carousing in the diner; and myself, goggled and begrimed, peering out of the engine cab at the tapering track, at the ruby or emerald point in the black distance. And then, in my sleep, I would see something totally different—a glass marble rolling under a grand piano or a toy engine lying on its side with its wheels still working gamely.

A change in the speed of the train sometimes interrupted the current of my sleep. Slow lights were stalking by; each, in passing, investigated the same chink, and then a luminous compass measured the shadows. Presently, the train stopped with a long-drawn Westinghousian sigh. Something (my brother's spectacles, as it proved next day) fell from above. It was marvelously exciting to move to the foot of one's bed, with part of the bedclothes following, in order to undo cautiously the catch of the window shade, which could be made to slide only halfway up, impeded as it was by the edge of the upper berth.

Like moons around Jupiter, pale moths revolved about a lone lamp. A dismembered newspaper stirred on a bench. Somewhere on the train one could hear muffled voices, somebody's comfortable cough. There was nothing particularly interesting in the portion of station platform before me, and still I could not tear myself away from it until it departed of its own accord.

Next morning, wet fields with misshapen willows along the radius of a ditch or a row of poplars afar, traversed by a horizontal band of milky-white mist, told one that the train was spinning through Belgium. It reached Paris at four p.m.; and even if the stay was only an overnight one, I had always time to purchase something—say, a little brass *Tour Eiffel*, rather roughly coated with silver paint—before we boarded at noon on the following day the Sud Express, which, on its way to Madrid, dropped us around ten p.m. at the La Négresse station of Biarritz, a few miles from the Spanish frontier.

2

Biarritz still retained its quiddity in those days. Dusty blackberry bushes and weedy *terrains à vendre* bordered the road that led to our villa. The Carlton was still being built. Some thirty-six years had to elapse before Brigadier General Samuel McCroskey would occupy the royal suite of the Hotel du Palais, which stands on the site of a former palace, where, in the sixties, that incredibly agile medium, Daniel Home, is said to have been caught stroking with his bare foot (in imitation of a ghost hand) the kind, trustful face of Empress Eugénie. On the promenade near the Casino, an elderly flower girl, with carbon eyebrows and a painted smile, nimbly slipped the plump torus of a carnation into the buttonhole of an intercepted stroller whose left jowl accentuated its royal fold as he glanced down sideways at the coy insertion of the flower.

Along the back line of the *plage*, various seaside chairs and stools supported the parents of straw-hatted children who were playing in front on the sand. I could be seen on my knees trying to set a found comb aflame by means of a magnifying glass. Men sported white trousers that to the eye of today would look as if they had comically shrunk in the washing; ladies wore, that particular season, light coats with silk-faced lapels, hats with big crowns and wide brims, dense embroidered white veils, frill-fronted blouses, frills at their wrists, frills on their parasols. The breeze salted one's lips. At a tremendous pace a stray golden-orange butterfly came dashing across the palpitating *plage*.

Additional movement and sound were provided by vendors hawking *cacahuètes*, sugared violets, pistachio ice cream of a heavenly green, cachou pellets, and huge convex pieces of dry, gritty, waferlike stuff that came from a red barrel. With a distinctness that no later superpositions have dimmed, I see that waffleman stomp along through deep mealy sand, with the heavy cask on his bent back. When called, he would sling it off his shoulder by a twist of its strap, bang it down on the sand in a Tower of Pisa position, wipe his face with his sleeve, and proceed to manipulate a kind of arrow-and-dial arrangement with numbers on the lid of the cask. The arrow rasped and whirred around. Luck was supposed to fix the size of a sou's worth of wafer. The bigger the piece, the more I was sorry for him.

The process of bathing took place on another part of the beach. Professional bathers, burly Basques in black bathing suits, were there to help ladies and children enjoy the terrors of the surf. Such a *baigneur* would place you with your back to the incoming wave and hold you by the hand as the rising, rotating mass of foamy, green water violently descended upon you from behind, knocking you off your feet with one mighty wallop. After a dozen of these tumbles, the *baigneur*, glistening like a seal, would lead his panting, shivering, moistly snuffling charge landward, to the flat foreshore, where an unforgettable old woman with gray hairs on her chin promptly chose a bathing robe from several hanging on a clothesline. In the security of a little cabin, one would be helped by yet another attendant to peel off one's soggy, sand-heavy bathing suit. It would plop onto the boards, and, still shivering, one would step out of it and trample on its bluish, diffuse stripes. The cabin smelled of pine. The attendant, a hunchback with beaming wrinkles, brought a basin of steaming-hot water, in which one immersed one's feet. From him I learned, and have preserved ever since in a glass cell of my memory, that "butterfly" in the Basque language is *misericoletea*—or at least it sounded so (among the seven words I have found in dictionaries the closest approach is *micheletea*).

3

On the browner and wetter part of the *plage*, that part which at low tide yielded the best mud for castles, I found myself digging, one day, side by side with a little French girl called Colette.

She would be ten in November, I had been ten in April. Attention was drawn to a jagged bit of violet mussel shell upon which she had stepped with the bare sole of her narrow long-toed foot. No, I was not English. Her greenish eyes seemed flecked with the overflow of the freckles that covered her sharp-featured face. She wore what might now be termed a playsuit, consisting of a blue jersey with rolled-up sleeves and blue knitted shorts. I had taken her at first for a boy and then had been puzzled by the bracelet on her thin wrist and the corkscrew brown curls dangling from under her sailor cap.

She spoke in birdlike bursts of rapid twitter, mixing governess English and Parisian French. Two years before, on the same *plage*, I had been much attached to the lovely, suntanned little daughter of a Serbian physician; but when I met Colette, I knew at once that this was the real thing. Colette seemed to me so much stranger than all my other chance playmates at Biarritz! I somehow acquired the feeling that she was less happy than I, less loved. A bruise on her delicate, downy forearm gave rise to awful conjectures. "He pinches as bad as my mummy," she said, speaking of a crab. I evolved various schemes to save her from her parents, who were *"des bourgeois de Paris"* as I heard somebody tell my mother with a slight shrug. I interpreted the disdain in my own fashion, as I knew that those people had come all the way from Paris in their blue-and-yellow limousine (a fashionable adventure in those days) but had drably sent Colette with her dog and governess by an ordinary coach train. The dog was a female fox terrier with bells on her collar and a most waggly behind. From sheer exuberance, she would lap up salt water out of Colette's toy pail. I remember the sail, the sunset, and the lighthouse pictured on that pail, but I cannot recall the dog's name, and this bothers me.

During the two months of our stay at Biarritz, my passion for Colette all but surpassed my passion for butterflies. Since my parents were not keen to meet hers, I saw her only on the beach; but I thought of her constantly. If I noticed she had been crying, I felt a surge of helpless anguish that brought tears to my own eyes. I could not destroy the mosquitoes that had left their bites on her frail neck, but I could, and did, have a successful fistfight with a red-haired boy who had been rude to her. She used to give me warm handfuls of hard candy. One day, as we were bending together over a starfish, and Colette's ringlets were tickling my ear, she suddenly turned toward me and kissed me on the cheek. So great was my emotion that all I could think of saying was, "You little monkey."

I had a gold coin that I assumed would pay for our elopement. Where did I want to take her? Spain? America? The mountains above Pau? *"Là-bas, là-bas, dans la montagne,"* as I had heard Carmen sing at the opera. One strange night, I lay awake, listening to the recurrent thud of the ocean and planning our flight. The ocean seemed to rise and grope in the darkness and then heavily fall on its face.

Of our actual getaway, I have little to report. My memory retains a glimpse of her obediently putting on rope-soled canvas shoes, on the lee side of a flapping tent, while I stuffed a folding butterfly net into a brown paper bag. The next glimpse is of our evading pursuit by entering a pitch-dark cinema near the Casino (which, of course, was absolutely out of bounds). There we sat, holding hands across the dog, which now and then gently jingled in Colette's lap, and were shown a jerky, drizzly, but highly exciting bullfight at San Sebastián. My final glimpse is of myself being led along the promenade by my tutor. His long legs move with a kind of ominous briskness and I can see the muscles of his grimly set jaw working under the tight skin. My bespectacled brother, aged nine, whom he happens to hold with his other hand, keeps trotting out forward to peer at me with awed curiosity, like a little owl.

Among the trivial souvenirs acquired at Biarritz before leaving, my favorite was not the small bull of black stone and not the sonorous seashell but something which now seems almost symbolic—a meerschaum penholder with a tiny peephole of crystal in its ornamental part. One held it quite close to one's eye, screwing up the other, and when one had got rid of the shimmer of one's own lashes, a miraculous photographic view of the bay and of the line of cliffs ending in a lighthouse could be seen inside.

And now a delightful thing happens. The process of re-creating that penholder and the microcosm in its eyelet stimulates my memory to a last effort. I try again to recall the name of Colette's dog—and, sure enough, along those remote beaches, over the glossy evening sands of the past, where each footprint slowly fills up with sunset water, here it comes, here it comes, echoing and vibrating: Floss, Floss, Floss!

Colette was back in Paris by the time we stopped there for a day before continuing our homeward journey; and there, in a fawn park under a cold blue sky, I saw her (by arrangement between our mentors, I believe) for the last time. She carried a hoop and a short stick to drive it with, and everything about her was extremely proper and stylish in an autumnal, Parisian, *tenue-de-ville-pour-fillettes* way. She took from her governess and slipped into my brother's hand a farewell present, a box of sugar-coated almonds, meant, I knew, solely for me; and instantly she was off, tap-tapping her glinting hoop through light and shade, around and around a fountain choked with dead leaves near which I stood. The leaves mingle in my memory with the leather of her shoes and gloves, and there was, I remember, some detail in her attire (perhaps a ribbon on her Scottish cap, or the pattern of her stockings) that reminded me then of the rainbow spiral in a glass marble. I still seem to be holding that wisp of iridescence, not knowing exactly where to fit it, while she runs with her hoop ever faster around me and finally dissolves among the slender shadows cast on the graveled path by the interlaced arches of its low looped fence.

SCENES FROM THE LIFE OF
A DOUBLE MONSTER

S OME years ago Dr. Fricke asked Lloyd and me a question that
I shall try to answer now. With a dreamy smile of scientific de-
lectation he stroked the fleshy cartilaginous band uniting us—
omphalopagus diaphragmo-xiphodidymus, as Pancoast has dubbed a
similar case—and wondered if we could recall the very first time either
of us, or both, realized the peculiarity of our condition and destiny. All
Lloyd could remember was the way our Grandfather Ibrahim (or
Ahim, or Ahem—irksome lumps of dead sounds to the ear of today!)
would touch what the doctor was touching and call it a bridge of gold.
I said nothing.

Our childhood was spent atop a fertile hill above the Black Sea on
our grandfather's farm near Karaz. His youngest daughter, rose of the
East, gray Ahem's pearl (if so, the old scoundrel might have taken better care of her) had been raped in a roadside orchard by our anonymous sire and had died soon after giving birth to us—of sheer horror
and grief, I imagine. One set of rumors mentioned a Hungarian peddler; another favored a German collector of birds or some member of
his expedition—his taxidermist, most likely. Dusky, heavily necklaced
aunts, whose voluminous clothes smelled of rose oil and mutton, attended with ghoulish zest to the wants of our monstrous infancy.

Soon neighboring hamlets learned the astounding news and began
delegating to our farm various inquisitive strangers. On feast days you
could see them laboring up the slopes of our hill, like pilgrims in
bright-colored pictures. There was a shepherd seven feet tall, and a
small bald man with glasses, and soldiers, and the lengthening shadows
of cypresses. Children came too, at all times, and were shooed away by
our jealous nurses; but almost daily some black-eyed, cropped-haired
youngster in dark-patched, faded-blue pants would manage to worm
his way through the dogwood, the honeysuckle, the twisted Judas

trees, into the cobbled court with its old rheumy fountain where little Lloyd and Floyd (we had other names then, full of corvine aspirates—but no matter) sat quietly munching dried apricots under a white-washed wall. Then, suddenly, the aitch would see an eye, the Roman two a one, the scissors a knife.

There can be, of course, no comparison between this impact of knowledge, disturbing as it may have been, and the emotional shock my mother received (by the way, what clean bliss there is in this deliberate use of the possessive singular!). She must have been aware that she was being delivered of twins; but when she learned, as no doubt she did, that the twins were conjoined ones—what did she experience then? With the kind of unrestrained, ignorant, passionately communicative folks that surrounded us, the highly vocal household just beyond the limits of her tumbled bed must, surely, have told her at once that something had gone dreadfully wrong; and one can be certain that her sisters, in the frenzy of their fright and compassion, showed her the double baby. I am not saying that a mother cannot love such a double thing—and forget in this love the dark dews of its unhallowed origin; I only think that the mixture of revulsion, pity, and a mother's love was too much for her. Both components of the double series before her staring eyes were healthy, handsome little components, with a silky fair fuzz on their violet-pink skulls, and well-formed rubbery arms and legs that moved like the many limbs of some wonderful sea animal. Each was eminently normal, but together they formed a monster. Indeed, it is strange to think that the presence of a mere band of tissue, a flap of flesh not much longer than a lamb's liver, should be able to transform joy, pride, tenderness, adoration, gratitude to God into horror and despair.

In our own case, everything was far simpler. Adults were much too different from us in all respects to afford any analogy, but our first coeval visitor was to me a mild revelation. While Lloyd placidly contemplated the awestruck child of seven or eight who was peering at us from under a humped and likewise peering fig tree, I remember appreciating in full the essential difference between the newcomer and me. He cast a short blue shadow on the ground, and so did I; but in addition to that sketchy, and flat, and unstable companion which he and I owed to the sun and which vanished in dull weather I possessed yet another shadow, a palpable reflection of my corporal self, that I always had by me, at my left side, whereas my visitor had somehow managed to lose his, or had unhooked it and left it at home. Linked Lloyd and Floyd were complete and normal; he was neither.

But perhaps, in order to elucidate these matters as thoroughly as they deserve, I should say something of still earlier recollections. Unless adult emotions stain past ones, I think I can vouch for the memory of a faint disgust. By virtue of our anterior duplexity, we lay originally front to front, joined at our common navel, and my face in those first years of our existence was constantly brushed by my twin's hard nose and wet lips. A tendency to throw our heads back and avert our faces as much as possible was a natural reaction to those bothersome contacts. The great flexibility of our band of union allowed us to assume reciprocally a more or less lateral position, and as we learned to walk we waddled about in this side-by-side attitude, which must have seemed more strained than it really was, making us look, I suppose, like a pair of drunken dwarfs supporting each other. For a long time we kept reverting in sleep to our fetal position; but whenever the discomfort it engendered woke us up, we would again jerk our faces away, in regardant revulsion, with a double wail.

I insist that at three or four our bodies obscurely disliked their clumsy conjunction, while our minds did not question its normalcy. Then, before we could have become mentally aware of its drawbacks, physical intuition discovered means of tempering them, and thereafter we hardly gave them a thought. All our movements became a judicious compromise between the common and the particular. The pattern of acts prompted by this or that mutual urge formed a kind of gray, evenly woven, generalized background against which the discrete impulse, his or mine, followed a brighter and sharper course; but (guided as it were by the warp of the background pattern) it never went athwart the common weave or the other twin's whim.

I am speaking at present solely of our childhood, when nature could not yet afford to have us undermine our hard-won vitality by any conflict between us. In later years I have had occasion to regret that we did not perish or had not been surgically separated, before we left that initial stage at which an ever-present rhythm, like some kind of remote tom-tom beating in the jungle of our nervous system, was alone responsible for the regulation of our movements. When, for example, one of us was about to stoop to possess himself of a pretty daisy and the other, at exactly the same moment, was on the point of stretching up to pluck a ripe fig, individual success depended upon whose movement happened to conform to the current ictus of our common and continuous rhythm, whereupon, with a very brief, chorealike shiver, the interrupted gesture of one twin would be swallowed and dissolved in the enriched ripple of the other's completed action. I say "enriched" because the ghost of the unpicked flower somehow seemed to be also there, pulsating between the fingers that closed upon the fruit.

There might be a period of weeks and even months when the guiding beat was much more often on Lloyd's side than on mine, and then a period might follow when I would be on top of the wave; but I cannot recall any time in our childhood when frustration or success in these matters provoked in either of us resentment or pride.

Somewhere within me, however, there must have been some sensitive cell wondering at the curious fact of a force that would suddenly sweep me away from the object of a casual desire and drag me to other, uncoveted things that were thrust into the sphere of my will instead of being consciously reached for and enveloped by its tentacles. So, as I watched this or that chance child which was watching Lloyd and me, I remember pondering a twofold problem: first, whether, perhaps, a single bodily state had more advantages than ours possessed; and second, whether *all* other children were single. It occurs to me now that quite often problems puzzling me were twofold: possibly a trickle of Lloyd's cerebration penetrated my mind and one of the two linked problems was his.

When greedy Grandfather Ahem decided to show us to visitors for money, among the flocks that came there was always some eager rascal who wanted to hear us talk to each other. As happens with primitive minds, he demanded that his ears corroborate what his eyes saw. Our folks bullied us into gratifying such desires and could not understand what was so distressful about them. We could have pleaded shyness; but the truth was that we never really *spoke* to each other, even when we were alone, for the brief broken grunts of infrequent expostulation that we sometimes exchanged (when, for instance, one had just cut his foot and had had it bandaged and the other wanted to go paddling in the brook) could hardly pass for a dialogue. The communication of simple essential sensations we performed wordlessly: shed leaves riding the stream of our shared blood. Thin thoughts also managed to slip through and travel between us. Richer ones each kept to himself, but even then there occurred odd phenomena. This is why I suspect that despite his calmer nature, Lloyd was struggling with the same new realities that were puzzling me. He forgot much when he grew up. I have forgotten nothing.

Not only did our public expect us to talk, it also wanted us to play together. Dolts! They derived quite a kick from having us match wits at checkers or *muzla*. I suppose had we happened to be opposite-sex twins they would have made us commit incest in their presence. But since mutual games were no more customary with us than conversation, we suffered subtle torments when obliged to go through the cramped motions of bandying a ball somewhere between our breast-bones or making believe to wrest a stick from each other. We drew wild applause by running around the yard with our arms around each other's shoulders. We could jump and whirl.

A salesman of patent medicine, a bald little fellow in a dirty-white Russian blouse, who knew some Turkish and English, taught us sentences in these languages; and then we had to demonstrate our ability to a fascinated audience. Their ardent faces still pursue me in my nightmares, for they come whenever my dream producer needs supers. I see again the gigantic bronze-faced shepherd in multicolored rags, the soldiers from Karaz, the one-eyed hunchbacked Armenian tailor (a monster in his own right), the giggling girls, the sighing old women, the children, the young people in Western clothes—burning eyes, white teeth, black gaping mouths; and, of course, Grandfather Ahem, with his nose of yellow ivory and his beard of gray wool, directing the proceedings or counting the soiled paper money and wetting his big thumb. The linguist, he of the embroidered blouse and bald head, courted one of my aunts but kept watching Ahem enviously through his steel-rimmed spectacles.

By the age of nine, I knew quite clearly that Lloyd and I presented the rarest of freaks. This knowledge provoked in me neither any special elation nor any special shame; but once a hysterical cook, a mustachioed woman, who had taken a great liking to us and pitied our plight, declared with an atrocious oath that she would, then and there, slice us free by means of a shiny knife that she suddenly flourished (she was at once overpowered by our grandfather and one of our newly acquired uncles); and after that incident I would often dally with an indolent daydream, fancying myself somehow separated from poor Lloyd, who somehow retained his monsterhood.

I did not care for that knife business, and anyway the manner of separation remained very vague; but I distinctly imagined the sudden melting away of my shackles and the feeling of lightness and nakedness that would ensue. I imagined myself climbing over the fence—a fence with bleached skulls of farm animals that crowned its pickets—and descending toward the beach. I saw myself leaping from boulder to boulder and diving into the twinkling sea, and scrambling back onto the shore and scampering about with other naked children. I dreamt of this at night—saw myself fleeing from my grandfather and carrying away with me a toy, or a kitten, or a little crab pressed to my left side. I saw myself meeting poor Lloyd, who appeared to me in my dream hobbling along, hopelessly joined to a hobbling twin while I was free to dance around them and slap them on their humble backs.

I wonder if Lloyd had similar visions. It has been suggested by doctors that we sometimes pooled our minds when we dreamed. One gray-blue morning he picked up a twig and drew a ship with three masts in the dust. I had just seen myself drawing that ship in the dust of a dream I had dreamed the preceding night.

An ample black shepherd's cloak covered our shoulders, and, as we squatted on the ground, all but our heads and Lloyd's hand was concealed within its falling folds. The sun had just risen and the sharp March air was like layer upon layer of semitransparent ice through which the crooked Judas trees in rough bloom made blurry spots of purplish pink. The long, low white house behind us, full of fat women and their foul-smelling husbands, was fast asleep. We did not say anything; we did not even look at each other; but, throwing his twig away, Lloyd put his right arm around my shoulder, as he always did when he wished both of us to walk fast; and with the edge of our common raiment trailing among dead weeds, while pebbles kept running from under our feet, we made our way toward the alley of cypresses that led down to the shore.

It was our first attempt to visit the sea that we could see from our hilltop softly glistening afar and leisurely, silently breaking on glossy rocks. I need not strain my memory at this point to place our stumbling flight at a definite turn in our destiny. A few weeks before, on our twelfth birthday, Grandfather Ibrahim had started to toy with the idea of sending us in the company of our newest uncle on a six-month tour through the country. They kept haggling about the terms, and had quarreled and even fought, Ahem getting the upper hand.

We feared our grandfather and loathed Uncle Novus. Presumably, after a dull forlorn fashion (knowing nothing of life, but being dimly aware that Uncle Novus was endeavoring to cheat Grandfather) we felt we should try to do something in order to prevent a showman from trundling us around in a moving prison, like apes or eagles; or perhaps we were prompted merely by the thought that this was our last chance to enjoy by ourselves our small freedom and do what we were absolutely forbidden to do; go beyond a certain picket fence, open a certain gate.

We had no trouble in opening that rickety gate, but did not manage to swing it back into its former position. A dirty-white lamb, with amber eyes and a carmine mark painted upon its hard flat forehead, followed us for a while before getting lost in the oak scrub. A little lower but still far above the valley, we had to cross the road that circled around the hill and connected our farm with the highway running along the shore. The thudding of hooves and the rasping of wheels came descending upon us; and we dropped, cloak and all, behind a bush. When the rumble subsided, we crossed the road and continued along a weedy slope. The silvery sea gradually concealed itself behind cypresses and remnants of old stone walls. Our black cloak began to feel hot and heavy but still we persevered under its protection, being afraid that otherwise some passerby might notice our infirmity.

We emerged upon the highway, a few feet from the audible sea—and there, waiting for us under a cypress, was a carriage we knew, a cartlike affair on high wheels, with Uncle Novus in the act of getting down from the box. Crafty, dark, ambitious, unprincipled little man! A few minutes before, he had caught sight of us from one of the galleries of our grandfather's house and had not been able to resist the temptation of taking advantage of an escapade which miraculously allowed him to seize us without any struggle or outcry. Swearing at the two timorous horses, he roughly helped us into the cart. He pushed our heads down and threatened to hurt us if we attempted to peep from under our cloak. Lloyd's arm was still around my shoulder, but a jerk of the cart shook it off. Now the wheels were crunching and rolling. It was some time before we realized that our driver was not taking us home.

Twenty years have passed since that gray spring morning, but it is much better preserved in my mind than many a later event. Again and again I run it before my eyes like a strip of cinematic film, as I have seen great jugglers do when reviewing their acts. So I review all the stages and circumstances and incidental details of our abortive flight—the initial shiver, the gate, the lamb, the slippery slope under our clumsy feet. To the thrushes we flushed we must have presented an extraordinary sight, with that black cloak around us and our two shorn heads on thin necks sticking out of it. The heads turned this way and that, warily, as at last the shoreline highway was reached. If at that moment some adventurous stranger had stepped onto the shore from his boat in the bay, he would have surely experienced a thrill of ancient enchantment to find himself confronted by a gentle mythological monster in a landscape of cypresses and white stones. He would have worshipped it, he would have shed sweet tears. But, alas, there was nobody to greet us there save that worried crook, our nervous kidnapper, a small doll-faced man wearing cheap spectacles, one glass of which was doctored with a bit of tape.

THE VANE SISTERS

1

I MIGHT never have heard of Cynthia's death, had I not run, that night, into D., whom I had also lost track of for the last four years or so; and I might never have run into D. had I not got involved in a series of trivial investigations.

The day, a compunctious Sunday after a week of blizzards, had been part jewel, part mud. In the midst of my usual afternoon stroll through the small hilly town attached to the girls' college where I taught French literature, I had stopped to watch a family of brilliant icicles drip-dripping from the eaves of a frame house. So clear-cut were their pointed shadows on the white boards behind them that I was sure the shadows of the falling drops should be visible too. But they were not. The roof jutted too far out, perhaps, or the angle of vision was faulty, or, again, I did not chance to be watching the right icicle when the right drop fell. There was a rhythm, an alternation in the dripping that I found as teasing as a coin trick. It led me to inspect the corners of several house blocks, and this brought me to Kelly Road, and right to the house where D. used to live when he was instructor here. And as I looked up at the eaves of the adjacent garage with its full display of transparent stalactites backed by their blue silhouettes, I was rewarded at last, upon choosing one, by the sight of what might be described as the dot of an exclamation mark leaving its ordinary position to glide down very fast—a jot faster than the thaw-drop it raced. This twinned twinkle was delightful but not completely satisfying; or rather it only sharpened my appetite for other tidbits of light and shade, and I walked on in a state of raw awareness that seemed to transform the whole of my being into one big eyeball rolling in the world's socket.

Through peacocked lashes I saw the dazzling diamond reflection of the low sun on the round back of a parked automobile. To all kinds of things a vivid pictorial sense had been restored by the sponge of the thaw. Water in overlapping festoons flowed down one sloping street and turned gracefully into another. With ever so slight a note of meretricious appeal, narrow passages between buildings revealed treasures of brick and purple. I remarked for the first time the humble fluting—last echoes of grooves on the shafts of columns—ornamenting a garbage can, and I also saw the rippling upon its lid—circles diverging from a fantastically ancient center. Erect, dark-headed shapes of dead snow (left by the blades of a bulldozer last Friday) were lined up like rudimentary penguins along the curbs, above the brilliant vibration of live gutters.

I walked up, and I walked down, and I walked straight into a delicately dying sky, and finally the sequence of observed and observant things brought me, at my usual eating time, to a street so distant from my usual eating place that I decided to try a restaurant which stood on the fringe of the town. Night had fallen without sound or ceremony when I came out again. The lean ghost, the elongated umbra cast by a parking meter upon some damp snow, had a strange ruddy tinge; this I made out to be due to the tawny red light of the restaurant sign above the sidewalk; and it was then—as I loitered there, wondering rather wearily if in the course of my return tramp I might be lucky enough to find the same in neon blue—it was then that a car crunched to a standstill near me and D. got out of it with an exclamation of feigned pleasure.

He was passing, on his way from Albany to Boston, through the town he had dwelt in before, and more than once in my life have I felt that stab of vicarious emotion followed by a rush of personal irritation against travelers who seem to feel nothing at all upon revisiting spots that ought to harass them at every step with wailing and writhing memories. He ushered me back into the bar that I had just left, and after the usual exchange of buoyant platitudes came the inevitable vacuum which he filled with the random words: "Say, I never thought there was anything wrong with Cynthia Vane's heart. My lawyer tells me she died last week."

2

_____

He was still young, still brash, still shifty, still married to the gentle, exquisitely pretty woman who had never learned or suspected anything about his disastrous affair with Cynthia's hysterical young sister, who in her turn had known nothing of the interview I had had with Cynthia when she suddenly summoned me to Boston to make me swear I would talk to D. and get him "kicked out" if he did not stop seeing Sybil at once—or did not divorce his wife (whom incidentally she visualized through the prism of Sybil's wild talk as a termagant and a fright). I had cornered him immediately. He had said there was nothing to worry about—had made up his mind, anyway, to give up his college job and move with his wife to Albany, where he would work in his father's firm; and the whole matter, which had threatened to become one of those hopelessly entangled situations that drag on for years, with peripheral sets of well-meaning friends endlessly discussing it in universal secrecy—and even founding, among themselves, new intimacies upon its alien woes—came to an abrupt end.

I remember sitting next day at my raised desk in the large classroom where a midyear examination in French Lit. was being held on the eve of Sybil's suicide. She came in on high heels, with a suitcase, dumped it in a corner where several other bags were stacked, with a single shrug slipped her fur coat off her thin shoulders, folded it on her bag, and with two or three other girls stopped before my desk to ask when I would mail them their grades. It would take me a week, beginning from tomorrow, I said, to read the stuff. I also remember wondering whether D. had already informed her of his decision—and I felt acutely unhappy about my dutiful little student as during 150 minutes my gaze kept reverting to her, so childishly slight in close-fitting gray, and kept observing that carefully waved dark hair, that small, small-flowered hat with a little hyaline veil as worn that season, and under it her small face broken into a cubist pattern by scars due to a skin disease, pathetically masked by a sunlamp tan that hardened her features, whose charm was further impaired by her having painted everything that could be painted, so that the pale gums of her teeth between cherry-red chapped lips and the diluted blue ink of her eyes under darkened lids were the only visible openings into her beauty.

Next day, having arranged the ugly copybooks alphabetically, I plunged into their chaos of scripts and came prematurely to Valevsky and Vane, whose books I had somehow misplaced. The first was dressed up for the occasion in a semblance of legibility, but Sybil's work displayed her usual combination of several demon hands. She had begun in very pale, very hard pencil which had conspicuously embossed the black verso, but had produced little of permanent value on the upper side of the page. Happily the tip soon broke, and Sybil continued in another, darker lead, gradually lapsing into the blurred thickness of what looked almost like charcoal, to which, by sucking the blunt point, she had contributed some traces of lipstick. Her work, although even poorer than I had expected, bore all the signs of a kind of desperate conscientiousness, with underscores, transposes, unnecessary footnotes, as if she were intent upon rounding up things in the most respectable manner possible. Then she had borrowed Mary Valevsky's fountain pen and added: "*Cette examain est finie ainsi que ma vie. Adieu, jeunes filles!* Please, *Monsieur le Professeur,* contact *ma soeur* and tell her that Death was not better than D minus, but definitely better than Life minus D."

I lost no time in ringing up Cynthia, who told me it was all over—had been all over since eight in the morning—and asked me to bring her the note, and when I did, beamed through her tears with proud admiration for the whimsical use ("Just like her!") Sybil had made of an examination in French literature. In no time she "fixed" two highballs, while never parting with Sybil's notebook—by now splashed with soda water and tears—and went on studying the death message, whereupon I was impelled to point out to her the grammatical mistakes in it and to explain the way "girl" is translated in American colleges lest students innocently bandy around the French equivalent of "wench," or worse. These rather tasteless trivialities pleased Cynthia hugely as she rose, with gasps, above the heaving surface of her grief. And then, holding that limp notebook as if it were a kind of passport to a casual Elysium (where pencil points do not snap and a dreamy young beauty with an impeccable complexion winds a lock of her hair on a dreamy forefinger, as she meditates over some celestial test), Cynthia led me upstairs to a chilly little bedroom, just to show me, as if I were the police or a sympathetic Irish neighbor, two empty pill bottles and the tumbled bed from which a tender, inessential body, that D. must have known down to its last velvet detail, had been already removed.

3

It was four or five months after her sister's death that I began seeing Cynthia fairly often. By the time I had come to New York for some vacational research in the Public Library she had also moved to that city, where for some odd reason (in vague connection, I presume, with artistic motives) she had taken what people, immune to gooseflesh, term a "cold water" flat, down in the scale of the city's transverse streets. What attracted me was neither her ways, which I thought repulsively vivacious, nor her looks, which other men thought striking. She had wide-spaced eyes very much like her sister's, of a frank, frightened blue with dark points in a radial arrangement. The interval between her thick black eyebrows was always shiny, and shiny too were the fleshy volutes of her nostrils. The coarse texture of her epiderm looked almost masculine, and, in the stark lamplight of her studio, you could see the pores of her thirty-two-year-old face fairly gaping at you like something in an aquarium. She used cosmetics with as much zest as her little sister had, but with an additional slovenliness that would result in her big front teeth getting some of the rouge. She was handsomely dark, wore a not too tasteless mixture of fairly smart heterogeneous things, and had a so-called good figure; but all of her was curiously frowzy, after a way I obscurely associated with left-wing enthusiasms in politics and "advanced" banalities in art, although, actually, she cared for neither. Her coily hairdo, on a part-and-bun basis, might have looked feral and bizarre had it not been thoroughly domesticated by its own soft unkemptness at the vulnerable nape. Her fingernails were gaudily painted, but badly bitten and not clean. Her lovers were a silent young photographer with a sudden laugh and two older men, brothers, who owned a small printing establishment across the street. I wondered at their tastes whenever I glimpsed, with a secret shudder, the higgledy-piggledy striation of black hairs that showed all along her pale shins through the nylon of her stockings with the scientific distinctness of a preparation flattened under glass; or when I felt, at her every movement, the dullish, stalish, not particularly conspicuous but all-pervading and depressing emanation that her seldom bathed flesh spread from under weary perfumes and creams.

Her father had gambled away the greater part of a comfortable fortune, and her mother's first husband had been of Slav origin, but otherwise Cynthia Vane belonged to a good, respectable family. For aught we know, it may have gone back to kings and soothsayers in the mists of ultimate islands. Transferred to a newer world, to a landscape of doomed, splendid deciduous trees, her ancestry presented, in one of its first phases, a white churchful of farmers against a black thunderhead, and then an imposing array of townsmen engaged in mercantile pursuits, as well as a number of learned men, such as Dr. Jonathan Vane, the gaunt bore (1780–1839), who perished in the conflagration of the steamer *Lexington* to become later an habitué of Cynthia's tilting table. I have always wished to stand genealogy on its head, and here I have an opportunity to do so, for it is the last scion, Cynthia, and Cynthia alone, who will remain of any importance in the Vane dynasty. I am alluding of course to her artistic gift, to her delightful, gay, but not very popular paintings, which the friends of her friends bought at long intervals—and I dearly should like to know where they went after her death, those honest and poetical pictures that illumined her living room—the wonderfully detailed images of metallic things, and my favorite, *Seen Through a Windshield*—a windshield partly covered with rime, with a brilliant trickle (from an imaginary car roof) across its transparent part and, through it all, the sapphire flame of the sky and a green-and-white fir tree.

4

Cynthia had a feeling that her dead sister was not altogether pleased with her—had discovered by now that she and I had conspired to break her romance; and so, in order to disarm her shade, Cynthia reverted to a rather primitive type of sacrificial offering (tinged, however, with something of Sybil's humor), and began to send to D.'s business address, at deliberately unfixed dates, such trifles as snapshots of Sybil's tomb in a poor light; cuttings of her own hair which was indistinguishable from Sybil's; a New England sectional map with an inked-in cross, midway between two chaste towns, to mark the spot where D. and Sybil had stopped on October the twenty-third, in broad daylight, at a lenient motel, in a pink and brown forest; and, twice, a stuffed skunk.

Being as a conversationalist more voluble than explicit, she never could describe in full the theory of intervenient auras that she had somehow evolved. Fundamentally there was nothing particularly new about her private creed since it presupposed a fairly conventional hereafter, a silent solarium of immortal souls (spliced with mortal antecedents) whose main recreation consisted of periodical hoverings over the dear quick. The interesting point was a curious practical twist that Cynthia gave to her tame metaphysics. She was sure that her existence was influenced by all sorts of dead friends each of whom took turns in directing her fate much as if she were a stray kitten which a schoolgirl in passing gathers up, and presses to her cheek, and carefully puts down again, near some suburban hedge—to be stroked presently by another transient hand or carried off to a world of doors by some hospitable lady.

For a few hours, or for several days in a row, and sometimes recurrently, in an irregular series, for months or years, anything that happened to Cynthia, after a given person had died, would be, she said, in the manner and mood of that person. The event might be extraordinary, changing the course of one's life; or it might be a string of minute incidents just sufficiently clear to stand out in relief against one's usual day and then shading off into still vaguer trivia as the aura gradually faded. The influence might be good or bad; the main thing was that its source could be identified. It was like walking through a person's soul, she said. I tried to argue that she might not always be able to determine the exact source since not everybody has a recognizable soul; that there are anonymous letters and Christmas presents which anybody might send; that, in fact, what Cynthia called "a usual day" might be itself a weak solution of mixed auras or simply the routine shift of a humdrum guardian angel. And what about God? Did or did not people who would resent any omnipotent dictator on earth look forward to one in heaven? And wars? What a dreadful idea—dead soldiers still fighting with living ones, or phantom armies trying to get at each other through the lives of crippled old men.

But Cynthia was above generalities as she was beyond logic. "Ah, that's Paul," she would say when the soup spitefully boiled over, or: "I guess good Betty Brown is dead" when she won a beautiful and very welcome vacuum cleaner in a charity lottery. And, with Jamesian meanderings that exasperated my French mind, she would go back to a time when Betty and Paul had not yet departed, and tell me of the showers of well-meant, but odd and quite unacceptable, bounties—beginning with an old purse that contained a check for three dollars which she picked up in the street and, of course, returned (to the aforesaid Betty Brown—this is where she first comes in—a decrepit colored woman hardly able to walk), and ending with an insulting proposal from an old beau of hers (this is where Paul comes in) to paint "straight" pictures of his house and family for a reasonable remuneration—all of which followed upon the demise of a certain Mrs. Page, a kindly but petty old party who had pestered her with bits of matter-of-fact advice since Cynthia had been a child.

Sybil's personality, she said, had a rainbow edge as if a little out of focus. She said that had I known Sybil better I would have at once understood how Sybil-like was the aura of minor events which, in spells, had suffused her, Cynthia's, existence after Sybil's suicide. Ever since they had lost their mother they had intended to give up their Boston home and move to New York, where Cynthia's paintings, they thought, would have a chance to be more widely admired; but the old home had clung to them with all its plush tentacles. Dead Sybil, how-ever, had proceeded to separate the house from its view—a thing that affects fatally the sense of home. Right across the narrow street a building project had come into loud, ugly, scaffolded life. A pair of fa-miliar poplars died that spring, turning to blond skeletons. Workmen came and broke up the warm-colored lovely old sidewalk that had a special violet sheen on wet April days and had echoed so memorably to the morning footsteps of museum-bound Mr. Lever, who upon retir-ing from business at sixty had devoted a full quarter of a century exclusively to the study of snails.

Speaking of old men, one should add that sometimes these posthu-mous auspices and interventions were in the nature of parody. Cynthia had been on friendly terms with an eccentric librarian called Porlock who in the last years of his dusty life had been engaged in examining old books for miraculous misprints such as the substitution of *l* for the second *h* in the word "hither." Contrary to Cynthia, he cared nothing for the thrill of obscure predictions; all he sought was the freak itself, the chance that mimics choice, the flaw that looks like a flower; and Cynthia, a much more perverse amateur of misshapen or illicitly con-nected words, puns, logographs, and so on, had helped the poor crank to pursue a quest that in the light of the example she cited struck me as statistically insane. Anyway, she said, on the third day after his death she was reading a magazine and had just come across a quotation from an imperishable poem (that she, with other gullible readers, believed to have been really composed in a dream) when it dawned upon her that "Alph" was a prophetic sequence of the initial letters of Anna Livia Plurabelle (another sacred river running through, or rather around, yet another fake dream), while the additional *h* modestly stood, as a pri-vate signpost, for the word that had so hypnotized Mr. Porlock. And I wish I could recollect that novel or short story (by some contempo-rary writer, I believe) in which, unknown to its author, the first letters of the words in its last paragraph formed, as deciphered by Cynthia, a message from his dead mother.

5

_____

I am sorry to say that not content with these ingenious fancies Cynthia showed a ridiculous fondness for spiritualism. I refused to accompany her to sittings in which paid mediums took part: I knew too much about that from other sources. I did consent, however, to attend little farces rigged up by Cynthia and her two poker-faced gentlemen friends of the printing shop. They were podgy, polite, and rather eerie old fellows, but I satisfied myself that they possessed considerable wit and culture. We sat down at a light little table, and crackling tremors started almost as soon as we laid our fingertips upon it. I was treated to an assortment of ghosts that rapped out their reports most readily though refusing to elucidate anything that I did not quite catch. Oscar Wilde came in and in rapid garbled French, with the usual anglicisms, obscurely accused Cynthia's dead parents of what appeared in my jottings as *"plagiatisme."* A brisk spirit contributed the unsolicited information that he, John Moore, and his brother Bill had been coal miners in Colorado and had perished in an avalanche at "Crested Beauty" in January 1883. Frederic Myers, an old hand at the game, hammered out a piece of verse (oddly resembling Cynthia's own fugitive productions) which in part reads in my notes:

> *What is this—a conjuror's rabbit,*
> *Or a flawy but genuine gleam—*
> *Which can check the perilous habit*
> *And dispel the dolorous dream?*

Finally, with a great crash and all kinds of shudderings and jiglike movements on the part of the table, Leo Tolstoy visited our little group and, when asked to identify himself by specific traits of terrene habitation, launched upon a complex description of what seemed to be some Russian type of architectural woodwork ("figures on boards—man, horse, cock, man, horse, cock"), all of which was difficult to take down, hard to understand, and impossible to verify.

I attended two or three other sittings which were even sillier but I must confess that I preferred the childish entertainment they afforded and the cider we drank (Podgy and Pudgy were teetotalers) to Cynthia's awful house parties.

She gave them at the Wheelers' nice flat next door—the sort of arrangement dear to her centrifugal nature, but then, of course, her own living room always looked like a dirty old palette. Following a barbaric, unhygienic, and adulterous custom, the guests' coats, still warm on the inside, were carried by quiet, baldish Bob Wheeler into the sanctity of a tidy bedroom and heaped on the conjugal bed. It was also he who poured out the drinks, which were passed around by the young photographer while Cynthia and Mrs. Wheeler took care of the canapés.

A late arrival had the impression of lots of loud people unnecessarily grouped within a smoke-blue space between two mirrors gorged with reflections. Because, I suppose, Cynthia wished to be the youngest in the room, the women she used to invite, married or single, were, at the best, in their precarious forties; some of them would bring from their homes, in dark taxis, intact vestiges of good looks, which, however, they lost as the party progressed. It has always amazed me the ability sociable weekend revelers have of finding almost at once, by a purely empiric but very precise method, a common denominator of drunkenness, to which everybody loyally sticks before descending, all together, to the next level. The rich friendliness of the matrons was marked by tomboyish overtones, while the fixed inward look of amiably tight men was like a sacrilegious parody of pregnancy. Although some of the guests were connected in one way or another with the arts, there was no inspired talk, no wreathed, elbow-propped heads, and of course no flute girls. From some vantage point where she had been sitting in a stranded mermaid pose on the pale carpet with one or two younger fellows, Cynthia, her face varnished with a film of beaming sweat, would creep up on her knees, a proffered plate of nuts in one hand, and crisply tap with the other the athletic leg of Cochran or Corcoran, an art dealer, ensconced, on a pearl-gray sofa, between two flushed, happily disintegrating ladies.

At a further stage there would come spurts of more riotous gaiety. Corcoran or Coransky would grab Cynthia or some other wandering woman by the shoulder and lead her into a corner to confront her with a grinning imbroglio of private jokes and rumors, whereupon, with a laugh and a toss of her head, she would break away. And still later there would be flurries of intersexual chumminess, jocular reconciliations, a bare fleshy arm flung around another woman's husband (he standing very upright in the midst of a swaying room), or a sudden rush of flirtatious anger, of clumsy pursuit—and the quiet half-smile of Bob Wheeler picking up glasses that grew like mushrooms in the shade of chairs.

After one last party of that sort, I wrote Cynthia a perfectly harmless and, on the whole, well-meant note, in which I poked a little Latin fun at some of her guests. I also apologized for not having touched her whiskey, saying that as a Frenchman I preferred the grape to the grain. A few days later I met her on the steps of the Public Library, in the broken sun, under a weak cloudburst, opening her amber umbrella, struggling with a couple of armpitted books (of which I relieved her for a moment), *Footfalls on the Boundary of Another World* by Robert Dale Owen, and something on "Spiritualism and Christianity"; when, suddenly, with no provocation on my part, she blazed out at me with vulgar vehemence, using poisonous words, saying—through pear-shaped drops of sparse rain—that I was a prig and a snob; that I only saw the gestures and disguises of people; that Corcoran had rescued from drowning, in two different oceans, two men—by an irrelevant coincidence both called Corcoran; that romping and screeching Joan Winter had a little girl doomed to grow completely blind in a few months; and that the woman in green with the freckled chest whom I had snubbed in some way or other had written a national best-seller in 1932. Strange Cynthia! I had been told she could be thunderously rude to people whom she liked and respected; one had, however, to draw the line somewhere and since I had by then sufficiently studied her interesting auras and other odds and ids, I decided to stop seeing her altogether.

6
————

The night D. informed me of Cynthia's death I returned after eleven to the two-story house I shared, in horizontal section, with an emeritus professor's widow. Upon reaching the porch I looked with the apprehension of solitude at the two kinds of darkness in the two rows of windows: the darkness of absence and the darkness of sleep.

I could do something about the first but could not duplicate the second. My bed gave me no sense of safety; its springs only made my nerves bounce. I plunged into Shakespeare's sonnets—and found myself idiotically checking the first letters of the lines to see what sacramental words they might form. I got FATE (LXX), ATOM (CXX), and, twice, TAFT (LXXXVIII, CXXXI). Every now and then I would glance around to see how the objects in my room were behaving. It was strange to think that if bombs began to fall I would feel little more than a gambler's excitement (and a great deal of earthy relief) whereas my heart would burst if a certain suspiciously tense-looking little bottle on yonder shelf moved a fraction of an inch to one side. The silence, too, was suspiciously compact as if deliberately forming a black backdrop for the nerve flash caused by any small sound of unknown origin. All traffic was dead. In vain did I pray for the groan of a truck up Perkins Street. The woman above who used to drive me crazy by the booming thuds occasioned by what seemed monstrous feet of stone (actually, in diurnal life, she was a small dumpy creature resembling a mummified guinea pig) would have earned my blessings had she now trudged to her bathroom. I put out my light and cleared my throat several times so as to be responsible for at least *that* sound. I thumbed a mental ride with a very remote automobile but it dropped me before I had a chance to doze off. Presently a crackle (due, I hoped, to a discarded and crushed sheet of paper opening like a mean, stubborn night flower) started and stopped in the wastepaper basket, and my bed table responded with a little click. It would have been just like Cynthia to put on right then a cheap poltergeist show.

I decided to fight Cynthia. I reviewed in thought the modern era of raps and apparitions, beginning with the knockings of 1848, at the hamlet of Hydesville, New York, and ending with grotesque phenomena at Cambridge, Massachusetts; I evoked the ankle bones and other anatomical castanets of the Fox sisters (as described by the sages of the University of Buffalo); the mysteriously uniform type of delicate adolescent in bleak Epworth or Tedworth, radiating the same disturbances as in old Peru; solemn Victorian orgies with roses falling and accordions floating to the strains of sacred music; professional impostors regurgitating moist cheesecloth; Mr. Duncan, a lady medium's dignified husband, who, when asked if he would submit to a search, excused himself on the ground of soiled underwear; old Alfred Russel Wallace, the naive naturalist, refusing to believe that the white form with bare feet and unperforated earlobes before him, at a private pandemonium in Boston, could be prim Miss Cook whom he had just seen asleep, in her curtained corner, all dressed in black, wearing laced-up boots and earrings; two other investigators, small, puny, but reasonably intelligent and active men, closely clinging with arms and legs about Eusapia, a large, plump elderly female reeking of garlic, who still managed to fool them; and the skeptical and embarrassed magician, instructed by charming young Margery's "control" not to get lost in the bathrobe's lining but to follow up the left stocking until he reached the bare thigh—upon the warm skin of which he felt a "teleplastic" mass that appeared to the touch uncommonly like cold, uncooked liver.

7

I was appealing to flesh, and the corruption of flesh, to refute and defeat the possible persistence of discarnate life. Alas, these conjurations only enhanced my fear of Cynthia's phantom. Atavistic peace came with dawn, and when I slipped into sleep the sun through the tawny window shades penetrated a dream that somehow was full of Cynthia.

This was disappointing. Secure in the fortress of daylight, I said to myself that I had expected more. She, a painter of glass-bright minutiae—and now so vague! I lay in bed, thinking my dream over and listening to the sparrows outside: Who knows, if recorded and then run backward, those bird sounds might not become human speech, voiced words, just as the latter become a twitter when reversed? I set myself to reread my dream—backward, diagonally, up, down—trying hard to unravel something Cynthia-like in it, something strange and suggestive that must be there.

I could isolate, consciously, little. Everything seemed blurred, yellow-clouded, yielding nothing tangible. Her inept acrostics, maudlin evasions, theopathies—every recollection formed ripples of mysterious meaning. Everything seemed yellowly blurred, illusive, lost.

LANCE

/

1
———

T HE name of the planet, presuming it has already received one, is immaterial. At its most favorable opposition, it may very well be separated from the earth by only as many miles as there are years between last Friday and the rise of the Himalayas—a million times the reader's average age. In the telescopic field of one's fancy, through the prism of one's tears, any particularities it presents should be no more striking than those of existing planets. A rosy globe, marbled with dusky blotches, it is one of the countless objects diligently revolving in the infinite and gratuitous awfulness of fluid space.

My planet's *maria* (which are not seas) and its *lacus* (which are not lakes) have also, let us suppose, received names; some less jejune, perhaps, than those of garden roses; others, more pointless than the surnames of their observers (for, to take actual cases, that an astronomer should have been called Lampland is as marvelous as that an entomologist should have been called Krautwurm); but most of them of so antique a style as to vie in sonorous and corrupt enchantment with place names pertaining to romances of chivalry.

Just as our Pinedales, down here, have often little to offer beyond a shoe factory on one side of the tracks and the rusty inferno of an automobile dump on the other, so those seductive Arcadias and Icarias and Zephyrias on planetary maps may quite likely turn out to be dead deserts lacking even the milkweed that graces our dumps. Selenographers will confirm this, but then, their lenses serve them better than ours do. In the present instance, the greater the magnification, the more the mottling of the planet's surface looks as if it were seen by a submerged swimmer peering up through semitranslucent water. And if certain connected markings resemble in a shadowy way the line-and-

632

hole pattern of a Chinese-checkers board, let us consider them geo-metrical hallucinations.

I not only debar a too definite planet from any role in my story—from the role every dot and full stop should play in my story (which I see as a kind of celestial chart)—I also refuse to have anything to do with those technical prophecies that scientists are reported to make to reporters. Not for me is the rocket racket. Not for me are the artificial little satellites that the earth is promised; landing starstrips for space-ships ("spacers")—one, two, three, four, and then thousands of strong castles in the air each complete with cookhouse and keep, set up by terrestrial nations in a frenzy of competitive confusion, phony gravita-tion, and savagely flapping flags.

Another thing I have not the slightest use for is the special-equipment business—the airtight suit, the oxygen apparatus—suchlike contraptions. Like old Mr. Boke, of whom we shall hear in a minute, I am eminently qualified to dismiss these practical matters (which any-way are doomed to seem absurdly impractical to future spaceshipmen, such as old Boke's only son), since the emotions that gadgets provoke in me range from dull distrust to morbid trepidation. Only by a heroic effort can I make myself unscrew a bulb that has died an inexplicable death and screw in another, which will light up in my face with the hideous instancy of a dragon's egg hatching in one's bare hand.

Finally, I utterly spurn and reject so-called science fiction. I have looked into it, and found it as boring as the mystery-story maga-zines—the same sort of dismally pedestrian writing with oodles of dia-logue and loads of commutational humor. The clichés are, of course, disguised; essentially, they are the same throughout all cheap reading matter, whether it spans the universe or the living room. They are like those "assorted" cookies that differ from one another only in shape and shade, whereby their shrewd makers ensnare the salivating con-sumer in a mad Pavlovian world where, at no extra cost, variations in simple visual values influence and gradually replace flavor, which thus goes the way of talent and truth.

So the good guy grins, and the villain sneers, and a noble heart sports a slangy speech. Star tsars, directors of Galactic Unions, are practically replicas of those peppy, red-haired executives in earthy earth jobs, that illustrate with their little crinkles the human interest stories of the well-thumbed slicks in beauty parlors. Invaders of Denebola and Spica, Virgo's finest, bear names beginning with Mac; cold scientists are usually found under Steins; some of them share with the superga-lactic gals such abstract labels as Biola or Vala. Inhabitants of foreign planets, "intelligent" beings, humanoid or of various mythic makes, have one remarkable trait in common: their intimate structure is never depicted. In a supreme concession to biped propriety, not only do centaurs wear loincloths; they wear them about their forelegs.

This seems to complete the elimination—unless anybody wants to discuss the question of time? Here again, in order to focalize young Emery L. Boke, that more or less remote descendant of mine who is to be a member of the first interplanetary expedition (which, after all, is the one humble postulate of my tale), I gladly leave the replacement by a pretentious "2" or "3" of the honest "1" in our "1900" to the capable paws of *Starzan* and other comics and atomics. Let it be 2145 A.D. or 200 A.A., it does not matter. I have no desire to barge into vested interests of any kind. This is strictly an amateur performance, with quite casual stage properties and a minimum of scenery, and the quilled remains of a dead porcupine in a corner of the old barn. We are here among friends, the Browns and the Bensons, the Whites and the Wilsons, and when somebody goes out for a smoke, he hears the crickets, and a distant farm dog (who waits, between barks, to listen to what we cannot hear). The summer night sky is a mess of stars. Emery Lancelot Boke, at twenty-one, knows immeasurably more about them than I, who am fifty and terrified.

2
———

Lance is tall and lean, with thick tendons and greenish veins on his suntanned forearms and a scar on his brow. When doing nothing—when sitting all at ease as he sits now, leaning forward from the edge of a low armchair, his shoulders hunched up, his elbows propped on his big knees—he has a way of slowly clasping and unclasping his handsome hands, a gesture I borrow for him from one of his ancestors. An air of gravity, of uncomfortable concentration (all thought is uncomfortable, and young thought especially so), is his usual expression; at the moment, however, it is a manner of mask, concealing his furious desire to get rid of a long-drawn tension. As a rule, he does not smile often, and besides, "smile" is too smooth a word for the abrupt, bright contortion that now suddenly illumes his mouth and eyes as the shoulders hunch higher, the moving hands stop in a clasped position, and he lightly stamps the toe of one foot. His parents are in the room, and also a chance visitor, a fool and a bore, who is not aware of what is happening—for this is an awkward moment in a gloomy house on the eve of a fabulous departure.

An hour goes by. At last the visitor picks up his top hat from the carpet and leaves. Lance remains alone with his parents, which only serves to increase the tension. Mr. Boke I see plainly enough. But I cannot visualize Mrs. Boke with any degree of clarity, no matter how deep I sink into my difficult trance. I know that her cheerfulness—small talk, quick beat of eyelashes—is something she keeps up not so much for the sake of her son as for that of her husband, and his aging heart, and old Boke realizes this only too well and, on top of his own monstrous anguish, he has to cope with her feigned levity, which disturbs him more than would an utter and unconditional collapse. I am somewhat disappointed that I cannot make out her features. All I manage to glimpse is an effect of melting light on one side of her misty hair, and in this, I suspect, I am insidiously influenced by the standard artistry of modern photography and I feel how much easier writing must have been in former days when one's imagination was not hemmed in by innumerable visual aids, and a frontiersman looking at his first giant cactus or his first high snows was not necessarily reminded of a tire company's pictorial advertisement.

In the case of Mr. Boke, I find myself operating with the features of an old professor of history, a brilliant medievalist, whose white whiskers, pink pate, and black suit are famous on a certain sunny campus in the Deep South, but whose sole asset in connection with this story (apart from a slight resemblance to a long-dead great-uncle of mine) is that his appearance is out of date. Now if one is perfectly honest with oneself, there is nothing extraordinary in the tendency to give to the manners and clothes of a distant day (which happens to be placed in the future) an old-fashioned tinge, a badly pressed, badly groomed, dusty something, since the terms "out of date," "not of our age," and so on are in the long run the only ones in which we are able to imagine and express a strangeness no amount of research can foresee. The future is but the obsolete in reverse.

In that shabby room, in the tawny lamplight, Lance talks of some last things. He has recently brought from a desolate spot in the Andes, where he has been climbing some as yet unnamed peak, a couple of adolescent chinchillas—cinder-gray, phenomenally furry, rabbit-sized rodents (*Hystricomorpha*), with long whiskers, round rumps, and petal-like ears. He keeps them indoors in a wire-screened pen and gives them peanuts, puffed rice, raisins to eat, and, as a special treat, a violet or an aster. He hopes they will breed in the fall. He now repeats to his mother a few emphatic instructions—to keep his pets' food crisp and their pen dry, and never forget their daily dust bath (fine sand mixed with powdered chalk) in which they roll and kick most lustily. While this is being discussed, Mr. Boke lights and relights a pipe and finally puts it away. Every now and then, with a false air of benevolent absent-mindedness, the old man launches upon a series of sounds and motions that deceive nobody; he clears his throat and, with his hands behind his back, drifts toward a window; or he begins to produce a tight-lipped tuneless humming; and seemingly driven by that small nasal motor, he wanders out of the parlor. But no sooner has he left the stage than he throws off, with a dreadful shiver, the elaborate structure of his gentle, bumbling impersonation act. In a bedroom or bathroom, he stops as if to take, in abject solitude, a deep spasmodic draft from some secret flask, and presently staggers out again, drunk with grief.

The stage has not changed when he quietly returns to it, buttoning his coat and resuming that little hum. It is now a matter of minutes. Lance inspects the pen before he goes, and leaves Chin and Chilla sitting on their haunches, each holding a flower. The only other thing that I know about these last moments is that any such talk as "Sure you haven't forgotten the silk shirt that came from the wash?" or "You remember where you put those new slippers?" is excluded. Whatever Lance takes with him is already collected at the mysterious and unmentionable and absolutely awful place of his zero-hour departure; he needs nothing of what we need; and he steps out of the house, empty-handed and hatless, with the casual lightness of one walking to the newsstand—or to a glorious scaffold.

3

Terrestrial space loves concealment. The most it yields to the eye is a panoramic view. The horizon closes upon the receding traveler like a trap door in slow motion. For those who remain, any town a day's journey from here is invisible, whereas you can easily see such transcendencies as, say, a lunar amphitheater and the shadow cast by its circular ridge. The conjuror who displays the firmament has rolled up his sleeves and performs in full view of the little spectators. Planets may dip out of sight (just as objects are obliterated by the blurry curve of one's own cheekbone); but they are back when the earth turns its head. The nakedness of the night is appalling. Lance has left; the fragility of his young limbs grows in direct ratio to the distance he covers.

From their balcony, the old Bokes look at the infinitely perilous night sky and wildly envy the lot of fishermen's wives.

If Boke's sources are accurate, the name "Lanceloz del Lac" occurs for the first time in Verse 3676 of the twelfth-century *Roman de la Charrette*. Lance, Lancelin, Lancelotik—diminutives murmured at the brimming, salty, moist stars. Young knights in their teens learning to harp, hawk, and hunt; the Forest Dangerous and the Dolorous Tower; Aldebaran, Betelgeuse—the thunder of Saracenic war cries. Marvelous deeds of arms, marvelous warriors, sparkling within the awful constellations above the Bokes' balcony: Sir Percard the Black Knight, and Sir Perimones the Red Knight, and Sir Pertolepe the Green Knight, and Sir Persant the Indigo Knight, and that bluff old party Sir Grummore Grummursum, muttering northern oaths under his breath. The field glass is not much good, the chart is all crumpled and damp, and: "You do not hold the flashlight properly"—this to Mrs. Boke.

Draw a deep breath. Look again.

Lancelot is gone; the hope of seeing him in life is about equal to the hope of seeing him in eternity. Lancelot is banished from the country of L'Eau Grise (as we might call the Great Lakes) and now rides up in the dust of the night sky almost as far as our local universe (with the balcony and the pitch-black, optically spotted garden) speeds toward King Arthur's Harp, where Vega burns and beckons—one of the few objects that can be identified by the aid of this goddam diagram. The sidereal haze makes the Bokes dizzy—gray incense, insanity, infinity-sickness. But they cannot tear themselves away from the nightmare of space, cannot go back to the lighted bedroom, a corner of which shows in the glass door. And presently *the* planet rises, like a tiny bonfire.

There, to the right, is the Bridge of the Sword leading to the Otherworld *("dont nus estranges ne retorne")*. Lancelot crawls over it in great pain, in ineffable anguish. "Thou shalt not pass a pass that is called the Pass Perilous." But another enchanter commands: "You shall. You shall even acquire a sense of humor that will tide you over the trying spots." The brave old Bokes think they can distinguish Lance scaling, on crampons, the verglased rock of the sky or silently breaking trail through the soft snows of nebulae. Boötes, somewhere between Camp X and XI, is a great glacier all rubble and icefall. We try to make out the serpentine route of ascent; seem to distinguish the light leanness of Lance among the several roped silhouettes. Gone! Was it he or Denny (a young biologist, Lance's best friend)? Waiting in the dark valley at the foot of the vertical sky, we recall (Mrs. Boke more clearly than her husband) those special names for crevasses and

Gothic structures of ice that Lance used to mouth with such professional gusto in his alpine boyhood (he is several light-years older by now); the *séracs* and the *schrunds*; the avalanche and its thud; French echoes and Germanic magic hobnailnobbing up there as they do in medieval romances.

Ah, there he is again! Crossing through a notch between two stars; then, very slowly, attempting a traverse on a cliff face so sheer, and with such delicate holds that the mere evocation of those groping fingertips and scraping boots fills one with acrophobic nausea. And through streaming tears the old Bokes see Lance now marooned on a shelf of stone and now climbing again and now, dreadfully safe, with his ice axe and pack, on a peak above peaks, his eager profile rimmed with light.

Or is he already on his way down? I assume that no news comes from the explorers and that the Bokes prolong their pathetic vigils. As they wait for their son to return, his every avenue of descent seems to run into the precipice of their despair. But perhaps he has swung over those high-angled wet slabs that fall away vertically into the abyss, has mastered the overhang, and is now blissfully glissading down steep celestial snows?

As, however, the Bokes' doorbell does not ring at the logical culmination of an imagined series of footfalls (no matter how patiently we space them as they come nearer and nearer in our mind), we have to thrust him back and have him start his ascent all over again, and then put him even farther back, so that he is still at headquarters (where the tents are, and the open latrines, and the begging, black-footed children) long after we had pictured him bending under the tulip tree to walk up the lawn to the door and the doorbell. As if tired by the many appearances he has made in his parents' minds, Lance now plows wearily through mud puddles, then up a hillside, in the haggard landscape of a distant war, slipping and scrambling up the dead grass of the slope. There is some routine rock work ahead, and then the summit. The ridge is won. Our losses are heavy. How is one notified? By wire? By registered letter? And who is the executioner—a special messenger or the regular plodding, florid-nosed postman, always a little high (he has troubles of his own)? Sign here. Big thumb. Small cross. Weak pencil. Its dull-violet wood. Return it. The illegible signature of teetering disaster.

But nothing comes. A month passes. Chin and Chilla are in fine shape and seem very fond of each other—sleep together in the nest box, cuddled up in a fluffy ball. After many tries, Lance had discovered a sound with definite chinchillan appeal, produced by pursing the lips and emitting in rapid succession several soft, moist *surpths*, as if taking sips from a straw when most of one's drink is finished and only its dregs are drained. But his parents cannot produce it—the pitch is wrong or something. And there is such an intolerable silence in Lance's room, with its battered books, and the spotty white shelves, and the old shoes, and the relatively new tennis racquet in its preposterously secure press, and a penny on the closet floor—and all this begins to undergo a prismatic dissolution, but then you tighten the screw and everything is again in focus. And presently the Bokes return to their balcony. Has he reached his goal—and if so, does he see us?

4
_____

The classical ex-mortal leans on his elbow from a flowered ledge to contemplate this earth, this toy, this teetotum gyrating on slow display in its model firmament, every feature so gay and clear—the painted oceans, and the praying woman of the Baltic, and a still of the elegant Americas caught in their trapeze act, and Australia like a baby Africa lying on its side. There may be people among my coevals who half expect their spirits to look down from heaven with a shudder and a sigh at their native planet and see it girdled with latitudes, stayed with meridians, and marked, perhaps, with the fat, black, diabolically curving arrows of global wars; or, more pleasantly, spread out before their gaze like one of those picture maps of vacational Eldorados, with a reservation Indian beating a drum here, a girl clad in shorts there, conical conifers climbing the cones of mountains, and anglers all over the place.

Actually, I suppose, my young descendant on his first night out, in the imagined silence of an inimaginable world, would have to view the surface features of our globe through the depth of its atmosphere; this would mean dust, scattered reflections, haze, and all kinds of optical pitfalls, so that continents, if they appeared at all through the varying clouds, would slip by in queer disguises, with inexplicable gleams of color and unrecognizable outlines.

But all this is a minor point. The main problem is: Will the mind of the explorer survive the shock? One tries to perceive the nature of that shock as plainly as mental safety permits. And if the mere act of imagining the matter is fraught with hideous risks, how, then, will the real pang be endured and overcome?

First of all, Lance will have to deal with the atavistic moment. Myths have become so firmly entrenched in the radiant sky that common sense is apt to shirk the task of getting at the uncommon sense behind them. Immortality must have a star to stand on if it wishes to branch and blossom and support thousands of blue-plumed angel birds all singing as sweetly as little eunuchs. Deep in the human mind, the concept of dying is synonymous with that of leaving the earth. To escape its gravity means to transcend the grave, and a man upon finding himself on another planet has really no way of proving to himself that he is not dead—that the naive old myth has not come true.

I am not concerned with the moron, the ordinary hairless ape, who takes everything in his stride; his only childhood memory is of a mule that bit him; his only consciousness of the future a vision of board and bed. What I am thinking of is the man of imagination and science, whose courage is infinite because his curiosity surpasses his courage. Nothing will keep him back. He is the ancient *curieux*, but of a hardier build, with a ruddier heart. When it comes to exploring a celestial body, his is the satisfaction of a passionate desire to feel with his own fingers, to stroke, and inspect, and smile at, and inhale, and stroke again—with that same smile of nameless, moaning, melting pleasure— the never-before-touched matter of which the celestial object is made. Any true scientist (not, of course, the fraudulent mediocrity, whose only treasure is the ignorance he hides like a bone) should be capable of experiencing that sensuous pleasure of direct and divine knowledge. He may be twenty and he may be eighty-five but without that tingle there is no science. And of that stuff Lance is made.

Straining my fancy to the utmost, I see him surmounting the panic that the ape might not experience at all. No doubt Lance may have landed in an orange-colored dust cloud somewhere in the middle of the Tharsis desert (if it is a desert) or near some purple pool— Phoenicis or Oti (if these are lakes after all). But on the other hand . . . You see, as things go in such matters, something is sure to be solved at once, terribly and irrevocably, while other things come up one by one and are puzzled out gradually. When I was a boy . . .

When I was a boy of seven or eight, I used to dream a vaguely recurrent dream set in a certain environment, which I have never been able to recognize and identify in any rational manner, though I have seen many strange lands. I am inclined to make it serve now, in order to patch up a gaping hole, a raw wound in my story. There was nothing spectacular about that environment, nothing monstrous or even odd: just a bit of noncommittal stability represented by a bit of level ground and filmed over with a bit of neutral nebulosity; in other words, the indifferent back of a view rather than its face. The nuisance of that dream was that for some reason I could not walk *around* the view to meet it on equal terms. There lurked in the mist a mass of something—mineral matter or the like—oppressively and quite meaninglessly shaped, and, in the course of my dream, I kept filling some kind of receptacle (translated as "pail") with smaller shapes (translated as "pebbles"), and my nose was bleeding but I was too impatient and excited to do anything about it. And every time I had that dream, suddenly somebody would start screaming behind me, and I awoke screaming too, thus prolonging the initial anonymous shriek, with its initial note of rising exultation, but with no meaning attached to it any more—if there *had* been a meaning. Speaking of Lance, I would like to submit that something on the lines of my dream— But the funny thing is that as I reread what I have set down, its background, the factual memory vanishes—has vanished altogether by now—and I have no means of proving to myself that there is any personal experience behind its description. What I wanted to say was that perhaps Lance and his companions, when they reached their planet, felt something akin to my dream—which is no longer mine.

5

And they were back! A horseman, clappity-clap, gallops up the cobbled street to the Bokes' house through the driving rain and shouts out the tremendous news as he stops short at the gate, near the dripping liriodendron, while the Bokes come tearing out of the house like two hystricomorphic rodents. They are back! The pilots, and the astrophysicists, and one of the naturalists, are back (the other, Denny, is dead and has been left in heaven, the old myth scoring a curious point there).

On the sixth floor of a provincial hospital, carefully hidden from newspapermen, Mr. and Mrs. Boke are told that their boy is in a little waiting room, second to the right, ready to receive them; there is something, a kind of hushed deference, about the tone of this information, as if it referred to a fairy-tale king. They will enter quietly; a nurse, a Mrs. Coover, will be there all the time. Oh, he's all right, they are told—can go home next week, as a matter of fact. However, they should not stay more than a couple of minutes, and no questions, please—just chat about something or other. *You* know. And then say you will be coming again tomorrow or day after tomorrow.

Lance, gray-robed, crop-haired, tan gone, changed, unchanged, changed, thin, nostrils stopped with absorbent cotton, sits on the edge of a couch, his hands clasped, a little embarrassed. Gets up wavily, with a beaming grimace, and sits down again. Mrs. Coover, the nurse, has blue eyes and no chin.

A ripe silence. Then Lance: "It was wonderful. Perfectly wonderful. I am going back in November."

Pause.

"I think," says Mr. Boke, "that Chilla is with child."

Quick smile, little bow of pleased acknowledgment. Then, in a narrative voice: *"Je vais dire ça en français. Nous venions d'arriver—"*

"Show them the President's letter," says Mrs. Coover.

"We had just got there," Lance continues, "and Denny was still alive, and the first thing he and I saw—"

In a sudden flutter, Nurse Coover interrupts: "No, Lance, no. No, Madam, please. No contacts, doctor's orders, *please*."

Warm temple, cold ear.

Mr. and Mrs. Boke are ushered out. They walk swiftly—although there is no hurry, no hurry whatever, down the corridor, along its shoddy, olive-and-ochre wall, the lower olive separated from the upper ochre by a continuous brown line leading to the venerable elevators. Going up (glimpse of patriarch in wheelchair). Going back in November (Lancelin). Going down (the old Bokes). There are, in that elevator, two smiling women and, the object of their bright sympathy, a girl with a baby, besides the gray-haired, bent, sullen elevator man, who stands with his back to everybody.

EASTER RAIN

T HAT day a lonely old Swiss woman named Joséphine, or Josefina
       Lvovna, as the Russian family she had once lived with for
       twelve years had dubbed her, bought half a dozen eggs, a black
brush, and two buttons of carmine watercolor. That day the apple trees
were in bloom. A cinema poster on the corner was reflected upside
down on the smooth surface of a puddle, and, in the morning, the
mountains on the far side of Lake Léman were all veiled in silky mist,
like the opaque sheets of rice paper that cover etchings in expensive
books. The mist promised a fair day, but the sun barely skimmed over
the roofs of the skewed little stone houses, over the wet wires of a toy
tram, and then dissolved once again into the haze. The day turned out
to be calm, with springtime clouds, but, toward evening, a weighty, icy
wind wafted down from the mountains, and Joséphine, on her way
home, broke into such a fit of coughing that she lost her balance for a
moment by the door, flushed crimson, and leaned on her tightly furled
umbrella, thin as a black walking stick.

It was already dark in her room. When she turned on the lamp, it illuminated her hands—thin hands with tight, glossy skin, ecchymotic
freckles, and white blotches on the fingernails.

Joséphine laid out her purchases on the table and dropped her coat
and hat on the bed. She poured some water into a glass and, putting
on a black-rimmed pince-nez that made her dark gray eyes look stern
beneath the thick funereal brows that grew together over the bridge of
her nose, began painting the eggs. For some reason the carmine watercolor would not stick. Perhaps she should have bought some kind of
chemical paint, but she did not know how to ask for it, and was too
embarrassed to explain. She thought about going to see a pharmacist
she knew—while she was at it, she could get some aspirin. She felt so

sluggish, and her eyeballs ached with fever. She wanted to sit quietly, think quietly. Today was the Russian Holy Saturday.

At one time, the peddlers on the Nevsky Prospect had sold a special kind of tongs. These tongs were very practical for fishing out the eggs from the hot, dark blue or orange liquid. But there were also the wooden spoons: They would bump lightly and compactly against the thick glass of the jars from which rose the heady steam of the dye. The eggs were then dried in piles, the red with the red, the green with the green. And they used to color them another way too, by wrapping them tightly in strips of cloth with decalcomanias tucked inside that looked like samples of wallpaper. After the boiling, when the manservant brought the huge pot back from the kitchen, what fun it was to unravel the cloth and take the speckled, marbled eggs out of the warm, damp fabric, from which rose gentle steam, a whiff of one's childhood.

The old Swiss woman felt strange remembering that, when she lived in Russia, she had been homesick, and sent long, melancholy, beautifully written letters to her friends back home about how she always felt unwanted, misunderstood. Every morning after breakfast she would go for a ride in the large open landau with her charge, Hélène. And next to the coachman's fat bottom, reminiscent of a gigantic blue pumpkin, was the hunched-over back of the old footman, all gold buttons and cockade. The only Russian words she knew were: "Coachman," "good," "fine," [*kutcher, tish-tish, nichevo* (*coachman, hush-hush, so-so,* all mispronounced.*)*]

She had left Petersburg with a dim sense of relief, just as the war was beginning. She thought that now she would delight endlessly in chatty evenings with her friends and in the coziness of her native town. But the reality turned out to be quite the opposite. Her real life—in other words, the part of life when one most keenly and deeply gets used to people and things—had passed by there, in Russia, which she had unconsciously grown to love and understand, and where God only knew what was going on now. . . . And tomorrow was Orthodox Easter.

Joséphine sighed loudly, got up, and closed the window more firmly. She looked at her watch, black on its nickel chain. She would have to do something about those eggs. They were to be a gift for the Platonovs, an elderly Russian couple recently settled in Lausanne, a town both native and foreign to her, where it was hard to breathe, where the houses were stacked at random, in disorder, helter-skelter, along the steep, angular streets.

She grew pensive, listening to the drone in her ears. Then she shook herself out of her torpor, poured a vial of purple ink into a tin can, and carefully lowered an egg into it.

The door opened softly. Her neighbor Mademoiselle Finard entered, quiet as a mouse. She was a thin little woman, a former governess herself. Her short-cropped hair was all silver. She was draped in a black shawl, iridescent with glass beads.

Joséphine, hearing her mouselike steps, awkwardly, with a newspaper, covered the can and the eggs that were drying on some blotting paper.

"What do you want? I don't like people simply coming in like that."

Mademoiselle Finard looked askance at Joséphine's anxious face and said nothing, but was deeply offended, and, without a word, left the room with the same mincing steps.

By now the eggs had turned a venomous violet. On an unpainted egg, she decided to draw the two Easter initials*, as had always been customary in Russia. The first letter, "X," she drew well, but the second she could not quite remember, and finally, instead of a "B," she drew an absurd, crooked "Я." When the ink had dried completely she wrapped the eggs in soft toilet paper and put them in her leather handbag.

But what tormenting sluggishness. . . . She wanted to lie down in bed, drink some hot coffee, and stretch out her legs. . . . She was feverish and her eyelids prickled. . . . When she went outside, the dry crackle of her cough began rising in her throat again. The streets were dark, damp, and deserted. The Platonovs lived nearby. They were seated, having tea, and Platonov, bald-pated, with a scanty beard, in a Russian serge shirt with buttons on the side, was stuffing yellow tobacco into cigarette papers when Joséphine knocked with the knob of her umbrella and entered.

"Ah, good evening, Mademoiselle."

She sat down next to them, and tactlessly, verbosely started discussing the imminent Russian Easter. She took the violet eggs out of her bag one by one. Platonov noticed the egg with the lilac letters "X Я" and burst out laughing.

"Whatever made her stick on those Jewish initials?"

His wife, a plump woman with a yellow wig and sorrowful eyes, smiled fleetingly. She started thanking Joséphine with indifference, drawing out her French vowels. Joséphine did not understand why they were laughing. She felt hot and sad. She began talking again, but she had the feeling that what she was saying was out of place, yet she could not restrain herself.

"Yes, at this moment there is no Easter in Russia. . . . Poor Russia! Oh, I remember how people used to kiss each other in the streets. And

*The Cyrillic letters X (Kh) and B (V) stand for *Khristos vorkresye*, "Christ has risen."

my little Hélène looked like an angel that day. . . . Oh, I often cry all night thinking of your wonderful country!"

The Platonovs always found these conversations unpleasant. They never discussed their lost homeland with outsiders, just as ruined rich men hide their poverty and become even haughtier and less approachable than before. Therefore, deep down, Joséphine felt that they had no love at all for Russia. Usually when she visited the Platonovs she thought that, if she only began talking of beautiful Russia with tears in her eyes, the Platonovs would suddenly burst into sobs and begin reminiscing and recounting, and that the three of them would sit like that all night reminiscing, crying, and squeezing each other's hands.

But in reality this never happened. Platonov would nod politely and indifferently with his beard, while his wife kept trying to find out where one could get some tea or soap as cheaply as possible.

Platonov began rolling his cigarettes again. His wife placed them evenly in a cardboard box. They had both intended to take a nap until it was time to leave for the Easter Vigils at the Greek church around the corner. They wanted to sit silently, to think their own thoughts, to speak only with glances and special, seemingly absent-minded smiles about their son, who had been killed in the Crimea, about Easter odds and ends, about their neighborhood church on Pochtamskaya Street. Now this chattering, sentimental old woman with her anxious dark gray eyes had come, full of sighs, and might well stay until they left the house themselves.

Joséphine fell silent, hoping avidly that she too might be asked to accompany them to church, and, afterward, to breakfast with them. She knew they had baked Russian Easter cakes the day before, and although she obviously could not eat any because she felt so feverish, still it would have been so pleasant, so warm, and so festive.

Platonov ground his teeth and, stifling a yawn, looked furtively at his wrist, at the dial under its little screen. Joséphine saw they were not going to invite her. She rose.

"You need a small rest, my dear friends, but there is something I want to say to you before I leave." And, moving close to Platonov, who also got up, she exclaimed in sonorous, fractured Russian, "Hath Christs rised!"

This was her last hope of eliciting a burst of hot, sweet tears, Easter kisses, an invitation to breakfast together. . . . But Platonov only squared his shoulders and said with a subdued laugh, "See, Mademoiselle, you pronounce Russian beautifully."

Once outside, she broke into sobs, and walked pressing her handkerchief to her eyes, swaying slightly, tapping her silken, canelike umbrella on the sidewalk. The sky was cavernous and troubled—the moon vague, the clouds like ruins. The angled feet of a curly-headed Chaplin were reflected in a puddle near a brightly lit cinema. And when Joséphine walked beneath the noisy, weeping trees beside the lake, which seemed like a wall of mist, she saw an emerald lantern glowing faintly at the edge of a small pier and something large and white clambering onto a black boat that bobbed below. She focused through her tears. An enormous old swan puffed itself up, flapped its wings, and suddenly, clumsy as a goose, waddled heavily onto the deck. The boat rocked; green circles welled over the black, oily water that merged into fog.

Joséphine pondered whether she should perhaps go to church anyway. But in Petersburg the only church she had ever gone to was the red Catholic one at the end of Morskaya Street, and she felt ashamed now to go into an Orthodox church, where she did not know when to cross herself or how one held one's fingers, and where somebody might make a comment. She felt intermittent chills. Her head filled with a confusion of rustling, of smacking trees, of black clouds, and Easter recollections: mountains of multicolored eggs, the dusky sheen of St. Isaac's. Deafened and woozy, she somehow managed to make it home and climb the stairs, banging her shoulder against the wall, and then, unsteadily, her teeth chattering, she began undressing. She felt weaker, and tumbled onto her bed with a blissful, incredulous smile.

A delirium, stormy and powerful as the surge of bells, took hold of her. Mountains of multicolored eggs scattered with rotund tapping sounds. The sun—or was it a golden-horned sheep made of creamery butter?—came tumbling through the window and began to grow, filling the room with torrid yellow. Meanwhile, the eggs scurried up and rolled down glossy little strips of wood, knocking against each other, their shells cracking, their whites streaked with crimson.

All night she lay delirious like that, and it was only the following morning that a still-offended Mademoiselle Finard came in, gasped, and ran off in panic to call a doctor.

"Lobar pneumonia, Mademoiselle."

Through the waves of delirium twinkled wallpaper flowers, the old woman's silver hair, the doctor's placid eyes—it all twinkled and dissolved. And again an agitated drone of joy engulfed her soul. The fable-blue sky was like a gigantic painted egg, bells thundered, and someone came into the room who looked like Platonov, or maybe like Hélène's father—and on entering he unfolded a newspaper, placed it on the table, and sat down nearby, glancing now at Joséphine, now at the white pages with a significant, modest, slightly cunning smile. Joséphine knew that in this paper there was some kind of wondrous news, but, try as she might, she could not decipher the Russian letters of the black headline. Her guest kept smiling and casting significant glances at her, and seemed on the very point of revealing the secret, to confirm the happiness that she foretasted—but the man slowly dissolved. Unconsciousness swept over her like a black cloud.

Then came another motley of delirious dreams: The landau rolled along the quay, Hélène lapped the hot bright color from a wooden spoon, the broad Neva sparkled expansively, and Czar Peter suddenly leapt off his bronze steed, the hooves of both its forelegs having simultaneously alighted. He approached Joséphine, and, with a smile on his green-tinted, stormy face, embraced her, kissed her on one cheek, then on the other. His lips were soft and warm, and when he brushed her cheek for the third time, she palpitated, moaning with bliss, spread out her arms, and suddenly fell silent.

Early in the morning, on the sixth day of her illness, after a final crisis, Joséphine came to her senses. A white sky shimmered brightly through the window and perpendicular rain was rustling and rippling in the gutters.

A wet branch stretched across the windowpane, and at its very end a leaf kept shuddering beneath the patter of the rain. The leaf leaned forward and let a large drop fall from the tip of its green blade. The leaf shuddered again, and again a moist ray rolled downward, then a long, bright earring dangled and dropped.

And it seemed to Joséphine as if the rainy coolness were flowing through her veins. She could not take her eyes off the streaming sky, and the pulsating, enraptured rain was so pleasant, the leaf shuddered so touchingly, that she wanted to laugh; the laughter filled her, though it was still soundless, coursing through her body, tickling her palate, and was on the very point of erupting.

To her left, in the corner, something scrabbled and sighed. Aquiver with the laughter that was mounting in her, she took her eyes off the window and turned her head. The little old woman lay facedown on the floor in her black kerchief. Her short-cropped silver hair shook angrily as she fidgeted, thrusting her hand under the chest of drawers, where her ball of wool had rolled. Black yarn stretched from the chest to the chair, where her knitting needles and a half-knitted stocking still lay.

Seeing Mademoiselle Finard's black hair, her squirming legs, her button boots, Joséphine broke out in peals of laughter, shaking as she gasped and cooed beneath her down comforter, feeling that she was resurrected, that she had returned from faraway mists of happiness, wonder, and Easter splendor.

Translated from the Russian by Dmitri Nabokov and Peter Constantine.

Notes

Following are my notes to the stories previously uncollected in English, together with Vladimir Nabokov's introductory notes to the stories collected in *A Russian Beauty and Other Stories* (1973), *Tyrants Destroyed and Other Stories* (1975), and *Details of a Sunset and Other Stories* (1976), all published by McGraw-Hill Book Company, New York, and in various translations around the world.

The notes to each story are arranged here in the order in which the stories appear in this volume; Nabokov wrote no notes for the individual stories in his first major collection in America, *Nabokov's Dozen* (Doubleday & Company, Garden City, New York, 1958); see, however, the appendix in this volume for his Bibliographical Note to that collection, along with his forewords to each collection published by McGraw-Hill.

I have tried, insofar as feasible, to establish a chronological order of composition. In those instances where only publication dates are available, they are used as a surrogate. My principal sources have been Nabokov's own notes, archive materials, and the invaluable research of Brian Boyd, Dieter Zimmer, and Michael Juliar. The reader will note occasional discrepancies in dating. Where such inconsistencies occur in Nabokov's own commentary, I have preferred not to alter the details of his texts.

Both Vladimir Nabokov and I have at times varied our systems of transliteration. The method set forth in Nabokov's translation of Alexander Pushkin's *Eugene Onegin* is probably the clearest and most logical of these variants. Except where accepted usage dictates a different form, or where Nabokov himself has digressed from that system, it is the one I have generally used.

Dmitri Nabokov

THE WOOD-SPRITE *(page 3)*

"The Wood-Sprite" *(Nezhit')* first appeared on January 7, 1921, in *Rul' (The Rudder)*, the Russian émigré newspaper in Berlin that had begun publication a little more than a month previously, and to which Nabokov would regularly contribute poems, plays, stories, translations, and chess problems. Only recently has the story been translated and published, with twelve other previously uncollected pieces, in *La Vénitienne et autres nouvelles* (Gallimard, 1990, trans. Bernard Kreise, ed. Gilles Barbedette), in *La Veneziana* (Adelphi, 1992, trans. and ed. Serena Vitale), in volumes 13 and 14 of *Vladimir Nabokov: Gesammelte Werke* (Collected Works; Rowohlt, 1989, trans. and ed. Dieter Zimmer), and in a two-volume Dutch edition (*De Bezige Bij*, 1995, 1996)—henceforth, together with the present English versions, referred to as the "current collections." While I translated most of the previously collected fifty-two stories under my father's supervision, I take full responsibility for the posthumous English translations of these thirteen.

"The Wood-Sprite" is the first story Nabokov published and one of the first he wrote. It was signed "Vladimir Sirin" (*sirin* is a bird of Russian fable as well as the modern hawk owl), the pseudonym that, in his youth, the author used for many of his works.

Nabokov's debut as a writer came when he was still a student at Trinity College, Cambridge (in May 1919 he had arrived in England with his family, abandoning Russia forever); he nurtured his passion for poetry, while also translating *Colas Breugnon*, a novella by Romain Rolland.

D.N.

RUSSIAN SPOKEN HERE   *(page 6)*

"Russian Spoken Here" (*Govoryat po-russki*) dates from 1923, most likely early in the year. It remained unpublished until the current collections.

The "Meyn Ried" mentioned in the story is Thomas Mayne Reid (1818–1883), author of adventure novels. "Mister Ulyanov" is Vladimir Ilyich Ulyanov, who entered history under the stage name V. I. Lenin. The GPU, originally known as the Cheka, and later designated by the acronyms NKVD, MVD, and KGB, was the Bolshevik political secret police. Among the books the "prisoner" was allowed to read were the *Fables* of Ivan Andreyevich Krylov (1768–1844) and *Prince Serebryaniy*, a popular historical novel by Aleksey Konstantinovich Tolstoy (1817–1875).

D.N.

SOUNDS   *(page 14)*

"Sounds" (*Zvuki*) was written in September 1923 and was published in my English translation in *The New Yorker* on August 14, 1995, and now in the current collections.

Nabokov did not resume writing stories until January 1923, two years after the publication of "The Wood-Sprite." In the interim he had finished his studies at Cambridge (in the summer of 1922). He was now living in Berlin, where his family had moved in October 1920, and where his father was assassinated on March 28, 1922. At the time he was composing "Sounds," Nabokov published two volumes of poetry and his Russian version of *Alice in Wonderland*. The story is, among other things, a transmuted evocation of a youthful love affair, almost certainly with his cousin Tatiana Evghenievna Segelkranz (the likely spelling of her military husband's name, cited incorrectly elsewhere), née Rausch, who also makes an appearance in *The Gift*.

D.N.

WINGSTROKE   *(page 25)*

"Wingstroke" (*Udar krïla*), written in October 1923, was published in *Russkoye Ekho (The Russian Echo)*, an émigré periodical in Berlin, in January 1924, and now in the current collections. Although the story is set in Zermatt, it refracts the recollection of a brief vacation Nabokov had taken in St. Moritz in December 1921, with his Cambridge friend Bobby de Calry.

We learn from a letter to his mother (who had moved to Prague late in 1923 while Nabokov remained in Berlin, where, in April 1924, he married Véra Slonim) that, in December 1924, he sent her a "continuation" of "Wingstroke," presumably in published form. To date, no trace of this piece has been found. My English translation was published, with one differently worded sentence, under the title "Wingbeat" in *The Yale Review*, vol. 80, nos. 1 and 2, April 1992.

D.N.

GODS *(page 44)*

Nabokov wrote "Gods" *(Bogi)* in October 1923. The story remained unpublished until the current collections.

Nabokov was working on what is probably his most important play, the five-act *Traghediya Gospodina Morna (The Tragedy of Mr. Morn)*, soon to be published for the first time by Ardis Press.

D.N.

A MATTER OF CHANCE *(page 51)*

"Sluchaynost'," one of my earliest tales, written at the beginning of 1924, in the last afterglow of my bachelor life, was rejected by the Berlin émigré daily *Rul'* ("We don't print anecdotes about cocainists," said the editor, in exactly the same tone of voice in which, thirty years later, Ross of *The New Yorker* was to say, "We don't print acrostics," when rejecting "The Vane Sisters") and sent, with the assistance of a good friend, and a remarkable writer, Ivan Lukash, to the Rigan *Segodnya*, a more eclectic émigré organ, which published it on June 22, 1924. I would never have traced it again had it not been rediscovered by Andrew Field a few years ago.

V.N., *Tyrants Destroyed and Other Stories*, 1975

THE SEAPORT *(page 60)*

"The Seaport" *(Port)*, written during the first months of 1924, appeared in *Rul'* on December 24 of the same year, and now in the current collections. This story was later published, with a handful of minor changes, in *Vozvrashchenie Chorba* (*The Return of Chorb*, Slovo, Berlin, 1930), Nabokov's first collection of short stories, which also included twenty-four poems. "The Seaport" has, in part, an autobiographical genesis: in July 1923, during a visit to Marseilles, Nabokov was fascinated by a Russian restaurant that he visited numerous times and where, among other things, two Russian sailors proposed that he embark for Indochina.

D.N.

REVENGE *(page 67)*

"Revenge" *(Mest')*, written in the spring of 1924, appeared in *Russkoye Ekho* on April 20, 1924, and now in the current collections.

D.N.

BENEFICENCE *(page 74)*

"Beneficence" *(Blagost')*, written in March 1924, was published in *Rul'* on April 28, 1924. Subsequently it appeared in *The Return of Chorb*, and now in the current collections.

D.N.

DETAILS OF A SUNSET *(page 79)*

I doubt very much that I was responsible for the odious title *("Katastrofa")* inflicted upon this story. It was written in June 1924 in Berlin and sold to the Riga émigré daily *Segodnya*, where it appeared on July 13 of that year. Still under that label, and no doubt with my indolent blessings, it was included in the collection *Soglyadatay*, Slovo, Berlin, 1930.

I have now given it a new title, one that has the triple advantage of corresponding to the thematic background of the story, of being sure to puzzle such readers as "skip descriptions," and of infuriating reviewers.

V.N., *Details of a Sunset and Other Stories*, 1976

THE THUNDERSTORM *(page 86)*

Thunder is *grom* in Russian, storm is *burya*, and thunderstorm is *groza*, a grand little word, with that blue zigzag in the middle.

"Groza," written in Berlin sometime in the summer of 1924, was published in August 1924 in the émigré daily *Rul'* and collected in the *Vozvrashchenie Chorba* volume, Slovo, Berlin, 1930.

V.N., *Details of a Sunset and Other Stories*, 1976

LA VENEZIANA *(page 90)*

"La Veneziana" *(Venetsianka)* was written mainly in September 1924; the manuscript is dated October 5 of that year. The story remained unpublished and untranslated until the current collections, becoming the title story for the French and Italian volumes. The recently completed English version was printed separately in a special edition celebrating the sixtieth birthday of Penguin, England, in 1995.

The painting by Sebastiano (Luciani) del Piombo (ca. 1485–1547) that almost certainly inspired the canvas described in the story is *Giovane romana detta Dorotea*, ca. 1512. Nabokov may have seen it at the Kaiser-Friedrich Museum (now the Staatliche Museen) in Berlin. Possibly the painter's birthplace—Venice—induced Nabokov to transform the lady from *"Romana"* to *"Veneziana."* And it is almost certainly the same artist's *Ritratto di donna*, which is in the Earl of Rador's collection at Longford Castle, to which Nabokov alludes in his brief mention of "Lord Northwick from London, the owner . . . of another painting by the same del Piombo."

D.N.

BACHMANN *(page 116)*

"Bakhman" was written in Berlin in October 1924. It was serialized in *Rul'*, November 2 and 4 of that year, and included in my *Vozvrashchenie Chorba* collection of short stories, Slovo, Berlin, 1930. I am told that a pianist existed with some of my invented musician's peculiar traits. In certain other respects he is related to Luzhin, the chess player of *The Defense* (*Zashchita Luzhina*, 1930), G. P. Putnam's Sons, New York, 1964.

V.N., *Tyrants Destroyed and Other Stories*, 1975

THE DRAGON *(page 125)*

"The Dragon" *(Drakon)*, written in November 1924, was published in a French translation by Vladimir Sikorsky, and now in the current collections.

D.N.

CHRISTMAS *(page 131)*

"Rozhdestvo" was written in Berlin at the end of 1924, published in *Rul'* in two installments, January 6 and 8, 1925, and collected in *Vozvrashchenie Chorba*, Slovo, Berlin, 1930. It oddly resembles the type of chess problem called "selfmate."

V.N., *Details of a Sunset and Other Stories*, 1976

A LETTER THAT NEVER REACHED RUSSIA *(page 137)*

Sometime in 1924, in émigré Berlin, I had begun a novel tentatively entitled *Happiness (Schastie)*, some important elements of which were to be reslanted in *Mashen'ka*, written in the spring of 1925 (published by Slovo, Berlin, in 1926, translated into English under the title of *Mary* in 1970, McGraw-Hill, New York, and reprinted in Russian from the original text, by Ardis and McGraw-Hill, in 1974). Around Christmas 1924, I had two chapters of *Schastie* ready but then, for some forgotten but no doubt excellent reason, I scrapped chapter 1 and most of 2. What I kept was a fragment representing a letter written in Berlin to my heroine who had remained in Russia. This appeared in *Rul'* (Berlin, January 29, 1925) as *"Pis'mo* (Letter) *v Rossiyu,"* and was collected in *Vozvrashchenie Chorba*, in Berlin, 1930. A literal rendering of the title would have been ambiguous and therefore had to be changed.

V.N., *Details of a Sunset and Other Stories*, 1976

THE FIGHT *(page 141)*

"The Fight" *(Draka)* appeared in *Rul'* on September 26, 1925; in the current collections; in a French translation by Gilles Barbedette; and in my English translation in *The New Yorker* on February 18, 1985.

D.N.

THE RETURN OF CHORB *(page 147)*

First published in two issues of the Russian émigré *Rul'* (Berlin), November 12 and 13, 1925. Reprinted in the collection *Vozvrashchenie Chorba*, Slovo, Berlin, 1930.

An English version by Gleb Struve ("The Return of Tchorb" by Vladimir Sirin) appeared in the anthology *This Quarter* (vol. 4, no. 4, June 1932), published in Paris by Edw. W. Titus. After rereading that version forty years later I was sorry to find it too tame in style and too inaccurate in sense for my present purpose. I have retranslated the story completely in collaboration with my son.

It was written not long after my novel *Mashen'ka (Mary)* was finished and is a good example of my early constructions. The place is a small town in Germany half a century ago. I notice that the road from Nice to Grasse where I imagined poor Mrs. Chorb walking was still unpaved and chalky with dust around 1920. I have skipped her mother's ponderous name and patronymic "Varvara Klimovna," which would have meant nothing to my Anglo-American readers.

V.N., *Details of a Sunset and Other Stories*, 1976

A GUIDE TO BERLIN *(page 155)*

Written in December 1925 in Berlin, *Putevoditel' po Berlinu* was published in *Rul'*, December 24, 1925, and collected in *Vozvrashchenie Chorba*, Slovo, Berlin, 1930.

Despite its simple appearance, this "Guide" is one of my trickiest pieces. Its translation has caused my son and me a tremendous amount of healthy trouble. Two or three scattered phrases have been added for the sake of factual clarity.

V.N., *Details of a Sunset and Other Stories*, 1976

A NURSERY TALE *(page 161)*

"A Nursery Tale" *(Skazka)* was written in Berlin in late May or early June 1926, and serialized in the émigré daily *Rul'* (Berlin), in the issues of June 27 and 29 of that year. It was reprinted in my *Vozvrashchenie Chorba* collection, Slovo, Berlin, 1930.

A rather artificial affair, composed a little hastily, with more concern for the tricky plot than for imagery and good taste, it required some revamping here and there in the English version. Young Erwin's harem, however, has remained intact. I had not reread my *"Skazka"* since 1930 and, when working now at its translation, was eerily startled to meet a somewhat decrepit but unmistakable Humbert escorting his nymphet in the story I wrote almost half a century ago.

V.N., *Tyrants Destroyed and Other Stories*, 1975

TERROR *(page 173)*

"Uzhas" was written in Berlin, around 1926, one of the happiest years of my life. The *Sovremennya Zapiski*, the Paris émigré magazine, published it in 1927 and it was included in the first of my three collections of Russian stories, *Vozvrashchenie Chorba*, Slovo, Berlin, 1930. It preceded Sartre's *La Nausée*, with which it shares certain shades of thought, and none of that novel's fatal defects, by at least a dozen years.

V.N., *Tyrants Destroyed and Other Stories*, 1975

RAZOR   *(page 179)*

"Razor" *(Britva)* first appeared in *Rul'* on September 16, 1926. *Mashen'ka (Mary)*, Nabokov's first novel, would be published approximately one month later. It was printed, in a French translation by Laurence Doll, in the introductory volume of the Dutch "Nabokov Library" (De Bezige Bij, 1991), and now in the current collections.

D.N.

THE PASSENGER   *(page 183)*

"Passazhir" was written in early 1927 in Berlin, published in *Rul'*, Berlin, March 6, 1927, and included in the collection *Vozvrashchenie Chorba*, by V. Sirin, Slovo, Berlin, 1930. An English translation by Gleb Struve appeared in *Lovat Dickson's Magazine*, edited by P. Gilchrist Thompson (with my name on the cover reading V. Nobokov [*sic*]-Sirin), vol. 2, no. 6, London, June 1934. It was reprinted in *A Century of Russian Prose and Verse from Pushkin to Nabokov*, edited by O. R. and R. P. Hughes and G. Struve, with the original *en regard*, New York, Harcourt, Brace, 1967. I was unable to use Struve's version in this volume for the same reasons that made me forgo his "Tchorb's Return" (see Introduction to it).

The "writer" in the story is not a self-portrait but the generalized image of a middlebrow author. The "critic," however, is a friendly sketch of a fellow émigré, Yuliy Ayhenvald, the well-known literary critic (1872–1928). Readers of the time recognized his precise, delicate little gestures and his fondness for playing with euphonically twinned phrases in his literary comments. By the end of the story everybody seems to have forgotten about the burnt match in the wineglass—something I would not have allowed to happen today.

V.N., *Details of a Sunset and Other Stories*, 1976

THE DOORBELL   *(page 189)*

The reader will be sorry to learn that the exact date of the publication of this story ["The Doorbell" *(Zvonok)*] has not been established. It certainly appeared in *Rul'*, Berlin, probably in 1927, and was republished in the *Vozvrashchenie Chorba* collection, Slovo, Berlin, 1930.

V.N., *Details of a Sunset and Other Stories*, 1976

AN AFFAIR OF HONOR   *(page 199)*

"An Affair of Honor" appeared under the title *"Podlets"* (The Cur), in the émigré daily *Rul'*, Berlin, around 1927, and was included in my first collection, *Vozvrashchenie Chorba*, Slovo, Berlin, 1930. The present translation was published in *The New Yorker*, September 3, 1966, and was included in *Nabokov's Quartet*, Phaedra, New York, 1966.

The story renders in a drab expatriate setting a belated variation on the romantic theme whose decline started with Chekhov's magnificent novella *Single Combat* (1891).

V.N., *A Russian Beauty and Other Stories*, 1973

THE CHRISTMAS STORY   *(page 222)*

"The Christmas Story" *(Rozhdestvenskiy rasskaz)* appeared in *Rul'*, December 25, 1928, and now in the current collections. In September 1928 Nabokov had published *Korol', dama, valet (King, Queen, Knave)*.

The story mentions several writers: the peasant-born Neverov (the pseudonym of Aleksandr Skobelev, 1886–1923); the "social realist" Maksim Gorky (1868–1936); the "populist" Vladimir Korolenko (1853–1921); the "decadent" Leonid Andreyev (1871–1919); and the "neo-realist" Evgeniy Chirikov (1864–1923).

D.N.

THE POTATO ELF   *(page 228)*

This is the first faithful translation of *"Kartofel'nyy el'f,"* written in 1929 in Berlin, published there in the émigré daily *Rul'* (December 15, 17, 18, and 19, 1929) and included in *Vozvrashchenie Chorba*, Slovo, Berlin, 1930, a collection of my stories. A very different English version (by Serge Bertenson and Irene Kosinska), full of mistakes and omissions, appeared in *Esquire*, December 1939, and has been reprinted in an anthology (*The Single Voice*, Collier, London, 1969).

Although I never intended the story to suggest a screenplay or to fire a scriptwriter's fancy, its structure and recurrent pictorial details do have a cinematic slant. Its deliberate introduction results in certain conventional rhythms—or in a pastiche of such rhythms. I do not believe, however, that my little man can move even the most lachrymose human-interest fiend, and this redeems the matter.

Another aspect separating "The Potato Elf" from the rest of my short stories is its British setting. One cannot rule out thematic automatism in such cases, yet on the other hand this curious exoticism (as being different from the more familiar Berlin background of my other stories) gives the thing an artificial brightness which is none too displeasing; but all in all it is not my favorite piece, and if I include it in this collection it is only because the act of retranslating it properly is a precious personal victory that seldom falls to a betrayed author's lot.

V.N., *A Russian Beauty and Other Stories*, 1973

The story was actually first published in *Russkoye Ekho* in April, 1924. It was reprinted in *Rul'* in 1929.

D.N.

THE AURELIAN   *(page 248)*

"The Aurelian" (1930) is from *Nabokov's Dozen*, 1958 (see Appendix).

A DASHING FELLOW   *(page 259)*

"A Dashing Fellow," *"Khvat"* in Russian, was first published in the early 1930s. The two leading émigré papers, *Rul'* (Berlin) and *Poslednie Novosti* (Paris), rejected it as improper and brutal. It appeared in *Segodnya* (Riga), exact date to be settled, and in 1938 was included in my collection of short stories *Soglyadatay* (Russkiya Zapiski, Paris). The present translation appeared in *Playboy* for December 1971.

V.N., *A Russian Beauty and Other Stories*, 1973

A BAD DAY *(page 268)*

"A Bad Day" (entitled in Russian *"Obida,"* the lexical meaning of which is "offense," "mortification," etc.) was written in Berlin in the summer of 1931. It appeared in the émigré daily *Poslednie Novosti* (Paris, July 12, 1931) and was included in my collection *Soglyadatay* (Paris, 1938), with a dedication to Ivan Bunin. The little boy of the story, though living in much the same surroundings as those of my own childhood, differs in several ways from my remembered self, which is really split here among three lads, Peter, Vladimir, and Vasiliy.

V.N., *Details of a Sunset and Other Stories*, 1976

THE VISIT TO THE MUSEUM *(page 277)*

"The Visit to the Museum" *(Poseshchenie muzeya)* appeared in the émigré review *Sovremennyya Zapiski*, LXVIII, Paris, 1939, and in my collection *Vesna v Fialte*, Chekhov Publishing House, New York, 1959. The present English translation came out in *Esquire*, March 1963, and was included in *Nabokov's Quartet*, Phaedra, New York, 1966.

One explanatory note may be welcomed by non-Russian readers. At one point the unfortunate narrator notices a shop sign and realizes he is not in the Russia of his past, but in the Russia of the Soviets. What gives that shop sign away is the absence of the letter that used to decorate the end of a word after a consonant in old Russia but is omitted in the reformed orthography adopted by the Soviets today.

V.N., *A Russian Beauty and Other Stories*, 1973

A BUSY MAN *(page 286)*

The Russian original *("Zanyatoy chelovek")*, written in Berlin between September 17 and 26, 1931, appeared on October 20 in the émigré daily *Poslednie Novosti*, Paris, and was included in the collection *Soglyadatay*, Russkiya Zapiski, Paris, 1938.

V.N., *Details of a Sunset and Other Stories*, 1976

TERRA INCOGNITA *(page 297)*

The Russian original of "Terra Incognita" appeared under the same title in *Poslednie Novosti*, Paris, November 22, 1931, and was reprinted in my collection *Soglyadatay*, Paris, 1938. The present English translation was published in *The New Yorker*, May 18, 1963.

V.N., *A Russian Beauty and Other Stories*, 1973

THE REUNION *(page 304)*

Written in Berlin in December 1931, published in January 1932 under the title *"Vstrecha" (Meeting)* in the émigré daily *Poslednie Novosti*, Paris, and collected in *Soglyadatay*, Russkiya Zapiski, Paris, 1938.

V.N., *Details of a Sunset and Other Stories*, 1976

LIPS TO LIPS *(page 312)*

Mark Aldanov, who was closer than I to the *Poslednie Novosti* (with which I conducted a lively feud throughout the 1930s), informed me, sometime in 1931 or 1932, that at the last moment, this story, "Lips to Lips" *(Usta k ustam)*, which finally had been accepted for publication, would not be printed after all. *"Razbili nabor"* ("They broke up the type"), my friend muttered gloomily. It was published only in 1956, by the Chekhov Publishing House, New York, in my collection *Vesna v Fialte*, by which time everybody who might have been suspected of remotely resembling the characters in the story was safely and heirlessly dead. *Esquire* published the present translation in its September 1971 issue.

V.N., *A Russian Beauty and Other Stories*, 1973

ORACHE *(page 325)*

"Lebeda" was first published in *Poslednie Novosti*, Paris, January 31, 1932; collected in *Soglyadatay*, Russkiya Zapiski, Paris, 1938. *Lebeda* is the plant *Atriplex*. Its English name, orache, by a miraculous coincidence, renders in its written form the *"ili beda,"* "or ache," suggested by the Russian title. Through the rearranged patterns of the story, readers of my *Speak, Memory* will recognize many details of the final section of chapter 9, *Speak, Memory*, Putnam's, New York, 1966. Amid the mosaic of fiction there are some real memories not represented in *Speak, Memory*, such as the passages about the teacher "Berezovski" (Berezin, a popular geographer of the day), including the fight with the school bully. The place is St. Petersburg, the time around 1910.

V.N., *Details of a Sunset and Other Stories*, 1976

MUSIC *(page 332)*

"Muzyka," a trifle singularly popular with translators, was written at the beginning of 1932, in Berlin. It appeared in the Paris émigré daily *Poslednie Novosti* (March 27, 1932) and in the collection of my stories *Soglyadatay*, published by the Russkiya Zapiski firm, in Paris, 1938.

V.N., *Tyrants Destroyed and Other Stories*, 1975

PERFECTION *(page 338)*

"Sovershenstvo" was written in Berlin in June 1932. It appeared in the Paris daily *Poslednie Novosti* (July 3, 1932) and was included in my collection *Soglyadatay*, Paris, 1938. Although I did tutor boys in my years of expatriation, I disclaim any other resemblance between myself and Ivanov.

V.N., *Tyrants Destroyed and Other Stories*, 1975

THE ADMIRALTY SPIRE *(page 348)*

Although various details of the narrator's love affair match in one way or another those found in my autobiographical works, it should be firmly borne in mind that the "Katya" of the present story is an invented girl. The *"Admiralteyskaya igla"* was written in May 1933, in Berlin, and serialized in *Poslednie Novosti*, Paris, in the issues of June 4 and 5 of that year. It was collected in *Vesna v Fialte*, Chekhov Publishing House, New York, 1956.

V.N., *Tyrants Destroyed and Other Stories*, 1975

THE LEONARDO   *(page 358)*

"The Leonardo" *(Korolyok)* was composed in Berlin, on the piney banks of the Grunewald Lake, in the summer of 1933. First published in *Poslednie Novosti*, Paris, July 23 and 24, 1933. Collected in *Vesna v Fialte*, New York, 1956.

Korolyok (literally: kinglet) is, or is supposed to be, a Russian cant term for "counterfeiter." I am deeply indebted to Professor Stephen Jan Parker for suggesting a corresponding American underground slang word which delightfully glitters with the kingly gold dust of the Old Master's name. Hitler's grotesque and ferocious shadow was falling on Germany at the time I imagined those two brutes and my poor Romantovski.

The English translation appeared in *Vogue*, April, 1973.

V.N., *A Russian Beauty and Other Stories*, 1973

IN MEMORY OF L. I. SHIGAEV   *(page 368)*

Andrew Field in his bibliography of my works says he has not been able to ascertain the exact date for *"Pamyati L. I. Shigaeva,"* written in the early 1930s in Berlin, and published probably in *Poslednie Novosti*. I am practically sure that I wrote it in the beginning of 1934. My wife and I were sharing with her cousin, Anna Feigin, the latter's charming flat in a corner house (Number 22) of Nestorstrasse, Berlin, Grunewald (where *Invitation to a Beheading* and most of *The Gift* were composed). The rather attractive, small devils in the story belong to a subspecies described there for the first time.

V.N., *Tyrants Destroyed and Other Stories*, 1975

THE CIRCLE   *(page 375)*

By the middle of 1936, not long before leaving Berlin forever and finishing *Dar (The Gift)* in France, I must have completed at least four-fifths of its last chapter when at some point a small satellite separated itself from the main body of the novel and started to revolve around it. Psychologically, the separation may have been sparked either by the mention of Tanya's baby in her brother's letter or by his recalling the village schoolmaster in a doomful dream. Technically, the circle which the present corollary describes (its last sentence existing implicitly before its first one) belongs to the same serpent-biting-its-tail type as the circular structure of the fourth chapter in *Dar* (or, for that matter, *Finnegans Wake*, which it preceded). A knowledge of the novel is not required for the enjoyment of the corollary which has its own orbit and colored fire, but some practical help may be derived from the reader's knowing that the action of *The Gift* starts on April 1, 1926, and ends on June 29, 1929 (spanning three years in the life of Fyodor Godunov-Cherdyntsev, a young émigré in Berlin); that his sister's marriage takes place in Paris at the end of 1926; and that her daughter is born three years later, and is only seven in June 1936, and not "around ten," as Innokentiy, the schoolmaster's son, is permitted to assume (behind the author's back) when he visits Paris in "The Circle." It may be added that the story will produce upon readers who are familiar with the novel a delightful effect of oblique recognition, of shifting shades enriched with new sense, owing to the world's being seen not through the eyes of Fyodor, but through those of an outsider less close to him than to old Russia's idealistic radicals (who, let it be said in passing, were to loathe Bolshevist tyranny as much as liberal aristocrats did).

"Krug" was published in 1936, in Paris, but the exact date and periodical (presumably, *Poslednie Novosti*) have not yet been established in bibliographic retrospect. It was reprinted twenty years later in the collection of my short stories *Vesna v Fialte*, Chekhov Publishing House, New York, 1956.

V.N., A Russian Beauty and Other Stories, 1973

A RUSSIAN BEAUTY   *(page 385)*

"A Russian Beauty" *(Krasavitsa)* is an amusing miniature, with an unexpected solution. The original text appeared in the émigré daily *Poslednie Novosti*, Paris, August 18, 1934, and was included in *Soglyadatay*, the collection of the author's stories published by Russkiya Zapiski, Paris, 1938. The English translation appeared in *Esquire* in April, 1973.

V.N., A Russian Beauty and Other Stories, 1973

BREAKING THE NEWS   *(page 390)*

"Breaking the News" appeared under the title *"Opoveshchenie"* (Notification) in an émigré periodical around 1935 and was included in my collection *Soglyadatay* (Russkiya Zapiski, Paris, 1938).

The milieu and the theme both correspond to those of "Signs and Symbols," written ten years later in English (see *The New Yorker*, May 15, 1948, and *Nabokov's Dozen*, Doubleday, 1958).

V.N., A Russian Beauty and Other Stories, 1973

TORPID SMOKE   *(page 396)*

"Torpid Smoke" *(Tyazhyolyy dym)* appeared in the daily *Poslednie Novosti*, Paris, March 3, 1935, and was reprinted in *Vesna v Fialte*, New York, 1956. The present translation has been published in *Triquarterly*, no. 27, Spring 1973. In two or three passages brief phrases have been introduced to elucidate points of habitus and locale, unfamiliar today not only to foreign readers but to the incurious grandchildren of the Russians who fled to western Europe in the first three or four years after the Bolshevist Revolution; otherwise the translation is acrobatically faithful—beginning with the title, which in a coarse lexical rendering that did not take familiar associations into account would read "Heavy Smoke."

The story belongs to that portion of my short fiction which refers to émigré life in Berlin between 1920 and the late thirties. Seekers of biographical tidbits should be warned that my main delight in composing those things was to invent ruthlessly assortments of exiles who in character, class, exterior features, and so forth were utterly unlike any of the Nabokovs. The only two affinities here between author and hero are that both wrote Russian verse and that I had lived at one time or another in the same kind of lugubrious Berlin apartment as he. Only very poor readers (or perhaps some exceptionally good ones) will scold me for not letting them into its parlor.

V.N., A Russian Beauty and Other Stories, 1973

RECRUITING *(page 401)*

"Nabor" was written in the summer of 1935 in Berlin. It appeared on August 18 of that year in *Poslednie Novosti*, Paris, and was included twenty-one years later in my *Vesna v Fialte* collection, published by the Chekhov Publishing House in New York.

V.N., *Tyrants Destroyed and Other Stories*, 1975

A SLICE OF LIFE *(page 406)*

The original title of this entertaining tale is *"Sluchay in zhizni."* The first word means "occurrence," or "case," and the last two "from life." The combination has a deliberately commonplace, newspaper nuance in Russian which is lost in a lexical version. The present formula is truer in English tone, especially as it fits so well my man's primitive jargon (hear his barroom maunder just before the fracas).

What was your purpose, sir, in penning this story, forty years ago in Berlin? Well, I did pen it (for I never learned to type and the long reign of the 3B pencil, capped with an eraser, was to start much later—in parked motorcars and motels); but I had never any "purpose" in mind when writing stories—for myself, my wife, and half a dozen dear dead chuckling friends. It was first published in *Poslednie Novosti*, an émigré daily in Paris, on September 22, 1935, and collected three years later in *Soglyadatay*, Russkiya Zapiski (Annales Russes, 51, rue de Turbigo, Paris, a legendary address).

V.N., *Details of a Sunset and Other Stories*, 1976

SPRING IN FIALTA *(page 413)*

"Spring in Fialta" is from *Nabokov's Dozen*, 1958 (see Appendix).

CLOUD, CASTLE, LAKE *(page 430)*

"Cloud, Castle, Lake" is from *Nabokov's Dozen*, 1958 (see Appendix).

TYRANTS DESTROYED *(page 438)*

"Istreblenie tiranov" was written in Mentone in spring or early summer 1938. It appeared in the *Russkiya Zapiski*, Paris, August 1938, and in my *Vesna v Fialte* collection of short stories, Chekhov Publishing House, New York, 1956. Hitler, Lenin, and Stalin dispute my tyrant's throne in this story—and meet again in *Bend Sinister*, 1947, with a fifth toad. The destruction is thus complete.

V.N., *Tyrants Destroyed and Other Stories*, 1975

LIK *(page 461)*

"Lik" was published in the émigré review *Russkiya Zapiski*, Paris, February 1939, and in my third Russian collection (*Vesna v Fialtre*, Chekhov Publishing House, New York, 1956). *"Lik"* reflects the miragy Riviera surroundings among which I composed it and attempts to create the impression of a stage performance engulfing

a neurotic performer, though not quite in the way that the trapped actor expected when dreaming of such an experience.

The present English translation appeared first in *The New Yorker*, October 10, 1964, and was included in *Nabokov's Quartet*, Phaedra Publishers, New York, 1966.

V.N., *Tyrants Destroyed and Other Stories*, 1975

MADEMOISELLE O   *(page 480)*

"Mademoiselle O" is from *Nabokov's Dozen*, 1958 (see Appendix).

VASILIY SHISHKOV   *(page 494)*

To relieve the dreariness of life in Paris at the end of 1939 (about six months later I was to migrate to America) I decided one day to play an innocent joke on the most famous of émigré critics, George Adamovich (who used to condemn my stuff as regularly as I did the verse of his disciples) by publishing in one of the two leading magazines a poem signed with a new pen name, so as to see what he would say, about that freshly emerged author, in the weekly literary column he contributed to the Paris émigré daily *Poslednie Novosti*. Here is the poem, as translated by me in 1970 (*Poems and Problems*, McGraw-Hill, New York):

THE POETS

> *From room to hallway a candle passes*
> *and is extinguished. Its imprint swims in one's eyes,*
> *until, among the blue-black branches,*
> *a starless night its contours finds.*
>
> *It is time, we are going away: still youthful,*
> *with a list of dreams not yet dreamt,*
> *with the last, hardly visible radiance of Russia*
> *on the phosphorent rhymes of our last verse.*
>
> *And yet we did know—didn't we?—inspiration,*
> *we would live, it seemed, and our books would grow*
> *but the kithless muses at last have destroyed us,*
> *and it is time now for us to go.*
>
> *And this not because we're afraid of offending*
> *with our freedom good people; simply, it's time*
> *for us to depart—and besides we prefer not*
> *to see what lies hidden from other eyes;*
>
> *not to see all this world's enchantment and torment,*
> *the casement that catches a sunbeam afar,*
> *humble somnambulists in soldier's uniform,*
> *the lofty sky, the attentive clouds;*
>
> *the beauty, the look of reproach; the young children*
> *who play hide-and-seek inside and around*
> *the latrine that revolves in the summer twilight;*
> *the sunset's beauty, its look of reproach;*

all that weighs upon one, entwines one, wounds one;
an electric sign's tears on the opposite bank;
through the mist the stream of its emeralds running;
all the things that already I cannot express.

In a moment we'll pass across the world's threshold
into a region—name it as you please:
wilderness, death, disavowal of language,
or maybe simpler: the silence of love;

the silence of a distant cartway, its furrow,
beneath the foam of flowers concealed;
my silent country (the love that is hopeless);
the silent sheet lightning, the silent seed.

Signed: Vasiliy Shishkov

The Russian original appeared in October or November 1939 in the *Russkiya Zapiski*, if I remember correctly, and was acclaimed by Adamovich in his review of that issue with quite exceptional enthusiasm. ("At last a great poet has been born in our midst," etc.—I quote from memory, but I believe a bibliographer is in the process of tracking down this item.) I could not resist elaborating the fun and, shortly after the eulogy appeared, I published in the same *Poslednie Novosti* (December 1939? Here again the precise date eludes me) my prose piece "Vasiliy Shishkov" (collected in *Vesna v Fialte*, New York, 1956), which could be regarded, according to the émigré reader's degree of acumen, either as an actual occurrence involving a real person called Shishkov, or as a tongue-in-cheek story about the strange case of one poet dissolving in another. Adamovich refused at first to believe eager friends and foes who drew his attention to my having invented Shishkov; finally, he gave in and explained in his next essay that I "was a sufficiently skillful parodist to mimic genius." I fervently wish all critics to be as generous as he. I met him, briefly, only twice; but many old literati have spoken a lot, on the occasion of his recent death, about his kindliness and penetrativeness. He had really only two passions in life: Russian poetry and French sailors.

V.N., *Tyrants Destroyed and Other Stories*, 1975

ULTIMA THULE and SOLUS REX (pages 500 and 523)

The winter of 1939–40 was my last season of Russian prose writing. In spring I left for America, where I was to spend twenty years in a row writing fiction solely in English. Among the works of those farewell months in Paris was a novel which I did not complete before my departure, and to which I never went back. Except for two chapters and a few notes, I destroyed the unfinished thing. Chapter 1, entitled "Ultima Thule," appeared in 1942 (*Novyy Zhurnal*, vol. 1, New York). It had been preceded by the publication of chapter 2, "Solus Rex," in early 1940 (*Sovremennyya Zapiski*, vol. 70, Paris). The present translation, made in February 1971 by my son with my collaboration, is scrupulously faithful to the original text, including the restoration of a scene that had been marked in the *Sovremennyya Zapiski* by suspension points.

Perhaps, had I finished my book, readers would not have been left wondering about a few things: was Falter a quack? Was he a true seer? Was he a medium whom the narrator's dead wife might have been using to come through with the blurry outline of a phrase which her husband did or did not recognize? Be that as it may, one thing is clear enough. In the course of evolving an imaginary country (which at first merely diverted him from his grief, but then grew into a self-contained artistic obsession), the widower becomes so engrossed in Thule that the latter starts to develop its own reality. Sineusov mentions in chapter 1 that he is moving from the Riviera to his former apartment in Paris; actually, he moves into a bleak palace on a remote northern island. His art helps him to resurrect his wife in the disguise of Queen Belinda, a pathetic act which does not let him triumph over death even in the world of free fancy. In chapter 3 she was to die again, killed by a bomb meant for her husband, on the new bridge across the Egel, a few minutes after returning from the Riviera. That is about all I can make out through the dust and debris of my old fancies.

A word about K. The translators had some difficulty about that designation because the Russian for "king," *korol*, is abbreviated as "Kr" in the sense it is used here, which sense can be rendered only by "K" in English. To put it rather neatly, my "K" refers to a chessman, not to a Czech. As to the title of the fragment, let me quote Blackburne, *Terms & Themes of Chess Problems* (London, 1907): "If the King is the only Black man on the board, the problem is said to be of the *'Solus Rex'* variety."

Prince Adulf, whose physical aspect I imagined, for some reason, as resembling that of S. P. Diaghilev (1872–1929), remains one of my favorite characters in the private museum of stuffed people that every grateful writer has somewhere on the premises. I do not remember the details of poor Adulf's death, except that he was dispatched, in some horrible, clumsy manner, by Sien and his companions, exactly five years before the inauguration of the Egel bridge.

Freudians are no longer around, I understand, so I do not need to warn them not to touch my circles with their symbols. The good reader, on the other hand, will certainly distinguish garbled English echoes of this last Russian novel of mine in *Bend Sinister* (1947) and, especially, *Pale Fire* (1962); I find those echoes a little annoying, but what really makes me regret its noncompletion is that it promised to differ radically, by the quality of its coloration, by the amplitude of its style, by something undefinable about its powerful underflow, from all my other works in Russian. The present translation of "Ultima Thule" appeared in *The New Yorker*, April 7, 1973.

V.N., *A Russian Beauty and Other Stories*, 1973

THE ASSISTANT PRODUCER *(page 546)*

"The Assistant Producer" is from *Nabokov's Dozen*, 1958 (see Appendix).

"THAT IN ALEPPO ONCE . . ." *(page 560)*

" 'That in Aleppo Once . . .' " is from *Nabokov's Dozen*, 1958 (see Appendix).

A FORGOTTEN POET *(page 569)*

"A Forgotten Poet" is from *Nabokov's Dozen*, 1958 (see Appendix).

TIME AND EBB *(page 580)*

"Time and Ebb" is from *Nabokov's Dozen*, 1958 (see Appendix).

CONVERSATION PIECE, 1945 *(page 587)*

"Conversation Piece, 1945" is from *Nabokov's Dozen*, 1958 (see Appendix).

SIGNS AND SYMBOLS *(page 598)*

"Signs and Symbols" is from *Nabokov's Dozen*, 1958 (see Appendix).

FIRST LOVE *(page 604)*

"First Love" is from *Nabokov's Dozen*, 1958 (see Appendix).

SCENES FROM THE LIFE OF A DOUBLE MONSTER
(page 612)

"Scenes from the Life of a Double Monster" is from *Nabokov's Dozen*, 1958 (see Appendix).

THE VANE SISTERS *(page 619)*

Written in Ithaca, New York, in February 1951. First published in the *Hudson Review*, New York, Winter 1959, and in *Encounter*, London, March 1959. Reprinted in the collection *Nabokov's Quartet*, Phaedra, New York, 1966.

In this story the narrator is supposed to be unaware that his last paragraph has been used acrostically by two dead girls to assert their mysterious participation in the story. This particular trick can be tried only once in a thousand years of fiction. Whether it has come off is another question.

V.N., *Tyrants Destroyed and Other Stories*, 1975

LANCE *(page 632)*

"Lance" is from *Nabokov's Dozen*, 1958 (see Appendix).

EASTER RAIN *(page 643)*

"Easter Rain" was published in the April 1925 issue of the Russian émigré magazine *Russkoe Ekho*, the only known extant copy of which was discovered in the 1990s. It was translated by Dmitri Nabokov and Peter Constantine.

Appendix

Following are Nabokov's Bibliographical Note to *Nabokov's Dozen* (Doubleday & Company, Garden City, New York, 1958) and his forewords to the three collections he published with McGraw-Hill, New York: *A Russian Beauty and Other Stories* (1973), *Tyrants Destroyed and Other Stories* (1975), and *Details of a Sunset and Other Stories* (1976).

Bibliographical Note to *Nabokov's Dozen* (1958)

"The Aurelian," "Cloud, Castle, Lake," and "Spring in Fialta" were originally written in Russian. They were first published (as *"Pilgram," "Oblako, ozero, bashnya,"* and *"Vesna v Fial'te"*) in the Russian émigré review *Sovremennyya Zapiski* (Paris, 1931, 1937, 1938) under my pen name V. Sirin and were incorporated in my collections of short stories (*Soglyadatay*, Russkiya Zapiski publisher, Paris, 1938, and *Vesna v Fial'te i drugie rasskazï*, Chekhov Publishing House, New York, 1956). The English versions of those three stories were prepared by me (who am alone responsible for any discrepancies between them and the original texts) in collaboration with Peter Pertzov. "The Aurelian" and "Cloud, Castle, Lake" came out in the *Atlantic Monthly*, and "Spring in Fialta" in *Harper's Bazaar*, and all three appeared among the *Nine Stories* brought out by New Directions in "Direction," 1947.

"Mademoiselle O" was originally written in French and was first published in the review *Mesures*, Paris, 1939. It was translated into English with the kind assistance of the late Miss Hilda Ward, and came out in the *Atlantic Monthly* and in the *Nine Stories*. A final, slightly different version, with stricter adherence to autobiographical truth, appeared as chapter 5 in my memoir *Conclusive Evidence*, Harper & Brothers, New York, 1951 (also published in England as *Speak, Memory*, by Victor Gollancz, 1952).

The remaining stories in the present volume were written in English. Of these, "A Forgotten Poet," "The Assistant Producer," " 'That in Aleppo Once . . .'," and "Time and Ebb" appeared in the *Atlantic Monthly* and in *Nine Stories;* "Conversation Piece" (as "Double Talk"), "Signs and Symbols," "First Love" (as "Colette"), and "Lance" came out first in *The New Yorker;* "Double Talk" was reprinted in *Nine Stories;* "Colette," in *The New Yorker* anthology and (as chapter 7) in *Conclu-*

sive Evidence; and "Scenes from the Life of a Double Monster" appeared in *The Reporter.*

Only "Mademoiselle O" and "First Love" are (except for a change of names) true in every detail to the author's remembered life. "The Assistant Producer" is based on actual facts. As to the rest, I am no more guilty of imitating "real life" than "real life" is responsible for plagiarizing me.

V.N.

Foreword to *a Russian Beauty and Other Stories* (1973)

The Russian originals of the thirteen Englished stories selected for the present collection were composed in western Europe between 1924 and 1940, and appeared one by one in various émigré periodicals and editions (the last being the collection *Vesna v Fialte*, Chekhov Publishing House, New York, 1956). Most of these thirteen pieces were translated by Dmitri Nabokov in collaboration with the author. All are given here in a final English form, for which I alone am responsible. Professor Simon Karlinsky is the translator of the first story.

V.N.

Foreword to *Tyrants Destroyed and Other Stories* (1975)

Of the thirteen stories in this collection the first twelve have been translated from the Russian by Dmitri Nabokov in collaboration with the author. They are representative of my carefree expatriate *tvorchestvo* (the dignified Russian word for "creative output") between 1924 and 1939, in Berlin, Paris, and Mentone. Bits of bibliography are given in the prefaces to them, and more information will be found in Andrew Field's *Nabokov: A Bibliography*, published by McGraw-Hill.

The thirteenth story was written in English in Ithaca, upstate New York, at 802 East Seneca Street, a dismal grayish-white frame house, subjectively related to the more famous one at 342 Lawn Street, Ramsdale, New England.

V.N., *December 31, 1974, Montreux, Switzerland*

Foreword to *Details of a Sunset and Other Stories* (1976)

This collection is the last batch of my Russian stories meriting to be Englished. They cover a period of eleven years (1924–1935); all of them appeared in the émigré dailies and magazines of the time, in Berlin, Riga, and Paris.

It may be helpful, in some remote way, if I give here a list of all my translated stories, as published, in four separate volumes in the U.S.A. during the last twenty years.

Nabokov's Dozen (New York, Doubleday, 1958) includes the following three stories translated by Peter Pertzov in collaboration with the author:

1. "Spring in Fialta" (*Vesna v Fial'te*, 1936)
2. "The Aurelian" (*Pil'gram*, 1930)
3. "Cloud, Castle, Lake" (*Oblako, ozero, bashnya*, 1937)

A Russian Beauty (New York, McGraw-Hill, 1973) contains the following thirteen stories translated by Dmitri Nabokov in collaboration with the author, except for the title translated by Simon Karlinsky in collaboration with the author:

4. "A Russian Beauty" (*Krasavitsa*, 1934)
5. "The Leonardo" (*Korolyok*, 1933)
6. "Torpid Smoke" (*Tyazhyolyy dym*, 1935)
7. "Breaking the News" (*Opoveshchenie*, 1935)
8. "Lips to Lips" (*Usta k ustam*, 1932)
9. "The Visit to the Museum" (*Poseshchenie muzeya*, 1931)
10. "An Affair of Honor" (*Podlets*, 1927)
11. "Terra Incognita" (same title, 1931)
12. "A Dashing Fellow" (*Khvat*, 1930)
13. "Ultima Thule" (same title, 1940)
14. "Solus Rex" (same title, 1940)
15. "The Potato Elf" (*Kartofel'nyy el'f*, 1929)
16. "The Circle" (*Krug*, 1934)

Tyrants Destroyed (New York, McGraw-Hill, 1975) includes twelve stories translated by Dmitri Nabokov in collaboration with the author:

17. "Tyrants Destroyed" (*Istreblenie tiranov*, 1938)
18. "A Nursery Tale" (*Skazka*, 1926)
19. "Music" (*Muzyka*, 1932)
20. "Lik" (same title, 1939)
21. "Recruiting" (*Nabor*, 1935)
22. "Terror" (*Uzhas*, 1927)
23. "The Admiralty Spire" (*Admiralteyskaya igla*, 1933)
24. "A Matter of Chance" (*Sluchaynost'*, 1924)
25. "In Memory of L. I. Shigaev" (*Pamyati L. I. Shigaeva*, 1934)
26. "Bachmann" (same title, 1924)
27. "Perfection" (*Sovershenstvo*, 1932)
28. "Vasiliy Shishkov" (same title, 1939)

Details of a Sunset (New York, McGraw-Hill, 1976) contains thirteen stories translated by Dmitri Nabokov in collaboration with the author:

29. "Details of a Sunset" (*Katastrofa*, 1924)
30. "A Bad Day" (*Obida*, 1931)
31. "Orache" (*Lebeda*, 1932)
32. "The Return of Chorb" (*Vozvrashchenie Chorba*, 1925)
33. "The Passenger" (*Passazhir*, 1927)
34. "A Letter That Never Reached Russia" (*Pis'mo v Rossiyu*, 1925)
35. "A Guide to Berlin" (*Putevoditel' po Berlinu*, 1925)
36. "The Doorbell" (*Zvonok*, 1927)
37. "The Thunderstorm" (*Groza*, 1924)
38. "The Reunion" (*Vstrecha*, 1932)
39. "A Slice of Life" (*Sluchay iz zhizni*, 1935)
40. "Christmas" (*Rozhdestvo*, 1925)
41. "A Busy Man" (*Zanyatoy chelovek*, 1931)

V.N., *Montreux, 1975*

ABOUT THE TRANSLATOR

Dmitri Nabokov was born in 1934 in Berlin and came to the United States as a young child with his parents. He graduated from Harvard, served in the U.S. Army, and then began the vocal studies that led him to become an opera and concert performer (as a basso) around the world. He has translated most of his father's Russian short stories and plays and many of his novels into English.

WOLF SOLENT

by John Cowper Powys

This rapturous novel of eros and ideas remains unrivaled in its risky balance of mysticism and comedy, ecstatic contemplation of nature, and unblinking observation of human folly and desire. Forsaking London for a village in Dorsetshire, *Wolf Solent* discovers a world of pagan splendor riddled by ancient scandals and resentments. This poetic young man meets two women—the sensuous beauty Gerda and the ethereal gamine Christie—who will become the sharers of his body and soul.

Fiction/Literature/0-375-70307-1

EVER AFTER

by Graham Swift

Dazzling in its structure and shattering in its emotional force, Graham Swift's *Ever After* spans two centuries and settings from the adulterous bedrooms of postwar Paris to the contemporary entanglements in the groves of academe. It is the story of Bill Unwin, a man haunted by the death of his beautiful wife and a survivor himself of a recent brush with mortality. And although it touches on Darwin and dinosaurs, bees and bridge builders, the true subject of *Ever After* is nothing less than the eternal question, "Why should things matter?"

Fiction/Literature/0-679-74026-0

THE NATURE OF BLOOD

by Caryl Phillips

At the center of *The Nature of Blood* is a young woman, a Nazi death camp survivor, devastated by the loss of everyone she loves. Her story is interwoven with a cast of characters from both the present and past: her uncle Stephan, Othello the Moorish general, three Jews in fifteenth-century Venice, and an Ethiopian Jew struggling for acceptance in contemporary Israel. Tracing these characters through disparate lands and centuries, Phillips creates an unforgettable group portrait of individuals overwhelmed by the force of European tribalism.

Fiction/Literature/0-679-77675-3

LOVES THAT BIND
by Julián Ríos

Emil haunts the streets of London with his heart in his hands, searching for the woman who has just abandoned him. Feeling at turns dejected and vengeful, he relishes memories of previous romances, the erotic details of which he reveals in twenty-six intricate letters addressed to his fugitive girlfriend. Emil's alphabetical list reveals that remarkably, each woman on it bears a striking resemblance to a memorable heroine from a classic novel of the twentieth century. And in every entry, Ríos echoes the writing style of each novelist. The result is a literary crossword puzzle that affirms its author's place in the pantheon of masters of the modern novel.

Fiction/Literature/0-375-70060-9

THE NEW LIFE
by Orhan Pamuk

The protagonist of Orhan Pamuk's fiendishly engaging novel is launched into a world of hypnotic texts and Byzantine conspiracies that whirl across the steppes and forlorn frontier towns of Turkey. Through the single act of reading a book, a young student is uprooted from his old life and identity. Within days he has fallen in love with the luminous and elusive Janan, witnessed the attempted assassination of a rival suitor, and forsaken his family to travel aimlessly through a nocturnal landscape of travelers' cafes and apocalyptic bus wrecks. The result is a wondrous marriage of the intellectual thriller and high romance.

Fiction/Literature/0-375-70171-0

THE REAL LIFE OF SEBASTIAN KNIGHT
by Vladimir Nabokov

The Real Life of Sebastian Knight is a perversely magical literary detective story—subtle, intricate, with a tantalizing climax—about the mysterious life of a famous writer. Many people knew things about Sebastian Knight as a distinguished novelist, but probably fewer than a dozen knew of the two love affairs that so profoundly influenced his career, the second one in a disastrous way. After Knight's death, his half brother sets out to penetrate the enigma of his life, starting with a few scanty clues in the novelist's private papers. His search proves to be a story as intriguing as any of his subject's own novels, as baffling, and, in the end, as uniquely rewarding.

Fiction/Literature/0-679-72726-4

THE THREE-ARCHED BRIDGE

by Ismail Kadare

In 1377, the Balkan peninsula is a bridge between cultures. On one side lies the flotsam of the receding Byzantine empire, an unruly alliance whose peoples quarrel in half a dozen tongues; on the other, the encroaching hordes of Ottoman Turkey. On the banks of a river somewhere in between these powers, another bridge is rising. When mysterious acts of sabotage halt construction of the three-arched bridge, a man suspected of the crimes is discovered walled up in the foundation, with only his head protruding from the stone. Is his death meant to deter other saboteurs or to appease the spirits of the river? Does it fulfill an ancient prophecy or predict further bloodshed? *The Three-Arched Bridge* is as powerful an evocation of a vanished world as *The Name of the Rose*.

Fiction/Literature/0-375-70094-3

THE CLUB DUMAS

by Arturo Pérez-Reverte

Lucas Corso, middle-aged, tired, and cynical, is a book detective, a mercenary hired to hunt down rare editions for wealthy and unscrupulous clients. When a well-known bibliophile is found hanged, leaving behind part of the original manuscript of Alexandre Dumas's *The Three Musketeers*, Corso is asked to authenticate the fragment. The task seems straightforward, but the unsuspecting Corso is soon drawn into a swirling plot involving devil worship, occult practices, and swashbuckling derring-do among a cast of characters bearing a suspicious resemblance to those of Dumas's masterpiece. Part mystery, part puzzle, part witty intertextual game, *The Club Dumas* is a wholly original intellectual thriller.

Fiction/Literature/0-679-77754-7

VINTAGE INTERNATIONAL
Available at your local bookstore, or call toll-free to order:
1-800-793-2665 (credit cards only).